By Gene Wolfe from Tom Doherty Associates

Novels
The Fifth Head of Cerberus
The Devil in a Forest
Peace
Free Live Free
Soldier of the Mist
Soldier of Arete
There Are Doors
Castleview
Pandora by Holly Hollander

Novellas
The Death of Doctor Island
Seven American Nights

Collections
Endangered Species
Storeys from the Old Hotel
Castle of Days
The Island of Doctor Death and Other Stories and Other Stories
Strange Travelers

The Book of the New Sun
Shadow and Claw
(comprising *The Shadow of the Torturer* and *The Claw of the Conciliator*)
Sword and Citadel
(comprising *The Sword of the Lictor* and *The Citadel of the Autarch*)
The Urth of the New Sun

The Book of the Long Sun
Litany of the Long Sun
(comprising *Nightside the Long Sun* and *Lake of the Long Sun*)
Epiphany of the Long Sun
(comprising *Caldé of the Long Sun* and *Exodus from the Long Sun*)

The Book of the Short Sun
On Blue's Waters
In Green's Jungles

EPIPHANY OF THE LONG SUN

Caldé of the Long Sun

AND

Exodus from the Long Sun

Gene Wolfe

A TOM DOHERTY ASSOCIATES BOOK

NEW YORK

EPIPHANY OF THE LONG SUN

This is an omnibus edition comprising the novels *Caldé of the
Long Sun,* copyright © 1994 by Gene Wolfe, and *Exodus from the
Long Sun,* copyright © 1996 by Gene Wolfe.

An Orb Edition
Published by Tom Doherty Associates, LLC
175 Fifth Avenue
New York, NY 10010

www.tor.com

ISBN 0-312-86072-2

First Orb Edition: November 2000

Printed in the United States of America

0 9 8 7 6 5 4 3 2 1

CONTENTS

Caldé of the Long Sun 7

Exodus from the Long Sun 317

About the Author 719

CALDÉ OF THE LONG SUN

For Todd Compton, classicist and rock musician.

Gods, Persons,

and Animals

Mentioned in the Text

N.B. In Viron, biochemical males are named after animals or animal products: Macaque, Mattak, OOSIK, and POTTO bear names of this type. Biochemical females are named for plants (most frequently flowers) or plant products: MUCOR, Nettle, ROSE, Teasel. Chemical persons, whether male or female, are named after metals and minerals: Moly, Sard, Shale. The names of major characters are given in CAPITALS in this listing.

A-man, a man representing all men.
Ah Lah, a forgotten god. (Perhaps an alternative name for the
   OUTSIDER.)
Aloe, a pious woman of the Sun Street Quarter.
Asphodella, a girl in the younger (prepubescent) group at the palaestra.
Aster, a girl in the older (pubescent) group at the palaestra.
AUK, the burly housebreaker who coached SILK in burglary; called
   "trooper" by HAMMERSTONE.
Babirousa, a smith's apprentice, one of MINT's volunteers.
Bass, the muscular bald man employed by Orchid.
Maytera *Betel,* the dark, sleepy-eyed sibyl noted by SILK during his
   enlightenment.
Bison, the big, black-bearded man who becomes MINT's chief
   lieutenant.
BLOOD, a wealthy dealer in drugs and women, at times an unpaid agent
   of the Ayuntamiento.

Bream, the thief who provides a white goat for Kypris at ROSE's final sacrifice.

Brocket, a distant cousin of MINT's.

Patera *Bull,* QUETZAL's prothonotary.

Bustard, AUK's older brother, now dead.

Cassava, a pious old woman of the Sun Street Quarter.

Cavy, one of the older (pubescent) boys at the palaestra.

CHENILLE, the tallest woman at Orchid's.

Major *Civet,* the officer who killed Doctor CRANE while trying to free SILK.

Doctor *CRANE,* the Trivigaunti spy who killed Councillor LEMUR, now dead.

Captain *DACE,* the skipper of the fishing boat commandeered by SCYLLA.

Dahlia, a student of MARBLE's, long ago.

Echidna, the Mother of the Gods; the most powerful goddess.

Sergeant *Eft,* Mattak's chief subordinate.

Eland, one of Urus's convict crew; he tamed and trained two tunnel gods.

Elodia, Gelada's former mistress.

Ermine, the owner of the highest-priced hotel in Viron.

Brigadier *Erne,* the commander of the Fourth Brigade of Viron's Civil Guard (formerly, the Caldé's Guard).

Femur, INCUS's much-older brother.

Gaur, one of Urus's convict crew.

Gayfeather, one of the older (pubescent) girls at the palaestra.

Captain *Gecko,* an officer on OOSIK's staff.

Gelada, the bowman in Urus's crew who shoots at CHENILLE.

Gib, the giant whose life was saved by AUK.

Ginger, one of the older (pubescent) girls at the palaestra.

Goral, an unemployed hostler, one of MINT's volunteers.

Patera *Gulo,* SILK's acolyte.

Corporal *HAMMERSTONE,* the soldier who (with Sergeant Sand) first arrested SILK in the tunnels, called "Stony" by CHENILLE.

Hart, a young layman of SILK's manteion.

Hierax, Echidna's second son, the god of death.

Holly, one of the older (pubescent) girls at the palaestra.

Horn, the student punished by ROSE for imitating SILK.

HYACINTH, the beautiful young woman at BLOOD's who persuaded CRANE to give SILK an azoth.

Patera *INCUS,* the black mechanic who repairs and reprograms HAMMERSTONE.

Iolar, the flier downed by *MUSK*'s eagle.

Patera *Jerboa,* the augur of the manteion on Brick Street.

Kingcup, the owner of a livery stable.

Kypris, the goddess of love, the first goddess to possess CHENILLE.

Councillor *LEMUR,* the leading member of the Ayuntamiento, killed by CRANE.

Liana, one of Zoril's subordinates.

Lily, AUK's mother, now dead.

Lime, MINT's chief female lieutenant.

Linsang, Liana's sweetheart.

Lion, the largest male among MUCOR's lynxes.

Councillor *LORIS,* the leader of the Ayuntamiento after the death of LEMUR.

Macaque, one of the older (pubescent) boys at the palaestra.

Mamelta, the sleeper arrested with SILK in the tunnels.

Mandrill, Gelada's cousin, now fled.

Maytera *MARBLE,* the sibyl who teaches the younger (prepubescent) children at the palaestra.

Marmot, an unemployed laborer, one of MINT's volunteers.

Cornet *Mattak,* OOSIK's son, a young cavalry officer.

Maytera *MINT,* the Sword of Echidna, the sibyl who teaches the older (pubescent) girls at the palaestra; called General MINT by the insurgents.

Maytera *Mockorange,* a sibyl at the manteion on Sun Street, now dead.

Molpe, Echidna's second daughter, goddess of the winds and of the lively arts.

Moly, HAMMERSTONE's lost sweetheart, a housemaid. (Short for Molybdenum.)

Patera *Moray,* the augur murdered by Eft.

MUCOR, the adolescent whose bedroom was invaded by SILK when he burglarized BLOOD's villa.

Murtagon, a famous artist.

MUSK, BLOOD's sadistic young killer; a competent tenor and a lover of raptorial birds.

Nettle, one of the older (pubescent) girls in Maytera MINT's class at the palaestra.

Oont, a porter.

Colonel *OOSIK,* the commander of the reserve brigade.

Orchid, the madame of a brothel owned by BLOOD.

OREB, a bird purchased by SILK as a victim but never sacrificed.

Orpine, Orchid's daughter, possessed by MUCOR and killed by CHENILLE.

The *OUTSIDER,* the god of the broken and the disparaged, whose realm lies outside the Whorl.

Pas, the Father of the Gods; the husband of Echidna and the father of SCYLLA, Molpe, TARTAROS, Hierax, Thelxiepeia, Phaea, and Sphigx.

Patera *Pike,* the elderly augur whose acolyte SILK became upon graduation from the schola, now dead.

Phaea, Echidna's fourth daughter, the goddess of food and healing.

Pork, the owner of the restaurant at which SILK dined with AUK.

Councillor *POTTO,* the member of the Ayuntamiento who (with Sand) interrogated SILK after his second arrest.

Patera *QUETZAL,* the ranking augur in Viron and for thirty-three years the head of its Chapter.

Quill, a poor student at the palaestra.

Patera *REMORA,* QUETZAL's coadjutor and presumed successor.

Rook, one of MINT's lieutenants.

Maytera *ROSE,* the sibyl who taught the older (pubescent) boys at the palaestra, now dead.

General *Saba,* the commander of the Trivigaunti airship and the troops it brings to Viron.

Sergeant *Sand,* HAMMERSTONE's squad leader.

Sard, the owner of a large pawnshop on Saddle Street.

Scale, one of Bison's lieutenants.

Private *Schist,* a soldier in Sand's squad.

Scleroderma, the fat woman who holds MINT's horse; the wife of a butcher in the Sun Street Quarter.

Captain *Scup,* the fishing-boat skipper employed by CRANE to watch the Pilgrims' Way.

SCYLLA, the firstborn of Echidna's children, and the patroness of Viron.

Private *Shale,* a soldier in Sand's squad.

Patera *Shell*, Patera Jerboa's acolyte; he attended the schola with SILK.

Caldé *SILK*, the augur of the manteion on Sun Street.

Generalissimo *Siyuf*, the commander of the armed forces of Trivigaunte.

Skink, the insurgent leader who attempts an all-out assault on the Palatine early Hieraxday night.

Sphigx, Echidna's youngest child, the patroness of Trivigaunte and the goddess of war.

Councillor *Tarsier*, one of the members of the Ayuntamiento.

TARTAROS, Echidna's eldest son, the god of night.

Teasel, a girl in MARBLE's class at the palaestra.

Thetis, a minor goddess to whom lost travelers pray.

Thelxiepeia, Echidna's third daughter, the goddess of learning and thus of magic and witchcraft.

Lieutenant *Tiger*, OOSIK's assistant operations officer.

Caldé *TUSSAH*, SILK's predecessor; he was assassinated by the Ayuntamiento. (Patera *Tussah*, presumably named for the caldé, is a member of INCUS's circle of black mechanics.)

Urus, a former associate of AUK's, sentenced to the pits.

Villus, a small boy in MARBLE's class at the palaestra.

Violet, a beautiful brunet at Orchid's, a friend of CHENILLE's.

Wo-Man, a woman representing all women.

Maytera *Wood*, the senior sibyl at the Brick Street manteion.

Wool, one of MINT's lieutenants.

Master *XIPHIAS*, a one-legged fencing teacher.

Yapok, a stableman, one of MINT's volunteers.

Zoril, a cabinetmaker, one of MINT's lieutenants.

Chapter 1

THE SLAVES OF SCYLLA

As unruffled by the disturbances shaking the city as by the furious thunderstorm that threatened with every gust to throw down its shiprock and return its mud brick to the parent mud, His Cognizance Patera Quetzal, Prolocutor of the Chapter of This Our Holy City of Viron, studied his present sere and sallow features in the polished belly of the silver teapot.

As at this hour each day, he swung his head to the right and contemplated his nearly noseless profile, made a similar inspection of its obverse, and elevated his chin to display a lengthy and notably wrinkled neck. He had shaped and colored face and neck with care upon arising, as he did every morning; nevertheless, there remained the possibility (however remote) that something had gone awry by ten: thus the present amused but painstaking self-examination.

"For I am a careful man," he muttered, pretending to smooth one thin white eyebrow.

A crash of thunder shook the Prolocutor's Palace to its foundations at the final word, brightening every light in the room to a glare; rain and hail drummed the windowpanes.

Patera Remora, Coadjutor of the Chapter, nodded solemnly. "Yes indeed, Your Cognizance. You are indeed a most—ah—advertent man."

Yet there was always that possibility. "I'm growing old, Patera. Even we careful men grow old."

Remora nodded again, his long bony face expressive of regret. "Alas, Your Cognizance."

"As do many other things, Patera. Our city . . . The Whorl itself grows old. When we're young, we notice things that are young, like ourselves. New grass on old graves. New leaves on old trees." Quetzal lifted his chin again to study his bulging reflection through hooded eyes.

"The golden season of beauty and—um—elegiacs, Your Cognizance." Remora's fingers toyed with a dainty sandwich.

"As we notice the signs of advancing age in ourselves, we see them in the Whorl. Just a few chems today who ever saw a man who saw a man who remembered the day Pas made the Whorl."

A little bewildered by the rapid riffle through so many generations, Remora nodded again. "Indeed, Your Cognizance. Indeed not." Surreptitiously, he wiped jam from one finger.

"You become conscious of recurrences, the cyclical nature of myth. When first I received the bacculus, I had occasion to survey many old documents. I read each with care. It was my custom to devote three Hieraxdays a month to that. To that alone, and to inescapable obsequies. I gave my prothonotary the straightest instructions to make no appointments for that day. It's a practice I recommend, Patera."

Thunder rattled the room again, lightning a dragon beyond the windows.

"I will, um, reinstitute this wise usage at once, Your Cognizance."

"At once, you say?" Quetzal looked up from the silver pot, resolved to repowder his chin at the first opportunity. "You may go to young Incus and so instruct him, if you want. Tell him now, Patera. Tell him now."

"That is—ah—unfeasible, I fear, Your Cognizance. I sent Patera Incus upon a—um—errand Molpsday. He has not—um—rejoined us."

"I see. I see." With a trembling hand, Quetzal raised his cup until its gilt rim touched his lips, then lowered it, though not so far as to expose his chin. "I want beef tea, Patera. There's no strength in this. I want beef tea. See to it, please."

Long accustomed to the request, his coadjutor rose. "I shall prepare it with my own hands, Your Cognizance. It will—ah—occupy only an, um, trice. Boiling water, an, um, roiling boil. Your Cognizance may rely upon me."

Slowly, Quetzal replaced the delicate cup in its saucer as he watched Remora's retreating back; he even spilled a few drops there, for he was, as he had said, careful. The measured closing of the door. Good. The clank of the latchbar. Good again. No one could intrude now without noise and a slight delay; he had designed the latching mechanism himself.

Without leaving his chair, he extracted the puff from a drawer on the other side of the room and applied flesh-toned powder delicately to the small, sharp chin he had shaped with such care upon arising. Swinging his head from side to side as before, frowning and smiling by turns, he studied the effect in the teapot. Good, good!

Rain beat against the windows with such force as to drive trickles of chill water through crevices in the casements; it pooled invitingly on the milkstone windowsills and fell in cataracts to soak the carpet. That, too, was good. At three, he would preside at the private sacrifice of twenty-one dappled horses, the now-posthumous offering of Councillor Lemur—one to all the gods for each week since rain more substantial than a shower had blessed Viron's fields. They could be converted to a thank offering, and he would so convert them.

Would the congregation know by then of Lemur's demise? Quetzal debated the advisability of announcing the fact if they did not. It was a question of some consequence; and at length, for the temporary relief the act afforded him, he pivoted his hinged fangs from their snug grooves in the roof of his mouth, snapping each gratefully into its socket and grinning gleefully at his distorted image.

The rattle of the latch was nearly lost in another crash of thunder, but he had kept an eye on the latchbar. There was a second and louder rattle as Remora, on the other side of the door, contended with the inconveniently shaped iron handle that would, when its balky rotation had been completed, laboriously lift the clumsy bar clear of its cradle.

Quetzal touched his lips almost absently with his napkin; when he spread it upon his lap again, his fangs had vanished. "Yes, Patera?" he inquired querulously. "What is it now? Is it time already?"

"Your beef tea, Your Cognizance." Remora set his small tray on the table. "Shall I—um—decant a cup for you? I have, er, obtained a clean cup for the purpose."

"Do, Patera. Please do." Quetzal smiled. "While you were gone, I was contemplating the nature of humor. Have you ever considered it?"

Remora resumed his seat. "I fear not, Your Cognizance."

"What's become of young Incus? You hadn't expected him to be gone so long?"

"No, Your Cognizance. I dispatched him to Limna." Remora spooned beef salts into the clean cup and added water from the small copper kettle he had brought, producing a fine plume of steam. "I am—

ah–moderately concerned. An, um, modicum of civil unrest last night, eh?" He stirred vigorously. "This–ah–stripling Silk. Patera Silk, alas. I know him."

"My prothonotary told me." With the slightest of nods, Quetzal accepted the steaming cup. "I'd have thought Limna would be safer."

"As would I, Your Cognizance. As did I."

A cautious sip. Quetzal held the hot, salty fluid in his mouth, drawing it deliciously through folded fangs.

"I sent him in search of a–ah, um–individual, Your Cognizance. A, er, acquaintance of this Patera Silk's. The Civil Guard is searching for Patera himself, hey? As are, er, certain others. Other–ah–parties. So I am told. This morning, Your Cognizance, I dispatched still others to look for young Incus. The rain, however, ah, necessitous, will hamper them all, hum?"

"Do you swim, Patera?"

"I, Your Cognizance? At the–um–lakeside, you mean? No. Or at least, not for many years."

"Nor I."

Remora groped toward a point he had yet to discern. "A healthful exercise, however. For those of, um, unaugmented years, eh? A hot bath before sacrifice, Your Cognizance? Or–I have it!–springs. There are, er, reborant springs at Urbs. Healing springs, most healthful. Possibly, while–ah–affairs are so–ah–unsettled here, eh?"

Quetzal shook himself. He had a way of quivering like a fat man when he did that, although on the few occasions when Remora had been obliged to lift him into bed, his body had in fact been light and sinuous. "The gods . . ." He smiled.

"Must be served, to be sure, Your Cognizance. I would be on the spot–ah–ensuring that the Chapter's interests were vigilantly safeguarded, hey?" Remora tossed lank black hair away from his eyes. "Each rite carried out with–um–"

"You must recall the story, Patera." Quetzal swayed from side to side, perhaps with silent mirth. "A-man and Wo-man like rabbits in a garden. The–what do you call them?" He held up a thin, blue-veined hand, palm cupped.

"A cobra, Your Cognizance?"

"The cobra persuaded Wo-man to eat fruit from his tree, miraculous fruit whose taste conferred wisdom."

Remora nodded, wondering how he might reintroduce the springs. "I recollect the—um—allegory."

Quetzal nodded more vigorously, a wise teacher proffering praise to a small boy. "It's all in the Writings. Or nearly all. A god called Ah Lah barred Wo-man and her husband from the garden." He ceased to speak, apparently wandering among thoughts. "We seem to have lost sight of Ah Lah, by the way. I can't recall a single sacrifice to him. No one ever asks why the cobra wanted Wo-man to eat his fruit."

"From sheer, er, wickedness, Your Cognizance? That is what I had always supposed."

Quetzal swayed faster, his face solemn. "In order that she would climb his tree, Patera. The man likewise. Their story's not over because they haven't climbed down. That's why I asked if you had considered the nature of humor. Is Patera Incus a strong swimmer?"

"Why, I've—ah—no notion, Your Cognizance."

"Because you think you know why the woman you sent him to look for visited the lake with our scamp Silk, whose name I see on walls."

"Why, er, Your Cognizance is—ah—great penetration, as always." Remora fidgeted.

"I saw it scratched on one five floors up, yesterday," Quetzal continued as though he had not heard, "and went wide."

"Disgraceful, Your Cognizance!"

"Respect for our cloth, Patera. I myself swim well. Not so well as a fish, but very well indeed. Or I did."

"I'm pleased to hear it, Your Cognizance."

"The jokes of gods are long in telling. That's why you ought to sift the records of the past on Hieraxdays, Patera. Today's Hieraxday. You'll learn to think in new and better ways. Thank you for my beef tea. Now go."

Remora rose and bowed. "As Your Cognizance desires."

His Cognizance stared past him, lost in speculation.

Greatly daring, Remora ventured, "I have often observed that your own way of thinking is somewhat—ah—unlike, as well as much more, um, select than that of most men."

There was no reply. Remora took a step backward. "Upon every—ah—topic whatsoever, Your Cognizance's information is quite, um, marvelous."

"Wait." Quetzal had made his decision. "The riots. Has the Alam-brera fallen?"

"What's that? The Alambrera? Why—ah—no. Not to my knowledge, Your Cognizance."

"Tonight." Quetzal reached for his beef tea. "Sit down, Patera. You're always jumping about. You make me nervous. It can't be good for you. Lemur's dead. Did you know it?"

Remora's mouth gaped, then snapped shut. He sat.

"You weren't. It's your responsibility to learn things."

Remora acknowledged his responsibility with a shamefaced nod. "May I inquire, Your Cognizance—?"

"How I know? In the same way I knew the woman you sent Incus after had gone to Lake Limna with Patera Caldé Silk."

"Your Cognizance!"

Once again, Quetzal favored Remora with his lipless smile. "Are you afraid I'll be arrested, Patera? Cast into the pits? You'd be Prolocutor, presumably. I've no fear of the pits." Quetzal's long-skulled, completely hairless head bobbed above his cup. "Not at my age. None."

"None the less, I implore Your Cognizance to be more—ah—circumspect."

"Why isn't the city burning, Patera?"

Caught by surprise, Remora glanced at the closest window.

"Mud brick and shiprock walls. Timbers supporting upper floors. Thatch or shingles. Five blocks of shops burned last night. Why isn't the whole city burning today?"

"It's raining, Your Cognizance," Remora summoned all his courage. "It's been raining—ah—forcibly since early this morning."

"Exactly so. Patera Caldé Silk went to Limna on Molpsday with a woman. That same day, you sent Incus there to look for an acquaintance of his. A woman, since you were reluctant to speak of it. Councillor Loris spoke through the glass an hour before lunch."

Remora tensed. "He told you Councillor Lemur was no longer among us, Your Cognizance?"

Quetzal swung his head back and forth. "That Lemur was still alive, Patera. There are rumors. So it would appear. He wanted me to denounce them this afternoon."

"But if Councillor Loris—ah—assures—"

"Clearly Lemur's dead. If he weren't, he'd speak to me in person. Or show himself at the Juzgado. Or both."

"Even so, Your Cognizance—"

Another crash of thunder made common cause with Quetzal's thin hand to interrupt.

"Can the Ayuntamiento prevail without him? That's the question, Patera. I want your opinion."

To give himself time to consider, Remora sipped his now-tepid tea. "Munitions, the–ah–thews of contention, are stored in the Alambrera, as well as in the, um, cantonment of the Civil Guard, east of the city."

"I know that."

"It is an, er, complex of great–um–redoubtability, Your Cognizance. I am informed that the outer wall is twelve cubits in–ah–laterality. Yet Your Cognizance anticipates its surrender tonight? Before venturing an opinion, may I enquire as to the source of Your Cognizance's information?"

"I haven't any," Quetzal told him. "I was thinking out loud. If the Alambrera doesn't fall in a day or so, Patera Caldé Silk will fail. That's my opinion. Now I want yours."

"Your Cognizance does me honor. There is also the–um–dormant army to consider. Councillor Lemur–ah–Loris will undoubtedly issue an–ah–call to arms, should the, um, situation, in his view, become serious."

"Your opinion, Patera."

Remora's cup rattled in its saucer. "As long as the–ah–fidelity of the Civil Guard remains–um–unblemished, Your Cognizance," he drew a deep breath, "it would appear to me, though I am assuredly no–um–master hand at matters military, that–ah, um–Patera Caldé cannot prevail."

Quetzal appeared to be listening only to the storm; for perhaps fifteen tickings of the coffin-shaped clock that stood beside the door, the howling of the wind and the lash of rain filled the room. At last he asked, "Suppose that you were to learn that part of the Guard's gone over to Silk already?"

Remora's eyes widened. "Your Cognizance has–?"

"No reason to think so. My question's hypothetical."

Remora, who had much experience of Quetzal's hypothetical questions, filled his lungs again. "I should then say, Your Cognizance, that should any such unhappy circumstance–ah–circumstances eventuate, the city would find itself amongst–ah–perilous waters."

"And the Chapter?"

Remora looked doleful. "Equally so, Your Cognizance, if not worse.

As an augur, Silk could well, ah, proclaim himself Prolocutor, as well as caldé."

"Really. He lacks reverence for you, my coadjutor?"

"No, Your Cognizance. Quite the, um, contrary."

Quetzal sipped beef tea in silence.

"Your Cognizance—ah—intends the Chapter to support the—um—host of, er, Patera Caldé?"

"I want you to compose a circular letter, Patera. You have nearly six hours. It should be more than enough. I'll sign it when we're through in the Grand Manteion." Quetzal stared down at the stagnant brown liquid in his cup.

"To all the clergy, Your Cognizance?"

"Emphasize our holy duty to bring comfort to the wounded and the Final Formula to the dying. Imply, but don't say—" Quetzal paused, inspired.

"Yes, Your Cognizance?"

"That Lemur's death ends the claim to rule the councillors had in the past. You say you know Patera Caldé Silk?"

Remora nodded. "I conversed with him at some—ah—extensively Scylsday evening, Your Cognizance. We discussed the financial—um—trials of his manteion, and—ah—various other matters."

"I don't, Patera. But I've read every report in his file, those of his instructors and those of his predecessor. Thus my recommendation. Diligent, sensitive, intelligent, and pious. Impatient, as is to be expected at his age. Respectful, which you now confirm. A tireless worker, a point his instructor in theonomy was at pains to emphasize. Pliable. During the past few days, he's become immensely popular. Should he succeed in subjugating the Ayuntamiento, he's apt to remain so for a year or more. Perhaps much longer. Charteral government by a young augur who'll need seasoned advisors to remain in office . . ."

"Indeed, Your Cognizance." Remora nodded energetically. "The same—ah—intuition had occurred to me."

With his cup, Quetzal gestured toward the nearest window. "We suffer a change in weather, Patera."

"An, um, profound one, Your Cognizance."

"We must acclimate ourselves to it. That's why I asked if young Incus swam. If you can reach him, tell him to strike out boldly. Have I made myself clear?"

Remora nodded again. "I will, um, strive to render the Chapter's wholehearted endorsement of an—ah—lawful and holy government apparent, Your Cognizance."

"Then go. Compose that letter."

"If the Alambrera doesn't—ah—hey?"

There was no indication that Quetzal had heard. Remora left his chair and backed away, at length closing the door behind him.

Quetzal rose, and an observer (had there been one) might have been more than a little surprised to see that shrunken figure grown so tall. As if on wheels, he glided across the room and threw open the broad casement that overlooked his garden, admitting pounding rain and a gust of wind that made his mulberry robe stand out behind him like a banner.

For some while he remained before the window, motionless, cosmetics streaming from his face in rivulets of pink and buff, while he contemplated the tamarind he had caused to be planted there twenty years previously. It was taller already than many buildings called lofty; its glossy, rain-washed leaves brushed the windowframe and now even, by the width of a child's hand, sidled into his bedchamber like so many timid sibyls, confident of welcome yet habitually shy. Their parent tree, nourished by his own efforts, was of more than sufficient size now, and a fount of joy to him: a sheltering presence, a memorial of home, the highroad to freedom.

Quetzal crossed the room and barred the door, then threw off his sodden robe. Even in this downpour the tree was safer, though he could fly.

The looming presence of the cliff slid over Auk as he sat in the bow, and with it a final whistling gust of icy rain. He glanced up at the beetling rock, then trained his needler on the augur standing to the halyard. "This time you didn't try anything. See how flash you're getting?" The storm had broken at shadeup and showed no signs of slackening.

Chenille snapped, "Steer for that," and pointed. Chill tricklings from her limp crimson hair merged into a rivulet between her full breasts to flood her naked loins.

At the tiller, the old fisherman touched his cap. "Aye, aye, Scaldin' Scylla."

They had left Limna on Molpsday night. From shadeup to shadelow, the sun had been a torrent of white fire across a dazzling sky; the wind, fair and strong at morning, had veered and died away to a breeze, to an occasional puff, and by the time the market closed, to nothing. Most of that afternoon Auk had spent in the shadow of the sail, Chenille beneath the shelter of the half deck; he and she, like the augur, had gotten badly sunburned just the same.

Night had brought a new wind, foul for their destination. Directed by the old fisherman and commanded to hold ever closer by the major goddess possessing Chenille, they had tacked and tacked and tacked again, Auk and the augur bailing frantically on every reach and often sick, the boat heeling until it seemed the gunnel must go under, a lantern swinging crazily from the masthead and crashing into the mast each time they went about, going out half a dozen times and leaving the three weary men below in deadly fear of ramming or being rammed in the dark.

Once the augur had attempted to snatch Auk's needler from his waistband. Auk had beaten and kicked him, and thrown him over the side into the churning waters of the lake, from which the old fisherman had by a miracle of resource and luck rescued him with a boathook. Shadeup had brought a third wind, this out of the southeast, a stormwind driving sheet after gray sheet of slanting rain before it with a lash of lightning.

"Down sail!" Chenille shrieked. "Loose that, you idiot! Drop the yard!"

The augur hurried to obey; he was perhaps ten years senior to Auk, with protruding teeth and small, soft hands that had begun to bleed almost before they had left Limna.

After the yard had crashed down, Auk turned in his seat to peer forward at their destination, seeing nothing but rainwet stone and evoking indignant squawks from the meager protection of his legs. "Come on out," he told Silk's bird. "We're under a cliff here."

"No out!"

Dry by comparison though the foot of the cliff was, and shielded from the wind, it seemed colder than the open lake, reminding Auk forcibly that the new summer tunic he had worn to Limna was soaked, his baggy trousers soaked too, and his greased riding boots full of water.

The narrow inlet up which they glided became narrower yet, damp black rock to left and right rising fifty cubits or more above the masthead. Here and there a freshet, born of the storm, descended in a slender line of silver to plash noisily into the quiet water. The cliffs united overhead, and the iron mast-cap scraped stone.

"She'll go," Chenille told the old fisherman confidently. "The ceiling's higher farther in."

"I'd 'preciate ter raise up that mains'l ag'in, ma'am," the old fisherman remarked almost conversationally, "an' undo them reefs. It'll rot if it don't dry."

Chenille ignored him; Auk gestured toward the sail and stood to the halyard with the augur, eager for any exercise that might warm him.

Oreb hopped onto the gunnel to look about and fluff his damp feathers. "Bird wet!" They were gliding past impressive tanks of white-painted metal, their way nearly spent.

"A *Sacred Window*! It *is*! There's a Window and an altar *right there*! Look!" The augur's voice shook with joy, and he released the halyard. Auk's kick sent him sprawling.

"Got ter break out sweeps, ma'am, if there's more channel."

"Mind your helm. Lay alongside the Window." To the augur Chenille added, "Have you got your knife?"

He shook his head miserably.

"Your sword then," she told Auk. "Can you sacrifice?"

"I've seen it done, Surging Scylla, and I got a knife in my boot. That might work better." As daring as Remora, Auk added, "But a bird? I didn't think you liked birds."

"That?" She spat into the water.

A fender of woven cordage thumped, then ground against stone. Their side lay within a cubit of the natural quay on which the tanks and the Window stood. "Tie us up." Chenille pointed to the augur. "You, too! No, the stern, you idiot. He'll take the bow."

Auk made the halyard fast, then sprang out onto the stone quay. It was wet, and so slimed that he nearly fell; in the watery light of the cavern, he failed to make out the big iron ring at his feet until he stepped on it.

The augur had found his ring sooner. He straightened up. "I–I *am* an *augur*, Savage Scylla. I've sacrificed to you and to all the Nine *many times*. I'd be *delighted*, Savage Scylla. With his knife . . ."

"Bad bird," Oreb croaked. "Gods hate." He flapped his injured wing as if to judge how far it might carry him.

Chenille bounded onto the slippery stone and crooked a finger at the old fisherman. "You. Come up here."

"I oughter—"

"You ought to do what you're told, or I'll have my thug kill you straight off."

It was a relief to Auk to draw his needler again, a return to familiar ground.

"*Scylla!*" the augur gasped. "A *human being?* Really—"

She whirled to confront him. "What were you doing on my boat? Who sent you?"

"Bad cut," Oreb assured her.

The augur drew a deep breath. "I am H-his *Eminence's* prothonotary." He smoothed his sopping robe as if suddenly conscious of his bedraggled appearance. "H-his E-e-eminence desired me to *l-locate* a particular y-y-young woman—"

Auk trained his needler on him.

"Y-you. Tall, red hair, and so forth. I *didn't* know it was you, Savage Scylla." He swallowed and added desperately, "H-his interest was ha-wholly friendly. H-his Eminence—"

"You are to be congratulated, Patera." Chenille's voice was smooth and almost courteous; she had an alarming habit of remaining immobile in attitudes no mere human being could have maintained for more than a few seconds, and she did so now, her pivoting head and glaring eyes seemingly the only living parts of her lush body. "You have succeeded splendidly. Perhaps you identified the previous occupant? You say this woman," she touched her chest, "was described to you?"

The augur nodded rapidly. "*Yes,* Savage Scylla. Fiery hair and—and s-skill with a *knife* and . . ."

Chenille's eyes had rolled backward into her skull until only the whites could be seen. "Your Eminence. Silk addressed him like that. You attended my graduation, Your Eminence."

The augur said hurriedly, "He wished me to *assure* her of our submission. Of the *Chapter's.* To offer our *advice* and *support,* and declare our *loyalty.* Information H-his Eminence had received indicated that—that you'd g-gone to the lake with Patera Silk. His Eminence is Patera's *superior.* He—I—we declare our *undying loyalty,* Savage Scylla."

"To Kypris."

There was that in Chenille's tone which rendered the words unanswerable. The augur could only stare at her.

"Bad man," Oreb announced virtuously. "Cut?"

"An augur? I hadn't considered it, but . . ."

The old fisherman hawked and spat. "If'n you're really Scaldin' Scylla, ma'am, I'd like ter say somethin'." He wiped his grizzled mustache on the back of his hand.

"I am Scylla. Be quick. We must sacrifice now if we're to sacrifice at all. My slave will arrive soon."

"I been prayin' and sacrificin' ter you all my life. You an' your pa's the only ones us fishermen pay mind to. I'm not sayin' you owe me anythin'. I got my boat, an' I had a wife and raised the boys. Always made a livin'. What I'm wantin' ter say is when I go you'll be losin' one of your own. It's goin' ter be one less here for you an' ol' Pas. Maybe you figure I took you 'cause the big feller's got his stitchin' gun. Fact is, I'd of took you anywheres on the lake soon as I knowed who you was."

"I must reintegrate myself in Mainframe," Chenille told him. "There may be new developments. Are you through?"

"Pretty nigh. The big feller, he does anythin' you want him, just like what I'd do in his britches. Only he b'longs ter Hierax, ma'am."

Auk started.

"Not ter you nor your pa neither. He maybe don't know it hisself, but he do. His bird an' that needler he's got, an' the big hanger-sword, an' his knife what he tells he's got in his boots, they all show it. You got ter know it better'n me. As fer this augur you're gettin' set ter offer me up, I fished him out o' the lake last night, and t'other day I seen another fished up. They do say—"

"Describe him."

"Yes'm." The old fisherman considered. "You was down in the cuddy then, I guess. When they'd got him out, I seen him look over our way. Lookin' at the bird, seemed like. Pretty young. Tall as the big feller. Yeller hair—"

"Silk!" Auk exclaimed.

"Pulled out of the water, you said?"

The fisherman nodded. "Scup's boat. I've knowed Scup thirty year."

"You may be right," Chenille told him. "You may be too valuable to sacrifice, and one old man is nothing anyway."

She strode toward the Window before whirling to face them again. "Pay attention to what I say, all three of you. In a moment, I'll depart from this whore. My divine essence will pass from her into the Sacred Window that I have caused to be put here, and be reintegrated with my greater divine self in Mainframe. Do you understand me? All of you?"

Auk nodded mutely. The augur knelt, his head bowed.

"Kypris, my mortal enemy and the enemy of my mother, my brothers, and my sisters—of our whole family, in fact—has been mischief-making here in Viron. Already she seems to have won to her side the meager fool this idiot—What's your name, anyhow?"

"Incus, Savage Scylla. I-I'm Patera *Incus.*"

"The fool this idiot calls His Eminence. I don't doubt that she intends to win over my Prolocutor and my Ayuntamiento too, if she can. The four of you, I include the whore after I'm through with her, are to see to it that she fails. Use threats and force and the power of my name. Kill anyone you need to, it won't be held against you. If Kypris returns, do something to get my attention. Fifty or a hundred children should catch my eye, and Viron's got plenty to spare."

She glared at each man in turn. "Questions? Let's hear them now, if there are any. Objections?"

Oreb croaked in his throat, one bright black eye trained warily upon her.

"Good. You're my prophets henceforth. Keep Viron loyal, and you'll have my favor. Believe nothing Kypris may tell you. My slave should be here shortly. He'll carry you there, and assist you. See the Prolocutor and talk to the commissioners in the Juzgado. Tell everyone who'll listen about me. Tell them everything I've said to you. I'd hoped that the Ayuntamiento's boat would be in this dock. It usually is. It isn't today, so you'll have to see the councillors for me. The old man can bring you back here. Tell them I mean to sink their boat and drown them all in my lake if my city goes over to Kypris."

Incus stammered, "A *th-theophany,* S-savage S-s-scylla, w-would—"

"Not convince your councillors. They think themselves too wise. Theophanies may be useful, however. Reintegrated, I may consider them."

She strode to the damp stone altar and sprang effortlessly to its top. "I had this built so your Ayuntamiento might offer private sacrifices and, when I chose, confer with me. Not a trace of ash! They'll pay for that as well.

"You." She pointed to Auk. "This augur Silk's plotting to overthrow them for Kypris. Help him, but show him where his duty lies. If he can't see it, kill him. You've my permission to rule yourself as my Caldé in that case. The idiot here can be Prolocutor under similar circumstances, I suppose."

She faced the Window and knelt. Auk knelt, too, pulling the fisherman down. (Incus was kneeling already.) Clearing his throat, Auk began the prayer that he had bungled upon the Pilgrims' Way, when Scylla had revealed her divine identity. "Behold us, lovely Scylla, woman of the waters—"

Incus and the fisherman joined in. "Behold our love and our need for thee. Cleanse us, O Scylla!"

At the name of the goddess, Chenille threw high her arms with a strangled cry. The dancing colors called the Holy Hues filled the Sacred Window with chestnut and brown, aquamarine, orange, scarlet, and yellow, cerulean blue and a curious shade of rose brushed with drab. And for a moment it seemed to Auk that he glimpsed the sneering features of a girl a year or two from womanhood.

Chenille trembled violently and went limp, slumping to the altar top and rolling off to fall to the dark and slimy stone of the quay.

Oreb fluttered over to her. "God go?"

The girl's face—if it had been a face—vanished into a wall of green water, like an onrushing wave. The Holy Hues returned, first as sunsparkles on the wave, then claiming the entire Window and filling it with their whirling ballet before fading back to luminescent gray.

"I think so," Auk said. He rose, and discovered that his needler was still in his hand; he thrust it beneath his tunic, and asked tentatively, "You all right, Jugs?"

Chenille moaned.

He lifted her into a sitting position. "You banged your head on the rock, Jugs, but you're going to be all right." Eager to do something for her, but unsure what he should do, he called, "You! Patera! Get some water."

"She throw?"

Auk swung at Oreb, who hopped agilely to one side.

"Hackum?"

"Yeah, Jugs. Right here." He squeezed her gently with the arm that supported her, conscious of the febrile heat of her sunburned skin.

"You came back. Hackum, I'm so glad."

The old fisherman coughed, striving to keep his eyes from Chenille's breasts. "Mebbe it'd be better if me an' him stayed on the boat awhile?"

"We're all going on your boat," Auk told him. He picked up Chenille.

Incus, a battered tin cup of water in his hand, asked, "You intend to *disobey?*"

Auk dodged. "She said to go to the Juzgado. We got to get back to Limna, then there's wagons to the city."

"She was sending someone, sending her slave she said, to take us there." Incus raised the cup and sipped. "She also said *I* was to be *Prolocutor.*"

The old fisherman scowled. "This feller she's sendin', he'll have a boat o' his own. Have ter, ter git out here. What becomes o' mine if we go off with him? She said fer me ter fetch the rest back ter see them councillors, didn't she? How'm I s'posed ter do that if I ain't got my boat?"

Oreb fluttered onto Auk's shoulder. "Find Silk?"

"You got it." Carrying Chenille, Auk strode across the quay to eye the open water between it and the boat; it was one thing to spring from the gunnel to the quay, another to jump from the quay to the boat while carrying a woman taller than most. "Get that rope," he snapped to Incus. "Pull it closer. You left too much slack."

Incus pursed his lips. "We cannot *possibly* disobey the instructions of the goddess."

"You can stay here and wait for whoever she's sending. Tell him we'll meet up with him in Limna. Me and Jugs are going in Dace's boat."

The old fisherman nodded emphatically.

"If *you* wish to disobey, my son, *I* will not attempt to prevent you. However—"

Something in the darkness beyond the last tank fell with a crash, and the scream of metal on stone echoed from the walls of the cavern. A new voice, deeper and louder than any merely human voice, roared, *"I bring her! Give her to me!"*

It was that of a talus larger than the largest Auk had ever seen; its virescent bronze face was cast in a grimace of hate, blinding yellow light glared from its eyes, and the oily black barrels of a flamer and a pair of buzz guns jutted from its open mouth. Behind it, the black dark at the back of the cavern had been replaced by a sickly greenish glow.

"I bring her! All of you! Give her to me!" The talus extended a lengthening arm as it rolled toward them. A steel hand the size of the altar from which she had fallen closed about Chenille and plucked her from Auk's grasp; so a child might have snatched a small and unloved doll from the arms of another doll. *"Get on my back! Scylla commands it!"*

A half dozen widely spaced rungs of bent rod laddered the talus's metal flank. Auk scrambled up with the night chough flapping ahead of him; as he gained the top, the talus's huge hand deposited Chenille on the sloping black metal before him.

"Hang on!"

Two rows of bent rods much like the steps of the ladder ran the length of the talus's back. Auk grasped one with his left hand and Chenille with his right. Her eyelids fluttered. "Hackum?"

"Still here."

Incus's head appeared as he clambered up; his sly face looked sick in the watery light. "By—by *Hierax!*"

Auk chuckled.

"You—You—Help me *up.*"

"Help yourself, Patera. You were the one that wanted to wait for him. You won. He's here."

Before Auk had finished speaking, Incus sprang onto the talus's back with astonishing alacrity, apparently impelled by the muscular arm of the fisherman, who clambered up a moment later. "You'd make a dimber burglar, old man," Auk told him.

"Hackum, where are we?"

"In a cave on the west side of the lake."

The talus turned in place, one wide black belt crawling, the other locked. Auk felt the thump of machinery under him.

Puffs of black smoke escaped from the joint between the upright thorax and long wagonlike abdomen to which they clung. It rocked, jerked, and skewed backward. A sickening sidewise skid ended in a geyser of icy water as one belt slipped off the quay. Incus clutched at Auk's tunic as their side of the talus went under, and for a dizzying second Auk saw the boat tossed higher than their heads.

The wave that had lifted it broke over them like a blow, a suffocating, freezing whorl that at once drained away; when Auk opened his eyes again Chenille was sitting up screaming, her dripping face blank with terror.

Something black and scarlet landed with a thump upon his sopping shoulder. "Bad boat! Sink."

It had not, as he saw when the talus heaved itself up onto the quay again; Dace's boat lay on its side, the mast unshipped and tossing like driftwood in the turbulent water.

Huge as a boulder, the talus's head swiveled around to glare at them, revolving until it seemed its neck must snap. *"Five ride! The small may go!"*

Auk glanced from the augur to the fisherman, and from him to the hysterical Chenille, before he realized who was meant. "You can beat the hoof if you want to, bird. He says he won't hurt you if you do."

"Bird stay," Oreb muttered. "Find Silk."

The talus's head completed its revolution, and the talus lunged forward. Yellow light glared back at them, reflected from the curved white side of the last tank, leaving the Sacred Window empty and dead looking behind them. Sallow green lights winked into being just above the talus's helmeted head, and the still-tossing waters of the channel congealed to rough stone as the cavern dwindled to a dim tunnel.

Auk put his arm around Chenille's waist. "Fancy a bit of company, Jugs?"

She wept on, sobs lost in the wind of their passage.

He released her, got out his needler, and pushed back the sideplate; a trickle of gritty water ran onto his fingers, and he blew into the mechanism. "Should be all right," he told Oreb, "soon as it dries out. I ought to put a couple drops of oil on the needles, though."

"Good girl," Oreb informed him nervously. "No shoot."

"Bad girl," Auk explained. "Bad man, too. No shoot. No go away, either."

"Bad bird!"

"Lily." Gently, he kissed Chenille's inflamed back. "Lie down if you want to. Lay your head in my lap. Maybe you can get a little sleep."

As he pronounced the words, he sensed that they came too late. The talus was descending, the tunnel angling downward, if only slightly.

The mouths of other tunnels flashed past to left and right, darker even than the damp shiprock walls. Drops of water clinging to the unchanging ceiling gleamed like diamonds, vanishing as they passed.

The talus slowed, and something struck its great bronze head, ringing it like a gong. Its buzz guns rattled and it spat a tongue of blue fire.

Chapter 2

SILK'S BACK!

"It would be better," Maytera Marble murmured to Maytera Mint, "if you did it, sib."

Maytera Mint's small mouth fell open, then firmly closed. Obedience meant obeying, as she had told herself thousands of times; obedience was more than setting the table or fetching a plate of cookies. "If you wish it, Maytera. High Hierax knows I have no voice, but I suppose I must."

Maytera Marble sighed to herself with satisfaction, a *hish* from the speaker behind her lips so soft that no ears but hers could hear it.

Maytera Mint stood, her cheeks aflame already, and studied the congregation. Half or more were certainly thieves; briefly she wondered whether even the images of the gods were safe.

She mounted the steps to the ambion, acutely conscious of the murmur of talk filling the manteion and the steady drum of rain on its roof; for the first time since early spring, fresh smelling rain was stabbing through the god gate to spatter the blackened altartop—though there was less now than there had been earlier.

Molpe, she prayed, Marvelous Molpe, for once let me have a voice. "Some—" Deep breath. "Some of you do not know me . . ."

Few so much as looked at her, and it was apparent that those who did could not hear her. How ashamed that gallant captain who had showed her his sword would be of her now!

Please Kypris! Sabered Sphigx, great goddess of war . . .

There was a strange swelling beneath her ribs; through her mind a swirl of sounds she had never heard and sights she had not seen: the rumbling hoofbeats of cavalry and the booming of big guns, the terrifying roars of Sphigx's lions, the silver voices of trumpets, and the sharp crotaline clatter of a buzz gun. A woman with a blood-stained rag about her head steadied the line: *Form up! Form up! Forward now! Forward! Follow me!*

With a wide gesture, little Maytera Mint drew a sword not even she could see. "*Friends!*" Her voice broke in the middle of the word.

Louder, girl! Shake these rafters!

"Friends, some of you don't know who I am. I am Maytera Mint, a sibyl of this manteion." She swept the congregation with her eyes, and saw Maytera Marble applauding silently; the babble of several hundred voices had stilled altogether.

"The laws of the Chapter permit sacrifice by a sibyl when no augur is present. Regrettably, that is the case today at our manteion. Few of you, we realize, will wish to remain. There is another manteion on Hat Street, a manteion well loved by all the gods, I'm sure, where a holy augur is preparing to sacrifice as I speak. Toward the market, and turn left. It's not far."

She waited hopefully, listening to the pattering rain; but not one of the five hundred or so lucky enough to have seats stood, and none of the several hundred standers in the aisles turned to go.

"Patera Silk did not return to the manse last night. As many of you know, Guardsmen came here to arrest him–"

The angry mutter from her listeners was like the growl of some enormous beast.

"That was yesterday, when Kind Kypris, in whose debt we shall always be, honored us for a second time. All of us feel certain that there has been a foolish error. But until Patera Silk comes back, we can only assume that he is under arrest. Patera Gulo, the worthy augur His Cognizance the Prolocutor sent to assist Patera Silk, seems to have left the manse early this morning, no doubt in the hope of freeing him."

Maytera Mint paused, her fingers nervously exploring the chipped stone of the ancient ambion, and glanced down at the attentive worshipers crouched on the floor in front of the foremost bench, and at the patchy curtain of watching faces that filled the narthex arch.

"Thus the duty of sacrifice devolves upon Maytera Marble and me. There are dozens of victims today. There is even an unspotted white bull for Great Pas, such a sacrifice as the Grand Manteion cannot often see." She paused again to listen to the rain, and for a glance at the altar.

"Before we begin, I have other news to give you, and most particularly to those among you who have come to honor the gods not only today but on Scylsday every week for years. Many of you will be saddened by what I tell you, but it is joyful news.

"Our beloved Maytera Rose has gone to the gods, in whose service she spent her long life. For reasons we deem good and proper, we have chosen not to display her mortal remains. That is her casket there, in front of the altar.

"We may be certain that the immortal gods are aware of her exemplary piety. I have heard it said that she was the oldest biochemical person in this quarter, and it may well have been true. She belonged to the last of those fortunate generations for which prosthetic devices remained, devices whose principles are lost even to our wisest. They sustained her life beyond the lives of the children of many she had taught as children, but they could not sustain it indefinitely. Nor would she have wished them to. Yesterday they failed at last, and our beloved sib was freed from the sufferings that old age had brought her, and the toil that was her only solace."

Some men standing in the aisles were opening the windows there; little rain if any seemed to be blowing in. The storm was over, Maytera Mint decided, or nearly over.

"So our sacrifice this morning is not merely that which we offer to the undying gods each day at this time if a victim is granted us. It is our dear Maytera Rose's last sacrifice, by which I mean that it is not just that of the white bull and the other beasts outside, but the sacrifice of Maytera herself.

"Sacrifices are of two kinds. In the first, we send a gift. In the second, we share a meal. Thus my dear sib and I dare hope it will not shock you when I tell you that my dear sib has taken for her use some of the marvelous devices that sustained our beloved Maytera Rose. Even if we were disposed to forget her, as I assure you we are not, we could never do so now. They will remind us both of her life of service. Though I know that her spirit treads the Aureate Path, I shall always feel that something of her lives on in my sib."

Now, or never.

"We are delighted that so many of you have come to honor her, as it is only right you should. But there are many more outside, men and women, children too, who would honor her if they could, but were unable to find places in our manteion. It seems a shame, for her sake and for the gods' as well.

"There is an expedient, as some of you must surely know, that can be adopted on such occasions as this. It is to move the casket, the altar, and the Sacred Window itself out into the street temporarily."

They would lose their precious seats. She half expected them to riot, but they did not.

She was about to say, "I propose—" but caught herself in time; the decision was hers, the responsibility for it and its execution hers. "That is what we will do today." The thick, leather-bound Chrasmologic Writings lay on the ambion before her; she picked it up. "Horn? Horn, are you here?"

He waved his hand, then stood so she could see him.

"Horn was one of Maytera's students. Horn, I want you to choose five other boys to help you with her casket. The altar and the Sacred Window are both very heavy, I imagine. We will need volunteers to move those."

Inspiration struck. "Only the very strongest men, please. Will twenty or thirty of the strongest men present please come forward? My sib and I will direct you."

Their rush nearly overwhelmed her. Half a minute later, the altar was afloat upon a surging stream of hands and arms, bobbing and rocking like a box in the lake as a human current bore it down the aisle toward the door.

The Sacred Window was more difficult, not because it was heavier, but because the three-hundred-year-old clamps that held it to the sanctuary floor had rusted shut and had to be hammered. Its sacred cables trailed behind it as it, too, was carried out the door, at times spitting the crackling violet fire that vouched for the immanent presence of divinity.

"You did wonderfully, sib. Just wonderfully!" Maytera Marble had followed Maytera Mint out of the manteion; now she laid a hand upon her shoulder. "Taking everything outside for a viaggiatory! However did you think of it?"

"I don't know. It was just that they were still in the street, most of them, and we were in there. And we couldn't let them in as we usually do. Besides," Maytera Mint smiled impishly, "think of all the blood, sib. It would've taken us days to clean up the manteion afterward."

There were far too many victims to pen in Maytera Marble's little

garden. Their presenters had been told very firmly that they would have
to hold them until it was time to lead them in, with the result that Sun
Street looked rather like the beast-sellers quarter in the market. How
many would be here, Maytera Mint wondered, if it hadn't been for the
rain? She shuddered. As it was, the victims and their presenters looked
soaked but cheerful, steaming in the sunshine of Sun Street.

"You're going to need something to stand on," Maytera Marble
warned her, "or they'll never hear you."

"Why not here on the steps?" Maytera Mint inquired.

"Friends . . ." To her own ears, her voice sounded weaker than ever
here in the open air; she tried to imagine herself a trumpeter, then a
trumpet. "Friends! I won't repeat what I said inside. This is Maytera
Rose's last sacrifice. I know that she knows what you've done for her,
and is glad.

"Now my sib and her helpers are going to build a sacred fire on the
altar. We will need a big one today—"

They cheered, surprising her.

"We'll need a big one, and some of the wood will be wet. But the
whole sky is going to be our god gate this afternoon, letting in Lord
Pas's fire from the sun."

Like so many brightly colored ants, a straggling line of little girls
had already begun to carry pieces of split cedar to the altar, where
Maytera Marble broke the smallest pieces.

"It is Patera Silk's custom to consult the Writings before sacrificing.
Let us do so too." Maytera Mint held up the book and opened it at random.

" 'Whatever it is we are, it is a little flesh, breath, and the ruling part.
As if you were dying, despise the flesh; it is blood, bones, and a network,
a tissue of nerves and veins. See the breath also, what kind of thing it is:
air, and never the same, but at every moment sent out and drawn in.
The third is the ruling part. No longer let this part be enslaved, no
longer let it be pulled by its strings like a marionette. No longer complain of your lot, nor shrink from the future.'

"Patera Silk has told us often that each passage in the Writings
holds two meanings at least." The words slipped out before she realized
that she could see only one in this one. Her mind groped frantically for
a second interpretation.

"The first seems so clear that I feel foolish explaining it, though it is my duty to explain it. All of you have seen it already, I'm sure. A part, two parts as the Chrasmologic writer would have it, of our dear Maytera Rose has perished. We must not forget that it was the baser part, the part that neither she nor we had reason to value. The better part, the part beloved by the gods and by us who knew her, will never perish. This, then, is the message for those who mourn her. For my dear sib and me, particularly."

Help me! Hierax, Kypris, Sphigx, please help!

She had touched the sword of the officer who had come to arrest Silk; her hand itched for it, and something deep within her, denied until this moment, scanned the crowd.

"I see a man with a sword." She did not, but there were scores of such men. "A fine one. Will you come forward, sir? Will you lend me your sword? It will be for only a moment."

A swaggering bully who presumably believed that she had been addressing him shouldered a path through the crowd. It was a hunting sword, almost certainly stolen, with a shell guard, a stag grip, and a sweeping double-edged blade.

"Thank you." She held it up, the polished steel dazzling in the hot sunshine. "Today is Hieraxday. It is a fitting day for final rites. I think it's a measure of the regard in which the gods held Maytera Rose that her eyes were darkened on a Tarsday, and that her last sacrifice takes place on Hieraxday. But what of us? Don't the Writings speak to us, too? Isn't it Hieraxday for us, as well as for Maytera? We know they do. We know it is.

"You see this sword?" The denied self spoke through her, so that she—the little Maytera Mint who had, for so many years, thought herself the only Maytera Mint—listened with as much amazement as the crowd, as ignorant as they of what her next word might be. "You carry these, many of you. And knives and needlers, and those little lead clubs that nobody sees that strike so hard. And only Hierax himself knows what else. But are you ready to pay the price?"

She brandished the hunting sword above her head. There was a white stallion among the victims; a flash of the blade or some note in her voice made him rear and paw the air, catching his presenter by surprise and lifting him off his feet.

"For the price is death. Not death thirty or forty years from now, but death now! Death today! These things say, *I will not cower to you! I am no slave, no ox to be led to the butcher! Wrong me, wrong the gods, and you die! For I fear not death or you!*"

The roar of the crowd seemed to shake the street.

"So say the Writings to us, friends, at this manteion. That is the second meaning." Maytera Mint returned the sword to its owner. "Thank you, sir. It's a beautiful weapon."

He bowed. "It's yours anytime you need it, Maytera, and a hard hand to hold it."

At the altar, Maytera Marble had poised the shallow bowl of polished brass that caught falling light from the sun. A curl of smoke arose from the splintered cedar, and as Maytera Mint watched, the first pale, almost invisible flame.

Holding up her long skirt, she trotted down the steps to face the Sacred Window with outstretched arms. "Accept, all you gods, the sacrifice of this holy sibyl. Though our hearts are torn, we, her siblings and her friends, consent. But speak to us, we beg, of times to come, hers as well as ours. What are we to do? Your lightest word will be treasured."

Maytera Mint's mind went blank—a dramatic pause until she recalled the sense, though not the sanctioned wording, of the rest of the invocation. "If it is not your will to speak, we consent to that, too." Her arms fell to her sides.

From her place beside the altar, Maytera Marble signaled the first presenter.

"This fine white he-goat is presented to . . ." Once again, Maytera Mint's memory failed her.

"Kypris," Maytera Marble supplied.

To Kypris, of course. The first three sacrifices were all for Kypris, who had electrified the city by her theophany on Scylsday. But what was the name of the presenter?

Maytera Mint looked toward Maytera Marble, but Maytera Marble was, strangely, waving to someone in the crowd.

"To Captivating Kypris, goddess of love, by her devout supplicant—?"

"Bream," the presenter said.

"By her devout supplicant Bream." It had come at last, the moment she had dreaded most of all. "Please, Maytera, if you'd do it, please . . . ?"

But the sacrificial knife was in her hand, and Maytera Marble raising the ancient wail, metal limbs slapping the heavy bombazine of her habit as she danced.

He-goats were supposed to be contumacious, and this one had long, curved horns that looked dangerous; yet it stood as quietly as any sheep, regarding her through sleepy eyes. It had been a pet, no doubt, or had been raised like one.

Maytera Marble knelt beside it, the earthenware chalice that had been the best the manteion could afford beneath its neck.

I'll shut my eyes, Maytera Mint promised herself, and did not. The blade slipped into the white goat's neck as easily as it might have penetrated a bale of white straw. For one horrid moment the goat stared at her, betrayed by the humans it had trusted all its life; it bucked, spraying both sibyls with its lifeblood, stumbled, and rolled onto its side.

"Beautiful," Maytera Marble whispered. "Why, Patera Pike couldn't have done it better himself."

Maytera Mint whispered back, "I think I'm going to be sick," and Maytera Marble rose to splash the contents of her chalice onto the fire roaring on the altar, as Maytera Mint herself had so often.

The head first, with its impotent horns. Find the joint between the skull and the spine, she reminded herself. Good though it was, the knife could not cut bone.

Next the hooves, gay with gold paint. Faster! Faster! They would be all afternoon at this rate; she wished that she had done more of the cooking, though they had seldom had much meat to cut up. She hissed, "You must take the next one, sib. Really, you must!"

"We can't change off now!"

She threw the last hoof into the fire, leaving the poor goat's legs ragged, bloody stumps. Still grasping the knife, she faced the Window as before. "Accept, O Kind Kypris, the sacrifice of this fine goat. And speak to us, we beg, of the days that are to come. What are we to do? Your lightest word will be treasured." She offered a silent prayer to Kypris, a goddess who seemed to her since Scylsday almost a larger self. "Should you, however, choose otherwise . . ."

She let her arms fall. "We consent. Speak to us, we beg, through this sacrifice."

On Scylsday, the sacrifices at Orpine's funeral had been ill-omened to say the least. Maytera Mint hoped fervently for better indicants today as she slit the belly of the he-goat.

"Kypris blesses . . ." Louder. They were straining to hear her. "Kypris blesses the spirit of our departed sib." She straightened up and threw back her shoulders. "She assures us that such evil as Maytera did has been forgiven her."

The goat's head burst in the fire, scattering coals: a presage of violence. Maytera Mint bent over the carcass once more, struggling frantically to recall what little she knew of augury—remarks dropped at odd moments by Patera Pike and Patera Silk, halfhearted lessons at table from Maytera Rose, who had spoken as much to disgust as to teach her.

The right side of the beast concerned the presenter and the augur who presided, the giver and the performer of the sacrifice; the left the congregation and the whole city. This red liver foretold deeds of blood, and here among its tangled veins was a knife, indicating the augur—though she was no augur—and pointing to a square, the square stem of mint almost certainly, and the hilt of a sword. Was she to die by the sword? No, the blade was away from her. She was to hold the sword, but she had already done that, hadn't she?

In the entrails a fat little fish (a bream, presumably) and a jumble of circular objects, necklaces or rings, perhaps. Certainly that interpretation would be welcomed. They lay close to the bream, one actually on top of it, so the time was very near. She mounted the first two steps.

"For the presenter. The goddess favors you. She is well pleased with your sacrifice." The goat had been a fine one, and presumably Kypris would not have indicated wealth had she not been gratified. "You will gain riches, jewels and gold particularly, within a short time."

Grinning from ear to ear, Bream backed away.

"For all of us and for our city, violence and death, from which good will come." She glanced down at the carcass, eager to be certain of the sign of addition she had glimpsed there; but it had gone, if it had ever existed. "That is all that I can see in this victim, though a skilled augur such as Patera Silk could see much more, I'm sure."

Her eyes searched the crowd around the altar for Bream. "The presenter has first claim. If he wishes a share in this meal, let him come forward."

Already the poor were struggling to get nearer the altar. Maytera Marble whispered, "Burn the entrails and lungs, sib!"

It was wise and good and customary to cut small pieces when the congregation was large, and there were two thousand in this one at least; but there were scores of victims, too, and Maytera Mint had little confidence in her own skill. She distributed haunches and quarters, receiving delighted smiles in return.

Next a pair of white doves. Did you share out doves or burn them whole? They were edible, but she remembered that Silk had burned a black cock whole at Orpine's last sacrifice. Birds could be read, although they seldom were. Wouldn't the giver be offended, however, if she didn't read these?

"One shall be read and burned," she told him firmly. "The other we will share with the goddess. Remain here if you would like it for yourself."

He shook his head.

The doves fluttered desperately as their throats were cut.

A deep breath. "Accept, O Kind Kypris, the sacrifice of these fine doves. And speak to us, we beg, of the times that are to come. What are we to do? Your lightest word will be treasured." Had she really killed those doves? She risked a peek at their lifeless bodies. "Should you, however, choose otherwise . . ."

She let her arms fall, conscious that she was getting more blood on her habit. "We consent. Speak to us, we beg, through this sacrifice."

Scraping feathers, skin, and flesh from the first dove's right shoulder blade, she scanned the fine lines that covered it. A bird with outspread wings; no doubt the giver's name was Swan or something of the sort, though she had forgotten it already. Here was a fork on a platter. Would the goddess tell a man he was going to eat dinner? Impossible! A minute drop of blood seemed to have seeped out of the bone. "Plate gained by violence," she announced to the presenter, "but if the goddess has a second message for me, I am too ignorant to read it."

Maytera Marble whispered, "The next presenter will be my son, Bloody."

Who was Bloody? Maytera Mint felt certain that she should recognize the name. "The plate will be gained in conjunction with the next presenter," she told the giver of the doves. "I hope the goddess isn't saying you'll take it from him."

Maytera Marble hissed, "He's bought this manteion, sib."

She nodded without comprehension. She felt hot and sick, crushed by the scorching sunlight and the heat from the blaze on the altar, and poisoned by the fumes of so much blood, as she bent to consider the dove's left shoulder blade.

Linked rings, frequently interrupted.

"Many who are chained in our city shall be set free," she announced, and threw the dove into the sacred fire, startling a little girl bringing more cedar. An old woman was overjoyed to receive the second dove.

The next presenter was a fleshy man nearing sixty; with him was a handsome younger one who hardly came to his shoulder; the younger man carried a cage containing two white rabbits. "For Maytera Rose," the older man said. "This Kypris is for love, right?" He wiped his sweating head with his handkerchief as he spoke, releasing a heavy fragrance.

"She is the goddess of love, yes."

The younger man smirked, pushing the cage at Maytera Mint.

"Well, roses stand for love," the older man said, "I think these should be all right."

Maytera Marble sniffed. "Victims in confinement cannot be accepted. Bloody, have him open that and hand one to me."

The older man appeared startled.

Maytera Marble held up the rabbit, pulling its head back to bare its throat. If there were a rule for rabbits, Maytera Mint had forgotten it; "We'll treat these as we did the doves," she said as firmly as she could.

The older man nodded.

Why, they do everything I tell them, she reflected. They accept anything I say! She struck off the first rabbit's head, cast it into the fire, and opened its belly.

Its entrails seemed to melt in the hot sunshine, becoming a surging line of ragged men with slug guns, swords, and crude pikes. The buzz gun rattled once more, somewhere at the edge of audibility, as one stepped over a burning rabbit.

She mounted the steps again, groping for a way to begin. "The message is very clear. Extraordinarily clear. Unusual."

A murmur from the crowd.

"We—mostly we find separate messages for the giver and the augur.

For the congregation and our city, too, though often those are together. In this victim, it's all together."

The presenter shouted. "Does it say what my reward will be from the Ayuntamiento?"

"Death." She stared at his flushed face, feeling no pity and surprised that she did not. "You are to die quite soon, or at least the presenter will. Perhaps your son is meant."

She raised her voice, listening to the buzz gun; it seemed strange that no one else heard it. "The presenter of this pair of rabbits has reminded me that the rose, our departed sib's nameflower, signifies love in what is called the language of flowers. He is right, and Comely Kypris, who has been so kind to us here on Sun Street, is the author of that language, by which lovers may converse with bouquets. My own nameflower, mint, signifies virtue. I have always chosen to think of it as directing me toward the virtues proper to a holy sibyl. I mean charity, humility, and—and all the rest. But *virtue* is an old word, and the Chrasmologic Writings tell us that it first meant strength and courage in the cause of right."

They stood in awed silence listening to her; she herself listened for the buzz gun, but it had ceased to sound if it had ever really sounded at all.

"I haven't much of either, but I will do the best I can in the fight to come." She looked for the presenter, intending to say something about courage in the face of death, but he had vanished into the crowd, and his son with him. The empty cage lay abandoned in the street.

"For all of us," she told them, "victory!" What silver voice was this, ringing above the crowd? "We must fight for the goddess! We will win with her help!"

How many remained. Sixty or more? Maytera Mint felt she had not strength enough for even one. "But I have sacrificed too long. I'm junior to my dear sib, and have presided only by her favor." She handed the sacrificial knife to Maytera Marble and took the second rabbit from her before she could object.

A black lamb for Hierax after the rabbit; and it was an indescribable relief to Maytera Mint to watch Maytera Marble receive it and offer it to the untenanted gray radiance of the Sacred Window; to wail and dance as she had so many times for Patera Pike and Patera Silk, to catch the lamb's blood and splash it on the altar—to watch Maytera cast the head into the fire, knowing that everyone was watching Maytera too, and that no one was watching her.

One by one, the lamb's delicate hoofs fed the gods. A swift stroke of the sacrificial knife laid open its belly, and Maytera Marble whispered, "Sib, come here."

Startled, Maytera Mint took a hesitant step toward her; Maytera Marble, seeing her confusion, crooked one of her new fingers. "Please!"

Maytera Mint joined her over the carcass, and Maytera Marble murmured, "You'll have to read it for me, sib."

Maytera Mint glanced up at the senior sibyl's metal face.

"I mean it. I know about the liver, and what tumors mean. But I can't see the pictures. I never could."

Closing her eyes, Maytera Mint shook her head.

"You must!"

"Maytera, I'm afraid."

Not so distant as it had been, the buzz gun spoke again, its rattle followed by the dull boom of slug guns.

Maytera Mint straightened up; this time it was clear that people on the edge of the crowd had heard the firing.

"Friends! I don't know who's fighting. But it would appear—"

A pudgy young man in black was pushing through the crowd, practically knocking down several people in his hurry. Seeing him, she knew the intense relief of passing responsibility to someone else. "Friends, neither my dear sib nor I will read this fine lamb for you. Nor need you endure the irregularity of sacrifice by sibyls any longer. Patera Gulo has returned!"

He was at her side before she pronounced the final word, disheveled and sweating in his wool robe, but transported with triumph. "You will, all you people—everybody in the city—have a real augur to sacrifice for you. Yes! But it won't be me. Patera Silk's back!"

They cheered and shouted until she covered her ears.

Gulo raised his arms for silence. "Maytera, I didn't want to tell you, didn't want to worry you or involve you. But I spent most of the night going around writing on walls. Talking to—to people. Anybody who'd listen, really, and getting them to do it, too. I took a box of chalk from the palaestra. *Silk for caldé! Silk for caldé! Here he comes!*"

Caps and scarves flew into the air. *"SILK FOR CALDÉ!"*

Then she caught sight of him, waving, head and shoulders emerging from the turret of a green Civil Guard floater—one that threw up dust as all floaters did, but seemed to operate in ghostly silence, so great was the noise.

"I am come!" the talus thundered again. *"In the service of Scylla! Mightiest of goddesses! Let me pass! Or perish!"* Both buzz guns spoke together, filling the tunnel with the wild shrieking of ricochets.

Auk, who had pulled Chenille flat when the shooting began, clasped her more tightly than ever. After a half minute or more the right buzz gun fell silent, then the left. He could hear no answering fire.

Rising, he peered over the talus's broad shoulder. Chems littered the tunnel as far as the creeping lights illuminated it. Several were on fire. "Soldiers," he reported.

"Men fight," Oreb amplified. He flapped his injured wing uneasily. "Iron men."

"The Ayuntamiento," Incus cleared his throat, "must have called out the *Army.*" The talus rolled forward before he had finished, and a soldier cried out as its belts crushed him.

Auk sat down between Incus and Chenille. "I think it's time you and me had a talk, Patera. I couldn't say much while the goddess was around."

Incus did not reply or meet his eyes.

"I got pretty rough with you, and I don't like doing that to an augur. But you got me mad, and that's how I am."

"Good Auk!" Oreb maintained.

He smiled bitterly. "Sometimes. What I'm trying to say, Patera, is I don't want to have to pitch you off this tall ass. I don't want to have to leave you behind in this tunnel. But I will if I got to. Back there you said you went out to the lake looking for Chenille. If you knew about her, didn't you know about me and Silk too?"

Incus seemed to explode. "How can you sit here talking about *nothing* when *men* are *dying* down there!"

"Before I asked you, you looked pretty calm yourself."

Dace, the old fisherman, chuckled.

"I was *praying* for them!"

Auk got to his feet again. "Then you won't mind jumping off to bring 'em the Pardon of Pas."

Incus blinked.

"While you're thinking that over," Auk frowned for effect and felt himself grow genuinely angry, "maybe you could tell me what your jefe wanted with Chenille."

The talus fired, a deafening report from a big gun he had not realized it possessed; the concussion of the bursting shell followed without an interval.

"You're *correct*." Incus stood up. His hand trembled as he jerked a string of rattling jet prayer beads from a pocket of his robe. "You're right, because Hierax has *prompted* you to recall *me* to my duty. I–I *go*."

Something glanced off the talus's ear and ricocheted down the tunnel, keening like a grief-stricken spirit. Oreb, who had perched on the crest of its helmet to observe the battle, dropped into Auk's lap with a terrified squawk. "Bad fight!"

Auk ignored him, watching Incus, who with Dace's help was scrambling over the side of the talus. Behind it, the tunnel stretched to the end of sight, a narrowing whorl of spectral green varied by fires.

When he caught sight of Incus crouched beside a fallen solder, Auk spat. "If I hadn't seen it . . . I didn't think he had the salt." A volley pelted the talus like rain, drowning Dace's reply.

The talus roared, and a gout of blue flame from its mouth lit the tunnel like lightning; a buzz gun supported its flamer with a long, staccato burst. Then the enormous head revolved, an eye emitting a pencil of light that picked out Incus's black robe. *"Return to me!"*

Still bent over the soldier, Incus replied, although Auk could not make out his words. Ever curious, Oreb fluttered up the tunnel toward them. The talus stopped and rolled backward, one of its extensile arms reaching for Incus.

This time his voice carried clearly. *"I'll* get back on if you take *him,* too."

There was a pause. Auk glanced behind him at the metal mask that was the talus's face.

"Can he speak!"

"Soon, I hope. I'm *trying* to repair him."

The huge hand descended, and Incus moved aside for it. Perched on the thumb, Oreb rode jauntily back to the talus's back. "Still live!"

Dace grunted doubtfully.

The hand swept downward; Oreb fluttered to Auk's shoulder. "Bird home!"

With grotesque tenderness fingers as thick as the soldier's thighs deposited him between bent handholds.

"Still live?" Oreb repeated plaintively.

Certainly it did not seem so. The fallen soldier's arms and legs, of painted metal now scratched and lusterless, lay motionless, bent at angles that appeared unnatural; his metal face, designed as a model of valor, was filled with the pathos that attaches to all broken things. Singled out inquiringly by one of Oreb's bright, black eyes, Auk could only shrug.

The talus rolled forward again as Incus's head appeared above its side. "I'm going to—he's not *dead*," the little augur gasped. "Not completely."

Auk caught his hand and pulled him up.

"I was—was just reciting the *liturgy*, you know. And I saw— The gods provide us such graces! I looked into his *wound*, there where the chest plate's sprung. They train us, you know, at the schola, to repair Sacred Windows."

Afraid to stand near the edge of the talus's back, he crawled across it to the motionless soldier, pointing. "I was quite good at it. And— And I've had occasion since to—to *help* various chems. *Dying* chems, you understand."

He took the gammadion from about his neck and held it up for Auk's inspection. "This is Pas's voided cross. You've seen it many times, I'm sure. But you can undo the catches and open up a chem with the pieces. *Watch.*"

Deftly he removed the sprung plate. There was a ragged hole near its center, through which he thrust his forefinger. "Here's where a flechette went in."

Auk was peering at the mass of mechanisms the plate had concealed. "I see little specks of light."

"Certainly you do!" Incus was triumphant. "What you're seeing is what *I* saw under this plate when *I* was bringing him the Pardon of Pas.

His primary cable had been severed, and those are the ends of the fibers. It's *exactly* as if your spinal cord were cut."

Dace asked, "Can't you splice her?"

"Indeed!" Incus positively glowed. "Such is the mercy of Pas! Such is his *concern* for us, his adopted sons, that here upon the back of this valiant talus is the one man who can *in actual fact* restore him to health and strength."

"So he can kill us?" Auk inquired dryly.

Incus hesitated, his eyes wary, one hand upraised. The talus was advancing ever more slowly now, so that the chill wind that had whistled around them before the shooting began had sunk to the merest breeze. Chenille (who had been lying flat on the slanted plate that was the talus's back) sat up, covering her bare breasts with her forearms.

"Why, ah, *no,*" Incus said at last. He took a diminutive black device rather like a pair of very small tongs or large tweezers from a pocket of his robe. "This is an opticsynapter, an *extremely* valuable tool. With it— Well, look there."

He pointed again. "That black cylinder is the triplex, the part corresponding to *your* heart. It's idling right now, but it pressurizes *his* working fluid so that he can move his limbs. The primary cable runs to his microbank—this big silver thing below the triplex—conveying instructions from his postprocessor."

Chenille asked, "Can you really bring him back to life?"

Incus looked frightened. "If he were *dead,* I could not, Superlative Scylla—"

"I'm not her. I'm me." For a moment it seemed that she might weep again. "Just me. You don't even know me, Patera, and I don't know you."

"I don't know you either," Auk said. "Remember that? Only I'd like to meet you sometime. How about it?"

She swallowed, but did not speak.

"Good girl!" Oreb informed them. Neither Incus nor Dace ventured to say anything, and the silence became oppressive.

With an arm of his gammadion, Incus removed the soldier's skull plate. After a scrutiny Auk felt sure had taken half an hour at least, he worked one end of a second gamma between two threadlike wires.

And the soldier spoke: "K-thirty-four, twelve. A-thirty-four, ninety-seven. B-thirty-four . . ."

Incus removed the gamma, telling Dace, "He was *scanning*, do you follow me? It's as if *you* were to consult a physician. He might listen to your chest and tell you to cough."

Dace shook his head. "You make this sojer well, an' he could kill all on board, like the big feller says. I says we shoves him over the side."

"He *won't*." Incus bent over the soldier again.

Chenille extended a hand to Dace. "I'm sorry about your boat, Captain, and I'm sorry I hit you. Can we be friends? I'm Chenille."

Dace took it in his own large, gnarled hand, then released it to tug the bill of his cap. "Dace, ma'am. I never did hold nothin' agin you."

"Thank you, Captain. Patera, I'm Chenille."

Incus glanced up from the soldier. "You asked whether I could restore *life*, my daughter. He isn't dead, merely unable to actuate those parts that require fluid. He's unable to move his head, his arms, and his legs, in other words. He can *speak*, as you've heard. He *doesn't* because of the shock he's suffered. That is my *considered* opinion. The problem is to reconnect all the severed fibers correctly. Otherwise, he'll move his *arms* when he *intends* to take a step." He tittered.

"I still says—" Dace began.

"In *addition*, I'll attempt to render him *compliant*. For our safety. It's not *legal*, but if we're to do as *Scylla* has commanded . . ." He bent over the recumbent soldier again.

Chenille said, "Hi, Oreb."

Oreb hopped from Auk's shoulder to hers. "No cry?"

"No more crying." She hesitated, nibbling her lower lip. "Other girls are always telling me how tough I am, because I'm so big. I think I better start trying to live up to it."

Incus glanced up again. "Wouldn't you like to borrow my *robe*, my daughter?"

She shook her head. "It hurts if anything touches me, and my back and shoulders are the worst. I've had men see me naked lots. Usually I've had a couple, though, or a pinch of rust. Rust makes it easy." She turned to Auk. "My name's Chenille, Bucko. I'm one of the girls from Orchid's."

Auk nodded, not knowing what to say, and at length said, "I'm Auk. Real pleased, Chenille."

·   ·   ·

That was the last thing he could remember. He was lying face down on a cold, damp surface, aware of pervasive pain and soft footsteps hastening to inaudibility. He rolled onto his back and sat up, then discovered that blood from his nose was dribbling down his chin.

"Here, trooper." The voice was unfamiliar, metallic and harshly resonant. "Use this."

A wad of whitish cloth was pressed into his hand; he held it gingerly to his face. "Thanks."

From some distance, a woman called, "Is that you?"

"Jugs?"

The tunnel was almost pitch dark to his left, a rectangle of black relieved by a single remote fleck of green. To his right, something was on fire—a shed or a big wagon, as well as he could judge.

The unfamiliar voice asked, "Can you stand up, trooper?"

Still pressing the cloth to his face, Auk shook his head.

There was someone nearer the burning structure, whatever it was: a short stocky figure with one arm in a sling. Others, men with dark and strangely variegated skins . . . Auk blinked and looked again.

They were soldiers, chems that he had sometimes seen in parades. Here they lay dead, their weapons beside them, eerily lit by the flames.

A small figure in black materialized from the gloom and gave him a toothy grin. "*I* had sped you to the *gods,* my son. I see *they* sent you back."

Through the cloth, Auk managed to say, "I don't remember meeting any," then recalled that he had, that Scylla had been their companion for the better part of two days, and that she had not been in the least as he had imagined her. He risked removing the cloth. "Come here, Patera. Have a seat. I got to have a word with you."

"Gladly. *I* must speak with *you,* as well." The little augur lowered himself to the shiprock floor. Auk could see the white gleam of his teeth.

"Was that really Scylla?"

"*You* know better than *I,* my son."

Auk nodded slowly. His head ached, and the pain made it difficult to think. "Yeah, only I don't know. Was it her, or just a devil pretending?"

Incus hesitated, grinning more toothily than ever. "This is *rather* difficult to explain."

"I'll listen." Auk groped his waistband for his needler; it was still in place.

"My son, if a devil were to *personate* a goddess, it would *become* that goddess, in a way."

Auk raised an eyebrow.

"Or that *god*. Pas, let us say, or *Hierax*. It would run a grave risk of merging into the total god. Or so the science of *theodaimony* teaches us."

"That's abram." His knife was still in his boot as well, his hanger at his side.

"Such are the *facts,* my son." Incus cleared his throat impressively. "That is to say, the facts as far as they can be expressed in purely *human* terms. It's there averred that devils do not often dare to personate the gods for *that very reason,* while the immortal gods, for their part, *never* stoop to personating devils."

"Hornbuss," Auk said. The man with the injured arm was circling the fire. Changing the subject, Auk asked, "That's our talus, ain't it? The soldiers got it?"

The unfamiliar voice said, "That's right, we got it."

Auk turned. There was a soldier squatting behind him. "I'm Auk," Auk said; he had reintroduced himself to Chenille with the same words, he remembered, before whatever had happened had happened. He offered his hand.

"Corporal Hammerstone, Auk." The soldier's grip stopped just short of breaking bones.

"Pleased." Auk tried to stand, and would have fallen if Hammerstone had not caught him. "Guess I'm still not right."

"I'm a little rocky myself, trooper."

"Dace and *that young woman* have been after me to have Corporal Hammerstone carry you, my son. I've *resisted* their importunities for *his* sake. He would *gladly* do it if I asked. He and I are the *best of friends.*"

"More than friends," Hammerstone told Auk; there was no hint of humor in his voice. "More than brothers."

"He would do *anything* for me. I'm tempted to *demonstrate* that, though I refrain. I prefer you to think about it for a while, always with some element of *doubt*. Perhaps I'm teasing you, merely *blustering*. What do you think?"

Auk shook his head. "What I think don't matter."

"Exactly. Because you *thought* that you could throw me from that filthy little boat with *impunity*. That I'd *drown*, and you would be well rid of me. We see *now*, don't we, how *misconceived* that was. You have forfeited any right to have your opinions heard with the *slightest* respect."

Chenille strode out of the darkness carrying a long weapon with a cylindrical magazine. "Can you walk now, Hackum? We've been waiting for you."

From his perch on the barrel, Oreb added, "All right?"

"Pretty soon," Auk told them. "What's that you got?"

"A launcher gun." Chenille grounded it. "This is what did for our talus, or that's what we think. Stony showed me how to shoot it. You can look, but don't touch."

Although pain prevented Auk from enjoying the joke, he managed, "Not till I pay, huh?"

She grinned wickedly, making him feel better. "Maybe not even then. Listen here, Patera. You too, Stony. Can I tell all of you what I've been thinking?"

"Smart girl!" Oreb assured them.

Incus nodded; Auk shrugged and said, "I'm not getting up for a while yet. C'mere, bird."

Oreb hopped onto his shoulder. "Bad hole!"

Chenille nodded. "He's right. We heard some real funny noises while I was back there looking for something to shoot, and there's probably more soldiers farther on. There's more lights up that way too though, and that might help."

Hammerstone said, "Not if we want to dodge their patrols."

"I guess not. But the thing is, Oreb could say what he did about anyplace down here, and he wouldn't be wrong. Auk, what I was going to tell you is I used to have a cute little dagger that I strapped onto my leg. It had a blade about as long as my foot, and I thought it was just right. I thought your knife or your needler or whatever should fit you, like shoes. You know what I'm saying?"

He did not, but he nodded nevertheless.

"Remember when I was Scylla?"

"It's whether you remember. That's what I want to know."

"I do a little bit. I remember being Kypris, too, maybe a little better. You didn't know about that, did you, Patera? I was. I was them, but underneath I was still me. I think it's like a donkey feels when somebody rides him. He's still him, Snail or whatever his name is, but he's you, too, going where you want to and doing what you want to do. And if he doesn't want to, he gets kicked till he does it anyhow."

Oreb cocked his head sympathetically. "Poor girl!"

"So pretty soon he gives up. Kick him and he goes, pull up and he stops, not paying a lot of attention either way. It was like that with me. I wanted rust really bad, and I kept thinking about it and how shaggy tired I was. And all at once it was like I'd been dreaming. I was in a manteion in Limna, then up on an altar in a cave and fit for sod. And I didn't remember anything, or if I did I wouldn't think about it. But when I was bumping out to the shrine, up on those high rocks, stuff started coming back. About being Kypris, I mean."

Incus sighed. "*Scylla* mentioned it, my daughter, so I did know. Sharing your *body* with the *goddess of love!* How I *envy* you! It must have been *wonderful!*"

"I guess it was. It wasn't nice. It wasn't fun at all. But the more I think, the more I think it really was wonderful in a abram sort of way. I'm not exactly like I used to be, either. I think when they left, the goddesses must have left some crumbs behind, and maybe they took some with them, too."

She picked up the launcher, running her fingers along the pins protruding from its magazine. "What I started to say was that after the talus got hit I saw I'd been wrong about things fitting, my dagger and all that. This stuff isn't really like shoes at all. The smaller somebody is, the bigger a shiv she needs. Scylla left that behind, I think, or maybe something I could use to see it myself.

"Anyway, Auk here plucks a dimber needler, but I doubt he needs it much. If I lived the way he does, and I close to do, I'd need it just about every day. So I found this launcher gun, and it's bigger. It was empty, but I found another one with the barrel flat where the talus had gone over it, and it was full. Stony showed me how you load and unload them."

Auk said, "I think I'll get something myself, a slug gun, anyhow. There's probably a bunch of 'em lying around."

Incus shook his head and reached for Auk's waist. "You'd better allow me to take your needler this time, my son."

At once Auk's arms were pinned from behind by a grip that was quite literally of steel.

With evident distaste, Incus lifted the front of Auk's tunic and took his needler from his waistband. "This wouldn't harm Corporal Hammerstone, but it would *kill* me, I suppose." He gave Auk a toothy smile. "Or *you,* my son."

"No shoot," Oreb muttered; it was a moment or two before Auk understood that he was addressing Chenille.

"If you see him with a *slug gun,* Corporal, you're to take it from him and break it *immediately.* A slug gun or any other such weapon."

"Ahoy, ahoy there!" The old fisherman was shouting and waving, silhouetted by orange flames from the burning talus. *"He says he's dyin'! Wants to talk to us!"*

Silk lifted himself until he could sit almost comfortably upon the turret, then waved both hands. His face was smeared with the mud of the storm, mud that was cracking and falling away now; the gaudy tunic that Doctor Crane had brought him in Limna was daubed with mud as well, and he wondered how many of those who waved and cheered and jumped and shouted around the floater actually recognized him.

SILK FOR CALDÉ!

SILK FOR CALDÉ!

Was there really to be a caldé again, and was this new caldé to be himself? Caldé was a title that his mother had mentioned occasionally, a carved head in her closet.

He looked up Sun Street, then stared. That was, surely, the silvergray of a Sacred Window, nearly lost in the bright sunshine—a Window in the middle of the street.

The wind carried the familiar odor of sacrifice—cedar smoke, burning fat, burning hair, and burning feathers, the mixture stronger than that of hot metal, hot fish-oil, and hot dust that wrapped the floater. Before the silver shimmer of the Window, a black sleeve slid down a thin arm of gray metal, and a moment later he caught sight of Maytera Marble's shining, beloved face below the waving, fleshlike hand. It seemed too good to be true.

"Maytera!" In the tumult of the crowd he could scarcely hear his own voice; he silenced them with a gesture, arms out, palms down. *"Quiet! Quiet, please!"*

The noise diminished, replaced by the troubled bleating of sheep and the angry hissing of geese; as the crowd parted before the floater, he located the animals themselves.

"Maytera! You're holding a viaggiatory sacrifice?"

"Maytera Mint is! I'm helping!"

"Patera!" Gulo was back, trotting alongside the floater, his black robe fallow with dust. "There are dozens of victims, Patera! Scores!"

They would have to sacrifice alternately if the ceremony were not to be prolonged till shadelow—which was what Gulo wanted, of course; the glory of offering so many victims, of appearing before so large a congregation. Yet he was not (as Silk reminded himself sharply) asking for more than his due as acolyte. Furthermore, Gulo could begin immediately, while he, Silk, would have to wash and change. "Stop," he called to the driver. "Stop right here." The floater settled to the ground before the altar.

Silk swung his legs from the turret to stand at the edge of the deck before it, admonished by a twinge from his ankle.

"*Friends!*" A voice he felt he should recognize at once, shrill yet thrilling, rang from the walls of every building on Sun Street. "This is Patera Silk! This is the man whose fame has brought you to the poorest manteion in the city. To the Window through which the gods look upon Viron again!"

The crowd roared approval.

"Hear him! Recall your holy errand, and his!"

Silk, who had identified the speaker at the fourth word, blinked and shook his head, and looked again. Then there was silence, and he had forgotten what he had been about to say.

An antlered stag among the waiting victims (an offering to Thelxiepeia, the patroness of divination, presumably) suggested an approach; his fingers groped for an ambion. "No doubt there are many questions you wish to ask the gods concerning these unsettled times. Certainly there are many questions I need to ask. Most of all, I wish to beg the favor of every god; and most of all to beg Stabbing Sphigx, at whose order armies march and fight, for peace. But before I ask the gods to speak to us, and before I beg their favor, I must wash and change into suitable clothes. I've been in a battle, you see—one in which good and brave men died; and before I return to our manse to scrub my face and hands and throw these clothes into the stove, I must tell you about it."

They listened with upturned faces, eyes wide.

"You must have wondered at seeing me in a Guard floater. Some of you surely thought, when you saw our floater, that the Guard intended to prevent your sacrifice. I know that, because I saw you drawing weapons and reaching for stones. But you see, these Guardsmen have endorsed a new government for Viron."

There were cheers and shouts.

"Or as I should have said, a return to the old one. They wish us to have a caldé—"

"Silk is caldé!" someone shouted.

"—and a return to the forms laid down in our Charter. I encountered some of these brave and devout Guardsmen in Limna, and because I was afraid we might be stopped by other units of the Guard, I foolishly suggested that they pretend I was their prisoner. Many of you will have anticipated what happened as a result. Other Guardsmen attacked us, thinking that they were rescuing me." He paused for breath.

"Remember that. Remember that you must not assume that every Guardsman you see is our enemy, and remember that even those who oppose us are Vironese." His eyes sought out Maytera Marble again. "I've lost my keys, Maytera. Is the garden gate unlocked? I should be able to get into the manse that way."

She cupped her hands (hands that might have belonged to a bio woman) around her mouth. "I'll open it for you, Patera!"

"Patera Gulo, proceed with the sacrifice, please. I'll join you as soon as I can."

Clumsily, Silk vaulted from the floater, trying to put as much weight as he could on his sound left leg; at once he found himself surrounded by well-wishers, some of them in green Civil Guard uniforms, some in mottled green conflict armor, most in bright tunics or flowing gowns, and more than a few in rags; they touched him as they might have touched the image of a god, in speeches blurted in a second or two declared themselves his disciples, partisans, and supporters forever, and carried him along like the rush of a rain-swollen river.

Then the garden wall was at his elbow, and Maytera Marble at the gate waving to him while the Guardsmen swung the butts of the slug guns to keep back the crowd. A voice at his ear said, "I shall come with you, My Caldé. Always now, you must have someone to protect you." It was the captain with whom he had breakfasted at four in the morning in Limna.

The garden gate banged shut behind them; on the other side Maytera Marble's key grated in the lock. "Stay here," the captain ordered a Guardsman in armor. "No one is to enter." He turned back to Silk, pointed toward the cenoby. "Is that your house, My Caldé?"

"No. It's over there. The triangular one." Belatedly, he realized that it did not appear triangular from the garden; the captain would think him mad. "The smaller one. Patera Gulo won't have locked the door. Potto got my keys."

"Councillor Potto, My Caldé?"

"Yes, Councillor Potto." Yesterday's pain rushed back: Potto's fists and electrodes, Sand's black box. Scrupulous answers that brought further blows and the electrodes at his groin. Silk pushed the memories away as he limped along the graveled path, the captain behind him and five troopers behind the captain, passing the dying fig in whose shadow the animals that were to die for Orpine's spirit had rested, the arbor in which he had spoken to Kypris and chatted with Maytera Marble, her garden and his own blackberries and wilting tomato vines, all in less time than his mind required to recognize and love them.

"Leave your men outside, Captain. They can rest in the shade of the tree beside the gate if they like." Were they doomed, too? From the deck of the floater he had talked of Sphigx; and those who perished in battle were accounted her sacrifices, just as those struck by lightning were said to have been offered to Pas.

The kitchen was exactly as he recalled it; if Gulo had eaten since moving into the manse, he had not done it here. Oreb's water cup still stood on the kitchen table beside the ball snatched from Horn. "If it hadn't happened, the big boys would have won," he murmured.

"I beg pardon, My Caldé?"

"Pay no attention—I was talking to myself." Refusing the captain's offer of help, he toiled at the pump handle until he could splash his face and disorderly yellow hair with cold water that he could not help imagining smelled of the tunnels, soap and rinse them, and rub them dry with a dish towel.

"You'll want to wash up a bit, too, Captain. Please do so while I change upstairs."

The stair was steeper than he remembered; the manse, which he had always thought small, smaller than ever. Seated on the bed that he had left unmade on Molpseday morning, he lashed its wrinkled sheets with Doctor Crane's wrapping.

He had told the crowd he would burn his tunic and loose brown trousers, but although soaked and muddy they were still practically new, and of excellent quality; washed, they might clothe some poor man for a year or more. He pulled the tunic off and tossed it into the hamper.

The azoth he had filched from Hyacinth's boudoir was in the waistband of the trousers. He pressed it to his lips and carried it to the window to examine it again. It had never been Hyacinth's, from what Crane had told him; Crane had merely had her keep it, feeling that her rooms were less likely to be searched than his own. Crane himself had received it from an unnamed khanum in Trivigaunte who had intended it as a gift for Blood. Was it Blood's, then? If so, it must be turned over to Blood without fail. There must be no more theft from Blood; he had gone too far in that direction on Phaesday.

On the other hand, if Crane had been authorized to dispose of it (as it seemed he had), it was his, since Crane had given it to him as Crane lay dying. It might be sold for thousands of cards and the money put to good use—but a moment's self-examination convinced him that he could never exchange it for money if he had any right to it.

Someone in the crowd beyond the garden wall had seen him standing at the window. People were cheering, nudging each other, and pointing. He stepped back, closed the curtains, and examined Hyacinth's azoth again, an object of severe beauty and a weapon worth a company of the Civil Guard—the weapon with which he had slain the talus in the tunnels, and the one she had threatened him with when he would not lie with her.

Had her need really been so great? Or had she hoped to make him love her by giving herself to him, as he had hoped (he recognized the kernel of truth in the thought) to make her love him by refusing? Hyacinth was a prostitute, a woman rented for a night for a few cards—that was to say, for the destruction of the mind of some forsaken, howling monitor like the one in the buried tower. He was an augur, a member of the highest and holiest of professions. So he had been taught.

An augur ready to steal to get just such cards as her body sold for. An augur ready to steal by night from the man from whom he had already bullied three cards at noon. One of those cards had bought Oreb and a cage to keep him in. Would three have bought Hyacinth? Brought her to this old three-sided cage of a manse, with its bolted doors and barred windows?

He placed the azoth on his bureau, put Hyacinth's needler and his beads beside it, and removed his trousers. They were muddier even than the tunic, the knees actually plastered with mud, though their color made their state less obvious. Seeing them, it struck him that augurs might wear black not in order that they might eavesdrop on the gods while concealed by the color of Tartaros, but because it made a dramatic background for fresh blood, and masked stains that could not be washed out.

His shorts, cleaner than the trousers but equally rain-soaked, followed them into the hamper.

Rude people called augurs butchers for good reason, and there was butchery enough waiting for him. Leaving aside his proclivity toward theft, were augurs really any better in the eyes of a god such as the Outsider than a woman like Hyacinth? Could they be better than the people they represented before the gods and still represent them? Bios and chems alike were contemptible creatures in the eyes of the gods, and ultimately those were the only eyes that mattered.

Eyes in the foggy little mirror in which he shaved caught his. As he stared, Mucor's deathly grin coalesced below them; in a travesty of coquetry, she simpered, "This isn't the first time I've seen you with no clothes on."

He spun around, expecting to see her seated on his bed; she was not there.

"I wanted to tell you about my window and my father. You were going to tell him to lock my window so I couldn't get out and bother you any more."

By that time he had recovered his poise. He got clean undershorts from the bureau and pulled them on, then shook his head. "I wasn't. I hoped that I wouldn't have to."

From beyond the bedroom door: *"My Caldé?"*

"I'll be down in a moment, Captain."

"I heard voices, My Caldé. You are in no danger?"

"This manse is haunted, Captain. You may come up and see for yourself if you like."

Mucor tittered. "Isn't this how you talk to them? In the glasses?"

"To a monitor, you mean?" He had been thinking of one; could she read his thoughts? "Yes, it's very much like this. You must have seen them."

"They don't look the same to me."

"I suppose not." With a considerable feeling of relief, Silk pulled on clean black trousers.

"I thought I'd be one for you."

He nodded in recognition of her consideration. "Just as you use your window and the gods their Sacred Windows. I had not thought of the parallel, but I should have."

Unreflected, her face in his mirror bobbed up and down. "I wanted to tell you it's no good any more, telling my father to lock my window. He'll kill you if he sees you, now. Potto said he had to, and he said he would."

The Ayuntamiento had learned that he was alive and in the city, clearly; it would learn that he was here soon, if it had not already. It would send loyal members of the Guard, might even send soldiers.

"So it doesn't matter. My body will die soon anyway, and I'll be free like the others. Do you care?"

"Yes. Yes, I do. Very much. Why will your body die?"

"Because I don't eat. I used to like it, but I don't any more. I'd rather be free."

Her face had begun to fade. He blinked, and nothing but the hollows that had been her eyes remained. A breath of wind stirred the curtains, and those hollows, too, were gone.

He said, "You must eat, Mucor. I don't want you to die." Hoping for a reply, he waited. "I know you can hear me. You have to eat." He had intended to tell her that he had wronged her and her father. That he would make amends, although Blood might kill him afterward. But it was too late.

Wiping his eyes, he got out his last clean tunic. His prayer beads and a handkerchief went into one trouser pocket, Hyacinth's needler into the other. (He would return it when he could, but that problematic moment at which they might meet again seemed agonizingly remote.) His waistband claimed the azoth; it was possible that augury would provide some hint of what he ought to do with it. He considered selling it again, and thought again of the howling face that had been so like Mucor's in his mirror, and shuddered.

Clean collar and cuffs on his second-best robe would have to do. And here was the captain, waiting at the foot of the stair and looking nearly as spruce as he had in that place—what had it been called? In the Rusty Lantern in Limna.

"I was concerned for your safety, My Caldé."

"For my reputation, you mean. You heard a woman's voice."

"A child's, I thought, My Caldé."

"You may search the upper floor if you wish, Captain. If you find a woman—or a child, either—please let me know."

"Hierax have my bones if I have thought of such a thing, My Caldé!"

"She is a child of Hierax's, certainly."

The Silver Street door was barred, as it should have been; Silk rattled the handle to make certain it was locked as well. The window was shut, and locked behind its bars.

"I can station a trooper in here, if you wish, My Caldé."

Silk shook his head. "We'll need every trooper you have and more, I'm afraid. That officer in the floater—"

"Major Civet, My Caldé."

"Tell Major Civet to station men to give the alarm if the Ayuntamiento sends its troopers to arrest me. They should be a street or two away, I suppose."

"Two streets or more, My Caldé, and there must be patrols beyond them."

"Very well, Captain. Arrange it. I'm willing to stand trial if I must, but only if it will bring peace."

"You are willing, My Caldé. We are not. Nor are the gods."

Silk shrugged and went into the sellaria. The Sun Street door was locked and barred. Two letters on the mantel, one sealed with the Chapter's knife and chalice, one with a flame between cupped hands; he dropped them into the large pocket of his robe. Both the Sun Street windows were locked.

As they hurried through the garden again and into the street, he found himself thinking of Mucor. And of Blood, who had adopted her; then of Highest Hierax, who had dropped from the sky a few hours ago for Crane and the solemn young trooper with whom he and Crane had talked in the Rusty Lantern. Mucor wanted to die, to yield to Hierax; and he, Silk, would have to save her if he could. Had it been wrong of him, then, to call her a child of Hierax?

Perhaps not. Women as well as men were by adoption the children of the gods, and no other god so suited Mucor.

Chapter 3

A TESSERA
FOR THE TUNNEL

"Bad thing," Oreb muttered, watching the burning talus to see whether it could hear him. When it did not react, he repeated more loudly, "Bad thing!"

"Shut up." Auk, too, watched it warily.

Chenille addressed it, stepping forward with her launcher ready. "We'd put out the fire if we could. If we had blankets or—or anything we could beat it out with."

"I die! Hear me!"

"I just wanted to say we're sorry." She glanced back at the four men, and Dace nodded.

"I serve Scylla! You must!"

Incus drew himself up to his full height. "You may rely upon *me* to do everything in my power to carry out the goddess's will. I speak here for my friend Corporal Hammerstone, as well as for myself."

"The Ayuntamiento has betrayed her! Destroy it!"

Hammerstone snapped to attention. "Request permission to speak, Talus."

The slender black barrel of one buzz gun trembled and the gun fired, its burst whistling five cubits above their heads and sending screaming ricochets far down the tunnel.

"Maybe you better not," Auk whispered. He raised his voice. "Scylla told us Patera Silk was trying to overthrow them, and ordered us to help him. We will if we can. That's Chenille and me, and his bird."

"Tell the Juzgado!"

"Right, she said to." Dace and Incus nodded.

A tongue of flame licked the talus's cheek. *"The tessera! Thetis! To the subcellar . . . "* An interior explosion rocked it.

Needlessly, Auk shouted, "Get back!" As they fled down the tunnel, fire veiled the great metal face.

"She's done fer now! She's goin' down!" Dace was slower even than Auk, who tottered on legs weaker than he had known since infancy.

A second muffled explosion, then silence except for the sibilation of the flames. Hammerstone, who had been matching strides with Auk, broke step to snatch up a slug gun. "This was a sleeper's," he told Auk cheerfully. "See how shiny the receiver is? Probably never been fired. I couldn't go back for mine 'cause I was supposed to watch you. Mine's had about five thousand rounds through it." He put the new slug gun to his shoulder and sighted down the barrel.

Oreb squawked, and Auk said, "Careful there! You might hit Jugs."

"Safety's on." Hammerstone lowered the gun. "You knew her before, huh?"

Auk nodded and slowed his pace enough to allow Dace to catch up. "Since spring, I guess it was."

"I had a girl myself once," Hammerstone told him. "She was a housemaid, but you'd never have guessed it to look at her. Pretty as a picture."

Auk nodded. "What happened?"

"I had to go on reserve. I went to sleep, and when I woke up I wasn't stationed in the city any more. Maybe I should've gone looking for Moly." He shrugged. "Only I figured by then she'd found somebody else. Just about all of them had."

"You'll find somebody, too, if you want to," Auk assured him. He paused to look back up the tunnel; the talus was still in view but seemed remote, a dot of orange fire no larger than the closest light. "You could be dead," he said. "Suppose Patera hadn't fixed you up?"

Hammerstone shook his head. "I can't ever pay him. I can't even show how much I love him, really. We can't cry. You know about that?"

"Poor thing!" Oreb sounded shocked.

Auk told him, "You can't cry either, cully."

"Bird cry!"

"You meatheads are always talking about how good us chems have it," Hammerstone continued. "Good means not being able to eat, and duty seventy-four, maybe a hundred and twenty, hours at a stretch. Good means sleeping so long the *Whorl* changes, and you got to learn new procedures for everything. Good means seven or eight tinpots after every woman. You want to try it?"

"Shag, no!"

Dace caught Auk's arm. "Thanks for waitin' up."

Auk shook him off. "I can't go all that fast myself."

More cheerfully Hammerstone said, "I could carry you both, only I'm not supposed to. Patera wouldn't like it."

Dace's grin revealed a dark gap from which two teeth were missing. "Mama, don't put me on no boat!"

Auk chuckled.

"He means well," Hammerstone assured them. "He cares about me. That's one reason I'd die for him."

Auk suppressed his first thought and substituted, "Don't you think about your old knot any more? The other soldiers?"

"Sure I do. Only Patera comes first."

Auk nodded.

"You got to consider the whole setup. Our top commander ought to be the caldé. That's our general orders. Only there isn't one, and that means all of us are stuck. Nobody's got the right to give an order, only we do it 'cause we've got to, to keep the brigade running. Sand's my sergeant, see?"

"Uh-huh."

"And Schist and Shale are privates in our squad. He tells me and I tell them. Then they go sure, Corporal, whatever you say. Only none of us feels right about it."

"Girl wait?" Oreb inquired. He had been eyeing Chenille's distant, naked back.

"Sooner or later," Auk told him. "Snuff your jaw. This is interesting."

"Take just the other day," Hammerstone continued, "I was watching a prisoner. A flap broke and I tried to handle it, and he got away from me. If everything was right, I'd've lost my stripes over that, see? Only it's not, so all I got was a chewing out from Sand and double from the major. Why's that?" He leveled a pipe-sized finger at Auk, who shook his head.

"I'll tell you. 'Cause both of them know Sand wasn't authorized to give anybody orders in the first place, and I could've told him dee-dee if I'd wanted to."

"Dee-dee?" Oreb peered quizzically at Hammerstone.

"You want the straight screw? I felt pretty bad when it happened, but it was a lot worse when I was talking to them. Not 'cause of anything they said. I've heard all that till I could sing it. 'Cause they didn't take my stripes. I never thought I'd say that, but that's what it was. They could've done it, only they didn't 'cause they knew they didn't have authority from the caldé, and I kept thinking, you don't have to tell me to wipe them off, I'll wipe them off myself. Only that would just have made them feel worse."

"I never liked working for anybody but me," Auk told him.

"You got to have somebody outside. Or anyhow I do. You feeling pretty good now?"

"Better'n I did."

"I been watching you, 'cause that's what Patera wants. And you can't hardly walk. You hit your head when the talus bought it, and we figured you were KIA. Patera sort of liked it at first. Only then, not so much. His essential nobility of character coming out. Know what I'm saying?"

Dace put in, "That big gal cryin' an' yellin' at him."

"Yeah, that too. Look here—"

"Wait a minute," Auk told them. "Chenille. She cried?"

Dace chuckled. "I felt sorrier fer her than fer you."

"She wasn't even there when I woke up!"

"She run off. I was over talkin' ter that talus, but I seen her."

"She was around when I came to," Hammerstone told Auk. "She had that launcher, only it was empty. There was another one, all smashed up, where we were. Maybe she brought it, I don't know. Anyhow, after I talked to Patera about you and a couple other things, I showed her how to disarm the bad one's magazine and load the SSMs in the good one."

Dace told Hammerstone, "She got her'n up the tunnel whilst the augur was fixin' you. This big feller, he was off watch, an' didn't nobody know rightly how bad he'd got hurt. When she come back an' seen he wasn't comin' 'round, she foundered."

Auk scratched his ear.

"You've broke your head-bone, big feller, don't let nobody tell you no different. I seen it afore. Feller on my boat got a rap from the boom. He laid in the cuddy couple nights 'fore we could fetch him ashore. He'd open the point an' talk, then sheer off down weather. We fetched him the doctor an' I guess he done all he was able but that feller died next day. You're in luck you wasn't hit no worse."

"What makes it good luck?" Hammerstone asked him.

"Why, stands ter reason, don't it? He don't want ter be dead, no more'n me!"

"All you meatheads talk like that. Only look at it. No more trouble and no more work. No more patrols through these tunnels looking everywhere for nothing and lucky to get a shot at a god. No more—"

"Shot god?" Oreb inquired.

"Yeah," Auk said. "What the shag are you talking about?"

"That's just what we call them," Hammerstone explained. "They're really animals. Kind of like a dog, only ugly where a real dog's all right, so we say it backwards."

"I've never seen any kind of shaggy animal down here."

"You haven't been down here long, either. You just think you have. There's bats and big blindworms, out under the lake especially. There's gods all around here, only there's five of us and me a soldier, and quite a few lights on this stretch. When we get to someplace darker, watch out."

"You don't mind dyin'," Dace reminded him. "That's what you says a little back."

"Now I do." Hammerstone pointed up the tunnel to Incus, a hundred cubits ahead. "That's what I was trying to tell you. Auk said he didn't need an outfit or a leader like Patera, or anything like that."

"I don't," Auk declared. "It's the shaggy truth."

"Then sit down right here. Go to sleep. Dace and me will keep going. You feel pretty sick, I can tell. You don't like walking. Well, there's no reason you've got to. I'll wait till we're about to lose sight of you, then I'll put a couple slugs in you."

"No shoot!" Oreb protested.

"I'll wait till you've settled down, see? You won't know it's coming. You'll get to thinking I'm not going to. What do you say?"

"No thanks."

"All right, here's what I been trying to get across. It doesn't sound that good to you. If I kept on about it, you'd say you had to take care of your girl, even when you're hurt so bad you can't hardly take care of yourself. Or maybe look out for your talking bird or something. Only it'd all be gas, 'cause you really don't want to, even when you know it makes more sense than what you're doing."

Sick and weak, Auk shrugged. "If you say so."

"It's not like that for us. Just sitting down somewhere down here and letting everything slow down till I go to sleep, and sleeping, with nobody ever coming by to wake me up, that sounds pretty good. It would sound all right to my sergeant, too, or the major. The reason we don't is we're supposed to look out for Viron. That means the caldé, 'cause he's the one that says what's good for Viron and what's not."

"Silk's supposed to be the new caldé," Auk remarked. "I know him, and that's what Scylla said."

Hammerstone nodded. "That'll be great if it happens, but it hasn't happened yet and maybe it never will. Only I've got Patera now, see? Right now I can walk in back of him like this and keep looking at him just about all the time, and he isn't even telling me not to look like he did at first. So I don't want to sit down and die any more than you do."

Oreb bobbed his approval. "Good! Good!"

Farther along the tunnel, Incus asked with some asperity, "Are you *sure* that's all, my daughter?"

"That's everything since Patera Silk shrived me, like I said," Chenille declared, "everything that I remember, anyhow." Apologetically she added, "That was Sphixday, so there wasn't time for a lot, and you said things I did when I was Kypris or Scylla don't count."

"Nor *do* they. The gods *can* do no evil. At least, not on *our* level." Incus cleared his throat and made sure that he was holding his prayer beads correctly. "That being the case, I bring to you, my daughter, the pardon of all the gods. In the name of *Lord Pas,* you are forgiven. In the name of *Divine Echidna,* you are forgiven. In the *glorious ever-efficacious* name of *Sparkling Scylla, loveliest* of goddesses and *firstborn* of the Seven and *ineffable patroness* of *this,* our—"

"I'm not her any more, Patera. That's Lily."

Incus, who had been seized by a sudden, though erroneous, presentiment, relaxed. "You are forgiven. In the name of *Molpe,* you are forgiven. In the name of *Tartaros,* you are forgiven. In the name of *Hierax,* you are forgiven."

He took a deep breath. "In the name of *Thelxiepeia,* you are forgiven. In the name of *Phaea,* you are forgiven. In the name of *Sphigx,* you are forgiven. And in the name of *all lesser gods,* you are forgiven. Kneel now, my daughter. I must trace the sign of addition over your head."

"I'd sooner Auk didn't see. Couldn't you just—"

"Kneel!" Incus told her severely, and by way of merited discipline added, *"Bow* your head!" She did, and he swung his beads forward and back, then from side to side.

"I hope he didn't see me," Chenille whispered as she got to her feet, "I don't think he's jump for religion."

"I dare say *not.*" Incus thrust his beads back into his pocket. "While you *are,* my daughter? If that's so, you've deceived me most completely."

"I thought I'd better, Patera. Get you to shrive me, I mean. We could've been killed back there when our talus fought the soldiers. Auk just about was, and the soldiers could have killed us afterwards. I don't think they knew we were on his back, and when he caught fire they were afraid he'd blow up, maybe. If they'd been right, we'd have got killed by that."

"They will return for their *dead,* eventually. I must say the prospect *concerns* me. What if we *encounter* them?"

"Yeah. We're supposed to get rid of the councillors?"

Incus nodded. "So *you,* possessed by Scylla, instructed us, my daughter. We are to displace *His Cognizance* as well." Incus permitted himself a smile, or perhaps could not resist it. "I am to have the office."

"You know what happens to people that go up against the Ayuntamiento, Patera? They get killed or thrown in the pits. All of them I ever heard of."

Incus nodded gloomily.

"So I thought I'd better get you to do it. Shrive me. I've got a day left, maybe. That's not a whole lot of time."

"Women, and *augurs,* are usually spared the ignominy of execution, my daughter."

"When they go up against the Ayuntamiento? I don't think so. Anyhow, I'd be locked up in the Alambrera or tossed in a pit. They eat the weak ones in the pits."

Incus, a full head shorter than she, looked up at her. "You've *never* struck me as *weak,* my daughter. And you *have* struck me, you know."

"I'm sorry, Patera. It wasn't personal, and anyhow you said it doesn't count." She glanced over her shoulder at Auk, Dace, and Hammerstone. "Maybe we'd better slow down, huh?"

"Gladly!" He had been hard put to keep up with her. "As I said, my daughter, what you did to me is not to be accounted *evil. Scylla* has every right to strike me, as a mother her child. Contrast that with that man *Auk's* behavior toward me. He seized me *bodily* and cast me into the lake."

"I don't remember that."

"Scylla did not order it, my daughter. He acted upon his own *evil impulse,* and were I to be asked to shrive him for it *again,* I am *far* from confident I could bring myself to do so. Do you find him attractive?"

"Auk? Sure."

"I confess *I* thought him a fine specimen when I first saw him. His features are *by no means* handsome, yet his *muscular masculinity* is both real and impressive." Incus sighed. "One *dreams* . . . I mean *a young woman* such as yourself, my daughter, not infrequently dreams of such a man. *Rough,* yet, one hopes, not entirely lacking inner *sensitivity.* When the *actual object* is encountered, however, one is *invariably* disappointed."

"He lumped me a couple of times while we were hoofing out to that shrine. Did he tell you about that?"

"About visiting a *shrine?"* Incus's eyebrows shot up. "Auk and yourself? No *indeed."*

"Lumping me, I meant. I thought maybe . . . Never mind. Once I sat down on one of those white rocks, and he kicked me. Kicked my leg, you know. I got pretty sore about that."

Incus shook his head, dismayed at Auk's brutality. "I should imagine *so,* my daughter. I, for one, am disinclined to criticize you for it."

"Only by-and-by I figured it out. See, Kypris had—you know, what Scylla did. It was at Orpine's funeral. Orpine's a dell I used to know." Transfering the launcher to her other hand, Chenille wiped her eyes. "I still feel really bad about her. I always will."

"Your grief does you *credit,* my daughter."

"Now she's lying in a box in the ground, and I'm walking in this one, only mine's a whole lot deeper. I wonder whether this is what being dead seems like to her? Maybe it is."

"Her *spirit* has doubtless united itself with the gods in Mainframe," Incus said kindly.

"Her spirit, sure, but what about her? What do you call this tunnel stuff? They make houses out of it, sometimes."

"The ignorant say *shiprock,* the learned *navislapis.*"

"A big shiprock box. That's what we're in, and we're just as buried as Orpine. What I was going to say is Kypris never told Auk, Patera. Not like Scylla. She told him right away, but he thought Kypris was me, and he liked her a lot. He gave me this ring, see? Then she talked to people in Limna and went in the manteion and went away. Went clear out of me and left me all alone in front of the Window. I was scared to death. I had some money and I kept buying red ribbon—"

"Brandy, my daughter?"

"Yeah. Throwing it down, trying to pretend it was rust because it's about the same color. It took a lot before I got over being scared, and then I still was, a little, way back in my head and deep down in my tripes. Then I saw Auk, this was still in Limna, so I hooked him because I was out of gelt, and I was just some drunk, some old drunk trull. So naturally he lumped me. He never did lump me as hard as Bass did once, and I'm sorry I lumped you. Aren't the gods supposed to care about us, Patera?"

"They *do,* my daughter."

"Well, Scylla didn't. She could've kept me out of the sun and kept my clothes so I wouldn't get so burned. We got hot when I was running for her and they got in our way, so she just tore them off and threw them down. My best winter gown."

Incus cleared his throat. "I have been meaning to speak to you about *that,* my daughter. Your *nudity.* Perhaps I ought to have done so when I shrove you. I foresaw, however, that you might misunderstand. I, *myself,* am sunburned, and nudity *is* wrong, you know."

"It gets bucks hot. Mine does, I mean, or Violet. I saw a buck practically jump the wall once when Violet took off her gown, and she wasn't really naked, either. She had on one of those real good bandeaus that hike up your tits when they look like they're just shoving them back."

"*Nudity,* my daughter," Incus continued gamely, "is wrong not only because it engenders concupiscent thoughts in weak men, but because it is *often* the occasion of *violent* attacks. Concupiscent thoughts are wrong in themselves, as I suggested, though they are not *seriously* evil. Violent *attacks,* on the other hand, *are* seriously evil. In the matter of concupiscent thoughts, the fault lies with you when by *intentional* nudity you give rise to them. In that of *violent attacks,* the fault lies with the *attacker.* He is obliged to *restrain* himself, no matter *how severe* a provocation is offered him. But I ask you to consider, my daughter, whether you wish *any* human spirit to be rejected by the immortal gods."

"Getting beat over the head the way they do," Chenille said positively, "that's the part I'd really hate."

Incus nodded, gratified. "There is *that,* as well. You must consider that the *men* most inclined to these attacks are *by no means* the most noble of my sex. To the *contrary!* You might actually be *killed.* Women frequently *are.*"

"I guess you're right, Patera."

"Oh, I *am,* my daughter. You may *rely* upon it. In our present company, your nudity does *little* harm, I would say. *I,* at least, am *proof* against it. So is the solder whose life I, by the grace and aid of *Fairest Phaea,* contrived to save. The captain of our boat—"

"Dace."

"Yes, *Dace.* Dace is *also* proof against it, or *nearly* so, I would imagine, by virtue of his advanced age. *Auk,* of whom I had entertained the gravest fears for your sake has *now,* by the intercession of *Divine Echidna,* who ever strives to safeguard the chastity of your sex as well as *my own,* been so severely injured that he is *most unlikely* to attack you or—"

"Auk? He wouldn't have to."

Incus cleared his throat again. "I forbear to dispute the matter, my daughter. Your reason or mine, though I *greatly* prefer *my own.* But consider this, *also.* We are to enter the *Juzgado,* using the tessera the talus supplied. Once there—"

"Is that what we're supposed to do when we get back? I guess it is, but I haven't been thinking about it, just about getting Auk to a doctor and all that. I know a good one. And sitting down and getting somebody nice to wash my feet, and some powder and rouge and some decent perfume, and drinks and something to eat. Aren't you hungry, Patera? I'm starving."

"I am not *wholly* unaccustomed to fasting, my daughter. To *revert* to our topic, we are to enter the Juzgado, or so that *talus* informed us as the claws of Hierax closed upon him. His instructions were *Scylla's,* he said, and I credit him. He told us the Ayuntamiento must be *destroyed,* as Scylla *herself* did upon that *unforgettable* occasion when she announced that she has chosen *me* her Prolocutor. The *talus* indicated that we were to announce her decision to the commissioners, and provided a *tessera* by which we are to *penetrate* the subcellar for that purpose. I must confess *I* had not known that such a subcellar existed, but presumably it does. *Consider* then, my daughter, that you will soon—"

"Thetis, that was it, wasn't it? I wondered what he meant when he said that. Does it work like a key? I've heard there are doors like that."

"*Ancient* doors," Incus informed her. "Doors constructed by *Great Pas* at the time he built the Whorl. The *Prolocutor's Palace* has such a door. Its tessera is known to me, though I may not reveal it."

"Thetis sounds like a god's name. Is it? I don't really know very much about any of the gods except the Nine. And the Outsider. Patera Silk told me a little about him."

"It is *indeed.*" Incus glowed with satisfaction. "In the *Writings,* my daughter, the mechanism by which we augurs are chosen is described in *beautiful* though *picturesque* terms. It is there said . . ." He paused. "I regret that I cannot *quote* the passage. I must paraphrase it, I'm afraid. But it is written there that *each* new year Pas brings is like a *fleet.* You are familiar with boats, my daughter. You were upon that *wretched* little fishing boat with *me,* after all."

"Sure."

"Each year, as I have indicated, is likened to a fleet of boats that are its days, *gallant* craft loaded with the *young men* of that year. Each of these day-boats is *obliged* to pass *Scylla* on its voyage to *infinity.* Some sail very near to her, while others remain at a greater *distance,* their youthful crews crowding the side *most distant* from her loving embrace. None of which *signifies.* From each of these boats, she selects the young men who most *please* her."

"I don't see—"

"*But,*" Incus continued impressively, "how is it that these *boats* pass her at all? Why do they not remain safe in harbor? Or sail *someplace else?* It is because there is a minor goddess whose function it is to direct them to her. *Thetis* is that goddess, and thus a most suitable *tessera* for us. A *key,* as you said. A *ticket* or *inscribed tile* that will admit *us* to the Juzgado, and incidentally *release* us from the cold and dark of these *horrid* tunnels."

"You think we might be close to the Juzgado now, Patera?"

Incus shook his head. "I do not know, my daughter. We traveled *some distance* on that *unfortunate* talus, and he went *very* fast. I dare *hope* we are beneath the city now."

"I doubt if we're much past Limna," Chenille told him.

Auk's head ached. Sometimes it seemed to him that a wedge had been pounded into it, sometimes it felt more like a spike; in either case, it hurt so much at times that he could think of nothing else, forcing himself to take one step forward like an automaton, one more weary step in a progression of weary steps that would never be over. When the ache subsided, as it did now and then, he became aware that he was as sick as he had ever been in his life and might vomit at any moment.

Hammerstone stalked beside him, his big, rubber-shod feet making less noise than Auk's boots as they padded over the damp shiprock of the tunnel floor. Hammerstone had his needler, and when the pain in his head subsided, Auk schemed to recover it, illusory schemes that were more like nightmares. He would push Hammerstone from a cliff into the lake, snatching his needler as Hammerstone fell, trip him as they scaled a roof, break into Hammerstone's house, find him asleep, and take his needler from Hammerstone's strong room. . . . Hammerstone falling headlong, somersaulting, rolling down the roof as he, Auk, fired needle after needle at him, viscous black fluid spurting from every wound to paint the snowy sheets and turn the water of the lake to black blood in which they drowned.

No, Incus had his needler, had it under his black robe; but Hammerstone had a slug gun, and even soldiers could be killed with slugs, which could and often did penetrate the mud-brick walls of houses, the thick bodies of horses and oxen as well as men, slugs that left horrible wounds.

Oreb fluttered on his shoulders, climbing with talon and crimson beak from one to the other. Peering through his ears Oreb glimpsed his thoughts; but Oreb could not know, no more than he himself knew, what those thoughts portended. Oreb was only a bird, and Incus could not take him from him, no more than his hanger, no more than his knife.

Dace had a knife as well. Under his tunic Dace had the old thick-bladed spear-pointed knife he had used to gut and fillet the fish they had caught from his boat, the knife that had worked so quickly, so surely, though it looked so unsuited to its task. Dace was not an old man at all, but a flunky and a toady to that old knife, a thing that carried it as Dace's old boat had carried them all when there was nothing inside it to make it go, carrying them as they might have been carried by a child's toy, toys that can shoot or fly because they are the right shape though hollow and empty as Dace's boat, as crank as the boat or solid as a potato; but Bustard would see to Dace.

His brother Bustard had taken his sling because he had slung stones at cats with it, and had refused to give it back. Nothing about Bustard had ever been fair, not his being born first though his name began with *B* and Auk's with *A,* not his dying first either. Bustard had cheated to the end and past the end, cheating Auk as he always did and cheating himself of himself. That was the way life was, the way death was. A man lived as long as you hated him and died on you as soon as you began to like him. No one but Bustard had been able to hurt him when Bustard was around; it was a privilege that Bustard reserved for himself, and Bustard was back and carrying him, carrying him in his arms again, though he had forgotten that Bustard had ever carried him. Bustard was only three years older, four in winter. Had Bustard himself been the mother that he, Bustard, professed to remember, that he, Auk, could not? Never could, never quite, Bustard with this big black bird bobbing on his head like a bird upon a woman's hat, its eyes jet beads, twitching and bobbing with every movement of his head, a stuffed bird mocking life and cheating death.

Bustards were birds, but bustards could fly—that was the Lily truth, for Bustard's mother had been Auk's mother had been Lily whose name had meant truth, Lily who had in truth flown away with Hierax and left them both; therefore he never prayed to Hierax, to Death or the God of Death, or anyhow very seldom and never in his heart, though Dace had said that he belonged to Hierax and therefore Hierax had snatched Bustard, the brother who had been a father to him, who had cheated him of his sling and of nothing else that he could remember.

"How you feelin', big feller?"

"Fine. I'm fine," he told Dace. And then, "I'm afraid I'm going to puke."

"Figure you might walk some?"

"It's all right, I'll carry him," Bustard declared, and by the timbre of his harsh baritone revealed Hammerstone the soldier. "Patera said I could."

"I don't want to get it on your clothes," Auk said, and Hammerstone laughed, his big metal body shaking hardly at all, the slug gun slung behind his shoulder rattling just a little against his metal back.

"Where's Jugs?"

"Up there. Up ahead with Patera."

Auk raised his head and tried to see, but saw only a flash of fire, a thread of red fire through the green distance, and the flare of the exploding rocket.

The white bull fell, scarlet arterial blood spilling from its immaculate neck to spatter its gilded hooves. Now, Silk thought, watching the garlands of hothouse orchids slide from the gold leaf that covered its horns.

He knelt beside its fallen head. Now if at all.

She came with the thought. The point of his knife had begun the first cut around the bull's right eye when his own glimpsed the Holy Hues in the Sacred Window: vivid tawny yellow iridescent with scales, now azure, now dove gray, now rose and red and thunderous black. And words, words that at first he could not quite distinguish, words in a voice that might almost have been a crone's, had it been less resonant, less vibrant, less young.

"Hear me. You who are pure."

He had assumed that if any god favored them it would be Kypris. This goddess's unfamiliar features overfilled the Window, her burning eyes just below its top, her meager lower lip disappearing into its base when she spoke.

"Whose city is this, augur?" There was a rustle as all who heard her knelt.

Already on his knees beside the bull, Silk contrived to bow. "Your eldest daughter's, Great Queen." The serpents around her face—thicker than a man's wrist but scarcely larger than hairs in proportion to her mouth, nose, and eyes, and pallid, hollow cheeks—identified her at once. "Viron is Scalding Scylla's city."

"Remember, all of you. You most of all, Prolocutor."

Silk was so startled that he nearly turned his head. Was it possible that the Prolocutor was in fact here, somewhere in this crowd of thousands?

"I have watched you," Echidna said. "I have listened."

Even the few remaining animals were silent.

"This city must remain my daughter's. Such was the will of her father. I speak everywhere for him. Such is my will. Your remaining sacrifices must be for her. For no one else. Disobedience invites destruction."

Silk bowed again. "It shall be as you have said, Great Queen." Momentarily he felt that he was not so much honoring a deity as surrendering to the threat of force; but there was no time to analyze the feeling.

"There is one here fit to lead. She shall be your leader. Let her step forth."

Echidna's eyes, hard and black as opals, had fastened on Maytera Mint. She rose and walked with small, almost mincing steps toward the awful presence in the Window, her head bowed. When she stood beside Silk, that head was scarcely higher than his own, though he was on his knees.

"You long for a sword."

If Maytera Mint nodded, her nod was too slight to be seen.

"You are a sword. Mine. Scylla's. You are the sword of the Eight Great Gods."

Of the thousands present, it was doubtful if five hundred had been able to hear most of what Maytera Marble, or Patera Gulo, or Silk himself had said; but everyone—from men so near the canted altar that their trouser legs were speckled with blood, to children held up by mothers themselves scarcely taller than children—could hear the goddess, could hear the peal of her voice and to a limited degree understand her, Great Echidna, the Queen of the Gods, the highest and most proximal representative of Twice-Headed Pas. As she spoke they stirred like a wheatfield that feels the coming storm.

"The allegiance of this city must be restored. Those who have suborned it must be cast out. This ruling council. Kill them. Restore my daughter's Charter. The strongest place in the city. The prison you call the Alambrera. Pull it down."

Maytera Mint knelt, and again the silver trumpet sounded. "I will, Great Queen!" Silk could hardly believe that it had emanated from the small, shy sibyl he had known.

At her reply the theophany was complete. The white bull lay dead beside him, one ear touching his hand; the Window was empty again, though Sun Street was still filled with kneeling worshipers, their faces blank or dazed or ecstatic. Far away—so distant that he, standing, could not see her—a woman screamed in an agony of rapture.

He raised his hands as he had when he had stood upon the floater's deck. "People of Viron!"

Half, perhaps, showed some sign of having heard.

"We have been honored by the Queen of the Whorl! Echidna herself—"

The words he had planned died in his throat as a searing incandescence smashed down upon the city like a ruinous wall. His shadow, blurred and diffused as shadows had always been under the beneficent radiance of the long sun, solidified to a pitch-black silhouette as sharp as one cut from paper.

He blinked and staggered beneath the weight of the white-hot glare; and when he opened his eyes again, it was no more. The dying fig (whose upper branches could be seen above the garden wall) was on fire, its dry leaves snapping and crackling and sending up a column of sooty smoke.

A gust fanned the flames, twisting and dissolving their smoke column. Nothing else seemed to have changed. A brutal-looking man, still on his knees by the casket before the altar, inquired, "W-was that more word from the gods, Patera?"

Silk took a deep breath. "Yes, it was. That was word from a god who is not Echidna, and I understand him."

Maytera Mint sprang to her feet—and with her a hundred or more; Silk recognized Gayfeather, Cavy, Quill, Aloe, Zoril, Horn and Nettle, Holly, Hart, Oont, Aster, Macaque, and scores of others. The silver trumpet that Maytera Mint's voice had become summoned all to battle. "Echidna has spoken! We have felt the wrath of Pas! To the Alambrera!"

The congregation became a mob.

Everyone was standing now, and it seemed that everyone was talking and shouting. The floater's engine roared. Guardsmen, some mounted, most on foot, called, "To me, everyone!" "To me!" "To the Alambrera!" One fired his slug gun into the air.

Silk looked for Gulo, intending to send him to put out the burning tree; he was already some distance away, at the head of a hundred or more. Others led the white stallion to Maytera Mint; a man bowed with clasped hands, and she sprang onto its back in a way Silk would not have thought possible. It reared, pawing the wind, at the touch of her heels.

And he felt an overwhelming sense of relief. "Maytera! *Maytera!*" Shifting the sacrificial knife to his left hand and forsaking the dignity augurs were expected to exhibit, he ran to her, his black robe billowing in the wind. "Take this!"

Silver, spring-green, and blood-red, the azoth Crane had given him flashed through the air as he flung it over the heads of the mob. The throw was high and two cubits to her left—yet she caught it, as he had somehow known she would.

"Press the bloodstone," he shouted, "when you want the blade!"

A moment later that endless aching blade tore reality as it swept the sky. She called, "Join us, Patera! As soon as you've completed the sacrifices!"

He nodded, and forced himself to smile.

The right eye first. It seemed to Silk that a lifetime had passed between the moment he had first knelt to extract the eye from its socket and the moment that he laid it in the fire, murmuring Scylla's short litany. By the time he had completed it, the congregation had dwindled to a few old men and a gaggle of small children watched by elderly women, perhaps a hundred persons in all.

In a low and toneless voice, Maytera Marble announced, "The tongue for Echidna. Echidna has spoken to us."

Echidna herself had indicated that the remaining victims were to be Scylla's, but Silk complied. "Behold us, Great Echidna, Mother of the Gods, Incomparable Echidna, Queen of this whorl—" (Were there others, where Echidna was not Queen? All that he had learned in the schola argued against it, yet he had altered her conventional compliment because he felt that it might be so.) "Nurture us, Echidna. By fire set us free."

The bull's head was so heavy that he could lift it only with difficulty; he had expected Maytera Marble to help, but she did not.

Vaguely he wondered whether the gold leaf on the horns would merely melt, or be destroyed by the flames in some way. It did not seem likely, and he made a mental note to make certain it was salvaged; thin though gold leaf was, it would be worth something. A few days before, he had been planning to have Horn and some of the others repaint the front of the palaestra, and that would mean buying paint and brushes.

Now Horn, the captain, and the toughs and decent family men of the quarter were assaulting the Alambrera with Maytera Mint, together with boys whose beards had not yet sprouted, girls no older, and young mothers who had never held a weapon; but if they lived . . .

He amended the thought to: if some lived.

"Behold us, lovely Scylla, wonderful of waters, behold our love and our need for thee. Cleanse us, O Scylla. By fire set us free."

Every god claimed that final line, even Tartaros, the god of night, and Scylla, the goddess of water. While he heaved the bull's head onto the altar and positioned it securely, he reflected that "by fire set us free" must once have belonged to Pas alone. Or perhaps to Kypris—love was a fire, and Kypris had possessed Chenille, whose hair was dyed flaming red. What of the fires that dotted the skylands beneath the barren stone plain that was the belly of the Whorl?

Maytera Marble, who should have heaped fresh cedar around the bull's head, did not. He did it himself, using as much as they would have used in a week before Kypris came.

The right front hoof. The left. The right rear and the left, this last freed only after a struggle. Doubtfully, he fingered the edges of his blade; they were still very sharp.

Not to read a victim as large as the bull would have been unthinkable, even after a theophany; he opened the great paunch and studied the entrails. "War, tyranny, and terrible fires." He pitched his voice as low as he dared, hoping that the old people would be unable to hear him. "It's possible I'm wrong. I hope so. Echidna has just spoken to us directly, and surely she would have warned us if such calamities awaited us." In a corner of his mind, Doctor Crane's ghost snickered. *Letters from the gods in the guts of a dead bull, Silk? You're getting in touch with your own subconscious, that's all.*

"More than possible that I'm wrong—that I'm reading my own fears into this splendid victim." Silk elevated his voice. "Let me repeat that

Echidna said nothing of the sort." Rather too late, he realized that he had yet to transmit her precise words to the congregation. He did so, interspersing every fact he could recall about her place at Pas's side and her vital role in superintending chastity and fertility. "So you see that Great Echidna simply urged us to free our city. Since those who have left to fight have gone at her behest, we may confidently expect them to triumph."

He dedicated the heart and liver to Scylla.

A young man had joined the children, the old women, and the old men. There was something familiar about him, although Silk, nearsightedly peering at his bowed head, was unable to place him. A small man, his primrose silk tunic gorgeous with gold thread, his black curls gleaming in the sunshine.

The bull's heart sizzled and hissed, then burst loudly—fulminated was the euchologic term—projecting a shower of sparks. It was a sign of civil unrest, but a sign that came too late; riot had become revolution, and it seemed entirely possible that the first to fall in this revolution had fallen already.

Indeed, laughing Doctor Crane had fallen already, and the solemn young trooper. This morning (only this morning!) he had presumed to tell the captain that nonviolent means could be employed to oust the Ayuntamiento. He had envisioned refusals to pay taxes and refusals to work, possibly the Civil Guard arresting and detaining officials who remained obedient to the four remaining councillors. Instead he had helped unleash a whirlwind; he reminded himself gloomily that the whirlwind was the oldest of Pas's symbols, and strove to forget that Echidna had spoken of "the Eight Great Gods."

With a last skillful cut he freed the final flap of hide from the bull's haunch; he tossed it into the center of the altar fire. "The benevolent gods invite us to join in their feast. Freely, they return to us the food we offer them, having made it holy. I take it that the giver is no longer present? In that case, all those who honor the gods may come forward."

The young man in the primrose tunic started toward the bull's carcass; an old woman caught his sleeve, hissing, "Let the children go first!" Silk reflected that the young man had probably not attended sacrifice since he had been a child himself.

For each, he carved a slice of raw bull-beef, presenting it on the point of the sacrificial knife—the only meat many of these children would taste for some time, although all that remained would be cooked tomorrow for the fortunate pupils at the palaestra.

If there was a tomorrow for the palaestra and its pupils.

The last child was a small girl. Suddenly bold, Silk cut her a piece substantially thicker than the rest. If Kypris had chosen to possess Chenille because of her fiery hair, why had she chosen Maytera Mint as well, as she had confided to him beneath the arbor before they went to Limna? Had Maytera Mint loved? His mind rejected the notion, and yet . . . Had Chenille, who had stabbed Orpine in a nimiety of terror, loved something beyond herself? Or did self-love please Kypris as much as any other sort? She had told Orchid flatly that it did not.

He gave the first old woman an even larger slice. These women, then the old men, then the lone young man, and finally, to Maytera Marble (the only sibyl present) whatever remained for the palaestra and the cenoby's kitchen. Where was Maytera Rose this morning?

The first old man mumbled thanks, thanking him and not the gods; he remembered then that others had done the same thing at Orpine's final rites, and resolved to talk to the congregation about that next Scylsday, if he remained free to talk.

Here was the last old man already. Silk cut him a thick slice, then glanced past him and the young man behind him to Maytera Marble, thinking she might disapprove—and abruptly recognized the young man.

For a moment that seemed very long, he was unable to move. Others were moving, but their motions seemed as labored as the struggles of so many flies in honey. Slowly, Maytera Marble inched toward him, her face back-tilted in a delicate smile; evidently she felt as he did: palaestra tomorrow was worse than problematical. Slowly, the last old man bobbed his head and turned away, gums bared in a toothless grin. Ardently, Silk's right hand longed to enter his trousers pocket, where the gold-plated needler Doctor Crane had given Hyacinth awaited it; but it would have to divest itself of the sacrificial knife first, and that would take weeks if not years.

The flash of oiled metal as Musk drew his needler blended with the duller gleam of Maytera Marble's wrists. The report was drowned by the screech of a wobbling needle, unbalanced by its passage through the sleeve of Silk's robe.

Maytera Marble's arms locked around Musk. Silk slashed at the hand that grasped the needler. The needler fell, and Musk shrieked. The old women were hurrying away (they would call it running), some herding children. A small boy dashed past Silk and darted around the casket, reappearing with Musk's needler precariously clutched in both hands and ridiculously trained upon Musk himself.

Two insights came to Silk simultaneously. The first was that Villus might easily fire by accident, killing Musk. The second, that he, Silk, did not care.

Musk's thumb dangled on a rag of flesh, and blood from his hand mingled with the white bull's. Still trying to comprehend the situation, Silk asked, "He sent you to do this, didn't he?" He pictured the flushed, perspiring face of Musk's employer vividly, although at that moment he could not recall his name.

Musk spat thick, yellow phlegm that clung to Silk's robe as Maytera Marble wrestled him toward the altar. Horribly, she bent him over the flames. Musk spat again, this time into her face, and struggled with such desperate strength that she was lifted off her feet.

Villus asked, "Should I shoot him, Maytera?" When she did not answer, Silk shook his head.

"This fine and living man," she pronounced slowly, "is presented to me, to Divine Echidna." Her hands, the bony blue-veined hands of a elderly bio, glowed crimson in the flames. "Mother of the Gods. Incomparable Echidna, Queen of the *Whorl*. Fair Echidna! Smile upon us. Send us beasts for the chase. Great Echidna! Put forth thy green grass for our kine . . ."

Musk moaned. His tunic was smoking; his eyes seemed ready to start from their sockets.

An old woman tittered.

Surprised, Silk looked for her and from her death's-head grin knew who watched through her eyes. "Go home, Mucor."

The old woman tittered again.

"Divine Echidna!" Maytera Marble concluded. "By fire set us free."

"Release him, Echidna," Silk snapped.

Musk's silk tunic was burning; so were Maytera Marble's sleeves. "Release him!"

The perverse self-forged discipline of the Orilla broke at last; Musk screamed and continued to scream, each pause and gasp followed by a scream weaker and more terrible. To Silk, tugging futilely at Maytera

Marble's relentless arms, those screams seemed the creakings of the wings of death, of the black wings of High Hierax as he flapped down the whorl from Mainframe at the East Pole.

Musk's needler spoke twice, so rapidly it seemed almost to stammer. Its needles scarred Maytera Marble's cheek and chin, and fled whimpering into the sky.

"Don't," Silk told Villus. "You might hit me. It won't do any good."

Villus started, then stared down in astonishment at the dusty black viper that had fastened upon his ankle.

"Don't run," Silk told him, and turned to come to his aid, thereby saving himself. A larger viper pushed its blunt head from Maytera Marble's collar to strike at his neck, missing by two fingers' width.

He jerked the first viper off Villus's ankle and flung it to one side, crouching to mark the punctures made by its fangs with the sign of addition, executed in shallow incisions with the point of the sacrificial knife. "Lie down and stay quiet," he told Villus. When Villus did, he applied his lips to the bleeding crosses.

Musk's screams ceased, and Maytera Marble faced them, her blazing habit slipping from her narrow shoulders; in each hand she brandished a viper. "I have summoned these children to me from the alleys and gardens of this treacherous city. Do you not know who I am?"

The familiarity of her voice left Silk feeling that he had gone mad. He spat a mouthful of blood.

"The boy is mine. I claim him. Give him to me."

Silk spat a second time and picked up Villus, cradling him in his arms. "None but the most flawless may be offered to the gods. This boy has been bitten by a poisonous snake and so is clearly unsuitable."

Twice Maytera Marble waved a viper before her face as if whisking away a fly. "Are you to judge that? Or am I?" Her burning habit fell to her feet.

Silk held out Villus. "Tell me why Pas is angry with us, O Great Echidna."

She reached for him, saw the viper she held as if for the first time, and raised it again. "Pas is dead and you a fool. Give me Auk."

"This boy's name is Villus," Silk told her. "Auk was a boy like this about twenty years ago, I suppose." When she said nothing more, he added, "I knew you gods could possess bios like us. I didn't know you could possess chems as well."

Echidna whisked the writhing viper before her face. "They are easier what mean these numbers? Why should we let you . . . ? My husband . . ."

"Did Pas possess someone who died?"

Her head swiveled toward the Sacred Window. "The prime calcula . . . His citadel."

"Get away from that fire," Silk told her, but it was too late. Her knees would no longer support her; she crumpled onto her burning habit, seeming to shrink as she fell.

He laid Villus down and drew Hyacinth's needler. His first shot took a viper behind the head, and he congratulated himself; but the other escaped, lost in the scorching yellow dust of Sun Street.

"You're to forget everything you just overheard," he told Villus as he dropped Hyacinth's needler back into his pocket.

"I didn't understand anyway, Patera." Villus was sitting up, hands tight around his bitten leg.

"That's well." Silk pulled her burning habit from under Maytera Marble.

The old woman tittered. "I could kill you, Silk." She was holding the needler that had been Musk's much as Villus had, and aiming it at Silk's chest. "There's councillors at our house now. They'd like that."

The toothless old man slapped the needler from her hand with his dripping slab of raw beef, saying sharply, "Don't, Mucor!" He put his foot on the needler.

As Silk stared, he fished a gammadion blazing with gems from beneath his threadbare brown tunic. "I ought to have made my presence known earlier, Patera, but I'd hoped to do it in private. I'm an augur too, as you see. I'm Patera Quetzal."

Auk stopped and looked back at the last of the bleared green lights. It was like leaving the city, he thought. You hated it–hated its nasty ugly ways, its noise and smoke and most of all its shaggy shitty itch for gelt, gelt for this and gelt for that until a man couldn't fart without paying. But when you rode away from it with the dark closing in on you and skylands you never noticed much in the city sort of floating around up there, you missed it right away and pulled up to look back at it from just about any place you could. All those tiny lights so far away, looking just like the lowest skylands after the market closed, over where it was night already.

From the black darkness ahead, Dace called, "You comin'?"

"Yeah. Don't get the wind up, old man."

He still held the arrow someone had shot at Chenille; its shaft was bone, not wood. A couple long strips of bone, Auk decided, running his fingers along it for the tenth or twelfth time, scarfed and glued together, most likely strips from the shinbone of a big animal or maybe even a big man. The nock end was fletched with feathers of bone, but the wicked barbed point was hammered metal. Country people hunted with arrows and bows, he had heard, and you saw arrows in the market. But not arrows like this.

He snapped it between his hands and let the pieces fall, then hurried down the tunnel after Dace. "Where's Jugs?"

"Up front ag'in with the sojer." Dace sounded as though he was still some distance ahead.

"Well, by Hierax! They almost got her the first time."

"They very nearly killed *me*." Incus's voice floated back through the darkness. "Have you forgotten *that*?"

"No," Auk told him, "only it don't bother me as much."

"No care," Oreb confirmed from Auk's shoulder.

Incus giggled. "Nor do *you* bother *me,* Auk. When I sent Corporal Hammerstone ahead of us, my *first* thought was that you would have to accompany him. Then I realized that there was no harm in *your* laggling behind. Hammerstone's task is not to *nurse you,* but to protect *me* from your *brutal* treatment."

"And thresh me out whenever you decide I need it."

"Indeed. Oh, *indeed.* But *mercy* and *forbearance* are much dearer to the *immortal gods* than sacrifice, Auk. If you wish to stay where you are, *I* will not seek to prevent you. Neither will my tall friend, who is, as we have seen, so much stronger than *yourself.*"

"Chenille ain't stronger than me, not even now. I doubt she's much stronger than you."

"But she possesses the best *weapon.* She insisted for *that* reason. For my own part, *I* was glad to have her *and* her weapon near the *redoubtable* corporal, and remote from *yourself.*"

Auk kicked himself mentally for having failed to realize that the launcher Chenille carried would flatten Hammerstone as effectively as any slug gun. Bitterly he mumbled, "Always thinking, ain't you."

"You refuse to call me *Patera,* Auk? Even *now,* you refuse me my title of respect?"

Auk felt weak and dizzy, afraid for Chenille and even for himself; but he managed to say, "It's supposed to mean you're my father, like Maytera meant this teacher I used to have was my mother. Anytime you start acting like a father, I'll call you that."

Incus giggled again. "We *fathers* are expected to curb the violent behavior of our offspring, and to teach them—I *do* hope you'll excuse a trifling bit of vulgarity—to teach them to wipe their *dirty, snotty little noses.*"

Auk drew his hanger; it felt unaccustomedly heavy in his hand, but the weight and the cold, hard metal of the hilt were reassuring. Hoarsely, Oreb advised, "No, no!"

Incus, having heard the hiss of the blade as it cleared the scabbard, called, *"Corporal!"*

Hammerstone's voice came from a distance, echoing through the tunnel. "Right here, Patera. I started dropping back as soon as I heard you and him talking."

"Hammerstone has no *light,* I fear. He tells me he lost it when he was *shot.* But he can see in the dark better than *we,* Auk. Better than *any* biological person, in fact."

Auk, who could see nothing in the pitch blackness, said, "I got eyes like a cat."

"*Do* you really. What have I in my *hand,* in that case?"

"My needler." Auk sniffed; there was a faint stench, as though someone were cooking with rancid fat.

"You're guessing." Hammerstone sounded closer. "You can't see Patera's needler 'cause he's not holding it. You can't see my slug gun either, but I see you and I got it aimed at you. Try to stick Patera with that thing, and I'll shoot you. Put it up or I'll take it away from you and bust it."

Faintly, Auk heard the big soldier's rapid steps. He was running, or at least trotting.

"Bird see," the night chough muttered in Auk's ear.

"You don't have to do that," Auk told Hammerstone. "I'm putting it up." To Oreb he whispered, "Where is he?"

"Come back."

"Yeah, I know. Is he as close as that shaggy butcher?"

"Near men. Men wait."

Auk called, "Hammerstone! Stop! Watch out!"

The running steps halted. "This better be good."

"How many men, bird?"

"Many." The night chough's bill clacked nervously. "Gods too. Bad gods!"

"Hammerstone, listen up! You can't see much better'n Patera. I know that."

"Spit oil!"

"Only I can. Between you and him, there's a bunch of culls, waiting quiet up against the wall. They got—"

The sound that filled the tunnel was half snarl and half howl. It was followed by a boom from Hammerstone's slug gun, and the ring of a hard blow on metal.

"Hit head," Oreb explained, and elaborated, "Iron man."

Hammerstone fired twice in quick succession, the echoing thunders succeeded by a series of hard, flat reports and the tortured shriekings of ricocheting needles.

"Get down!" Auk reached for a place where he thought Dace might be, but his hand met only air.

A scream. Auk shouted, "I'm coming, Jugs!" and found that he was running already, sprinting sightless through darkness thicker than the darkest night, his hanger blade probing the blackness before him like a beggar's white stick.

Oreb flapped overhead. "Man here!"

Auk slashed wildly again and again, half crouched, still advancing, his left hand groping frantically for the knife in his boot. His blade struck something hard that was not the wall, then bit deep into flesh. Someone who was not Chenille yelped with pain and surprise.

Hammerstone's slug gun boomed, close enough that the flash lit the vicinity like lightning: a naked skeletal figure reeled backward with half its face gone. Auk slashed again and again and again. The third slash met no resistance.

"Man dead!" Oreb announced excitedly. "Cut good!"

"Auk! Auk, help me! Help!"

"I'm coming!"

"Watch out!" Oreb warned, *sotto voce.* "Iron man."

"Get outta my way, Hammerstone!"

From his left, Oreb croaked, "Come Auk."

His blade rang upon metal. He ducked, certain Hammerstone would swing at him. Then he was past, and Oreb exclaiming from some distance, "Here girl! Here Auk! Big fight!"

"Auk! Get him off me!"

A new voice nearly as harsh as Oreb's demanded, "Auk? Auk from the Cock?"

"Shag yes!"

"Pas piss. Wait a minute."

Auk halted. "Jugs, you all right?"

There was no reply.

Someone moaned, and Hammerstone fired again. Auk yelled, "Don't fight unless they do, anybody. Old man, where are you?" His own fighting frenzy had drained away, leaving him weaker and sicker than ever. "Jugs?"

Oreb seconded him. "Girl say. All right? No die?"

"No! I'm not all right." Chenille gasped for breath. "He hit me with something, Auk. He knocked me down and tried to . . . You know. Get it free. I'm pretty beat up, but I'm still alive, I guess."

The darkness faded, as sudden as shadeup and as faint. A dozen stades along the tunnel, one of the crawling lights was slowly rounding a corner. As Auk watched fascinated, it came into full view, a gleaming pinprick that rendered plain all that had been concealed.

Chenille was sitting up some distance away. Seeing Auk, the naked, starved-looking man standing over her raised both hands and backed off. Auk went to her and tried to help her up, discovering (just as Silk had a moment before) that his hand was encumbered by his knife. Gritting his teeth against pain that seemed about to tear his head to bits, he stooped and returned the knife to his boot.

"He grabbed my launcher in the dark. Hit me with a club or something."

Examining her scalp in the dim light, Auk decided the dark splotch was a bleeding bruise. "You're shaggy lucky he didn't kill you."

The naked man smirked. "I could of. I wasn't tryin' to."

"I ought to kill you," Auk told him. "I think I will. Go get your launcher, Jugs."

Behind Auk, Incus said, "He intended to take her by *force,* I dare say. I warned her on that *very* point. To force *any* woman is wrong, my son. To force yourself upon a *prophetess—*" Striding forward, the little augur leveled Auk's big needler. "I *too* am of half a mind to kill you, for *Scylla's* sake."

"Patera got both gods," Hammerstone announced proudly. "A couple of you meatheads, too."

"Wait up, Patera. We got to talk to him." Auk indicated the naked man by a jab of his gory hanger. "What's your name?"

"Urus. Look, Auk, we used to be a dimber knot. Remember that sweatin' ken? You went in through the back while I kept the street for you."

"Yeah. I remember you. You got the pits. That was—" Auk tried to think, but found only pain.

"Only a couple months ago, 'n I got lucky." Urus edged closer, hands supplicating. "If I'd of knowed it was you, Auk, this whole lay would of gone different. We'd of helped you, me 'n my crew. Only I never had no way to know, see? This cully Gelada, all he said was her 'n him." He indicated Chenille and Incus by quick gestures. "A tall piece out of the piece pit 'n a runt cull with her, see, Auk? He never said nothin' about no sojer. Nothin' about you. Soon's I twigged the sojer walkin', I was fit to beat hoof, only by then he was goin' back."

Chenille began, "How come—"

"Because you ain't got anything on, Jugs." Auk sighed. "They take their clothes before they shove 'em in. I thought everybody knew that. Sit down. You too, Patera, Hammerstone. Old man, you coming?"

Oreb added his own throaty summons. "Old man!"

There was no reply from the ebbing darkness.

"Sit down," Auk told them again. "We're all tired out—shaggy Hierax knows I am—and we've probably got a long way to go before we find dinner or a place to sleep. I got a few questions for Urus here. Most likely the rest of you got some too."

"*I* do, certainly."

"All right, you'll get your chance." Auk seated himself gingerly on the cold floor of the tunnel. "First, I ought to tell you that what he said's lily, but it don't mean a lot. I know maybe a hundred culls I can trust a little, only not too much. Before they threw him in the pits, he used to be one of 'em, and that's all it ever was."

Incus and Hammerstone had sat down together as he spoke; cautiously, Urus sat, too, after receiving a permissive nod.

Auk leaned back, his eyes shut and his head spinning. "I said everybody'd get their chance. I only got this one first, then the rest of you can go ahead. Where's Dace, Urus?"

"Who's that?"

"The old man. We had a old man with us, a fisherman. His name's Dace. You do for him?"

"I didn't do for anybody." Urus might have been a league away. Hammerstone's voice: "Why'd they throw you in the pit?" Chenille's: "That doesn't matter now. What are you doing here? That's what I want to know. You're supposed to be in a pit, and you thought I'd been in one. Was it no clothes, like Auk said?" Incus: "My son, I have been *considering* this. You could *hardly* have foreseen that I, an augur, would be *armed*." "I didn't even know you was one. That cully Gelada, he said there was this long mort, and a little cull with her. That's all we knew when we started pullin' lights down." "It was this *Gelada* who shot the bone arrow at *me*, I take it." "Not at you, Patera. At her. She had a launcher, he said, so he shot, only he missed. He's got this bow pasted up out of bones, only he's not as good with it as he thinks. Auk, all I want's to get out, see? You take me up, anyplace, 'n that's it. I'll do anythin' you say."

"I was wondering," Auk murmured.

Incus: "I *fired* twenty times at least. There were *beastly animals,* and *men* as well." Chenille: "You could've killed all of us, you know that? Just shooting Auk's needler like that in the dark. That was abram." Hammerstone: "Not me." "If I had *not,* my daughter, I might very well have died *myself.* Nor was I firing at *random.* I *knew!* Though I might as well have been *blind.* That was *wonderful.* Truly *miraculous. Scylla* must have been at my side. They *rushed* upon me to kill me, all of them, but *I* killed *them* instead."

Auk opened his eyes to squint into the darkness behind them. "They killed Dace, maybe. I dunno. In a minute I'm going to see."

Chenille prepared to rise. "You feel awful, don't you? I'll go."

"Not now, Jugs. It's still dark back there. Urus, you said your culls took down lights. That was to make a dark stretch here so you could get behind us, right?"

"That's it, Auk. Gelada got up on my shoulders to pull four down, 'n Gaur run them on back. They spread out lookin' for dark. You know about that?"

Auk grunted.

"Only they don't go real fast. So we figured we'd wait flat to the side till you went by. Her, I mean, 'n this runt augur cully. That's all we figured there was." "And jump on me from in back!" "What'd you of done?" (Auk sensed, though he could not see, Urus's outspread hands.) "You shot a rocket at Gelada. If it hadn't been for the bend, you coulda done for our whole knot." "Bad man!" (That was Oreb.)

Auk opened his eyes once more. "Three or four, anyhow. Hammerstone, didn't you say something about a couple animals Patera shot?"

"Tunnel gods," Hammerstone confirmed. "Like dogs, like I told you, only not nice like dogs."

"I got to go back," Auk muttered. "I got to see what's happened to the old man, and I want to have a look at these gods. Urus, you're one, and I did for one, so that makes two. Hammerstone says Patera got a couple, that's four. Anybody else do for any?"

Hammerstone: "Me. One. And one Patera'd shot was still flopping around, so I shot him again."

"Yeah, I think I heard that. So that's five. Urus, don't give me clatter, I'm telling you. How many'd you have?"

"Six, Auk, 'n the two bufes."

"Counting you?"

"That's right, countin' me, 'n that's the lily word."

"I'm going back there," Auk repeated, "soon as the lights get there and I feel better. Anybody that wants to come with me, that's all right. Anybody that wants to go on, that's all right, too. But I'm going to look at the gods and see about Dace." He closed his eyes again.

"Good man!"

"Yeah, bird, he was." Auk waited for someone to speak, but no one did. "Urus, they threw you in the pits. Do they really throw them? I always wondered."

"Only if you get their backs up. If you don't, you can ride down in the basket."

"That's how they feed you? Put your slum in this basket and let it down?"

" 'N water jars, sometimes. Only mostly we got to catch our own when it rains."

"Keep talking."

"It ain't as bad as you think. Anyhow mine ain't. Mostly we get along, see? 'N the new ones comin' in are stronger."

"Unless they get thrown. They'd have broken legs and so forth, I guess."

"That's lily, Auk."

"Then you kill 'em right off and eat 'em while they're still fat?"

Someone (Incus, Auk decided) gasped.

"Not all the time, 'n that's lily. Not if it's somebody that somebody knows. We wouldn't of et you, see."

"So you got stuck in a pit, riding down in this basket, and you're a bully cull, or used to be. Found out they'd been digging, didn't you?" Auk opened his eyes, resolving to keep them open.

"That's it. They meant to dig out, see? Over till they fetched the big wall, then down underneath, deep as they had to. Ours is about the deepest, see? One of the real old 'uns 'n one that's near the wall. They'd dig with bones, two culls at once, 'n more carryin' it out in their hands. The rest'd watch for Hoppy 'n tramp it down when it was scattered 'round. They told me all about it."

Hammerstone asked, "You hit this tunnel when you went to go under the wall?"

Urus nodded eagerly. "They did, that's the right of it. They told me. And the shiprock—it's shiprock there, it is in lots of places—it was cracked, see? 'N they scraped the dirt out, hopin' to get through, 'n saw the lights. They got wild then, that's what they said. So they fetched rocks 'n chipped away at the shiprock, just a snowflake, like, for your wap, till you can wiggle through."

Incus grinned, exposing his protruding teeth more than ever. "I *begin* to comprehend your plight, my son. When you had *accessed* these horrid tunnels, you found yourself *unable* to reach the *surface*. Is that not correct? The fact of the matter? *Pas's* justice on you?"

"Yeah, that's it, Patera." With an ingratiating grimace, Urus leaned toward Incus, appearing almost to abase himself. "Only look at it, Patera. You shot a couple friends of mine just a minute ago, didn't you? You didn't lend 'em no horse to Mainframe, did you?"

Incus shook his head, plump cheeks quivering. "I thought it best to let the gods judge for *themselves* in this instance, my son. As I would in *yours,* as well."

"All right, I was fixin' to kill you. That's lily, see? I'm not tryin' to bilk you over it. Only now you 'n me ought to forget about all that, see Patera? Put it right behind us like what Pas'd want us to do. So how about it?" Urus held out his hand.

"My son, when you possess such a needler as *this,* I shall consent to a truce *gladly.*"

Auk chuckled. "How far you gone, Urus? Looking for a way out?"

"Pretty far. Only there's queer cheats in these tunnels, see? 'N there's various ones, too. Some's full of water, or there's cave-ins. Some ends up against doors."

Chenille said, "I can tell you something about the doors, Hackum, next time we're alone."

"That's the dandy, Jugs. You do that." Painfully, Auk clambered to his feet. Seeing that the blade of his hanger was still fouled with blood, he wiped it on the hem of his tunic and sheathed it. "Things in these tunnels, huh? What kinds of things?"

"There's sojers like him down this way." Urus pointed to Hammerstone. "They'll shoot if they see you, so you got to keep listenin' for 'em. That was how I knowed he was a sojer in the dark, see? They don't make much noise, not even when they're marchin', but they don't sound like you 'n me, neither, 'n sometimes you can hear when their guns hit up against 'em. Then there's bufes, what he calls gods, 'n they can be devils. Only this cull Eland caught a couple little 'uns 'n kind of tamed 'em, see? We had 'em with us. There's big machines, sometimes, too. Some's tall asses, only not all. Some won't row you if you don't rouse 'em."

"That all?"

"All I ever seen, Auk. There's stories 'bout ghosts 'n things, but I don't know."

"All right." Auk turned to address Incus, Hammerstone, and Chenille. "I'm going to go back there and have a look for Dace, like I said."

He strolled slowly along the tunnel toward the lingering darkness, not stopping until he reached the point at which the men and beasts shot by Incus lay. Squatting to examine them more closely, he contrived to glance toward the group he had left. No one had followed him, and he shrugged. "Just you and me, Oreb."

"Bad things!"

"Yeah, they sure are. He called 'em bufes, but a bufe's a watchdog, and Hammerstone was right. These ain't real dogs at all."

A crude bludgeon, a stone lashed with sinew to a fire-blackened bone, lay near one of the convicts Incus had shot. Auk picked it up to look at, then tossed it away, wondering how close the man had gotten to Incus before he fell. If Incus had been killed, he, Auk, would have gotten his needler back. But what might Hammerstone have done?

He examined more curiously the one he had cut down with his hanger. He had stolen the hanger originally, had worn it largely for show, had sharpened it once only because he used it now and then to cut rope or prize open drawers, had taken two lessons from Master Xiphias out of curiosity; now he felt that he possessed a weapon he had never known was his.

The radiance of the creeping lights was noticeably dimmer here; it would be some time before the section in which he had left the old fisherman was well lit. He drew his hanger and advanced cautiously. "You sing out if you see anything, bird."

"No see."

"But you can see in this, can't you? Shag, I can see, too. I just can't see good."

"No men." Oreb snapped his bill and fluttered from Auk's right shoulder to his left. "No things."

"Yeah, I don't see much either. I wish I could be sure this was the spot."

Most of all, he wished that Chenille had come. Bustard was walking beside him, big and brawny; but it was not the same. If Chenille had not cared enough to come, there was no point going—no point in anything.

How'd you get yourself into this, sprat, Bustard wanted to know.

"I dunno," Auk muttered. "I forget."

Give me the pure keg, sprat. You want me to winnow you out? If I'm going to help, I got to know.

"Well, I liked him. Patera, I mean. Patera Silk. I think the Ayuntamiento got him. I thought, well, I'll go out to the lake tonight, meet 'em in Limna, and they'll be glad to see me for the gelt, for a dimber dinner and drinks, and maybe a couple uphill rooms for us after. He won't touch her, he's a augur—"

"Bad talk!"

"He's a augur, and she'll have a couple with her dinner and feel like she owes me for it and the ring, owes for both, and it'll be nice."

What'd I tell you about hooking up with some dell, sprat?

"Yeah, sure, brother. Whatever you say. Only then he was gone and she was fuddled, and I got hot and lumped her and went looking. Only everybody say's he's going to be caldé, the new caldé—Patera. That would be somebody to know, if he pulls it off."

"Girl come!"

Never mind that. So now you're going back here, back the way we come, for this Silk butcher?

"Yeah, for Silk, because he'd want me to. And for him, too, for Dace, the old man that owned our boat."

You've snaffled a sackful like him. You don't even have his shaggy boat.

"Patera'd want me to, and I liked him."

This much?

"Hackum? Hackum!"

He's waitin', you know. That buck Gelada's waitin' for us in the dark next to the old man's body, sprat. He had a bow. Didn't any of 'em back there have no bow.

"Girl come," Oreb repeated.

Auk swung around to face her. "Stand clear, Jugs!"

"Hackum, there's something I've got to tell you, but I can't yell it."

"He can see us, Jugs. Only we can't see him. Not even the bird can see him from here where it's brighter, looking into the dark. Where's your launcher?"

"I had to leave it with Stony. Patera didn't want me to go. I think he thought I might try to kill them with it once I got off a ways."

Auk glanced to his right, hoping to consult Bustard; but Bustard had gone.

"So I said, we're not going to do anything like that. We don't hate you. But he said you did."

Auk shook his head, the pain there a crimson haze. "He hates me, maybe. I don't hate him."

"That's what I told him. He said very well my daughter—you know how he talks—leave *that* with us, and I shall believe you. So I did. I gave it to Stony."

"And came after me without it to tell me about the shaggy doors."

"Yes!" She drew nearer as she spoke. "It's important, really important, Hackum, and I don't want that cully that knocked me down to hear it."

"Is it about what the tall ass said?"

Chenille halted, dumbfounded.

"I heard, Jugs. I was right there behind you, and doors are my business. Doors and windows and walls and roofs. You think I'd miss that?"

She shook her head. "I guess not."

"I guess not, too. Stay back where you'll be safe." He turned away, hoping she had not seen how sick and dizzy he was; the darkening tunnel seemed to spin as he stared into its black maw, a pinwheel that had burned out, or the high rear wheel of a deadcoach, all ebony and black iron, rolling down a tarred road to nowhere. "I know you're in there, Gelada, and you got the old man with you. You listen here. My name's Auk, and I'm a pal of Urus's. I'm not here for a row. Only I'm a pal of the old man's, too."

His voice was trailing away. He tried to collect such strength as remained. "What we're going to do pretty soon now, we're going to go back to your pit with Urus."

"Hackum!"

"Shut up." He did not bother to look at her. "That's 'cause I can get you through one of these iron doors down here that you can't solve. I'm going to talk to 'em in your pit. I'm going to say anybody that wants out, you come with me and I'll get you out. Then we'll go to that door and I'll open it, and we'll go on out. Only that's it. I ain't coming back for anybody."

He paused, waiting for some reply. Oreb's bill clacked nervously.

"You and the old man come here and you can come with us. Or let him go and head back to the pit yourself, and you can come along with the rest if you want to. But I'm going to look for him."

Chenille's hand touched his shoulder, and he started.

"You in this, Jugs?"

She nodded and put her arm through his. They had taken perhaps a hundred more steps into the deepening darkness when an arrow whizzed between their heads; she gasped and held him more tightly than ever.

"That's just a warning," he told her. "He could have put it in us if he'd wanted to. Only he won't, because we can get him out and he can't get out himself."

He raised his voice as before. "The old man's finished, ain't he, Gelada? I got you. And you think when I find out, it's all in the tub. That's not how it'll be. Everything I said still goes. We got a augur with us, the little cull you saw with Jugs here when you shot at her. Just give us the old man's body. We'll get him to pray over it and maybe bury it somewhere proper, if we can find a place. I never knew you, but maybe you knew Bustard, my brother. Buck that nabbed the gold Molpe Cup? You want us to fetch Urus? He'll cap for me."

Chenille called, "He's telling the truth, Gelada, really he is. I don't think you're here any more, I think you ran off down the tunnel. That's what I'd have done. But if you are, you can trust Auk. You must have been down in the pit a real long time, because everybody in the Orilla knows Auk now."

"Bird see!" Oreb muttered.

Auk walked slowly into the deepening twilight of the tunnel. "He got his bow?"

"Got bow!"

"Put it down, Gelada. You shoot me, you're shooting the last chance you'll ever get."

"Auk?" The voice from the darkness might have been that of Hierax himself, hollow and hopeless as the echo from a tomb. "That your name? Auk?"

"That's me. Bustard's brother. He was older than me."

"You got a needler? Lay it down."

"I don't have one." Auk sheathed his hanger, pulled off his tunic, and dropped it to the tunnel floor. With uplifted arms, he turned in a complete circle. "See? I got the whin, and that's all I got." He drew his hanger again and held it up. "I'm leaving it right here on my gipon. You can see Jugs don't have anything either. She left her launcher back there with the soldier." Slowly he advanced into the darkness, his hands displayed.

There was a sudden glimmer a hundred paces up the tunnel. "I got a darkee," Gelada called. "Burns bufe drippin's."

He puffed the flame again, and this time Auk could hear the soft exhalation of his breath. "I should've figured," he muttered to Chenille.

"We don't like to use 'um much." Gelada stood, a stick figure not much taller than Incus. "Keep 'um shut up mostly. Wick 'bout snuffed. Culls bring 'um down 'n leave 'um."

When Auk, walking swiftly through the dark, said nothing, he repeated, "Burn drippin's when the oil's gone."

"I was thinking you'd make 'em out of bones," Auk said conversationally. "Maybe twist the wicks out of hair." He was close now, near enough to see Dace's shadowy body lying at Gelada's feet.

"We do that sometimes, too. Only hair's no good. We braid 'um out o' rags."

Auk halted beside the body. "Got him back there, didn't you? His kicks are messed some."

"Dragged 'im far as I could. 'E's a grunter."

Auk nodded absently. Silk had once told him, as the two had sat at dinner in a private room in Viron, that Blood had a daughter, and that Blood's daughter's face was like a skull, was like talking to a skull though she was living and Bustard was dead (Bustard whose face really was a skull now) was not like that. Her father's face, Blood's flabby face, was not like that either, was soft and red and sweating even when he was saying that this one or that one must pay.

But this Gelada's too was a skull, as if he and not Blood were the mort Mucor's father, was as beardless as any skull or nearly, the grayish white of dirty bones even in the stinking yellow light of the dark lantern—a talking cadaver with a little round belly, elbows bigger than its arms, and shoulders like a towel horse, the dark lantern in its hand and its small bow, like a child's bow, of bone wound with rawhide, lying at its feet, with an arrow next to it, with Dace's broad-bladed old knife next to that, and Dace's old head, the old cap it always wore gone, his wild white hair like a crone's and the clean white bones of his arm half-cleaned of flesh and whiter than his old eyes, whiter than anything.

"You crank, Auk?"

"Yeah, a little." Auk crouched beside Dace's body.

"Had the shiv on 'im." Stooping swiftly, Gelada snatched it up. "I'm keepin' it."

"Sure." The sleeve of Dace's heavy, worn blue tunic had been cut away, and strips cut from his forearm and upper arm. Oreb hopped from Auk's shoulder to scrutinize the work, and Auk warned him, "Not your peck."

"Poor bird!"

"Had a couple bits, too. You can have 'um when you get me out."

"Keep 'em. You'll need 'em up there."

From the corner of his eye, Auk saw Chenille trace the sign of addition. "High Hierax, Dark God, God of Death . . ."

"He show much fight?"

"Not much. Got behind 'im. Got my spare string 'round 'is neck. There a art to that. You know Mandrill?"

"Lit out," Auk told him without looking up. "Palustria's what I heard."

"My cousin. Used to work with 'im. How 'bout Elodia?"

"She's dead. You, too." Auk straightened up and drove his knife into the rounded belly, the point entering below the ribs and reaching upward for the heart.

Gelada's eyes and mouth opened wide. Briefly, he sought to grasp Auk's wrist, to push away the blade that had already ended his life. His dark lantern fell clattering to the naked shiprock with Dace's old knife, and darkness rushed upon them.

"Hackum!"

Auk felt Gelada's weight come onto the knife as Gelada's legs went limp. He jerked it free and wiped the blade and his right hand on his thigh, glad that he did not have to look at Gelada's blood at that moment, or meet a dead man's empty, staring eyes.

"Hackum, you said you wouldn't hurt him!"

"Did I? I don't remember."

"He wasn't going to do anything to us."

She had not touched him, but he sensed the nearness of her, the female smell of her loins and the musk of her hair. "He'd already done it, Jugs." He returned his knife to his boot, located Dace's body with groping fingers, and slung it across his shoulders. It felt no heavier than a boy's. "You want to bring that darkee? Could be good if we can figure a way to light it."

Chenille said nothing, but in a few seconds he heard the tinny rattle of the lantern.

"He killed Dace. That'd be enough by itself, only he ate him some, too. That's why he didn't talk at first. Too busy chewing. He knew we'd want the old man's body, and he wanted to fill up."

"He was starving. Starving down here." Chenille's voice was barely above a whisper.

"Sure. Bird, you still around?"

"Bird here!" Feathers brushed Auk's fingers; Oreb was riding atop Dace's corpse.

"If you were starving, you might have done the same thing, Hackum."

Auk did not reply, and she added, "Me, too, I guess."

"It don't signify, Jugs." He was walking faster, striding along ahead of her.

"I don't see why not!"

"Because I had to. He'd have done it too, like I said. We're going to the pit. I told him so."

"I don't like that, either." Chenille sounded as though she were about to weep.

"I got to. I got too many friends that's been sent there, Jugs. If some's in this pit and I can get 'em out, I got to do it. And everybody in the pit's going to find out. Maybe Patera wouldn't tell 'em, if I asked nice. Maybe Hammerstone wouldn't. Only Urus would for sure. He'd say this cull, he did for a pal of Auk's and ate him, too, and Auk never done a thing. When I got 'em out, it'd be all over the city."

A god laughed behind them, faintly but distinctly, the meaningless, humorless laughter of a lunatic; Auk wondered whether Chenille had heard it. "So I had to. And I did it. You would've too, in my shoes."

The tunnel was growing lighter already. Ahead, where it was brighter still, he could see Incus, Hammerstone, and Urus still seated on the tunnel floor, Hammerstone with Chenille's launcher across his steel lap, Incus telling his beads, Urus staring back up the tunnel toward them.

"All right, Hackum."

Here were his hanger and his tunic. He laid down Dace's corpse, sheathed the hanger, and put on his tunic again.

"Man good!" Oreb's beak snapped with appreciation.

"You been eating off him? I told you about that."

"Other man," Oreb explained. "My eyes."

Auk shrugged. "Why not?"

"Let's get out of here. Please, Hackum." Chenille was already several steps ahead.

He nodded and picked up Dace.

"I've got this bad feeling. Like he's still alive back there or something."

"He ain't." Auk reassured her.

As they reached the three who had waited, Incus pocketed his beads. "I would gladly have brought the *Pardon of Pas* to our late comrade. But his spirit has *flown.*"

"Sure," Auk said. "We were just hoping you'd bury him, Patera, if we can find a place."

"It's *Patera* now?"

"And before. I was saying Patera before. You just didn't notice, Patera."

"Oh, but I *did,* my son." Incus motioned for Hammerstone and Ursus to rise. "I would do what I *can* for our unfortunate comrade in any case. Not for your sake, my son, but for *his.*"

Auk nodded. "That's all we're asking, Patera. Gelada's dead. Maybe I ought to tell everybody."

Incus was eyeing Dace's body. "You cannot bear such a weight *far,* my son. Hammerstone will have to carry him, I suppose."

"No," Auk said, his voice suddenly hard. "Urus will. Come're, Urus. Take it."

Chapter 4

THE PLAN OF PAS

"I'm sorry you did that, Mucor," Silk said mildly.

The old woman shook her head. "I wasn't going to kill you. But I could've."

"Of course you could."

Quetzal had picked up the needler; he brushed it with his fingers, then produced a handkerchief with which to wipe off the white bull's blood. The old woman turned to watch him, her eyes widening as her death's-head grin faded.

"I'm sorry, my daughter," Silk repeated. "I've noticed you at sacrifice now and then, but I don't recall your name."

"Cassava." She spoke as though in a dream.

He nodded solemnly. "Are you ill, Cassava?"

"I . . ."

"It's the heat, my daughter." To salve his conscience, he added, "Perhaps. Perhaps it's the heat, in part at least. We should get you out of the sun and away from this fire. Do you think you can walk, Villus?"

"Yes, Patera."

Quetzal held out the needler. "Take this, Patera. You may need it." It was too large for a pocket; Silk put it in his waistband beneath his tunic, where he had carried the azoth. "Farther back, I think," Quetzal told him. "Behind the point of the hip. It will be safer there and just as convenient."

"Yes, Your Cognizance."

"This boy shouldn't walk." Quetzal picked up Villus. "He has poison in his blood at present, and that's no little thing, though we may hope there's only a little poison. May I put him in your manse, Patera? He should be lying down, and this poor woman, too."

"Women are not—but of course if Your Cognizance—"

"They are with my permission," Quetzal told him. "I give it. I also permit you, Patera, to go into the cenoby to fetch a sibyl's habit. Maytera here," he glanced down at Maytera Marble, "may regain consciousness at any moment. We must spare her as much embarrassment as we can." With Villus over his shoulder, he took Cassava's arm. "Come with me, my daughter. You and this boy will have to nurse each other for a while."

Silk was already through the garden gate. He had never set foot in the cenoby, but he thought he had a fair notion of its plan: sellaria, refectory, kitchen, and pantry on the lower floor; bedrooms (four at least, and perhaps as many as six) on the upper floor. Presumably one would be Maytera Marble's, despite the fact that Maytera Marble never slept.

As he trotted along the graveled path, he recalled that the altar and Sacred Window were still in the middle of Sun Street. They should be carried back into the manteion as soon as possible, although that would take a dozen men. He opened the kitchen door and found himself far from certain of even that necessity. Pas was dead—no less a divine personage than Echidna had declared it—and he, Silk, could not imagine himself sacrificing to Echidna again, or so much as attending a sacrifice honoring her. Did it actually matter, save to those gods, if the altar of the gods or the Window through which they so rarely condescended to communicate were ground beneath the wheels of dung carts and tradesmen's wagons?

Yet this was blasphemy. He shuddered.

The cenoby kitchen seemed almost familiar, in part, he decided, because Maytera Marble had often mentioned this stove and this woodbox, these cupboards and this larder; and in part because it was, although cleaner, very much like his own.

Upstairs he found a hall that was an enlarged version of the landing at the top of the stair in the manse, with three faded pictures decorating its walls: Pas, Echidna, and Tartaros bringing gifts of food, progeny, and prosperity (here mawkishly symbolized by a bouquet of marigolds) to a wedding; Scylla spreading her beautiful unseen mantle over a traveler drinking from a pool in the southern desert; and Molpe, perfunctorily disguised as a young woman of the upper classes, approving a much older and poorer woman's feeding pigeons.

Momentarily he paused to examine the last. Cassava might, he decided, have posed for the old woman; he reflected bitterly that the flock she fed could better have fed her, then reminded himself that in a sense they had—that the closing years of her life were brightened by the knowledge that she, who had so little left to give, could still give something.

A door at the end of the hall was smashed. Curious, he went in. The bed was neatly made and the floor swept. There was water in a ewer on the nightstand, so this was certainly Maytera Mint's room or Maytera Rose's, or perhaps the room in which Chenille had spent Scylsday night. An icon of Scylla's hung on the wall, much darkened by the votive lamps of the small shrine before it. And here was—yes—what appeared to be a working glass. This was Maytera Rose's room, surely. Silk clapped, and a monitor's bloodless face appeared in its gray depths.

"Why has Maytera Rose never told me she had this glass?" Silk demanded.

"I have no idea, sir. Have you inquired?"

"Of course not!"

"That may well be the reason, sir."

"If you—" Silk rebuked himself, and found that he was smiling. What was this, compared to the death of Doctor Crane or Echidna's theophany? He must learn to relax, and to think.

When the manteion had been built, a glass must have been provided for the use of the senior sibyl as well as the senior augur; that was natural enough, and in fact praiseworthy. The senior augur's glass, in what was now Patera Gulo's room, was out of order and had been for decades; this one, the senior sibyl's, was still functioning, perhaps only because it had been less used. Silk ran his fingers through his disorderly yellow hair. "Are there more glasses in this cenoby, my son?"

"No, sir."

He advanced a step, wishing that he had a walking stick to lean upon. "In this manteion?"

"Yes, sir. There is one in the manse, sir, but it is no longer summonable."

Silk nodded to himself. "I don't suppose you can tell me whether the Alambrera has surrendered?"

Immediately the monitor's face vanished, replaced by the turreted building and its flanking walls. Several thousand people were milling before the grim iron doors, where a score of men attempted to batter their way in with what seemed to be a building timber. As Silk watched, two Guardsmen thrust slug guns over the parapet of a turret on the right and opened fire.

Maytera Mint galloped into view, her black habit billowing about her, looking no bigger than a child on the broad back of her mount. She gestured urgently, the newfound silver trumpet that was her voice apparently sounding retreat, although Silk could not distinguish her words; the terrible discontinuity that was the azoth's blade sprang from her upraised hand, and the parapet exploded in a shower of stones.

"Another view," the monitor announced smoothly.

From a vantage point that appeared to be fifteen or twenty cubits above the street, Silk found himself looking down at the mob before the doors; some turned and ran; others were still raging against the Alambrera's stone and iron. The sweating men with the timber gathered themselves for a new assault, but one fell before they began it, his face a pulpy mask of scarlet and white.

"Enough," Silk said.

The monitor returned. "I think it safe to say, sir, that the Alambrera has not surrendered. If I may, I might add that in my judgment it is not likely to do so before the arrival of the relief force, sir."

"A relief force is on the way?"

"Yes, sir. The First Battalion of the Second Brigade of the Civil Guard, sir, and three companies of soldiers." The monitor paused. "I cannot locate them at the moment, sir, but not long ago they were marching along Ale Street. Would you care to see it?"

"That's all right. I should go." Silk turned away, then back. "How were you—there's an eye high up on a building on the other side of Cage Street, isn't there? And another over the doors of the Alambrera?"

"Precisely, sir."

"You must be familiar with this cenoby. Which room is Maytera Marble's?"

"Less so than you may suppose, sir. There are no other glasses in this cenoby, sir, as I told you. And no eyes save mine, sir. However, from certain remarks of my mistress's, I infer that it may be the second door on the left, sir."

"By your mistress you mean Maytera Rose? Where is she?"

"Yes, sir. My mistress has abandoned this land of trials and sorrows for a clime infinitely more agreeable, sir. That is to say, for Mainframe, sir. My lamented mistress has, in short, joined the assembly of the immortal gods."

"She's dead?"

"Precisely so, sir. As to the present whereabouts of her remains, they are, I believe, somewhat scattered. This is the best I can do, sir."

The monitor's face vanished again, and Sun Street sprang into view: the altar (from which Musk's fire-blackened corpse had partially fallen); and beyond it, Maytera Marble's naked metal body, sprawled near a coffin of softwood stained black.

"Those were her final rites," Silk muttered to himself. "Maytera Rose's last sacrifice. I never knew."

"Yes, sir, I fear they were." The monitor sighed. "I served her for forty-three years, sir, eight months, and five days. Would you care to view her as she was in life, sir? Or the last scene it was my pleasure to display to her? As a species of informal memorial, sir? It may console your evident grief, sir, if I may be so bold."

Silk shook his head, then thought better of it. "Is some god prompting you, my son? The Outsider, perhaps?"

"Not that I'm aware of, sir."

"Last Phaesday I encountered a very cooperative monitor," Silk explained. "He directed me to his mistress's weapons, something that I wouldn't—in retrospect—have supposed a monitor would normally do. I have since concluded that he had been ordered to assist me by the goddess Kypris."

"A credit to us all, sir."

"He would not say so, of course. He had been enjoined to silence. Show me that scene, the last your mistress saw."

The monitor vanished. Choppy blue water stretched to the horizon; in the mid-distance, a small fishing boat ran close-hauled under a lowering sky. A black bird (Silk edged closer) fluttered in the rigging, and a tall woman, naked or nearly so, stood beside the helmsman. A movement of her left hand was accompanied by a faint crimson flash.

Silk stroked his cheek. "Can you repeat the order Maytera Rose gave you that led you to show her this?"

"Certainly, sir. It was, 'Let's see what that slut Silk foisted on us is doing now.' I apologize, sir, as I did to my mistress, for the meager image of the subject. There was no nearer point from which to display it, and the focal length of the glass through which I viewed it was at its maximum."

Hearing Silk's approach, Maytera Marble turned away from the Window and tried to cover herself with her new hands. With averted eyes, he passed her the habit he had taken from a nail in the wall of her room, saying, "It doesn't matter, Maytera. Not really."

"I know, Patera. Yet I feel . . . There, it's on."

He faced her and held out his hand. "Can you stand up?"

"I don't know, Patera. I—I was about to try when you came. Where is everyone?" Harder than flesh, her fingers took his. He heaved with all his strength, reawakening the half-healed wounds left by the beak of the white-headed one.

Maytera Marble stood, almost steadily, and endeavored to shake the dust from her long, black skirt, murmuring, "Thank you, Patera. Did you get—? Thank you very much."

He took a deep breath. "I'm afraid you must think I've acted improperly. I should explain that His Cognizance the Prolocutor personally authorized me to enter your cenoby to bring you that. His Cognizance is here; he's in the manse at the moment, I believe."

He waited for her to speak, but she did not.

"Perhaps if you got out of the sun."

She leaned heavily on his arm as he led her through the arched gateway and the garden to her accustomed seat in the arbor.

In a voice not quite like her own, she said, "There's something I should tell you. Something I should have told you long ago."

Silk nodded. "There's something I should have told you long ago, too, Maytera—and something new that I must tell you now. Please let me go first; I think that will be best."

It seemed she had not heard him. "I bore a child once, Patera. A son, a baby boy. It was . . . Oh, very long ago."

"Built a son, you mean. You and your husband."

She shook her head. "Bore him in blood and pain, Patera. Great Echidna had blinded me to the gods, but it wasn't enough. So I suffered, and no doubt he suffered, too, poor little mite, though he had done nothing. We nearly died, both of us."

Silk could only stare at her smooth, metal face.

"And now somebody's dead, upstairs. I can't remember who. It will come to me in a moment. I dreamt of snakes last night, and I hate snakes. If I tell you now, I think perhaps I won't have that dream again."

"I hope not, Maytera," he told her. And then, "Think of something else, if you can."

"It was . . . was not an easy confinement. I was forty, and had never borne a child. Maytera Betel was our senior then, an excellent woman. But fat, one of those people who lose nothing when they fast. She became horribly tired when she fasted, but never thinner."

He nodded, increasingly certain that Maytera Marble was possessed again, and that he knew who possessed her.

"We pretended I was becoming fat, too. She used to tease me about it, and our sibs believed her. I'd been such a small woman before."

Watching carefully for her reaction, Silk said, "I would have carried you, Maytera, if I could; but I knew you'd be too heavy for me to lift."

She ignored it. "A few bad people gossiped, but that was all. Then my time came. The pains were awful. Maytera had arranged for a woman in the Orilla to care for me. Not a good woman, Maytera said, but a better friend in time of need than many good women. She told me she'd delivered children often, and washed her hands, and washed me, and told me what to do, but it would not come forth. My son. He wouldn't come into this world, though I pressed and pressed until I was so tired I thought I must die."

Her hand—he recognized it now as Maytera Rose's—found his. Hoping it would reassure her, he squeezed it as hard as he could.

"She cut me with a knife from her kitchen that she dipped in boiling water, and there was blood everywhere. Horrible! Horrible! A doctor came and cut me again, and there he was, covered with my blood and dripping. My son. They wanted me to nurse him, but I wouldn't. I knew that she'd blinded me, Ophidian Echidna had blinded me to the gods for what I'd done, but I thought that if I didn't nurse it she might relent and let me see her after all. She never has."

Silk said, "You don't have to tell me this, Maytera."

"They asked me to name him, and I did. They said they'd find a family that wanted a child and would take him, and he'd never find out, but he did, though it must have taken him a long while. He spoke to Marble, said she must tell me he'd bought it, and his name. When I heard his name, I knew."

Silk said gently, "It doesn't matter any more, Maytera. That was long ago, and now the whole city's in revolt, and it no longer matters. You must rest. Find peace."

"And that is why," Maytera Marble concluded. "Why my son Bloody bought our manteion and made all this trouble."

The wind wafted smoke from the fig tree to Silk's nose, and he sneezed.

"May every god bless you, Patera." Her voice sounded normal again.

"Thank you," he said, and accepted the handkerchief she offered.

"Could you bring me water, do you think? Cool water?"

As sympathetically as he could, he told her, "You can't drink water, Maytera."

"Please? Just a cup of cool water?"

He hurried to the manse. Today was Hieraxday, after all; no doubt she wished him to bless the water for her in Hierax's name. Later she would sprinkle it upon Maytera Rose's coffin and in the corners of her bedroom to prevent Maytera's spirit from troubling her again.

Cassava was sitting in the kitchen, in the chair Patera Pike had used at meals. Silk said, "Shouldn't you lie down, my daughter? It would make you feel better, I'm sure, and there's a divan in the sellaria."

She stared at him. "That was a needler, wasn't it? I gave you a needler. Why'd I have a thing like that?"

"Because someone gave it to you to give me." He smiled at her. "I'm going to the Alambrera, you see, and I'll need it." He worked the pump-handle vigorously, letting the first rusty half-bucketful drain away, catching the clear, cold flood that followed in a tumbler, and presenting it to Cassava. "Drink this, please, my daughter. It should make you feel better."

"You called me Mucor," she said. "Mucor." She set the untasted tumbler on the kitchen table and rubbed her forehead. "Didn't you call me Mucor, Patera?"

"I mentioned Mucor, certainly; she was the person who gave you the needler to give to me." Studying her puzzled frown, Silk decided it would be wise to change the subject. "Can you tell me what has become of His Cognizance and little Villus, my daughter?"

"He carried him upstairs, Patera. He wanted him to lie down, like you wanted me."

"Doubtless he'll be down shortly." Silk reflected that the Prolocutor had probably intended to bandage Villus's leg, and lost some time searching for medical supplies. "Drink that water, please. I'm sure it will make you feel better." He filled a second tumbler and carried it outside.

Maytera Marble was sitting in the arbor just as he had left her. Pushing aside the vines, he handed her the tumbler, saying, "Would you like me to bless this for you, Maytera?"

"It won't be necessary, Patera."

Water spilled from the lip; rills laced her fingers, and rain pattered upon the black cloth covering her metal thighs. She smiled.

"Does that make you feel better?" he asked.

"Yes, much better. Much cooler, Patera. Thank you."

"I'll be happy to bring you another, if you require it."

She stood. "No. No, thank you, Patera. I'll be all right now, I think."

"Sit down again, Maytera, please. I'm still worried about you, and I have to talk to you."

Reluctantly, she did. "Aren't there others hurt? I seem to remember others—and Maytera Rose, her coffin."

Silk nodded. "That's a part of what I must talk to you about. Fighting has broken out all over the city."

She nodded hesitantly. "Riots."

"Rebellion, Maytera. The people—some at least—are rising against the Ayuntamiento. There won't be any burials for several days, I'm afraid; so when you're feeling better, you and I must carry Maytera's coffin into the manteion. Is it very heavy?"

"I don't think so, Patera."

"Then we should be able to manage it. But before we go, I ought to tell you that Villus and an old woman named Cassava are in the manse with His Cognizance. I can't stay here, nor will he be able to, I'm sure; so I intend to ask him to allow you to enter to care for them."

Maytera Marble nodded.

"And our altar and Window are still out in the street. I doubt that it will be possible for you to get enough help to move them back inside until the city is at peace. But if you can, please do."

"I certainly will, Patera."

"I want you to stay and look after our manteion, Maytera. Maytera Mint's gone; she felt it her duty to lead the fighting, and she answered duty's call with exemplary courage. I'll have to go soon as well. People are dying—and killing others—to make me caldé, and I must put a stop to that if I can."

"Please be careful, Patera. For all our sakes."

"Yet this manteion is still important, Maytera. Terribly important." (Doctor Crane's ghost laughed aloud in a corner of Silk's mind.) "The Outsider told me so, remember? Someone must care for it, and there's no one left but you."

Maytera Marble's sleek metal head bobbed humbly, oddly mechanical without her coif. "I'll do my best, Patera."

"I know you will." He filled his lungs. "I said there were two things I had to tell you. You may not recall it, but I did. When you began to speak, I found there were a great many more. Now I must tell you those two, and then we'll carry Maytera into the manteion, if we can. The first is something I should have said months ago. Perhaps I did; I know I've tried. Now I believe—I believe it's quite likely I may be killed, and I must say it now, or be silent forever."

"I'm anxious to hear it, Patera." Her voice was soft, her metal mask expressionless and compassionate; her hands clasped his, hard and wet and warm.

"I want to say—this is the old thing—that I could never have stood it here if it hadn't been for you. Maytera Rose and Maytera Mint tried to help, I know they did. But you have been my right arm, Maytera. I want you know that."

Maytera Marble was staring at the ground. "You're too kind, Patera."

"I've loved three women. My mother was the first. The third . . ." He shrugged. "It doesn't matter. You don't know her, and I doubt that I'll ever see her again." A pillar of swirling dust rose above the top of the garden wall, to be swept away in a moment.

"The second thing, the new one, is that I can't remain the sort of augur I've been. Pas—Great Pas, who ruled the whole Whorl like a father—is dead, Maytera. Echidna herself told us. Do you remember that?"

Maytera Marble said nothing.

"Pas built our whorl, as we learn from the Writings. He built it, I believe, to endure for a long, long time, but not to endure indefinitely in his absence. Now he's dead, and the sun has no master. I believe that the

Fliers have been trying to tame it, or perhaps only trying to heal it. A man in the market told me once that his grandfather had spoken of them, saying their appearance presaged rain; so all my life, and my mother's, and her parents', too, have been lived under their protection, while they wrestled the sun."

Silk peered through the wilting foliage overhead at the dwindling golden line, already narrowed by the shade. "But they've failed, Maytera. A Flier told me yesterday, with what was almost his final breath. I didn't understand then; but I do now, or at least I believe I may. Something happened in the street that made it unmistakable. Our city, and every other, must help if it can, and prepare for worse times than we've ever known."

Quetzal's tremulous old voice came from outside the arbor. "Excuse me, Patera. Maytera." The wilting vines parted, and he stepped inside. "I overheard what you said. I couldn't help it, it's so quiet. You'll pardon me, I hope?"

"Of course, Your Cognizance." Both rose.

"Sit down, my daughter. Sit, please. May I sit beside you, Patera? Thank you. Everyone's hiding indoors, I imagine, or gone off to join the fighting. I've been upstairs in your manse, Patera, and I looked out your window. There isn't a cart in the street, and you can hear shooting."

Silk nodded. "A terrible thing, Your Cognizance."

"It is, as I overheard you say earlier, Patera. Maytera, you are, from all I've heard and read in our files, a woman of sound sense. A woman outstanding for that valuable quality, in fact. Viron's at war with itself. Men and women, and even children, are dying as we speak. They call us butchers for offering animal blood to the gods, though they're only animals and die quickly for the highest of purposes. Now the gutters are running with wasted human blood. If we're butchers, what will they call themselves when it's over?" He shook his head. "Heroes, I suppose. Do you agree?"

Maytera Marble nodded mutely.

"Then I ask you, how can it be ended? Tell me, Maytera. Tell us both. My coadjutor fears my humor, and I myself fear at times that I overindulge it. But I was never more serious."

She muttered something inaudible.

"Louder, Maytera."

"Patera Silk must become our caldé."

Quetzal leaned back in the little rustic seat. "There you have it. Her reputation for good sense is entirely justified, Patera Caldé."

"Your Cognizance!"

Maytera Marble made Quetzal a seated bow. "You're too kind, Your Cognizance."

"Maytera. Suppose I maintain that yours isn't the only solution. Suppose I say that the Ayuntamiento has governed us before and can govern us again. We need only submit. What's wrong with that?"

"There'd be another rebellion, Your Cognizance, and more riots." Maytera Marble would not meet Silk's eyes. "More fighting, new rebellions every few years until the Ayuntamiento was overthrown. I've watched discontent grow for twenty years, Your Cognizance, and now they're killing, Patera says. They'll be quicker to fight next time, and quicker again until it never really stops. And—and . . ."

"Yes?" Quetzal motioned urgently. "Tell us."

"The soldiers will die, Your Cognizance, one by one. Each time the people rise, there will be fewer soldiers."

"So you see." His head swung about on its wrinkled neck as he spoke to Silk. "Your supporters must win, Patera Caldé. Stop wincing when I call you that, you've got to get used to it. They must, because only their victory will bring Viron peace. Tell Loris and the rest they can save their lives by surrendering now. Lemur's dead, did you know that?"

Swallowing, Silk nodded.

"With Lemur gone, a few smacks of your quirt will make the rest trot anywhere you want. But you must be caldé, and the people must see you are."

"If I may speak, Your Cognizance?"

"Not to tell me that you, an anointed augur, will not do what I, your Prolocutor, ask you to, I trust."

"You've been Prolocutor for many years, Your Cognizance. Since long before I was born. You were Prolocutor in the days of the last caldé."

Quetzal nodded. "I knew him well. I intend to know you better, Patera Caldé."

"I was a child when he died, Your Cognizance, a child just learning to walk. A great many things must have happened then that I've never heard of. I mention it to emphasize that I'm asking out of ignorance. If you would prefer not to answer, no more will be said about the matter."

Quetzal nodded. "If it were Maytera here inquiring, or your acolyte, let's say, or even my coadjutor, I might refuse exactly as you suggest. I can't imagine a question asked by our caldé that I wouldn't feel it was my duty to answer fully and clearly, however. What's troubling you?"

Silk ran his fingers through his hair. "When the caldé died, Your Cognizance, did you—did anyone—protest the Ayuntamiento's decision not to hold an election?"

Quetzal nodded, as if to himself, and passed a trembling hand across his hairless scalp, a gesture similar to Silk's yet markedly different. "The short answer, if I intended nothing more than a short answer, would be yes. I did. So did various others. You deserve more than a short answer, though. You deserve a complete explanation. In the meantime, that lucky young man's body lies half consumed on the altar. I saw it from your window. You indicate that you're not inclined to plead your office to excuse disobedience. Will you follow me into the street and help me do what can be done there? When we're finished, I'll answer you fully."

Crouched behind the remaining wall of a fire-gutted shop, Maytera Mint studied her subordinates' faces. Zoril looked fearful, Lime stunned, and the big, black-bearded man (she found she had forgotten his name, if she had ever heard it) resolute. "Now, then," she said.

Why it's just like talking to the class, she thought. No different at all. I wish I had a chalkboard.

"Now then, we've just had news, and it's bad news, I don't intend to deny that. But it isn't unexpected news. Not to me, and I hope to none of you. We've got Guards penned up in the Alambrera, where they're supposed to pen up other people."

She smiled, hoping they appreciated the irony. "Anyone would expect that the Ayuntamiento would send its people help. Certainly I expected it, though I hoped it wouldn't be quite so prompt. But it's come, and it seems to me that we can do any of three things." She held up three fingers. "We can go on attacking the Alambrera, hoping we can take it before they get here." One finger down. "We can withdraw." Another finger down. "Or we can leave the Alambrera as it is and fight the reinforcements before they can get inside." The last finger down. "What do you suggest, Zoril?"

"If we withdraw, we won't be doing what the goddess said for us to."

The black-bearded man snorted.

"She told us to capture the Alambrera and tear it down," Maytera Mint reminded Zoril. "We've tried, but we haven't been able to. What we've got to decide, really, is should we go on trying until we're interrupted? Or rest awhile until we feel stronger, knowing that they'll be stronger too? Or should we see to it that we're not interrupted. Lime?"

She was a lank woman of forty with ginger-colored hair that Maytera Mint had decided was probably dyed. "I don't think we can think *only* about what the goddess said. If she just wanted it torn down, she could have done it herself. She wants *us* to do it."

Maytera Mint nodded. "I'm in complete agreement."

"We're mortals, so we've got to do it as mortals." Lime gulped. "I don't have as many people following me as the rest of you, and most of mine are women."

"There's nothing wrong with that," Maytera Mint assured her. "So am I. So is the goddess, or at least she's female like us. We know she's Pas's wife and seven times a mother. As for your not having lots of followers, that's not the point. I'd be happy to listen to somebody who didn't have any, if she had good, workable ideas."

"What I was trying to say—" A gust of wind carried dust and smoke into their council; Lime fanned her face with one long, flat hand. "Is most of mine don't have much to fight with. Just kitchen knives, a lot of them. Eight, I think it is, have needlers, and there's one who runs a stable and has a pitchfork."

Maytera Mint made a mental note.

"So what I was going to say is they're feeling left out. Discouraged, you know?"

Maytera Mint assured her that she did.

"So if we go home, I think some will stay there. But if we can beat these new Hoppies that're coming, they could get slug guns. They'd feel better about themselves, and us, too."

"A very valid point."

"Bison here—"

Maytera Mint made another note: "Bison" was clearly the black-bearded man; she resolved to use his name whenever she could until it was fixed in her memory.

"Bison thinks they won't fight. And they won't, not the way he wants them to. But if they had slug guns, they'd shoot all day if you told them to, Maytera. Or if you told them to go someplace and Hoppies tried to stop them."

"You're for attacking the relief column, Lime?"

Lime nodded.

Bison said, "She's for it as long as somebody else does the fighting. I'm for it, too, and we'll do the fighting."

"The fighting among ourselves, you mean, Bison?" Maytera Mint shook her head. "That sort of fighting will never bring back the Charter, and I'm quite sure it isn't what the goddess intended. But you're in favor of attacking the relief column? Good, so am I! I'm not sure I know what Zoril wants, and I'm not sure he knows. Even so, that's a clear majority. Where would you suggest we attack it, Bison?"

He was silent, fingering his beard.

"We'll lose some stragglers. I realize that. But there are steps we can take to keep from losing many, and we might pick up some new people as well. Zoril?"

"I don't know, Maytera. I think you ought to decide."

"So do I, and I will. But it's foolish to make decisions without listening to advice, if there's time for it. I think we should attack right here, when they reach the Alambrera."

Bison nodded emphatically.

"In the first place, we don't have much time to prepare, and that will give us the most."

Bison said, "People are throwing stones at them from the rooftops. The messenger told us that, too, remember? Maybe they'll kill a few Hoppies for us. Let's give them a chance."

"And perhaps some of their younger men will come over to us. We ought to give them as much opportunity as we can to do that." Inspired by the memory of games at the palaestra, she added, "When somebody changes sides, it counts twice, one more for us and one fewer for them. Besides, when they get here the Guards in the Alambrera will have to open those big doors to let them in." Their expressions showed that none of them had thought of that, and she concluded, "I'm not saying that we'll be able to get inside ourselves. But we might. Now then, how are we going to attack?"

"Behind and before, with as many men as we can," Bison rumbled.

Lime added, "We need to take them by surprise, Maytera."

"Which is another reason for attacking here. When they get to the Alambrera, they'll think they've reached their goal. They may relax a little. That will be the time for us to act."

"When the doors open." Bison drove a fist into his palm.

"Yes, I think so. What is it, Zoril?"

"I shouldn't say this. I know what everybody's going to think, but they've been shooting down on us from the walls and the high windows. Just about everybody we've lost, we've lost like that." He waited for contradiction, but there was none.

"There's buildings across the street as high as the wall, Maytera, and one just a little up the street that's higher. I think we ought to have people in there to shoot at the men on the wall. Some of mine that don't have needlers or slug guns could be on the roofs, too, throwing stones like the messenger talked about. A chunk of shiprock falling that far ought to hit as hard as a slug, and these Hoppies have got armor."

Maytera Mint nodded again. "You're right. I'm putting you in charge of that. Get some people—not just your own, some of the older boys and girls particularly—busy right away carrying stones and bricks up there. There must be plenty around after the fires.

"Lime, your women are no longer fighters unless they've got needlers or slug guns. We need people to get our wounded out of the fight and take care of them. They can use their knives or whatever they have on anyone who tries to interfere with them. And that woman with the pitchfork? Go get her. I want to talk to her."

A fragment of broken plaster caught Maytera Mint's eye. "Now, Bison, look here." Picking it up, she scratched two widely spaced lines on the fire-blackened wall behind her. "This is Cage Street." With speed born of years of practice, she sketched in the Alambrera and the buildings facing it.

· · · ·

There was still a good deal of cedar left, and the fire on the altar had not quite gone out. Silk heaped fresh wood on it and let the wind fan it for him, sparks streaking Sun Street.

Quetzal had taken charge of Musk's corpse, arranging it decently beside Maytera Rose's coffin. Maytera Marble, who had gone to the cenoby for a sheet, had not yet returned.

"He was the most evil man I've ever known." Silk had not intended to speak aloud, but the words had come just the same. "Yet I can't help feeling sorry for him, and for all of us, as well, because he's gone."

Quetzal murmured, "Does you credit, Patera Caldé," and wiped the blade of the manteion's sacrificial knife, which he had rescued from the dust.

Vaguely, Silk wondered when he had dropped it. Maytera Rose had always taken care of it, washing and sharpening it after each sacrifice, no matter how minor; but Maytera Rose was gone, as dead as Musk.

After he had cut the sign of addition in Villus's ankle, of course, when he had knelt to suck out the poison.

When he had met Blood on Phaesday, Blood had said that he had promised someone—had promised a woman—that he would pray at this manteion for her. Suddenly Silk knew (without in the least understanding how he knew) that the "woman" had been Musk. Was Musk's spirit lingering in the vicinity of Musk's body and prompting him in some fashion? Whispering too softly to be heard? Silk traced the sign of addition, knowing that he should add a prayer to Thelxiepeia, the goddess of magic and ghosts, but unable to do so.

Musk had bought the manteion for Blood with Blood's money; and Musk must have felt, in some deep part of himself that all his evil actions had not killed, that he had done wrong—that he had by his purchase offended the gods. He had asked Blood to pray for him, or perhaps for them both, in the manteion that he had bought; and Blood had promised to do it.

Had Blood kept his promise?

"If you'd help with the feet, Patera Caldé?" Quetzal was standing at the head of Maytera Rose's coffin.

"Yes, of course, Your Cognizance. We can carry that in."

Quetzal shook his head. "We'll lay it on the sacred fire, Patera Caldé. Cremation is allowed when burial is impractical. If you would . . . ?"

Silk picked up the foot of the coffin, finding it lighter than he had expected. "Shouldn't we petition the gods, Your Cognizance? On her behalf?"

"I already have, Patera Caldé. You were deep in thought. Now then, as high as you can, then quickly down upon the fire. Without dropping it, please. One, two, *three!*"

Silk did as he was told, then stepped hurriedly away from the lengthening flames. "Possibly we ought to have waited for Maytera, Your Cognizance."

Quetzal shook his head again. "This way is better, Patera Caldé. It would be better for you to keep from looking at the fire, too. Do you know why coffins have that peculiar shape, by the way? Look at me, Patera Caldé."

"To allow for the shoulders, Your Cognizance, or so I've heard."

Quetzal nodded. "That's what everyone's told. Would this sibyl of yours need extra room for her shoulders? Look at me, I said."

Already the thin, stained wood was blackening honestly, charring as the flames that licked it brought forth new flames. "No," Silk said, and looked away again. (It was strange to think that this bent, bald old man was in fact the Prolocutor.) "No, Your Cognizance. Nor would most women, or many men."

There was a stench of burning flesh.

"They do it so that we, the living, will know at which end the head lies, when the lid's on. Coffins are sometimes stood on end, you see. Patera!"

Silk's gaze had strayed to the fire again. He turned away and covered his eyes.

"I would have saved you that if I could," Quetzal told him, and Maytera Marble, arriving with the sheet, inquired, "Saved him from what, Your Cognizance?"

"Saved me from seeing Maytera Rose's face as the flames consumed it," Silk told her. He rubbed his eyes, hoping that she would think he had been rubbing them before, that he had gotten smoke in them.

She held out one end of the sheet. "I'm sorry I took so long, Patera. I–I happened to see my reflection. Then I looked for Maytera Mint's mirror. My cheek is scratched."

Silk took corners of the sheet in tear-dampened fingers; the wind tried to snatch it from him, but he held it fast. "So it is, Maytera. How did you do it?"

"I have no idea!"

To his surprise, Quetzal lifted Musk's half-consumed body easily. Clearly, this venerable old man was stronger than he appeared. "Spread it flat and hold it down," he told them. "We'll lay him on it and fold it over him."

A moment more, and Musk, too, rested among the flames.

"It's our duty to tend the fire until both have burned. We don't have to watch, and I suggest we don't." Quetzal had positioned himself between Silk and the altar. "Let us pray privately for the repose of their spirits."

Silk shut his eyes, bowed his head, and addressed himself to the Outsider, without much confidence that this most obscure of gods heard him or cared about what he said, or even existed.

"And yet I know this." (His lips moved, although no sound issued from them.) *"You are the only god for me. It is better for me that I should give you all my worship, though you are not, than that I should worship Echidna or even Kypris, whose faces I have seen. Thus I implore your mercy on these, our dead. Remember that I, whom once you signally honored, ought to have loved them both but could not, and so failed to provide the impetus that might have brought them to you before Hierax claimed them. Mine therefore is the guilt for any wrong they have done while they have known me. I accept it, and pray you will forgive them, who burn, and forgive me also, whose fire is not yet lit. Obscure Outsider, be not angry with us, though we have never sufficiently honored you. All that is outcast, discarded, and despised is yours. Are this man and this woman, who have been neglected by me, to be neglected by you as well? Recall the misery of our lives and their deaths. Are we never to find rest? I have searched my conscience, Outsider, to discover that in which I have displeased you. I find this: That I avoided Maytera Rose whenever I could, though she might have been to me the grandmother I have never known; and that I hated Musk, and feared him too, when he had not done me the least wrong. Both were yours, Outsider, as I now see; and for your sake I should have been loving with both. I renounce my pride, and I will honor their memories. This I swear. My life to you, Outsider, if you will forgive this man and this woman whom we burn today."*

Opening his eyes he saw that Quetzal had already finished, if he had ever prayed. Soon Maytera Marble raised her head as well, and he inquired, "Would Your Cognizance, who knows more about the immortal gods than anyone else in the Whorl, instruct me regarding the Outsider? Though he's enlightened me, as I informed your coadjutor, I would be exceedingly grateful if you could tell me more."

"I have no information to give, Patera Caldé, regarding the Outsider or any other god. What little I have learned in the course of a long life, regarding the gods, I have tried to forget. You saw Echidna. After that, can you ask me why?"

"No, Your Cognizance." Silk looked nervously at Maytera Marble.

"I didn't, Your Cognizance. But I saw the Holy Hues and heard her voice, and it made me wonderfully happy. I remember that she exhorted all of us to purity and confirmed Scylla's patronage, nothing else. Can you tell me what else she said?"

"She told your sib to overthrow the Ayuntamiento. Let that be enough for you, Maytera, for the present."

"Maytera Mint? But she'll be killed!"

Quetzal's shoulders rose and fell. "I think we can count on it, Maytera. Before Kypris manifested here on Scylsday, the Windows of our city had been empty for decades. I can't take credit for that, it wasn't my doing. But I've done everything in my power to prevent theophanies. It hasn't been much, but I've done what I could. I proscribed human sacrifice, and got it made law, for one thing. I admit I'm proud of that."

He turned to Silk. "Patera Caldé, you wanted to know if I protested when the Ayuntamiento failed to hold an election to choose a new caldé. You were right to ask, more right than you knew. If a new caldé had been elected when the last died, we wouldn't have had that visit from Echidna today."

"If Your Cognizance—"

"No, I want to tell you. There are many things you have to know as caldé, and this is one. But the situation wasn't as simple as you may think. What do you know about the Charter?"

"Next to nothing, Your Cognizance. We studied it when I was a boy—that is to say, our teacher read it to us and answered our questions. I was ten, I think."

Maytera Marble said, "We're not supposed to teach it now. It was dropped from all the lesson plans years ago."

"At my order," Quetzal told them, "when even mentioning it became dangerous. We have copies at the Palace, however, and I've read it many times. It doesn't say, Patera Caldé, that an election must be held on the death of the caldé, as you seem to believe. What it really says is that the caldé is to hold office for life, that he may appoint his successor, and that a successor is to be elected if he dies without having done it. You see the difficulty?"

Uneasily, Silk glanced up and down the street, seeing no one near enough to overhear. "I'm afraid not, Your Cognizance. That sounds quite straightforward to me."

"It does *not* say that the caldé must announce his choice, you'll notice. If he wants to keep it secret, he can do it. The reasons are so obvious I hesitated to explain them."

Silk nodded. "I can see that it would put them both in an uncomfortable position."

"In a very dangerous one, Patera Caldé. Partisans of the successor might assassinate the caldé, while those who'd hoped to become caldé would be tempted to murder the successor. When the last caldé's will was read, it was found to designate a successor. I remember the exact wording. It said, 'Though he is not the son of my body, my son will succeed me.' What do you make of that?"

Silk stroked his cheek. "It didn't name this son?"

"No. I've given you the entire clause. The caldé had never married, as I should have told you sooner. As far as anybody knew, he had no sons."

Maytera Marble ventured, "I never knew about this, Your Cognizance. Didn't the son tell them?"

"Not that I know of. It's possible he did and was killed secretly by Lemur or one of the other councillors, but I doubt it." Quetzal selected a long cedar split and poked the sinking fire. "If they'd done that, I'd have heard about it by this time. Probably much sooner. No public announcement was made, you understand. If there'd been one, pretenders would have put themselves forward and made endless trouble. The Ayuntamiento searched in secret. To be frank, I doubt that the boy would have lived if they'd found him."

Silk nodded reluctantly.

"If it had been a natural son, they could've used medical tests. As it was, the only hope was to turn up a record. The monitors of every glass that could be located were queried. Old documents were read and reread, and the caldé's relatives and associates interrogated, all without result. An election should have been held, and I urged one repeatedly because I was afraid we'd have a theophany from Scylla unless something was done. But an election would have been illegal, as I had to admit. The caldé had designated his successor. They simply couldn't find him."

"Then I'll have no right to office if it's forced on me."

"Hardly. In the first place, that was a generation ago. It's likely the adopted son's dead if he ever existed. In the second, the Charter was written by the gods. It's a document expressing their will regarding our governance, nothing more. It's clear they're displeased with the present state of things, and you're the only alternative, as Maytera told you."

Quetzal handed the sacrificial knife to Maytera Marble. "I think we can go now, Maytera. You must stay. Watch the fire until it goes out. When it does, carry the ashes into your manteion and dispose of them as usual. You may notice bones or teeth among them. Don't touch them, or treat them differently from the rest of the ashes in any way."

Maytera Marble bowed.

"Purify the altar as usual. If you can get people to help you, take it back into the manteion. Your Sacred Window, too."

She bowed again. "Patera has already instructed me to do so, Your Cognizance."

"Fine. You're a good sensible woman, Maytera, as I said. I was glad to see that you had resumed your coif when you went back to your cenoby. You've my permission to enter the manse. There's an old woman there. I think you'll find she's well enough to go home. There's a boy on one of the beds upstairs. You can leave him there or carry him into your cenoby to nurse, if that will be more convenient. See to it that he doesn't exert himself, and that he drinks a lot of water. Get him to eat, if you can. You might cook some of this meat for him."

Quetzal turned to Silk. "I want to look in on him again, Patera, while Maytera's busy with the fire. I'm also going to borrow a spare robe I saw up there, your acolyte's, I suppose. It looked too short for you, but it should fit me, and when we meet the rebels—perhaps we should call them servants of the Queen of the Whorl, some such. When we meet them, it may help if they know who I am as well as who you are."

Silk said, "I feel certain Patera Gulo would want you to have anything that can be of any assistance whatsoever to you, Your Cognizance."

As Quetzal tottered away, Maytera Marble asked, "Are you going to help Maytera Mint, Patera? You'll be in frightful danger, both of you. I'll pray for you."

"I'm much more worried about you than about myself," Silk told her. "More, even, than I am about her—she must be under Echidna's protection, in spite of what His Cognizance said."

Maytera Marble lifted her head in a slight, tantalizing smile. "Don't fret about me. Maytera Marble's taking good care of me." Unexpectedly, she brushed his cheek with warm metal lips. "If you should see my boy Bloody, tell him not to worry either. I'll be all right."

"I certainly will, Maytera." Silk took a hasty step back. "Good-bye, Maytera Rose. About those tomatoes—I'm sorry, truly sorry about everything. I hope you've forgiven me."

"She passed away yesterday, Patera. Didn't I tell you?"

"Yes," Silk mumbled. "Yes, of course."

Auk lay on the floor of the tunnel. He was tired—tired and weak and dizzy, he admitted to himself. When had he slept last? Dayside on Molpsday, after he'd left Jugs and Patera, before he went to the lake, but he'd slept on the boat a dog's right before the storm. Her and the butcher had been tired, too, tireder than him though they hadn't been knocked on the head. They'd helped in the storm, and Dace was dead. Urus hadn't done anything, would kill him if he got the chance. He pictured Urus standing over him with a bludgeon like the one he had seen, and sat up and stared around him.

Urus and the soldier were talking quietly. The soldier called, "I'm keeping an eye out. Go back to sleep, trooper."

Auk lay down again, though no soldier could be a friend to somebody like him, though he'd sooner trust Urus though he didn't trust Urus at all.

What day was it? Thelxday. Phaesday, most likely. Grim Phaea, for food and healing. Grim because eating means killing stuff to eat, and it's no good pretending it don't. Stuff like Gelada'd killed Dace with his bad arm and the string around his neck. That's why you ought to go to manteion once in a while. Sacrifice showed you, showed the gray ram dying and its blood thrown in the fire, and poor people thanking Phaea or whatever god it was for "this good food." Grim because healing hurts more than dying, the doctor cuts you to make you well, sets the bone and it hurts. Dace said a bone in his head was broken, was cracked or something, he was cracked for sure and it was probably true because he got awful dizzy sometimes, couldn't see good sometimes, even stuff right in front of him. A white ram, Phaea, if I get over this.

It should've been a black ram. He'd promised Tartaros a black ram, but the only one in the market had cost more than he had, so he'd bought the gray one. That was before last time, before Kypris had promised them it'd be candy, before the ring for Jugs, the anklet for Patera. It had been why his troubles started, maybe, because his ram had been the wrong color. They dyed those black rams anyhow. . . .

Up the tree and onto the roof, then in through the attic window, but he was dizzy, dizzy and the tree already so high its top touched the shade, brushed the shaggy shade with dead leaves rustling, rustling, and the roof higher, Urus whistling, whistling from the corner because the Hoppies were practically underneath this shaggy tree now.

He stood on a limb, walked out on it watching the roof sail away with all the black peaked roofs of Limna as the old man's old boat put out with Snarling Scylla at the helm, Scylla up in Jugs's head not taking up room but pulling her strings, jerking her on reins, digging spurred heels in, Spurred Scylla a gamecock spurring Jugs to make her trot. A little step and another and the roof farther than ever, higher than the top of the whole shaggy tree and his foot slipped where Gelada's blood wet the slick silvery bark and he fell.

He woke with a start, shaking. Something warm lay beside him, close but not quite touching. He rolled over, bringing his legs up under her big soft thighs, his chest against her back, an arm around her to warm her and it, cupping her breast. "By Kypris, I love you, Jugs. I'm too sick to shag you, but I love you. You're all the woman I'll ever want."

She didn't talk, but there'd been a little change in her breathing, so he knew she wasn't asleep even if she wanted him to think so. That was dimber by him, she wanted to look at it and he didn't blame her, wouldn't want a woman who wouldn't look because a woman like that got you nabbed sooner or later even if she didn't mean to.

Only he'd looked at it already, had looked all that he'd ever need to while he was rolling over. And he slept beside her quite content.

"I shocked you, Patera Caldé. I know I did. I could see it in your face. My eyes aren't what they were, I'm afraid. I'm no longer good at reading expressions. But I read yours."

"Somewhat, Your Cognizance." Together, they were walking up a deserted Sun Street, a tall young augur and a stooped old one side-by-side, Silk taking a slow step for two of Quetzal's lame and unsteady ones.

"Since you left the schola, Patera Caldé, since you came to this quarter, you've prayed that a god would come to your Window, haven't you? I feel sure you have. All of you do, or nearly all. Who did you hope for? Pas or Scylla?"

"Scylla chiefly, Your Cognizance. To tell the truth, I scarcely thought about the minor gods then. I mean the gods outside the Nine—no god is truly minor, I suppose. Scylla seemed the most probable. It was only on Scylsdays that we had a victim, for one thing; and she's the patroness of the city, after all."

"She'd tell you what to do, which was what you wanted." Quetzal squinted up at Silk with a toothless smile he found disconcerting. "She'd fill your cash box, too. You could fix up those old buildings, buy books for your palaestra, and sacrifice in the grand style every day."

Reluctantly, Silk nodded.

"I understand. Oh, I understand. It's perfectly normal, Patera Caldé. Even commendable. But what about me? What about me, not wanting gods to come at all? That isn't, is it? It isn't, and it's bothering you."

Silk shook his head. "It's not my place to judge your acts or your words, Your Cognizance."

"Yet you will." Quetzal paused to peer along Lamp Street, and seemed to listen. "You will, Patera Caldé. You can't help it. That's why

I've got to tell you. After that, we're going to talk about something you probably think that you learned all about when you were a baby. I mean the Plan of Pas. Then you can go off to Maytera what'shername."

"Mint, Your Cognizance."

"You can go off to help her overthrow the Ayuntamiento for Echidna, and I'll be going off to find you more people to do it with, and better weapons. To begin—"

"Your Cognizance?" Silk ran nervous fingers through his haystack hair, unable to restrain himself any longer. "Your Cognizance, did you know Great Pas was dead? Did you know it already, before she told us today?"

"Certainly. We can start there, Patera Caldé, if that's troubling you. Would you have talked about it from the ambion of the Grand Manteion if you'd been in my place? Made a public announcement? Conducted ceremonies of mourning and so forth?"

"Yes," Silk said firmly. "Yes, I would."

"I see. What do you suppose killed him, Patera Caldé? You're an intelligent young fellow. You studied hard at the schola, I know. Your instructors' reports are very favorable. How could the Father of the Gods die?"

Faintly, Silk could hear the booming of slug guns, then a long, concerted roar that might almost have been thunder.

"Building falling," Quetzal told him. "Don't worry about that now. Answer my question."

"I can't conceive of such a thing, Your Cognizance. The gods are immortal, ageless. It's their immortality that makes them gods, really, more than anything else."

"A fever," Quetzal suggested. "We mortals die of fevers every day. Perhaps he caught a fever?"

"The gods are spiritual beings, Your Cognizance. They're not subject to disease."

"Kicked in the head by a horse. Don't you think that could have been it?"

Silk did not reply.

"I'm mocking you, Patera Caldé, of course I am. But not idly. My question's perfectly serious. Echidna told you Pas is dead, and you can't help believing her. I've known it for thirty years, since shortly after his death, in fact. How did he die? How could he?"

Silk combed his disorderly yellow hair with his fingers again.

"When I was made Prolocutor, Patera Caldé, we had a vase at the Palace that had been thrown on the Short Sun Whorl, a beautiful thing. They told me it was five hundred years old. Almost inconceivable. Do you agree?"

"And priceless, I would say, Your Cognizance."

"Lemur wanted to frighten me, to show me how ruthless he could be. I already knew, but he didn't know I did. I think he thought that if I did I'd never dare oppose him. He took that vase from its stand and smashed it at my feet."

Silk stared down at Quetzal. "You—you're serious, Your Cognizance? He actually did that?"

"He did. Look, now. That vase was immortal. It didn't age. It was proof against disease. But it could be destroyed, as it was. So could Pas. He couldn't age, or even fall sick. But he could be destroyed, and he was. He was murdered by his family. Many men die like that, Patera Caldé. When you're half my age, you'll know it. Now a god has, too."

"But, Your Cognizance . . ."

"Viron's isolated, Patera Caldé. All the cities are. He gave us floaters and animals. No big machines that could carry heavy loads. He thought that would be best for us, and I dare say he was right. But the Ayuntamiento's not isolated. The caldé wasn't either, when we had one. Did you think he was?"

Silk said, "I realize we have diplomats, Your Cognizance, and there are traveling traders and so forth—boats on the rivers, and even spies."

"That's right. As Prolocutor, I'm no more isolated than he was. Less, but I won't try to prove that. I'm in contact with religious leaders in Urbs, Wick, and other cities, cities where his children have boasted of killing Pas."

"It was the Seven, then, Your Cognizance? Not Echidna? Was Scylla involved?"

Quetzal had found prayer beads in a pocket of Gulo's robe; he ran them through his fingers. "Echidna was at the center. You've seen her, can you doubt it? Scylla, Molpe, and Hierax were in it. They've said so at various times."

"But not Tartaros, Thelxiepeia, Phaea, or Sphigx, Your Cognizance?" Silk felt an irrational surge of hope.

"I don't know about Tartaros and the younger gods, Patera Caldé.

But do you see why I didn't announce it? There would have been panic. There will be, if it becomes widely known. The Chapter will be destroyed and the basis of morality gone. Imagine Viron with neither. As for public observances, how do you think Pas's murderers would react to our mourning him?"

"We—" Something tightened in Silk's throat. "We, you and I, Your Cognizance. Villus and Maytera Marble, all of us are—were his children too. That is to say, he built the whorl for us. Ruled us like a father. I . . ."

"What is it, Patera Caldé?"

"I just remembered something, Your Cognizance. Kypris—you must know there was a theophany of Kypris at our manteion on Scylsday."

"I've had a dozen reports. It's the talk of the city."

"She said she was hunted, and I didn't understand. Now I believe I may."

Quetzal nodded. "I imagine she is. The wonder is that they haven't been able to corner her in thirty years. She can't be a tenth as strong as Pas was. But it can't be easy to kill even a minor goddess who knows you're trying to. Not like killing a husband and father who trusts you. Now you see why I've tried to prevent theophanies, don't you, Patera Caldé? If you don't, I'll never be able to make it clear."

"Yes, Your Cognizance. Of course. It's—horrible. Unspeakable. But you were right. You are right."

"I'm glad you realize it. You understand why we go on sacrificing to Pas? We must. I've tried to downgrade him somewhat. Make him seem more remote than he used to. I've emphasized Scylla at his expense, but you're too young to have realized that. Older people complain, sometimes."

Silk said nothing, but stroked his cheek as he walked.

"You have questions, Patera Caldé. Or you will have when you've digested all this. Don't fear you may offend me. I'm at your disposal whenever you want to question me."

"I have two," Silk told him. "I hesitate to pose the first, which verges upon blasphemy."

"Many necessary questions do." Quetzal cocked his head. "This isn't one, but do you hear horses?"

"Horses, Your Cognizance? No."

"I must be imagining it. What are your questions?"

Silk walked on in silence for a few seconds to collect his thoughts.

At length he said, "My original two questions have become three, Your Cognizance. The first, for which I apologize in advance, is, isn't it true that Echidna and the Seven love us just as Pas did? I've always felt, somehow, that Pas loved them, while they love us; and if that is so, will his death—terrible though it is—make a great deal of difference to us?"

"You have a pet bird, Patera Caldé. I've never seen it, but so I've been told."

"I had one, Your Cognizance, a night chough. I've lost him, I'm afraid, although it may be that he's with a friend. I'm hoping he'll return to me eventually."

"You should have caged him, Patera Caldé. Then you'd still have him."

"I liked him too much for that, Your Cognizance."

Quetzal's small head bobbed upon its long neck. "Just so. There are people who love birds so much they free them. There are others who love them so much they cage them. Pas's love of us was of the first kind. Echidna's and the Seven's is of the other. Were you going to ask why they killed Pas? Is that one of your questions?"

Silk nodded, "My second, Your Cognizance."

"I've answered it. What's the third?"

"You indicated that you wished to discuss the Plan of Pas with me, Your Cognizance. If Pas is dead, what's the point of discussing his plan?"

Hoofbeats sounded faintly behind them.

"A god's plans do not die with him, Patera Caldé. He is dead, as Serpentine Echidna told us. We are not. We were to carry Pas's plan out. You said he ruled us as a father. Do a father's plans benefit him? Or his children?"

"Your Cognizance, I just remembered something! Another god, the Outsider—"

"Pateras!" The horseman, a lieutenant of the Civil Guard in mottled green conflict armor, pushed up his visor. "Are you—you there, Patera. The young one. Aren't you Patera Silk?"

"Yes, my son," Silk said. "I am."

The lieutenant dropped the reins. His hand appeared slow as it jerked his needler from the holster, yet it was much too quick to permit Silk to draw Musk's needler. The flat crack of the shot sounded an instant after the needle's stinging blow.

Chapter 5

MAIL

They had insisted she not look for herself, that she send one of them to do it, but she felt she had already sent too many others. This time she would see the enemy for herself, and she had forbidden them to attend her. She straightened her snowy coif as she walked, and held down the wind-tossed skirt of her habit—a sibyl smaller and younger than most, gowned (like all sibyls) in black to the tops of her worn black shoes, out upon some holy errand, and remarkable only for being alone.

The azoth was in one capacious pocket, her beads in the other; she got them out as she went around the corner onto Cage Street, wooden beads twice the size of those Quetzal fingered, smoothed and oiled by her touch to glossy chestnut.

First, Pas's gammadion: *"Great Pas, Designer and Creator of the Whorl, Lord Guardian of the Aureate Path, we—"*

The pronoun should have been *I,* but she was used to saying them with Maytera Rose and Maytera Marble; and they, praying together in the sellaria of the cenoby, had quite properly said "we." She thought: But I'm praying for all of us. For all who may die this afternoon, for Bison and Patera Gulo and Bream and that man who let me borrow his sword. For the volunteers who'll ride with me in a minute, and Patera Silk and Lime and Zoril and the children. Particularly for the children. For all of us, Great Pas.

"We acknowledge you the supreme and sovereign . . ."

And there it was, an armored floater with all its hatches down turning onto Cage Street. Then another, and a third. A good big space between the third and the first rank of marching Guardsmen because of the dust. A mounted officer riding beside his troopers. The soldiers would be in back (that was what the messenger had reported) but there was no time to wait until they came into view, though the soldiers would be the worst of all, worse even than the floaters.

Beads forgotten, she hurried back the way she had come.

Scleroderma was still there, holding the white stallion's reins. "I'm coming too, Maytera. On these two legs since you won't let me have a horse, but I'm coming. You're going, and I'm bigger than you."

Which was true. Scleroderma was no taller, but twice as wide. "Shout," she told her. "You're blessed with a good, loud voice. Shout and make all the noise you can. If you can keep them from seeing Bison's people for one second more, that may decide it."

A giant with a gape-toothed grin knelt, hands clasped to help her mount; she put her left foot in them and swung into the saddle, and although she sat a tall horse, the giant's head was level with her own. She had chosen him for his size and ferocious appearance. (Distraction—distraction would be everything.) Now it struck her that she did not know his name. "Can you ride?" she asked. "If you can't, say so."

"Sure can, Maytera."

He was probably lying; but it was too late, too late to quiz him or get somebody else. She rose in her stirrups to consider the five riders behind her, and the giant's riderless horse. "Most of us will be killed, and it's quite likely that all of us will be."

The first floater would be well along Cage Street already, halted perhaps before the doors of the Alambrera; but if they were to succeed, their diversion would have to wait until the marching men behind the third floater had closed the gap. It might be best to fill the time.

"Should one of us live, however, it would be well for him—or her—to know the names of those who gave their lives. Scleroderma, I can't count you among us, but you are the most likely to live. Listen carefully."

Scleroderma nodded, her pudgy face pale.

"All of you. Listen, and try to remember."

The fear she had shut out so effectively was seeping back now. She bit her lip; her voice must not quaver. "I'm Maytera Mint, from the Sun Street manteion. But you know that. You," she pointed to the rearmost rider. "Give us your name, and say it loudly."

"Babirousa!"

"Good. And you?"

"Goral!"

"Kingcup!" The woman who had supplied horses for the rest.

"Yapok!"

"Marmot!"

"Gib from the Cock," the giant grunted, and mounted in a way that showed he was more accustomed to riding donkeys.

"I wish we had horns and war drums," Maytera Mint told them. "We'll have to use our voices and our weapons instead. Remember, the idea is to keep them, the crews of the floaters especially, looking and shooting at us for as long as we can."

The fear filled her mind, horrible and colder than ice; she felt sure her trembling fingers would drop Patera Silk's azoth if she tried to take it from her pocket; but she got it out anyway, telling herself that it would be preferable to drop it here, where Scleroderma could hand it back to her.

Scleroderma handed her the reins instead.

"You have all volunteered, and there is no disgrace in reconsidering. Those who wish may leave." Deliberately she faced forward, so that she would not see who dismounted.

At once she felt that there was no one behind her at all. She groped for something that would drive out the fear, and came upon a naked woman with yellow hair—a wild-eyed fury who was not herself at all—wielding a scourge whose lashes cut and tore the gray sickness until it fled her mind.

Perhaps because she had urged him forward with her heels, perhaps only because she had loosed his reins, the stallion was rounding the corner at an easy canter. There, still streets ahead though not so far as they had been, were the floaters, the third settling onto the rutted street, with the marching troopers closing behind it.

"For Echidna!" she shouted. "The gods will it!" Still she wished for war drums and horns, unaware that the drumming hooves echoed and re-echoed from each shiprock wall, that her trumpet had shaken the street. "Silk is Caldé!"

She jammed her sharp little heels in the stallion's sides. Fear was gone, replaced by soaring joy. *"Silk is Caldé!"* At her right the giant was firing two needlers as fast as he could pull their triggers.

"Down the Ayuntamiento! Silk is Caldé!"

The shimmering horror that was the azoth's blade could not be held on the foremost floater. Not by her, certainly not at this headlong gallop. Slashed twice across, the floater wept silvery metal as the street before it erupted in boiling dust and stones exploded from the gray walls of the Alambrera.

Abruptly, Yapok was on her right. To her left, Kingcup flailed a leggy bay with a long brown whip, Yapok bellowing obscenities, Kingcup shrieking curses, a nightmare witch, her loosed black hair streaming behind her.

The blade again, and the foremost floater burst in a ball of orange flame. Behind it, the buzz guns of the second were firing, the flashes from their muzzles mere sparks, the rattle of their shots lost in pandemonium. "Form up," she shouted, not knowing what she meant by it. Then, *"Forward! Forward!"*

Thousands of armed men and women were pouring from the buildings, crowding through doorways and leaping from windows. Yapok was gone, Kingcup somehow in front of her by half a length. Unseen hands snatched off her coif and plucked one flapping black sleeve.

The shimmering blade brought a gush of silver from the second floater, and there were no more flashes from its guns, only an explosion that blew off the turret—and a rain of stones upon the second floater, the third, and the Guardsmen behind it, and lines of slug guns booming from rooftops and high windows. But not enough, she thought. Not nearly enough, we must have more.

The azoth was almost too hot to hold. She took her thumb off the demon and was abruptly skyborne as the white stallion cleared a slab of twisted, smoking metal at a bound. The guns of the third floater were firing, the turret gun not at her but at the men and women pouring out of the buildings, the floater rising with a roar and a cloud of dust and sooty smoke that the wind snatched away, until the blade of her azoth impaled it and the floater crashed on its side, at once pathetic and comic.

To Silk's bewilderment, his captors had treated him with consideration, bandaging his wound and letting him lie unbound in an outsized bed with four towering posts which only that morning had belonged to some blameless citizen.

He had not lost consciousness so much as will. With mild surprise, he discovered that he no longer cared whether the Alambrera had surrendered, whether the Ayuntamiento remained in power, or whether the long sun would nourish Viron for ages to come or burn it to cinders. Those things had mattered. They no longer did. He was aware that he might die, but that did not matter either; he would surely die, whatever happened. If eventually, why not now? It would be over—over and done forever.

He imagined himself mingling with the gods, their humblest servitor and worshiper, yet beholding them face-to-face; and found that there was only one whom he desired to see, a god who was not among them.

"Well, well, well!" the surgeon exclaimed in a brisk, professional voice. "So you're Silk!"

He rolled his head on the pillow. "I don't think so."

"That's what they tell me. Somebody shoot you in the arm, too?"

"No. Something else. It doesn't matter." He spat blood.

"It does to me, that's an old dressing. It ought to be changed." The surgeon left, returning at once (it seemed) with a basin of water and a sponge. "I'm taking that ultrasonic diathermic wrapping on your ankle. We've got men who need it a lot more than you do."

"Then take it, please," Silk told him.

The surgeon looked surprised.

"What I mean is that 'Silk' has become someone a great deal bigger than I am—that I'm not what is meant when people say, 'Silk.'"

"You ought to be dead, Patera," the surgeon informed him somewhat later. "It'll do less damage if I open up the exit wound, instead of going in where the needle did. I'm going to turn you over. Did you hear that? I'm going to turn you over. Keep your nose and mouth to the side so you can breathe."

He did not, but the surgeon moved his head for him.

Abruptly he was sitting almost upright with a quilt around him while the surgeon stabbed him with another needle. "It's not as bad as I thought, but you need blood. You'll feel a lot better with more blood in you."

A dark flask dangled from the bedpost like a ripe fruit.

Someone he could not see was seated beside his bed. He turned his head and craned his neck to no avail. At last he extended a hand toward the visitor; and the visitor took it between his own, which were large and hard and warm. As soon as their hands touched, he knew.

You said you weren't going to help, he told the visitor. You said I wasn't to expect help from you, yet here you are.

The visitor did not reply, but his hands were clean and gentle and full of healing.

"Are you awake, Patera?"

Silk wiped his eyes. "Yes."

"I thought you were. Your eyes were closed, but you were crying."

"Yes," Silk said again.

"I brought a chair. I thought we might talk for a minute. You don't mind?" The man with the chair was robed in black.

"No. You're an augur, like me."

"We were at the schola together, Patera. I'm Shell—Patera Shell now. You sat behind me in canonics. Remember?"

"Yes. Yes, I do. It's been a long time."

Shell nodded. "Nearly two years." He was thin and pale, but his small shy smile made his face shine.

"It was good of you to come and see me, Patera—very good." Silk paused for a moment to think. "You're on the other side, the Ayuntamiento's side. You must be. You're taking a risk by talking to me, I'm afraid."

"I was." Shell coughed apologetically. "Perhaps— I don't know, Patera. I—I haven't been fighting, you know. Not at all."

"Of course not."

"I brought the Pardon of Pas to our dying. To your dying, too, Patera, when I could. When that was done, I helped nurse a little. There aren't enough doctors and nurses, not nearly enough, and there was a big battle on Cage Street. Do you know about it? I'll tell you if you like. Nearly a thousand dead."

Silk shut his eyes.

"Don't cry, Patera. Please don't. They've gone to the gods. All of them, from both sides, and it wasn't your fault, I'm sure. I didn't see the battle, but I heard a great deal about it. From the wounded, you know. If you'd rather talk about something else—"

"No. Tell me, please."

"I thought you'd want to know, that I could describe it to you and it would be something that I could do for you. I thought you might want me to shrive you, too. We can close the door. I talked to the captain, and he said that as long as I didn't give you a weapon it would be all right."

Silk nodded. "I should have thought of it myself. I've been involved with so many secular concerns lately that I've been getting lax, I'm afraid." There was a bow window behind Shell; noticing that it displayed only black night and their own reflected images, Silk asked, "Is this still Hieraxday, Patera?"

"Yes, but its after shadelow. It's about seven-thirty, I think. There's a clock in the captain's room, and it was seven-twenty-five when I went in. Seven-twenty-five by that clock, I mean, and I wasn't there long. He's very busy."

"Then I haven't neglected Thelxiepeia's morning prayers." Briefly, he wondered whether he could bring himself to say them when morning came, and whether he should. "I won't have to ask forgiveness for that when you shrive me. But first, tell me about the battle."

"Your forces have been trying to capture the Alambrera, Patera. Do you know about that?"

"I knew they had gone to attack it. Nothing more."

"They were trying to break down the doors and so on. But they didn't, and everybody inside thought they had gone away, probably to try to take over the Juzgado."

Silk nodded again.

"But before that, the government—the Ayuntamiento, I mean—had sent a lot of troopers, with floaters and so on and a company of soldiers, to drive them away and help the Guards in the Alambrera."

"Three companies of soldiers," Silk said, "and the Second Brigade of the Guard. That's what I was told, at any rate."

Shell nearly bowed. "Your information will be much more accurate than mine, I'm sure, Patera. They had trouble getting through the city, even with soldiers and floaters, although not as much as they expected. Do you know about that?"

Silk rolled his head from side to side.

"They did. People were throwing things. One man told me he was hit by a slop jar thrown out of a fourth-floor window." Shell ventured an apologetic laugh. "Can you imagine? What will the people who live up there do tonight, I wonder? But there wasn't much serious resistance, if you know what I mean. They expected barricades in the street, but there was nothing like that. They marched through the city and stopped in front of the Alambrera. The troopers were supposed to go in while the soldiers searched the buildings along Cage Street."

Silk allowed his eyes to close again, visualizing the column described by the monitor in Maytera Rose's glass.

"Then," Shell paused for emphasis, "General Mint herself charged them down Cage Street, riding like a devil on a big white horse. From the other way, you see. From the direction of the market."

Surprised, Silk opened his eyes. "*General* Mint?"

"That's what they call her. The rebels—your people, I mean." Shell cleared his throat. "The fighters loyal to the Caldé. To you."

"You're not offending me, Patera."

"They call her General Mint and she's got an azoth. Just imagine! She chopped up the Guard's floaters horribly with it. This trooper I talked to had been the driver of one, and he'd seen everything. Do you know how the Guard's floaters are on the inside, Patera?"

"I rode in one this morning." Silk shut his eyes again, striving to remember. "I rode inside until the rain stopped. Later I rode on it, sitting on the . . . Up on that round part that has the highest buzz gun. It was crowded inside, not at all comfortable, and we'd put the bodies in there— but it was better than being out in the rain, perhaps."

Shell nodded eagerly, happy to agree. "There are two men and an officer. One of the men drives the floater. He was the one I talked to. The officer's in charge. He sits beside the driver, and there's a glass for the officer, though some don't work any more, he said. The officer has a buzz gun, too, the one that points ahead. There's another man, the gunner, up in the round thing you sat on. It's called the turret."

"That's right. I remember now."

"General Mint's azoth cut right into their floater and killed their officer, and stopped one of the rotors. That's what this driver said. It had seemed to me that if an azoth could do that, it could cut right through the doors of the Alambrera and kill everyone in there, but he said they won't. That's because the doors are steel and three fingers thick, but a floater's armor is aluminum because it couldn't lift that much. It couldn't float at all, if it were made out of iron or steel."

"I see. I didn't know that."

"There was cavalry following General Mint. About a troop is what he said. I asked how many that was, and it's a hundred or more. The others had needlers and swords and things. His floater had fallen on its side, but he crawled out through the hatch. The gunner had already gotten out, he said, and their officer was dead, but as soon as he got out himself, someone rode him down and broke his arm. That's why he's here, and without the gods' favor he would've been killed. When he got up again, there were rebels—I mean—"

"I know what you mean, Patera. Go on, please."

"They were all around him. He said he would have climbed back in their floater, but it was starting to burn, and he knew that if the fire didn't go out their ammunition would explode, the bullets for the buzz guns. He wasn't wearing armor like the troopers outside, just a helmet, so he pulled it off and threw it away, and the—your people thought he was one of them, most of them. He said that sometimes swords would cut the men's armor. It's polymeric, did you know that, Patera? Sometimes they silver it, private guards and so on do, like a glazier silvers the back of a mirror. But it's still polymeric under that, and the troopers' is painted green like a soldier."

"It will stop needles, won't it?"

Shell nodded vigorously. "Mostly it will. Practically always. But sometimes a needle will go through the opening for the man's eyes, or where he breathes. When it does that, he's usually killed, they say. And sometimes a sword will cut right through their armor, if it's a big heavy sword, and the man's strong. Or stabbing can split the breastplate. A lot of your people had axes and hatchets. For firewood, you know. And some had clubs with spikes through them. A big club can knock down a trooper in armor, and if there's a spike in it, the spike will go right through." Shell paused for breath.

"But the soldiers aren't like that at all. Their skin's all metal, steel in the worst places. Even a slug from a slug gun will bounce off a soldier sometimes, and nobody can kill or even hurt a soldier with a club or a needler."

Silk said, I know, I shot one once, then realized that he had not spoken aloud. I'm like poor Mamelta, he thought—I have to remember to speak, to breathe out while I move my lips and tongue.

"One told me she saw two men trying to take a soldier's slug gun. They were both holding onto it, but he lifted them right off their feet and threw them around. This wasn't the driver but a woman I talked to, one of your people, Patera. She had her washing stick, and she got behind him and hit him with it, but he shook off the two men and hit her with the slug gun and broke her shoulder. A lot of your people had gotten slug guns from troopers by then, and they were shooting at the soldiers with them. Somebody shot the one fighting her. She would've been killed if it hadn't been for that she said. But the soldiers shot a lot of them, too, and chased them up Cheese Street and a lot of other streets. She tried to fight, but she didn't have a slug gun, and with her shoulder she couldn't have shot one if she'd had it. A slug hit her leg, and the doctors here had to cut it off."

"I'll pray for her," Silk promised, "and for everyone else who's been killed or wounded. If you see her again, Patera, please tell her how sorry I am that this happened. Was Maytera—was General Mint hurt?"

"They say not. They say she's planning another attack, but nobody really knows. Were you wounded very badly, Patera?"

"I don't believe I'm going to die." For seconds that grew to a minute or more, Silk stared in wonder at the empty flask hanging from the bedpost. Was life such a simple thing that it could be drained from a man as red fluid, or poured into him? Would he eventually discover that he held a different life, one which longed for a wife and children, in a house that he had never seen? It had not been his own blood—not his own life— surely. "I believed I was, not long ago. Even when you came, Patera. I didn't care. Consider the wisdom and mercy of the god who made us so that when we're about to die we no longer fear death!"

"If you don't think you're going to die—"

"No, no. Shrive me. The Ayuntamiento certainly intends to kill me. They can't possibly know I'm here; if they did, I'd be dead already." Silk pushed aside his quilt.

Hurriedly, Shell replaced it. "You don't have to kneel, Patera. You're still ill, terribly ill. You've been badly hurt. Turn your head toward the wall, please."

Silk did so, and the familiar words seemed to rise to his lips of their own volition. "Cleanse me, Patera, for I have given offense to Pas and to other gods." It was comforting, this return to ritual phrases he had memorized in childhood; but Pas was dead, and the well of his boundless mercy gone dry forever.

. . .

"Is that all, Patera?"

"Since my last shriving, yes."

"As penance for the evil you have done, Patera Silk, you are to perform a meritorious act before this time tomorrow." Shell paused and swallowed. "I'm assuming that your physical condition will permit it. You don't think it's too much? The recitation of a prayer will do."

"Too much?" With difficulty, Silk forced himself to keep his eyes averted. "No, certainly not. Too little, I'm sure."

"Then I bring to you, Patera Silk, the pardon of all the gods—"

Of *all* the gods. He had forgotten that aspect of the Pardon, fool that he was! Now the words brought a huge sense of relief. In addition to Echidna and her dead husband, in addition to the Nine and truly minor gods like Kypris, Shell was empowered to grant amnesty for the Outsider. For all the gods. Hence he, Silk, was forgiven his doubt.

He turned his head so that he could see Shell. "Thank you, Patera. You don't know—you can't—how much this means to me."

Shell's hesitant smile shone again. "I'm in a position to do you another favor, Patera. I have a letter for you from His Cognizance." Seeing Silk's expression, he added quickly, "It's only a circular letter, I'm afraid. All of us get a copy." He reached into his robe. "When I told Patera Jerboa you had been captured, he gave me yours, and it's about you."

The folded sheet Shell handed him bore the seal of the Chapter in mulberry-colored wax; beside it, a clear, clerkly hand had written: "Silk, Sun Street."

"It's a very important letter, really," Shell said.

Silk broke the seal and unfolded the paper.

30th Nemesis 332
To the Clergy of the Chapter,
Both Severally and Collectively

Greetings in the name of Pas, in the name of Scylla, and in the names of all gods! Know that you are ever in my thoughts, as in my heart.

The present disturbed state of Our Sacred City obliges us to be even more conscious of our sacred duty to minister to the dying, not only to those amongst them with whose recent actions we may sympathize, but to all those to whom, as we apprehend, Hierax may swiftly reveal his compassionate power. Thus it is that I implore you this day to cultivate the perpetual and indefatigable—

Patera Remora composed this, Silk thought; and as though Remora sat before him, he saw Remora's long, sallow, uplifted face, the tip of the quill just brushing his lips as he sought for a complexity of syntax that would satisfy his insatiate longing for caution and precision.

The perpetual and indefatigable predisposition toward mercy and pardon whose conduit you so frequently must be.

Many of you have appealed for guidance in these most disturbing days. Nay, many appeal so still, even hourly. Most of you will have learned before you read this epistle of the lamented demise of the presiding officer of the Ayuntamiento.

The late Councillor Lemur was a man of extraordinary gifts, and his passing cannot but leave a void in every heart. How I long to devote the remainder of this necessarily curtailed missive to mourning his passing. Instead, for such are the exactions of this sad whorl, the whorl that passes, my duty to you requires that I forewarn you without delay against the baseless pretexts of certain vile insurgents who would have you to believe that they act in the late Councillor Lemur's name.

Let us set aside, my beloved clergy, all fruitless debate regarding the propriety of an intercaldean caesura spanning some two decades. That the press of unhappy events then rendered an interval of that kind, if not desirable, then unquestionably attractive, we can all agree. That it represented, to judgments not daily schooled to the nice discriminations of the law, a severe strain upon the elasticity of our Charter, we can agree likewise, can we not? The argument is wholly historical now. O beloved, let us resign it to the historians.

What is inarguable is that this caesura, to which I have had reason to refer above, has attained to its ordained culmination. It cannot, O my beloved clergy, as it should not, survive the grievous loss which it has so recently endured. What, then, we may not illegitimately inquire, is to succeed that just, beneficent and ascendant government so sadly terminated?

Beloved clergy, let us not be unmindful of the wisdom of the past, wisdom which lies in no less a vehicle than our own Chrasmologic Writings. Has it not declared, *"Vox populi, vox dei"?* Which is to say, in the will of the masses we may discern words of Pas's. At the present critical moment in the lengthy epic of Our Sacred City, Pas's grave words are not to be mistaken. With many voices they cry out that the time has arrived for a precipitate return to that Charteral guardianship which once our city knew. Shall it be said of us that we stop our ears to Pas's words?

Nor is their message so brief, and so less than mistakable. From forest to lake, from the proud crown of the Palatine to the humblest of alleys they proclaim him. O my beloved clergy, with what incommunicable joy shall I do so additionally. For Supreme Pas has, as never previously, espoused for our city a caldé from within our own ranks, an anointed augur, holy, pious, and redolent of sanctity.

May I name him? I shall, yet surely I need not. There is not one amongst you, Beloved Clergy, who will not know that name prior to mine overjoyed acclamation. It is Patera Silk.

Again I say, Patera Silk!

How readily here might I inscribe, let us welcome him and obey him as one of ourselves. With what delight shall I inscribe in its place, let us welcome him and obey him, for he is one of ourselves!

May every god favor you, beloved clergy. Blessed be you in the Most Sacred Name of Pas, Father of the Gods, in that of Gracious Echidna, His Consort, in those of their Sons and their Daughters alike, this day and forever, in the name of their eldest child, Scylla, Patroness of this, Our Holy City of Viron. Thus say I, Pa. Quetzal, Prolocutor.

As Silk refolded the letter, Shell said, "His Cognizance has come down completely on your side, you see, and brought the Chapter with him. You said—I hope you were mistaken in this, Patera, really I do. But you said a minute ago that if the Ayuntamiento knew you were here they'd have you shot. If that's true—" He cleared his throat nervously.

"If it's true, they'll have His Cognizance shot too. And—and some of the rest of us."

"The coadjutor," Silk said, "he drafted this. He'll die as well, if they can get their hands on him." It was strange to think of Remora, that circumspect diplomatist, tangled and dead in his own web of ink.

Of Remora dying for him.

"I suppose so, Patera." Shell hesitated, plainly ill at ease. "I'd call you—use the other word. But it might be dangerous for you."

Silk nodded slowly, stroking his cheek.

"His Cognizance says you're the first augur, ever. That—it came as a shock to—to a lot of us, I suppose. To Patera Jerboa, he said. He says it's never happened before in his lifetime. Do you know Patera Jerboa, Patera?"

Silk shook his head.

"He's quite elderly. Eighty-one, because we had a little party for him just a few weeks ago. But then he thought, you know, sort of getting still and pulling at his beard the way he does, and then he said it was sensible enough, really. All the others, the previous—the previous—"

"I know what you mean, Patera."

"They'd been chosen by the people. But you, Patera, you were chosen by the gods, so naturally their choice fell upon an augur, since augurs are the people they've chosen to serve them."

"You yourself are in danger, Patera," Silk said. "You're in nearly as much danger as I am, and perhaps more. You must be aware of it."

Shell nodded miserably.

"I'm surprised they let you in here after this."

"They—the captain, Patera. I—I haven't . . ."

"They don't know."

"I don't think so, Patera. I don't think they do. I didn't tell them."

"That was wise, I'm sure." Silk studied the window as he had before, but as before saw only their reflections, and the night. "This Patera Jerboa, you're his acolyte? Where is he?"

"At our manteion, on Brick Street."

Silk shook his head.

"Near the crooked bridge, Patera."

"Way out east?"

"Yes, Patera." Shell fidgeted uncomfortably. "That's where we are now, Patera. On Basket Street. Our manteion's that way," he pointed, "about five streets."

"I see. That's right, they lifted me into something—into some sort of cart that jolted terribly. I remember lying on sawdust and trying to cough. I couldn't, and my mouth and nose kept filling with blood." Silk's index finger drew small circles on his cheek. "Where's my robe?"

"I don't know. The captain has it, I suppose, Patera."

"The battle, when General Mint attacked the floaters on Cage Street, was that this afternoon?"

Shell nodded again.

"About the time I was shot, perhaps, or a little later. You brought the Pardon to the wounded. To all of them? All those in danger of death, I mean?"

"Yes, Patera."

"Then you went back to your manteion—?"

"For something to eat, Patera, a bite of supper." Shell looked apologetic. "This brigade—it's the Third. They're in reserve, they say. They don't have much. Some were going into people's houses, you know, and taking any food they could find. There's supposed to be food coming in wagons, but I thought—"

"Of course. You returned to your manse to eat with Patera Jerboa, and this letter had arrived while you were gone. There would have been a copy for you, too, and one for him."

Shell nodded eagerly. "That's right, Patera."

"You would have read yours at once, of course. My copy—this one— it was there as well?"

"Yes, Patera."

"So someone at the Palace knew I had been captured, and where I'd been taken. He sent my copy to Patera Jerboa instead of to my own manteion in the hope that Patera Jerboa could arrange to get it to me, as he did. His Cognizance was with me when I was shot; there's no reason to conceal that now. While my wounds were being treated, I was wondering whether he had been killed. The officer who shot me may not have recognized him, but if he did . . ." Silk let the thought trail away. "If they don't know about this already—and I think you're right, they can't know yet, not here at any rate—they're bound to find out soon. You realize that?"

"Yes, Patera."

"You must leave. It would probably be wise for you and Patera Jerboa to leave your manteion, in fact—to go to a part of the city controlled by General Mint, if you can."

"I—" Shell seemed to be choking. He shook his head desperately.

"You what, Patera?"

"I don't want to leave you as long as I can be of—of help to you. Of service. It's my duty."

"You have been of help," Silk told him. "You've rendered invaluable service to me and to the Chapter already. I'll see you're recognized for it, if I can." He paused, considering.

"You can be of further help, too. On your way out, I want you to speak to this captain for me. There were two letters in a pocket of my robe. They were on the mantel this morning; my acolyte must have put them there yesterday. I haven't read them, and your giving me this one has reminded me of them." Somewhat tardily, he thrust the letter under his quilt. "One had the seal of the Chapter. It may have been another copy of this, though that doesn't seem very likely, since this one has today's date. Besides, they wouldn't have sent this to Patera Jerboa this evening, in that case."

"I suppose not, Patera."

"Don't mention them to the captain. Just say I'd like to have my robe—all of my clothes. Ask for my clothes and see what he gives you. Bring them to me, my robe particularly. If he mentions the letters, say that I'd like to see them. If he won't give them to you, try to find out what was in them. If he won't tell you, return to your manteion. Tell Patera Jerboa that I, the caldé, order him to get himself and you—are there sibyls, too?"

Shell nodded. "There's Maytera Wood—"

"Never mind their names. That you and he and they are to lock up the manteion and leave as quickly as possible."

"Yes, Patera." Shell stood, very erect. "But I won't go back to our manteion straight away, no matter what the captain says. I—I'm coming back. Back here to see you and tell you what he said, and try to do something more for you, if I can. Don't tell me not to, please, Patera. I'll only disobey."

To his surprise, Silk found that he was smiling. "Your disobedience is better than the obedience of many people I've known, Patera Shell. Do what you think right; you will anyway, I feel certain."

Shell left, and the room seemed empty as soon as he was out the door. Silk's wound began to throb, and he made himself think of something else. How proudly Shell had announced his intention to disobey, while his lip trembled! It reminded Silk of his mother, her eyes shining with tears of joy at some only too ordinary childhood feat. *Oh, Silk! My son, my son!* That was how he felt now. These boys!

Yet Shell was no younger. They had entered the schola together, and Shell had sat at the desk in front of his own when an instructor insisted on alphabetical seating; they had been anointed on the same day, and both had been assigned to assist venerable augurs who were no longer able to attend to all the demands of their manteions.

Shell, however, had not been enlightened by the Outsider—or had not had a vein burst in his head, as Doctor Crane would have had it. Shell had not been enlightened, had not hurried to the market, had not encountered Blood. . . .

He had been as young as Shell when he had talked to Blood and plucked three cards out of Blood's hand, not knowing that somewhere below a monitor was mad and howling for want of those cards—as young or nearly, because Shell might have done it, too. Again Silk smelled the dead dog in the gutter and the stifling dust raised by Blood's floater, saw Blood wave his stick, tall, red faced, and perspiring. Silk coughed, and felt that a poker had been plunged into his chest.

Somewhat unsteadily, he crossed the room to the window and raised the sash to let in the night wind, then surveyed his naked torso in the mirror over the bureau, a much larger one than his shaving mirror back at the manse.

A dressing half concealed the multicolored bruise left by Musk's hilt. From what little anatomy he had picked up from the victims he had sacrificed, he decided that the needle had missed his heart by four fingers. Still, it must have been good shooting by a mounted man.

With his back to the mirror, he craned his neck to see as much as possible of the dressing on his back; it was larger, and his back hurt more. He was conscious of a weak wrongness deep in his chest, and of the effort he had to make to breathe.

Clothing in the drawers of the bureau: underwear, tunics, and carelessly folded trousers—under these last, a woman's perfumed scarf. This was a young man's room, a son's; the couple who owned the house would have a bedroom on the ground floor, a corner room with several windows.

Chilled, he returned to the bed and drew up the quilt. The son had left without packing, otherwise the drawers would be half empty. Perhaps he was fighting in Maytera Mint's army.

Some part of Kypris had entered her, and that fragment had made the shy sibyl a general—that, and Echidna's command. For a moment he wondered what fragment it had been, and whether Echidna had realized Maytera possessed it. It was the element that had freed Chenille from rust, presumably; they would be part and parcel of the same thing. Kypris had told him she was hunted, and His Cognizance had called it a wonder that she had not been killed long ago. Echidna and her children, hunting the goddess of love, must soon have learned that love is more than perfumed scarves and thrown flowers. That there is steel in love.

A young woman had thrown that scarf from a balcony, no doubt. Silk tried to visualize her, found she wore Hyacinth's face, and thrust the vision back. Blood had wiped his face with a peach-colored handkerchief, a handkerchief more heavily perfumed than the scarf. And Blood had said . . .

Had said there were people who could put on a man like a tunic. He had been referring to Mucor, though he, Silk, had not known it then—had not known that Mucor existed, a girl who could dress her spirit in the flesh of others just as he, a few moments before, had been considering putting on the clothes of the son whose room this was.

Softly he called, "Mucor? Mucor?" and listened; but there was no phantom voice, no face but his own in the mirror above the bureau. Closing his eyes, he composed a long formal prayer to the Outsider, thanking him for his life, and for the absence of Blood's daughter. When it was complete, he began a similar prayer to Kypris.

Beyond the bedroom door, a sentry sprang to attention with an audible clash of his weapon and click of his heels.

Shadeup woke Auk, brilliant beams of the long sun piercing his tasseled awnings, his gauze curtains, his rich draperies of puce velvet, and the grimed glass of every window in the place, slipping past his lowered blinds of split bamboo, the warped old boards someone else had nailed up, his colored Scylla, and his shut and bolted shutters; through wood, paper, and stone.

He blinked twice and sat up, rubbing his eyes. "I feel better," he announced, then saw that Chenille was still asleep, Incus and Urus both sleeping, Dace and Bustard sound asleep as well, and only big Hammerstone the soldier already up, sitting crosslegged with Oreb on his shoulder and his back against the tunnel wall. "That's good, trooper," Hammerstone said.

"Not good," Auk explained. "I don't mean that. Better. Better than I did, see? That feels better than good, 'cause when you're feeling good you don't even think about it. But when you feel the way I do, you pay more attention than when you're feeling good. I'm a dimberdamber nanny nipper." He nudged Chenille with the toe of his boot. "Look alive, Jugs. Time for breakfast!"

"What's the matter with *you*?" Incus sat up as though it had been he and not Chenille who had been thus nudged.

"Not a thing," Auk told him. "I'm right as rain." He considered the matter. "If it does, I'll go to the Cock. If it don't, I'll do some business on the hill. Slept with my boots on." He seated himself beside Chenille. "You too? You shouldn't do that, Patera. Bad on the feet."

Untying their laces, he tugged off his boots, then pulled off his stockings. "Feel how wet these are. Still wet from the boat. Wake up, old man! From the boat and the rain. If we had that tall ass again, I'd make him squirt fire for me so I could dry 'em. Phew!" He hung the stockings over the tops of his boots and pushed them away.

Chenille sat up and began to take off her jade earrings. "Ooh, did I dream!" She shuddered. "I was lost, see? All alone down here, and this tunnel I was in kept going deeper both ways. I'd walk one way for a long, long while, and it would just keep going down. So I'd turn around and walk the other way, only that way went down, too, deeper and deeper all the time."

"Recollect that the *immortal gods* are always with you, my daughter," Incus told her.

"Uh-huh. Hackum, I've got to get hold of some clothes. My sunburn's better. I could wear them, and it's too cold down here without any." She grinned. "A bunch of new clothes, and a double red ribbon.

After that, I'll be ready for ham and half a dozen eggs scrambled with peppers."

"Watch out," Hammerstone warned her, "I don't think your friend's ready for inspection."

Auk rose, laughing. "Look at this," he told Hammerstone, and kicked Urus expertly, bending up his bare toes so that Urus's ribs received the ball of his foot.

Urus blinked and rubbed his eyes just as Auk had, and Auk realized that he himself was the long sun. He had awakened himself with his own light, light that filled the whole tunnel, too dazzlingly bright for Urus's weak eyes.

"The way you been carrying the old man," he told Urus, "I don't like it." He wondered whether his hands were hot enough to burn Urus. It seemed possible; they were ordinary when he wasn't looking at them, but when he did they glowed like molten gold. Stooping, he flicked Urus's nose with a forefinger, and when Urus did not cry out, jerked him to his feet.

"When you carry the old man," Auk told him, "you got to do it like you love him. Like you were going to kiss him." It might be a good idea to make Urus really kiss him, but Auk was afraid Dace might not like it.

"All right," Urus said. "All right."

Bustard inquired, How you feelin', sprat?

Auk pondered. "There's parts of me that work all right," he declared at length, "and parts that don't. A couple I'm not set about. Remember old Marble?"

Sure.

"She told us she could pull out these lists. Out of her sleeve, like. What was right and what wasn't. With me, it's one thing at a time."

"I can do that," Hammerstone put in. "It's perfectly natural."

Chenille had both earrings off, and was rubbing her ears. "Can you put these in your pocket, Hackum? I got no place to carry them."

"Sure," Auk said. He did not turn to look at her.

"I could get a couple cards for them at Sard's. I could buy a good worsted gown and shoes, and eat at the pastry cook's till I was ready to split."

"Like, there's this dimber punch," Auk explained to Urus. "I learned it when I wasn't no bigger than a cobbler's goose, and I always did like it a lot. You don't swing, see? Culls always talk about swinging at you, and they do. Only this is better. I'm not sure it still works, though."

His right fist caught Urus square in the mouth, knocking him backward into the shiprock wall. Incus gasped.

"You sort of draw your arm up and straighten it out," Auk explained. Urus slumped to the tunnel floor. "Only with your weight behind it, and your knuckles level. Look at them." He held them out. "If your knuckles go up and down, that's all right, too. Only it's a different punch, see?" Not as good, Bustard said. "Only not as good," Auk confirmed.

I kin walk, big feller, he don't have to carry me, nor kiss me neither.

The dead body at his feet, Auk decided, must be somebody else. Urus, maybe, or Gelada.

Maytera Marble tried to decide how long it had been since she had done this, entering *roof,* and when that evoked only a flood of dripping ceilings and soaked carpets, *attic.*

A hundred and eighty-four years ago.

She could scarcely believe it—did not wish to believe it. A graceful girl with laughing eyes and industrious hands had climbed this same stair, as she still did a score of times every day, walked along this hall, and halted beneath this odd-looking door overhead, reaching up with a tool that had been lost now for more than a century.

She snapped her new fingers in annoyance, producing a loud and eminently satisfactory clack, then returned to one of the rooms that had been hers and rummaged through her odds-and-ends drawer until she found the big wooden crochet hook that she had sometimes plied before disease had deprived her of her fingers. Not these fingers, to be sure.

Back in the hall, she reached up as the girl who had been herself had and hooked the ring, wondering whimsically whether it had forgotten how to drop down on its chain.

It had not. She tugged. Puffs of dust emerged from the edges of the door above her head. The hall would have to be swept again. She hadn't been up there, no one had—

A harder tug, and the door inclined reluctantly downward, exposing a band of darkness. "Am I going to have to swing on you?" she asked. Her voice echoed through all the empty rooms, leaving her sorry she had spoken aloud.

Another tug evoked squeals of protest, but brought the bottom of the door low enough for her to grasp it and pull it down; the folding stair that was supposed to slide out when she did yielded to a hard pull.

I'll oil this, she resolved. I don't care if there isn't any oil. I'll cut up some fat from that bull and boil it, and skim off the grease and strain it, and use that. Because this *isn't* the last time. It *is not.*

She trotted up the folding steps in an energetic flurry of black bombazine.

Just look how good my leg is! Praise to you, Great Pas!

The attic was nearly empty. There was never much left when a sibyl died; what there was, was shared among the rest in accordance with her wishes, or returned to her family. For half a minute, Maytera Marble tried to recall who had owned the rusted trunk next to the chimney, eventually running down the whole list—every sibyl who had ever lived in the cenoby—without finding a single tin trunk among the associated facts.

The little gable window was closed and locked. She told herself that she was being foolish even as she wrestled its stubborn catch. Whatever it was that she had glimpsed in the sky while crossing the playground was gone, must certainly be gone by this time if it had ever existed.

Probably it had been nothing but a cloud.

She had expected the window to stick, but the dry heat of the last eight months had shrunk its ancient wood. She heaved at it with all her strength, and it shot up so violently that she thought the glass must break.

Silence followed, with a pleasantly chill wind through the window. She listened, then leaned out to peer up at the sky, and at last (as she had planned the whole time, having a lively appreciation of the difficulty of proving a negative after so many years of teaching small boys and girls) she stepped over the sill and out onto the thin old shingles of the cenoby roof.

Was it necessary to climb to the peak? She decided that it was, necessary for her peace of mind at least, though she wondered what the quarter would say if somebody saw her there. Not that it mattered, and most were off fighting anyhow. It wasn't as noisy as it had been during the day, but you could still hear shots now and then, like big doors shutting hard far away. Doors shutting on the past, she thought. The cold wind flattened her skirt against her legs as she climbed, and would have snatched off her coif had not one hand clamped it to her smooth metal head.

There were fires, as she could see easily from the peak, one just a few streets away. Saddle Street or String Street, she decided, probably Saddle Street, because that was where the pawnbrokers were. More fires beyond it, right up to the market and on the other side, as was to be expected. Darkness except for a few lighted windows up on Palatine Hill.

Which meant, more surely than any rumor or announcement, that Maytera Mint had not won. Hadn't won yet. Because the Hill would burn, would be looted and burned as predictably as the sixth term in a Fibonacci series of ten was an eleventh of the whole. With the Civil Guard beaten, nothing—

Before she could complete the thought, she caught sight of it, way to the south. She had been looking west toward the market and north to the Palatine, but it was over the Orilla . . . No, leagues south of that, way over the lake. Hanging low in the southern sky and, yes, opposing the wind in some fashion, because the wind was in the north, was blowing cold out of the north where night was new, because the wind must have come up, now that she came to think of it, only a few minutes before while she had been in the palaestra cutting up the last of the meat and carrying it down to the root cellar. She had come upstairs again and found her hoarded wrapping papers blown all over the kitchen, and shut the window.

So this thing—this huge thing, whatever it might be—had been over the city or nearly over it when she had glimpsed it above the back wall of the ball court. And it wasn't being blown south any more, as a real cloud would be; if anything, it was creeping north toward the city again, was creeping ever so slowly down the sky.

She watched for a full three minutes to make sure.

Was creeping north like a beetle exploring a bowl, losing heart at times and retreating, then inching forward again. It had been here, had been over the city, before. Or almost over it, when the wind had risen— had been taken unawares, as it seemed, and blown away over the lake; and now it had collected its strength to return, wind or no wind.

So briefly that she was not sure she had really seen it, something flashed from the monstrous dark flying bulk, a minute pinprick of light, as though someone in the shadowy skylands behind it had squeezed an igniter.

Whatever it might be, there was no way for her to stop it. It would come, or it would not, and she had work to do, as she always did. Water, quite a lot of it, would have to be pumped to fill the wash boiler. She picked her way back to the gable, wondering how much additional damage she had done to a roof by no means tight to begin with.

She would have to carry wood in, enough for a big fire in the stove. Then she could wash the sheets from the bed she had died in and hang them out to dry. If Maytera Mint came back (and Maytera Marble prayed very fervently that she would) she could cook breakfast for her on the same fire, and Maytera Mint might even bring friends with her. The men, if there were any, could eat in the garden; she would carry one of the long tables and some chairs out of the palaestra for them. Luckily there was still plenty of meat, though she had cooked some for Villus and given more to his family when she had carried him home.

She stepped back into the attic and closed the window.

Her sheets would be dry by shadeup. She could iron them and put them back on her bed. She was still senior sibyl—or rather, was again senior sibyl, so both rooms were hers, though she probably ought to move everything into the big one.

Descending the folding steps, she decided that she would leave them down until she oiled them. She could cut off some fat and boil it in a saucepan while the wash water was getting hot; the boiler wouldn't take up the whole stove. By shadeup, the thing in the air would be back, perhaps; if she stood in the middle of Silver Street she might be able to see it quite clearly then, if she had time.

Auk felt sure they had been tramping through this tunnel forever, and that was funny because he could remember when they had turned off the other one to go down this one that they had been going down since Pas built the Whorl, Urus spitting blood and carrying the body, himself behind them in case Urus needed winnowing out, Dace and Bustard so they could talk to him, then Patera with the big soldier with the slug gun who had told them how to walk and made him do it, and last Chenille in Patera's robe, with Oreb and her launcher. Auk would rather have walked with her and had tried to, but it was no good.

He looked around at her. She waved friendly, and Bustard and Dace had gone. He thought of asking Incus and the soldier what had become of them but decided he didn't want to talk to them, and she was too far in back for a private chat. Bustard had most likely gone on ahead to look things over and taken the old man with him. It would be like Bustard, and if Bustard found something to eat he'd bring him back some.

Pray to Phaea, Maytera Mint instructed him. Phaea is the food goddess. Pray to her, Auk, and you will surely be fed. He grinned at her. "Good to see you, Maytera! I been worried about you." May every god smile upon you, Auk, this day and every day. Her smile turned the cold damp tunnel into a palace and replaced the watery green glow of the crawling light with the golden flood that had awakened him. Why should you worry about me, Auk? I have served the gods faithfully since I was fifteen. They will not abandon me. No one has less reason to worry than I. "Maybe you could get some god to come down here and walk with us," Auk suggested.

Behind him, Incus protested, "*Auk,* my son!"

He made a rude noise and looked around for Maytera Mint, but she was gone. For a minute he thought she might have run ahead to talk to Bustard, then realized that she had gone to fetch a god to keep him company. That was the way she'd always been. The least little thing you happened to mention, she'd jump up and do it if she could.

He was still worried about her, though. If she was going to Mainframe to fetch a god, she'd have to pass the devils that made trouble for people on the way, telling lies and pulling them off the Aureate Path. He should have asked her to go get Phaea. Phaea and maybe a couple pigs. Jugs would like some ham, and he still had his hanger and knife. He could kill a pig and cut it up, and dish up her ham. Shag, he was hungry himself and Jugs couldn't eat a whole pig. They'd save the tongue for Bustard, he'd always liked pig's tongue. It was Phaesday, so Maytera would most likely bring Phaea, and Phaea generally brought at least one pig. Gods generally brought whatever animal theirs was, or anyhow, pretty often.

Pigs for Phaea. (You had to get them all right if you wanted to learn the new stuff next year.) Pigs for Phaea and lions or anyhow cats for Sphigx. Who'd eat a cat? Fish for Scylla, but some fish would be all right. Little birds for Molpe, and the old 'un had limed perches for 'em, salted 'em, and made sparrow pie when he'd got enough. Bats for Tartaros, and owls and moles.

Moles?

Suddenly and unpleasantly it struck Auk that Tartaros was the underground god, the god for mines and caves. So this was his place, only Tartaros was supposed to be a special friend of his and look what had happened to him down here, he had made Tartaros shaggy mad at him somehow because his head hurt, his head wasn't right, something kept sliding and slipping up there like a needler that wouldn't chamber right no matter how much you oiled it and made sure every last needle was as straight as the sun. He reached under his tunic for his, but it wasn't right at all—was so wrong, in fact, that it wasn't there, though Maytera Mint was his mother and in need of him and it.

"Poor Auk! Poor Auk!" Oreb circled above his head. The wind from his laboring wings stirred Auk's hair, but Oreb would not settle on his shoulder, and soon flew back to Chenille.

It wasn't there any more and neither was she. Auk wept.

The captain's salute was much smarter than his torn and soiled green uniform. "My men are in position, My General. My floater is patrolling. To reinforce the garrison by stealth is no longer possible. Nor will reinforcement at the point of the sword be possible, until we are dead."

Bison snorted, tilting back the heavy oak chair that was temporarily his.

Maytera Mint smiled. "Very good, Captain. Thank you. Perhaps you had better get some rest now."

"I have slept, My General, though not long. I have eaten as well, as you, I am told, have not. Now I inspect my men at their posts. When my inspection is complete, perhaps I shall sleep another hour, with my sergeant to wake me."

"I'd like to go with you," Maytera Mint told him. "Can you wait five minutes?"

"Certainly, My General. I am honored. But . . ."

She looked at him sharply. "What is it, Captain? Tell me, please."

"You yourself must sleep, My General, and eat as well. Or you will be fit for nothing tomorrow."

"I will, later. Please sit down. We're tired, all of us, and you must be exhausted." She turned back to Bison. "We have a principle in the Chapter, for sibyls like me and augurs like Patera Silk. Discipline, it's called, and it comes from an old word for pupil or student. If you're a teacher, as I am, you must have discipline in the classroom before you can teach anything. If you don't, they'll be so busy talking among themselves that they won't hear a thing that you say, and draw pictures instead of doing the assignment."

Bison nodded.

Recalling an incident from the year before, Maytera Mint smiled again. "Unless you've *told* them to draw pictures. If you've told them to draw, they'll write each other notes."

The captain smoothed his small mustache. "My General. We have discipline also, we officers and men of the Civil Guard. The word is the same. The practice, I dare say, not entirely different."

"I know, but I can't use you to patrol the streets and stop the looting. I wish I could, Captain. It would be very convenient, and no doubt effective. But to many people the Guard is the enemy. There would be a rebellion against our rebellion, and that's exactly what we cannot afford."

She turned back to Bison. "You understand why this is needed, don't you? Tell me."

"We're robbing ourselves," he said.

His beard made it difficult to read his expression, but she tried and decided he was uncomfortable. "What you say is true. The people whose houses and shops are being looted are our people, too, and if they have to stay there to defend them, they can't fight for us. But that isn't all, is it? What else did you want to say?"

"Nothing, General."

"You must tell me everything." She wanted to touch him, as she would have touched one of the children at that moment, but decided it might be misconstrued. "Telling me everything when I ask you to is discipline as well, if you like. Are we going to let the Guard be better than we are?"

Bison did not reply.

"But it's really more important than discipline. Nothing is more important to us now than my knowing what you think is important. You and the captain here, and Zoril, and Kingcup, and all the rest."

When he still said nothing, she added, "Do you want us to fail, so you won't be embarrassed, Bison? That is what is going to happen if we won't share concerns and information: we will fail the gods and die. All of us, probably. Certainly I will, because I will fight until they kill me. What is it?"

"They're burning, too," he blurted. "The burning's worse than the looting, a lot worse. With this wind, they'll burn down the city if we don't stop them. And—and . . ."

"And what?" Maytera Mint nibbled her underlip. "And put out the fires that are raging all around the city already, of course. You're right, Bison. You always are." She glanced at the door. "Teasel? Are you still out there? Come in, please. I need you."

"Yes, Maytera."

"We're telling one another we should rest, Teasel. It seems to be the convention of this night. You're not exempt. You were quite ill only a few days ago. Didn't Patera Silk bring you the Peace of Pas?"

Teasel nodded solemnly; she was a slender, pale girl of thirteen, with delicate features and lustrous black hair. "On Sphixday, Maytera, and I started getting better right away."

"Sphixday, and this is Hieraxday." Maytera Mint glanced at the blue china clock on the sideboard. "Thelxday in a few hours, so we'll call it Thelxday. Even so, less than a week ago you were in imminent danger of death, and tonight you're running errands for me when you ought to be in bed. Can you run one more?"

"I'm fine, Maytera."

"Then find Lime. Tell her where I am, and that I want to see her just as soon as she can get away. Then go home and go to bed. *Home,* I said. Will you do that, Teasel?"

Teasel curtsied, whirled, and was gone.

"She's a good, sensible girl," Maytera Mint told Bison and the captain. "Not one of mine. Mine are older, and they're off fighting or nursing, or they were. Teasel's one of Maytera Marble's, very likely the best of them."

Both men nodded.

"Captain, I won't keep you waiting much longer. Bison, I had begun to talk about discipline. I was interrupted, which served me right for being so long-winded. I was going to say that out of twenty boys and girls, you can make eighteen good students with discipline. I can, and you could too. In fact you would probably be better at it than I am, with a little practice." She sighed, then forced herself to sit up straight with her shoulders back.

"Of the remaining two, one will never be a good student. He doesn't have it in him, and all you can do is stop him from unsettling the others. The other one doesn't need discipline at all, or at least that's how it seems. Pas's own truth is that he's already disciplined himself before you ever called the class to order. Do you understand me?"

Bison nodded.

"You're one of those. If you weren't, you wouldn't be my surrogate now. Which you are, you know. If I am killed, you must take charge of everything."

Bison grinned, big white teeth flashing in the thicket of his black beard. "The gods love you, General. Your getting killed's one thing I don't have to worry about."

She waited for a better answer.

"Hierax forbid," Bison said at last. "I'll do my best if it happens."

"I know you will, because you always do. What you have to do is find others like yourself. We don't have enough time to establish real discipline, though I wish very much that we did. Choose men with needlers, we won't need slug guns for this—older men, who won't loot themselves when they're sent to stop looters. Organize them in groups of four, designate a leader for each group, and have them tell—Don't forget this, it's extremely important. Have them tell everyone they meet that looting and burning have to stop, and they'll shoot anyone they find doing either."

She rose. "We'll go now, Captain. I want to see how you've arranged this. I've a great deal to learn and very little time to learn it in."

Horn and Nettle, he with a captured slug gun and she with a needler, had stationed themselves outside the street door.

"Horn, go in the house and find yourself a bed," Maytera Mint told him. "That is an order. When you wake up, come back here and relieve Nettle if she's still here. Nettle, I'm going around the Alambrera with the captain. I'll be back soon."

The wind that chilled her face seemed almost supernatural after so many months of heat; she murmured thanks to Molpe, then recalled that the wind was fanning the fires Bison feared, and that it might—that in some cases it most certainly would—spread fire from shop to stable to manufactory. That there was a good chance the whole city would burn while she fought the Ayuntamiento for it.

"The Ayuntamiento. They aren't divine, Captain."

"I assure you, I have never imagined that they were, My General." He guided her down a crooked street whose name she had forgotten, if she had ever known it; around its shuttered store fronts the wind whispered of snow.

"Since they aren't," she continued, "they can't possibly resist the will of the gods for long. It is Echidna's will, certainly. I think we can be sure it's Scylla's too."

"Also that of Kypris," he reminded her. "Kypris spoke to me, My General, saying that Patera Silk must be caldé. I serve you because you serve him, him because he serves her."

She had scarcely heard him. "Five old men. Four, if His Cognizance is right, and no doubt he is. What gives them the courage?"

"I cannot guess, My General. Here is our first post. Do you see it?"

She shook her head.

"Corporal!" the captain called. Hands clapped, and lights kindled across the street; a gleaming gun barrel protruded from a second-floor window. The captain pointed. "We have a buzz gun for this post, as you see, My General. A buzz gun because the street offers the most direct route to the entrance. The angle affords us a longitudinal field of fire. Down there," he pointed again, "a step or two more, and we could be fired upon from an upper window of the Alambrera."

"They could come down this street, straight across Cage, and go into the Alambrera?"

"That is correct, My General. Therefore we will not go farther. This way, please. You do not object to the alley?"

"Certainly not."

How strange the service of the gods was! When she was only a girl, Maytera Mockorange had told her that the gods' service meant missing sleep and meals, and had made her give that response each time she was asked. Now here she was; she hadn't eaten since breakfast, but by Thelxiepeia's grace she was too tired to be hungry.

"The boy you sent off to bed." The captain chuckled. "He will sleep all night. Did you foresee that, My General? The poor girl will have to remain at her post until morning."

"Horn? No more than three hours, Captain, if that."

The alley ended at a wider steet. Mill Street, Maytera Mint told herself, seeing the forlorn sign of a dark coffee shop called the Mill. Mill Street was where you could buy odd lengths of serge and tweed cheaply.

"Here we are out of sight, though not hidden from sentries on the wall. Look." He pointed again. "Do you recognize it, My General?"

"I recognize the wall of the Alambrera, certainly. And I can see a floater. Is it yours? No, it can't be, or they'd be shooting at it, and the turret's missing."

"It is one of those you destroyed, My General. But it is mine now. I have two men in it." He halted. "Here I leave you for perhaps three minutes. It is too dangerous for us to proceed, but I must see that all is well with them."

She let him trot away, waiting until he had almost reached the disabled floater before she began to run herself, running as she had so often pictured herself running in games with the children at the palaestra, her skirt hiked to her knees and her feet flying, the fear of impropriety gone who could say where.

He jumped, caught the edge of the hole where the turret had been, pulled himself up and rolled over, vanishing into the disabled floater. Seeing him, she felt less confident that she could do it too.

Fortunately she did not have to; when she was still half a dozen strides away, a door opened in its side. "I did not think you would remain behind, My General," the captain told her, "though I dared hope. You must not risk yourself in this fashion."

She nodded, too breathless to speak, and ducked into the floater. It was cramped yet strangely roofless, the crouching Guardsmen clearly ill at ease, trained to snap to attention but compressed by circumstance. "Sit down," she ordered them, "all of you. We can't stand on formality in here."

That word *stand* had been unwisely chosen, she reflected. They sat anyway, with muttered thanks.

"This buzz gun, you see, My General," the captain patted it, "once it belonged to the commander of this floater. He missed you, so it is yours."

She knew nothing about buzz guns and was curious despite her fatigue. "Does it still operate? And do you have," at a loss, she waved a vague hand, "whatever it shoots?"

"Cartridges, My General. Yes, there are enough. It was the fuel that exploded in this floater, you see. They are not like soldiers, these floaters. They are like taluses and must have fish oil or palm-nut oil for their engines. Fish oil is not so nice, but we employ it because it is less costly. This floater carried sufficient ammunition for both guns, and there is sufficient still."

"I want to sit there." She was looking at the officer's seat. "May I?"

"Certainly, My General." The captain scrambled out of her way.

The seat was astonishingly comfortable, deeper and softer than her bed in the cenoby, although its scorched upholstery smelled of smoke. Not astonishing, Maytera Mint told herself, not really. To be expected, because it had been an officer's seat, and the Ayuntamiento treated officers well, knowing that its power rested on them; that was something to keep in mind, one more thing she must not forget.

"Do not touch the trigger, My General. The safety catch is disengaged." The captain reached over her shoulder to push a small lever. "Now it is engaged. The gun will not fire."

"This spiderweb thing." She touched it instead. "Is it what you call the sight?"

"Yes, the rear sight, My General. The little post you see at the end of the barrel, that is the front sight. The gunner aligns the two, so that he sees the top of the post in one or another of the small rectangles."

"I see."

"Higher rectangles, My General, if the target is distant. To left or right if there is a strong wind, or because the gun favors one side or another."

She leaned back in the seat and allowed herself, for no more than a second or two, to close her eyes. The captain was saying something about night vision, short bursts hitting more than long ones, about fields of fire.

Fire was eating up somebody's home while he talked, and Lime (if Teasel had found her quickly and she hadn't been far) was looking for her right now, going from sentry post to post to post to post. Looking for her and asking people at each post whether they had seen her, whether they knew where the next one was and whether they would take her there because of the fires, because Bison had known, had rightly known that the fires must be put out but had been afraid to say it because he had known his people couldn't do it, could not, men and women who had fought so long and hard already all day, fight fires tonight and fight again tomorrow. Bison who made her feel so strong and competent, whose thick and curling black beard was longer than her hair. Maytera Mockorange had warned her about going without her coif, which was not just against the rule but stimulating to a great many men who were aroused by the sight of women's hair, particularly if long. She had lost her coif somewhere, had gone without it though her hair was short, though it had been cropped short on the first day, all of it.

She fled Maytera Mockorange's anger down dark cold halls full of sudden turnings until she found Auk, who reminded her that she was to bring him the gods.

"I am Colonel Oosik, Caldé," Silk's visitor informed him. He was a big man, so tall and broad that Shell was hidden by his green-uniformed bulk.

"The officer who directs this brigade," Silk offered his hand. "In command. Is that what you say? I'm Patera Silk."

"You have familiarized yourself with our organization." Oosik sat down in the chair Shell had carried in earlier.

"Not really. Are those my clothes you have?"

"Yes." Oosik held them up, an untidy black bundle. "We will speak of them presently, Caldé. If you have made no study of our organization charts, how is it you know my position?"

"I saw a poster." Silk paused, remembering. "I was going to the lake with a woman named Chenille. The poster announced the formation of a reserve brigade. It was signed by you, and it told anyone who wanted to join it to apply to Third Brigade Headquarters. Patera Shell was kind enough to look in on me a few minutes ago, and he happened to mention that this was the Third Brigade. After he had gone, I recalled your poster."

Shell said hurriedly, "The colonel was in the captain's room when I got there, Patera. I told them I'd wait, but he made me come in and asked what I wanted, so I told him."

"Thank you," Silk said. "Please return to your manteion at once, Patera. You've done everything that you can do here tonight." Trying to freight the words with significance, he added, "It's already late. Very late."

"I thought, Patera—"

"Go," Oosik tugged his drooping mustache. "Your caldé and I have delicate matters to discuss. He understands that. So should you."

"I thought—"

"Go!" Oosik had scarcely raised his voice, yet the word was like the crack of a whip. Shell hurried out.

"Sentry! Shut the door."

The mustache was tipped with white, Silk observed; Oosik wound it about his index finger as he spoke. "Since you have not studied our organization, Caldé, you will not know that a brigade is the command of a general, called a brigadier."

"No." Silk admitted. "I've never given it any thought."

"In that case no explanation is necessary. I had planned to tell you, so that each of us would know where we stand, that though I am a mere colonel, an officer of field grade," Oosik released his mustache to touch the silver osprey on his collar, "I command my brigade exactly as a brigadier would. I have for four years. Do you want your clothes?"

"Yes. I'd like to get dressed, if you'll let me."

Oosik nodded, though it was not clear whether his nod was meant to express permission or understanding. "You are nearly dead, Caldé. A needle passed through your lung."

"Nevertheless, I'd feel better if I were up and dressed." It was a lie, although he wished fervently that it were true. "I'd be sitting on this bed then, instead of lying in it; but I've got nothing on."

Oosik chuckled. "You wish your shoes as well?"

"My shoes and my stockings. My underwear, my trousers, my tunic, and my robe. Please, Colonel."

The corners of the mustache tilted upward. "Dressed, you might easily escape, Caldé. Isn't that so?"

"You say I'm near death, Colonel. A man near death might escape, I suppose; but not easily."

"We have handled you roughly here in the Third, Caldé. You have been beaten. Tortured."

Silk shook his head. "You shot me. At least, I suppose that it was one of your officers who shot me. But I've been treated by a doctor and installed in this comfortable room. No one has beaten me."

"With your leave." Oosik peered at him. "Your face is bruised. I assumed that we had beaten you."

Silk shook his head, pushing back the memory of hours of interrogation by Councillor Potto and Sergeant Sand.

"You do not wish to explain the source of your bruises. You have been fighting, Caldé, a shameful thing for an augur. Or boxing. Boxing would be permissible, I suppose."

"Through my own carelessness and stupidity, I fell down a flight of stairs," Silk said.

To his surprise, Oosik roared with laughter, slapping his knee. "That is what our troopers say, Caldé," he wiped his eyes, still chuckling, "when one has been beaten by the rest. He says he fell down the barracks stairs, almost always. They don't want to confess that they've cheated their comrades, you see, or stolen from them."

"In my case it's the truth." Silk considered. "I had been trying to steal, though not to cheat, two days earlier. But I really did fall down steps and bruise my face."

"I am happy to hear you haven't been beaten. Our men do it sometimes without orders. I have known them to do it when it was contrary to their orders, as well. I punish them for that severely, you may be sure. In your case, Caldé," Oosik shrugged. "I sent out an officer because I required better information concerning the progress of the battle before the Alambrera than my glass could give me. I had made provisions for wounded and for prisoners. I needed to learn whether they would be sufficient."

"I understand."

"He came back with you." Oosik sighed. "Now he expects a medal and a promotion for putting me in this very difficult position. You understand my problem, Caldé?"

"I'm not sure I do."

"We are fighting, you and I. Your followers, a hundred thousand or more, against the Civil Guard, of which I am a senior officer, and a few thousand soldiers. Either side may win. Do you agree?"

"I suppose so," Silk said.

"Let us say, for the moment, that it is mine. I do not intend to be unfair to you, Caldé. We will discuss the other possibility in a moment. Say that the victory is ours, and I report to the Ayuntamiento that you are my prisoner. I will be asked why I did not report it earlier, and I may be court-martialed for not having reported it. If I am fortunate, my career will be destroyed. If I am not, I may be shot."

"Then report it," Silk told him, "by all means."

Oosik shook his head again, his big face gloomier than ever. "There is no right course for me in this, Caldé. No right course at all. But there is one that is clearly wrong, that can lead only to disaster, and you have advised it. The Ayuntamiento has ordered that you be killed on sight. Do you know that?"

"I had anticipated it." Silk discovered that his hands were clenched beneath the quilt. He made himself relax.

"No doubt. Lieutenant Tiger should have killed you at once. He didn't. May I be frank? I don't think he had the stomach for it. He denies it, but I don't think he had the stomach. He shot you. There you lay, an augur in an augur's robe, gasping like a fish and bleeding from the mouth. One more shot would be the end." Oosik shrugged. "No doubt he thought you would die while he was bringing you in. Most men would have."

"I see," Silk said. "He'll be in trouble now if you tell the Ayuntamiento that you have me, alive."

"*I* will be in trouble." Oosik tapped his chest with a thick forefinger. "I will be ordered to kill you, Caldé, and I will have to do it. If we lose after that, your woman Mint will have me shot, if she doesn't light upon something worse. If we win, I will be marked for life. I will be the man who killed Silk, the augur who was, as the city firmly believes, chosen by Pas to be caldé. If it is wise, the Ayuntamiento will disavow my actions, court-martial me, and have me shot. No, Caldé, I will not report that I hold you. That is the last thing that I will do."

"You said that the Guard and the Army—I've been told there are seven thousand soldiers—are fighting the people. What is the strength of the Guard, Colonel?" Silk strove to recall his conversation with Hammerstone. "Thirty thousand, approximately?"

"Less."

"Some Guardsmen have deserted the Ayuntamiento. I know that for a fact."

Oosik nodded gloomily.

"May I ask how many?"

"A few hundred, perhaps, Caldé."

"Would you say a thousand?"

For half a minute or more, Oosik did not speak; at last he said, "I am told five hundred. If that is correct, almost all have come from my own brigade."

"I have something to show you," Silk said, "but I have to ask you for a promise first. It's something that Patera Shell brought me, and I want you to give me your word that you won't harm him or the augur of his manteion, or any of their sibyls. Will you promise?"

Oosik shook his head. "I cannot disobey if I am ordered to arrest them, Patera."

"If you're not ordered to." It should give them ample time to leave, Silk thought. "Promise me that you won't do anything to them on your own initiative."

Oosik studied him. "You are offering your information very cheaply, Caldé. We don't bother you religious, except under the most severe provocation."

"Then I have your word as an officer?"

Oosik nodded, and Silk took the Prolocutor's letter from under his quilt and handed it to him. He unbuttoned a shirt pocket and got out a pair of silver-rimmed glasses, shifting his position slightly so that the light fell upon the letter.

In the silence that followed, Silk reviewed everything Oosik had said. Had he made the right decision? Oosik was ambitious—had probably volunteered to take charge of the reserve brigade as well as his own in the hope of gaining the rank and pay to which his position entitled him. He might be, in fact he almost certainly was, underestimating the fighting capabilities of soldiers like Sand and Hammerstone; but he was sure to know a great deal about those of the Civil Guard, in which he had spent his adult life; and he was considering the possibility that the Ayuntamiento would lose. The Prolocutor's letter, with its implications of increased support for Maytera Mint, might tilt the balance.

Or so Silk hoped.

Oosik looked up. "This says Lemur's dead."

Silk nodded.

"There have been rumors all day. What if your Prolocutor is simply repeating them?"

"He's dead." Silk made the statement as forceful as he could, fortified by the knowledge that for once there was no need to hedge the truth. "You've got a glass, Colonel. You must. Ask it to find Lemur for you."

"You saw him die?"

Silk shook his head, saying, "I saw his body, however," and Oosik returned to the letter.

Too much boldness could ruin everything; it would be worse than useless to try to make Oosik say or do anything that could be brought up against him later. Oosik put down the letter. "The Chapter is behind you, Caldé. I suspected as much, and this makes it very plain."

"It is now, apparently." Here was a chance for Oosik to declare himself. "If you suspected it before you read that letter, Colonel, it was doubly kind of you to let Patera Shell in to see me."

"I didn't, Caldé. Captain Gecko did."

"I see. But you'll keep your promise?"

"I am a man of honor, Caldé." Oosik refolded the letter and put it in his pocket with his glasses. "I will also keep this. Neither of us would want anyone else to read it. One of my officers, particularly."

Silk nodded. "You're welcome to."

"You want your clothes back. No doubt you would like to have the contents of your pockets as well. Your beads are in there, I think. I imagine you would like to tell them as you lie here."

"I would, yes. Very much."

"There are needlers, too. One is like the one with which you were shot. There is also a smaller one that seems to have belonged to a woman named Hyacinth."

"Yes," Silk said again.

"I see. I know her, if she is the Hyacinth I'm thinking of. An amiable girl, as well as a very beautiful one. I lay with her on Phaesday."

Silk shut his eyes.

"I did not set out to give you pain, Caldé. Look at me. I'm old enough to be your father, or hers. Do you imagine she sends me love letters?"

"Is that . . . ?"

"What one of the letters in your pocket is?" Oosik nodded solemnly. "Captain Gecko told me the seals had not been broken when he found them. Quite frankly, I doubted him. I see that I should not have. You have not read them."

"No," Silk said.

"Captain Gecko has, and I. No one else. Gecko can be discreet if I order it, and a man of honor must be a man of discretion, also. Otherwise he is worse than useless. You did not recognize her seal?"

Silk shook his head. "I've never gotten a letter from her before."

"Caldé, I have never gotten one at all." Oosik tugged his mustache. "You would be well advised to keep that before you. Many letters from women over the years, but never one from her. I say again, I envy you."

"Thank you," Silk said.

"You love her." Oosik leaned back in his chair. "That is not a question. You may not know it, but you do." His voice softened. "I was your age once, Caldé. Do you realize that in a month it may be over?"

"In a day it may be over," Silk admitted. "Sometimes I hope it will be."

"You fear it, too. You need not say so. I understand. I told you I knew her and it gave you pain, but I do not want you to think, later, that I have been less than honest. I am being equally honest now. Brutally honest with myself. My pride. I am nothing to her."

"Thank you again," Silk said.

"You are welcome. I do not say that she is nothing to me. I am not a man of stone. But there are others, several who are much more. To explain would be offensive."

"Certainly you don't have to go into details unless you want me to shrive you. May I see her letter?"

"In a moment, Caldé. Soon I will give it to you to keep. I think so, at least. There is one further matter to be dealt with. You chanced to mention a woman called Chenille. I know a woman of that name, too. She lives in a yellow house."

Silk smiled and shook his head.

"That does not pain you at all. She is not the Chenille you took to the lake?"

"I was amused at myself—at my stupidity. She told me she had entertained colonels; but until you said you knew her, it had never entered my mind that you were almost certain to be one of them. There can't be a great many."

"Seven besides myself." Oosik rummaged in the bundle of clothing and produced Musk's big needler and Hyacinth's small, gold-plated one. After holding them up so that Silk could see them, he laid them on the windowsill.

"The little one is hers," Silk said. "Hyacinth's. Could you see that it's returned to her?"

Oosik nodded. "I shall send it by a mutual acquaintance. What about the large one?"

"The owner's dead. I suppose it's mine now."

"I am too well mannered to ask if you killed him, but I hope he was not one of our officers."

"No," Silk said, "and no. I confess I was tempted to kill him several times—as he was undoubtedly tempted to kill me—but I didn't. I've only killed once, in self-defense. May I read Hyacinth's letter now?"

"If I can find it." Oosik fumbled through Silk's clothes again, then held up both the letters Silk had taken from the mantel in the manse that morning. "This other is from another augur. You have no interest in it?"

"Not as much, I'm afraid. Who is it?"

"I have forgotten." Oosik extracted the letter from its envelope and unfolded it. " 'Patera Remora, Coadjutor.' He wishes to see you, or he did. You were to come to his suite in the Prolocutor's Palace yesterday at three. You are more than a day late already, Caldé. Do you want it?"

"I suppose so," Silk said; and Oosik tossed it on the bed.

Oosik rose, holding out Hyacinth's letter. "This one you will not wish to read while I watch, and I have urgent matters to attend to. I may look in on you again, later this evening. Much later. If I am too busy, I will see you in the morning, perhaps." He tugged his mustache. "Will you think me a fool if I say I wish you well, Caldé? That if we were no longer opponents I should consider your friendship an honor?"

"I'd think you were an estimable, honorable man," Silk told him, "which you are."

"Thank you, Caldé!" Oosik bowed, with a click of his booted heels.

"Colonel?"

"Your beads. I had forgotten. You will find them in a pocket of the robe, I feel sure." Oosik turned to go, but turned back. "A matter of curiosity. Are you familiar with the Palatine, Caldé?"

Silk's right hand, holding Hyacinth's letter, had begun to tremble; he pressed it against his knee so that Oosik would not see it. "I've been there." By an effort of will, he kept his voice almost steady. "Why do you ask?"

"Often, Caldé?"

"Three times, I believe." It was impossible to think of anything but Hyacinth; he could as easily have said fifty, or never. "Yes, three times—once to the Palace, and twice to attend sacrifice at the Grand Manteion."

"Nowhere else?"

Silk shook his head.

"There is a place having a wooden figure of Thelxiepeia. As an augur, you may know where it is."

"There's an onyx image in the Grand Manteion—"

Oosik shook his head. "In Ermine's, to the right as one enters the sellaria. One sees an arch with greenery beyond it. At the rear, there is a pool with goldfish. She stands by it holding a mirror. The lighting is arranged so that the pool is reflected in her mirror, and her mirror in the pool. It is mentioned in that letter." Oosik turned upon his heel.

"Colonel, these needlers—"

He paused at the door. "Do you intend to shoot your way to freedom, Caldé?" Without waiting for Silk's reply he went out, leaving the door ajar behind him. Silk heard the sentry come to attention, and Oosik say, "You are dismissed. Return to the guardroom immediately."

Silk's hands were still shaking as he unfolded Hyacinth's letter; it was on stationery the color of heavy cream, scrawled in violet ink, with many flourishes.

O My Darling Wee Flea:

    I call you so not only because of the way you sprang from my window, but because of the way you hopped into my bed! How your lonely bloss has longed for a note from you!!! You might have sent one by the kind friend who brought you my gift, you know!

That had been Doctor Crane, and Doctor Crane was dead—had died in his arms that very morning.

Now you have to tender me your thanks and so much more, when next we meet! Don't you know that little place up on the Palatine where Thelx holds up a mirror? *Hieraxday*.

                                          Hy

Silk closed his eyes. It was foolish, he told himself. Utterly foolish. The semiliterate scribbling of a woman whose education had ended at fourteen, a girl who had been given to her father's superior as a household servant and concubine, who had scarcely read a book or written a letter, and was trying to flirt, to be arch and girlish and charming on paper. How his instructors at the schola would have sneered!

Utterly foolish, and she had called him darling, had said she longed for him, had risked compromising herself and Doctor Crane to send him this.

He read it again, refolded it, and returned it to its envelope, then pushed aside the quilt and got up.

Oosik had intended him to go, of course—had intended him to escape, or perhaps to be killed escaping. For a few seconds he tried to guess which. Had Oosik been insincere in speaking of friendship? Oosik was capable of any quantity of double-dealing, if he was any judge of men.

It did not matter.

He took his clothing from the chair and spread it on the bed. If Oosik intended him to escape, he must escape as Oosik intended. If Oosik intended him to be killed escaping, he must escape just the same, doing his best to remain alive.

His tunic was crusted with his own blood and completely unwearable; he threw it down and sat on the bed to pull on his undershorts, trousers, and stockings. When he had tied his shoes, he rose and jerked open a drawer of the bureau.

Most of the tunics were cheerful reds and yellows; but he found a blue one, apparently never worn, so dark that it might pass for black under any but the closest scrutiny. He laid it on the pillow beside the letters, and put on a yellow one. The closet yielded a small traveling bag. Slipping both letters into a pocket, he rolled up his robe, stuffed it into the bag, and put the dark blue tunic on top of it.

The magazine status pin of the big needler indicated it was loaded; he opened the action anyway, trying to recall how Auk had held his that night in the restaurant, and remembering at the last moment Auk's adjuration to keep his finger off the trigger. The magazine appeared to be full of long, deadly looking needles, or nearly full. Auk had said his needler held how many? A hundred or more, surely; and this big needler that had been Musk's must hold at least as many if not more. It was possible, of course, that it had been disabled in some way.

There was no one in the hall outside. Silk closed the door, and after a moment's thought put the quilt against its bottom and shut the window, then sat down on the bed, sick and horribly weak. When had he eaten last?

Very early that morning, in Limna, with Doctor Crane and that captain whose name he had never learned or had forgotten, and the captain's men. Kypris had granted another theophany, had appeared to them, and to Maytera Marble and Patera Gulo, and they had been full of the wonder of it, all three of them newly come to religious feeling, and feeling that no one had ever come to it before. He had eaten a very good omelet, then several slices of hot, fresh bread with country butter, because the cook, roused from sleep by a trooper, had popped the loaves that had been rising overnight into the oven. He had drunk hot, strong coffee, too; coffee lightened with cream the color of Hyacinth's stationery and sweetened with honey from a white, blue-flowered bowl passed to him by Doctor Crane, who had been putting honey on his bread. Now Doctor Crane was dead, and so was one of the troopers, the captain and the other trooper most likely dead too, killed in the fighting before the Alambrera.

Silk lifted the big needler.

Someone had told him that he, too, should be dead—he could not remember whether it had been the surgeon or Colonel Oosik. Perhaps it had been Shell, although it did not seem the sort of thing that Shell would say.

The needler would not fire. He tugged its trigger again and returned it to the windowsill, congratulating himself on having resolved to test it; saw that he had left the safety catch on, pushed it off, took aim at a large bottle of cologne on the dresser, and squeezed the trigger. The needler cracked in his hand like a bullwhip and the bottle exploded, filling the room with the clean scent of spruce.

He reapplied the safety and thrust the needler into his waistband under the yellow tunic. If Musk's needler had not been disabled, there was no point in testing Hyacinth's small one, too. He made sure its safety catch was engaged, forced himself to stand, and dropped it into his trousers pocket.

One thing more, and he could go. Had the young man whose bedroom this was never written anything here? Looking around, he saw no writing materials.

What of the owner of the perfumed scarf? She would write to him, almost certainly. A woman who cared enough to drop a silk scarf from her window would write notes and letters. And he would keep them, concealing them somewhere in this room and replying in notes and letters of his own, though perhaps less frequently. The study, if there was one, would belong to his father. Even a library would not be sufficiently private. He would write to her here, surely, sitting–where?

There had been no chair in the room until Shell brought one. The occupant could only have sat on the bed or the floor, assuming that he had sat at all. Silk sat down again, imagined that he held a quill, pushed aside the chair Shell had put in front of the little night table, and pulled it over to him. Its shallow drawer held a packet of notepaper, a discolored scrap of flannel, a few envelopes, four quills, and a small bottle of ink.

Choosing a quill, he wrote:

Sir, events beyond my control have forced me to occupy your bedchamber for several hours, and I fear I have broken a bottle of your cologne, and stained your sheets. In extreme need, I have, in addition, appropriated two of your tunics and your smallest traveling bag. I am heartily sorry to have imposed on you in this fashion. I am compelled, as I indicated.

When peace and order return to our city, as I pray that they soon will, I will endeavor to locate you, make restitution, and return your property. Alternately, you may apply to me, at any time you find convenient. I am Pa. Silk, of Sun Street

For a long moment he paused, considering, the feathery end of the gray goose-quill tickling his lips. Very well.

With a final dip into the ink, he added a comma and the word *Caldé* after "Sun Street," and wiped the quill.

Restoring the quilt to the bed, he opened the door. The hall was still empty. Back stairs brought him to the kitchen, in which it appeared at least a company had been foraging for food. The back door opened on what seemed, from what he could see by skylight, to be a small formal garden; a white-painted gate was held shut by a simple hook.

Outside on Basket Street, he stopped to look back at the house he had left. Most of its windows were lit, including one on the second floor whose lights were dimming; his, no doubt. Distant explosions indicated the center of the city as well as anything could.

An officer on horseback who might easily have been the one who had shot him galloped past without taking the least notice. Two streets nearer the Palatine, a hurrying trooper carrying a dispatch box touched his cap politely.

The box might contain an order to arrest every augur in the city, Silk mused; the galloping officer might be bringing Oosik word of another battle. It would be well, might in fact be of real value, for him to read those dispatches and hear the news that the galloping officer brought.

But he had already heard, as he walked, the most important news, news pronounced by the muzzles of guns: the Ayuntamiento did not occupy all the city between this remote eastern quarter and the Palatine. He would have to make his way along streets in which Guardsmen and Maytera Mint's rebels were slaughtering each other, return to the ones that he knew best—and then, presumably, cross another disputed zone to reach the Palatine.

For the Guard would hold the Palatine if it held anything, and in fact the captain had indicated only that morning that a full brigade had scarcely sufficed to defend it Molpsday night. Combatants on both sides would try to prevent him; he might be killed, and the exertions he was making this moment might kill him as surely as any slug. Yet he had to try, and if he lived he would see Hyacinth tonight.

His free hand had begun to draw Musk's needler. He forced it back to his side, reflecting grimly that before shadeup he might learn some truths about himself that he would not prefer to ignorance. Unconsciously, he increased his pace.

Men thought themselves good or evil; but the gods—the Outsider especially—must surely know how much depended upon circumstance. Would Musk, whose needler he had nearly drawn a few seconds before, have been an evil man if he had not served Blood? Might not Blood, for that matter, be a better man with Musk gone? He, Silk, had sensed warmth and generosity in Blood beneath his cunning and his greed, potentially at least.

Something dropped from the sky, lighting on his shoulder so heavily he nearly fell. " 'Lo Silk! Good Silk!"

"Oreb! Is it really you?"

"Bird back." Oreb caught a lock of Silk's hair in his beak and gave it a tug.

"I'm very glad–immensely glad you've returned. Where have you been? How did you get here?"

"Bad place. Big hole!"

"It was I who went into the big hole, Oreb. By the lake, in that shrine of Scylla's, remember?"

Oreb's beak clattered. "Fish heads?"

Chapter 6

THE BLIND GOD

Oreb had eyed Dace's corpse hopefully when Urus let it fall to the tunnel floor and spun around to shout at Hammerstone. "Why we got to find him? Tell me that! Tell me, an' I'll look till I can't shaggy walk, till I got to crawl–"

"Pick it up, you." Without taking his eyes off Urus, Hammerstone addressed Incus. "All right if I kill him, Patera? Only I won't be able to carry them both and shoot."

Incus shook his head. "He has a *point,* my son, so let us consider it. *Ought* we, as he inquires, continue to search for our friend Auk?"

"I'll leave it up to you, Patera. You're smarter than all of us, smarter than the whole city'd be if you weren't living there. I'd do anything you say, and I'll see to it these bios do, too."

"*Thank* you, my son." Incus, who was exceedingly tired already, lowered himself gratefully to the tunnel floor. "Sit *down,* all of you. We shall discuss this."

"I don't see why." Tired herself, Chenille grounded her launcher. "Stony there does whatever you tell him to, and he could do for me and Urus like swatting flies. You say it and we'll do it. We'll have to."

"Sit *down.* My daughter, can't you see how very *illogical* you're being? You *maintain* that you're forced to obey in *all things,* yet you will not oblige even the simplest request."

"All right." She sat; and Hammerstone, laying a heavy hand on Urus, forced him to sit, too.

"Where Auk?" Oreb hopped optimistically across the damp gray shiprock. "Auk where?" Although he could not have put the feeling into words, Oreb felt that he was nearer Silk when he was with Auk than in any other company. The red girl was close to Silk as well, but she had once thrown a glass at him, and Oreb had not forgotten.

"*Where* indeed?" Incus sighed. "My daughter, you invite me to be a *despot,* but what you say is true. I might lord it over you both if I chose. I need not lord it over our friend. *He* obeys me very willingly, as you have seen. But I am *not,* by inclination, training, or *native character* inclined toward despotism. A holy augur's part is to lead and to advise, to *conduct* the laity to rich fields and *unfailing* springs, if I may put it thus *poetically.*

"So *let us* review our position and take *council,* one with another. Then I will lead us in prayer, a fervent and *devout* prayer, let it be, to all the Nine, *imploring* their guidance."

"Then we'll decide?" Urus demanded.

"Then *I* will decide, my son." By an effort, Incus sat up straighter. "But *first,* allow me to dispel certain fallacies that have already crept into our deliberations." He addressed himself to Chenille. "*You,* my daughter, seek to accuse me of despotism. It is *impolite,* but courtesy itself must at times give way to the *sacred duty* of *correction.* May I remind you that *you,* for the space of nearly *two days, tyrannized* us all aboard that miserable boat? Tyrannized *me* largely by means of our unfortunate friend, for whom we have already searched, as I would think, for nearly half a day?"

"I'm not saying we ought to stop, Patera. That was him." She pointed to Urus. "I want to find him."

"Be *quiet,* my daughter. I am not yet finished with *you.* I shall come to *him* soon enough. *Why,* I inquire, did you so tyrannize us? I say–"

"I was possessed! Scylla was in me. You know that."

"No, no, my daughter. It won't *do.* It is what you have *maintained,* deflecting all criticism of your conduct with the same *shabby* defense. It shall serve you no longer. You were *domineering, oppressive,* and *brutal.* Is that characteristic of *Our Surging Scylla?* I affirm that it is *not.* As we have trudged on, I have reviewed all that is recorded of *her,* both in the *Chrasmologic Writings* and in our *traditions* likewise. *Imperious?* One can but agree. *Impetuous* at times, perhaps. But *never* brutal, oppressive, or *domineering.*" Incus sighed again, removed his shoes, and caressed his blistered feet.

"*Those* evil traits, I say, my daughter, *cannot* have been *Scylla's.* They were present *in you* when she arrived, and so deeply rooted that she found it, I dare say, quite impossible to *expunge* them. *Some* there are, or so I have heard it said, who actually *prefer* domineering women, *unhappy* men twisted by nature beyond the natural. Our poor friend Auk, with all his manifest excellencies of *strength* and *manly* courage, is one of those unfortunates, so it would seem. I am *not,* my daughter, and I thank Sweet Scylla for it! Understand that for *my* part, and for our tall friend's here, as I dare to say, we have not sought Auk for your sake, but for *his own.*"

"Talk talk," Oreb muttered.

"As for *you,*" Incus shifted his attention to Urus, "*you* appear to believe that it is only because of my loyal friend *Hammerstone* that you obey me. Is that not so?"

Urus stared sullenly at the tunnel wall to the left of Incus's face.

"You are *silent,*" Incus continued. "Talk and more talk, complains our small *feathered* companion, and again, talk, talk and *talk.* Not impossibly you concur. No, my son, you *deceive* yourself, as you have deceived yourself throughout what I feel *certain* must have been a most unhappy life." Incus drew Auk's needler and leveled it at the silent Urus. "I have but little *need* of my tall friend Hammerstone, where *you* are concerned, and should this endless *talk* that you complain of end, you may find yourself less pleased *than ever* with that which succeeds it. I invite a *comment.*"

Urus shook his head. Hammerstone clenched his big fists, clearly itching to batter him insensible.

"Nothing? In that case, my son, I am going to take the opportunity to tell you something of *myself,* because I have been pondering *that,* with many other things, while we walked, and it will bear upon what I mean to do, as you will see.

"I was born to poor yet *upright* parents, their *fifth* and *final* child. At the time they were *wed,* they had made *solemn pledge* to Echidna that they would furnish the immortal gods with an augur or a sibyl, the ripest *fruit* of their union and the most *perfect* of all *thank offerings* for it. Of my older brothers and sisters, I shall say nothing. *Nothing,* that is to say, except that there was nothing to be hoped for from *them.* No more *holy piety* was to be discovered in the four of them than in four of those *horrid beasts* with which you, my son, proposed to attack us. I was born some *seven years* after my youngest sibling, Femur. Conceive of my parents' *delight,* I invite you, when the passing *days, weeks, months,* and *years* showed ever more plainly my *predilection* for a life of *holy contemplation,* of *worship* and *ritual,* far from the *bothersome exigencies* that trouble the hours of most men.

The schola, if I may say it, welcomed me with *arms outspread.* Its *warmth* was no less than that with which I, in my turn, rushed to *it.* I was together *pious* and *brilliant,* a combination not often found. *Thus endowed,* I gained the friendship of *older men* of tastes like to *my own,* who were to extend themselves *without stint* in my behalf following my *designation.*

"I was informed, and you may conceive of my *rapture,* my *delight,* that no less a figure than the *coadjutor* had agreed to make me his prothonotary. With all my heart I entered into my *duties,* drafting and summarizing letters and depositions, stamping, filing, and retrieving files, managing his *calendar of appointments,* and a hundred like tasks."

Incus fell silent until Chenille said, "By Thelxiepeia I could sleep for a week!" She leaned back against the tunnel wall and closed her eyes.

"Where Auk?" Oreb demanded, but no one paid him the least attention.

"We are all *exhausted,* my daughter. I not *less* than you, and perhaps with more *reason,* because my legs are not so *long,* nor am I, by a decade and *more,* so young, nor so well fed."

"I'm not even a little bit well fed, Patera." Chenille did not open her eyes. "I guess none of us are. I haven't had anything but water since forever."

"When we were on that *wretched* little fishing boat, you *appropriated* to yourself what food you *wished,* and *all* that you wished, my daughter. You left to *Auk* and Dace, and even to *me,* an anointed augur, only such *scraps* as you disdained. But you have *forgotten* that, or say you have. I wish that I might forget it, too."

"Fish heads?"

Chenille shrugged, her eyes still closed. "All right, Patera, I'm sorry. I don't suppose we'll ever find any food down here, but if we do, or when we get back home, I'll let you have first pick."

"I would *refuse* it, my daughter. That is the *point* I am *striving* to make. I became His Eminence's prothonotary, as I said. I entered the *Prolocutor's Palace,* not as an awestruck *visitor,* but as an *inhabitant.* Each morning I sacrificed *one squab* in the *private chapel* below the reception hall, chanting my prayers to empty chairs. Afterward, I enjoyed that same *bird* at my luncheon. *Upon a monthly basis,* I shrove Patera Bull, His Cognizance's prothonotary, as *he me.* That was the whole compass of my duties as an augur.

"But from time to time, His Eminence assigned to *me* such errands as he felt, or *feigned* to feel, overdifficult for a *boy*. One such brought me to that miserable village of *Limna,* as you know. I was to search for *you,* my daughter, and it was my *ill luck* to succeed. Your own life, I suppose, has been, I will not say *adventurous,* but *tumultuous.* Is that not so?"

"It's had its ups and downs," Chenille conceded.

"*Mine* had not, with the result that I had assumed myself *incapable.* Had some god informed me," Incus paused to thrust Auk's needler back into his waistband, then contemplated his scabbed hands, "that I should be forced to serve as the *entire crew* of a fishing vessel, *bailing, making sail, reefing,* and all the rest, and this during a *tempest* as severe as any the Whorl has ever seen, I should have called it *quite impossible,* declaring roundly that I should *die* within an hour. I would have informed this wholly supposititious divinity that I was a man of *intellect,* now largely affecting to be a man of prayer, for my early piety had long since given way to an advancing *skepticism.* Had he suggested that I might *yet* become a man of action, I would have declared it to be *beneath* me, and thought myself profound."

Urus said, "Well, if you didn't have a needler 'n this big chem, we'd see."

Incus nodded his agreement, his round, plump little face serious and his protuberant teeth giving him something of the look of a resolute chipmunk. "We would *indeed.* Therefore, I shall *kill* you, Urus my son, or order Hammerstone to, whenever it appears that I am liable to lose either."

"Bad man!" It was not immediately apparent whether Oreb intended Incus or Urus.

Chenille said, "You don't really mean that, Patera."

"Oh, but I *do,* my daughter. Tell them, Corporal. Do I mean what I say?"

"Sure, Patera. See, Chenille, Patera's a bio like you, and bios like you and him are real easy to kill. You can't take chances, or him either. You got a prisoner, he's got to toe the line every minute, 'cause if you let him get away with anything, that's it. If it was up to me, I'd kill him right now, and not chance something happening to Patera."

"We need him to show us how to get to the pit, and that door that opens into the cellar of the Juzgado."

"Only we're not going to either one now, are we? And I know where the Juzgado is if I can get myself located. So why shouldn't I quiet him down?" As if by chance, Hammerstone's slug gun was pointing in Urus's direction; his finger found its trigger.

"We *have not* been going to the pit, I am happy to say," Incus told them. "It was *Auk* who wished to go there, for no good reason that *I* could ever understand. *Unfortunately,* we haven't been going to the Juzgado, *either,* though it was to the Juzgado that Surging Scylla directed us. *I* am the sole person present who *recollects* her instructions, possibly. But I *assure* you it is so."

"All right," Chenille said wearily, "I believe you."

"As you *ought,* my daughter, because it was *through your mouth* that Scylla spoke. That very *fact* brings me to another point. She made Auk, Dace, and *myself* her prophets, specifying that I am to replace His Cognizance as *Prolocutor.* Dace has *departed* this whorl, so grievously infected by *evil,* for the richer life of Mainframe. Succoring Scylla might recall him *if she chose,* perhaps. I *cannot.* If our search for *Auk* is to be given up, or at least *postponed,* and I confess there is *much* that appeals to *me* in that, only *I* remain of Scylla's three.

"Earlier, *bedeviled* by multiple interruptions, I *strove* to explain my position. Because neither of you has *patience* for that explanation, though it would occupy but a *few moments* at most, I shall *state* it. Pay *attention,* both of you."

Incus's voice strengthened. "I have awakened to *myself,* both as *man* and as *augur.* A servant of *Men,* if you will. A servant of the *gods,* most particularly. You are three. One loves, two *hate* me. I am not unaware of it."

"I don't hate you," Chenille protested. "You let me wear this when I got cold. Auk doesn't hate you either. You just think that."

"*Thank you,* my daughter. I was about to remark that from what I've learned from my brother augurs concerning manteions, the proportion implied is the one most frequently seen, though our *congregation* is so much less numerous. Very well, *my good people,* I accept it. I shall do my best for each and for all, nonetheless, trusting in a reward from the east."

"See?" Hammerstone nudged Chenille. "What'd I tell you? The greatest man in the *Whorl.*"

Oreb cocked his head at Incus. "Where Auk?"

"Nowhere to be found in that shining city we name *Reason,* I fear," Incus told him half humorously. "He hailed someone. *I* saw him do it, though there was no one to be seen. After saluting this *unseen being,* he dashed away. Our good corporal pursued him, as you saw, but lost him in the *darkness*."

"These green lights don't work the way people think, see, Chenille. People think they just crawl around all the time and don't care where they're at, only they're not really like that. If it's bright one way and dark the other, they'll head for the dark, see? Real slow, but that's how they go. It's what keeps them spread out."

Chenille nodded. "Urus said something about that."

"In a little place, they get everything worked out among themselves after a while and don't hardly move except to get away from the windows in the daytime, but in a big place like this they don't ever settle down completely. Only they don't ever go down much, 'cause if they did, they'd get stepped on and broken real fast."

"Lots of these tunnels slope down besides the one Auk ran down," she objected, "and I've seen lights in them."

"Depends on how dark it is down there, and how steep the slope is. If it's too steep, they won't go in there at all."

"It was pretty steep," Chenille conceded, "and we went down it quite a ways, but later we took that one that went up, remember? It didn't go up as steep as the dark one went down, and it had lights, but it climbed like that for a long time."

"I *think,* my daughter—"

"So what I've been wondering is would Auk have gone back up like we did? He was kind of out of it."

"He was *deranged*," Incus declared positively. "I would hope that condition was only temporary, but temporary or *not,* he was not *rational*."

"Yeah, and that's why we took the tunnel that angled back up that I was talking about, Patera. We're not abram and we knew we wanted to get back up to the surface, besides finding Auk. But if Auk was abram ... To let you have the lily word, all you bucks seem pretty abram to me, mostly, so I didn't pay much attention. Only if he was, maybe he'd just keep on going down, because that's easier. He was running like you say, and it's pretty easy to run downhill."

"There *may* be something in what you suggest, my daughter. We must keep it in mind, *if* our discussion concludes that we should continue our pursuit.

"Now, may *I* sum up? The *question* is whether we are to continue, or to break off our search, *at least temporarily,* and attempt to return to the surface. Allow *me,* please, to state both cases. I shall strive for *concision.* If any of you has an *additional point,* you are free to advance it when I have *concluded.*

"It would seem to me that there is only one *cogent* reason to *protract* our search, and I have touched upon that *already.* It is that Auk is one of the *triune prophets* commissioned by *Scylla.* As a *prophet* he is a *theodidact* of *inestimable* value, as was Dace. It is for that reason, and for it alone, that I *instructed* Hammerstone to pursue him following his precipitate departure. It is for that reason *solely* that I have prolonged the pursuit so far. For *I,* also, am such a prophet. The only such prophet remaining, as I have said."

"He's one of us," Chenille declared. "I was with him at Limna before Scylla possessed me, and I remember him a little on the boat. We can't just go off and leave him."

"Nor do *I* propose to do so, my daughter. Hear me out, I beg you. We are *exhausted and famished.* When we return to the *surface* with Scylla's messages, in *fulfillment* of her will, we can gain rest and food. *Furthermore,* we can enlist others in the search. We will–"

Urus interrupted. "You said we could put in stuff of our own, right? All right, how about me? Do I get to talk, or are you goin' to have the big chem shoot me?"

Incus smiled gently. "You must understand, my son, that as your spiritual guide, I love *you* no less and no more than the others. I have threatened your life only as the *law* does, for your correction. *Speak.*"

"Well, I don't love Auk, only if you want to get him back it looks to me like you're goin' about it wrong. He wanted us to go to the pit, remember? So maybe now that he's gone off by himself that's where. We could go 'n see, 'n there's lots of bucks there that know these tunnels as well as me, so why not tell 'em what happened 'n get 'em to look too?"

Incus nodded, his face thoughtful. "It *is* a suggestion worthy of consideration."

"They'll eat us," Chenille declared.

"Fish head?" Oreb fluttered to her shoulder.

"Yeah, like you'd eat a fish head, Oreb. Only we'd have to have fish heads to do it."

"They won't eat me," Hammerstone told her. "They won't eat anybody I say not to eat, either, while I'm around."

"Now let us *pray.*" Incus was on his knees, hands clasped before him. "Let us petition the *immortal gods,* and Scylla *particularly,* to rescue both Auk and *ourselves,* and to guide us in the ways they would have us go."

"I twigged you don't buy that any more."

"I have *encountered* Scylla," Incus told Urus solemnly. "I have seen for myself the *majesty* and *power* of that very great goddess. How could I lack belief now?" He contemplated the voided cross suspended from his prayer beads as if he had never seen it before. "I have suffered, too, on that wretched boat and in these *detestable* tunnels. I have been in terror of my life. It is hunger and fear that direct us toward the gods, my son. I have learned that, and I wonder that *you,* suffering as you clearly have, have not turned to them long ago."

"How do you know I haven't, huh? You don't know a shaggy thing about me. Maybe I'm holier than all of you."

Tired as she was, Chenille giggled.

Incus shook his head. "No, my son. It won't do. I am a *fool,* perhaps. Beyond dispute I have not infrequently been a fool. But not such a fool as that." More loudly he added, "On your *knees.* Bow your heads."

"Bird pray! Pray Silk!"

Incus ignored Oreb's hoarse interruption, his right hand making the sign of addition with the voided cross. "Behold us, lovely Scylla, *wonderful* of *waters.* Behold our love and our need for thee. Cleanse us, O Scylla!" He took a deep breath, the inhalation loud in the whispering silence. "Your prophet is bewildered and dismayed, Scylla. Wash clear my *eyes* as I implore you to cleanse my *spirit.* Guide me in this confusion of darkling passages and obscure responsibilities." He looked up, mouthing: *"Cleanse us, O Scylla."*

Chenille, Hammerstone, and even Urus dutifully repeated, "Cleanse us, O Scylla."

Bored, Oreb had flown up to grip a rough stone protrusion in his red claws. He could see farther even than Hammerstone through the yellow-green twilight that filled the tunnel, and clinging thus to the ceiling, his vantage point was higher; but look as he might, he saw neither Auk or Silk. Abandoning the search, he peered hungrily at Dace's corpse; its half-open eyes tempted him, though he felt sure he would be chased away.

Below, the black human droned on: "Behold us, fair Phaea, *lady of the larder.* Behold our love and our need for thee. *Feed* us, O Phaea! Famished we wander in need of your nurture." All the humans squawked, "Feed us, O Phaea!"

"Talk talk," Oreb muttered to himself; he could talk as well as they, but it seemed to him that talking was of small benefit in such situations.

"Behold us, fierce Sphigx, *woman of war.* Behold our love and our need for thee. *Lead* us, O Sphigx! We are lost and dismayed, O Sphigx, hemmed *all about* by danger. Lead us in the ways we should go." And all the humans, "Lead us, O Sphigx!"

The black one said, "Let us now, with heads bowed, put ourselves in *personal communion* with the Nine." He and the green one and the red one looked down, and the dirty one got up, stepped over the dead one, and trotted softly away.

"Man go," Oreb muttered, congratulating himself on having hit on the right words; and because he liked announcing things, he repeated more loudly, "Man go!"

The result was gratifying. The green one sprang to his feet and dashed after the dirty one. The black one shrieked and fluttered after the green one, and the red one jiggled after them both, faster than the black one but not as fast as the first two. For as long as it might have taken one of his feathers to float to the tunnel floor, Oreb preened, weighing the significance of these events.

He had liked Auk and had felt that if he remained with Auk, Auk would lead him to Silk. But Auk was gone, and the others were not looking for him any more.

Oreb glided down to a convenient perch on Dace's face and dined, keeping a wary eye out. One never knew. Good came of bad, and bad of good. Humans were both, and changeable in the extreme, sleeping by day yet catching fish whose best parts they generously shared.

And—so on. His crop filled, Oreb meditated on these points while cleaning his newly bright bill with his feet.

The dead one had been good. There could be no doubt about that. Friendly in the reserved fashion Oreb preferred alive, and delicious, dead. There was another one back there, but he was no longer hungry. It was time to find Silk in earnest. Not just look. Really find him. To leave this green hole and its living and dead humans.

Vaguely, he recalled the night sky, the gleaming upside-down country over his head, and the proper country below.

The wind in trees. Drifting along with it looking for things of inter-est. It was where Silk would be, and where he could be found. Where a bird could fly high, see everything, and find Silk.

Flying was not as easy as riding the red one's launcher, but flying downwind through the tunnel permitted rests in which he had only to keep his wings wide and sail along. There were twinges at times, reminding him of the blue thing that had been there. He had never understood what it was or why it had stuck to him.

Downwind along this hole and that, through a little hole (he landed and peered into it cautiously before venturing in himself) and into a big one where dirty humans stretched on the ground or prowled like cats, a hole lidded like a pot with the remembered sky of night.

Sword in hand, Master Xiphias stood at the window looking at the dark and empty street. Go home. That was what they'd told him.

Go home, though it had not been quite so bluntly worded. That dunce Bison, a fool who couldn't hold a sword correctly! That dunce Bison, who seemed in charge of everything, had come by while he was arguing with that imbecile Scale. Had smiled like friend and admired his sword, and had only pretended—pretended!—to believe him when he had stated (not boasting, just supplying a plain, straightforward answer in response to direct, uninvited questions) that he had killed five troop-ers in armor in Cage Street.

Then Bison had—the old fencing master grinned gleefully—had gaped like a carp when he, Xiphias, had parted a thumb-thick rope dan-gling from his, Bison's, hand. Had admired his sword and waved it around like the ignorant boy he was, and had the gall to say in many sweet words, go home like Scale says, old man. We don't need you tonight, old man. Go home and eat, old man. Go home and sleep. Get some rest, old man, you've had a big day.

Bison's sweet words had faded and blown away, lighter and more fragile than the leaves that whirled up the empty street. Their import, bitter as gall, remained. He had been fighting—had been a famous fight-ing man—when Bison was in diapers. Had been fighting before Scale's mother had escaped her kennel to bump tails with some filthy garbage-eating cur.

Xiphias turned his back to the window and sat on the sill, his head in his hands, his sword at his feet. He was no longer what he had been thirty years ago, perhaps. No longer what he had been before he lost his leg. But there wasn't a man in the city—not one!—who dared cross blades with him.

A knock at the front door, floating up the narrow stair from the floor below.

There would be no students tonight; his students would be fighting on one side or the other; yet somebody wanted to see him. Possibly Bison had realized the gravity of his error and come to implore him to undertake some almost suicidal mission. He'd go, but by High Hierax they'd have to beg first!

He picked up his sword to return it to its place on the wall, then changed his mind. In times like these—

Another knock.

There had been somebody. A new student down for tonight, came with Auk, tall, left-handed. Had studied with somebody else but wouldn't admit it. Good though. Talented! Gifted, in fact. Couldn't be here for his lesson, could he? With the city like this?

A third knock, almost cursory. Xiphias returned to the window and peered out.

Silk sighed. The house was dark; when he had been here before, the second floor had blazed with light. He had been foolish to think that the old man might be home after all.

He knocked for the last time and turned away, only to hear a window thrown open above him. "It's you! Good! Good!" The window banged down. With speed that was almost comic, the door flew wide. "Inside! Inside! Bolt it, will you? Is that a bird? A pet bird? Upstairs!" Xiphias gestured largely with a saber, his shadow leaping beside him; whipped by the night wind, his wild white hair seemed to possess a life of its own.

"Master Xiphias, I need your help."

"Good man?" Oreb croaked.

"A very good man," Silk assured him, hoping he was right; he caught the good man's arm as he turned away. "I know I was supposed to come tonight for another lesson, Master Xiphias. I haven't. I can't, but I need your advice."

"Been called out? Have to fight? What did I tell you? What weapons?"

"I'm very tired. Is there a place where we can sit down?"

"Upstairs!" The old man bounded up them himself just as he had on Sphixday night. Wearily, Silk followed.

"Lesson first!" Lights kindled at the sound of the old man's voice, brightened as he beat the wall with a foil.

The traveling bag now held only the yellow tunic, yet it seemed as heavy as a full one; Silk dropped it into a corner. "Master Xiphias—"

He snatched down another foil and beat the wall with that as well. "Been fighting?"

"Not really. In a manner of speaking I have, I suppose."

"Me too!" Xiphias tossed Silk the second foil. "Killed five. Ruins you, fighting! Ruins your technique!"

Oreb squawked, "Look out!" and flew as Silk ducked.

"Don't cringe!" Another whistling cut, this one rattling on the bamboo blade of Silk's foil. "What do you need, lad?"

"A place to sit." He was tired, deadly tired; his chest throbbed and his ankle ached. He parried and parried again, sickened by the realization that the only way to get this mad old man to listen was to defeat him or lose to him; and to lose (it was as if a god had whispered it) tonight was death: the thing in him that had kept him alive and functioning since he had been shot would die at his defeat, and he soon after.

Feinting and lunging, Silk fought for his life with the bamboo sword.

Its hilt was just long enough for him to grip it with both hands, and he did. Cut right and left and right again, beating down the old man's guard. He was still stronger than any old man, however strong, however active, and he drove him back and again back, slashing and stabbing with frenzied speed.

"Where'd you learn that two-handed thrust, lad? Aren't you left-handed?"

Dislodged from his waistband, Musk's needler fell to the mat. Silk kicked it aside and snatched a second foil from the wall, parrying with one, then the other, attacking with the free foil, right, left, and right again. A vertical cut, and suddenly Xiphias's foot was on his right-hand foil. The blunt tip of Xiphias's foil thumped his wound, bringing excruciating pain.

"What'll you charge, lad? For the lesson?"

Silk shrugged, trying to hide the agony that lightest of blows had brought. "I should pay you, sir. And you won."

"Silk win!" Oreb proclaimed from the grip of a yataghan.

Silk die, Silk thought. So be it.

"I learned, lad! Know how long it's been since I had a student who could teach me anything? I'll pay! Food? You hungry?"

"I think so." Silk leaned upon his foil; in the same way that faces from his childhood swam into his consciousness, he recalled that he had once had a walking stick with the head of a lioness carved on its handle—had leaned upon it like this the last time he had been here, although he could not remember where he had acquired such a thing or what had become of it.

"Bread and cheese? Wine?"

"Wonderful." Retrieving the traveling bag, he followed the old man downstairs.

The kitchen was at once disorderly and clean, glasses and dishes and bowls, pots and ladles anywhere and everywhere, an iron bread-pan already in the chair Xiphias offered, as if it fully expected to join in their conversation, though it found itself banished to the woodbox. Mismatched glasses crashed down on the table so violently that for a moment Silk felt sure they had broken.

"Have some? Red wine from the veins of heroes! Care for some?" It was already gurgling into Silk's glass. "Got it from a student! Fact! Paid wine! Ever hear of such a thing? Swore it was all good! Not so! What do you think?"

Silk sipped, then half emptied his glass, feeling that he was indeed drinking from the flask that had dangled from his bedpost, drinking new life.

"Bird drink?"

He nodded, and when he could find no napkin patted his mouth with his handkerchief. "Could we trouble you for a cup of water, Master Xiphias, for Oreb here?"

The pump at the sink wheezed into motion. "You been out? City in an uproar! Dodging! Throwing stones! Haven't thrown stones since I was a sprat! Had a sling! You too? Better armed!" Crystal water rushed forth like the old man's words until he had filled a battered tankard. "This new cull, Silk! Going to show 'em! We'll see . . . Fighting, fighting!

Threw stones, ducked and yelled! Five with my sword. I tell you? Know how to make a sling?"

Silk nodded again, certain that he was being gulled but unresentful.

"Me too! Used to be good with one!" The tankard arrived with a cracked green plate holding a shapeless lump of white-rinded cheese only slightly smaller than Silk's head. "Watch this!" Thrown from across the room, a big butcher knife buried its blade in the cheese.

"You asked whether I'd been out much tonight."

"Think there's any real fighting now?" Abruptly, Xiphias found himself siding with Bison. "Nothing! Nothing at all! Snipers shooting shadows to keep awake." He paused, his face suddenly thoughtful. "Can't see the other man's blade in the dark, can you? Interesting. Interesting! Have to try it! A whole new field! What do you think?"

The sight and the rich, corrupt aroma of the cheese had awakened Silk's appetite. "I think that I'll have a piece," he replied with sudden resolution. He was about to die—very well, but no god had condemned him to die hungry. "Oreb, you like cheese, too, I know. It was one of the first things you told me, remember?"

"Want a plate?" It came with a quarter of what must have been a gargantuan loaf on a nicked old board, and a bread knife nearly as large as Auk's hanger. "All I've got! You eat at cookshops, mostly? I do! Bad now! All shut!"

Silk swallowed. "This is delicious cheese and wonderful wine. I thank you for it, Master Xiphias and Feasting Phaea." Impelled by habit, the last words had left his lips before he discovered that he did not mean them.

"For my lesson!" The old man dropped into a chair. "Can you throw, lad? Knives and whatnot? Like I just did?"

"I doubt it. I've never tried."

"Want me to teach you? You're an augur?"

Silk nodded again as he sliced bread.

"So's this Silk! You know Bison? He told me! Told us all!" Xiphias raised his glass, discovered he had neglected to fill it, and did so. "Funny, isn't it? An augur! Heard about him? He's an augur too!"

Although his mouth watered for the bread, Silk managed, "That's what they say."

"He's here! He's there! Everybody knows him! Nobody knows where he is! Going to do away with the Guard! Half's on his side already! Ever hear such nonsense in your life? No taxes, but he'll dig canals!" Master Xiphias made a rude noise. "Pas and the rest! Could they do all that people want by this time tomorrow? You know they couldn't!"

Oreb hopped back onto Silk's shoulder. "Good drink!"

He chewed and swallowed. "You should have some of this cheese, too, Oreb. It's marvelous."

"Bird full."

Xiphias chortled. "Me too, Oreb! That's his name? Ate when I got home! Ever see a shoat? Like that! All the meat, half the bread, and two apples! Why'd you go out?"

Silk patted his lips. "That was what I came to talk to you about, Master Xiphias. I was on the East Edge—"

"You walked?"

"Walked and ran, yes."

"No wonder you're limping! Wanted to sit, didn't you? I remember!"

"There was no other way by which I might hope to reach the Palatine," Silk explained, "but there were Guardsmen all along one side of Box Street, and the rebels—General Mint's people—had three times as many on the other, young men mostly, but women and even children, too, though the children were mostly sleeping. I had trouble getting across."

"I'll lay you did!"

"Maytera—General Mint's people wanted to take me to her when they found out who I was. I had a hard time getting away from them, but I had to. I have an appointment at Ermine's."

"On the Palatine? You should've stayed with the Guard! Thousands there! Know Skink? Tried about suppertime! Took a pounding! Two brigades! Taluses, too!"

Silk persevered. "But I must go there, without fighting if I can. I must get to Ermine's." Before he could rein in his tongue he added, "She might actually be there."

"See a woman, eh, lad?" Xiphias's untidy beard rearranged itself in a smile. "What if I tell old what'shisname? Old man, purple robe?"

"I had hoped—"

"I won't! I won't! Forget everything anyhow, don't I? Ask anybody! We going tomorrow? Need a place to sleep?"

"Day sleep," Oreb advised.

"Tonight," Silk told the old man miserably, "and only I am going. But it has to be tonight. Believe me, I would postpone it until morning if I could."

"Drinking wine? No more for us!" Xiphias recorked the bottle and set it on the floor beside his chair. "Watch your bird! Watch and learn! Knows more than you, lad!"

"Smart bird!"

"Hear that? There you are!" Xiphias bounced out of his chair. "Have an apple? Forgot 'em! Still a few." He opened the oven door and banged it shut. "Not in there! Had to move 'em! Cooked the meat! Where's Auk?"

"I've no idea, I'm afraid." Silk cut himself a second, smaller piece of cheese. "I hope he's home in bed. May I put that apple you're looking for in my pocket? I appreciate it very much—I feel a great deal better—but I must go. I wanted to ask whether you knew a route to the Palatine that might be safer than the principal streets—"

"Yes, lad! I do, I do!" Triumphantly, Xiphias displayed a bright red apple snatched from the potato bin.

"Good man!"

"And whether you could teach me a trick that might get me past the fighters on both sides. I knew there must be such things, and Auk would certainly know them; but it's a long way to the Orilla, and I wasn't sure that I'd be able to find him. It occurred to me that he'd probably learned many from someone else, and that you were a likely source."

"Need a teacher? Yes, you do! Glad you know it! Where's your needler, lad?"

For a moment Silk was nonplussed. "My—? Right here in my pocket." He held it up much as Xiphias had the apple. "It isn't actually mine, however. It belongs to the young woman I'm to meet at Ermine's."

"Big one! I saw it! Fell out of your pants! Left it upstairs! Want me to get it? Eat your cheese!"

Xiphias darted through the kitchen door, and Silk heard him clattering up the stair. "We must go, Oreb." He rose and dropped the apple into a pocket of his robe. "He intends to go with us, and I can't permit it." For a second his head spun; the walls of the kitchen shook like jelly and revolved like a carousel before snapping back into place.

A dark little hallway beyond the kitchen door led to the stair, and the door by which they had entered the house. He steadied himself against the newel post, half hoping to hear the old man on the floor above or even to see him descending again, but the old house could not have been more silent if he and Oreb had been alone in it; it puzzled him until he recalled the canvas mats on the floor of the salon.

Unbolting the door, he stepped into the empty, skylit street. The tunnels through which he had trudged for so many weary hours presumably underlay the Palatine, as they seemed to underlie everything; but they would almost certainly be patrolled by soldiers like the one from whom he had escaped. He knew of no entrance except Scylla's lakeshore shrine in any case, and was glad at that moment that he did not. A big hole, Oreb had said. Was it possible that Oreb, also, had wandered in those dread-filled tunnels?

Shuddering at the memories he had awakened, Silk limped away toward the Palatine with renewed determination, telling himself that his ankle did not really hurt half so much as he believed it did. His gaze was on the rutted potholed street, for he knew that despite what he might tell himself, twisting his ankle would put an end to walking; but regardless of all the self-discipline he brought to bear, his thoughts threaded the tunnels once more, and hand-in-hand with Mamelta reentered that curious structure (not unlike a tower, but a tower thrust into the ground instead of rising into the air) that she had called a ship, and again beheld below it emptiness darker than any night and gleaming points of light that the Outsider—at his enlightenment!—had indicated were whorls, whorls outside the whorl, to which dead Pas and deathless Echidna, Scylla and her siblings had never penetrated.

You was goin' to get me out. Said you would. Promised.

Auk, who could not quite see Gelada, heard him crying in the wind that filled the pitch-black tunnel, while Gelada's tears dripped from the rock overhead. The two-card boots he had always kept well greased were sodden above the ankle now. "Bustard?" he called hopefully. "Bustard?"

Bustard did not reply.

You had the word, you said. Get me out o' here. "I saw you that time, off to one side." Unable to remember when or where he had said it last, Auk repeated, "I got eyes like a cat."

It was not quite true because Gelada had vanished when he had turned his head, yet it seemed a good thing to say. Gelada might walk wide if he thought he was being watched.

Auk? That your name? Auk? "Sure. I told you." Where's the Juzgado, Auk? Lot o' doors down here. Which 'uns that 'un, Auk? "I dunno. Maybe the same word opens 'em all."

This was the widest tunnel he had seen, except he couldn't see it. The walls to either side were lost in the dark, and he might, for all he knew, be walking at a slant, might run into the wall slantwise with any step. From time to time he waved his arms, touching nothing. Oreb flapped ahead, or maybe it was a bat, or nothing.

(Far away a woman's voice called, *"Auk? Auk?"*)

The tunnel wall was aglow now, but still dark, dark with a peculiar sense of light—a luminous blackness. The toe of one boot kicked something solid, but his groping fingers found nothing.

"Auk, my noctolater, are you lost?"

The voice was near yet remote, a man's, deep and laden with sorrow.

"No, I ain't. Who's that?"

"Where are you going, Auk? Truthfully."

"Looking for Bustard." Auk waited for another question, but none came. The thing he had kicked was a little higher than his knees, flat on top, large and solid feeling. He sat on it facing the luminous dark, drew up his legs, and untied his boots. "Bustard's my brother, older than me. He's dead now, took on a couple Hoppies and they killed him. Only he's been down here with me a lot, giving me advice and telling me stuff, I guess because this is under the ground and it's where he lives on account of being dead."

"He left you."

"Yeah, he did. He generally does that if I start talking to somebody else." Auk pulled off his right boot; his foot felt colder than Dace had after Gelada killed him. "What's a noctolater?"

"One who worships by night, as you worship me."

Auk looked up, startled. "You a god?"

"I am Tartaros, Auk, the god of darkness. I have heard you invoke me many times, always by night."

Auk traced the sign of addition in the air. "Are you standing over there in the dark talking to me?"

"It is always dark where I stand, Auk. I am blind."

"I didn't know that." Black rams and lambs, the gray ram when Patera Silk got home safely, once a black goat, first of all the pair of bats he'd caught himself, surprised by day in the dark, dusty attic of the palaestra and brought to Patera Pike, all for this blind god. "You're a god. Can't you make yourself see?"

"No." The hopeless negative seemed to fill the tunnel, hanging in the blackness long after its sound had faded. "I am an unwilling god, Auk. The only unwilling god. My father made me do this. If, as a god, I might have healed myself, I would have obeyed very willingly, I believe."

"I asked my mother . . . Asked Maytera to bring a god down here to walk with us. I guess she brought you."

"No," Tartaros said again; then, "I come here often, Auk. It is the oldest altar we have."

"This I'm sitting on? I'll get off."

(Again the woman's voice: *"Auk? Auk?"*)

"You may remain. I am also the sole humble god, Auk, or nearly."

"If it's sacred . . ."

"Wood was heaped upon it, and the carcasses of animals. You profane it no more than they. When the first people came, Auk, they were shown how we desired to be worshiped. Soon, they were made to forget. They did, but because they had seen what they had seen, a part of them remembered, and when they found our altars on the inner surface, they sacrificed as we had taught them. First of all, here."

"I haven't got anything," Auk explained. "I used to have a bird, but he's gone. I thought I heard a bat a little while ago. I'll try to catch one, if you'd like that."

"You think me thirsty for blood, like my sister Scylla."

"I guess. I was with her awhile." Auk tried to remember when that had been; although he recalled incidents—seeing her naked on a white stone and cooking fish for her—the days and the minutes slipped and slid.

"What is it you wish, Auk?"

Suddenly he was frightened. "Nothing really, Terrible Tartaros."

"Those who offer us sacrifice always wish something, Auk. Often, many things. Rain, in your city and many others."

"It's raining down here already, Terrible Tartaros."

"I know, Auk."

"If you're blind . . . ?"

"Can you see it, Auk?"

He shook his head. "It's too shaggy dark."

"But you hear it. Hear the slow splash of the falling drops kissing the drops that fell."

"I feel it, too," Auk told the god. "Every once in a while one goes down the back of my neck."

"What is it you wish, Auk?"

"Nothing, Terrible Tartaros." Shivering, Auk wrapped himself in his own arms.

"All men wish for something, Auk. Most of all, those who say they wish for nothing."

"I don't, Terrible Tartaros. Only if you want me to, I'll wish for something for you. I'd like something to eat."

Silence answered him.

"Tartaros? Listen, if this's a altar I'm sitting on and you're here talking to me, shouldn't there be a Sacred Window around here someplace?"

"There is, Auk. You are addressing it. I am here."

Auk took off his left boot. "I got to think about that."

Maytera Mint had taught him all about the gods, but it seemed to him that there were really two kinds, the ones she had told about, the gods in his copybook, and the real ones like Scylla when she'd been inside Chenille, and this Tartaros. The real kind were a lot bigger, but the ones in his copybook had been better, and stronger somehow, even if they were not real.

"Terrible Tartaros?"

"Yes, Auk, my noctolater, what is it you wish?"

"The answers to a couple questions, if that's all right. Lots of times you gods answer questions for augurs. I know I'm not no augur. So is it all right for me to ask you, 'cause we haven't got one here?"

Silence, save for the ever-present splashings, and the woman's voice, sad and hoarse and very far away.

"How come I can't see your Window, Terrible Tartaros? That's my first one, if that's all right. I mean, usually they're sort of gray, but they shine in the dark. So am I blind, too?"

Silence fell again. Auk chafed his freezing feet with his hands. Those hands had glowed like molten gold, not long ago; now they were not even warm.

"I guess you're waiting for the other question? Well, what I wanted to know is how come I hear words and everything? At this palaestra I went to, Maytera said when we got bigger we wouldn't be able to make sense out of the words if a god ever came to our Sacred Window, just sort of know what he meant and maybe catch a couple of words once in a while. Then when Kypris came, it was just like what Maytera'd said it was going to be. Sometimes I felt like I could practically see her, and there was a couple words she said that I heard just as clear as I ever heard anybody, Terrible Tartaros. She said *love* and *robbery,* and I knew it. I knew both those words. And I knew she was telling us it was all right, she loved us and she'd protect us, only we had to believe in her. But when you talk, it's like you were a man just like me or Bustard, standing right here with me."

No voice replied. Auk let out his breath with a whoosh, and put his freezing fingers in armpits for a moment or two, and then began to wring out his stockings.

"You yourself have never seen a god in a Window, Auk my nocto-later?"

Auk shook his head. "Not real clear, Terrible Tartaros. I sort of saw Kindly Kypris just a little, though, and that's good enough for me."

"Your humility becomes you, Auk."

"Thanks." Lost in thought, Auk reflected on his own life and character, the limp stocking still in his hand. At length he said, "It's never done me a lot of good, Terrible Tartaros, only I guess I never really had much."

"If an augur sees the face and hears the words of a god, Auk, he sees and hears because he has never known Woman. A sibyl, also, may see and hear a god, provided that she has not known Man. Children who have never known either may see us as well. That is the law fixed by my mother, the price that she demanded for accepting the gift my father offered. And though her law does not function as she intended in every instance, for the most part it functions well enough."

"All right," Auk said.

"The faces we had as mortals have rotted to dust, and the voices we once possessed have been still for a thousand years. No augur, no sibyl in the *Whorl,* has ever seen or heard them. What your augurs and sibyls see, if they see anything, is the self-image of the god who chooses to be seen. You say that you could nearly make out the face of my father's concubine. The face you nearly saw was her own image of herself, her self as she imagines that self to appear. I feel confident that it was a beautiful face. I have never met any woman more secure in her own vanity. In the same fashion, we sound to them as we conceive our voices to sound. Have I made myself clear to you, Auk?"

"No, Terrible Tartaros, 'cause I can't see you."

"What you see, Auk, is that part of me which can be seen. That is to say, nothing. I came blind from the womb, Auk, and because of it I am incapable of formulating a visual image for you. Nor can I show you the Holy Hues, which are my brother's and my sisters' thoughts before they have coalesced. Nor can I exhibit to you any face at all, whether lovely or terrible. You see the face I envision when I think upon my own. That is to say, nothing. When I depart, you will behold once more the luminous gray you mention."

"I'd rather you stayed around awhile, Terrible Tartaros. If Bustard ain't going to come back, I like having you with me." Auk licked his lips. "Probably I oughtn't to say this, but I don't mean any harm by it."

"Speak, Auk, my noctolater."

"Well, if I could scheme out some way to help you, I'd do it."

There was silence again, a silence that endured so long that Auk feared that the god had returned to Mainframe; even the distant woman's voice was silent.

"You asked by what power you hear my words as words, Auk, my noctolater."

He breathed a sigh of relief. "Yeah, I guess I did."

"It is not uncommon. My mother's law has lost its hold on you, because there is something amiss with your mind."

Auk nodded. "Yeah, I know. I fell off our tall ass when he got hit with a rocket, and I guess I must've landed on my head. Like, it don't bother me that Bustard's dead, only he's down here talking to me. Only I know it would've in the old days. I don't worry about Jugs, either, like I ought to. I love her, and maybe that cull Urus's trying to jump her right now, but she's a whore anyhow." Auk shrugged. "I just hope he don't hurt her."

"You cannot live in these tunnels, Auk, my noctolater. There is no food for you here."

"Me and Bustard'll try to get out, soon as I find him," Auk promised.

"If I were to possess you, I might be able to heal you, Auk."

"Go ahead, then."

"We would be blind, Auk. As blind as I. Because I have never had eyes of my own, I could not look out through yours. But I shall go with you, and guide you, and use your body to heal you, if I can. Look upon me, Auk."

"There's nothing to see," Auk protested.

But there was: a stammering light so filled with hope and pleasure and wonder that Auk would willingly have seen nothing else, if only he could have watched it forever.

"If you're actually Patera Silk," the young woman at the barricade told him, "they'll kill you the minute you step out there."

"No step," Oreb muttered. And again, "No step."

"Very possibly they would," Silk conceded. "As in fact they almost certainly will—unless you're willing to help."

"If you're Silk you wouldn't have to ask me or my people for anything." Uneasily she studied the thin, ascetic face revealed by the bright skylight. "If you're Silk, you are our commander and even General Mint must answer to you. You could just tell us, and we'd have to do whatever you said."

Silk shook his head. "I am Silk, but I can't prove that here. You would have to find someone you trust who knows me and can identify me, and that would consume more time than I have; so I'm begging you instead. Assume—though I swear to you that this is contrary to fact—that I am not Silk. That I am—this, of course, is entirely factual—a poor young augur in urgent need of your assistance. If you won't help me for my sake, or for that of the god I serve, do so for your own, I implore you."

"I can't launch an attack without an order from Brigadier Bison."

"You shouldn't," Silk told her, "with one. There's an armored floater behind those sandbags. I can see the turret above them. If your people attacked, they would be advancing into its fire, and I've seen what a buzz gun can do."

The young woman drew herself up to her full height, which was a span and a half less than his own. "We will attack if we are ordered to do so, Caldé."

Oreb bobbed his approbation. "Good girl!"

Looking at the sleeping figures behind the barricade, children of fifteen and fourteen, thirteen and even twelve, Silk shook his head.

"They're pretty young." (The young woman could not have been more than twenty herself.) "But they'll fight if they're led, and I'll lead them." When Silk said nothing, she added, "That's not all. I've got a few men, too, and some slug guns. Most of the women—the other women, I ought to say—are working in the fire companies. You were surprised to find me in command, but General Mint's a woman."

"I am surprised at that, as well," Silk told her.

"Men want to fight a male officer. Besides, the women of Trivigaunte are famous troopers, and we women of Viron are in no way inferior to them!"

Recalling Doctor Crane, Silk said, "I'd like to believe that our men are as brave as theirs, as well."

The young woman was shocked. "They're slaves!"

"Have you been there?"

She shook her head.

"Neither have I. Surely then it's pointless for us to discuss their customs. A moment ago you called me Caldé. Did you mean that . . . ?"

"Lieutenant. I'm Lieutenant Liana now. I used the title as a courtesy, nothing more. If you want my opinion, I think you're who you say you are. An augur wouldn't lie about that, and there's the bird. They say you've got a pet bird."

"Silk here," the bird informed her.

"Then do as I ask. Do you have a white flag?"

"For surrender?" Liana was offended. "Certainly not!"

"To signal a truce. You can make one by tying a white rag to a stick. I want you to wave it and call to them, on the other side. Tell them there's an augur here who's brought the pardon of Pas to your wounded. That's entirely true, as you know. Say he wants to cross and do the same for theirs."

"They'll kill you when they find out who you are."

"Perhaps they won't find out. I promise you that I won't volunteer the information."

Liana ran her fingers through her tousled hair; it was the same gesture he used in the grip of indecision. "Why me? No, Caldé, I can't let you risk yourself."

"You can," he told her. "What you cannot do is maintain that position with even an appearance of logic. Either I am Caldé or I am not. If I am, it is your duty to obey any order I give. If I'm not, the life of the Caldé is not at risk."

A few minutes later, as she and a young man called Linsang helped him up the barricade, Silk wondered whether he had been wise to invoke logic. Logic condemned everything he had done since Oosik had handed him Hyacinth's letter. When Hyacinth had written, the city had been at peace, at least relatively. She had no doubt expected to shop on the Palatine, stay the night at Ermine's, and return—

"No fall," Oreb cautioned him.

He was trying not to. The barricade had been heaped up from any-thing and everything: rubble from ruined buildings, desks and counters from shops, beds, barrels, and bales piled upon one another without any order he could discern.

He paused at the top, waiting for a shot. The troopers behind the sandbag redoubt had been told he was an augur, and might know of the Prolocutor's letter by this time. Seeing Oreb, they might know which augur he was, as well.

And shoot. It would be better, perhaps, to fall backward toward Liana and Linsang if they did—better, certainly, to jump that way if they missed.

No shot came; he began a cautious descent, slightly impeded by the traveling bag. Oosik had not killed him because Oosik had taken the long view, had been at least as much politician as trooper, as every high-ranking officer no doubt had to be. The officer commanding the redoubt would be younger, ready to obey the orders of the Ayun-tamiento without question.

Yet here he was.

Once invoked, logic was like a god. One might entreat a god to visit one's Window; but if a god came it could not be dismissed, nor could any message that it vouchsafed mankind be ignored, suppressed, or denied. He had invoked logic, and logic told him that he should be in bed in the house that had become Oosik's temporary headquarters—that he should be getting the rest and care he needed so badly.

"He knew I'd go, Oreb." Something closed his throat; he coughed and spat a soft lump that could have been mucus. "He'd read her letter before he came in, and he's seen her." Silk found that he could not, even now, bring himself to mention that Oosik had lain with Hyacinth. "He knew I'd go, and take his problem with me."

"Man watch," Oreb informed him.

He paused again, scanning the sandbag wall but unable to distinguish, at this distance, rounded sandbags from helmeted heads. "As long as they don't shoot," he muttered.

"No shoot."

This stretch of Gold Street had been lined with jewelers, the largest and richest shops nearest the Palatine, the richest of all clinging to the skirts of the hill itself, so that their patrons could boast of buying their bangles "uphill." Most of the shops were empty now, their grills and bars torn from their fronts by a thousand arms, their gutted interiors guarded only by those who had died defending or looting them. Beyond the redoubt, other richer shops waited, still intact. Silk tried and failed to imagine the children over whose recumbent bodies he had stepped looting them. They would not, of course. They would charge, fight, and very quickly die at Liana's order, and she with them. The looters would follow—if they succeeded. This body (Silk crouched to examine it) was that of a boy of thirteen or so; one side of his face had been shot away.

He had not been on Gold Street often; but he was certain that it had never been this long, or half this wide.

Here a trooper of the Guard and a tough-looking man who might have been the one who had questioned him after Kypris's theophany lay side-by-side, their knives in each other's ribs.

"Patera!" It was the rasping voice that had answered Liana's hail.

"What is it, my son?"

"Hurry up, will you!"

He broke into a trot, though not without protest from his ankle. When he had feared a shot at any moment, this lowest slope of the Palatine had been very steep; now he was scarcely conscious of its grade.

"Here. Grab my hand."

The Guard's redoubt was only half the height of the rebel barricade, although it was (as Silk saw when he had scrambled to the top) rather thicker. Its front was nearly sheer, its back stepped for the troopers who would fire over it.

The one who had helped him up said, "Come on. I don't know how long he'll last."

Silk nodded, out of breath from his climb and afraid he had torn the stitches in his lung. "Take me to him."

The trooper jumped from the sandbag step; Silk followed more circumspectly. There were sleepers here as well, a score of armored Guardsmen lying in the street wrapped in blankets that were probably green but looked black in the skylight.

"They going to rush us, over there?" the trooper asked.

"No. Not tonight, I'd say—tomorrow morning, perhaps."

The trooper grunted. "Slugs'll go right through a lot of that stuff in their fieldwork. I been lookin' it over, and there's a lot of furniture in there. Boards no thicker than your thumb in junk like that. I'm Sergeant Eft."

They shook hands, and Silk said, "I was thinking the same thing as I climbed over it, Sergeant. There are heavier things as well, though, and even the chairs and so forth must obstruct your view."

Eft snorted. "They got nothin' I want to see."

That could not be said of the Guard, as Silk realized as soon as he looked past the floater. A talus had been posted at an intersection a hundred paces uphill, its great, tusked head (so like that of the one he had killed beneath Scylla's shrine that he could have believed them brothers) swiveling to peer down each street in turn. Liana would have been interested in it, he thought, if she did not know about it already.

"In here." Eft opened the door of one of the dark shops; his voice and the thump of the door brightened lights inside, where troopers stripped of parts of their armor and more or less bandaged lay on blankets on a terrazzo floor. One moaned, awakened by the noise or the lights; two, it seemed, were not breathing. Silk knelt by the nearest, feeling for a pulse.

"Not him. Over here."

"All of them," Silk said. "I'm going to bring the Pardon of Pas to all of them, and I won't do it en masse. There's no justification for that."

"Most's already had it. He has."

Silk looked up at the sergeant, but there was no judging his truthfulness from his hard, ill-favored face. Silk rose. "This man's dead, I believe."

"All right, we'll get him out of here. Come over here. He's not." Eft was standing beside the man who had moaned.

Silk knelt again. The injured man's skin was cold to his touch. "You're not keeping him warm enough, Sergeant."

"You a doctor, too?"

"No, but I know something about caring for the sick. An augur must."

"No hurt." Oreb hopped from Silk's shoulder to the injured man's chest. "No blood."

"Leave him alone, you silly bird."

"No hurt!" Oreb whistled. "No blood!"

A bald man no taller than Liana stepped from behind one of the empty showcases. Although he held a slug gun, he was not in armor or even in uniform. "He—he isn't, Patera. Isn't wounded. At least he doesn't—I couldn't find a thing. I think it must be his heart."

"Get a blanket," Silk told Eft. "Two blankets. Now!"

"I don't take orders from any shaggy butcher."

"Then his death will be on your head, Sergeant." Silk took his beads from his pocket. "Bring two blankets. Three wouldn't be too many. The men watching the rebels can spare theirs, surely. Three blankets and clean water."

He bent over the injured man, his prayer beads dangling in the approved fashion from his right hand. "In the names of all the gods you are forgiven forever, my son. I speak here for Great Pas, for Divine Echidna, for Scalding Scylla, for Marvelous Molpe . . ."

The names rolled from his tongue, each with its sonorous honorific, names empty or freighted with horror. Pas, whose Plan the Outsider had endorsed, was dead; Echidna a monster. The ghost that haunted Silk's mind now, as he spoke and swung his beads, was not Doctor Crane's but that of the handsome, brutal chem who had believed himself Councillor Lemur.

"The monarch wanted a son to succeed him," the false Lemur had said. "Scylla was as strong-willed as the monarch himself but female. Her father allowed her to found our city, however, and many others. She founded your Chapter as well, a parody of the state religion of her own whorl. His queen bore the monarch another child, but she was worse yet, a fine dancer and a skilled musician, but female, too, and subject to fits of insanity. We call her Molpe. The third was male, but no better than the first two because he was born blind. He became that Tartaros to whom you were recommending yourself, Patera. You believe he can see without light. The truth is that he cannot see by daylight. Echidna conceived again, and bore another male, a healthy boy who inherited his father's virile indifference to the physical sensations of others to the point of mania. We call him Hierax now—"

And this boy over whom he bent and traced sign after sign of addition was nearly dead. Possibly—just possibly—he might derive comfort from the liturgy, and even strength. The gods whom he had worshiped might be unworthy of his worship, or of anyone's; but the worship itself must have counted for something, weighed in some scales somewhere, surely. It had to, or else the Whorl was mad.

"The Outsider likewise forgives you, my son, for I speak here for him, too." A final sign of addition and it was over. Silk sighed, shivered, and put away his beads.

"The other one didn't say that," the civilian with the slug gun told him. "That last."

He had waited so long in fear of some such remark that it came now as an anticlimax. "Many augurs include the Outsider among the minor gods," he explained, "but I don't. His heart? Is that what you said? He's very young for heart problems."

"His name's Cornet Mattak. His father's a customer of mine." The little jeweler leaned closer. "That sergeant, he killed the other one."

"The other—?"

"Patera Moray. He told me his name. We chatted awhile when he'd said the prayers of the Pardon, and I—I— And I—" Tears flooded the jeweler's eyes, abrupt and unexpected as the gush from a broken jar. He took out a blue handkerchief and blew his nose.

Silk bent over the cornet again, searching for a wound.

"I said I'd give him a chalice. To catch the blood, you know what I mean?"

"Yes," Silk said absently. "I know what they're for."

"He said theirs was yellow pottery, and I said—said—"

Silk rose and picked up the small traveling bag. "Where is his body? Are you certain he's dead?" Oreb fluttered back to his shoulder.

The jeweler wiped his eyes and nose. "Is he dead? Holy Hierax! If you'd seen him, you wouldn't ask. He's out in the alley. That sergeant came in while we were talking and shot him. In my own store! He dragged him out there afterward."

"Show him to me, please. He brought the Pardon of Pas to all these others? Is that correct?"

Leading Silk past empty display cases toward the back of the shop, the jeweler nodded.

"Cornet Mattak hadn't been wounded then?"

"That's right." The jeweler pushed aside a black velvet curtain, revealing a narrow hallway. They passed a padlocked iron door and stopped before a similar door that was heavily barred. "I said when all this is over and things have settled down, I'll give you a gold one. I was still emptying out my cases, you see, while he was bringing them the Pardon. He said he'd never seen so much gold, and they were saving for a real gold chalice. They had one at his manteion, he said, before he came, but they'd had to sell it."

"I understand."

The jeweler took down the second bar and stood it against the wall. "So I said, when this is over I'll give you one to remember tonight by. I've got a nice one that I've had about a year, plain gold but not plain looking, you know what I mean? He smiled when I said that."

The iron door swung open with a creak of dry hinges that reminded Silk painfully of the garden gate at the manse.

"I said, you come into the strong room with me, Patera, and I'll show it to you. He put his hand on my shoulder then and said, my son, don't consider yourself bound by this. You haven't sworn by a god, and—and—"

"Let me see him." Silk stepped outside into the alley.

"And then the sergeant came in and shot him," the jeweler finished. "So don't you go back inside, Patera."

In the chill evil-smelling darkness, someone was murmuring the prayer that Silk himself had just completed. He caught the names of Phaea and Sphigx, followed by the conventional closing phrase. The voice was an old man's; for an eerie moment, Silk felt that it was Patera Pike's.

His eyes had adjusted to the darkness of the alley by the time the kneeling figure stood. "You're in terrible danger here," Silk said, and bit back the stooped figure's title just in time.

"So are you, Patera," Quetzal told him.

Silk turned to the jeweler. "Go inside and bar the door, please. I must speak to the—to my fellow augur. Warn him."

The jeweler nodded, and the iron door closed with a crash, leaving the alley darker than ever.

For a few seconds, Silk assumed that he had simply lost sight of Quetzal in the darkness; but he was no longer there. Patera Moray—of an age, height, and weight indeterminable without more light—lay on his back in the filthy mud of the alley, his beads in his hands and his arms neatly folded across his torn chest, alone in the final solitude of death.

Chapter 7

WHERE THELX
HOLDS UP A MIRROR

Silk stopped to look at Ermine's imposing façade. Ermine's had been built as a private house, or so it appeared—built for someone with a bottomless cardcase and a deep appreciation of pillars, arches, friezes, and cornices and the like; features he had previously seen only as fading designs painted on the otherwise stark fronts of shiprock buildings were real here in a jungle of stone that towered fully five stories. A polished brass plaque of ostentatiously modest proportions on the wide green front door announced: "Ermine's Hôtel."

Who, Silk wondered almost idly, had Ermine been? Or was he still alive? If so, might Linsang be a poor relation—or even a rich one who had turned against the Ayuntamiento? And what about Patera Gulo? Stranger things had happened.

Though he felt cold, his hands were clammy; he groped for his robe before remembering that it was back in the borrowed traveling bag with the borrowed blue tunic, and wiped his hands on the yellow one he was wearing instead.

"Go in?" Oreb inquired.

"In a minute." He was procrastinating and knew it. This was Ermine's, the end of dreams, the shadeup of waking. If he was lucky, he would be recognized and shot. If he was not, he would find Thelxiepeia's image and wait until Ermine's closed, for even Ermine's must close sometime. An immensely superior servant would inform him icily that he would have to leave. He would stand, and look about him one last time, and try to hold the servant in conversation to gain a few moments more.

After that, he would have to go. The street would be gray with morning and very cold. He would hear Ermine's door shut firmly behind him, the snick of the bolt and the rattle of the bar. He would look up and down the street and see no Hyacinth, and no one who could be carrying a message from her.

Then it would be over. Over and dead and done with, never to live again. He would recall his longing as something that had once occupied an augur whose name chanced to be his, Silk, a name not common but by no means outlandish. (The old caldé, whose bust his mother had kept at the back of her closet, had been—what? Had he been Silk, too? No, Tussah; but tussah was another costly fabric.) He would try to bring peace and to save his manteion, fail at both, and die.

"Go in?"

He wanted to say that they were indeed going in, but found himself too dismayed to speak. A man with a pheasant's feather in his hat and a fur cape muttered, "Pardon me," and shouldered past. A footman in livery (presumably the supercilious servant envisioned a few seconds before) opened the door from inside.

Now. Or not at all. Leave or send a message. Preserve the illusion.

"Are you coming in, sir?"

"Yes," Silk said. "Yes, I am. I was wondering about my pet, though. If there are objections, I'll leave him outside."

"None, sir." A faint, white smile touched the footman's narrow lips like the tracery of frost upon a windowpane. "The ladies not infrequently bring animals, sir. Boarhounds, sir. Monkeys. Your bird cannot be worse. But, sir, the door . . ."

It was open, of course. The night was chill, and Ermine's would be comfortably warm, rebellion or no rebellion. Silk climbed the steps to the green door, discovering that Liana's barricade had been neither higher nor steeper.

"This is your first visit to Ermine's, I take it, sir?"

Silk nodded. "I'm to meet a lady here."

"I quite understand, sir. This is our anteroom, sir." There were sofas and stiff-looking chairs. "It is principally for the removal of one's outer garments, sir. They are left in the cloakroom. You may check your bag there, if you so desire. There is no hospitality here in the anteroom, sir, but one can observe all the guests who enter or depart."

"Good man?" Oreb studied the footman through one bright, black eye. "Like bird?"

"Tonight, sir," the footman leaned nearer Silk, and his voice became confidential, "I might be able to fetch you some refreshment myself, however. We've little patronage tonight. The unrest."

"Thank you," Silk said. "Thank you very much. But no."

"Beyond the anteroom, sir, is our sellaria. The chairs are rather more comfortable, sir, and there is hospitality as well. Some gentlemen read."

"Suppose I go into your sellaria and turn to the right," Silk inquired, "where would I be then?"

"In the Club, sir. Or if one turns less abruptly, in the Glasshouse, sir. There are nooks, sir. Benches and settees. There is hospitality, sir, but it is infrequent."

"Thank you," Silk said, and hurried away.

Strange to think that this enormous room, a room that held fifty chairs or more, with half that many diminutive tables and scores of potted plants, statues, and fat-bellied urns, should be called by the same name as his musty little sitting room at the manse. Swerving to his right he wound among them, worrying that he had turned too abruptly and feeling that he walked in a dream through a house of giants—while politely declining the tray proffered by a deferential waiter. All the chairs he saw were empty; a table with a glass top scarcely bigger than the seat of a milking stool held wads of crumpled paper and a sheet half covered with script, the only signs of human habitation.

A wall loomed before him like the face of a mountain, or more accurately, like a fog bank through rents in which might be glimpsed scenes of unrelated luxury that were in truth its pictures. He veered left, and after another twenty strides caught sight of a marble arch framing a curtain of leaves.

It had been as warm as he had expected in the sellaria; passing through the arch he entered an atmosphere warmer still, humid, and freighted with exotic perfumes. A moth with mauve-and-gray wings larger than his palms fluttered before his face to light on a purple flower the size of a soup tureen. A path surfaced with what seemed precious stones, narrower even than the graveled path through the garden of his manteion, vanished after a step or two among vines and dwarfish trees. The music of falling water was everywhere.

"Good place," Oreb approved.

It was, Silk thought. It was stranger and more dreamlike than the sellaria, but more friendly and more human, too. The sellaria had been a vision of opulence bordering on nightmare; this was a gentler one of warmth and water, sunshine and lush fertility, and though this glass-roofed garden might be used for vicious purposes, sunshine and fertility, water and warmth were things in themselves good; their desirability could only be illustrated more clearly by the proximity of evil. "I like it," he whispered to Oreb. "Hyacinth must too, or she wouldn't have told me to meet her here, where all this would surely dim the beauty of a woman less lovely."

The sparkling path divided. He hesitated, then turned to his right. A few steps more, and there was no light save that from the skylands floating above the Whorl. "His Cognizance would like this as much as we do, I believe, Oreb. I've been in his garden at the Palace, and this reminds me of it, though that's an open-air garden, and this can't be nearly as large."

Here was a seat for two, masterfully carved from a single block of myrtle. He halted to stare at it, longing to sit but restrained by the fear that he would be unable to stand again. "We have to find this image of Thelxiepeia," he muttered, "and there must be places to sit there. Hyacinth won't come. She's at Blood's in the country, she's bound to be. But we can rest there awhile."

A new voice, obsequious and affected, murmured, "I *beg* your pardon, sir."

"Yes, what is it?" Silk turned.

A waiter had come up behind him. "I'm rather embarrassed, sir. I really don't know quite how to phrase it."

"Am I not supposed to be in here now?" As Silk asked, he resolved not to leave without a fight; they might overwhelm him with a mob of waiters and footmen, but they would have to—no mere order or argument would suffice.

"Oh, no, sir!" The waiter looked horrified. "It's quite all right."

The desperate struggle Silk had visualized faded into the mist of unactualized eventualities.

"There is a gentleman, sir. A very tall gentleman, sir, with a long face? Rather a sad face, if I may say so, sir. He's in the Club."

"No go," Oreb announced firmly.

"He would not give me his name, sir. He said it was not relevant." The waiter cleared his throat. "He would not give your name either, sir, but he described you. He said that I was to say nothing if you were with someone, sir. I was only to offer to bring you and anyone who might be in your company refreshment, for which he would pay. But that if I found you alone, I was to invite you to join him."

Silk shook his head. "I have no idea who this gentleman is. Do you?"

"No, sir. He is not a regular patron, sir. I don't think I've ever seen him before."

"Do you know the figure of Thelxiepeia, waiter? Here in the Glass-house?"

"Certainly, sir. The tall gentleman instructed me to look for you there, sir."

Colonel Oosik was tall, Silk reflected, though so massive that his height had not been very noticeable; but Oosik could scarcely be called long-faced. Since only he and Captain Gecko had read Hyacinth's letter, the long-faced man was presumably Gecko. "Tell him I can't join him in the Club," Silk said, choosing his words. "Express my regrets. Tell him I'll be at the figure of Thelxiepeia, and I'm alone. He may speak to me there if he chooses."

"Yes, sir. Thank you, sir. May I get you anything, sir? I could bring it there."

Silk shook his head impatiently.

"Very well, sir. I will deliver your message."

"Wait a moment. What time is it?"

The waiter looked apologetic. "I have no watch, sir."

"Of course not. Neither do I. Approximately."

"I looked at the barman's clock, sir, only a minute or two before I came here. It was five until twelve then, sir."

"Thank you," Silk said, and sat down on the carved wooden seat without a thought about the difficulty of getting up.

Hieraxday, Hyacinth's letter said. He tried to recall her exact words and failed, but he remembered their import. She had mentioned no time, perhaps intending late afternoon, when she would have finished her shopping. The barman's clock was in the Club, no doubt; and the Club would be a drinking place, primarily for men—a rich man's version of the Cock, where he had found Auk. The waiter was unlikely to have glanced at the barman's clock after speaking to the long-faced man, whoever he was; so it had probably been ten minutes or more since he had noticed the time. Hieraxday was past. This was Thelxday, and if Hyacinth had waited for him (which was highly unlikely) he had not come.

"Hello, Jugs," Auk said, emerging from the darkness of a side tunnel. "He wants us to work on Pas's Plan."

Chenille whirled. "Hackum! I've been looking all over for you!" She ran to him, surprising him, threw her arms around him, and wept.

"Now," he said. "Now, now, Jugs. Now, now." She had been unhappy, and he knew it and knew that in some ill-defined and troubling way it was his fault, although he had meant her no harm, had wished her well and thought of her with kindness when he had thought of her at all. "Excuse," he muttered, and let go of Tartaros's hand to embrace her with both arms.

When at last she ceased sobbing, he kissed her as tenderly as he could, a kiss she returned passionately. She wiped her eyes, sniffled, and gulped, "Oh, Hierax! Hackum, I missed you so much! I've been so lonesome and scared. Hug me."

This baffled him, because he already was. He tried, "I'm sorry, Jugs," and when it seemed to do no good, "I won't ever leave you again unless you want me to."

She nodded and swallowed. "It's all right, as long as you keep coming back."

He noticed her ring. "Didn't I give you that?"

"Yeah, thanks." Stepping back, she held it up to show it off better, although the bleared greenish lights could never do it justice. "I love it, but you can have it back anytime if you need the gelt."

"I'm flush, but I gave it to you?"

"You forget, huh?" She looked at him searchingly. "On account of hitting your head. Or maybe a god got you like Kypris did me? It's still pretty hard for me to remember lots of things that happened when she was boss, or Scylla."

Auk shook his head, and found that it no longer ached. "I've never had no god bossing me, Jugs, or wanted to either. That's lily. I never even knew about Kypris, but you were a lot different when you were Scylla."

"Some of that was me, I think. Hold me tighter, won't you? I'm really cold."

"Your sunburn don't hurt any more?"

She shook her head. "Not much. I'm starting to peel a little. The bird was pulling on the peels before he left, only I made him stop."

Auk looked around. "Where is he?"

"With Patera and Stony, I guess. That Urus beat the hoof and they took off after him. Me, too, only we came to a split in the tunnel, you know?"

"Sure. I've seen a lot of them."

"And then I thought, they're not going to look for Auk anymore, and that's what I want to do. So I sort of slowed down, and when they went one way I went the other. I guess the bird went with them."

"That was you I heard calling me."

Chenille nodded. "Yeah. I yelled until my pipe gave out. Oh, Hackum, I'm so glad I found you!"

"We found you," he told her seriously. "Why I ran off, Jugs . . ." He fell silent, massaging his big jaw.

"You saw somebody, Hackum. Or anyhow you thought you did. I could see that, and Patera said so, too."

"Yeah. My brother Bustard. He's dead, see? Only he was down here talking to me. I was going to say he wasn't really, I just sort of dreamed it, only now I'm not so sure. Maybe he was. Know what I mean?"

The gray shiprock walls seemed to press in upon her. "I think so, Hackum."

"Then he went away, and I missed him a lot, just like when he died. So then when I saw him again, maybe it was a couple, three hours later, I waved and yelled and tried to catch up, only I never did. Then I got lost, but I didn't care because I was looking for Bustard, and he could've been anywhere. Then I ran into this god. Into Tartaros. Mostly I call him Terrible Tartaros, 'cause I can't say the other right."

"You met a god, Hackum? Like you'd meet somebody in the street, you mean?"

"Sort of." Auk sat down on the tunnel floor. "Jugs, will you sit on my lap, the way you used to do in the old days? I'd like that."

"All right." She did, laying her launcher flat, crossing her long legs, and leaning back in his arms. "This is really better, Hackum. It's a lot warmer. Except I don't do it much any more because I know I'm a pretty good load. Orchid says I'm getting fat. She's been telling me for a couple of months now."

He held her closer, reveling in her softness. "She's fat. Real fat. Not you, Jugs."

"Thanks. This god you met. Tartaros, right? He's for you like Kypris is for us."

"Yeah, except he's one of the Seven."

"I know that. Tarsday."

"He's got a whole bunch of stuff besides us. The main thing is, he's the night god. Anywhere it's dark, that's a special place for him. Sleep and dreams, too. I mean, any god can send a dream if he wants to, but the regular kind that seem like nobody sent 'em are his. I call him Terrible Tartaros 'cause you had to say terrible or the other, or Maytera'd stomp you. I'd lay he could cut up rough, but he's been a bob cull with me. He came along to show how to find you and get out of here, and all that. He's next to us right now, only you can't see him 'cause he's blind."

"You mean he's here with us?" Chenille's eyes were wide.

"Yeah, he's sitting right here with me, only I wouldn't try to reach over and feel. Maybe he wouldn't do anything—"

She had already, waving her free arm through the empty space on Auk's right.

He shook her, not roughly. "Don't, Jugs. I told you."

"He's not there. There's nothing there."

"All right, there's nothing there. I was shaving you."

"You shouldn't do that." She got up. "You don't know how shaggy scared I am down here, or how shaggy hungry."

Auk rose too. "Yeah, it wasn't very funny, I guess. I'm sorry, Jugs. I won't do it again. C'mon."

"Where are we going?"

"Out."

"Really, Hackum?"

"Sure. You're hungry. So am I. We're going to go out and get a dimber dinner, probably at Pork's or one of those places. After that, we can rent a room and get a little rest. He says I got to rest. After that, maybe we'll do what Scylla said, only I don't know. I'll have to ask him."

"Tartaros? That's who you're talking about? You really met him?"

"Yeah. It's real dark in there and pretty wet. Water's sort of raining through the roof. If you saw it, you probably didn't go in, but there's nothing in there that'll hurt you. I don't think so, anyhow."

"I've still got this lantern that Gelada had, Hackum, only there's no way to light it."

"We don't have to," he told her. "It's not very far."

"You said we were going out."

"It's on our way." He stopped and faced her. "Only we'd be going even if it wasn't, 'cause he's got something to show us. He just told me, see? Now listen up."

She nodded, drawing Incus's robe around her.

"This's a real god. Tartaros, just like I told you. My head's not right 'cause I got a bruise in there and a big gob of blood, too, he says. He's trying to fix it, and I been feeling better ever since he started. Only we got to do like he says, so you're coming if I got to carry you."

"Wood girl," Oreb called. "Here girl!"

Silk sat up; the "girl" might be Hyacinth. If there was the least chance, one in a thousand or ten million—if there was any chance at all—he had to go. He made himself stand, picked up the bag, coughed, spat, and stumbled away. The path wound right then left, dropped into a tiny vale, and forked. White as ghosts, enormous blossoms dripped moisture. "I'm coming, Oreb. Tell her I'm coming."

"Here, here!"

The bird sounded very near. He stepped off the glittering path, his feet sinking in soft soil, and parted the leaves; the face that stared into his own might have been that of a corpse, hollow-cheeked and dull-eyed. He gasped, and saw its bloodless lips part. Oreb flew to him, becoming two birds.

He advanced another step, sparing the crowding plants as much as he could, and found himself standing upon red stones that bordered a clear pool no bigger than a tablecloth, which a path approached from the opposite side.

"Here girl!" Oreb hopped to the wooden figure's head and rapped it smartly with his beak.

"Yes," Silk said, "that's Thelxiepeia." No other goddess had those tilted eyes, and a carved marmoset perched upon the figure's shoulder. He tapped his reflected face with a finger and clapped his hands, but no monitor appeared in the silvered globe she held. "It's just a mirror," he told Oreb. "I hoped it might be a glass—that Hyacinth might call me on it."

"No call?"

"No call on this, alas." With help from a friendly tree, he walked the stony rim of the pool to a swinging seat facing the water. Here, as Oosik had said, one saw the pool reflected in Thelxiepeia's mirror, and her mirror reflected in it.

Hieraxday had been the day for dying and for honoring the dead. Crane had died; but he, Silk, had done neither. Today, Thelxday, was the day for crystal gazing and casting fortunes, for tricks and spells, and for hunting and trapping animals; he resolved to do none of those things, leaned back in the swing, and closed his eyes. Thelxiepeia was at once the cruelest and kindest of goddesses, more mercurial even than Molpe, though she was said—it would be why her image was here—to favor lovers. Love was the greatest of enchantments; if Echidna and her children succeeded in killing Kypris, Thelxiepeia would no doubt, would doubtless . . .

Become the goddess of love in a century or less, said the Outsider, standing not behind Silk as he had in the ball court, but before him—standing on the still water of the pool, tall and wise and kind, with a face that nearly came into focus. *I would claim her in that case, long before the end. As I have so many others. As I am claiming Kypris even now because love always proceeds from me, real love, true love. First romance.*

The Outsider was the dancing man on a toy, and the water the polished toy-top on which he danced with Kypris, who was Hyacinth and Mother, too. *First romance,* sang the Outsider with the music box. *First romance.* It was why he was called the Outsider. He was outside—

"I, er, hope and—ah—trust I'm not disturbing you?"

Silk woke with a start and looked around wildly.

"Man come," Oreb remarked. "Bad man." Oreb was perched on a

stone beside Thelxiepeia's pool; when he had concluded his remarks, he pecked experimentally at a shining silver minnow that darted away in terror.

"Names are not—um—requisite, eh? I know who you are. You know me, hey? Let that be enough for both of us."

Silk recognized his swaying visitor, started to speak, and assimilating what had been said remained silent.

"Capital. I—ah—we are taking a risk, you and I. An—ah—rash gamble. Simply by, urp, being where we belong. Here on the hill, eh?"

"Won't you sit down?" Silk struggled to his feet.

"No. I—ah—no." His visitor belched again, softly. "Thank you. I have been waiting in the—ah—bar. Where, ump, I have been compelled to buy drinks. And—um—drink. Standing's best. Um, at present, eh? I'll just, er, lean on this, if I may. But please—ah—be seated yourself, Pa—" He covered his mouth with his hand. "Seated by all means. It is I who should—and I do. I, um, am. As you see, eh?"

Silk resumed his place in the swing. "May I ask—"

His visitor raised a hand. "How I knew I should find you here? I did not, Pa— Did not. Nothing of the sort. But while I was—rup!—sitting in that, er, whatchamacallit, I observed you to enter the room. Not the—um—one I sat in, that, ah, darksome and paneled drinking place, hey? The other. The outer room, much bigger."

"The sellaria," Silk supplied.

"Ah—quite. I, um, went to the door. Spied upon you." The visitor shook his head in self-reproach.

"It was excusable, surely, under the circumstances. I have recently done far worse things."

"Good of you to say so. I—um—waylaid that waiter. You spoke with him."

Silk nodded.

"I had, um, observed you to pass under—ah—through the arch. I had never had the, er, pleasure myself, eh? I, ah, apprehended that it was—ah, is—some sort of garden, however. I inquired about it. He, um, indicated that it was—is, I surmise—employed for, um, discussions of a—ah—amorous nature."

"You knew that I would be here, at this particular spot." Silk found it extremely inconvenient to be unable to say *Your Eminence*. "You told him to look for me here."

"No, no!" His visitor shook his head emphatically. "I, ah, antici- pated you might, um, possibly have an appointment. As he had, um, inadverted. But I—ah—in addition, um, however, ah, considered that you might wish to, um, petition the immortal gods. As I, ah, myself. I inquired about such a place in this, um, conservatory. He mentioned the present, ah, xylograph." The visitor smiled. "That's the spot, I told him. That's where you'll find him. Would you mind if I, um, sat myself, now? There by you? I'm—ah—quite fatigued."

"Please do." Hastily, Silk moved to one side.

"Thank you—ah—thank you. Most thoughtful. I have had no sup- per. Hesitated to order anything in—ah—that place. With the wine. Parsi- mony. Foolish—ah—imbecile, actually."

"Catch fish," Oreb suggested.

Silk's visitor ignored him. "I've funds, eh? You?"

"No, nothing."

"Here, Pa— My boy. Hold out your hands." Golden cards showered into Silk's lap. "No, no! Take them! Others—ah—more. Where they came from, eh? Wait for the waiter. Buy yourself a bit of food. For me, ah, in addition. I am, um, in need. Of help. Of—ah—succor. Such is, um, the long and short of it. I cast myself—um. Ourselves. I—we—cast our- selves upon your—ah—commiseration."

Silk looked searchingly at Thelxiepeia, who returned his look with wooden aplomb. Was this enchanted gold that would (figuratively at least) melt at a touch? If not, what had he done to earn her favor? "Thank you," he managed at last. "If I can be of any service to Your—to you, I will be only too happy to oblige you." He counted them by touch: seven cards.

"They came to the Palace. To the—ah—Palace itself, if you can, um, credit that." His visitor sat with his head in his hands. "I was, um, din- ing. At dinner. In came a, ah, page, eh? One of the boys who runs with messages for us, hey? You do that?"

"No. I know of them, of course."

"Some of us did, eh? I, myself. Many years ago. We—ah—matricu- late to schola. Ah—afterwards. Some of us. Fat little boy. Not I. He was. Is. Said they'd arrest me. Arrest His Cognizance! I said, ah, balderdash. Ate my sweet, eh? They—um—arrived. Unannounced. Officer—um—cap- tain, lieutenant, something. Troopers with him, Guardsmen every- where, eh? Looked everywhere for His Cog— Turned the whole place upside down. Couldn't find him though. Took me. Bound my hands. Me! Hands tied behind me under my robe."

"I'm very sorry," Silk said sincerely.

"They, er, carried me to the headquarters of the Fourth Brigade. A temporary headquarters. Do I make myself–ah–intelligible? Brigadier's house. No more–ah–titular generals in the Civil Guard, hey? No generalissimo any more. Only this, er, brigadiers. Quizzed me, eh? Hours and hours. Absolutely. Old Quetzal's letter, hey? You know about it?"

"Yes, I've seen it."

"I–ah–composed it. I didn't–ah–inform the brigadier, eh? Didn't 'fess up. Would have shot me, eh? We–ah–I'd expected trouble. Labored to phrase it softly. His– He wouldn't hear of it." His visitor looked around at Silk with the expression of a whipped hound, his breath thick with wine. "You apprehend whom I–ah–intend?"

"Of course."

"He sent it back. Twice. Hadn't happened in years, eh? The third stuck. 'How readily here might I, ah, inscribe–' Yes, inscribe. Ah, 'Let us welcome him and obey him as one of ourselves. With what delight do– shall I inscribe in its place, let us welcome him and, ump, obey him, for he is one of ourselves!' That's what got the third draft past His–ah–past the person known to us both, eh? So I–um–presume. Proud of it, hey? Still am. Still am."

"With reason," Silk told him. "But the Civil Guard can't have cared for it. I'm surprised they let you go." He yawned and rubbed his eyes, discovering that he felt somewhat better, refreshed by his few moments of sleep.

"Talked my way out, hey? Eloquent. No one speaks of me like that. Dull at the ambion, eh? What they say. I know, I know. Eloquent tonight, though. Swim or sink, and I did, Pa–I did. Go between. Peacemaker. End rebellion. Used their glass to talk to Councillor Loris. Harmless, ump! Let him go. Bad feeling in the ranks, hey? Augurs shot, eh? A sibyl, too. The– um–missive. Lay clothing, as you, er, wise. Fearful still. Terribly frightened. Not, er, shamed by the accusation–admission. Still afraid, sitting in there sipping. Looking over my shoulder, hey? Afraid they'd come for me. Sprang up like a rabbit when a porter dropped something in the street."

"I suppose that every man is frightened when his life is threatened. It's very much to Your–to your credit that you are willing to admit it."

"You will–ah–assist me? If you can?"

Oreb looked up from his fishing. "Watch out!"

"I'm tired and very weak," Silk said, "but yes, I will. Will we have to walk far?"

"Won't have to walk at all." His visitor thrust his hand beneath his cream-colored tunic. "I've, ah, informed you it wasn't me they wanted, eh? After old Quetzal, actually. The Prolocutor. His Cognizance. Signed the letter, hey?"

Silk nodded.

"They'd have shot him, eh? Earlier. Earlier. When they—ah—constrained me. That was then, hum? This is—er—the present instant. After midnight. Nearly one, eh? Nearly one. Late when they released me. I've said it? Suppertime—after suppertime, really. They know your—um—profession. Vocation, hey? Mint's a sibyl. You take my meaning?"

"Of course," Silk said.

His visitor produced an elegant ostrich-skin pen case. "On the other side, old Quetzal is, hey? Unmistakable. The letter shows it. And there is that—ah, um—other matter. Vocation, eh? Brigadier thinks he and I might arrange an—urp—hiatus in hostilities. A truce, hey? His word. Been one already, eh? So why not?"

Silk straightened up. "There has? That's wonderful!"

"Little thing, eh? Few hundred involved. Didn't last. But an augur—see the connection? This augur, one of our—ah—of the Chapter's own, crossed the lines. One side to the other, eh? Got them to stop shooting so he could. Colonel's son, wounded. Nearly dead. This—ah—holy augur brought him the Pardon. So far so good? Rebels—ah—tendered an extension. Both sides, um, sweep up bodies. Claim their dead, hey? They did. So why not longer? Old Quetzal might do it. Respected by both sides. Man of peace. You follow me?"

Silk nodded to himself.

"If your, ah, supporters learn the brigadier sent me, eh? What then? Shoot, eh? Possibly. Very possibly. So I require some, um, document from you, Pa— From, ah, you. Signed," the visitor's voice faded to a whisper, "with your—ah—as the—um—your civil title."

"I see. Certainly."

"Capital!" He took a sheaf of paper from the pen case. "These, um, fanciful leathers are not—ah—conducive to penmanship. But the paper should help, hey? I'll hold the ink bottle for you. Brief, ah, inconsiderable. Concise. The, um, bearer, eh? Respect his—ah—um . . ."

"No shoot," Oreb suggested.

He handed Silk a quill. "Point suit you? Not too fine, eh? My prothonotary, Pa–Incus. You know him?"

"I met him once when I was trying to see you."

"Ah? Hm."

The pen case braced on both knees, Silk dipped the quill.

"He–ah–Incus. He points them for me. Had him do it, ah, Molpsday. Too fine, though. Hairsplitters. I shall rid myself of Incus, ah, presently. Could be dead this moment. 'Mongst the gods, eh? Haven't laid eyes on him for days. Gave him a–um–errand. Never came back. All this unrest."

Bent above the paper, Silk hardly heard him.

To General Mint, her officers and troopers.

The bearer, Patera Remora, is authorized by me and by . . .

Silk looked up. "To whom did you speak? Who was this brigadier who released you?"

"Brigadier, er, Erne. Signed for me, too, eh? His side."

Brigadier Erne to negotiate a truce. Please show him every courtesy.

The wavering tip of the quill stopped and began to blot; there seemed to be no more to say. Silk forced it to move on.

If the whereabouts of His Cognizance the Prolocutor are known to you, please conduct the bearer to him in order that he may assist His Cognizance in conducting negotiations.

Oreb dropped a struggling goldfish and pinned it with one foot. "No shoot," he repeated. "Man hide."

I hold you responsible for the safety of the bearer, and that of His Cognizance. Both are to be permitted to pass unharmed. Their movements are not to be restricted in any fashion.

A truce made and kept in good faith is greatly to be desired.

I am Pa. Silk, of Sun Street, Caldé

"Capital! Yes, capital, Pa—Thank you!"

With his beak pointed to the glass roof, Oreb gulped down a morsel of goldfish and announced loudly, "Good man!"

"There is a—um—dispenser in here someplace." The visitor retrieved his pen case and took out a silver shaker. "If you require sand, eh?"

Silk shuddered, added the date, blew upon the paper, then spat congealing blood into the moss at his feet.

"I thank you. I have—ah—so expressed myself, um, previously, I, er, recognize. I am, um, in your, ah, books, eh? Your debtor."

Silk handed him the safe-conduct.

"I, ah, surmise that I can stand now, er, walk. All the rest. Taken a bit dizzy there, eh? For an, er, momentarily." He climbed to his feet, holding tightly to the chain from which their seat was suspended. "I shall partake of an, er, morsel of food, I believe. An, um, collation. Much as I should like—ah—may be imprudent . . ."

"I had a good supper," Silk told him, "and it might be dangerous for us to be seen together. I'll stay here."

"I, um, consider it would be best myself." His visitor released the chain and smiled. "Better, hey? Be all right with a bite to eat. Too much wine. I—ah—concede it. More than I ought. Frightened, but the wine made it worse. To think that we, ump, we pay—" He fell silent. Slowly his smile widened to a death's-head rictus. "Hello, Silk," he said. "They made me find you."

Silk nodded wearily. "Hello, Mucor."

"It's smoky in here. All smoky."

For a moment he did not understand what she meant.

"Dark, Silk. Like falling down steps."

"The fumes of the wine, I suppose. Who made you find me?"

"The councillors will burn me again."

"Torture, unless you do as they say?" Silk tried to keep the anger he felt out of his voice. "Do you know their names, these councillors who threaten to burn you?"

The visitor's grinning head bobbed. "Loris. Tarsier. Potto. My father said not, but the soldier made him go."

"I see. His Eminence—the man you're possessing—told me he'd talked with Councillor Loris through a glass. Is that why you possessed him when you were sent to look for me?"

"I had to. They burned me like Musk."

"Then you were right to obey, to keep from being burned again. I don't blame you at all."

"We're going to kill you, Silk."

Foliage beside the pool shook, spraying crystal droplets as warm as blood; a white-haired man stepped into view. In one hand he held a silver-banded cane with which he had parted the leaves. The other poised a saber, its slender blade pointed at the visitor's heart.

"Don't!" Silk told him.

"No stick," Oreb added with the air of one who clarifies a difficult situation.

"You're Silk yourself, lad! You're him!"

"I'm afraid I am. If you left your place of concealment to protect me, I would be somewhat safer if you didn't speak quite so loudly." Silk turned his attention back to the death-mask that had supplanted his visitor's face. "Mucor, how are you supposed to kill me? This man has Musk's needler now; he followed me here to return it to me, I imagine. Do you—does the man you're possessing have a weapon?"

"I'll tell them, and they'll come."

"I see. And if you won't, they'll burn you."

The visitor's head bobbed again. "It brings me back. I can't stay gone when they burn me."

"We must get you out of there." Silk raised the ankle he had broken jumping from Hyacinth's window and rubbed it. "I've said you're like a devil—I told Doctor Crane that, I know. I thought it, too, when I saw the dead sleepers; I forgot that devils, who torment others, are themselves tormented."

The saber inched forward. "Shall I kill him, lad?"

"No. He's as good a chance for peace as our city has, and I doubt that killing him would ensure Mucor's silence. You can do no good here."

"I can protect you, lad!"

"Before I left you, I knew that I'd meet Hierax tonight." Silk's face was somber. "But there's no reason for you to die with me. If you've tracked me through half the city to return the needler I dropped, give it to me and go."

"This, too!" He held out the silver-banded cane. "Lame, aren't you?

Lame when we fought! Take it!" He threw the cane to Silk, then drew Musk's needler and tossed it into Silk's lap as well. "You're the caldé, lad? The one they tell about?"

"I suppose I am."

"Auk told me! How'd I forget that? Gave your name! I didn't know until this fellow said it. Councillors! Loris? Going to kill you?"

"And Potto and Tarsier." Silk laid Musk's needler aside, thought better of it, and put it into his waistband. "I'm glad that you brought that up. I'd lost sight of it, and it strains probability. Mucor, do you have to return to Loris right away? I'd like you to do me a favor, if you can."

"All right."

"Thank you. First, did Councillor Loris tell you about the man you're possessing? Did he ask you to find him?"

"I know him, Silk. He talks to the man who's not there."

"To Pas, you mean. Yes, he does, I'm sure. But Loris told you. Did he say why?"

The visitor's head shook. "I have to go soon."

"Go to Maytera Mint first—to General Mint, they're the same person." Silk's forefinger traced a circle on his cheek. "Tell her where I am, and that they'll come here to kill me. Then tell Maytera Marble—"

"Girl go," Oreb remarked.

The corpse-grin was indeed fading. Silk sighed again and rose. "Sheath that sword, please. We've no need of it."

"Possession? That's what you call this, lad?"

"Yes. He'll come to himself in a moment."

Silk's visitor caught hold of the chain to steady himself. "You proferred a comment, Pa—? I was taken, ah, vertiginous again, I fear. Please accept my—um—unreserved apology. This—ah—gentleman is . . . ?"

"Master Xiphias. Master Xiphias teaches the sword, Your Eminence. Master Xiphias, this is His Eminence Patera Remora, Coadjutor of the Chapter."

"Really, ah, Patera, you might be more circumspect, hey?"

Silk shook his head. "We're past all that, I'm afraid, Your Eminence. You're in no danger. I doubt that you ever were. My own is already so great that it wouldn't be much greater if you and Master Xiphias were to run up to the first Guardsman you could find and declare that Caldé Silk was at Ermine's awaiting arrest."

"Really! I–ah–"

"You spoke to Councillor Loris, so you told me, through Brigadier Erne's glass."

"Why, er, yes."

"For a moment–while you were dizzy, Your Eminence–I thought that Loris might have told you where to find me; that a certain person in the household he's visiting had told him that I might be here, or had confided in someone else who did. It could have come about quite innocently–but it can't be true, since Loris sent someone to you in order to locate me. Clearly the information traveled the other way: you knew that I might come here tonight. I doubt that you actually told Loris that you knew where to find me; you couldn't have been that certain I'd be here. You said something that led him to think you knew, however. In his place, I'd have ordered Brigadier Erne to have you followed. Thanks to some careless remarks of mine Tarsday, he didn't need to. Will you tell me–quickly, please–how you got your information?"

"I swear–warrant you, Patera–"

"We'll have to talk about it later." Silk stood up less steadily than Remora had, leaning on the silver-banded cane. "A moment ago I told Master Xiphias not to kill you; I'm not certain it would have been wrong for me to have told him to go ahead, but I don't have time for questions–we must go before the Guard gets here. You, Master Xiphias, must return home. You're a fine swordsman, but you can't possibly protect me from a squad of troopers with slug guns. You, Your Eminence, must go to Maytera Mint. Don't bother filling your belly. If–"

"Girl come!" Oreb flew to Silk's shoulder, fluttered his wings, and added, "Come quick!"

For a wasted second, Silk stared at Remora, searching for signs of Mucor in his face. Hyacinth was in sight before he heard the rapid pattering of her bare feet on the path of false gems and saw her, mouth open and dark eyes bright with tears above the rosy confusion of a gossamer dishabille, her hair a midnight cloud behind her as she ran.

She stopped. It was as if the sight of him had suspended her in amber. "You're here! You're really here!"

By Thelxiepeia's spell she was in his arms, suffocating him with kisses. "I didn't–I knew you couldn't come, but I had to. Had to, or I'd never know. I'd always think–"

He kissed her, clumsy but unembarrassed, trying to say by his kiss that he, too, had been forced by something in himself stronger than himself.

The pool and the miniature vale that contained it, always dark, grew darker still. Looking up after countless kisses, he saw idling fish of mottled gold and silver, black, white, and red, hanging in air above the goddess's upraised hand, and for the first time noticed light streaming from a lamp of silver filigree in the branches of a stunted tree. "Where did they go?" he asked.

"Was—somebody—else here?" She gasped for breath and smiled, giving him sweeter pain than he had ever known.

"His Eminence and a fencing master." Silk felt that he should look around him, but would not take his eyes from hers.

"They must have done the polite thing," she kissed him again, "and left quietly."

He nodded, unable to speak.

"So should we. I've got a room here. Did I tell you?"

He shook his head.

"A suite, really. They're all suites, but they call them rooms. It's a game they play, being simple, pretending to be a country inn." She sank to her knees with a dancer's grace, her hand still upon his arm. "Will you kneel by the pool here with me? I want to look at myself, and I want to look at you, too, at the same time." Abruptly, the tears overflowed. "I want to look at *us*."

He knelt beside her.

"I knew you couldn't come," a tear fell, creating a tiny ripple, "so I have to see us both. See you beside me."

As in the ball court (though perhaps only because he had experienced it there) it seemed that he stood outside time.

And when they breathed again and turned to kiss, it seemed to him that their reflections remained as they had been in the quiet water of the pool, invisible but forever present. "We—I have to go," he told her. It had taken an enormous effort to say it. "They know I'm here, or they soon will if they don't already. They'll send troopers to kill me, and if you're with me, they'll kill you, too."

She laughed, and her soft laughter was sweeter than any music. "Do you know what I went through to get here? What Blood will do to me if he finds out I took a floater? By the time I got onto the hill, past the checkpoints and sentries— Are you sick? You don't look at all well."

"I'm only tired." Silk sat back on his heels. "When I thought about having to run again, I felt . . . It will pass." He believed it as soon as he had said it, himself persuaded by the effort he had made to compel her belief.

She rose, and gave him her hand. "By the time I got to Ermine's, I thought I'd been abram to come at all, drowning in a glass of water. I didn't even look in here," happy again, she smiled, "because I didn't want to see there wasn't anyone waiting. I didn't want to be reminded of what a putt I'd been. I got my room and started getting ready for bed, and then I thought—I thought—"

He embraced her; from a perch over the filigree lamp, Oreb croaked, "Poor Silk!"

"What if he's there? What if he's *really down there,* and I'm up here? I'd unpinned my hair and taken off my makeup, but I dived down the stairs and ran through the sellaria, and you were here, and it's only a dream but it's the best dream that ever was."

He coughed. This time the blood was fresh and red. He turned aside and spat it into a bush with lavender flowers and emerald leaves and felt himself falling, unable to stop.

He lay on moss beside the pool. She was gone; but their reflections remained in the water, fixed forever.

When he opened his eyes again, she was back with an old man whose name he had forgotten, the waiter who had offered him wine in the sellaria, the one who had told him of Remora, the footman who had opened the door, and others. They rolled him onto something and picked him up, so that he seemed to float somewhere below the level of their waists, looking up at the belly of the vast dark thing that had come between the bright skylands and the glass roof. His hand found hers. She smiled down at him and he smiled too, so that they journeyed together, as they had on the deadcoach in his dream, in the companionable silence of two who have overcome obstacles to be together, and have no need of noisy words, but rest—each in the other.

Chapter 8

PEACE

Maytera Marble smiled to herself, lifting her head and cocking it to the right. Her sheets were clean at last, and so was everything else—Maytera Mint's things, a workskirt that had been badly soiled at the knees, and the smelly cottons she had dropped into the hamper before dying.

After strenuous pumping, she rinsed them in the sink and wrung them out. Her dipper transferred most of the sink water to the wash boiler before she took out the old wooden stopper and let the rest drain away; when it had cooled, the water in the wash boiler could be given to her suffering garden.

With her clever new fingers, she scooped the white bull's congealing fat from the saucepan. A rag served for a strainer; a chipped cup received the semiliquid grease. Wiping her hands on another rag, she considered the tasks that still confronted her: grease the folding steps first, or hang out this wash?

The wash, to be sure; it could be drying while she greased the steps. Very likely, it would be dry or nearly dry by the time she finished.

Beyond the doorway, the garden was black with storm. That wouldn't do! Rain (though Pas knew how badly they needed it) would spot her clean sheets. Fuming, she put aside the wicker clothes-basket and stepped out into the night, a hand extended to catch the first drops.

At least it wasn't raining yet; and the wind (now that she came to think of it, it had been windier earlier) had fallen. Peering up at the storm cloud, she realized with a start that it was not a real cloud at all—that what she had taken for a cloud was in fact the uncanny flying thing she had glimpsed above the wall, and even stared at from the roof.

A memory so remote that it seemed to have lain behind her curved metal skull stirred at this, her third view. Dust flew, as dust always does when something that has remained motionless for a long time moves at last.

"Why don't you dust it?" (Laughter.)

She would have blinked had she been so built. She looked down again, down at her dark garden, then up (but reasonably and prudently up only) at the pale streaks of her clotheslines. They were still in place, though sometimes the children took them for drover's whips and jump ropes. Started upward thus prudently and reasonably, her gaze continued to climb of its own volition.

"Why don't you dust it?"

Laughter filled her as the summer sunshine of a year long past descends gurgling to fill a wineglass, then died away.

Shaking her head, she went back inside. It was a trifle windy yet to hang out wash, and still dark anyway. Sunshine always made the wash smell better; she would wait till daylight and hang it out before morning prayer. It would be dry after.

When had it been, that sun-drenched field? The jokes and the laughter, and the overhanging, overawing shadow that had made them fall silent?

Grease the steps now, and scrub them, too; then it would be light out and time to hang the wash, the first thin thread of the long sun cutting the skylands in two.

She mounted the stair to the second floor. Here was that picture again, the old woman with her doves, blessed by Molpe. A chubby postulant whose name she could not recall had admired it; and she, thin, faceless, old Maytera Marble, flattered, had said that she had posed for Molpe. It was almost the only lie she had ever told, and she could still see the incredulity in that girl's eyes, and the shock. Shriven of that lie again and again, she nevertheless told Maytera Betel at each shriving—Maytera Betel, who was dead now.

She ought to have brought something, an old paintbrush, perhaps, to dab on her grease with. Racking her brain, she recalled her toothbrush, retained for decades after the last tooth had failed. (She wouldn't be needing *that* any more!) Opening the broken door to her room . . . She should fix this, if she could. Should try to, anyhow. They might not be able to afford a carpenter.

Yet it seemed tonight that she remembered the painter, the little garden at the center of his house, and the stone bench upon which the old woman (his mother, really) had sat earlier. Posing gowned and jeweled as the goddess with a stephane, the dead butterfly pinned in her hair.

It had been embarrassing, but the painter had wonderful brushes, not in the least like this worn toothbrush of hers, whose wooden handle had cracked so badly, whose genuine boar bristles, once so proudly black, had faded to gray.

She pushed the old toothbrush down into the bull's soft, white fat, then ran it energetically along the sliding track.

She could not have been a sibyl then, only the sibyls' maid; but the artist had been a relative of the Senior Sibyl's, who had agreed to let her pose. Chems could hold a pose much longer than bios. All artists, he had said, used chems when they could, although he had used his mother for the old woman because chems never looked old. . . .

She smiled at that, tilting her head far back and to the right. The hinges, then the other track.

He had given them the picture when it was done.

She had a gray smear on one black sleeve. Dust from the steps, most likely. Filthy. She beat the sleeve until the dust was gone, then started downstairs to fetch her bucket and scrub brush. Had the bull's grease done what it was supposed to? Perhaps she should have paid for real oil. She lifted the folding steps tentatively. The grease had certainly helped. All the way up!

Gratifyingly smooth, so she had saved three cardbits at least, perhaps more. How had she gotten them down? With the crochet hook, that was it. But if she did not push the ring up she would not need it. The steps would have to come down again anyway when she scrubbed them, and she itched to see them work as they should. An easy tug on the ring, and down they slid with a puff of dust that was hardly noticeable.

"Why don't you dust it?"

Everyone had laughed, and she had too, though she had been so shy. He had been tall and—what was it? Five-point-two-five times stronger than she, with handsome steel features that faded when she tried to see them again.

All nonsense, really.

Like believing she had posed, after she had told Maytera over and over that she had lied. She would never have taken these new parts if . . . Though they were hers, to be sure.

One more time up the steps. One final time, and here was her old trunk.

She opened the gable window and climbed out onto the roof. If the neighbors spied her, they would be shocked out of their wits. *Trunk* evoked only her earlier search for its owner.

Footlocker, that was it. Here was a list of the dresses she had worn before they had voted to admit her. Her perfume. The commonplace book that she had kept for the mere pleasure of writing in it, of practicing her hand. Perhaps if she went back into the attic and opened her footlocker, she would find them all, and would never have to look at the thrumming thing overhead again.

Yet she did.

Enormous, though not so big you couldn't see the skylands on each side of it. Higher up and farther west now, over the market certainly and nosing toward the Palatine, its long axis bisected by Cage Street, where convicts were no longer exposed in cages. Its noise was almost below her threshold of hearing, the purr of a mountain lion as big as a mountain.

She should go back down now. Get busy. Wash or cook—though she was dead, and Maytera Betel and the rest dead, too, and Maytera Mint gone only Pas knew where, and nobody left to cook for unless the children came.

Enormous darkness high overhead, blotting the sun-drenched field, the straggling line of servants in which she had stood, and the soldiers' precise column. She had seen it descend from the sky, at first a fleck of black that had seemed no bigger than a flake of soot; had said, "It looks so dirty." A soldier had overheard her and called, "Why don't you dust it?"

Everyone had laughed, and she had laughed, too, though she had been humiliated to tears, had tears been possible for her. Angry and defiant, she had met his eyes and sensed the longing there.

And longed.

How tall he had been! How big and strong! So much steel!

Winged figures the size of gnats sailed this way and that below the vast, dark bulk; something streaked up toward them as she watched—flared yellow, like bacon grease dripping into the stove. Some fell.

.   .   .

"Here we are," Auk told Chenille. It was a break in the tunnel wall.

"This leads into the pit?"

"That's what he says. Let me go first, and listen awhile. Beat the hoof if it sounds a queer lay."

She nodded, resolving that she and her launcher would have something to say about any queer lay, watched him worm his way through (a tight squeeze for shoulders as big as his), listened for minutes that seemed like ten, then heard his booming laugh, faint and far away.

It was a tight squeeze for her as well, and it seemed her hips would not go through. She wriggled and swore, recalling Orchid's dire warnings and that Orchid's were twice—at least twice!—the size of hers.

The place she was trying so hard to get into was a pit in the pit, apparently—as deep as a cistern, with no way to go higher, though Auk must have found one since he was not there.

Her hips scraped through at last. Panting as she knelt on the uneven soil, she reached back in and got her launcher.

"You coming, Jugs?" He was leaning over the edge, almost invisible in the darkness.

"Sure. How do I get out of here?"

"There's a little path around the sides." He vanished.

There was indeed—a path a scant cubit wide, as steep as a stair. She climbed cautiously, careful not to look down, with Gelada's lantern rattling on the barrel of her launcher. Above, she heard Auk say, "All right, maybe I will, but not till she gets here. I want her to see him."

Then her head was above the top and she was looking at the pit, a stade across, its reaches mere looming darkness, its sheer sides faced with what looked like shiprock. A wall rose above it on the side nearest her. She stared up at it without comprehension, turned her head to look at the shadowy figures around Auk, and looked up at it again before she recognized it as the familiar, frowning wall of the Alambrera, which she was now seeing from the other side for the first time.

Auk called, "C'mere, Jugs. Still got that darkee?"

A vaguely familiar voice ventured, "Might be better not to light it, Auk."

"Shut up."

She took Gelada's lantern off the barrel of her launcher and advanced hesitantly toward Auk, nearly falling when she tripped over a roll of rags in the darkness.

Auk said, "You do it, Urus. Keep it pretty near shut," and one of the men accepted the lantern from her.

The acrid smell of smoke cut through the prevailing reek of excrement and unwashed bodies; a bearded man with eyes like the sockets in a skull had removed the lid of a firebox. He puffed the coals it held until their crimson glow lit his face—a face she quickly decided she would rather not have seen. A wisp of flame appeared. Urus held the lantern to it, then closed the shutter, narrowing the yellow light to a beam no thicker than her forefinger.

"You want it, Auk?"

"I got no place to put it," Auk told him; and Chenille, edging nearer, saw that he had his hanger in his right hand and a slug gun in his left. The blade of the hanger was dark with blood. "Show her Patera first," he said.

On legs as thin as sticks, the shadowy figures parted; a pencil of light settled on a dark bundle that stared up at her with Incus's agonized eyes. A rag covered his mouth.

"Looks cute, don't he?" Auk chuckled.

She ventured, "He really is an augur . . ."

"He shot a couple of 'em with my needler, Jugs. It got 'em mad, and they jumped him. We'll cut him loose in a minute, maybe. Urus, show her the soldier."

Hammerstone was bound as well, though no rag had been tied over his mouth; she wondered whether it would work on a chem anyway, and decided that it might not. "I'm sorry, Stony," she said. "I'll get you out of this. Patera, too."

"They were going to stab him in the throat," Hammerstone told her. "They'd grabbed him from behind." He spoke slowly and without rancor, but there was a whorl of self-loathing in his voice. "I got careless."

"Those ropes are made out of that muscle in the back of your leg," Auk told her conversationally. "That's what they got him tied up with. They're pretty strong, I guess."

Neither she nor Hammerstone replied.

"Only I don't think they'd hold him. Not if he really tried. It'd take chains. Big ones, if you ask me."

"Hackum, maybe I shouldn't say this—"

"Go ahead."

"What if they jump you and me like they did Patera?"

"I was going to tell you why Hammerstone here don't break loose. Maybe I ought to do that first."

"Because you've got his slug gun?"

"Uh-huh. Only they had it then, see? They got hold of Incus, and they made Hammerstone give it to 'em. It takes a lot to kill a soldier, but a slug gun'll do it. So'll that launcher you got."

She scarcely heard him. When she had struggled through the narrow opening in the side of the tunnel, the deep humming from above had so merged with the rush of blood in her ears that she had assumed it was one with it; now she realized that it actually proceeded from the dark bulk in the sky that she (like Maytera Marble) had thought a cloud. She peered up at it, astonished.

"We'll get to that in a minute," Auk told her, looking upward too. "Terrible Tartaros says it's a airship. That's a thing kind of like the old man's boat, see? Only it sails through the air instead of water. The Rani of Trivigaunte's invaded Viron. That's another reason for us to do like he showed us down there—"

Hammerstone heaved himself upright, throwing aside four stick-limbed men who tried to hold him down. The sinews that bound his wrists and ankles broke in a rattattoo of poppings, like the burning of a string of firecrackers.

Almost casually, Auk thrust his hanger into the ground at his feet and leveled the slug gun. "Don't try it."

"We got to fight," Hammerstone told him. "Patera and me. We got to defend the city."

Reluctantly, Chenille trained the launcher Hammerstone had taught her to load and fire at his broad metal chest. He knelt to tear off Incus's gag, snapping the cords that had secured Incus's hands and feet between his fingers.

"Look! Look!" Urus shouted and pointed, then futilely directed the beam of Gelada's lantern upward. Others around him shouted and pointed, too.

Another voice, remote but louder than the loudest merely human voice silenced them, filling the pit with its thunder: *"Convicts, you are free! Viron has need of every one of you. In the name of all the—in the Outsider's name, forget your quarrel with the Civil Guard, which now supports our Charter. Forget any quarrel you may have with your fellow citizens. Most of all, forget every quarrel among yourselves!"*

Chenille grasped Auk's elbow. "That's Patera Silk! I recognize his voice!"

Auk could only shake his head, unbelieving. Something–a tumbling, flying thing that appeared, incredibly, to have a turret and a buzz gun–had cleared the parapet of the wall and was drifting into the pit, lower and lower, an armed floater blown upwind by a wind that was none, hundreds of cubits above the Alambrera.

Chenille's launcher was snatched from her hands and fired as soon as it had left them, Hammerstone aiming at the immense shape far above the floater, directing a single missile at it (or perhaps at the winged figures that streamed from it like smoke), and watching it expectantly to observe the strike and correct his aim.

"There Auk!" thundered a hoarse voice from the floater tumbling slowly overhead. *"Here girl!"*

A second missile, and Auk was firing the slug gun that had been Hammerstone's, too, shooting winged troopers who swooped and soared above the pit firing slug guns of their own.

A minute dot of black fell from the vast flying thing Auk had called an airship. She saw it streak through the milling cloud of winged troopers. An instant later, the dark wall of the Alambrera exploded with a force that rocked the whorl.

Silk stood in his boyhood bedroom, looking down at the boy who had been himself. The boy's face was buried in his pillow; by an effort of will he made it look toward him; each time it turned, its features dissolved in mist.

He sat down on the sill of the open window, conscious of the borage growing under it and of lilacs and violets beyond it. A copybook lay open, waiting, on the sleeping boy's small table; there were quills beside it, their ends more or less chewed. He ought to write, he knew–tell this boy who had been himself that he was taking his blue tunic, and leave him advice that would be of help in the troubles to come.

Yet he could not settle upon the right words, and he knew that the boy would soon wake. It was shadeup, and he would be late at his palaestra; already Mother approached the bed.

What could he say that would have meaning for this boy? That this boy might recall more than a decade later?

Mother shook his shoulder, and Silk felt his own shoulder touched; it was strange she could not see him.

Fear no love, he wrote; and then: *Carry out the Plan of Pas.* But Mother's hand was shaking him so hard that the final words were practically unreadable; *of Pas* faded from the soft, blue-lined paper as he watched. Pas was, after all, a thing of the past. Like the boy.

Xiphias and the Prolocutor were standing at the foot of the boy's bed, which had become his own.

He blinked.

As if to preside over a sacrifice at the Grand Manteion, the Prolocutor wore mulberry vestments crusted with diamonds and sapphires, and held the gold baculus that symbolized his authority; Xiphias had what appeared to be an augur's black robe folded over his arm. It seemed the wildest of dreams.

His blankets were pushed away; and the surgeon, standing next to his bed beside Hyacinth, rolled him onto his side and bent to pull off the bandages he had applied earlier. Silk managed to smile up at Hyacinth, and she smiled in return—a shy, frightened smile that was like a kiss.

From the other side of the bed, Colonel Oosik inquired, "Can you speak, Caldé?"

He could not, though it was his emotions that kept him silent.

"He talked to me last night before he went to sleep," Hyacinth told Oosik.

"Silk talk!" Oreb confirmed from the top of a bedpost.

"Please don't sit up." The surgeon laid his hand—a much larger and stronger one than the hand that had awakened him—upon Silk's shoulder to prevent it.

"I can speak," he told them. "Your Cognizance, I very much regret having subjected you to this."

Quetzal shook his head and told Hyacinth, "Perhaps you'd better get him dressed."

"No time to dawdle, lad!" Xiphias exclaimed. "Shadeup in an hour! Want them to start shooting again?"

Then the surgeon who had held him down was helping him to rise, and Hyacinth (who smelled better than an entire garden of flowers) was helping him into a tunic. "I did this for you last Phaesday night, remember?"

"Do I still have your azoth?" he asked her. And then, "What in the Whorl's going on?"

"They sent Oosie to kill you. He just came back and he doesn't want to."

Silk was looking, or trying to look, into the corners of the room. Gods and others who were not gods waited there, he felt certain, watching and nearly visible, their shining heads turned toward him. He remembered climbing onto Blood's roof and his desperate struggle with the white-headed one, Hyacinth snatching his hatchet from his waistband. He groped for it, but hatchet and waistband had vanished alike.

Quetzal muttered, "Somebody will have to tell him what to tell them. How to make peace."

"I don't expect you to believe me, Your Cognizance—" Hyacinth began.

"Whether I believe you or not, my child, will depend on what you say."

"We didn't! I swear to you by Thelxiepeia and Scalding Scylla—"

"For example. If you were to say that Patera Caldé Silk had violated his oath and disgraced his vocation, I would not believe you."

Standing upon the arm of his mother's reading chair, he had studied the caldé's head, carved by a skillful hand from hard brown wood. "Is this my father?" Mother's smile as she lifted him down, warning him not to touch it. "No, no, that's my friend the caldé." Then the caldé was dead and buried, and his head buried, too—buried in the darkest reaches of her closet, although she spoke at times of burning it in the big black kitchen stove and perhaps believed eventually that she had. It was not well to have been a friend of the caldé's.

"I know our Patera Caldé Silk too well for that," Quetzal was telling Hyacinth. "On the other hand, if you were to say that nothing of the kind had taken place, I would believe you implicitly, my child."

Xiphias helped Silk to his feet, and Hyacinth pulled up a pair of unbleached linen drawers that had somehow appeared around his ankles and were new and clean and not his at all, and tied the cord for him.

"Caldé . . ."

At that moment, the title sounded like a death sentence. He said, "I'm only Patera— Only Silk. Nobody's caldé now."

Oosik stroked his drooping, white-tipped mustache. "You fear that because my men and I are loyal to the Ayuntamiento, we will kill you. I understand. It is undoubtedly true, as this young woman has said . . ."

In the presence of the Prolocutor, Oosik was pretending he did not know Hyacinth, exactly as he himself had tried to pretend he was not caldé; Silk found wry amusement in that.

"–and already you have almost perished in this foolish fighting," Oosik was saying. "Another dies now, even as we speak. On our side or yours, it does not matter. If it was one of us, we will kill one of you soon. If one of you, you will kill one of us. Perhaps it will be me. Perhaps my son, though he has already–"

Xiphias interrupted him. "Couldn't get home, lad! Tried to! Big night attack! Still fighting! Didn't think they'd try that. You don't mind my coming back to look out for you?"

Kneeling with his trousers, Hyacinth nodded confirmation. "If you listen at the window, you can still hear shooting."

Silk sat on the rumpled bed again and pushed his feet into the legs. "I'm confused. Are we still at Ermine's?"

She nodded again. "In my room."

Oosik had circled the bed to hold his attention. "Would it not be a great thing, Caldé, if we–if you and I, and His Cognizance–could end this fighting before shadeup?"

With less confidence in his legs than he tried to show, Silk stood to pull up and adjust his waistband. "That's what I'd hoped to do." He sat as quickly as he could without loss of dignity.

"We will–"

Quetzal interposed, "We must strike fast. We can't wait for you to recover, Patera Caldé. I wish we could. You were startled to see me vested like this. My clothes always shock you, I'm afraid."

"So it seems, Your Cognizance."

"I'm under arrest, too, technically. But I'm trying to bring peace, just as you are."

"We've both failed, in that case, Your Cognizance."

Oosik laid his hand upon Silk's; it felt warm and damp, thick with muscle. "Do not burden yourself with reproaches, Caldé. No! Success is possible still. Who had you in mind as commander of your Civil Guard?"

The gods had gone, but one–perhaps crafty Thelxiepeia, whose day was just beginning–had left behind a small gift of cunning. "If anyone could put an end to this bloodshed, he would surely deserve a greater reward than that."

"But if that were all the reward he asked?"

"I'd do everything I could to see that he obtained it."

"Wise Silk!" Oreb cocked a bright black eye approvingly from the bedpost.

Oosik smiled. "You are better already, I think. I was greatly concerned for you when I saw you." He looked at the surgeon. "What do you think, Doctor? Should our caldé have more blood?"

Quetzal stiffened, and the surgeon shook his head.

"Achieving peace, Caldé, may not be as difficult as you imagine. Our men and yours must be made to understand that loyalty to the Ayuntamiento is not disloyalty to you. Nor is loyalty to you disloyalty to the Ayuntamiento. When I was a young man we had both. Did you know that?"

Xiphias exclaimed, "It's true, lad!"

"There is a vacancy on the Ayuntamiento. Clearly it must be filled. On the other hand, there are councillors presently in the Ayuntamiento. Their places are theirs. Why ought they not retain them?"

A compromise; Silk thought of Maytera Mint, small and heartrendingly brave upon a white stallion in Sun Street. "The Alambrera—?"

"Cannot be permitted to fall. The morale of your Civil Guard would not survive so crushing a humiliation."

"I see." He stood again, this time with more confidence; he felt weak, yet paradoxically strong enough to face whatever had to be faced. "The poor, the poorest people of our quarter especially, who began the insurrection, are anxious to release the convicts there. They are their friends and relatives."

Quetzal added, "Echidna has commanded it."

Oosik nodded, still smiling. "So I have heard. Many of our prisoners say so, and a few even claim to have seen her. I repeat, however, that a successful assault on the Alambrera would be a disaster. It cannot be permitted. But might not our caldé, upon his assumption of office, declare a general amnesty? A gesture at once generous and humane?"

"I see," Silk repeated. "Yes, certainly, if it will end the fighting—if there's even the slightest chance that it will end it. Must I come with you, Generalissimo?"

"You must do more. You must address both the insurgents and our own men, forcefully. It can be begun here, from your bed. I have a means of transmitting your voice to my troops, defending the Palatine. Afterward we will have to put you in a floater and take you to the Alambrera, in order that both our men and Mint's may see you, and see for themselves that there is no trickery. His Cognizance has agreed to go with you to bless the peace. Many know already that he has sided with you. When it is seen that my brigade has come over to you as a body, the rest will come as well."

Oreb crowed, "Silk win!" from the bedpost.

"I'm coming, too," Hyacinth declared.

"You must understand that there is to be no surrender, Caldé. Viron will have chosen to return to its Charter. A caldé–yourself–and an Ayuntamiento."

Oosik turned ponderously to Quetzal. "Is that not the system of government stipulated by Scylla, Your Cognizance?"

"It is, my son, and it is my fondest desire to see it reinstated."

"If we're paraded through the city in this floater," Silk said, "many of the people who see us are certain to guess that I've been wounded." In the nick of time he remembered to add, "Generalissimo."

"Nor will we attempt to conceal it, Caldé. You yourself have played a hero's part in the fighting! I must tell Gecko to work that into your little speech."

Oosik took two steps backward. "Now someone must attend to all these things, I fear, and there is no one capable of it but myself. Your pardon, my lady." He bowed. "Your pardon, Caldé. I will return shortly. Your pardon, Your Cognizance."

"Bad man?" mused Oreb.

Silk shook his head. "No one who ends murder and hatred is evil, even if he does it for his own profit. We need such people too much to let even the gods condemn them. Xiphias, I sent you away last night at the same time that I sent away His Eminence. Did you leave at once?"

The old fencing master was shamefaced. "Did you say at once, lad?"

"I don't think so. If I did, I don't recall it."

"I'd brought you this, lad, remember?" He bounded to the most remote corner of the room and held up the silver-banded cane. "Valuable!" He parried an imaginary opponents's thrust. "Useful! Think I'd let them leave it behind in that garden?"

Hyacinth said, "You followed when we carried him up here, didn't you? I saw you watching us from the foot of the stairs, but I didn't know you from a rat then."

"I understand." Silk nodded almost imperceptibly. "His Eminence left at once, I imagine. I had told him to find you if he could, Your Cognizance. Did he?"

"No," Quetzal said. With halting steps, he made his way to a red velvet chair and sat, laying the baculus across his knees. "Does it matter, Patera Caldé?"

"Probably not. I'm trying to straighten things out in my mind, that's all." Silk's forefinger traced pensive circles on his beard-rough cheek. "By this time, His Eminence may have reached Maytera Mint—reached General Mint, I should say. It's possible they have already begun to work out a truce. I hope so, it could be helpful. Mucor reached her in any event; and when General Mint heard Mucor's message, she attacked the Palatine hoping to rescue me—I ought to have anticipated that. My mind wasn't as clear as it should be last night, or I would never have told her where I was."

Hyacinth asked, "Mucor? You mean Blood's abram girl? Was she here?"

"In a sense." Silk found that by staring steadfastly at the yellow goblets and chocolate cellos that danced across the carpet, it was possible to speak to Hyacinth without choking, and even to think in a patchy fashion about what he said. "I met her Phaesday night, and I talked to her in the Glasshouse before you found me. I'll explain about her later, though, if I may—it's appalling and rather complex. The vital point is that she agreed to carry a message to General Mint for me, and did it. Colonel Oosik's brigade was being held in reserve when I spoke to him earlier; when the attack came, it must have been brought up to strengthen the Palatine."

Hyacinth nodded. "That's what he told me before we woke you. He said it was lucky for you because Councillor Loris ordered him to send somebody to kill you, but he came himself instead and brought you a doctor."

"I operated on you yesterday, Caldé," the surgeon told Silk, "but I don't expect you to remember me. You were very nearly dead." He was horse-faced and balding; his eyes were rimmed with red, and there were bloodstains on his rumpled green tunic.

"You can't have had much sleep, Doctor."

"Four hours. I wouldn't have slept that much, if my hands hadn't started to shake. We have over a thousand wounded."

Hyacinth sat on the bed next to Silk. "That's about what we got, too—four hours, I mean. I must look a hag."

He made the error of trying to verify it, and discovered that his eyes refused to leave her face. "You are the most beautiful woman in the whorl," he said. Her hand found his, but she indicated Quetzal by a slight tilting of her head.

Quetzal had been dozing—so it appeared—in the red chair; he looked up as though she had pronounced his name. "Have you a mirror, my child? There must be a mirror in a suite like this."

"There's a glass in the dressing room, Your Cognizance. It'll show you your reflection if you ask." Hyacinth nibbled at her full lower lip. "Only I ought to be in there getting dressed. Oosie will come back in a minute, I think, with a speech for Patera and one of those ear things."

Quetzal rose laboriously with the help of his baculus, and Silk's heart went out to him. How feeble he was! "I've had four hours sleep, Your Cognizance; Hyacinth less than that, I'm afraid, and the doctor here about the same; but I don't believe Your Cognizance can have slept at all."

"People my age don't need much, Patera Caldé, but I'd like a mirror. I have a skin condition. You've been too well bred to remark upon it, but I do. I carry paint and powder now like a woman, and fix my face whenever I get the chance."

"In the balneum, Your Cognizance." Hyacinth rose, too. "There's a mirror, and I'll dress while you're in there."

Quetzal tottered away. Hyacinth paused with one hand on the latch-bar, clearly posing but so lovely that Silk could have forgiven her things far worse. "You men think it takes women a long while to get dressed, but it won't take *me* long this morning. Don't go without me."

"We won't," Silk promised, and held his breath until the boudoir door closed behind her.

"Bad thing," Oreb muttered from a bedpost.

Xiphias displayed the silver-banded cane to Silk. "Now I can show you this, lad! Modest? Proper? Augur can't wear a sword, right? But you can carry this! Had a stick first time you came, didn't you?"

"Bad thing!" Oreb dropped down upon Silk's shoulder.

"Yes, I had a walking stick then. It's gone now, I'm afraid. I broke it."

"Won't break this! Watch!" Between Xiphias's hands, the cane's head separated from its brown wooden shaft, exposing a straight, slender, double-edged blade. "Twist, and pull them apart! You try it!"

"I'd much rather put them back together." Silk accepted the cane from him; it seemed heavy for a walking stick, and somewhat light for a sword. "It's a bad thing, as Oreb says."

"Nickel in that steel! Chrome, too! Truth! Could parry an azoth! Believe that?"

Silk shuddered. "I suppose so. I had an azoth once and couldn't cut through a steel door with it."

The azoth reminded him of Hyacinth's gold-plated needler; hurriedly, he put his hand in his pocket. "Here it is. I've got to return this to her. I was afraid that it would be gone, somehow, though I can't imagine who might have taken it, except Hyacinth herself." He laid it on the peach-colored sheet.

"I gave your big one back, lad. Still got it?"

Silk shook his head, and Xiphias began to prowl around the room, opening cabinets and examining shelves.

"This cane will be useful, I admit," Silk told him, "but I really don't require a needler."

Xiphias whirled to confront him, holding it out. "Going to make peace, aren't you?"

"I hope to, Master Xiphias, and that's exactly–"

"What if they don't like the way you're making it, lad? Take it!"

"Here you are, Caldé." Oosik bustled in with a sheet of paper and a black object that seemed more like a flower molded from synthetic than an actual ear. "I'll turn it on before I pass it to you, and all you'll have to do is talk into it. Do you understand? My loudspeakers will repeat everything that you say, and everyone will hear you. Here's your speech."

He handed Silk the paper. "It would be best for you to read it over first. Insert some thoughts of your own if you like. I would not deviate too far from the text, however."

Words crawled across the sheet like ants, some bearing meaning in their black jaws, most with none. *The insurgent forces. The Civil Guard. The rebellion. The commissioners and the Ayuntamiento. The Army. The arms in the Alambrera. The insurgents and the Guard. Peace.*

There it was at last. *Peace.*

"All right." Silk let the sheet fall into his lap.

Oosik signaled to someone in the outer room, waited for a reply that soon came, cleared his throat, and held the ear to his lips. "This is Generalissimo Oosik of the Caldé's Guard. Hear me all ranks, and especially you rebels. You're fighting us because you want to make Patera Silk caldé, but Caldé Silk is with us. He is with the Guard, because he knows that we are with him. Now you soldiers. Your duty is to obey our caldé. He is sitting here beside me. Hear his instructions."

Silk wanted his old chipped ambion very badly; his hands sought it blindly as he spoke, rattling the paper. "My fellow citizens, what Generalissimo Oosik has just told you is true. Are we not—" The words seemed predisposed to hide behind his trembling fingers.

"Are we not, every one of us, citizens of Viron? On this historic day, my fellow citizens—" The type blurred, and the next line began a meaningless half sentence.

"Our city is in great danger," he said. "I believe the whole whorl's in great danger, though I can't be sure."

He coughed and spat clotted blood on the carpet. "Please excuse me. I've been wounded. It doesn't matter, because I'm not going to die. Neither are you, if only you'll listen."

Faintly, he heard his words re-echoed in the night beyond Ermine's walls: *"You'll listen."* The loudspeakers Oosik had mentioned, mouths with stentorian voices, had heard him in some fashion, and in some fashion repeated his thoughts.

The door of the balneum opened. Framed in the doorway, Quetzal gave him an encouraging nod, and Oreb flew back to his post on the bedpost.

"We can't rebel against ourselves," Silk said. "So there is no rebellion. There is no insurrection, and none of you are insurgents. We can fight among ourselves, of course, and we've been doing it. It was necessary, but the time of its necessity is over. There is a caldé again—I am your caldé. We needed rain, and we have gotten rain." He paused to look across the room at the rich smoke-gray drapes. "Master Xiphias, will you open that window for me, please? Thank you."

He drew a deep and somewhat painful breath of cool, damp air. "We've had rain, and if I'm any judge of weather, we'll get more. Now let's have peace—it's a gift we can provide ourselves, one more precious than rain. Let's have peace."

(What was it the captain had said whole ages ago in that inn?) "Many of you are hungry. We plan to buy food with city funds and sell it to you cheaply. Not free, because there are always people who will waste anything free. But very cheaply, so that even beggars will be able to buy enough. My Guard will release the convicts from the pits. Generalissimo Oosik, His Cognizance the Prolocutor, and I are going to the Alambrera this morning, and I'll order it. All convicts are pardoned as of this moment—I pardon them. They'll be hungry and weak, so please share whatever food you have with them."

He recalled his own hunger, hunger at the manse and worse hunger underground, gnawing hunger that had become a sort of illness by the time Mamelta located the strange, steaming meals of the underground tower. "We had a poor harvest this year," he said. "Let us pray, every one of us, for a better one next year. I've prayed for that often, and I'll pray for it again; but if we want to have enough to eat for the rest of our lives, we must have water for our fields when the rains fail.

"There are ancient tunnels under the city. Some of you can confirm that because you've come upon them while digging foundations. They reach Lake Limna—I know that, because I've been in them. If we can break through near the lake—and I'm sure we can—we can use them to carry water to the farms. Then we'll all have plenty of food, cheaply, for a long time." He wanted to say, until it's time for us to leave this whorl behind us, but he bit the words back, pausing instead to watch the gray drapes sway in the breeze and listen to his own voice through the open window.

"If you have been fighting for me, don't use your weapons again unless you're attacked. If you're a Guardsman, you have sworn that you'll obey your officers." (He could not be sure of that, but it was so probable that he asserted it boldly.) "Ultimately, that means Generalissimo Oosik, who commands both the Guard and the Army. You've already heard what he has to say. He's for peace. So am I."

Oosik pointed to himself, then to the ear; and Silk added, "You'll hear him again, very soon."

He felt that the shade should be up by now—indeed that it was past that time, the hour of first light, and time for the morning prayer to

Thelxiepeia; yet the city beyond the gray drapes was still twilit. "To you whose loyalty is to the Ayuntamiento, I have two things to say. The first is that you're fighting—dying, many of you—for an institution that needs no defense. Neither I nor Generalissimo Oosik nor General Mint desires to destroy it. So why shouldn't there be peace? Help us make peace!

"The second is that the Ayuntamiento was created by our Charter. Were it not for our Charter, it would have no right to exist, and wouldn't exist. Our Charter grants to you—to you, the people of Viron, and not to any official—the right to choose a new caldé whenever the position is vacant. It then makes the Ayuntamiento subject to the caldé you have chosen. I need not tell you that our Charter proceeds from the immortal gods. All of you know that. Generalissimo Oosik and I have been consulting His Cognizance the Prolocutor on this matter of the caldé and the Ayuntamiento. He is here with us, and if I have misinformed you he will correct me, I feel certain."

With his left hand Quetzal accepted the ear; his right traced a trembling sign of addition. "Blessed be you in the Most Sacred Name of Pas, the Father of the Gods, in that of Gracious Echidna, His consort, in those of the Sons and their Daughters alike, this day and forever, in the name of their eldest child, Scylla, Patroness of this—"

He continued to speak, but Silk's attention deserted him; the door of the dressing room had opened. Hyacinth stepped through it, radiantly lovely in a flowing gown of scarlet silk. In a low voice she said, "The glass in there just told me the Ayuntamiento's offering ten thousand to anybody who kills you and two thousand each for Oosie and His Cognizance. I thought you should know."

Silk nodded and thanked her; Oosik muttered, "It was only to be expected."

"Consider, my children," Quetzal was saying, "how painful it must be to Succoring Scylla to see the sons and daughters of the city that she founded clawing one another's eyes. She has provided everything we require. First of all our Charter, the foundation of peace and justice. If we wish to regain her favor we need only return to it. If we wish to reclaim the peace we have lost, again we need only return to her Charter. We wish justice, I know. I wish it myself, and the wish for it has been planted in every bosom by Great Pas. Even the worst of us wish to live in holiness, too. Perhaps there are a few ingrates who don't, but they are very few. We wish all these things, and we can make them ours by one simple act. Let us return to our Charter. That is what the gods desire. Let us accept this anointed augur, Patera Caldé Silk. The gods desire that, too. To conform to Sustaining Scylla's Charter, we must have a caldé, and the smallest of our children know on whom the choice has fallen. If you have any doubts on these topics, my children, I beg you to consult the anointed augur into whose care you are given. There is one, you know, in every quarter. Or you may consult the next you see, or any holy sibyl. They will tell you that the path of duty is not difficult but simple and plain."

Quetzal paused, exhaling with a slight hiss. "Now, my children, a most painful matter. Word has come to me that devils in human shape are seeking our destruction. Falsely and evilly, they promise money they have not got and will not pay, for our blood. Do not believe their lies. Their lies offend the gods. Anyone who slays good men for money is worse than a devil, and anyone who slays for money he will never see is a fool. Worse than a fool, a dupe."

Oosik reached for the ear, but Quetzal shook his head. "My children, it will soon be shadeup. A new day. Let it be a day of peace. Let us stand together. Let us stand by the gods, by their Charter, and by the Caldé they have chosen for us. I bid you farewell for the present, but soon I hope to talk to you face-to-face and bless you for the peace you've given our city. Now I believe Generalissimo Oosik wants to speak to you again."

Oosik cleared his throat. "This is the Generalissimo. Operations against the rebels are canceled, effective at once. Every officer will be held responsible for his obedience to my order and for the actions of his troopers or soldiers, as the case may be. Caldé Silk and His Cognizance are going through the city on one of our floaters. I expect every officer, every trooper, and every soldier to receive them in a manner fully in accordance with loyalty and good discipline.

"My Caldé, have you anything further to say?"

"Yes, I do." Silk leaned toward him, speaking into the ear. "Please stop fighting. It was needful, as I said; but it's become senseless. Stop them if you can, Maytera Mint. General Mint, please stop them. Peace is within our grasp—from the moment we accept it, all of us have won."

He straightened up, savoring the wonder of the ear. It really does look like a black flower, he thought, a flower meant to bloom at night; and because it's bloomed, shadeup is on the way, even if the night looks nearly as dark as ever.

To the ear he added, "We'll be with you in a few minutes, on the floater Generalissimo Oosik told you about. Don't shoot us, please. We certainly won't shoot you. No one will." He turned to Oosik for confirmation, and Oosik nodded vigorously.

"Not even if you shoot me. I'll stand up if I can, so you can see me." He paused. Was there more to say?

Attenuated like distant thunder, his words flew back to him through the window, an ebbing storm: *"Can see me."*

"Those who fought for Viron will be rewarded, regardless of the side on which they fought. Maytera Marble, if you can hear this, please come to the floater. I need you badly, so please come. Auk, too, and Chenille." Had Kypris possessed Hyacinth, rendering her irresistible? Could she possess two women simultaneously? For a second he pondered the question among the remembered faces of his teachers at the schola. He ought to end this, he thought, by invoking the gods; but the time-worn honorifics caught in his throat.

"Until I see you," he said at last, "please pray for me—for our city, and for all of us. Pray to Kind Kypris, who is love. Pray especially to the Outsider, because he is the god whose time is coming and I am the help he's sent us."

He let the hand that held the ear fall, and Oosik took it from him. "For which we all give thanks," Oosik said, and Oreb muttered, "Watch out."

No one spoke after that. Although Oosik and his surgeon, Xiphias, and Quetzal were all present, the bedroom felt empty. Beyond the window, a hush hung over the Palatine. No street vendor hawked his wares and no gun spoke.

Peace.

Peace here, at least; for those on the Palatine and those surrounding it, there was peace. Incredible as it seemed, hundreds—thousands—had ceased fighting, merely because he, Silk, had told them to.

He felt better; perhaps peace, like blood, made one feel better. He was stronger, though he was still not strong. The surgeon had poured blood—more blood—into him while he slept, and that sleep must have been something akin to a coma, because the needle had not awakened him. Another's blood–another's life–had let him live, though he had been certain the night before that he would die that night. Premonitions born of weakness could be frustrated, clearly; he would have to remember that. With friends to help, a man could make his own fate.

Chapter 9

VICTORY

Xiphias, it transpired, had gone to the Palace, bringing back one of Remora's fine robes. It fit Silk surprisingly well, although it carried in its soft fabric a suggestion of somber luxury he found detestable. "They won't know you outside of this, lad," Xiphias said. He, shaking his head, wondered how they could possibly know him in it.

Oosik returned. "I have had more lights mounted on your floater, Caldé. There will be a flag on its antenna as well. Most will be on you, two on the flag." Without waiting for a reply, he asked the surgeon, "Is he ready?"

"He shouldn't walk far," the surgeon said.

"I can walk around the city if need be," Silk told them.

Hyacinth declared, "He should lie down again till it's time to go," and to please her, he did.

Within half a minute, it seemed, Xiphias and the surgeon were lowering him into a litter. Hyacinth walked beside him as she had when the waiters had carried him out of the Glasshouse, and it seemed to him that his mother's garden walked with her; from the other side, Quetzal asperged him with benedictions, his robe of mulberry velvet contributing the mingled smells of frankincense and something else to the cool and windy dark. At his ears, the *frou-frou-frou* of Hyacinth's skirt and the *whish-shish* of Quetzal's robe sounded louder than the snap of Oosik's flag. Troopers saluted, clicking their heels. One knelt for Quetzal's blessing.

"It would be better," Oosik said, "if you did not have to be carried into the floater, Caldé. Can you do it?"

He could, of course, rising from the litter with the help of Xiphias's cane. A volley of shots crackled in the distance; it was followed by a faint scream, rarefied and unreal. "Men fight," Oreb commented.

"Some do," Silk told him. "That's why we're going."

The entry port let spill a sallow light; the surgeon was crouching inside to help him in. "Blood's floater was open," Silk remarked, remembering. "There was a transparent canopy—a top that you could see through almost as well as air—but when it was down, you could stand up."

"You can stand in this, too," the surgeon said, "right here." He steered Silk toward the spot. "See? You're under the turret here."

Straightening up, Silk nodded. "I rode in one of these yesterday—on the outside, when the rain stopped. It wasn't nearly as roomy as this." Corpses, including Doctor Crane's, had taken up most of the space inside.

"We took out a lot of ammo, Caldé," the trooper at the controls told him.

Silk nearly nodded again, although the trooper could not see his head. He had found the ladder he recalled, a spidery affair of metal rods, and was climbing cautiously but steadily toward the open hatch at the top of the turret.

"Bad thing," Oreb informed him nervously. "Thing shine."

To his own astonishment Silk smiled. "This buzz gun, you mean?" It was dull black, but the open breech revealed bright steel. "They won't shoot us with it, Oreb. They won't shoot anyone, I hope."

The surgeon's voice floated up from below. "There's a saddle for the gunner, Caldé, and things to put your feet in."

"Stirrups." That voice had been Oosik's, surely.

Silk swung himself onto the leather-covered seat, almost but not quite losing his grip on Xiphias's cane. There were officers on horseback around the floater, and what seemed to be a full company of troopers standing at ease half a street behind it. The footman who had admitted him to Ermine's was watching everything from his station by the door; Silk waved to him with the cane, and he waved in return, his grin a touch of white in the darkness.

It's going to rain again, Silk thought. I don't believe we've had a morning this dark since spring.

Quetzal's head rose at his elbow. "I'm going to be beside you, Patera Caldé. They're finding a box for me to stand on."

With as much firmness as he could muster, Silk said, "I can't possibly sit while Your Cognizance stands."

A hatch opened at the front of the floater; Oosik's head and shoulders emerged, and he spoke to someone inside.

Quetzal touched Silk's hand with cold, dry fingers that might have been boneless. "You're wounded, Patera Caldé, and weaker than you think. Stay seated. That is my wish." His head rose to the level of Silk's own.

"As Your Cognizance desires." With both hands on the rim of the hatch, Silk heaved up his unwontedly uncooperative body. For an instant the effort seemed too great; his heart pounded and his arms shook; then one foot found a corner of the box on which Quetzal stood, and he was able to hoist himself enough to sit on the coaming of the open turret hatch. "The gunner's seat remains for Your Cognizance," he said.

The floater lifted beneath them, gliding forward. Louder than the roar of its engine, Oosik's voice seemed to reach into every street in the city: *"People of Viron! Our new caldé is coming among you as we promised. At his side is His Cognizance the Prolocutor, who has confirmed that Caldé Silk has the favor of all the gods. Hail him! Follow him!"*

Brilliant white lights glared to left and right, less than an arm's length away, more than half blinding him.

"Girl come!" Oreb exclaimed.

A black civilian floater had nosed between their floater and the troopers, and was pushing through the mounted officers. Hyacinth stood on its front seat beside the driver; and while Silk watched openmouthed, she stepped over what seemed to be a low invisible barrier, and onto the waxed and rounded foredeck. "Your stick!" she called.

Silk tightened the handle, leaned as far back as he dared, and held it out to her; the civilian floater advanced until its cowling touched the back of the floater upon which he rode.

And Hyacinth leaped, her scarlet skirt billowing about her bare legs in the updraft from the blowers. For an instant he was certain she would fall. Then she had grasped the cane and stood secure on the sloping rear deck of his floater, waving in triumph to the mounted officers, most of whom waved in return or saluted. As the floater in which she had come turned away and vanished into the twilight beyond the lights on their own, Silk recognized the driver who had returned him to his manse Phaesday night.

Hyacinth gave him a mischievous grin. "You look like you've seen a ghost. You didn't expect company, did you?"

"I thought you were inside. I should've–I'm sorry, Hyacinth. Terribly sorry."

"You ought to be." He had to put his ear to her lips to hear her, and she nipped and kissed it. "Oosie sent me away. Don't tell him I'm up here."

Lost in the wonder of her face, Silk could only gasp.

Quetzal raised the baculus to bestow a benison, although Silk could see no one beyond the glare that enveloped the three of them except the mounted officers. The roar of their floater was muted now; an occasional grating hesitation suggested that its cowling was actually scraping the cobbles.

"You said you took a floater," Silk told Hyacinth. "I thought you meant that you just, well, took it."

"I wouldn't know how to make one go." Sitting, she edged nearer, grasping the coaming of the turret hatch. "Would you? But that driver's my friend, and I gave him a little money."

They rounded a corner, and innumerable throats cheered from the dimness beyond the lights. Someone shouted, "We've gone over to Silk!"

A thrown chrysanthemum brushed his cheek, and he waved.

Another voice shouted, "Live the caldé!" It brought a storm of cheering, and Hyacinth waved and smiled as if she herself were that caldé, evoking a fresh outburst. "Where are we going? Did Oosie tell you?"

"To the Alambrera." Silk had to shout to make himself heard. "We'll free the convicts. The Juzgado afterward."

A jumble of boxes and furniture opened to let them pass–Liana's barricade.

Beside him, Quetzal invoked the Nine: "In the name of Marvelous Molpe, you are blessed. In the name of Tenebrous Tartaros . . ." They trust the gods, Silk thought, all these wretched men; and because they do, they have made me their leader. Yet I feel I can't trust any god at all, not even the Outsider.

As if they had been chatting over lunch, Quetzal said, "Only a fool would, Patera Caldé."

Silk stared.

"Didn't I tell you that I've done everything I could to prevent theophanies? Those we call gods are nothing more than ghosts. Powerful ghosts, but only because they entailed that power to themselves in life."

"I–" Silk swallowed. "I wasn't aware that I had spoken aloud, Your Cognizance. I apologize; my remark was singularly inappropriate." Oreb stirred apprehensively on his shoulder.

"You didn't, Patera Caldé. I saw your face, and I've had lots of practice. Don't look at me or your young woman. Look at the people. Wave. Look ahead. Smile."

Both waved, and Silk tried to smile as well. His eyes had adjusted to the lights well enough now for him to glimpse indistinct figures beyond the mounted officers, many waving slug guns just as he waved the cane. Through clenched teeth he ventured, "Echidna told us Pas was dead. Your Cognizance confirmed it."

"Dead long ago," Quetzal agreed, "whoever he really was, poor old fellow. Murdered by his family, as was inevitable." Deftly he caught a bouquet. "Blessings on you, my children. Blessings, blessings. . . . May Great Pas and the immortal gods smile upon you and all that you own, forever!"

"Silk is caldé! Long live Silk!"

Hyacinth told him happily, "We're getting a real tour of the city!"

He nodded, feeling his smile grow warm and real.

"Look at them, Patera Caldé. This is their moment. They have bled for this."

"Peace!" Silk called to the shadowy crowds, waving the cane. "Peace!"

"Peace!" Oreb confirmed, and hopped up onto Silk's head flapping his wings. The day was brightening at last, Silk decided, in spite of the storm-black cloud hanging over the city. How appropriate that shadeup should come now—peace and sunlight together! A cheering woman waved an evergreen bough, the symbol of life. He waved in return, meeting her eyes and smiling, and she seemed ready to swoon with delight.

"Don't start throwing flowers to yourself," Hyacinth told him with mock severity. "They'll be blaming you soon enough."

"Then let's enjoy this while we can." Seeing the woman with the bough had recalled one of the ten thousand things the Outsider had shown him—a hero riding through some foreign city while a cheering crowd waved big fanlike leaves. Would Echidna and her children kill the Outsider too? With a flash of insight, he felt sure they were already trying.

"Look! There's Orchid, throwing out the house."

A light directed at the flag showed her plainly, leaning so far from the second-story window through which Kypris had called to him that it seemed she might fall any moment. They were floating down Lamp Street, clearly; the Alambrera could not be far.

As Hyacinth blew Orchid a kiss, something whizzed past Silk's ear, striking the foredeck like a gong. A high whine and a booming explosion were followed by the rattle of a buzz gun. Somebody shouted for someone to come down, and someone inside the floater caught his injured ankle and pulled.

He looked up instead, to where something new and enormous that was not a cloud at all filled the sky. Another whine, louder, mounting ever higher, until Lamp Street exploded in front of them, peppering his face and throwing something solid at his head.

Oosik shouted, "Faster!" and disappeared down his hatch, slamming it behind him.

"Inside, Patera Caldé!"

He scooped Hyacinth into his arms instead, dropping the cane into the floater. It was racing now, careering along Lamp Street and scattering people like chaff. She shrieked.

Here was Cage Street, overlooked by the despotic wall of the Alambrera. Hanging in the air in front of it was a single trooper with wings— a female trooper, from the bulge at her chest—who leveled a slug gun. He slid off the coaming and dropped, still holding Hyacinth, onto the men below.

They sprawled in a tangle of arms and legs, like beetles swept into a jar. Someone stepped on his shoulder and swarmed up the spidery ladder. The turret hatch banged shut. At the front of the floater Oosik snapped, "Faster, Sergeant!"

"We're getting a vector now, sir."

Silk tried to apologize, to tug Hyacinth's scarlet skirt (about which Hyacinth herself seemed to care not a cardbit) over her thighs, and to stand in a space in which he could not possibly have stood upright, all at once. Nothing succeeded.

Something struck the floater like a sledge, sending it yawing into something else solid; it rolled and plunged and righted itself, its straining engine roaring like a wounded bull. Reeking of fish, a wisp of oily black smoke writhed through the compartment.

"Faster!" Oosik shouted.

The turret gun spoke as if in response, a clatter that went on and on, as though the turret gunner were intent on massacring the whole city.

Scrambling across Xiphias and the surgeon, Silk peered over Oosik's shoulder. Fiery red letters danced across his glass: VECTOR UNACCEPTABLE.

Something banged the slanted foredeck above their heads, and the thunder of the engine rose to a deafening crescendo; Silk felt that he had been jerked backwards.

Abruptly, their motion changed.

The floater no longer rocked or raced. The noise of the engine waned until he could distinguish the high-pitched song of the blowers. It ascended to an agonized scream and faded away. A red light flared on the instrument panel.

For the second time in a floater, Silk felt that he was truly floating; it was, he thought, like the uncanny sensation of the moving room in which he had ridden with Mamelta.

Behind him, Hyacinth gasped. A strangely shaped object had risen from Oosik's side. Before Silk recognized it, it had completed a leisurely quarter revolution, scarcely a span in front of his nose. It was a large needler, similar to the one in his own waistband; and it had bobbed up like a cork, unimpelled, from Oosik's holster.

"Look! Look! They're picking us up!" Hyacinth's full breasts pressed his back as she stared at the glass.

He plucked Oosik's needler out of the air and returned it to its holster. When he looked at the glass again, it showed a sprawling pattern of crooked lines, enlivened here and there by crimson sparks. It looked, he decided, like a city in the skylands, except that it seemed much closer. Intrigued, he undogged the hatchcover over Oosik's seat and threw it back. As he completed the motion, both his feet left the floor; he snatched at the hatch dog, missed it by a finger, and drifted up like Oosik's needler until someone inside caught his foot.

The pattern he had seen in the glass was spread before him without limit here: a twilit skyland city, ringed by sun-bright brown fields and huddled villages; and to one side, a silver mirror anchored by a winding, dun-colored thread. Oreb fluttered from his shoulder as he gaped and disappeared into the twilight.

"We're flying." Incredulity and dismay turned the words to a sigh that dwindled with the black bird. Silk coughed, spat congealed blood, and tried again. "We are flying upside down. I see Viron and the lake, even the road to the lake."

Quetzal spoke from inside the floater. "Look behind us, Patera Caldé."

They were nearer now, so near that the vast dark belly of the thing roofed out the sky. Beneath it, suspended by cables that appeared no thicker than gossamer, dangled a structure like a boat with many short oars; Silk's lungs had filled and emptied before he realized that the oars were the barrels of guns, and half a minute crept by before he made out the blood-red triangle on its bottom. "Your Cognizance . . ."

"You don't understand why they're not shooting at us." Quetzal shook himself. "I imagine it's only that they haven't noticed us yet. A wind is forcing them to hold their airship parallel to the sun, so they're peering down at a dark city. At the moment our floater's presenting its narrowest aspect to them. But we're turning, and soon they'll be looking straight down at us. Let's duck inside and shut the hatch."

The glass showed Lake Limna now. Watching its shoreline creep from one corner to the other, Silk thought of Oosik's needler; their floater seemed to be tumbling through the sky in the same dilatory fashion.

Clinging to him, Hyacinth whispered, "You're not afraid at all, are you? Are we up terribly high?" She trembled.

"Of course I am; when I was out there, I was terrified." He examined his emotional state. "I'm still badly frightened; but thinking about what's happening—how it can possibly have come about except by a miracle—keeps my mind off my fear." Watching the glass, he tried to describe the airship.

"Pulling us up, lad! That's what she said! Think we could cut it?"

"There's nothing to cut; if there were, they'd know where we were and shoot us, I believe. This is something else. Was it you who held my foot, by the way? Thank you."

Xiphias shook his head and indicated the surgeon.

"Thank you," Silk repeated. "Thank you very much indeed, Doctor." He grasped the operator's shoulder. "You said we were getting a vector. Exactly what does that mean?"

"It's a message you get if you float too fast, My Caldé, either north or south. You're supposed to slow down. The monitor's supposed to make you if you don't, but that doesn't work any more on this floater."

"I see." Silk nodded, encouragingly he hoped. "Why are you supposed to slow down?"

Oosik put in, "Going too fast north makes you feel as if someone were shoveling sand on you. It is not good for you, and makes everyone in the floater slow to react. Going south too fast makes you giddy. It feels like swimming."

Almost too softly to be heard, Quetzal inquired, "Do you know the shape of the Whorl, Patera Caldé?"

"The whorl? Why, it's cylindrical, Your Cognizance."

"Are we on the outside of the cylinder, Patera Caldé? Or on the inside?"

"We're inside, Your Cognizance. If we were outside, we'd fall off."

"Exactly. What is it that holds us down? What makes a book fall if you drop it?"

"I can't remember the name, Your Cognizance," Silk said, "but it's the tendency that keeps a stone in a sling until it is thrown."

Hyacinth had released him; now her hand found his, and he squeezed it. "As long as the boy keeps twirling his sling, the stone in it can't fall out. The Whorl turns—I see! If the stone were a—a mouse and the mouse ran in the direction the sling was going, it would be held in place more securely, as though the sling were being twirled faster. But if the mouse were to run the other way, it would be as if the sling weren't twirling fast enough. It would fall out."

"Gunner!" Oosik was staring at the glass. "Your gun should bear." As he flicked off his own buzz gun's safety, the red triangle crept into view.

"Trivigaunte," Hyacinth whispered. "Sphigx won't let them make pictures of anything. That mark's on their flag."

Auk stood, unable for a moment to recall where he was or why he had come. Had he fallen off a roof? Salt blood from his lips trickled into his mouth. A man with arms and legs no thicker than kindling and a face like a bearded skull dashed past him. Then another and another.

"Don't be afraid," the blind god whispered. "Be brave and act wisely, and I will protect you." He took Auk's hand, not as Hyacinth had put her own hand into Silk's a few minutes before, but as an older man clasps a younger's at a crisis.

"All right," Auk told him. "I ain't scared, only kind of shook up." The blind god's hand felt good in his own, big and strong, with long powerful fingers; he could not think of the blind god's name and was embarrassed by his failure.

"I am Tartaros, and your friend. Tell me everything you see. You may speak or not, as you wish."

"There's a big hole with smoke coming out in the middle of the wall," Auk reported. "That wasn't there before, I'm pretty sure. There's some dead culls around besides the ones Patera killed and the one I killed. One's a trooper, like, only a mort it looks like. Her wings broke, I guess, maybe when she hit the ground. Everything's brown, the wings and pants and a kind of a bandage, like, over her boobs."

"Brown?"

Auk looked more closely. "Not exactly. Yellowy-brown, more like. Dirt color. Here comes Chenille."

"That is well. Comfort her, Auk my noctolater. Is the airship still overhead?"

"Sure," Auk said, implying by his tone that he did not require a god to coach him in such elementary things. "Yeah, it is." Chenille rushed into his arms.

"It's all right, Jugs," he told her. "Going to be candy. You'll see. Tartaros is a dimber mate of mine." To Tartaros himself, Auk added, "There's this hoppy floater that's falling in the pit, only slow, while it shoots. That's up there, too. And there's maybe a couple hundred troopers like the dead mort flying around, way up."

The blind god gave his hand a gentle tug. "We emerged from a smaller pit into this one, Auk. If you see no other way out, it would be well to return to the tunnel. There are other egresses, and I know them all."

"Just a minute. I lost my whin. I see it." Releasing Chenille, Auk hurried over, jerked his hanger from the mire, and wiped the blade on his tunic.

"*Auk,* my son—"

He shooed Incus with the hanger. "You get back in the tunnel, Patera, before you get hurt. That's what Tartaros says, and he's right."

The floater was descending faster now, almost as though it were really falling. Watching it, Auk got the feeling it was, only not straight down the way other things fell. Until the last moment, it seemed it might come to rest upright; but it landed on the side of its cowling and tumbled over.

Something much higher was falling much faster, a tiny dot of black that seemed almost an arrow by the time it struck the ruined battlement of the Alambrera's wall, which again erupted in a gout of flame and smoke. This time masses of shiprock as big as cottages were flung up like chaff. Auk thought it the finest sight he had seen in his life.

"Silk here!" Oreb announced proudly, dropping onto his shoulder. "Bird bring!" A hatch opened at the front of the fallen floater.

"Hackum!" Chenille shouted. "Hackum, come on! We're going back in the tunnel!"

Auk waved to silence her. The wall of the Alambrera had taken its death blow. As he watched, cracks raced down it to reappear as though by magic in the shiprock side of the pit. There came a growl deeper than any thunder. With a roar that shook the ground on which he struggled to stand, the wall and the side of the pit came down together. Half the pit vanished under a scree of stones, earth, and shattered slabs. Coughing at the dust, Auk backed away.

"Hole break," Oreb informed him.

When he looked again, several men and a slender woman in scarlet were emerging from the overturned floater; its turret gun, unnaturally canted but pointing skyward, was firing burst after burst at the flying troopers.

"Return to the woman," the blind god told him. "You must protect her. A woman is vital. This is not."

He looked for Chenille, but she was gone. A few skeletal figures were disappearing into the hole from which he and she had emerged into the pit. Men from the floater followed them; through the billowing dust he could make out a white-bearded man in rusty black and a taller one in a green tunic.

"Silk here!" Oreb circled above two fleeing figures.

Auk caught up with them as they started down the helical track;

Silk was hobbling fast, helped by a cane and the woman in scarlet. Auk caught her by the hair. "Sorry, Patera, but I got to do this." Silk's hand went to his waistband, but Auk was too quick—a push on his chest sent him reeling backward into the lesser pit.

"Listen!" urged the blind god beside Auk; he did, and heard the rising whine of the next bomb a full second before it struck the ground.

Silk looked down upon the dying augur's body with joy and regret. It was—had been—himself, after all. Quetzal and a smaller, younger augur knelt beside it, with a woman in an augur's cloak and a third man nearly as old as Quetzal.

Beads swung in sign after sign of addition: "I convey to you, Patera Silk my son, the forgiveness of all the gods."

"Recall now the words of Pas—"

It was good; and when it was over, he could go. Where? It didn't matter. Anywhere he wished. He was free at last, and though he would miss his old cell now and then, freedom was best. He looked up through the shiprock ceiling and saw only earth, but knew that the whole whorl was above it, and the open sky.

"I pray you to forgive us, the living," the smaller augur said, and again traced the sign of addition, which could not—now that he came to think of it—ever have been Pas's. A sign of addition was a cross; he remembered Maytera drawing one on the chalkboard when he was a boy learning to do sums. Pas's sign was not the cross but the voided cross. He reached for his own at his neck, but it was gone.

The older augur: "I speak here for Great Pas, for Divine Echidna, for Scalding Scylla."

The younger augur: "For Marvelous Molpe, for Tenebrous Tartaros, for Highest Hierax, for Thoughtful Thelxiepeia, for Fierce Phaea, and for Strong Sphigx."

The older augur: "Also for all lesser gods."

The shiprock gave way to earth, the earth to a clearer, purer air than he had ever known. Hyacinth was there with Auk; in a slanting mass of stones, broken shiprock rolled and slid to reveal a groping steel hand. Glorying, he soared.

The Trivigaunti airship was a brown beetle, infinitely remote, the Aureate Path so near he knew it could not be his final destination.

He lighted upon it, and found it a road of tinsel down a whorl no bigger than an egg. Where were the lowing beasts? The spirits of the other dead? There! Two men and two women. He blinked and stared and blinked again.

"Oh, Silk! My son! Oh, son!" She was in his arms and he in hers, melting in tears of joy. "Mother!" "Silk, my son!"

The whorl was filth and stink, futility and betrayal; this was everything—joy and love, freedom and purity.

"You must go back, Silk. He sends us to tell you."

"You must, my lad." A man's voice, the voice of which Lemur's had been a species of mockery. Looking up he saw the carved brown face from his mother's closet.

"We're your parents." He was tall and blue-eyed. "Your fathers and your mothers."

The other woman did not speak, but her eyes spoke truth.

"You were my mother," he said. "I understand." He looked down at his own beautiful mother. "You will always be my mother. Always!"

"We'll be waiting, Silk my son. All of us. Remember."

Something was fanning his face.

He opened his eyes. Quetzal was seated beside him, one long, bloodless hand swinging as regularly and effortlessly as a pendulum. "Good afternoon, Patera Caldé. I would guess, at least, that it may be afternoon by now."

He lay on dirt, staring up at a shiprock ceiling. Pain stabbed his neck; his head, both arms, his chest, both legs, and his lower torso ached, each in its separate, painful way.

"Lie quietly. I wish I had water to offer you. How are you feeling?"

"I'm back in my dirty cage." Too late, he remembered to add *Your Cognizance*. "I didn't know it was a cage, before."

Quetzal pressed down on his shoulder. "Don't sit up yet, Patera Caldé. I'm going to ask a question, but you are not to put it to the test. It is to be a matter for discussion only. Do you agree?"

"Yes, Your Cognizance." He nodded, although nodding took immense effort.

"This is my question. We are only to speak of it. If I were to help you up, could you walk?"

"I believe so, Your Cognizance."

"Your voice is very weak. I've examined you and found no broken bones. There are four of us besides yourself, but—"

"We fell, didn't we? We were in a Civil Guard floater, spinning over the city. Did I dream that?"

Quetzal shook his head.

"You and I and Hyacinth. And Colonel Oosik and Oreb. And . . ."

"Yes, Patera Caldé?"

"A trooper—two troopers—and an old fencing master that someone had introduced me to. I can't remember his name, but I must have dreamed that he was there as well. It's too fantastic."

"He is some distance down the tunnel now, Patera Caldé. We have been troubled by the convicts you freed."

"Hyacinth?" Silk struggled to sit up.

Quetzal held him down, his hands on both shoulders. "Lie quietly or I'll tell you nothing."

"Hyacinth? For—for the sake of all the gods! I've got to know!"

"I dislike them, Patera Caldé. So do you. Why should either of us tell anyone anything for their sake? I don't know. I wish I did. She may be dead. I can't say."

"Tell me what happened, please."

Slowly, Quetzal's hairless head swung from side to side. "It would be better, Patera Caldé, for you to tell me. You've been very near death. I need to know what you've forgotten."

"There's water in these tunnels. I was in them before, Your Cognizance. In places there was a great deal."

"This is not one of those places. If you have recovered enough to grasp how ill you are and keep a promise, I'll find some. Do you remember blessing the crowds with me? Tell me about that."

"We were trying to bring peace—peace to Viron. Blood had bought it—Musk, but Musk was only a tool of Blood's."

"Had bought the city, Patera Caldé?"

Silk's mouth opened and closed again.

"What is it, Patera Caldé?"

"Yes, Your Cognizance, he has. He, and others like him. I hadn't thought of that until you asked. I'd been confusing the things."

"What things, Patera Caldé?"

"Peace and saving my manteion. The Outsider asked me to save it, and then the insurrection broke out, and I thought I would have saved it if only I could bring peace, because the people made me caldé, and I would save it by an order." For a second or two, Silk lay silent, his eyes half closed. "Blood—men like Blood—have stolen the city, every part of it except the Chapter, and the Chapter has resisted only because you are at its head, Your Cognizance. When you're gone . . ."

"When I die, Patera Caldé?"

"If you were to die, Your Cognizance, they'd have it all. Musk actually signed the papers. Musk was the owner of record—the man whose body we burned on the altar, Your Cognizance. I remember thinking how horrible it would be if Musk were the real owner and clenching my teeth—puffing myself up with courage I've never really had and telling myself over and over that I couldn't allow it to happen."

"You're the only man in Viron who doubts your courage, Patera Caldé."

Silk scarcely heard him. "I was wrong. Badly mistaken. Musk wasn't the danger, was never the danger, really. There are scores of Musks in the Orilla, and Musk loved birds. Did I tell you that, Your Cognizance?"

"No, Patera Caldé. Tell me now, if you wish."

"He did. Mucor told me he liked birds, and he'd brought her a book about the cats she carried for Blood. When he saw Oreb, he said I'd gotten him because I wanted to be friends, which wasn't true, and threw his knife at him. He missed, and I believe he intended to miss. Blood, with his money and his greed for more, has done Viron more harm than all the Musks. Everything I've done has been trying to pry bits of the city from Blood. I was trying to save my manteion, I said; but you can't save just one manteion—I can't save our quarter and nothing else. I see that now. And yet I like Blood, or at least I would like to like him."

"I understand, Patera Caldé."

"Little pieces—the manteion, and Hyacinth and Orchid, and Auk, because Auk matters so much to Maytera Mint. Auk . . ."

"Yes, Patera Caldé?"

"Auk pushed me, Your Cognizance. We had been together in the floater, Hyacinth and I. Your Cognizance, too, and—and others. We were coming down, and Colonel Oosik—"

"You've made him Generalissimo Oosik," Quetzal reminded Silk gently.

"Yes. Yes, I did. He passed me the ear, and I talked to the convicts, telling them they were free, and then we hit the ground. We opened a hatch and Hyacinth and I climbed out–"

"I'm satisfied, Patera Caldé. Promise me you won't try to stand until I come back, and I'll look for water."

Silk detained him, clasping one boneless, bloodless hand. "You can't tell me what's happened to her, Your Cognizance?"

Again Quetzal's head swung from side to side, a slow and almost hypnotic motion.

"Then Auk has her, I don't know why, and I must get her back from him. What happened to me, Your Cognizance?"

"You were buried alive, Patera Caldé. When the floater crashed, some of us climbed out. I did, as you see, and you and your young woman, as you say. The fencing master, too, and your physician. I'm sure of those. The convicts were running to a hole in the ground to escape the shooting and explosions. Do you remember them?"

This time Silk was able to nod without much difficulty, although his neck was stiff and painful.

"There was a ramp down the side of the hole, and a break in this tunnel at the bottom. The fencing master and I ducked through. Almost at once there was another explosion, and the hole fell in behind us. We were lucky to have gotten in. Do you know my coadjutor's prothonotary, Patera Caldé?"

"I've met him, Your Cognizance. I don't know him well."

"He's here. I was surprised to see him, and he to see me. There is a woman with him called Chenille who says she knows you. They went into the tunnel yesterday, at Limna. They had been trying to reach the city."

"Chenille, Your Cognizance? A tall woman? Red hair?"

"Exactly so. She's an extraordinary woman. Soon after the explosion, the convicts attacked us. They were friendly at first, but soon demanded we give them Patera and the woman. We refused, and Xiphias killed four. Xiphias is the fencing master. Am I making myself clear?"

"Perfectly, Your Cognizance."

"We tried to dig our way out and found you. We thought you were dead, and Patera and I brought you the Peace of Pas. Eventually we stopped digging, having realized that the effort was hopeless. For a dozen men with shovels and barrows, two days might be enough."

"I understand, Your Cognizance."

"By then I was exhausted, though I had dug less than the woman. The others left to look for another way out. She and Patera are famished, and they have a tessera that they believe will admit them to the Juzgado. They promised to return for your body and me. I prayed for you after they had gone."

"Your Cognizance distrusts the gods."

"I do." Quetzal nodded, his hairless head bobbing on its long neck. "I know them for what they are. But consider. I believe in them. I have faith. You mentioned your quarter. How many there really believe in the gods? Half?"

"Less than that, I'm afraid, Your Cognizance."

"What about you, Patera Caldé? Look into your heart."

Silk was silent.

"I'll give you my thoughts, Patera Caldé. This young man believes, and he loves the gods even after seeing Echidna. I too believe, though I distrust them. He would want me to pray for him, and that's my office. I've done it often, hoping I wouldn't be heard. This time it's possible one will restore him, to prove she's not as bad as I think."

Faint yet unmistakable, the crack of a needler echoed down the tunnel.

"That will be Patera, Patera Caldé. We've been lucky in the matter of weapons. Xiphias has a sword, and had a small needler he said was yours. You left it on your bed, and he took charge of it for you. He gave it to the woman. We found a large one in your waistband. Patera took it, surprising me again. Our clergy have hidden depths."

In spite of pain and weakness, Silk smiled. "Some do, perhaps, Your Cognizance."

"Last night before you saw me in the alley, Patera Caldé, I met your acolyte, young Gulo. He is most embarrassed."

"I'm sorry to hear that, Your Cognizance."

"You shouldn't be. His uncle is a major in the Second Brigade. One uncle of many. Were you aware of it?"

"No, Your Cognizance. I don't know much about Patera."

"Neither do I, though he was one of our copyists until my coadjutor sent him to you. He commands several thousand now. It's a great responsibility for someone so young. More join every hour, he tells me, because they know he's your acolyte."

Silk managed to swallow. "I hope he won't waste their lives, Your Cognizance."

"So do I. I asked if it was hard. He said he discussed each operation with those who would have to fight. He finds them sensible, and he knows something of war from his uncle's table talk. He fights in the front rank afterward, he says."

"Your Cognizance mentioned that he was embarrassed."

"So he is, Patera Caldé." Quetzal shook himself, lifting one corner of his mouth by the thickness of a thread. "He has captured his uncle. Our clergy have hidden depths. The older man is humiliated. It's an awkward situation, I'm afraid, but I was amused."

"So am I, Your Cognizance. Thank you."

Quetzal rose. "We'll find our own amusing, when we find our way out. May I look for water?"

"Of course, Your Cognizance."

"You won't try to stand until I'm back? Give me your word, Patera Caldé."

Silk sat up.

"Please, Patera—"

"I have to go with you, Your Cognizance. I have to find water, wash, and drink, so I can do whatever I can for Viron and Hyacinth. You've got nothing to carry water in, and all four of you couldn't possibly carry me far."

"You've been suffocated, Patera Caldé." Quetzal bent over him. "We merely thought you dead, and I shouldn't have hinted at a miracle. No god can turn back death, and if they could, no god would to please us. You were still alive when we dug you out. You revived naturally—"

Unaided, Silk staggered to his feet. "I had a cane, Your Cognizance. Master Xiphias gave it to me. I didn't need it then, or at least not much. Now I do."

Quetzal offered him the baculus. "Use this."

"Never, Your Cognizance. Councillor Lemur called me— No, I won't."

The tunnel behind them was nearly choked with earth; a trampled path led Silk to an opening in the wall. "Is this where you found me, Your Cognizance? In there?"

"Yes, Patera Caldé. But if your young woman is in there, she is surely dead by now."

"I realize that." Silk put his head through the opening, "and I believe she's in the pit with Auk, anyway; but Master Xiphias values that cane, I need it, and it's probably very close to the place where you found me." He began to work his shoulders through.

"Be careful, Patera Caldé."

The wall was shiprock, little more than a cubit thick. Beyond it lay a cavity hollowed from the tumbled soil that seemed utterly dark. When Silk tried to stand, he found his head capped by a rough dome; earth and small stones showered him invisibly. "This could collapse any moment," he told the swaying figure in the tunnel.

"So it could, Patera Caldé. Come out, please."

His questing fingers had come upon stubby protuberances he assumed were roots. Exploring his pockets, he discovered the cards Remora had given him and used one to scrape away the soil. One root wore a ring. He cleared away more soil until he could get a firm grip on the hand, tugged, dug farther, and tugged again.

"There are new sounds in this tunnel, Patera Caldé. You had better leave that place."

"I've found someone, Your Cognizance. Somebody else." Silk hesitated, unwilling to trust his judgment. "I don't think it's Hyacinth. The hand is too big."

"Then it doesn't matter whose it is. We must go."

Getting a firm grip on the arm, Silk heaved with all the strength that remained to him, and was rewarded by a cataract of earth and a dead man's embrace.

I'm robbing a grave, he thought, spitting grit and wiping his eyes. Robbing this man's grave from below—stealing his grave as well as his body.

It should have been at least as amusing as Gulo's uncle the major, but was not. Holding onto the jagged edge of the opening in the tunnel wall, he succeeded in pulling his own partially buried body free. Back in the tunnel (suddenly very glad of its cold, sighing airs and watery lights) he was able to extract the corpse from the loose soil that had reclaimed it. Quetzal was nowhere to be seen.

"He's gone to look for water," Silk muttered. "Perhaps water could revive you the way something revived me," but the dead man's ears were stopped with earth. As he cleaned the pitiful face, Silk added, "I'm sorry, Doctor."

He searched his pockets again; his beads were not there, left behind with his own worn and dirty robe at Ermine's. It seemed a very long time ago.

He wriggled back into the dark cavity beyond the tunnel wall. Hyacinth had bathed him in their bedroom at Ermine's, undressing him, and scrubbing and drying him bit by bit. He ought to have been embarrassed (he told himself); but he had been too exhausted to feel anything beyond vague satisfaction, a weak pleasure at finding himself the object of so beautiful a woman's attention. Now all her concern had been undone, and Remora's fine robe, scarcely worn, ruined.

"You returned me to life, Outsider," Silk murmured as he resumed digging, "I wish you'd cleaned me up, too." But the Outsider had doubtless been, as Doctor Crane had maintained, no more than a vein's bursting.

Or had Doctor Crane—who had thought himself, or at any rate called himself, an agent of the Rani—been in truth an agent of the Outsider? Doctor Crane had made it possible for him to proceed in his attempt to save the manteion despite his broken ankle; and Doctor Crane had freed him when he had been taken by the Ayuntamiento. It was conceivable, even likely, that Doctor Crane's skepticism had been a test of faith.

Had he passed?

Weighing that question, he dug harder than ever, making the dark, evil-smelling earth fly. If he had, he would almost certainly be tested again, after this surrender to doubt.

The card struck something hard. At first he assumed it was a stone, but it was too smooth; another half minute's work bared the new find: a slender hook. As soon as he grasped it to pull it free, he knew that he had found the silver-banded cane Xiphias had brought to Ermine's for him.

Without warning, brilliant light flooded the cavity. He turned away from it, covering his eyes.

"I see you in there. Come on out."

There was something familiar about the harsh voice, but it was not until its owner said, "Put your hands where I can see them," that Silk recognized it as Sergeant Sand's.

.   .   .

Sitting the white stallion in the middle of Fisc Street, Maytera Mint surveyed the advancing ranks. Every one of those soldiers would be worth three of her best, but they were few. Hearteningly few, and the troopers from Trivigaunte had come. Just a few hundred now, but thousands more were on the way.

"Fire and fall back," she called softly, adding under her breath, "Gracious Echidna, grant that I be heard by our people but not by those soldiers." Then, a trifle louder, "Not too quickly. But not too slowly, either. This isn't the time to impress me. Don't get yourselves killed."

The first-level metal rank was practically within slug-gun range. She wheeled her stallion and cantered off, hearing the firing break out behind her, the *whiz . . . bang!* of missiles and the dull booming of slug guns.

Someone cried out.

I told them to, she reminded herself. I emphasized it in the briefing.

Yet she knew the wound had been real. She reined in the stallion and turned to look again: behind the soldiers, Rook's blocking force was straggling into position. Too early, she thought. Far too early. You never appreciated men like Bison and the captain—men who helped you make plans and carried them out—until you got something like this.

One long cable had been looped around each pillar of the Corn Exchange; it was not taut yet, nor should it have been. She risked a glance up at the towering façade, another at Wool and his bullock men, motionless in the shadows half a street away. He and they stood ready beside their animals, waiting for her signal.

The bullock men trusted her. So did the ragged men and women who were shooting and retreating as she had taught them. Shooting and dying, because they had trusted a weak woman—trusted her because Brocket had taught her to ride when she was a child.

She clapped heels to the stallion's sides. He had been used long and hard yesterday, yet he surged forward, a foaming wave of strength. Patera Silk's azoth was in her hand; she thumbed the demon.

Seeing its terrible blade split the sky, Wool's bullock men prodded their animals. The cable tightened, a slithering monster of steel and silence, Echidna's greatest serpent.

The soldiers halted and faced about at a loud command, their officer having seen Rook's force and detected the trap. They would have to attack in earnest now, but her own voice (she told herself) was incapable of launching troops against the enemy. Her voice would not inspire anyone, so her person must. She neck-reined the stallion, and the silver trumpet that was her voice in fact echoed from every wall.

Five chains away, the blade of the azoth wrecked a fusion generator, and the soldier whose heart it had been died.

Forward! Past her own disorderly line. Another soldier down, and another! Forward!

The stallion stumbled, crying out like a man in pain.

A half-dozen soldiers dashed forward. The stallion fell, too weak to stand; it seemed to her that the street itself had struck her, casting all its clods and ridges at her at once. Steel hands laid hold of her, and bios wrestled with chems in a desperate foolish fight. A woman three times her size swung a wrecking bar. The soldier she struck, struck her with the butt of his slug gun; she fell backward and did not rise.

Maytera Mint struggled in a soldier's grasp. The azoth was gone—No! Was under her shoe. He lifted her, his arms clamping her like tongs; she stamped on the azoth with all her strength, and its lancing point sheared off his foot. Smoking black fluid spurted from the stump of his leg, slippery as so much grease. They fell, and his grip weakened.

She tore herself away, stooping for the azoth, and ran, nearly falling again, pursued with terrifying speed until the façade of the Corn Exchange frowned above her and she whirled to cut down a soldier whose blazing, arcing halves tumbled at her feet. "Run! Run! Save yourselves!"

Her people streamed past in full flight, though to her, her voice was a powerless wail.

"Hierax, accept my spirit." The azoth's blade struck the first pillar, and it shattered like glass. Another, and the façade seemed to hang in air, an ominous cloud of grimy brick.

A soldier leveled his slug gun, firing an instant before her blade split his skullplate. She felt the slug tear her habit, smelled the powder smoke, and fled, slashing wildly at a third pillar without breaking stride—stopped and turned back, hot tears streaming. "You gods, for *twenty years*! Now let me go!"

The weightless, endless blade came up. The weightless, endless blade came down. And the façade of the Corn Exchange was coming down too, falling like a picture, nearly whole and almost maintaining its graceless design as it fell, its stone sills falling neither faster nor slower than its tons of brick and timber. Her right hand, still clutching the azoth, had begun the sign of addition when Rook grabbed her from behind and dashed away with her.

Chapter 10

CALDÉ SILK

"Let me go," Maytera Marble insisted Phaesday morning. "They won't shoot me."

Generalissimo Oosik regarded her through his left eye alone; his right was concealed by a patch of surgical gauze. He shrugged. General Saba, the commander from Trivigaunte, pursed pendulous lips. "We've wasted a shaggy hole too much time on this country house already, when nobody can say—"

"You're quite wrong, my daughter," Maytera Marble told her firmly. "Mucor can and does. Our Patera Silk is a prisoner in there, just as the Ayuntamiento claims."

"Spirits!"

"Only hers, really. I'd never seen anyone possessed until she began doing it to our students. I find it very upsetting." She beckoned Horn. "You've made me a white flag? Wonderful! Such a nice long stick, too. Thank you!"

General Saba snorted.

"You don't like my bringing our boys and girls."

"Children shouldn't have to fight."

"Certainly not." Maytera Marble nodded solemn agreement. "But they were, and some have been killed. They'd run off with General Mint, you see, almost all of them. I tried to think who might help me after Mucor left, and our students were the only ones I could think of. Horn and a few others are really mature enough already, more grown up than a great many adults. It got them away from the city, too, where the worst fighting was." She looked to Oosik for support, but found none.

"Where it still is," General Saba snapped. "Where the troops we've got out here are badly needed."

"They were fighting your girls, some of them, as well as our Army, and some are dead. Have I told you that? Some are dead, some hurt very badly. Ginger's had her hand blown off, I'm told. No doubt some of your girls are hurt as well."

"Which is why—"

"You said we're wasting time." Maytera Marble sniffed; she had acquired a devastating sniff. "I couldn't agree more. It will only take a minute to shoot me, if they do. Then you can attack at once. But if they don't, I may be able to talk to the councillors in there. They can order the Army and the Guards who are still fighting you—"

"The Second," Oosik supplied.

"Yes, the Second Brigade and our Army." Maytera Marble bowed in humble appreciation of his information. "Thank you, my son. The councillors could order them to give up, but no one knows whether there are really councillors in the Juzgado." Without waiting for a reply, she accepted the flag from Horn.

"I'm coming with you, Sib."

"You are not!"

He followed her nearly as far as the shattered gate just the same, ignoring a pterotrooper who shouted for him to stay back, and watched unhappily as she picked her way through its tumbled stones and twisted bars, somberly clad but conveniently short-skirted in Maytera Rose's best habit.

Two dead taluses smoked and guttered on the close-mown grassway between the gate and the villa. A few steps past the first, General Saba's adjutant sprawled face down beside her own flag of truce. Disregarding all three, Maytera Marble cut across the lush lawn toward the porticoed entrance, keeping well clear of the fountain to avoid its windblown spray.

This was Bloody's house, she reminded herself, this grand place. This was where the little man with oily hair had come from, the one she and Echidna had offered to her. It had been practically impossible, for a time, for her to remember being Echidna; now the image of the little man's agonized face had returned, framed by flame as she forced him down onto the altar fire. Would Divine Echidna help her now, in gratitude for that sacrifice? The Echidna she had pictured at prayer over so many years might have condemned her because of it.

But there had been no shot yet.

No missile. No sounds at all, save the soughing of the wind and the snapping of the rag on the stick she held. How young she felt, and how strong!

If she stopped here, if she looked back at Horn, would they shoot, killing her and waking the children? The children were asleep, most of them. Or at least they were supposed to be, back there beneath the leaf-less mulberries. The summer's unrelenting heat, the desert heat that she had hated so much, had deserted just when the children needed it, leav-ing them to sleep in the deepening chill of an autumn already half spent, to shiver huddled together like piglets or puppies in unroofed houses with broken windows and slug-pocked, fire-scarred walls, though most of them had liked that better than their studies, they said: had preferred killing Ayuntamientados and pillaging their dead.

A mottled green face appeared at the window next to the big door. Only the face, Maytera Marble noted with a little shiver of relief. No slug gun, and no launcher.

"I've come to see my son, my son," she called. "My son Bloody. Tell him his mother's here."

Shallow stone steps led up to a wide veranda. Before she put her foot on the last, the door swung back. Through it she saw soldiers, and bios in silvered armor. (Bios got up like chems, as she put it to herself, because chems were braver.) Behind them stood another bio, tall and red-faced.

"Good morning, Bloody," she said. "Thank you for bringing those white bunnies. May Kypris smile upon you."

Blood grinned. "You've changed a little, Mama." Some of the armored men laughed.

"Yes, I have. When we can talk in private, I'll tell you all about it."

"We thought you wanted to cut a deal for Hoppy."

"I do." Maytera Marble surveyed the hall; though she knew little about art, she suspected that the misty landscape facing her was a Murta-gon. "I want to talk about that. We've knocked down a good deal of your wall, I'm afraid, Bloody, and I'd like to see your beautiful house spared."

Two soldiers stood aside, and Blood came to meet her. "So would I, Mama. I'd like to see us spared, too."

"Is that why you didn't shoot? You killed that poor woman General Saba sent, so why not me? Perhaps I shouldn't ask."

Blood glanced to his right. "A shag-up over there. *We* didn't shoot the fussock with the flag, and I want that settled right now. If there's a question about it, there's no point in talking. I didn't shoot her, and didn't tell anybody to. None of the boys did, either, and they didn't get anybody to do it. Is that clear? Will you say Pas to that, nothing back?"

Maytera Marble cocked and lifted her head, thus raising an eyebrow. "Someone shot her from a window of your house, Bloody. I saw it."

"All right, you saw it, and Trivigaunte's going to make somebody pay. I don't blame them. What I'm saying is that it shouldn't be me or the boys. We didn't do it, and that's not open to argument. I want that settled before the cut."

Maytera Marble put a hand on his shoulder. "I understand, Bloody. Do you know who did? Will you point them out to us?"

Blood hesitated, his apoplectic face growing redder than ever. "If . . ." His eyes shifted toward a soldier almost too swiftly to be seen. "Yes, absolutely." Several of the armored men muttered agreement.

"In that case it's accepted by our side," Maytera Marble told him. "I'll report to my principals, Generalissimo Oosik and General Saba, that you had nothing to do with it and are anxious to testify against the guilty parties. Who are they?"

Blood ignored the question. "Good. Fine. They won't attack while I'm talking to you?"

"Of course not." Silently, Maytera Marble prayed that she was being truthful.

"You'd probably like to sit. I know I would. Come in here, and I think we can settle this."

He showed her into a paneled drawing room and shut the door firmly. "My boys are getting edgy," he explained, "and that gets me edgy around them."

"They're my grandchildren?" Maytera Marble sank into a tapestry chair too deep and too soft for her. "Your sons?"

"I don't have any. You said you were my mother. I guess you meant you came to talk for her."

"I am your mother, Bloody." Maytera Marble studied him, finding traces of her earlier self in his heavy, cunning face, as well as far too many of his father. "I suppose you've seen me since you found out who

I was or had somebody look at me and describe me, and now you don't recognize me. I understand. You're my son, just the same."

He grasped the advantage by reflex. "Then you wouldn't want to see me killed, or would you?"

"No. No, I wouldn't." She let her stick and white flag fall to the carpet. "If I had been willing to have you die, everything would have been a great deal easier. Don't you see that? You should. You, of all people."

She paused, considering. "I was an old woman before you found out who I was, and I think I must have looked older. I was already forty when you were born. That's terribly old for a bio mother."

"She came a few times when I was little. I remember her."

"Every three months, Bloody. Once in each season, if I could get away alone that often. We were supposed to go out in pairs, and usually we had to."

"She's dead? My mother?"

"Your foster mother? I don't know. I lost track of her when you were nine."

"I mean y–! Rose. Maytera Rose, my real mother."

"Me." Maytera Marble tapped her chest, a soft click.

"It was her funeral sacrifice. The other sibyl said so."

"We burned parts of her," Maytera Marble conceded. "But mostly those were parts of me in her coffin. Of Marble, I mean, though I've kept her name. It makes things easier, with the children particularly. And there's still a great deal of my personality left."

Blood rose and went to a window. The dull green turret of a Guard floater showed above a half-ruined section of wall. "You mind if I open this?"

"Certainly not. I'd prefer it."

"I want to hear if they start shooting, so I can stop it."

She nodded. "My thought exactly, Bloody. Some of the children have slug guns, and nearly all the rest have needlers. Perhaps I should have taken them, but I was afraid we'd need them on the walk out." She sighed, the weary *hish* of a mop across a terazzo floor. "The worst would have hidden theirs anyway, though none of the children are really bad."

"I remember when she lost her arm," Blood told her. "She used to pat me on the head and say, you know, my, he's getting big. One day it was a hand like yours–"

"It was this one." Maytera Marble displayed it.

"So I asked her what happened. I didn't know she was my mother then. She was just a sibyl that came sometimes. My mother would have tea and cookies."

"Or sandwiches." Maytera Marble supplemented his account. "Very good sandwiches, too, though I was always careful not to eat more than a fourth of one. Bacon in the fall, cheese in winter, pickled burbot and chives on toast in spring, and curds and watercress in summer. Do you remember, Bloody? We always gave you one."

"Sometimes it was all I got," Blood said bitterly.

"I know. That's why I never ate more than a fourth."

"Is that really the same hand?" Blood eyed it curiously.

"Yes, it is. It's hard to change hands yourself, Bloody, because you have to do it one-handed. It was particularly hard for me, because by then I already had a great many new parts. Or rather, I had reclaimed a great many old ones. They worked better, that was why I wanted them, but I wasn't used to the new assembly yet, which made changing hands harder. It would have been wasteful to burn them, though. They were in much better condition than my old ones."

"Even if it is, I'm not going to call you Mother."

Maytera Marble smiled, lifting her head and inclining it to the right as she always did. "You have already, Bloody. Out there. You called me Mama. It sounded wonderful."

When he said nothing, she added, "You said you were going to open that window. Why don't you?"

He nodded and raised the sash. "That's why I bought your manteion, do you know about that? I wasn't just a sprat nobody wanted any more. I had money and influence, and I got word my mother was dying. I hadn't spoken to her in fifteen, twenty years, but I asked Musk, and he said if I really wanted to get even it might be my last chance. I saw the sense in that, so we went, both of us."

"To get even, Bloody?" Maytera Marble lifted an eyebrow.

"It doesn't matter. I was sitting with her, see, and she needed something, so I sent Musk. Then I said something and called her Mom, and she said your mother's still alive, I tried to be a mother to you, Blood, and I swore I wouldn't tell."

Turning from the window to face Maytera Marble, he added, "She wouldn't, either. But I found out."

"And bought our manteion to torment me, Bloody?"

"Yeah. The taxes were in arrears. I'm real close to the Ayuntamiento. I guess you know that already or you wouldn't have come out here shooting."

"You have councillors here, staying with you. Loris, Tarsier, and Potto. That was one reason I wanted to talk."

Blood shook his head. "Tarsier's gone. Who told you?"

"Like your foster mother, I've sworn not to tell."

"One of my people? Somebody in this house?"

"My lips are sealed, Bloody."

"We'll get into that later, maybe. Yeah, I've got them staying here. It's not the first time, either. When I found out about you—if you're who you say you are—I talked to Loris, just one friend to another, and he let me have it for taxes. Know how much it was? Twelve hundred and change. I was going to leave you hanging, keep talking about tearing the whole thing down. Then Silk came out here. The great Caldé Silk himself! Nobody would believe that now, but he did. He solved my house like a thief. By Phaea, he *was* a thief."

Maytera Marble sniffed. It was at once a devastating and a confounding sniff, the sniff of a destroyer of cities and a confronter of governments; Blood winced, and she enjoyed it so much that she sniffed again. "So are you, Bloody."

"Lily." Blood swallowed. "Only your Silk's no better, is he? Not a dog's right better. So I saw a chance to turn a few cards and have a little fun by making the whole wormy knot of you squirm. I'd got your manteion for twelve hundred like I told you, just a little thank-you from Councillor Loris, and I was going to tell Silk thirteen hundred, then double that." Blood crossed the room to an inlaid cabinet, opened it, and poured gin and water into a squat glass.

"Only when I'd talked to him a little, I made it thirteen *thousand,* because he really thought those old buildings in the middle of that slum were priceless. And I said I'd sell them back to him for twenty-six thousand."

Blood chuckled and sat down again. "I'm not really a bad host, Mama. If I thought that you'd drink it, I'd stand you a drink, even after you called me a thief."

"I was speaking of fact, Bloody, not calling names. Here in private you may call me a trull or a trollop any other such filthy sobriquet. That is what I am, or at any rate what I've been, although no man but your father ever touched me."

"Not me," Blood told her. "I'm above all that."

"But not above defrauding that poor boy because he valued the things given to his care, and was so foolish as to imagine you wouldn't lie to an augur."

Blood grinned. "If I were above that, Mama, I'd be as poor as he is. Or as he was, anyhow. I don't remember how much time I gave him to come up with the gelt. A couple of weeks, maybe, or something like that. Then when I had him crawling, I said that if he brought me something next week or whatever, I might let him have a little more time. Then after a couple days, I sent Musk to tell him I had to have it all right away. I figured he'd come out here again and beg me for more time, see? It looked like it was going to be a nice little game, the kind I like best."

Maytera Marble nodded sympathetically. "I understand. I suppose all of us play wicked little games like that from time to time. I have, I know. But yours is over, Bloody. You've won. You have him here, a prisoner in your house. The person who told me that the councillors were here told me that, too. You have me as well. You say you wanted to avenge yourself on the foster mother we found for you, and you bought our manteion so you could avenge yourself on me, because I gave you life and tried to see that you were taken care of."

Blood stared at her and licked his lips.

"You've won both games. Perhaps all three. So go ahead, Bloody. A single shot should kill me, and I saw a lot of slug guns out there in your foyer. Then the Trivigauntis can kill you for killing General Saba's adjutant, or Generalissimo Oosik can shoot you for shooting me. Possibly you'll be given your choice. Would you rather die justly? Or unjustly?"

When Blood did not reply, she added, "Perhaps you ought to ask your friend Musk about it. He advises you, from what you've said. Where is he, anyway?"

"He stayed behind after we brought the doves. He said he had a couple things to take care of, and he doesn't get into town very often. I thought maybe your side picked him up when he tried to come home."

Maytera Marble shook her head.

Blood took a liberal swallow from his glass. "I wasn't going to shoot you, Mama, and I didn't shoot her. You agreed to that already. Let's pin it down. In about an hour, the Guard could knock this house down and kill everybody. I know that. They're not doing it because they know we've got Silk in here. Isn't that right?"

Maytera Marble nodded. "Free him, turn him over to me, Bloody, and we'll go away and leave you alone."

"It's not that easy. He's here all right, right here in my house. But it's the councillors and their soldiers who've got him, not me."

"Then I must speak with them. Take me to them."

"I'll bring them in here," Blood told her, "they're all over." Under his breath he added, "It's still my hornbussing house, by Phaea's feast!"

Potto opened the door at the top of the cellar steps and crooked his finger at Sand. "Bring him up, Sergeant. We're getting them all together."

Sand saluted with a crash of titanium heels, his slug gun vertical before his face. "Yes, Councillor!" He nudged Silk with the toe of his right foot, and Silk rose.

He fell as he attempted to mount from the second step to the third, and again halfway up. "Here," Sand told him, and returned Xiphias's stick.

"Thank you," Silk murmured. And then, "I'm sorry. My legs feel a trifle weak, I'm afraid."

Potto said cheerfully, "We're going to try to give you back to your friends, Patera, if we can get them to take you." Grabbing the front of Remora's ruined robe, he jerked Silk up the remaining step. "You'd like to lie down again, wouldn't you? Get in a little nap? Maybe something to eat? Help us, and you'll get it."

He released Silk so suddenly that he fell a third time. "Has he tried to escape again, Sergeant?"

Silk did not hear Sand's reply; he was thinking about a great many things. Among them, names.

His own and Sand's were similar—each had four letters, each contained a single vowel, and each began with an *S*. They could not be related, however, because Sand was a chem and he a bio. Yet they were related by the similarity of their names. Not inconceivably (he found it a tantalizing idea), Sand was a cognate, a version of himself in some whorl of a higher order. Many things the Outsider had shown him seemed to imply that there were such whorls.

Sand prodded him from behind with the barrel of his slug gun, and he staggered against a wall.

Since chems were never augurs, it could not be that Sand had been meant to be an augur. Was it possible then, that he, Silk, had been meant to be a Guardsman? If he were a Guardsman instead of a failed augur, the many correspondences (already so marked) linking them would be much more perfect, and thus this inferior whorl they inhabited more perfect, too.

But, no, his mother had wanted him to enter the Juzgado, to become a clerk there like Hyacinth's father and perhaps rise to commissioner. How glowingly she had spoken of a political career, almost up until the day he left for the schola.

"This way," Potto told him, and pushed him through a door and into a gorgeous room full of lounging soldiers and armored men. "Is that the caldé?" one of the men asked another; the second nodded.

He was in politics at last, as his mother had wished.

He had pulled a chair over to her closet and stood on the seat to examine the caldé's bust on its dark, high shelf; and she, finding him there intent upon it, had lifted it down for him, dusted it, and set it on her dressing table where he could see it better—wonder at the wide, flat cheeks, the narrow eyes, the high, rounded forehead, and the generous mouth that longed to speak. The caldé's carved countenance rose again before his mind's eye, and it seemed to him that he had seen it someplace else only a day or two before.

Streaming sunlight, and cheeks that were not smooth wood but blotched and lightly pocked. Was it possible he had once seen the caldé in person, perhaps as an infant?

"Now listen to me." Potto was standing before him, his plump, pleasant face half a head lower than Silk's own.

. . . had seen the caldée outside, because even without his lost glasses he had noticed the powder on the cheeks and the flaws that the powder tried to cover—had seen him, in that case, under the auspices of the Outsider, in a sense.

Blood and Maytera Marble were sitting side-by-side when Potto shoved Silk into the room; he was so surprised to see her that for a moment he failed to notice Chenille, Xiphias, and a drooping augur lined up against the wall.

A still handsome elderly man standing by the fireplace said, "I'm Councillor Loris. I take it you're Silk?"

"Patera Silk. His Cognizance the Prolocutor has not yet accepted my resignation. May I sit down?"

Loris ignored the last. "You're the insurgent caldé."

"Others have called me caldé, but I'm not involved in an insurrection." Potto pushed him to the wall beside Chenille.

Loris smiled, his blue eyes glinting like chips of ice; and the seduction of his craggy wisdom was so great that even a mocking smile made it almost irresistible. "You killed my Cousin Lemur, did you, Caldé?"

Silk shook his head.

Maytera Marble said, "I don't know these others, except Chenille. Shouldn't I introduce myself?"

"I'll do it," Blood told her, "it's my house." With a slight start, Silk realized that Blood was in the chair he had occupied a week earlier, and that this was the same room.

"This is Councillor Loris," Blood began unnecessarily, "the new presiding officer of the Ayuntamiento. This other councillor's Councillor Potto."

"Caldé Silk and Councillor Potto are old acquaintances," Loris purred. "Isn't that right, Caldé?"

"I don't know this soldier myself," Blood continued, and paused to sip his drink. "It probably doesn't matter."

"Sergeant Sand," Silk told him. "He and Councillor Potto interrogated me Tarsday. It was very painful, and I suppose it's quite possible they're going to do it again."

Sand came to attention and appeared about to speak, but Silk stopped him with a gesture. "You were only doing your duty, Sergeant. I understand. In justice to you, I ought to add that you had treated me well earlier."

Potto said, "We won't need you here, Sergeant. You know what to do." Sand looked at Silk, saluted, executed an about-face, and left, shutting the door behind him.

"A very handsome young man," Maytera Marble remarked. "I was sorry to hear that he behaved badly toward you, Patera."

Blood indicated her with his glass. "This holy sibyl's Maytera Rose—"

Chenille tittered nervously. Maytera Marble said, "I'm Maytera Marble, Bloody. Remember? I explained about that. Chenille and I have met, and naturally Patera knows me well."

"Patera *Silk,* she means," elucidated the small augur in the corner. "I, *too,* am entitled to the honorific, as well as my more customary ones. Caldé, I have been appointed the new *Prolocutor* of *Viron* by *Subleviating Scylla,* who during that same *theophany* confirmed *you* as its caldé. Am *I,* as I *dare hope,* the first to—"

Silk managed to smile. "It's a pleasure to see you again, Patera."

Chenille blurted, "Why weren't you dead? I've just been standing here . . . We couldn't, none of us—"

Xiphias cackled. "He's a tough one! Student of mine, too! Truth!"

Silk said, "Maytera, do you know Master Xiphias? Master Xiphias is teaching me to fence. Master Xiphias, this holy sibyl is Maytera Marble. She's the senior sibyl now at my—Of the manteion on Sun Street."

Maytera Marble added softly, "I'm also the representative of our Generalissimo Oosik and the Trivigauntis's General Saba, Patera. I've come to arrange your release."

His voice thick with mock sincerity, Loris said, "We hold the key to the crisis now, you see, the generous gods having flung the ring into our laps. How foolish are those who scorn the power of the immortal gods!"

A black shape darted through the open window, landing with a thump on Silk's shoulder. "Bird back!"

"Oreb!" Silk looked around at him, surprised and more pleased than he would have been willing to admit.

"*Scourging Scylla,*" ignoring Oreb, Incus had leveled his forefinger at Loris, "has given *you* nothing."

"In that case, we have gained our present advantage by merit." Loris smiled. "We thank the undying, evergenerous gods for our talents."

Oreb cocked an inquiring head. "Good gods?"

"She will *destroy* all of you, should you harm *either* of the holy augurs present, or this *sibyl.* We are *sacred.*"

"We'll risk her wrath if need be. Old man, stop reaching for your sword. It's gone. Were you thinking of overpowering us?"

Xiphias shook his head. "Think I don't know there's soldiers out there?"

"You could not even if there were none." Loris took a bookend from the mantle; it shattered between his fingers with a sharp report and an explosion of snowy chips. The door flew open, revealing Sand and two other soldiers with leveled slug guns. Oreb whistled.

Potto told them, "It's all right. Shut it."

"Caldé Silk is a strong young man, but he's been severely wounded. You are an old one, unarmed, and not as strong as you suppose. Our new Prolocutor's not physically imposing. Need I continue?"

Silk said, "I can understand how you came to be in the tunnel, Master Xiphias—both you and His Cognizance. You ran for cover just as Hyacinth and I did—"

Blood interrupted. "You've got her? Where is she?"

"I don't. I had her, if you like. We were separated." Turning back to Xiphias, Silk continued, "After you dug me out of the loose soil, you went down the tunnel to look for water with Chenille and Patera, leaving His Cognizance with me—with my body, as you thought. Is that right?"

Xiphias nodded.

"Only we didn't think your body," Chenille told Silk. "We knew you were alive. His Cognizance said there was a pulse, only we didn't understand how you could be alive after getting buried like that."

Loris rattled what remained of the bookend in his hand. "What puzzles me—excuse my interrupting your conference—is your mention of His Cognizance. I take it you don't refer to our friend, but to the actual head of the Chapter? Was he in the tunnel with you, Caldé?"

"Yes, he was. Perhaps I shouldn't have mentioned it."

Potto said happily, "He's an old man. One of the patrols will pick him up, Cousin."

"A clever old man." Loris looked grim. "A troublemaker."

Privately, Silk was trying to reconcile Quetzal's telling Chenille that he, Silk, was alive with his saying that they had thought him dead. He had lied in one or the other, but why?

"Bad thing!" Oreb told everyone.

Silk ventured, "A patrol headed by Sergeant Sand—one like the patrol that arrested me originally, I suppose—must have come across Master Xiphias, Patera Incus, and Chenille. I was surprised to see them here, but I believe I understand now. Sand must have sent the other man back here with them and gone on alone until he found me, perhaps because he'd heard my voice—I'd been talking to His Cognizance. Is that correct?"

"Where is this tunnel, Patera?" Maytera Marble asked. "Are you talking about a tunnel underneath the house?"

Potto grinned at her, displaying gleaming teeth.

Blood put down his drink. "Yeah, we're right over it, Mama, and it hooks up with a bunch of others."

Loris told her, "That's the first item you ought to pass on to your principals, Maytera. They think they have us like rats in a cauldron. Nothing could be further from the truth. We can leave this house, and them, whenever we wish."

Blood added, "Only I don't want to. It's my house."

She looked thoughtful, a finger pressed to her cheek.

"Bad hole." Oreb ruffled his feathers apprehensively. Chenille whispered, "Your bird was down there with us. Auk had him on the boat."

"You're sunburned!" Inwardly, Silk reproached his own stupidity. "I've been looking at you–gaping actually, I suppose. I hope you'll excuse it, but I couldn't imagine how your face had gotten so red, so close to the red-brown color of a wood-carving my mother used to have."

"She wore *nothing* on the boat," Incus interposed. "Then my robe. Maytera *forced* them to give her that gown."

Loris snapped, "Is this germane?"

"Perhaps not," Silk admitted. "It's just that Chenille has reminded me of a childhood incident, Councillor."

Loris waved aside Chenille's sunburn, tossing the largest fragment of the bookend onto the rosewood end table at Maytera Marble's elbow. "Marble? Isn't that your name, Maytera? The caldé just reminded us of that."

"It is."

"That was what this knickknack was, I'd say. Real marble from the Short Sun Whorl, precisely like you." For an instant, Loris's face was no longer attractive. "I'll leave that chunk there so you don't forget it."

"I shan't," Maytera Marble promised. "It would be wise for you to keep in mind that you're surrounded by thousands of well-armed troops, Councillor. I suppose most people in my position would be inclined to exaggerate their numbers, but I won't. I'll tell you the truth, so you won't be able to say that you were deceived, or even misled, afterward. There are two companies of Trivigaunti pterotroopers, almost the entire Third Brigade of the Civil Guard, and elements of the

Fourth. I asked Generalissimo Oosik what he meant by 'elements' and he said four floaters and the heavy weapons company. Besides all those, there are about five thousand of Maytera Mint's people, with more arriving from the city all the time. They've heard that Patera Silk's in here, and they want to charge the house. When I left, General Saba and Generalissimo Oosik were afraid they might not be able to prevent them without using Guardsmen and creating more friction."

"Fight now?" Oreb inquired.

Smiling, Maytera Marble turned to Silk. "That's the bird I saw hopping into your kitchen when Doctor Crane was treating you, isn't? Later on my glass, and on your shoulder like that in the garden. I knew I'd seen him before."

"No, little bird, no fighting. Not now, or not yet. But Generalissimo Oosik told me quite frankly that if there's no way to stop Maytera Mint's insurgents from attacking short of firing on them, he'll stand back and let them do it. You see, I confided to the children that your master was in here. They seem to have told a great many other people before we left the city, so the whole thing's my fault. I feel very badly indeed about that, and I'm trying to make amends."

Blood added, "But she won't say who told her. Or have you changed your mind about that, Mama?"

"Certainly not. I gave my word."

Loris, who had been leaning against the mantel, left it to stand in front of Maytera Marble. "This little conference has already run too long. Allow me to tell you what we want, Maytera. Then you can go back out there and repeat it to the Trivigauntis and Mint's five thousand rioters, if there are actually that many, which I am ungentlemanly enough to doubt. Our position is not negotiable. You accept our terms or we'll kill these prisoners, Silk included, and crush the rebellion."

"You have *no* authority—"

Potto's fist striking Incus's cheek sounded almost as loud as the breaking of the bookend.

"So, we've come to that." Maytera Marble smoothed the black skirt covering her metal thighs. "It will be needlers and knives next, no doubt."

Silk said, "I warn you, Councillor Potto, not to do that again."

"Or you'll break my neck?" Potto's smile was that of a fat boy contemplating a stolen pie. "Beat little butcher, big butcher bark? We've had some games of strength already. If you've forgotten them, I can teach you the rules again."

Incus spat blood. "The just *gods* avenge the wrongs of *augurs*. A doom . . ."

Potto lifted his hand, and Incus fell silent.

"No hit," Oreb suggested.

"The gods may or may not," Silk murmured. "I don't know, and if I were forced to choose, I'd probably say that they did nothing of the sort."

Loris applauded with a sardonic smile; a half-second too late, Potto joined him.

Abruptly Silk's voice dominated the room. "The law does, however. Maytera told you how many troops Generalissimo Oosik has, saying—very fairly and reasonably, I thought—that she didn't want you to feel you'd been tricked when all this is over. You should have listened more carefully."

"Tell 'em!" Xiphias put in.

"I'm attempting to." Silk nodded, mostly (it appeared) to himself. "Because it will be over soon. There will be a trial, and you, Councillor Potto, and you, Councillor Loris, will hear Maytera, Chenille, Master Xiphias, and Patera Incus testify to what they saw and heard—and felt, as well—to a judge who will no longer be afraid of you."

Potto giggled and glanced at Loris. "Is this what they picked to replace us?"

Surprising everyone, Blood said, "Yeah, I didn't get it at first, but I'm starting to."

Maytera Marble told Potto, "All human things wear out and must be replaced eventually, Councillor."

"Not me!"

"I'd think you'd welcome it. How long have you toiled, worrying and planning, for our ungrateful city? Fifty years? Sixty?"

"Longer!" Potto dropped into a gilt settee.

Silk inquired, "Councillor, do you—not the authentic Potto down in your underwater boat, but you yourself to whom I speak—recall the Short Sun Whorl? Councillor Loris implied that marble could be quarried there. I don't know anything about antiques, but I've heard that it is a stone that's never found in its natural state in our whorl."

"I'm not that old."

Loris snapped, "I was about to outline our demands. I'd like to get on with it."

Maytera Marble left her chair to stand beside Silk. "Do, Councillor, please."

"As I said, they're not negotiable. The following five conditions embody them, and we're prepared to accept nothing less." Loris fished a square of paper from an inner pocket and unfolded it with a snap.

"First, Silk must declare publicly, without reservation, that he is not and has never been caldé, that Viron has none, and that the Ayuntamiento alone is its sole governing body."

To bring peace I'll be happy to, Silk told him; and only when he had completed the final word realized that he had not spoken aloud.

"Second, there must be no new election of councillors. Vacant seats are to remain vacant, and the present members of the Ayuntamiento are to remain in office.

"Third, the Rani of Trivigaunte must withdraw her troops from Vironese territory and furnish us with hostages—whom we will name—against further interference in our affairs.

"Fourth, the Civil Guard must surrender its treasonous officers to us, the Ayuntamiento, for trial and punishment.

"Fifth and last, the rioters must surrender their arms, which will be collected by the Army."

Through bruised lips, Incus muttered, "I suggest you *pray* long and hard over this, my son, and *sacrifice*. The *wisdom* of the gods has not enlightened your *councils*."

"We don't need it," Potto told him.

"When *Splenetic Scylla* learns—"

Maytera Marble interrupted. "What have you to offer the Rani, the rioters, as you call them, and the Guard in return?"

"Peace and a general amnesty. The captives you see here, including Silk, will be released unharmed."

"I see." Maytera Marble laid a hand on Silk's shoulder. "I'm very disappointed. It was I who persuaded General Saba and Generalissimo Oosik that you were reasonable men. They listened because of the courage of my sib General Mint. And because of her victories, of which we're all very proud, if I don't offend the good gods who gave them to her by saying so. Now I find that by interceding for you I've squandered all the credit she's earned us."

Loris began, "If you think us unreasonable now—"

"I do. You say Patera Silk isn't really caldé. What good is his declaration then? What do you want him to tell the people? That the augur of the Sun Street manteion says that your Ayuntamiento is to continue to govern the city? You'll only make yourselves ridiculous."

Potto snapped, "Why didn't you laugh?"

"Caldé?" Loris smiled. "Those are our demands. The Prolocutor hasn't freed you from your vows, you said, the implication being that you want him to. Are you willing to resign this caldéship you've never really had as well?"

"Yes, I'd like nothing better." Silk had been leaning on Xiphias's silver-banded cane; he straightened up as he spoke. "I did not choose to become involved in politics, Councillor. Politics chose me."

"Good Silk," Oreb explained.

Loris returned his attention to Maytera Marble. "You heard that. You'll want to tell Oosik what you heard."

"Unfortunately," Silk continued, "the remainder of your terms are not feasible. Take the second. The people demand that government return to our Charter, the foundation of the law; and the law requires elections to fill the empty seat in the Ayuntamiento."

"We ought to kill you," Potto told him. "I will."

"In which case you would no longer hold the caldé. The people— the rioters, as you call them—will choose a new one, no doubt a much better and more effective one than I am, since they could hardly do worse."

He waited for someone else to speak, but no one did; at length he added, "I'm not an advocate, Councillors—I wish I were. If I were, I could easily imagine myself defending you on nearly every charge that could be brought against you thus far. You suspended the Charter, but I believe there was some uncertainty regarding the wishes of the old caldé, and it was long ago in any case. You tried to put down the riots, but in that you were doing your duty. You questioned Mamelta and me when we were detained for violating a military area, which could easily be justified."

"He *hit* me!" Incus exclaimed. "An *augur*!"

Silk nodded. "That is an individual matter, concerning Councillor Potto alone, and I was considering the Ayuntamiento as a whole—or rather, what remains of that whole. But what you say, Patera, is quite right; and it's an indication of the road along which this Ayuntamiento is traveling. I'd like to persuade Councillor Loris, its presiding officer, to turn back before it's too late."

Loris fixed him with a malevolent stare. "Then you won't accede to our demands? I can call in the soldiers at once and get this over with."

Silk shook his head. "I can't accede. Nor can I speak for the Rani of Trivigaunte, obviously; but I can and do speak for Viron; and for Viron all of your demands, except the one for my resignation, are out of the question."

"Nevertheless," Maytera Marble put in, "General Mint and Generalissimo Oosik may accede to them, in part at least, to save Patera Silk. May I speak to him in private?"

"Don't be ridiculous!"

"It isn't ridiculous, I must. Don't you see that General Mint and Generalissimo Oosik and all the rest of them are only acting on the authority of Patera Silk? When I report that I've seen him and tell them you've recognized him as caldé, they will certainly want to know whether he's willing to agree to your terms. They'll have to know what he wants them to do, but they won't pay the least attention to it unless I can say that he told me in private. Let me talk to him, and I'll go back and talk to Generalissimo Oosik and General Saba. Then, if we're lucky, we'll have real peace in place of this truce."

"We have not recognized him as caldé," Loris told her coldly. "I invite you to retract that."

"But you have! You've called him Caldé several times in my presence, and I could see you congratulating yourselves on having the caldé. You even called him the key to the crisis. You're threatening to shoot *him* because *he* won't agree to your precious five demands. If he's the caldé, that's only cruel. If he isn't, it's idiotic."

She raised her hands and time-smoothed face to Loris in supplication. "He's terribly weak. I've been watching him while the rest of us were talking, and if it weren't for his stick I think he would have fallen. Can't you let him sit down? And tell everyone else to leave? A quarter of an hour should be enough."

Blood rose, swaying a little. "Over here, Patera. Take my seat. This's a good chair, better than the one you had in here that other time."

"Thank you," Silk said. "Thank you very much. I owe you a great deal, Blood." Chenille, next to him, took his arm; he wanted to assure her he did not need her help, but stumbled on the carpet before he could speak, eliciting an unhappy squawk from Oreb.

"Get the rest of them out," Loris told Potto.

Xiphias paused in the doorway, showing Silk both his hands, then twisting one slightly and separating them.

Chenille kissed his forehead, the brush of her lips the silken touch of a butterfly's wing—and was gone, violently pulled away by Potto, who left with her and shut the door.

Maytera Marble reoccupied the chair beside the one that had been Blood's. "Well," she said.

Silk nodded. "Well indeed. You did very well, Maytera. Much better than I. But before we talk about—all of the things we'll have to talk about, I'd like to ask a question. One foolish question, or perhaps two. Will you indulge me?"

"Certainly, Patera. What is it?"

Silk's forefinger traced small circles on his cheek. "I know nothing about women's clothes. You must know a great deal more—at least, I hope you do. You got Councillor Loris to bring Chenille her gown?"

"She was naked under that augur's robe," Maytera Marble explained, "and I refused to talk about anything else until they got her dressed. Bloody called in one of the maids, and she and Chenille went with a soldier to find her some clothes. They weren't gone long."

Silk nodded, his face thoughtful.

"It's too small for her, but the maid said it was the largest in the house, and it's only a little bit too small."

"I see. I was wondering whether it belonged to a woman I met here."

"You and Bloody were talking about her, Patera." Maytera Marble sounded ill at ease. "He asked you where she was, and you said you'd gotten separated."

Silk nodded again.

"I don't want to pry into your personal affairs."

"I appreciate that. Believe me, Maytera, I appreciate it very much." He hesitated, staring through the open window at the wind-rippled green lawn before he spoke again. "I thought it might be one of Hyacinth's, as I said. In fact, I rather hoped it was; but it couldn't be. It almost fits Chenille, as you say, and Hyacinth's much smaller." The circles, which had ceased to spin, reappeared. "What do you call that fabric?"

"It's chen. . . . Why, I see what you're getting at, and you're right, Patera! That gown's chenille, exactly like her name!"

"Not silk?"

Maytera Marble snapped her fingers. "I know! She must have told the maid her name, and it suggested the gown."

"She kissed me as she left," he remarked. "I certainly didn't invite it, but she did. You must have seen it."

"Yes, Patera. I did."

"I suppose she wanted to signal that she was with us—that she supported us. Master Xiphias made a gesture of the same sort, probably something to do with swordplay. Anyway, her kiss made me think of silk, of the fabric I mean, for some reason. It seemed strange, but I thought perhaps her skirt had brushed my hand. You say it's actually called chenille?"

"Chenille *is* silk, Patera. Or anyway the best chenille is, and the other is something else that's supposed to look like silk. Chenille is a kind of yarn, made of silk, that's furry-looking like a caterpillar. If they weave cloth of it, that's called chenille too. It's a foreign word that means caterpillar, and silk threads are spun by silkworms, which are a kind of caterpillar. But I'm sure you know that."

"I must speak to her," he said. "Not now, but when we're alone, and as soon as I can."

"Good girl!"

"Yes, Oreb. Indeed she is." Silk returned his attention to Maytera Marble. "A moment ago when you spoke to Loris, you didn't want us to leave this room. Would you mind telling me why?"

"Was I as transparent at that?"

"No, you weren't transparent at all; but I know you, and if you'd really been so worried about me, you would have asked him to let us talk in a bedroom where I could lie down, and to send for a doctor. I don't suppose Blood's got one, now that Doctor Crane's dead; but Loris might have been able to supply one, or to send someone for one of the Guard's doctors under a flag of truce, like that white flag next to your chair."

Maytera Marble looked grave. "I should have asked him to do that. I can still ask, Patera. I'll go out and find him. It won't take a moment."

"No, I'm fine. By Phaea's favor—" It was too late to call back the conventional phrase. "I'll recover. Why did you want to stay here?"

"Because of this window." Maytera Marble waved a hand at it. "Bloody had opened it while we were in here by ourselves, and I worried the whole time that someone would get cold and shut it. You must know Mucor, Patera. She said you sent her to me."

Silk nodded. "She's Blood's adopted daughter."

"Adopted? I didn't know that. She said she was Bloody's daughter. That was Hieraxday night, terribly late. . . . Do you know Asphodella, Patera?"

Silk smiled. "Oh, yes. A lively little thing."

"That's her. I'd done the wash, you see, and I wanted to pour the dirty water on my garden. Plants actually like dirty water with soapsuds in it better than clean. It sounds wrong, I know, but they do."

"If you say so, I'm sure it must be true."

"So I was pouring out the water, so much for each row, when Asphodella pulled my skirt. I said what are you doing out so late, child? And she told me she'd gone with the others to fight, but Horn had sent her back—"

"Cat come!" Oreb warned. Silk looked for it, seeing none.

"Horn had sent her home, and quite right, too, if you ask me, Patera. So now she wanted to know if there'd be palaestra on Thelxday."

"Then," Silk said slowly, "her face changed. Is that it, Maytera?"

"Yes. Exactly. Her face became, well, horrible. She saw I was frightened, as I certainly was, and said don't be afraid, Grandmother. My name's Mucor, I'm Blood's daughter." Maytera Marble paused, not certain that he understood. "Have I told you Bloody's my son, Patera? Yes, I know I did, right after we sacrificed in the street."

"He was Maytera Rose's," Silk said carefully. "You, I know, are also Maytera Rose—at least, at times."

"All the time, Patera." Maytera Marble laughed. "I've integrated our software. As far as we sibyls are concerned, I'm your best friend and worst enemy, all in one."

He stirred uncomfortably in Blood's comfortable chair. "I was never Maytera Rose's enemy, I hope."

"You thought I was yours, though, Patera. Perhaps I was, a little."

He leaned toward her, his hands folded over the crook of Xiphias's cane. "Are you now, Maytera? Please be completely frank with me."

"No. Your friend and well-wisher, Patera."

Oreb applauded, flapping his wings. "Good girl!"

She added, "Even if I were entirely Maytera Rose, I'd do all I could to get you out of this."

Silk let himself fall back. It was astonishing how soft these chairs of Blood's were. He remembered (vividly now) how badly he had wanted to rest in his chair, to sleep in it, when he had talked with Blood in this very room. Yet this one was better, just as Blood had promised: yielding where it should, firm where firmness was desirable. He stroked one wide arm, its maroon leather as smooth as butter beneath his touch.

"They let me lie down after I was captured," he confided to Maytera Marble. "Sand did. I'd had to walk all the way to this house, and it was a very long way. It had seemed long when Auk and I rode donkeys; and walking with Sand's gun at my back, it seemed a great deal longer; but once we arrived, once we'd climbed up through the hatch into the cellar, he let me lie down on the floor. He isn't a bad man, really–just a disciplined soldier obeying bad men. There's good in Loris, too, and even in Potto. I know you must sense it, just as I do, Maytera; otherwise you'd never have spoken to Potto as you did. That's why–one reason, anyway–I don't feel that this situation from which you're trying to rescue me is as bad as it appears, though I'll always be grateful."

"Cat! Cat!" Oreb flew from Silk's shoulder to the head of an alabaster bust of Thelxiepeia.

Maytera Marble smiled. "There's no cat in here, you pretty bird."

"You were telling me about this room," Silk reminded her, "and meeting Mucor. I wish you'd continue with that. It may be significant."

"I–Patera, I want to tell you first about meeting you. It won't take long, and it may be more important, maybe a lot more important. You still think about the day you came to our manteion, I know. You've mentioned it several times."

He nodded.

"Patera Pike was there, and you loved and respected him, but a man wants a woman to talk to. Most men do, anyway, and you did. You'd been raised by your mother, and we could see how you missed her."

"I still do," Silk admitted.

"Don't feel bad about that, Patera. No one should ever be ashamed of love."

Maytera Marble paused to collect her thoughts; her rapid scan was back, and she reveled in it. "We were three sibyls, I was about to say.

Maytera Mint was still young and pretty, but so shy that she ran from you whenever she could. When she couldn't, she would hardly speak. Maybe she guessed what had happened to me long ago. I've sometimes thought that, and you were young and good-looking, as you still are."

He began a question, but thought better of it.

"I won't tell you who Bloody's father was, Patera. I've never told anybody and I won't tell now. But I will tell you this. He never knew. I don't think he even suspected."

Silk filled his lungs with the cool, clean breeze from the window. "I slept with a woman last night, Maytera. With Hyacinth, the woman Blood asked about."

"I'm sorry you told me."

"I wanted to. I've wanted—I want so badly, still, to tell people who don't know, although a great many people know already. His Cognizance and Master Xiphias and Generalissimo Oosik."

"And me." Maytera Marble's forefinger tapped her metal chest through her habit. "I knew. Or rather, I guessed, as anybody would, and I wish that you'd left it like that. Some things aren't improved by talking about them."

Oreb broke off his inverted examination of Thelxiepeia's features to applaud Maytera Marble. "Smart girl!"

"We were three sibyls, as I said. But Maytera Mint wasn't there for you Patera, so I was the only ones left. I was old. I don't think you ever grasped how old. My faces had gone long before you were born. You never realized they weren't there, did you?"

"What are you talking about? Your face is where it ought to be, Maytera. I'm looking at it."

"This?" She drummed her fingers on it, a quick metallic *tap-tap-tap*. "This is my faceplate, really. I used to have a face like yours. I would say like Dahlia's, but she was before your time. Like Teasel's or Nettle's, and there were things in it, little bits of alnico, that let me really smile or frown when I moved them with the coils behind my faceplate. But all that's gone except for the coils."

"It's a beautiful face," Silk insisted, "because it's yours."

"My other face wasn't, and what it was showed in your own every time you saw it. I resented that, and you resented my resentment and turned to me to ease your loneliness. But we were much more alike than you realized, not that I've ever cared, myself, for machines like this. I never thought they could be people, really, no matter how many times they said they were. Now I'm just a message written on those teeny gold doodads you see in cards. But I'm still me, a person, because I always was."

Silk fumbled Remora's ruined robe for a handkerchief, and finding none blotted his eyes on his sleeve.

"I didn't tell you that to make you feel sorry for me, Patera. Neither of me were easy to love, no more than I am now. You were able to love one just the same, and not very many men could have, not even many augurs. I thought that if you knew how you came to love and not like me, it might help you some other time with some other woman."

"It will, I know." Silk sighed. "Thank you, Maytera. With myself, most of all."

"Let's not talk about it any more. What do you think of the Ayuntamiento's terms? Still what you told Loris?"

Silk made a last dab at his eyes, feeling the grit in the cloth, knowing that he was dirtying his already-soiled face and not caring. "I suppose so."

Maytera Marble nodded. "They're perfectly hopeless. Not a single thing for Trivigaunte, and why should the Guard hand over its senior officers, why should Generalissimo Oosik allow it? But if we offered trials, regular ones with judges—"

"Man back!" A big hand glittering with rings had appeared on the windowsill. It was followed by a yellow-sleeved arm and a whiff of musk rose.

"That's why you wanted to stay here." Silk stood up a trifle unsteadily, helped by the cane, and crossed the room to the window. "So your son could join us."

"Why no, Patera. Not at all."

Leaning over the sill, Silk spoke to Blood. "Here, hold onto my hand. I'll help you up."

"Thanks," Blood said. "I should have brought a stool or something."

"Take mine, too, Bloody." Maytera Marble braced one foot on the sill in imitation of Silk.

Flushed redder than ever with exertion, Blood's face rose on the other side of the window. With a grunt and a heave, he tumbled into the room.

"Now for my granddaughter. She'll be easy after Bloody." Bending over the sill again, Maytera Marble clasped skeletally thin hands and lifted in an emaciated young woman with a seared cheek.

"Poor girl!"

Silk nodded his agreement as he returned to his chair. "Hello, Mucor. Sit down, please, so that I may sit. We're neither of us strong."

"Needlers're no good 'gainst the soldiers," Blood puffed. He brushed off the front of his tunic and reached beneath it. "So I'm giving you this, Caldé Silk."

"This" was an azoth, its long hilt rough with rubies and chased with gold; its sharply curved guard was more elaborate than that of the one Doctor Crane had given him at Hyacinth's urging, and diamonds ringed its pommel.

Silk resumed his seat. "I should have anticipated that. Doctor Crane told me you had two."

"Don't you want it?" Blood did not trouble to hide his surprise.

"No. Not now, at least."

"It's worth—"

"I know what it's worth, and how effective a weapon it can be in a strong hand like yours. At the moment, I don't have one, though that's the least of my reasons for refusing."

Silk settled back in his chair. "I asked your daughter to sit down, and she was good enough to oblige me. I can't invite you to sit in your house, and I'm very aware that I'm occupying your former seat; but there are many others."

Blood sat.

"Thank you. Maytera—"

"Cat come!"

It did, almost before Oreb's agitated whoop, springing lightly over the windowsill to land noiselessly in the middle of the room and glare at Blood with eyes like burning amber. Maytera Marble gathered her skirts as if it were a mouse; Silk asked, "Is that Lion? I seem to remember him."

The lynx turned its glare on him and nodded.

"Patera's been making everybody sit," Maytera Marble told Mucor.

"It would be nicer if you had your big kitty sit too, Darling. I wouldn't mind him so much then."

Lion lay down obediently, dividing his attention between Blood and Oreb.

"Sphigx bless you." Maytera Marble traced the sign of addition. "I—it's rather amusing now that I come to think of it, the sort of thing the children enjoy. Patera thought I wanted this window open so your Papa could come in, and I said, no, I hadn't even thought of it, which was the plain truth. I wanted it opened because you told me the first time, Darling, not to stay in rooms with the doors and windows shut, because you might have to drop in again, and that would make it harder. So I was happy when he opened this one, and now you've come in through it, and your long-legged kitty, too."

"I didn't know she could take over an animal like that." Blood had his thumb on the demon. "We didn't know she had any power left till Lemur taped the caldé talking to Crane, but it sounds like she's been paying visits to both of you."

"Sneaking outside the window, Bloody? You shouldn't do that."

"I didn't."

"A listening device." Silk sighed. "I'm disappointed. I'd thought there might be a secret door behind one of these big paintings. When I was a sprat, boys' books were full of them, but I've never actually seen one."

"You knew I'd come?"

"I surmised you might. Do you want the entire thing?"

Maytera Marble sniffed loudly. "I do, Patera."

"I wish you wouldn't make that noise," he told her.

"Then I won't, or at least not very often. But Bloody's my son, and I meant I have a right to know."

"All right, the entire thing." Silk leaned back in his chair, eyes half closed. "On Hieraxday, I walked some distance through the city with His Cognizance, and from the East Edge to Ermine's; it was about evenly divided between Maytera Mint's insurgents and the Guard. I slept at Ermine's for a few hours, as I told you; when I woke up, half the Guard seemed to have gone over to Maytera Mint."

Maytera Marble said, "All of it but the Second, I'm told."

"Good. Before I was brought here, I was in the tunnels or in the cellar, so I didn't see much; but there were councillors here. It seemed likely they were directing their forces in person, and I didn't think they'd do that unless the situation was critical. Then too, you told me you'd walked out here with the children and mentioned a general from Trivigaunte—"

"General Saba. A very good woman at heart, from what I saw of her, though quite large and rather prone to obstinacy."

"I assume it was her airship that attacked us when His Cognizance and I were riding in Oosik's floater."

"Her airship's been over the city, certainly. It's been shooting and dropping explosives. It's huge."

"Your Doctor Crane was a spy from Trivigaunte," Silk told Blood. "You must know that by now. He told me once, joking, that if I were in need of rescue all I'd have to do was kill him. He had a device in his chest that let others find him and told them whether his heart was beating. He was shot Hieraxday morning, due to a misunderstanding. I imagine the attack on us resulted from a similar mix-up—the Trivigauntis had been told the Guard was opposing us. When they saw a Guard floater surrounded by officers on horseback, they attacked it."

"I don't see what this has to do with me," Blood grunted.

"It has everything to do with you," Silk told him, "and I was right about it, too—the only thing I've been completely right about. You were fighting in a losing cause; this house was about to be destroyed, and you might easily be wounded or killed. You knew about the tunnels, and no doubt you've been down there. So have I, as I've said—more than I like. I couldn't imagine your leaving this house in flames and trudging off underground unless there were no alternative."

"I worked shaggy hard to get this place."

"Don't swear, Bloody. It doesn't become you."

"I did! Your kind thinks it's easy. One wrong move and you're packed for Mainframe, day after day, and nobody to help me I could trust till I found Musk, nobody at all. It'd kill both of you in a week. Shag yes, it would! Twelve years I did it before I ever took my first crap in this place."

"Bloody!"

"It's only a guess," Silk admitted, "and I can't pretend an intimate familiarity with your mental processes; but I'd imagine you've been looking for an opportunity to change sides since sometime last night."

"What's the shaggy Ayuntamiento ever done for me? Worked me

for payoffs and favors every month. Shut me down to make themselves look good. What the shag do I owe them?"

"I've no idea. Then—about an hour ago, perhaps—your mother entered the picture, ostensibly and no doubt principally to help me, but clearly with influence on the other side and eager to save you as well. So when I realized Maytera wanted us to stay in this room, I expected you to step from behind a picture." Silk smiled and shrugged apologetically.

Mucor surprised them all by asking, "Would you like me to see what they're doing?"

"I'd rather have you eat something," Silk told her, "but I don't suppose there's anything in here. Go ahead, if Lion will behave himself."

He waited for her reply, but none came.

"Girl go." Oreb's croak was scarcely audible. "No here." Lion stretched himself on the floor and closed his eyes.

"Actually, I was surprised you didn't come sooner," Silk told Blood conversationally, "but of course you had to fetch Mucor and get her dressed—perhaps even clean her up a bit with the help of one of your maids, and I hadn't allowed for that. The point that puzzles me is that Mucor seems to have felt it necessary to send Lion ahead of her."

"Did she?" Blood eyed his adopted daughter curiously.

"So it seems. Oreb—my bird, up there—must have glimpsed him or, more likely heard him, because he told us several times that there was a cat about."

"She probably didn't realize that the soldiers wouldn't be afraid of him," Maytera Marble suggested.

"Bad cat," Oreb muttered.

"Not too loud," Silk cautioned him, "he might hear you."

"It was nice of you to join us, Bloody." Maytera Marble smoothed her skirt. "It's to your advantage, no doubt, just as Patera says. But you're taking a big risk just the same."

Blood stood. "I know it. You don't think much of me, do you, Caldé?"

"I think a great deal of your shrewdness," Silk told him. "I'd be glad to have your cunning mind on our side. I'm aware that you have no morals."

"Colonel Oosik," Blood gestured with the azoth. "He's your man, from what I've heard. This General Saba's there for the Rani, Colonel Oosik for you."

"Generalissimo Oosik."

Blood snorted. "You trust him and you won't trust me, but I've had him in my pocket for years."

Maytera Marble said, "Sit down, Bloody. Or are you going to do something?"

"I want a drink, but since the caldé doesn't want it, I think I'll hang onto my azoth as long as that cat's in here. Will you fix me one, Mama?"

"Certainly." She rose. "A little more gin, I imagine?"

Silk began, "If it's not too much trouble, Maytera—"

"And ice. There's ice behind the big doors underneath."

"I'll be happy to. Brandy, or—" she examined bottles. "Here's a nice red wine, Patera."

"Just water and ice, please. The same for Mucor, I think."

Blood shook his head. "No ice, Mama. She'll throw it. Believe me, I know."

"Poor bird!"

"A cup of plain water for Oreb, if you would, Maytera. I believe he'll come down to drink it if you leave it on top of the cabinet."

"Plain water for Oreb." Revealing two fingers' width of silvery leg as she stood on tiptoe, she put a brimming tumbler on the cabinet. "Soda water and ice for Patera, and ice, gin, and soda water for you, Bloody. Soda water without ice for my granddaughter. It's nice and cool, though." As she placed the final tumbler before Mucor, she added, "I must say she doesn't look as if you've been taking good care of her."

Blood picked up his drink. "We've got to force-feed her, mostly, and she tears off her clothes."

"Who was her mother?" Silk asked.

"She never had one." Blood sipped his drink and eyed it with disfavor. "You know about frozen embryos? You can buy them now and then if you want them, but you don't always get what you paid for."

Recalling dots of rotting flesh, Silk shuddered.

"The old caldé, Tussah his name was, was supposed to have done it. That leaked out after he died. So I decided to give it a try. Buy myself an embryo with spooky powers. I got one of the girls to carry it."

"And you were actually able to purchase such a thing? An embryo that would develop into someone with Mucor's powers?"

Blood nodded unhappily. "Like I said, you don't always get what you pay for, but I was careful and I did. She's got the stuff, but she's crazy. Always has been."

"You engaged a specialist to operate on her brain."

"Sure, trying to cure her, only it didn't work. If it had, I'd be caldé."

"She's been my friend," Silk told him, "a difficult one, perhaps, but helpful just the same. She likes me, I believe, and the good god knows I'd like to help her in return."

Oreb caught at the phrase. "Good god?"

"The Outsider, I ought to have said."

Mucor herself said, "They're arguing about you." Her voice sounded faint and far away; the tumbler Maytera Marble had filled for her waited untouched on the low table before her.

Silk sipped from his own, careful not to drink too much too fast. "Men and women breed children from their bodies on impulse. We augurs rail against it; but although inexcusable, it is at least understandable. They are swept away by the emotions of the moment; and if they weren't, perhaps the whole Whorl would stand empty. Adoption, on the other hand, is a considered act, consummated only with the assistance of an advocate and a judge. Thus an adoptive parent cannot say, 'I didn't know what I was doing,' or 'I didn't think it would happen.' Worthless though those protestations are, he has no claim to them."

"You think I knew she'd turn out like this? She was a baby." Blood glared at his daughter. "I'm twice your age, Patera, maybe more. When you're as old as I am, maybe you'll have a few little things that you regret too."

"There are many already."

"You think there are. Women, you mean. Hy. Oh shag it, what's the use?" Blood set his drink aside and wiped his damp left hand on his thigh. "I don't care much for them. Neither would you, if you'd been in my business as long as I have. I started when I was seven or eight, just a dirty little sprat going up to men in the market. Anyhow, Mucor's the only child I'll ever have, probably."

Maytera Marble told him, "She's the only granddaughter I'll ever have, too, Bloody. If you won't take proper care of her, I will."

Blood looked angrier than ever. "Like you did me?"

"It would be better if we kept our voices down," Silk said. "You're not supposed to be here."

"I wish I wasn't." A smile twisted Blood's mouth. "That would be the elephant, wouldn't it? Shot for trying to pick up a couple bits down at the market. Hey, Patera, you want to meet my sister? She'll give you some hot mutton."

"Bloody, don't!"

"It's pretty late to tell me that, Mama. Or don't you think so?"

Without waiting for an answer, he turned to Silk. "I'm going to outline a deal. If you take it, I'm in, and I'll do everything I can to get you out of here in one piece."

Silk opened his mouth to speak.

"When I say you, that's you and the other augur, the old man, Mama here, and that big piece from Orchid's. Even your bird. All of you. All right?"

"Certainly."

"If you don't take it, I'm out the window, understand? No hard feelings, but no deal either."

"You could be shot going out the window, too, Bloody," Maytera Marble warned him. "I'm surprised that you weren't, you and my granddaughter, before you got back inside."

Blood shook his head. "There's a truce, remember? And I'll stick the azoth back under my tunic. They aren't going to shoot an unarmed man and a girl that never even come close to the wall."

"As good as a secret passage." Maytera Marble's eyes gleamed with amusement.

"Right, it is." Blood went to the window. "Now here's what I say, Caldé. I'll come over to you and Mint, gun, goat, and gut, and try to see to it that all of us get clear. When we do, I'll sign over your manteion to you for one card and other considerations, as we say, and you can owe me the card."

He waited for Silk to speak, but Silk said nothing.

"After we get out, I'm still your bucky. I've done plenty of favors for the Ayuntamiento, see? I can help you too, and I will, everything that I can. I've got Mucor, remember," Blood nodded toward her, "and I know what she can do now. Lemur's crowd never got anything half as good as that."

Silk sipped from his tumbler.

"More talk," Oreb muttered; it was not clear whether it was a suggestion or a complaint.

"Here's all I want from you, Caldé. No gelt, just three things.

Firstly, I get to hang onto my other property. That means my real estate, my accounts at the fisc, and the rest. Number two, I stay in business. I'm not asking you to make it legal. I don't even want you to. Only you don't shut me down, see? Last, I don't have to pay anybody anything above regular taxes. I'll open my books to you, but no more payoffs on top of that. You understand what I'm telling you?"

Blood leaned against the window frame. "Look it over, and you'll see I'm making you as good a deal as anybody could ask for. I'm giving you my complete, unlimited support, plus some valuable property, and all I want from you is that you leave me alone. Let me keep what's mine and earn my living, and don't come down on me any harder than you do on anybody else. What do you say?"

For a few seconds, Silk did not say anything. The tramp of rubber-shod metal feet came faintly from the wide foyer on the other side of the carved walnut door, punctuated by Potto's strident tones; embroidered hangings stirred, whispering, in the cool wind from the window.

"I've been expecting to be tested." Silk glanced at his tumbler, surprised to find that he had drunk more than half his soda water. "Tested by the Outsider. He's been testing me physically, and I felt quite confident that he would soon take my measure morally as well. When you began, I was certain this was it. But this is so easy!"

Lion raised his head to look at him inquiringly, then rose, stretched, and padded over to rub his muscled, supple body against Silk's knees.

Maytera Marble shook her finger at her son. "What you've been doing is very wrong, Bloody. You sell rust, don't you? I thought so."

"To begin," Silk told Blood, "you must turn my manteion over to me—you're going to do that right now. If you didn't bring along the deed, you can go out that window and get it. I'll wait."

"I brought it," Blood admitted. He fished a folded paper from an inner pocket of his tunic.

"Good. My manteion, for three cards."

Blood crossed the room to an inlaid escritoire; after a time, Mucor stood as well, her mouth working silently as though she were pronouncing the labored scratchings of Blood's pen.

"I'm not much of a scholar," he said at length, "but here you are, Patera. I had to sign for Musk, but it should be all right. I've got his power of advocacy."

The ink was not yet dry; Silk waved the deed gently as he read.

"Fine." He took three of Remora's cards from his pocket and handed them to Blood.

"You're to do everything in your power to end the fighting without further loss of life," he told Blood, "and so am I. If I'm caldé when it's over, as you obviously expect, you will be prosecuted for any crimes you may have committed, in accordance with the law. No unfair advantage will be taken beyond that which I just took. That's a large concession, but I make it. I warn you, however, that nothing that you may have done will be overlooked, either. If you're found guilty on any charge, as I expect that you will be, I'll ask the court to take into consideration whatever assistance you've rendered our city in this time of crisis. Am I making myself clear?"

Blood glowered. "You extorted that property from me. You took it under false pretences."

"I did." Silk nodded agreement. "I committed a crime to right the wrong done to the people of our quarter by an earlier one. Why should men like you be free to do whatever you wish whenever you wish, guaranteed that you yourself will never be victimized? You may, if you choose, complain about what I've done when peace has been restored. You have a witness in the person of your mother."

He gave the lynx a last pat before pushing him away. "I wouldn't advise you to call your adopted daughter, however. She's not competent to testify, and she might tell the court about the nativity of her pets."

"You had better not ask me to testify, either, Bloody," Maytera Marble told him. "I'd have to tell the judge that you tried to bribe our caldé."

"They're coming," Mucor announced to Silk. "Councillor Loris has finished talking to Councillor Tarsier through the glass. They've decided to kill you and send your body back with the woman that killed Musk."

Silk froze, his eyes on Blood.

Oreb squawked, "Watch out!"

Instinctively, Maytera Marble reached out to her son, a plea for forgiveness and understanding.

His grip on the azoth tightened, and the shimmering horror that was its blade divided the cosmos, leaving Maytera Marble on one side and the hand she had held out to him on the other. It dropped to the carpet as the hideous discontinuity swung up, showering them with plaster and sundered lath. Silk shouted a warning; absurdly, he tried to shield her from Blood's downward cut with Xiphias's cane.

Its thin wooden casing exploded in blazing splinters; but the azoth's blade sprang back from the double-edged steel blade the casing had concealed, having notched it to the spine.

It seemed to Silk then that his arm moved of itself–that he merely watched it, a spectator fully as horrified as she, and fully as separated from his arm's acts. As the door flew in with a crash, that arm swung the ruined blade.

From behind Sergeant Sand and a second soldier equally large, Potto barked, *"Shoot him!"*

The notched blade slid forward, penetrating Blood's throat as readily as the manteion's old bone-handled sacrificial knife had ever entered that of a ram.

"Shoot the caldé?" Sand's hand caught the other soldier's slug gun.

Blood's knees buckled as the light left his eyes. The double-edged blade, scarlet to within a hand's breadth of the notch with Blood's own blood, retreated from his throat.

"Yes, the caldé!"

For a moment it seemed to Silk that Maytera Marble should have knelt to catch Blood's blood; perhaps it seemed so to her as well, for she crouched, her remaining hand extended to her son as he fell.

Silk turned, the sword still in his hand. Sand's slug gun was no longer pointed at him, if it had ever been. Sand fired, and the second soldier a fraction of a second after him. Potto fell, his cheerful face slack with surprise.

"Take this, Patera." Maytera Marble was pressing Blood's azoth into his free hand. "Take it before I kill you with it."

He did, and she took Xiphias's ruined sword from him, and with its crook wedged between her small black shoes, contrived to wipe its blade with a big handkerchief that she shook from her sleeve.

There was a clash of heels and a crash of weapons as Sand and the second soldier saluted. Soldiers and men in silvered armor peering around them began to salute as well. Silk nodded in response, and when that seemed inadequate traced the sign of addition in the air.

Epilogue

It had been hastily erected, Caldé Silk reflected, studying the triumphal arch that spanned the Alameda—very hastily. But surely this new generalissimo from Trivigaunte would understand the situation, would realize the difficulties they had labored under in organizing a formal welcome in a city still at war with what remained of its Ayuntamiento, and make allowances.

Now, this wind.

It stirred yellow dust from the gutters, whistled among the chimneys, and shook the ramshackle arch until it trembled like an aspen. Flowers covering the arch would have been nice, but that moment of searing heat on Hieraxday had made flowers out of the question. So much the better, Silk thought; this wind would surely have stripped off every petal an hour ago. Even as he watched, a long streamer of colored paper pulled free, becoming a flying jade snake that mounted to the sky.

There the Trivigaunte airship fought its straining tether, so high that its vast bulk appeared, if not festive, at least unthreatening. From that airship, it should be simple to gauge the advance of Generalissimo Siyuf's troops. Silk wished that there had been time to arrange for signals of some sort: a flag hung from the gondola when she entered the city, for example, or a smoke pot lit to warn that she had been delayed. Rather to his own surprise, he discovered that he was eager to go up in the airship himself, to see Viron like the skylands again, and travel among the clouds as the Fliers did.

There were a lot of them out today, riding this cold wind. More, he decided, than he had ever seen before. A whole flock, like a flight of storks, was just now appearing from behind the airship. What city sent them forth to patrol the length of the sun, and what good did those patrols do? Speculation about the Fliers had been dismissed as bootless at the schola, until the Ayuntamiento had condemned them as spies.

Had the Ayuntamiento known? Did Councillor Loris, who wielded what authority remained to it, know now?

Might it not be possible to track Fliers in the airship, anchor at last at that fabled city, learn its name, and offer whatever assistance in its sacred labor Viron and Trivigaunte could provide?

(Buried, he had been wherever he had thought to be.)

A fresh gust, colder and wilder than any before it, roared up the Alameda, shaking its raddled poplars like rats. To his right General Saba stiffened, while he himself shivered without shame. He was wearing the Cloak of Lawful Governance over his augur's robe; it fell to his shoe-tops and was of the thickest tea-colored velvet, stiff with gold thread. He ought to have been awash in his own perspiration; he found himself wishing ardently for some sort of head-covering instead. General Saba had a dust-colored military cap and Generalissimo Oosik beyond her a tall helmet of green leather topped with a plume, but he had nothing.

He recalled the broad-brimmed straw hat he had worn while repairing the roof of the manteion—which would be missing more shingles, surely, thanks to this wind. He had pulled that hat down so that Blood's talus could not identify him later, and it had known him by that.

(Dead by his hand, Blood and the talus both.)

He had lost that recollected hat somehow. Might not this wind return it to him? All sorts of rubbish was blowing about, and stranger things had happened.

His wound throbbed. Mentally he pushed it aside, forcing himself to fill his lungs with cold air.

The shade had not climbed far yet, but what should have been a bright streak of purest gold seemed faint, and flushed with brownish purple. The Aureate Path was empty and failing visibly, signally the end of mankind's dream of paradise, of some inconceivable fraternity with its gods. For one vivid instant he remembered Iolar, the dying Flier. But no doubt the sun was merely dimmed at the moment, stained and darkened by dust. Winter was long overdue in any event. Was Maytera Mint, who would be so conspicuously absent from this, her victory parade, cold too? Wherever she was?

Was Hyacinth? Silk shivered again.

Far away, a band struck up, and ever so faintly he heard, or seemed to hear, the sound of bugles, the tramp of marching feet, and the clatter of cavalry.

That was a good sign, surely.

Exodus from the Long Sun

For Paul and Vicki Marxen
—we go way back.

Gods, Persons,

and Animals

Mentioned in the Text

N.B. The names of Trivigauntis, Fliers, and gods do not adhere to the Vironese conventions. As in *Caldé of the Long Sun*, the names of major characters are given in CAPITALS.

Colonel *ABANJA*, SIYUF's spymaster.
Aer, SCIATHAN's lover, a Flier.
Aster, a former classmate of NETTLE's.
AUK, the prophet of TARTAROS.
Maytera *Betel*, the big dark woman with sleepy eyes whom SILK was shown during his first enlightenment, now dead.
Colonel *Bison*, MINT's chief subordinate.
Blood, ROSE's son and MUCOR's adoptive father, a crime lord; he was killed by SILK.
Bluebell, one of the women at Orchid's.
Bongo, the trained baboon SILK noticed when buying OREB.
CHENILLE, Tussah's natural daughter.
Chamomile, Swallow's assistant.
Doctor *Crane*, a subordinate of ABANJA's; his death caused SIYUF to send Saba's airship to Viron.
Dace, a fisherman killed by one of Urus's gang.
Dahlia, a student at the palaestra on Sun Street long ago.
Desmid, one of POTTO's spycatchers, now dead.
ECHIDNA, the goddess who conspired to murder PAS, her husband.
Eland, a convicted murderer.
Feather, a small boy who attended the Sun Street palaestra.

Patera *Feeler*, a proverbial carper.

Fulmar, a member of Incus's circle of black mechanics.

Councillor *Galago*, a surviving member of the Ayuntamiento.

Gib, the giant who bought Bongo.

Ginger, a young woman who lost a hand in the insurrection.

Goldcrest, a former classmate of NETTLE's.

Grian, the Flier who escaped the Trivigauntis.

Guan, the man with the slug gun, a subordinate of SPIDER's.

Major *Hadale*, the officer who places SABA under arrest.

Corporal HAMMERSTONE, INCUS's dearest friend.

Hart, a friend of HORN's, wounded in the fighting.

Hide, one of NETTLE's twin sons.

Hierax, ECHIDNA's younger son, the god of death.

Holly, a former classmate of NETTLE's.

Hoof, one of NETTLE's twin sons.

HORN, the colonist who undertook to write *The Book of Silk*.

Hossaan, see *Willet*.

HYACINTH, the estranged wife of Serval.

HYRAX, the dead man in the doorway.

Patera INCUS, the augur who supplants REMORA.

Patera *Jerboa*, the augur of the Brick Street manteion.

Kerria, a boy of four.

Councillor *Kingcup*, the new member of the Ayuntamiento chosen by MINT.

Kit, a former pupil at SILK's palaestra.

Kypris, PAS's mistress, the goddess of love.

Councillor *Lemur*, the presiding officer of the Ayuntamiento, killed by Crane. (Also the bio of the same name.)

Sergeant *Linsang*, one of MINT's volunteers.

Lijam, the Minister of War of Trivigaunte; she is a political ally of SIYUF's.

Lion, the largest of MUCOR's lynxes.

Councillor *Loris*, Lemur's successor.

Macaque, a former classmate of HORN's.

Maytera *Maple*, the youngest sibyl at Jerboa's manteion.

Maytera MARBLE, formerly the maid-of-all-work Magnesia.

Marl, Fulmar's elderly manservant.

Marrow, the greengrocer who becomes a leader of the colonists on Blue.

Private *Matar*, one of SABA's pterotroopers.

Cornet *Mattak*, a young officer who was attacked by an inhumu.

Mear, one of the Fliers killed by the Trivigauntis.

Maytera MINT, the Sword of Echidna, also known as General MINT.

Maytera *Mockorange*, MINT's preceptress long ago.

Molpe, Echidna's mad daughter, the goddess of the winds.

Moly, HAMMERSTONE's lost sweetheart, a housemaid. (Short for Molybdenum.)

Moorgrass, the woman who prepared the body of Orchid's daughter for burial.

MUCOR, the young woman grown from a frozen embryo purchased by Blood.

Murtagon, a famous artist, now dead.

Musk, Blood's lover and chief subordinate, killed by MARBLE.

NETTLE, HORN's wife, a former student at SILK's palaestra.

Councillor *Newt*, the new member of the Ayuntamiento chosen by POTTO.

Private *Nizam*, a young pterotrooper who is fond of animals.

Generalissimo *Oosik*, the commander of the armed forces of Viron, appointed by SILK.

Orchid, the madam of a brothel on Lamp Street.

OREB, a night chough, SILK's pet bird.

The OUTSIDER, the god of gods.

Paca, the dead man in the tunnel.

PAS, the digitized personality of a tyrant.

Peeper, a turnkey at the Juzgado.

Petal, see *Titi*.

Phaea, Echidna's fat daughter.

Patera *Pike*, the elderly augur whose acolyte SILK was, now dead.

Poppy, a friend of CHENILLE's at Orchid's.

Councillor POTTO, a surviving member of the Ayuntamiento.

Patera QUETZAL, a male of the inhumi, native to Green.

Patera REMORA, the lanky augur who expected to succeed QUETZAL.

General *Rimah*, SIYUF's chief of staff.

Rook, one of MINT's subordinates.

Maytera ROSE, the elderly sibyl whose personality has merged with MARBLE's, now dead.

General SABA, the Trivigaunti possessed by MUCOR at SILK's dinner party.

Sergeant *Sand,* HAMMERSTONE's squad leader.

Sard, a pawnbroker; his shop is on Saddle Street, not far from Orchid's yellow house.

Private *Schist,* a soldier in Sand's squad.

SCIATHAN, the Flier captured by the Trivigauntis.

SCLERODERMA, the author of a much briefer account of the exodus from Viron and the events leading up to it.

Scylla, ECHIDNA's eldest child, the goddess of water.

Captain *Serval,* the officer who pretended to arrest SILK in Limna, usually called "the captain."

Sewellel, the dead man in the abandoned guardroom.

Private *Shale,* a soldier in Sand's squad.

Patera *Shell,* Jerboa's acolyte.

Shrike, SCLERODERMA's husband, a butcher.

Sigada, see *Crane.*

Silah, a daughter of the Rani of Trivigaunte.

Caldé *SILK,* the young augur grown from the frozen embryo purchased by Tussah.

Sinew, NETTLE's eldest son.

Major *Sirka,* the officer in charge of the Trivigaunti advance party.

Generalissimo *SIYUF,* the commander of the armed forces of Trivigaunte.

General *Skate,* a subordinate of Oosik's, the nominal commander of the Caldé's Guard.

Major *Skin,* a subordinate of Bison's.

Skink, one of MINT's subordinates, crippled in the fighting.

Private *Slate,* a soldier in Sand's squad.

Sphigx, ECHIDNA's youngest daughter, the goddess of war.

SPIDER, POTTO's chief spycatcher.

Sumaire, one of the Fliers killed by the Trivigauntis.

Director *Swallow,* the head of the manufactory that builds taluses.

Councillor *Tarsier,* a surviving member of the Ayuntamiento.

TARTAROS, ECHIDNA's older son, the god of darkness.

Teasel, a girl who was attacked by an inhumu.

Thelxiepeia, ECHIDNA's third daughter, the goddess of learning.

Tick, the catachrest SILK rejected before buying OREB.

Titi, one of SPIDER's spycatchers, now dead.

Thyone, a minor goddess, invoked by those who tell fortunes by
    throwing the lees of wine.
Commissioner *Trematode,* the Vironese city official overseeing
    diplomacy, ceremony, and protocol.
Trotter, the owner of a drinking den near the Juzgado.
Caldé *Tussah,* SILK's predecessor, thought to have been murdered.
Urus, a former confederate of AUK's.
Villus, the small boy who scratched MARBLE's face with Musk's needler.
Violet, the second tallest woman at Orchid's.
Willet, the floater driver who brought Hyacinth to Ermine's to meet
    SILK.
Maytera *Wood,* the oldest sibyl at Jerboa's manteion.
Wool, a subordinate of MINT's, now dead; he was in charge of the oxen
    used to pull down the Corn Exchange.
Master *Xiphias,* SILK's self-appointed bodyguard.

Chapter 1

BACK FROM DEATH

An eerie silence overhung the ruined villa. Listening for the closing of a slug gun's bolt, Maytera Mint heard only the groan of the wind and the irregular snapping of the flag of truce she held.

"On Phaesday they were *in situ*," Patera Remora conceded. "The Ayuntamiento, eh?"

They had come abreast of a dead talus, its painted steel sides blistered by fire and blackened by smoke; she caught a whiff of fish oil, despite the wind.

"Might be repaired, eh, General?" Remora pushed back a lock of lank black hair that had fallen over his eyes. "Not like we biochemicals, hey? Still we—ah—dispatch their spirits to Mainframe. Not identical in the, um, revivified one, perhaps. Amongst the new parts."

"Or they really haven't any," Maytera Mint murmured. She had stopped to wait for Remora, and was taking the opportunity to study the windows of the house that had been Blood's.

Her remark bordered on heresy, but Remora thought it most prudent to return to his earlier topic. "If they're not here, eh? Loris and the rest? Will, ah, Buffalo—"

"Bison." She turned back to Remora, her face pinched and the tip of her delicate nose red with cold. "Colonel Bison."

"Um, precisely. Will Colonel Bison," Remora waved vaguely at the ruined wall, "and his—ah—troopers await our return back there?"

"You heard my instructions, Your Eminence."

"But if we're some time, eh? The front door is broken. Shattered, in fact."

Maytera Mint, who had noted it as they passed through the ruined gateway, nodded.

"So it's not a matter of knocking, hey? Not a mere matter of knocking at all." Remora brightened. "Knock on the frame, eh? We could do that. Wait a bit. Polite."

"I will go inside," she told him firmly, "and search. I would not presume to dictate Your Eminence's course of action. If I can get in touch with the Ayuntamiento, I'll ask them to send for you. If I can't, I may be able to learn where we can. As for Colonel Bison, he's completely loyal, my best officer. My only concern is that he may send in a patrol to look for us, though I have forbidden it."

"I, um, apprehend your position," Remora said, rejoining her. "If one does not expect obedience, one will not, ah, be obeyed. Memorized it in schola, all of us did. Still, if he were to depart? Decamp. Our, um, withdrawal to the city could be hazardous, hey? Laborious, likewise."

"That's not the question." She forgot for a moment that Remora was the second highest dignitary of the Chapter. "The question is whether the enemy's back. There are no bodies."

"These, ah—"

"These taluses. It would take ten yoke of oxen to drag them away, I suppose. No dead bios or chems."

"The, ah, Army, eh? To the Caldé. So I understood."

"Some soldiers went over to him, yes. Others who hadn't heard about him didn't, and were fighting their comrades here."

Remora nodded. "Unfortunate. Um, tragic."

"When this man Blood's bodyguards learned Caldé Silk had killed him, some attacked him and his soldiers. That's when Generalissimo Oosik and General Saba stormed the house."

"Lovely, hum?" Remora harbored a sneaking admiration for architecture as others cherish a vice. "Even, ah, despoiled. Pity. Pity. More so, possibly. No pretensions now. No more vulgar display. Wreckage more—um—romantic? Poetic." He favored Blood's torn lawns with a toothy smile.

Maytera Mint drew her soiled habit more tightly about her and for the hundredth time wished for her coif. "If we were to walk a little faster, Your Eminence, we could get out of this wind, whether the Ayuntamiento's come back or not."

"Of course, of course."

"And though I don't concede that Bison–"

"Those–um–corpses, General." Catching up, Remora strode along beside her, his lanky legs making a single step of two of hers. "You were about to, er, um, propose that we afford them an–ah–sanctified burial? It would be most inconvenient, I fear. Most inopportune!"

"Granted. But there must have been bodies, and I'd think more than a few. The Ayuntamiento's soldiers and this man's bodyguards would have been shooting from these windows."

Maytera Mint paused, drawing on her recent experiences to visualize the scene. "Floaters would have rushed the gate, and Guardsmen and General Saba's pterotroopers must have swarmed through every break in the wall. Then my troopers from the city, thousands of them. Some must have been killed, I'd think at least a hundred. Some of the bodyguards and soldiers must have been killed too. See that line of pockmarks? Buzz-gun fire. A floater's turret gun raked the front of the house."

"I, ah–"

For once she interrupted him. "We would have taken away our dead, or I hope we would. But what about theirs? They were retreating under fire, going down into the tunnels Sand talked about. Would they have dragged bodies along with them? I find it hard to believe, Your Eminence."

"If I may." Remora cleared his throat. "It seems to me that you have, ah, disposed of the, um, dead yourself, though I confess that I am no great hand at matters military."

"Nor I. I was appointed by Echidna, you must have heard of that. What little I know I've picked up as I went along."

"Defeating commanders vastly more–ah–schooled. I would conjecture, leastwise, that there must be something like our schola for the officers of the, er, Caldé's Guard. As we call them now, eh, General? The Civil Guard we used to phrase it, hey? Admirable, I, um, insist."

"I've lost to them, too, Your Eminence. Lost nearly as often as I've won." They were passing Scylla's fountain, now sheathed in ice.

"Though no great hand," Remora repeated, "I offer the, um, this hypothesis. Would not well regulated troops inter their dead? The generalissimo's men are, ah, proficient, to be sure, and we–ah–furnish a chaplain to each brigade. The, um, desiderata of that. Conduct military obsequies. Subsequently, please to follow me here, Mayt–General.

Would not such, er, troopers compel the, ah, your own, though not then under, as it were, your eye—"

"Make them bury the rest? Possibly." Maytera Mint, who was very tired, forced herself to stand straighter and square her shoulders. "More likely no compulsion was needed. If they had not thought of it themselves, seeing the Guard and Saba's pterotroopers loading their dead to take back to the city would suggest it. But what about the enemy dead? Where are they?"

"Within this desolate, ah, mansion. I dare say. They would not have abandoned its shelter, hey? Shot through its windows. You—um—proposed it yourself."

She pointed with the stick that held her white flag. "See where the wall's fallen? You can look into several rooms, and there's not a single body in any of them."

"Yet, ah—"

"Through the doorway, too." They had nearly reached the steps of Blood's portico. "That door would have been defended more strongly than any other point, and I can look right into the sellaria. There's not a one. Where are they?"

"I would, er, hazard that the victorious troops disposed of them afterward."

She shook her head vigorously. "Troopers who've won are never anxious to get the bodies of those they've killed out of sight, Your Eminence. Never! I've seen that much more often than I like. They're proud, and it's good for their morale. Yesterday Major Skin was begging, literally begging me, not to have bodies that had lain in the streets for days carted off. If the bodies are gone, it's because their friends came back for them. It would be interesting to see if there are graves behind the house. That's where they'd be, I imagine. By the wall, as far as possible from the road. Do you know if there are gardens in back?"

"I have never, um, had the pleasure." Remora started up the steps. "Nor has His Cognizance, I think. He, um, confided it to me a year or two past. We had been—um—dissecting? Decrying this, er, Blood's influence. Was never a, um, visitor within these—ah—despoiled walls."

"Neither have I, Your Eminence." Maytera Mint hiked up her skirt and started up the steps.

"To be sure. To be sure, General. I regret it. Regret it now. I will not dissemble, nor, um, ever. Seldom. To have seen this in its days of prosperity would–prosperity and peace, eh? The contrast 'twixt memory and the, um, less happy present. Do you follow me? Whereas one can now but picture . . . See that picture? Fine. Very fine indeed, eh? Torn. Might be refurbished yet, in skillful hands. Like the tali, eh?"

"I suppose." She had glanced at the ruined furniture, and was studying the shadowy doorways of further rooms. "He kept women here, didn't he? This bad man Blood who owned the house. Women–women who . . ."

"Enough, enough! Do not, um, perturb yourself, Maytera. General. A few such. An, er, select contingent. So I was given to understand upon the occasion of our–um–my *tête-à-tête,* eh? With old Quetzal. Do I, um, scandalize you? With His Cognizance. I am, ah, betimes inclined to be overfree. To presume upon an old friendship. A failing, I concede." Remora advanced to study the damaged Murtagon.

"Was this where it happened?"

"Where the women–ah?" He glanced back at her with a half smile. "No indeed."

"Where Caldé Silk killed this man Blood, and Sergeant Sand killed Councillor Potto."

"We've finer ones at the Palace, hey? Still it's nice and might be–ah–emended. In an, um, one of the anterooms as I understand it, General. May I ask why you wish to know? A, um, monument of some kind, possibly? A dedicational tablet of, er, bronze?"

"Because we know that the man who owned this house died in it, Your Eminence," Maytera Mint explained. "This Blood, with Councillor Potto. If their bodies aren't here, they've been removed by someone, and I'd think that if Generalissimo Oosik or even General Saba had done it I'd have heard. A councillor's body? Everyone would be arguing about what should be done with it, and I would certainly have heard."

Her tone grew crisp. "Now if you'll oblige me."

Remora, who was not used to being asked for favors in that peremptory fashion, looked around sharply.

"There seems to be no one here, though my informants . . . Never mind. Do you agree?"

"There is certainly no one in this room at present except–ah–ourselves. With regard to the, er, remainder of the, um, building, I–hum–further investigation."

"I've been listening carefully and heard nothing. The bodies may be in plain view or hidden by furniture or whatnot." Rather tardily Maytera Mint added, "Your Eminence. I'll search the rooms on this side. I'd like you to search the other. We needn't bother with the rest of the house, I think."

"If there are no, er, bodies, General," Remora smoothed the truant lock into place, "shall we return to the city—ah—forthwith? Might be wise, eh? We have no way of knowing what has transpired in our absence, hey?"

She nodded. "Agreed. We'll know then that they've been here and may return later. I'll leave one of Bison's officers to watch, with a few troopers. If we *do* find a body, either one, it should be safe to assume that the Ayuntamiento's troops have never come back at all. We can go back to the city at once and forget about this house."

"Wisely, er, spoken." Remora was already hurrying toward the first of his assigned rooms. "I shall inform you promptly should I discover a—ah—the mortal remains."

The anteroom Maytera Mint entered had, it appeared, been the owner's study. A massive mahogany desk, lavishly carved, stood against one wall, and there were shelves of books, mostly (she scanned the titles on a shelf at the level of her eyes) erotic if not pornographic: *Three Maids and Their Mistress, The Astonishing Exploits of a Virile Young Man and His Donkey, His Resistance Overcome* . . .

She turned away. What had it been like to be here under such a master? She tried and failed to picture the lives of the women who had endured it. They had been bad women, as the whorl judged, but that only meant that they had commanded defenses greatly inferior to her own.

Strange, how she had come to think in military metaphors during the past few days.

The desk drawers seemed apt to tell her a good deal about the owner, who counted for nothing now, and nothing about the Ayuntamiento and those who served it. She opened a drawer at random anyway, glanced at the papers it had held—all of them concerned in some fashion with money—shut it, and made sure no corpse lay concealed in the leg hole.

"General!"

Turning so quickly that the long, black skirt of her habit billowed about her, she hurried out of the study and across the sellaria. "What is it, Your Eminence?"

He met her at the doorway, visibly struggling to conceal his pleasure. "I have the–ah–it is my unhappy duty–"

"You've found a body. Whose?"

"The, um, late councillor's, I believe. If, perhaps, you would not care–"

"To see it? I must! Your Eminence, I've seen hundreds of bodies since this began. Thousands." There had been a time when she had found it nearly impossible to cut the throat of a goat; as she pushed past Remora, she reflected that she would find that difficult still, and find it literally impossible to cut a man's, even an enemy's. Yet she had made plans and given orders that had clogged entire streets with corpses.

"I took the, um, responsibility? The–ah–presumption of, er, tidying him up. On his back now, eh? Folded the arms, prior to calling you."

Potto lay almost at her feet, his arms crossed in such a way as to hide the wound Sand's slug had made just below his sternum. The graying hair that he had worn long trailed over Blood's lush carpet, and Maytera Mint found herself muttering, "He looks surprised."

"Doubtless he–ah–was." Remora cleared his throat. "Caught unawares, hey? Shot by one of his own. All in a, um, trice. So my prothonotary tells me. He–ah–Incus is his name, General. Patera Incus. He has, um, fallen prey in some–ah–wise to the notion that he's old Quetzal–"

She knelt beside the corpse, traced the sign of addition, and opened its card case.

"Mad, I fear. Deranged. Bit of rest, eh? He'll come to himself soon enough. General–ah–?"

"In the first place," Maytera Mint explained, "There may be papers of value in here. In the second, there's money, ten cards or so, and we need that very badly."

"I, ah, see."

Cards and papers vanished into her wide sleeve. "Where's the blood? Did you clean up his blood before you called to me, Your Eminence?"

"Through the heart, eh?" Remora's nasal tones sounded slightly strangled. "Not much bleeding then, eh? So I am–ah–apprised."

Gently at first, then with increased vigor, Maytera Mint rubbed the councillor's cheek. "This's a chem!"

"I—um—"

She looked up at Remora. "You knew."

"I—ah—suspected."

"You rolled him over, you said, Your Eminence. You folded his arms. You must have known."

"Then? Oh, yes, I—ah—confirmed, eh? I had, um, and—ah—Quetzal, eh? Old Quetzal. Wouldn't tell. Asked him once. More, actually. He, ah, er, wouldn't. Confides in me, eh? Nearly everything. Very, ah, delicate points. Sensitive matters, finances. Everything. But he—ah—wouldn't."

Suddenly Remora was on his knees beside her. "General—ah—General. Alone here, hey? No one but, er, ourselves. May I call you Maytera?"

She ignored it. "There'll be the question of burial. A dozen questions, really. You must have realized I'd find out."

"I—ah—did. Indeed. Not so swiftly, however. You are most—er—perspicacious."

"Then why didn't you say so? Why all that nonsense about blood?"

"Because I—Incus. Patera Incus. And old Quetzal, eh? My position is, er, delicate. Imperiled. Maytera, hear me, I—ah—beg you. Yes, beg. Implore."

She nodded. "I'm listening. What is it?"

"Incus, my prothonotary. Was. You know him?"

She shook her head. "Just tell me."

"He's been appointed Prolocutor. By, um, Scylla. He says it, I mean. Credits it himself, eh? Convinced. Spoke to him yesterday, but he—you . . ."

"Me?" For a second, Maytera Mint felt she was missing some vital clue. It dawned upon her, and she rocked backward to sit cross-legged on the carpet, her head in her hands.

"Maytera? Er, General?"

She looked up at Remora. "I was appointed by Echidna, in front of thousands of people. Is that it, Your Eminence?"

Remora's mouth opened and shut silently.

"So you know it happened. All those witnesses. And I've been successful, as you say. The victorious commander, chosen for us by the gods. Even Bison and the captain talk like that, and then there's Patera Silk."

Remora nodded miserably.

"Everyone says he's been appointed by Great Pas to be our caldé, even Maytera Marble. He's been successful, too, so it looks like the gods have decided to choose leaders for us, and if this Patera Incus is going to be the new Prolocutor, he'll want to pick his own coadjutor."

"Nor—ah—um—worse. If he—ah—old Quetzal, you know. Resourceful. Cunning. Seen it myself, hundreds of times, eh? Ayuntamiento had the force, but he'd get 'round them. Get 'round Lemur and Loris, all of them. Old man, hey? Foolish old man. What they think. His Cognizance. Quetzal. But sly, Mayt—General. Very sly. Deep."

She made a small sound of encouragement.

"Compromise. I—ah—sense it. I am not, um, clever, General. Try to be, indeed. Try. Some have said—well, it pares no parsnips. But not like old Quetzal. Experienced, though. My—ah—self. Conferences, negotiations. And I wind it. Wind it already. Be coadjutor, Incus. Obvious, eh? First thing anybody would, er, formulate. Old Quetzal would—ah—visualize? Comprehend the whole before Incus finished. Old man. Die soon, hey? A year, two years, to—ah—fit yourself into the position, Patera. I'll be gone. I can, um, hear him as I—we—speak. So I didn't dare, eh? Tell you. You see my predicament? The—ah—Loris. Galago. All the rest. Chems, every one of them. I suspected it for years. Meeting with this one, that one, entire days, sometimes. Saw them up close. Quetzal knows, he must."

"But His Cognizance wouldn't talk about it?"

"No. Ah—no. Too sensitive. Even for me, eh? He, Incus. I told you?"

"You told me he says Scylla's made him Prolocutor."

"He, um, offered me . . ."

One bony hand pushed back the straying lock, and Maytera Mint saw how violently that hand shook. "He offered you . . . ?"

"An—ah—appointment. A position. He was," Remora swallowed, "not abusive. It was not, I judge, his intent to be—ah—disparage. He said that I—I refused, to be sure. His prothonotary. His, ah, I—I—I . . ."

Maytera Mint nodded. "I see."

"We have been, er, companions, Maytera. Coworkers—ah—partners in peace, hey? Son and daughter of the Chapter. We have conferred, and the same—um—consecrated vision has inspired us both. I well—ah—recol-

lect our first meeting. You averred with—um—coruscant eyes that peace
was your, er, sole desire once you had—ah, um—executed the will of the
gods. I affirmed? Avowed that it was mine likewise. In concert we have
conferred with Brigadier Erne and the caldé. You are a hero, um, hero-
ine to the—ah—populace. There is talk of a statue, hey? A word from
you, your support . . ."

"Be quiet," she told him. "I haven't had a moment to get used to the
idea that the Ayuntamiento's made up of chems, and now this."

"If I, ah—"

"Be quiet, I said!" She drew a deep breath, running the fingers of
both hands through her short brown hair. "To begin with, no, you may
not call me Maytera. Not in private, and not any other time. If His Cognizance will release me, I mean to return to secular life. I," another
breath, "may marry. We'll see. As for you, if this Patera Incus has in fact
been named Prolocutor by Scylla, then he *is* Prolocutor, regardless of
any arrangement that he and Patera Quetzal may make. I can readily
imagine a younger man of great sanctity deferring to a much older one.
Viewed in a certain light, it would be an act of noble self-renunciation.
But it wouldn't alter the fact. He would be our Prolocutor, though he
wasn't called so. Since he proposed that you become his prothonotary,
plainly you're not to be coadjutor any longer. No doubt Patera Quetzal
is, in solemn truth, coadjutor. That being so, I'll call you Patera."

"My dear young woman!"

Her look silenced him. "I'm not your dear young woman, or anyone's. I'm thirty-six, and I assure you that for a woman it's no longer
young. Call me General, or I'll make your life a great deal less pleasant
than it has been."

A door at the far end of the room opened, and someone who was
neither Mint nor Remora applauded. "Brava, my dear young general!
Simply marvelous! You ought to be on the stage."

He waddled over to them, a short, obese man with bright blue eyes,
a cheerful round face, and hair so light as to be nearly blond. "But as for
accepting an Ayuntamiento of chems, you need not trouble. I'm no
chem, though I confess that the object before you is something of the
kind."

Remora gasped, having recognized him.

"This augur and I are old—I really can't say friends. Acquaintances.
You, I feel sure, are the rebels' famous General Mint." The stranger gig-

gled. "Presumably you aim at supreme power, which would make you the Govern-Mint. I like that! I'm Councillor Potto. Curtain. Did you wish to speak to me?"

For a fleeting moment in which his heart nearly stopped, it seemed to Silk that he had seen Hyacinth among the cheering pedestrians. Before he could shout to his bearers, the woman turned her head and the illusion ended. He had been ready, he realized as he settled back among the cushions, to spring out of the litter.

I need my glasses, he thought. My old ones, which I can't possibly get back, or some new ones.

Oreb fluttered on his shoulder. "Good Silk!"

"Crazed Silk," he told his bird. "Mad and foolish Silk. I mistook another woman for her."

"No see."

"My own thought exactly. Several times I've dreamed my mother was alive. Have I told you about that?"

Oreb whistled.

"For a minute or two after I woke up, I believed it, and I was so happy. This was like that." Leaning from the right side of the litter, he addressed the head bearer. "You needn't go so fast. You'll wear yourselves out."

The man grinned and bobbed his head.

Silk settled back again. Their speed was increasing. No doubt the bearers felt it a question of honor; when one carried the caldé, one ran. Otherwise ordinary people who had never had the privilege of carrying the caldé's litter might think him on an errand of no importance. Which would never do; if his errand were of no importance, neither were his bearers.

"I've got twenty Guardsmen looking for her," he told Oreb. "That's not enough, since they didn't find her, but it's all we could spare with the Fourth Brigade holding out on the north side, and the Ayuntamiento in the tunnels."

Mention of the tunnels made Oreb croak unhappily.

At what amounted to a dead run, the litter swayed, yawed, and swerved off Sun Street onto Lamp. Leaning out Silk said, "Music Street—I thought I made it clear. A block east."

The head bearer's head bobbed as before.

"If twenty Guardsmen can't find her, Oreb, I certainly can't; and last night I didn't. We didn't, I ought to say. So we need help, and I can think of three places—no, four—where we may get it. Today we're going to try them all. Most of the fires are out, and Maytera Mint and Oosik can actually fight better without me in the way; so although the physician says I should be in bed, and I'm not supposed to have a minute to myself, I intend to take as many hours as necessary."

Yawing as before, the litter turned onto a still narrower street that Silk did not recognize.

"It's up to the gods, I'm afraid. I don't trust them—not even the Outsider, who seems to trust me—but they may smile on us yet."

"Find girl?"

He had lost his desire to talk, but the intensity of his emotions drove the words forth. "What did he *want* with her!" As he spoke, the litter sped past a shop with a zither and a dusty bassoon in its window.

But Caldé Silk of Viron did not see them.

"This is the kitchen?" Maytera Mint looked around her in surprise. It was the largest that she had ever seen.

"There are, ah, alternatives," Remora ventured. "Still entire, eh? Equally, hum, unsigned by Sabered Sphigx."

"I find it cozy," Potto declared. "For one thing, there's food, though your troops, my dear young General, made off with a lot. I like food, even if I can't eat it. For another, I'm a good host, eager for the comfort of my guests, and it's easy to heat. Behold this noble stove and laden woodbox. I'm happily immune to drafts, but you aren't. I'm determined to make you comfortable. Those other rooms offer the chilly attractions of a society beauty. This will provide warmth and tea, even soup." He giggled. "All the solid virtues of an old nurse. Besides, there are a great many sharp knives, and I'm always encouraged by the presence of sharp knives."

"You can't be here alone," Maytera Mint said.

Potto grinned. "Do you propose to attack me if I am?"

"Certainly not."

"You have an azoth, the famous one given you by Silk. I won't search you for it now."

"I left it with Colonel Bison. If I had come armed after calling for a truce, you'd be entitled to kill me."

"I am anyhow," Potto told her. He picked up a stick of firewood and snapped it between his hands. "The rules of war protect armies and their auxiliaries. Yours is a rebellion, not a war, and rebels get no such protection. Patera there knows that's the truth. Look at his face."

"I—ah—assert the privilege of my cloth."

"You can. You haven't fought, so you're entitled to it. The General has and isn't. It's all very simple."

When neither replied, Potto added, "Speaking of cloth, I forgot to say that the rules apply only to soldiers and those auxiliaries who wear their city's uniform, as General Saba does. You, my dear General, don't. The upshot is that though I can't offer violence to your armies as long as the truce holds, I'm entitled to break both your leggies if I want to, and even to wring your necky. Sit down, there's a cozy little table right over there. I'll build a fire and put the kettle on."

They sat, Remora tucking the rich overrobe he wore around his legs, Maytera Mint as she might have in the cenoby, her delicate hands folded in her lap, and her head bowed.

Potto filled one of the stove's fireboxes and stroked a stick of kindling. It burst into flame, not merely at one end like a torch, but along its entire length. He tossed it into the firebox and shoved the firebox back in place with an angry grinding of iron.

"He, um, intrigues to separate us," Remora whispered. "A—ah—hallowed? Elementary stratagem, General. I shall, um, cleave to you, eh? If you in, ah, analogous fashion—"

"Maytera. Call me Maytera, please, Your Eminence, when we're alone."

"Indeed. Indeed! O, ah, *soror neque enim ignari sumus ante malorum. O passi graviora, dabit Pas his quoque finem.*"

Potto was filling a teakettle. Without turning his head, he said, "I have sharp ears. Don't say I didn't warn you."

Maytera Mint looked up. "Then I'm spared the necessity of raising my voice. Are you really Councillor Potto? We came to negotiate with the Ayuntamiento, not with anyone we chanced to meet. If you are, whose body was that?"

"Yes." Potto put the kettle on the stove. "Mine. Have you more questions?"

"Certainly. Are you willing to stop all this bloodshed?"

"It bothers you, doesn't it?" He pulled out a stout stool and sat down so heavily the floor shook.

"Seeing good and brave troopers die? Watching someone who was eager to obey me a few seconds ago writhing and bleeding in the street? It does!"

"Well, it doesn't me, and I don't understand why it should you. I never have. Call it a gift. There are people who can listen to music all evening, then go home and write everything down, and others who can run faster and farther than a horse. Did you know that? Mine's a less amazing gift, though it's brought me success. I don't feel pain I don't feel. Is that what you call a tautology? It's what life has taught me. I give it to you for nothing."

Remora nodded, his long face longer than ever. "I, er, vouchsafe it might be included under that—ah—rubric."

"Councillor."

"Why—ah—indeed. I had no, um, intention—"

"Thanks. I'm the only member who forced his way in, or had to. Did you know that, either of you?"

Maytera Mint shook her head.

"We're all related, as you can see from our names. Lemur and Loris were brothers. Lemur's dead. You don't have to look surprised, I know you know. He packed the Ayuntamiento with relatives, back before Patera here was born. I came to him. I approached him forthrightly and fairly. He'd brought in Galago, a second cousin by courtesy. I was much closer, and I said so. He said he'd take it under advisement. A week later—there'd been this and that, you know, nothing serious—he tried to have me killed. I saw to it that the man's flesh was served to us at dinner, and dessert was his head in lemon sherbert. Lemur jerked away from it, and I scooped up a little sherbet with my fingers and ate it. I took the oath next day. Councillor Potto. My cousins soon discovered that I was a useful friend, not just an unpleasant relative."

Maytera Mint nodded. "You're proud of being useful, as everyone who is, is entitled to be. Now you have a chance to be of great service to our whole city."

"We have, ah, ventured forth in good faith," Remora put in. "The general has come unarmed. My—ah—vocation prohibits weapons. Such, at least, is my own opinion, though the—our caldé's may differ. I ask you, Councillor, whether you, er, similarly. Are we intermediaries? Or, um, captives?"

"You want to go before your tea's ready?" Potto waved in the direction of the door. "Make the experiment, Patera."

"My duty, um, confines me."

"Then you're a prisoner, but not mine. Dear young General Mint, wouldn't you like to know how I manage to be alive in the kitchen and dead in the drawing room?"

"There were two of you, clearly." She had taken her big wooden prayer beads from her pocket; she ran them through her fingers, comforted by their familiar shapes.

"No, only one, and that one is neither here nor there. As we aged, Cousin Tarsier made us new bodies out of chems. Lemur got the first one, and the rest of us later as we came to need them, bodies we can work from our beds. I can't enjoy food, but I eat. I'm feeding intravenously right now."

"What became of the chems?" Maytera Mint managed to keep her voice steady. "Of their minds?"

"I thought you were going to ask me whether he made the others more than one."

"No. Clearly he did, or someone did. But you got this body from another person. And—and changed it to look like you? You must have. Did he consent to any of that?"

"The logical question is whether there are two of all of us." Potto struck the table with his fist. "You didn't even ask how I got the wood to burn. How am I supposed to deal with someone who won't stick to the point?"

Remora began, "I, ah—" But Potto was not through. "By sticking with the point myself. That's it! I may soon stick with one so well that it sticks out your back." He turned to Remora. "Yes, Patera. You were about to say . . . ?"

"I was, um, speculating, Councillor, upon how you ignited that wood so, er, effortlessly. I, um, hope that you will, um, consent to—ah—illuminate that matter for us."

"I am not going to sit here teaching a butcher chemistry. Can't either of you understand that once I've told you what I want, I don't want it? What are *you* doing here anyway? Dear General Mint's the leader, after Silk. Why are you here?"

"To, er, mediate. We, um, His Cognizance and, hum—"

"To bring peace," Maytera Mint declared. "Caldé Silk has offered to let all of you keep your seats under the Charter. Considering all that's happened, I think it very generous."

"For life?"

Remora touched her arm, and she found it easy to interpret the gesture. "Is there a provision for life tenure? If so, I imagine it might be invoked." Remora shook his head; the motion was slight, but she saw it.

Potto smiled; it was so unexpected that she wondered for a moment whether she had unwittingly promised a return to power.

Seeing it, Remora positively beamed. "Better! Oh, indeed! Must be friends, eh? Friends can make peace, foes, er, unable."

"You misunderstand my expression, Patera."

"I, um, hail and approve it. Time—ah—sufficient for understanding, er, presently. Maybe I put forward a proposal, Councillor? General? My wish, a heartfelt suggestion. That we—ah—solemnly convene at the present moment, offering our prayer to the Nine. Our petition, if you will, that—"

"Shut up," Potto snapped. "I've got the key, and you go on blathering. Caldé Silk sent you, General. Is that right?"

"He would approve of my coming, certainly. For days we've been trying to reach you councillors on our glasses. I thought we might try this."

When Potto did not reply, she added, "His Eminence was chosen as an intermediary by your Brigadier Erne and our caldé. Soon after, as I understand it, His Cognizance offered his help as well. We were and are overjoyed. I would hope—"

"You can't speak for him," Potto told her. "You may think you can, or that Patera here can, but you can't. I've known him a long time, and there's not a more malicious and unpredictable person in the city. Not even me. You're a general, General?"

She nodded. "Appointed by Divine Echidna in a theophany. My instructions," she amended them mentally in the interests of peace, "were to tear down the Alambrera and see to it that Viron remained loyal to Scylla. If you're asking my position in the command structure, Caldé Silk is the head of our government, civil as well as military. Generalissimo Oosik is our supreme military commander. I am in charge of the armed populace, and General Skate commands the Caldé's Guard."

Potto tittered. "Then you've a firm grasp of the military situation. I don't. Lemur was our military man. Explain our circumstances to me, General, so we can start together."

"You're serious?"

He rocked with silent merriment. "Never more."

"As you wish. After Ophidian Echidna's theophany, we had about thirty thousand troopers. Not that there were that many witnesses, or half that many, but a great many who heard what had happened from others joined us. Some were Guardsmen, none, I think, above captain. You, the Ayuntamiento, called out the Army, giving you something like seven thousand soldiers, besides the twenty-four thousand troopers of your Civil Guard."

"Go on," Potto told her. "None of this is quite right, but it's interesting."

"My figures for the Guard come from Generalissimo Oosik, who was certainly in a position to know. Those for the Army, from Sergeant Sand, the leader of those brave soldiers who saw that true loyalty lay in siding with the caldé."

Potto was still grinning. "Excuse the interruption."

"I was about to say that since then we've gained strength, and you've lost it. By shadelow, we had nearly reached our present total of about fifty thousand. I'm referring to my own troops here. That night, every brigade of your Civil Guard went over to the caldé except the Fourth. The Fourth and the Third, which was the generalissimo's, had been holding the Palatine. The Fourth, commanded by Brigadier Erne, was driven from it next day, and into the northern suburbs."

"Where it still is."

"That's correct. We had fires all over the city to fight, hundreds of them, and we've been busy trying to get ourselves organized. When the Alambrera surrendered, we got thousands of slug guns and hundreds of thousands of rounds of ammunition. We had to see to it that they went to people of good character. Furthermore, there's a feeling that the Fourth Brigade might come over to our side in another day or two. Caldé Silk and Generalissimo Oosik think so, and so do I. I'm told that His Cognizance is of the same opinion."

Remora cleared his throat. "It was, hmp!, Brigadier Erne who, um, entreated me to—ah—initiate? To set in motion these negotiations. I, er, thereafter—shortly thereafter—sought out the caldé, whom, um, approved likewise. I can—am able and—ah—authorized. The Brigadier's viewpoint."

"Not now," Potto told him. "General, could you crush the Fourth Brigade? Suppose Silk ordered it."

"Certainly, in two or three hours. Less if I had a few taluses and floaters, as well as my people. But we'd rather not, obviously, in view of the loss of—"

"Not to me!" Potto chortled. "It's not obvious to me! Is the bloodshed really what's bothering you?"

"I should think it would bother anyone."

"Well, you're right, but you're wrong too. The bloodshed wouldn't bother me, but why shouldn't you take five thousand prime troopers if you can get them? We would. Are those the only reasons, General?"

"I'll be frank. There's another aspect. You, by which I mean the Ayuntamiento, are down in the tunnels with most of the Army and a few troopers."

"Nearly a thousand."

"Setting them aside, you must have about seven thousand soldiers down there."

Potto's grin widened.

"More? Very well, if you say so. Seven thousand was our estimate. In any case, if we got deeply involved in an attack on the Fourth, which shouldn't be our primary objective anyway, you might make a sortie from the tunnels and strike us from behind. According to reports I've had, it takes at least four of my troopers to match a soldier, which means that your seven thousand—that's the figure we discussed—are equivalent to twenty-eight thousand of mine. We didn't feel we could risk it. I should say that we don't feel we can as yet."

Potto nodded rather too enthusiastically. "Someplace in all that verbiage was a morsel that seemed intelligent, my dear General. You said our Guard, or what's left, wasn't what you really wanted to destroy. That it was us. Why don't you come down after us?"

Remora looked deeply distressed. "Do you, er, Councillor . . . Is this—ah—productive?"

"I think so. You'll see. Answer me if you can, General."

"Because the tunnels are too defensible. I haven't been in them, but they've been described to me. A dozen soldiers could hold a place like that against a hundred troopers. If we've got to, we'll find a way, digging shafts and so on. But we'd rather not, which is why I'm here. Also there's another consideration. You spoke of destroying the Fourth. Clearly, we don't want to. Still less do we want to destroy the Army, which is of immense value to our city. We know that—"

"You are an amazing woman." Potto pushed his stool back and crossed the big kitchen to the stove. "A woman who talks sense whenever it suits her but can't hear a kettle boil."

"Women generally talk sense, if men will listen to it."

"Those who are generals generally do, anyway. You're right about the Fourth, and right about the Army and not tackling the tunnels, though you really don't understand the situation at all. I'm our head spy, did you know that? I was in charge of Lemur's spies, and now I've got Loris's." Potto tittered. "Who are generally the same, General, and mine. Do you really think all the troopers in the city are yours or ours? You simply can't be that simple!" He lifted the big copper teakettle off the stove; it was spurting steam.

Maytera Mint pursed her lips.

"There are, um, an—ah—minuscule? Likewise. Token, eh? An—ah—few hundred . . ."

"Two hundred, more or less," she supplied. "Two hundred Trivigaunti pterotroopers commanded by General Saba, who also commands the airship. Two hundred's a very small force, as His Eminence says, though with supporting fire from the airship even a small force might accomplish a great deal. General Saba has offered her help when we move against the Fourth, by the way."

"How kind." Potto had carried the steaming teakettle to their table.

"Not to you, Councillor. I realize that. But to us it is. It's a gesture of good will from the Rani to the new government of Viron, and as such is greatly appreciated."

"Your diplomacy flourishes." He raised the teakettle.

"It does. It's in its infancy, but it does." Maytera Mint stood. "We need a teapot, and tea. Sugar, milk, and a lemon, if His Eminence takes lemon. I'll look for them."

"I was about to ask you if my face looks dusty."

"I beg your pardon, Councillor?"

"Whether it's dusty. Look carefully, will you? Maybe we should go to a window, where the light will be better."

"I don't see any dust." She was struck, unexpectedly and unpleasantly, by the lack of warmth in that face, which seemed so animated. Maytera Marble's familiar metal mask held a whorl of humility and compassion; this, for all its seeming plumpness and high color, was as cold as Echidna's serpents.

"It's been packed away for years, you see." Leaning back at an impossible angle, Potto scratched the tip of his nose with the steaming spout of the teakettle. "I'm the youngest member of the Ayuntamiento, dear General. Did you know that?"

Maytera Mint shook her head.

"Just the same, they thought this seemed too young, and asked me to replace it." He contrived to lean even farther backward. A trickle of boiling water escaped the spout. "You don't know about the Rani's horde, either. Do you?"

"What about it?"

"My face?" Potto jabbed the spout toward it. "It was in storage. I said that, why didn't you listen? Now I can't see as clearly as I did. I may have dust in my eyes."

Before Maytera Mint could stop him, he raised the teakettle and tilted it. Seething water cascaded down onto his nose and eyes. Remora exclaimed, "Oh, you gods!" as Maytera Mint jumped back from the hissing spray.

"There. That ought to do it." Straightening up, Potto regarded her through wide blue eyes again, blinking hard to clear them of boiling drops. "That's much better. I can see everything. I hope you can, too, my dear young General. The Rani's horde has already set out, and there's sixty thousand foot and fifteen thousand cavalry. I haven't the luxury of an airship to keep watch on Viron's enemies, but I do the best I can. Seventy-five thousand battle-hardened troopers, with their support troops, a supply train of fifteen thousand camels, and a labor battalion of ten thousand men." Potto turned to Remora. "Trivigaunte's men are of your school, Patera. No weapons. Or anyway they're supposed to be."

Remora had regained his composure. "If this extensive and, ah, formidable force is—ah—marching? Marching, you said, eh? Then I take it that it can't be marching here, or you—um—the Ayuntamiento, more formally. Terms of surrender, hey?"

Potto tittered.

Maytera Mint squared her shoulders. "I wouldn't laugh, Councillor. His Eminence is entirely correct. If the Rani is sending us a force of that size, your cause is doomed."

"It's just as I feared," Potto told her. He held up the teakettle. "Do you think it's cooled too much?"

"To make tea?" She took an involuntary step backward. "I doubt it."

"To wash eyes, so they can see. I think you're right. Boiling water stays hot for a long time."

"I came under a flag of truce!"

He reached for her, moving much faster than so fat a man should have been able to. She whirled and ran, feeling his fingertips brush her habit, reached the door a hand's breadth ahead of him, and flung herself through. An arm hooked her like a lamb; another pinned her own arms to her sides. Her face was crushed against musty cloth.

Sounding near, Potto said, "Bring her back in here."

Not so near, words failed Remora. "You cannot—I mean to say simply cannot—woman's a sibyl! You, you—"

"Oh, be quiet," Potto told him. "Bend her over backwards, Spider. Make her look up at this."

Abruptly there was light and air. The man who had caught her was as tall as Remora and as wide as Potto; he held her by her hair and dropped to one knee, pulling her across the other.

"My son." Looking up at his heavy, unshaven chin, she found it horribly hard to keep from sounding frightened. "Do you realize what you're doing?"

The man, presumably Spider, glanced to one side, presumably at Potto. "How's this, Councillor?"

She rolled her eyes without finding him, and the thick fingers would not let her turn her head.

His voice came from a distance. "I'm putting the kettle back. We can't have it cooling off while I give you the rules."

Remora entered her field of view, seeming as lofty as a tower when he bent above them. "If there is—ah—Maytera. General. Anything I can do . . . ?"

"There is," she said. "Let Bison know what happened."

"Go back to your seat," Potto told Remora, and he vanished. "Didn't you wonder, my dear General," it was Potto's cheerful, round face opposite Spider's now, "how I happened to be so near my own corpse? Or what became of Blood's? Blood was stabbed by your friend Silk. Let's not call him Caldé. We're no longer being so polite."

"Let me up, and I'll be happy to ask you."

"It won't be necessary. Blood's body has been hauled away already, you see. And you do see, don't you? At present. I ordered that my own wasn't to be touched, because I think we may be able to fix it. I came in person to pick it up, with a few of my most trusted spy catchers. Spider's their jefe. I'd use soldiers, but they're awfully sensitive, it seems, to mention of a caldé, though you wouldn't think it to look at them."

From a distance, Remora called, "Councillor? Councillor!"

She shut her eyes. If she was never to see again, the last thing she saw should not be the high smoke-grimed ceiling of the kitchen in this ruined villa. Echidna, rather, her face filling the Sacred Window. Her mother's face. Bison's, with its quick eyes and curling black beard. Her room in the cenoby. Children playing, Maytera Marble's group because she had always wanted them instead of the older girls this year and the older boys before Patera Pike died. Auk's face, so ugly and serious, more precious than a stack of cards. Bison's. Cage Street, and the floaters firing as the white stallion thundered toward them.

"Did you hear that, my dear General?"

"Hear what?" Maytera Mint opened her eyes, remembering too late that scalding water might be poured into them.

"Tell her, Patera! Tell her!" Potto was giggling like a girl of twelve, giggling so hard that he could hardly talk.

"I—ah—um—proposed an, er, substitution."

"He wants to take your place. Really, it's too funny."

She tried to speak, and found that her eyes were filling with hot tears, irony so cheap and obvious as to be unbearable. "No, Your Eminence. But . . . But thank you."

"He, um, Potto. Councillor. He wishes to, um, secure your—ah—collaboration, hey? I, um, endeavored to point out that to, er, spare me you would, eh? Whatever he wants."

"I can already make you do anything I want." Potto was back. He held the teakettle over her. "What I'm trying to do is what she's done for years. Educate." Giggling, he covered his mouth with his free hand. "Wash the dust out. Clarify her vision. Have I explained the rules?"

"Er—no."

"Then I will. I have to. You want to save her, Patera?"

She could actually hear Remora's teeth chatter. She had always supposed the business about chattering teeth was a sort of verbal convention, like hair standing on end.

"You made your offer, and I said no. But you can save me the trouble of washing her eyes."

"I, um, every effort."

"I'm going to ask questions. Educational questions. If her answers are right, we postpone the eyebath. Or if yours are. Ready? Spider, what about you? When you see the kettle tip, you'll have to hold her tight and keep your hands clear."

"Any time, Councillor."

"I'll start with an easy one. That's the best way, don't you think? If you really want children to learn. If you aren't just showing off. Did you know Silk's friend Doctor Crane?"

She shut her eyes again, finding it difficult to think. "Know him? No. Maytera Marble mentioned him once, the nice doctor who let her ride in his litter. I don't think I ever saw him. I'm sure I haven't met him."

"And you never will. He's dead." Potto sounded pleased. "Your turn, Patera. What about you?"

"Crane, eh? A doctor? Can't, um, place him."

"He was a spy. Let's give the poor fellow his due. He was a master spy, some say the Rani's best. Trivigaunte had more spies in Viron than any other city. It still does, though they have no jefe now. Why do you think that is, Maytera? More spies than Urbs or Palustria?"

"All I can do is guess." Her mouth was dry; she tried unsuccessfully to swallow. "The Rani's a woman, but all the other cities near ours have male rulers. She may have been more sensitive to the danger you and your cousins presented."

"Not bad. Can you improve on that, Patera?"

"I, ah, cheating."

Potto giggled. "Double credit for it. Go ahead."

"His Cognizance, eh? He told me. Not in so many words, eh? No mountains. First, um, er—"

"Objective," Potto supplied.

"Indeed. Next, ah, year. Spring. Not long now, hey, Councillor? Winter has, um, commenced."

"General, this is your area of expertise. Say another force is opposing yours, which is larger. Would you rather fight your way across a mountain range or a desert?"

"I'd want to see the desert," she hedged.

"You can't see either one, and if you won't answer you won't see anything." The teakettle tilted a little.

"Then I prefer the desert."

"Why?"

"Because fighting in mountains would be like fighting in tunnels. There would be narrow passes, in which we'd have to go at the enemy head-on. In a desert we could get around them."

"Correct. Patera, I haven't been giving you many chances, so you first. Two cities I'll call Viron and Trivigaunte are separated by a lake and a desert. A big lake, though it's been getting smaller and turning brackish. That's the situation, and here's the question. If the easiest city for Viron to attack is Trivigaunte, what's easiest for Trivigaunte? Think carefully."

"For, ah, them?" Remora's voice quavered. "Us, I should say. Viron."

"Do you agree, my dear General?"

She had begun a short prayer to Echidna while Remora was speaking; after murmuring the final phrase she said, "There could be other answers, but that's the most probable. Viron."

"I'm putting the kettle on again," Potto told her. "Not because you've passed, but because you may fail right here, and I want the water hot enough to do the job. Listen carefully, because we're going from geography to arithmetic. Listen, and think. Are you ready?"

She compelled her mind and lips. "I suppose so."

Potto tittered. "Are you, Patera?"

"Ah . . . I wish, Councillor—"

"Save it for later. It's time for arithmetic. The Rani of Trivigaunte has seventy-five thousand crack troopers in Viron. The so-called caldé's general has fifty thousand untrained ones, and the traitor commanding the Caldé's Guard has about eighteen thousand fit for duty, of doubtful loyalty. If these numbers have you mixed up, I don't blame you. Would you like me to stop here and repeat them, General?"

"Let me hear the rest."

"We're getting to the crux. Rani, seventy-five thousand. You, fifty thousand. Oosik, eighteen thousand. All these are troopers, armed bios. Now then, the Ayuntamiento, which opposes all three of them, has eight thousand two hundred soldiers and a thousand troopers underground, and another five thousand on the surface. The question is, *who rules Viron?* Answer, Patera."

"The—ah—you do. The Ayuntamiento."

"One drop for that," Potto said. "I'll fetch the kettle."

Maytera Mint squeezed her eyes shut, clenching her teeth as a single scalding drop struck her forehead. Locked in a private nightmare of fear and pain, she heard the opening of the door as if it were leagues away. A new voice spoke in the reedy tones of an old man: "What's this?"

Remora, overjoyed: *"Your Cognizance!"*

Almost carelessly, Potto said: "This is a nice surprise, I had men posted. Another prisoner's welcome, just the same."

She squinted upward. The sere old face over hers was one she had seen only at a distance; she had not realized then how its eyes glittered.

"Release her!" Quetzal snapped. "Let her go. Now!"

She tried to smile as Spider inquired, "Councillor?"

"Class dismissed for the present. It may resume soon, so think about the material." He sounded angry.

Spider stood, and she fell to the floor.

"I've talked to your cousin Loris," Quetzal told Potto, "and I've come to give you the news I brought him. If you decide to detain me afterward, it's the risk I run."

Potto spoke to Spider. "This old fox is the Prolocutor. If that's going to bother you, say so."

"Anything you want, Councillor."

"He's worth two of the general and ten of the butcher. Don't forget it. Old man, what tricks have you cooked up?" Maytera Mint scrambled to her feet, trying not to step on the hem of her habit.

"No tricks, Councillor. There was a theophany during my sacrifice at the Grand Manteion." Simultaneously, Maytera Mint received the impression that Quetzal was never excited, and that he was excited now.

Potto snorted and set his steaming teakettle on the table. "Another one? Who was it this time? Sphigx?"

Quetzal shook his head. "Pas."

"Pas is dead!"

Quetzal turned from Potto. "Great Pas, Maytera. Lord Pas, the Father of the Seven. If it wasn't him, it was his ghost. Which in point of fact is what the god himself said."

Chapter 2

His Name Is Hossaan

He himself had shut this door from inside and shot the bolt; it had been the final action of his exorcism. But if this door (the obscure side door of what had been a manteion, and what many passers-by no doubt assumed was a manteion still) was used to admit patrons who did not want to be seen entering Orchid's, there should be someone to answer his knock. By summer habit, he squinted up to gauge the width of the narrowing sun; it was masked by clouds dark with rain or snow, and the awe-inspiring mummy-colored bulk of the Trivigaunti airship.

He knocked again. His bearers had put down the litter and were making themselves comfortable. Did he dare risk their seeing him pound on a door to which nobody came? What would Commissioner Newt have to say about the effect on his prestige and popularity? What would Oosik say? Would it replace the fighting as the talk of the city?

He was smiling at the thought when the door was opened by a small and markedly unattractive woman with a faded rag over her graying hair. "Come—uh. It ain't anymore, Patera."

"I am Orchid's spiritual advisor," Silk told her firmly. "Admit me." The woman backed away; he stepped inside and bolted the door behind him. "Take me to her."

"I'm cleaning up in here." She eyed Oreb with disfavor.

Silk conceded privately that the former manteion could use a cleaning. He glanced up at the stage to see whether the new backdrop was as blasphemous as the one he had cut down, and was illogically pleased to find that it was merely obscene.

"She'll be in her room. She might not be up yet."

"Take me to her," he repeated, and added, "At once!"

"I won't knock." The small woman sounded frightened.

"Never mind. I remember the way." He pushed past her and strode across the former manteion with scarcely a twinge from his ankle. Here was the step on which he had sat to talk to Musk. Musk was dead now. The memory of Musk's tortured face returned.

The courtyard beyond the manteion was deserted but by no means empty, littered with scraps of food over which crows and pigeons squabbled, spilled liquors, bottles, and broken glass. Oreb, bigger than the biggest crow, watched fascinated, cocking his head this way and that.

Orpine's naked corpse had sprawled on this wooden stair. There was no point in looking for bloodstains today, or in trying not to step on such stains as might be present. Silk climbed, his eyes resolutely fixed on the gallery above.

What faith he'd had then! That Silk would be praying now, as confident as a child that the gods heard each word, a prayer to Molpe as patroness of the day, and one to Pas, who was as dead as Crane, Orpine, and Musk. Most of all, that earlier Silk would have prayed devoutly to the Outsider, though the Outsider had warned that he would send no aid.

Yet the Outsider had come with healing when he had lain near death. And to be more accurate (Silk paused at the top of the steps, remembering) the Outsider had not actually said that he would get no help, but warned him to expect none—which was not precisely the same thing.

Buoyed by the thought, he walked along the creaking gallery to the door that Crane had opened when he came out to examine Orpine's body, and was about to open it himself when it was opened from within.

He blinked, gasped, and blinked again. Oreb, whom few things surprised, whistled before croaking, " 'Lo, girl."

"Hi, Oreb. Hello, Patera. All the blessings on you this afternoon and all that."

Silk smiled, finding it easier than he had expected; there was nothing to be gained by berating her, surely. "Chenille, it's good to see you. I've been wondering where you were. I have people searching for you and Auk."

"You thought I was finished with this." The expression of her coarse, flat-cheeked face was by no means easy to read, but she sounded despondent.

"I hoped you were," Silk said carefully. "I still hope you are—that last night was the last night." If the gods did not care, why should he? He thrust the thought aside.

"Nobody last night, Patera. There wasn't enough to keep the other dells busy. You're thinking how about rust, aren't you? I can tell from the way you look at me. Not since the funeral. Come on in." She stepped back.

He entered, careful not to brush her jutting breasts.

"Now you're wondering how long it'll last. Me too. You didn't know I was a regular mind reader, did you?" She smiled, and the smile made him want to put his arms around her.

He nodded instead. "You're very perceptive. I was."

Oreb felt he had been left out long enough. "Where Auk?"

"I don't know. You want to come to my room, Patera? You can sit, and we could talk like we did that other time."

"I must speak to Orchid—but if you wish it."

"We don't have to. Come on, she's probably about dressed. Her room's up this way." Chenille led him along a corridor he recalled only vaguely. "Maybe I could come by tomorrow to talk? Only you're not at the place on Sun Street anymore, are you?"

"No," Silk said, "but I'm going there when I leave here. Would you like to come?" When Chenille did not reply, he added, "I have a litter; I've been trying to spare my ankle."

She was shocked. "You can't let people see me with you!"

"We'll put the curtains down."

"Then we could talk in there, huh? All right."

Silk, too, had come to a decision. "I'd like to have you with me when I speak to Orchid. Will you do it?"

"Sure, if you want me." She stopped before Orchid's door. "Only I hope you're not going to get her mad."

Recalling the small woman's fear, Silk knocked. "Were you leaving just now, Chenille? We can arrange to meet later, if this is inconvenient."

She shook her head. "I saw you out my window and put this gown on, that's all."

Orchid's door had opened. Orchid, in a black peignoir that reminded Silk vividly of the pink one she had worn when she had admitted him with Crane, was staring open mouthed.

He tore his own gaze from her gaping garment. "May I speak with you when you've finished dressing, Orchid? It's urgent; I wouldn't have troubled you otherwise."

Numbly, the fat woman retreated.

"Come on, Patera." Chenille led the way in. "She can put on a, you know, more of a wrap-up." To Orchid she added, "He's gimp, remember? Maybe you could invite him to sit."

Orchid had recovered enough to tug at the lace-decked edges of the peignoir, covering bulging flesh that would reappear the moment she released them. "I—you're the caldé now. The new one. Everybody's talking about you."

Oreb offered proof. "Say Silk!"

"I'm afraid I am. I'm still the same man, however, and I need your help."

Chenille said firmly, "Have a seat, Patera."

"Yeah, sit down. Do I call you Caldé or Patera?"

"I really prefer to stand as long as you and Chenille are standing. May I say it's pleasant to see you again? Pleasant to see you both. I've been looking for Chenille, as I told her, and I've met so many new people—commissioners at the Juzgado and so forth—that you seem like old friends."

"Good friends." Chenille dropped onto the green-velvet couch. "I'll never forget how you stood up to the councillors at Blood's." She turned to Orchid. "I told you about it, right?"

"Yeah, but I never thought I'd see you again, Caldé. I mean to talk to."

He grasped the opportunity. "You saw me when Hyacinth and I were riding through the city, and we saw you. Have you seen Hyacinth since then?"

Orchid shook her head as she sat down beside Chenille.

Gratefully, Silk sat too. "I mean her no harm—none whatsoever. I merely wish to find her."

"I'm sure you don't, Caldé. I'd tell you if I knew."

Chenille said, "You're going to ask me in a minute. I can't remember how long it's been since I saw Hy. A couple months. Maybe longer than that."

"No girl?" Oreb inquired.

Silk looked around at him. "Chenille is only one of the people we've been trying to find, actually. Now I'm hoping to find out something about the others."

"I'll call you Caldé," Orchid announced. "It feels easier. A hoppy was here asking about Hy. Did you know that?"

"I sent him, indirectly at least."

"He wanted to know about Chen, too. And Auk." Orchid glanced at Chenille, afraid that she was revealing too much.

"But you told him nothing. I can't blame you. In your place I would probably have done the same."

Orchid struggled to her feet. "I'm forgetting my manners. Maybe you'd like a glass of wine? I remember that time when you said you were sorry you only had water, but water was what I wanted right then. You got some for me, and good water too. You've got a good well."

"No wine, thank you. You told the Guardsman who came here that you didn't know where Hyacinth, or Chenille, or Auk was. I know you must have, because any information you provided him would have been reported to me, with its source. As I said, I would very likely have acted just as you did, if I had been in your place. This afternoon it occurred to me that you might tell me more than you'd tell someone you didn't know or trust, so I came in person. I take it that Chenille was already here when he arrived to question you. Was that yesterday?"

Orchid nodded. Chenille said, "It's my fault, Patera. I asked her not to tell anybody." For perhaps five seconds she was silent, nibbling at her lower lip. "Because of that other man. You know who I mean, Patera? He was at Blood's, too, and he didn't get shot like the fat one. The tall one. He saw me, and he heard my name."

Silk's forefinger drew small circles on his cheek. "Do you think he knew enough about you to search for you here?"

"I don't know. I've tried to remember everything Blood said, and I don't remember anything about that. Only he might have said something before or after or maybe even something I've forgotten. He'd seen me, and knew who I was."

"In that case," Silk said slowly, "I'm surprised that you came back here."

Orchid poured a pony of brandy. "It isn't as dumb as you think, Caldé. If somebody came around, we'd tell her so she'd have time to hide. We did with the hoppy, didn't we, Chen?"

"That's right, Patera. Anyhow I pretty much had to. I didn't have any money—"

"I must speak to you about that; remind me after we leave."

"Except a little here, and my jewelry's here, except for this ring." She held up her hand to display it, and the ruby glowed like a coal from the forge. "I think it's worth a deck, and so does Orchid."

Orchid nodded emphatically.

"Only Auk gave it to me, and I told him I'd never sell it. I won't, either. Remember when you and me talked in the front room of your little house, Patera?"

"Yes, I do. I'm surprised that you do, however."

"I didn't to start, but after a while it came back. What I was going to say is I had my best pieces on, my jade earrings and the necklace, only it got lost when my good wool gown did."

Silk nodded. "Patera Incus said Maytera Marble had made Blood give you the chenille one you had on there."

"Uh-huh. I'll tell you about losing the other one and my necklace some other time. What I was going to say is they hurt my ears, down in the tunnel. I took them off and gave them to Auk, and he put them in his pocket." She fell silent, her chest heaving dramatically.

"When I find Auk, I'll remind him to return them to you."

"There's something I've got to tell you about him, too. You won't believe me, but I've got to tell you just the same. Only not now."

"All right. Tell me when you feel ready to do so." Silk turned back to Orchid. "Permit me to ask again. Do you know where Hyacinth is? Do you have any idea at all?"

Shaking her head, Orchid passed her brandy to Chenille. "Drink it, you'll feel better." Freed of the stem, Orchid's beringed fingers clenched. "Patera, I need a favor and I need it bad. Ever since I saw you in the hall I've been trying to think of a good way to ask. If I knew anything that would help you find Hy, I'd tell you and ask for my favor. I don't, but I got connections and they know places the hoppies never heard of. I'll get them on it as quick as I can."

Oreb flew from Silk's shoulder to Chenille's. "Where Auk?"

"My question exactly," Silk said. "You told the Guardsman you didn't know where Hyacinth was, and you were telling him the truth. You lied when you told him that you didn't know where Chenille was. What about Auk?"

Orchid shook her head. "I've got a couple culls asking. He's got Chen's bobbers, like she says. We know he's around. We've talked to bucks that saw him. Isn't that right?"

Chenille nodded.

"But nobody seems to know where he dosses. A friend of mine told him I wanted to see him, and he said maybe he'd come later, but he hasn't." Orchid tapped her forehead. "He's cank, they say. Talking clutter."

"Let me know if he comes, will you please? Immediately."

"Absolutely, Caldé. You can count on it. Want me to keep him here until you get here?"

"He'll stay," Chenille interposed. "He'll be in my room."

"Yes, I do," Silk told Orchid. "You've offered me several favors, and I want them all. I want very much to learn where Hyacinth is. I want to learn where Auk is, too, and I want you to keep him here if he comes. He used to come here often, I know. You said you required a favor from me. I'll help you if I can. What is it?"

"Blood's dead. That's what Chen says, and it's all over town anyhow. They say—am I stepping in it?"

Chenille swallowed a sip of brandy. "They say you killed him, Patera. That's what some people told me out at his house before the fighting was over."

Orchid took a step toward Silk. "I own this." Her voice was husky with emotion. "This house of mine. But I bought it with money Blood gave me, and I had to sign a paper."

Belatedly, Silk rose too. "What did it say?"

"I don't know. It was at his place in the country. Once in a while he'd come to town and see people, but mostly he sent word and you went out there to see him. If he liked you, he'd send his floater for you. That was the first time in my life I got to ride in one."

Recalling his trip from Blood's villa to the manteion on Sun Street, Silk nodded. "Go on."

"We talked about, you know, what sort of house I'd found, where it was and how big and the girls I'd got lined up. Then he pulled out a paper and said sign this. I did, and he stuck it away again and gave me the money. I got the deed, and it's in my name, but now he's dead and I don't know about the paper. I want to keep my house. It would kill me to lose it. That's lily. With him gone, I don't know where I stand, but I'd feel a lot better knowing I had the caldé in my corner."

"He is." Silk started toward the door. "You have my word, Orchid; but I must go—we must, if Chenille's coming."

"I've got to get my coat." She was already on her feet. "Your litter's around back? On Music? I'll meet you."

As he rattled down the wooden steps, Silk could not be sure he had told her it was, or that he had replied at all.

"If you don't want to, they won't make you," Auk told his listeners. "You think the gods are a bunch of hoppies? They don't push anybody around. Why should they? When they want to do you a good turn, they say do this and this, 'cause it's going to be good, you're going to like it. Only if you say it's a queer lay, they say dimber by us, we'll give it to somebody else. Remember Kypris? She didn't say go uphill and solve all those kens. She said if you want to, go to it and I'll keep the street. This is like that. I'm not here to make anybody do anything. Neither's Tartaros."

One of his listeners asked, "What've we got to do now?"

The blind god whose hand was upon Auk's shoulder whispered, "Tell him to make ready."

"To start with, you got to get yourself set," Auk said. "Get used to it. You'll be going to a new place. It'll be better, real nice, but all the stuff you're used to will be down the chute. Even the sun'll be different, a short sun that won't ever go out. You got to think about it, and that's why I'm here, to start you culls thinking. You want to think about what to take, and who to take with you, and talk to 'em. If you're like me, you're going to want pals. Tell 'em. Every man's got to have a woman, too, and every woman's got to take a man. Just sprats don't have to have anybody."

A big-nosed woman shouted, "Over here!" and Auk's listeners drifted away, forming two long lines, slug guns at the ready.

"That went well," Tartaros whispered.

"They didn't believe me." Wearily, Auk started back down the tunnel; this one was open to the sky, as most were on this level. The walls were walls, but had doors and windows in them. He was still trying to make up his mind whether that made things better or worse.

"Men come slowly to belief," the god whispered, "nor is that to be deplored. Some have taken the first step already, because you urged it."

Auk felt a glow of satisfaction. "If you figure that was enough, what we did back there, dimber with me. Think I ought to steal something for her to eat? I said I would."

"You must steal more cards, as well."

Auk steered the blind god around a hoppy's corpse, its eyes and mouth black with cold-numbed flies. "You won't let me spend 'em, Terrible Tartaros."

"We will have need of many cards, and quickly. Have I not made it clear to you?"

"Yeah, to fix up a lander." Auk smiled at the thought. "I guess you did."

"That is well. Your mind is mending. Steal food, if you wish, Auk, and more cards where you can."

As their litter jogged down Sun Street Chenille said, "I'd like you to shrive me. Will this take long enough?"

"That will depend on how much you have to tell me." Silk was acutely aware of her hip pressing his own. He recalled a rule forbidding sibyls from riding in a litter with a man; he was beginning to feel that there should be another—strictly enforced—against augurs riding with women. "Certainly it would be more regular to do it in the manteion, where we would not be pressed for time."

"You know what I'm afraid of? I'm afraid of some goddess getting in me again. You don't know about Scylla, do you?"

"I've spoken with Patera Incus. He told me that Scylla had possessed you—it was one of the reasons I was anxious to find you—and that she, through you, had appointed him Prolocutor."

Chenille nodded, the motion of her head almost ghostly in the tightly curtained litter. "I remember that a little. Only he talked about it so much after she let me go that I can't be sure exactly what I said. Auk could tell you."

"I'll ask when we find him; but the Prolocutorship is a concern of the Chapter's, not the civil government's. In other words, I have no more say in the matter than any other member of the clergy, and none at all as caldé. Was Auk the only other person present?"

"Dace, but he's dead."

"I see. I refrained from asking Patera about witnesses. As I said, it's a matter that concerns me only as one augur among many. It may be that I'll no longer be an augur at all when the matter comes before the clergy."

Silk was silent for a moment, his eyes vague. "If what Patera reports is true, and I'm inclined to credit him, it's unfortunate that Scylla didn't make her wish known at a time when other augurs, or sibyls, were present. Most of the—"

Chenille interrupted. "I wouldn't mind if it was Kypris again. It might be nice. Only Scylla was really rough. That's how I lost my gown and my good jade necklace. I'd go out to the lake and look for it, only I'm pretty sure somebody's found it by this time. Anyway, isn't there someplace where we could do it besides in the manteion? Kypris got me when I was in there, and Scylla when I was in her shrine at the lake. I'm going to try to stay away from places like that for a while."

"I see. If you don't look at the Sacred Window, you can't be possessed—so Kypris implied, at least." Too late, Silk recalled that there was no Window in Scylla's shrine. "It may be that there are other means, of course," he finished lamely, "or that only she is limited in that fashion."

"Don't you bucks ever get possessed?"

"Certainly we do. In fact, it's much more usual, or so the Chrasmologic Writings imply. Men are normally possessed by male gods, such as Pas, Tartaros, Hierax, and the Outsider, or such minor male gods at Catamitus. That is true of enlightenment as well. I myself was enlightened by the Outsider, not Pas, though it would appear that common report attributes my enlightenment to Pas." Silk forbore mentioning that Pas was dead.

"The reason I was asking—"

Their litter stopped, lowered gently to an uneven surface. Oreb pushed the curtain aside with his beak, and was gone.

"I'll be here a while," Silk told the head bearer. "It might be best if I were to pay you now."

The head bearer made an awkward bow with one eye on his men, who were helping Chenille out of the litter. "We'll wait, Caldé. No trouble."

Silk got out his cardcase. "May I give you something so you can refresh yourselves while you wait?"

"We'll be all right." The head bearer backed away.

"As you wish."

The garden gate was unlocked; Silk opened it for Chenille. "I was afraid you'd give them too much," she whispered as she passed. "They'd get drunk."

That explained the head bearer's refusal, Silk decided as he reclosed the gate; it would not do for the bearers of the caldé's litter to be drunk. He made a mental note to allow for the propensity of the lowest classes to drink too much.

"Is anybody here?" Chenille looked about her at the arbor and the wells, the berry brambles and wilted tomato vines under the windows of the manse, the seared fig and the leafless little pear, and the spaded black soil that had been Maytera Marble's struggling garden.

"At the moment? I can't say. I assume that Patera Gulo's still off fighting—or at any rate off watching what's left of Erne's brigade. Maytera Marble's probably in the cenoby; we'll find out when I've shriven you."

"You won't hold us long with a handful of men," Maytera Mint told Spider. "Colonel Bison has five hundred."

Spider chuckled. He was, as she had concluded a half hour before, rather too well suited to his name, a man who made her think of a fat, hairy spider watching its web in a dirty corner.

Quetzal said, "He's taking us down into the tunnels."

Spider opened a door as Quetzal spoke, revealing a flight of rough steps descending into darkness. "You know about those, old man?"

"I just came up from them. Did you hear me tell Potto I'd talked to Loris?"

"Councillor Potto to you." Spider gestured with a needler; he was two full heads taller. "Now get down there before I kick you down."

"I can't walk fast, my son." Quetzal tottered toward the steps. "I'll delay you and the others."

There had been a note in his quavering old voice that gave Maytera Mint a surge of irrational confidence. "The Nine avenge wrongs done to augurs and sibyls," she warned Spider, "and their vengeance is swift and terrible. What they might do to someone who maltreats the Prolocutor, I shudder to think."

Spider grinned, showing remarkably crooked teeth. "That's lily, General. So don't you shove him down and run. Stir it, now. The tall cully behind you, and me behind him. We're all going to wait nice till Councillor Potto and my knot fetch along his dead body."

She started down the steps, one hand on a wooden rail that seemed both grimy and insecure. Behind her, Remora said, "This is where, ah, the caldé, eh? The cellar, in which, um–"

"Sergeant Sand," she told him. The dull gleam that had been Quetzal's hairless head had disappeared into the darkness; she quickened her pace, although the steps were steep and high, and she was afraid of falling. "Sergeant Sand held the caldé down here for six hours or more. He told me about it."

Remora bumped her from behind. "Sorry! Ah–pushed."

"Keep moving," Spider growled.

The sound of their voices had kindled a dull green light some distance down the steps; in the dimness she could make out ranked shelves of dusty jars, and what seemed to be abandoned machinery. Involuntarily she murmured, "He's gone."

Spider heard her. "Who is?"

"His Cognizance." She halted, speaking over her shoulder. "Look for yourself. He should be on the stair in front of me, but he's not." At the last words, the bright bird called *hope* sang in her heart.

"There you are!" Maytera Marble exclaimed as Silk emerged from the chilly privacy of the vine-draped arbor. "There's a man here looking for you, Patera. I said you weren't here, but he says you've got a litter on Sun Street."

Silk sighed. "It's been like this since Phaesday. No doubt it's extremely urgent."

"That's just what he said, Patera." Maytera Marble nodded vigorously, her metal face luminous in the gray daylight. "And it must be. He came in a floater."

Chenille's smile turned to a stare. "Hello, Maytera. What happened to your hand?"

"How good of you to ask!" She displayed her stump of arm. "My hand's fine, my daughter. I've got it in a drawer, wrapped up in a clean towel. It's the rest of–we should go, Patera. He's waiting for you in front of the cenoby. He came in through the garden and knocked at your manse. I thought he was looking for Patera Gulo."

"I was shriving Chenille," Silk explained. "I'm afraid we didn't hear him."

"I did," Chenille declared, "only I thought it was on the street. It was while I was telling you about–" He silenced her, a finger to his lips.

"His name is Hossaan," Maytera Marble continued. "He's foreign, I think, but he says he knows you. He gave you a ride once, and he was on a boat with you out on the lake. Now where are you–? Oh, I forgot. He can't go through there."

The last words were spoken to Silk's back. At a limping run, he vanished into the narrow opening between the northwest corner of the manteion and the southwest corner of the cenoby.

"There's a gate," Maytera Marble explained to Chenille, "That opens onto the children's playground from Silver Street. But you and I can go through the cenoby."

She mounted the back step and opened the kitchen door. "My granddaughter's in here. I had just fixed her a bite when I saw that man. Do you know her?"

"Your granddaughter?" Chenille shook her head.

"Perhaps you'd enjoy a little boiled beef too?" Maytera Marble lowered her voice. "I think it's good for her to talk with other bio girls. She's been, well, sheltered, I suppose you could call it. And I have something to say to Patera before that man makes off with him. I have a favor to ask him, a great big one."

On Silver Street, Silk was already speaking to "That man." "I haven't been looking for you," he said. "It was stupid of me, incredibly stupid. I've had Guardsmen out combing the city for Hyacinth and some other people, but you had slipped my mind completely."

"We can talk in my floater, Caldé." Hossaan was slight and swarthy, with vigilant eyes. "It'll be more private and get us out of this wind."

"Thank you." Stepping into the floater, Silk let himself sink into its black-leather upholstery.

The translucent canopy went up with a muted sigh, and the freezing gusts that had been punishing Viron ended, if only for them.

"If your Guardsmen had looked, they would've found me." Hossaan smiled as he took his place in the front seat. "These things aren't easy to hide."

"I suppose not. I ran to see you as soon as I realized who you were because I want to ask where Hyacinth is. You brought her to Ermine's on Hieraxday to meet me."

Hossaan nodded.

"From your name—Maytera Marble told me that—you're a Trivigaunti. Is that right? Doctor Crane said once that you were his second in command. Most of the spies he employed seem to have been Vironese, but it would be natural for him to have a few from his own city, people he could trust completely."

"Only me, Caldé. You're right, though. More of us would have made us a lot more effective."

"Do you know where Hyacinth is?"

"No. I wish I did." Hossaan drew a deep breath. "You know, Caldé, you've taken a load off my shoulders. I thought I'd have to find out how much you knew and make sure you didn't learn more than you had to. It turns out you knew everything."

Silk shook his head. "Not at all. Doctor Crane and I made an agreement. I told him all I'd learned or guessed about his activities, and in return he answered my questions about them. I had guessed very little, and he told me very little more, not even his real name."

"It was Sigada." Hossaan smiled bitterly. "It means he was supposed to be handsome and humble."

"But he was neither. Thank you." Silk nodded. "Sigada. I'll always remember him as Doctor Crane, but I'm glad to know how he remembered himself. You weren't called Hossaan when you were at Blood's, I'm sure."

"No. Willet."

"I see. You didn't give that name to Maytera Marble; you gave her your real one. You can't have known that Doctor Crane had told me about you, because you can't have talked to him between our conversation Tarsday afternoon and his death on Hieraxday morning."

"I told you I didn't know how much you knew, Caldé."

"That's right." Futilely, Silk groped in a pocket of his robe. "Do you know, I don't have any prayer beads now? When I was a poor augur, I had beads in my pocket but no money. Now I have money, but no beads."

"An improvement. You can buy some."

"If I can find the time when the shops are open, and get into one without being mobbed. You said you were going to tell me no more than you had to; but plainly you intended to tell me you were a Trivigaunti spy."

"That's right. I was going to tell you because you would have known it from the news I came to give you. Generalissimo Siyuf is coming to reinforce you, with thousands of troopers. I just found out about it myself." Hossaan twisted in his seat until he was face-to-face with Silk. "It means your victory is assured, Caldé. If you're not defeated before she arrives, it will be impossible for you to be defeated at all." There was a timid tap on the canopy, and Hossaan said, "It's the sibyl."

Turning, Silk saw Maytera Marble's metal face, hardly a span from his. "Let her in, please. I can't imagine myself saying anything I wouldn't want her to know—or hearing any such news or confidence, except in shriving."

The canopy retraced, and Maytera Marble entered, her long black skirt and wide sleeves flapping in the wind. "I spoke to you, Patera, but you couldn't hear me."

"No," Silk said. "No, Maytera, I couldn't." He motioned to Hossaan and the canopy enclosed them as before.

"I don't want to interrupt, but seeing you in this machine I thought you might be about to leave. And . . . and . . ."

"I suppose we are, but not without Chenille. I want to take her with me. Is she in the cenoby?"

Maytera Marble nodded. "I'll go get her in a moment, Patera. She's eating."

"But first you want to tell me something. Is it about her, or," Silk hesitated, "your granddaughter, Maytera?"

"I wanted to ask you for something, Patera, actually. I realize that you and this foreign gentleman were conferring, and that it's important. But this won't take long. I'll ask and go."

"Hossaan is from Trivigaunte," Silk told her, "like your friend General Saba. They're our allies, as you must know, and I've just learned from Hossaan that they're sending more troops to help us."

"Why, that's wonderful!" Maytera Marble smiled, her head back and inclined to the right. "But after news like that my little problem will seem terribly insignificant, I'm afraid."

"I'm certain it won't, Maytera. You're not the sort who bothers others with insignificant problems." To Hossaan, Silk added, "Now I want to say that Maytera was to me what you were to Doctor Crane, but she was far more. I came to this manteion straight from the schola, and I'd been here only a bit over a year when Patera Pike died. Maytera saved me from making a fool of myself at least once a day." He paused, remembering. "Though I wish it had been more, because I did make a fool of myself often, in spite of all that she could do."

"I intrigued against you, too," Maytera Marble confessed. "I didn't hate you, or at least I told myself I didn't. But I obstructed and embarrassed you in small ways, telling myself that it was for your own good." Her voice grew urgent. "I don't have the *right* to ask favors. I know that, but—"

"Of course you do!"

"I can't manage it myself. I wish I could. I've prayed for the means, but I can't. Do you know Marl, Patera?"

"I don't think so." Silk, who knew few chems, exhausted his mental list quickly. "She—?"

"He, Patera."

"He can't attend our sacrifices. I can't even remember the last time I saw a chem there—except you, of course."

"There aren't many left," Hossaan put in, "here or in my own city. Is he a soldier?"

Maytera Marble shook her head. "He's a valet. He works for a man called Fulmar. I don't see him often at all, but I went over yesterday, my granddaughter and I did, and . . ."

"Go on, Maytera."

"I showed him my hand. The one that my—you know . . ."

Silk nodded, he hoped encouragingly. "It's better not to dwell on that, Maytera, I'm sure. You showed him your hand."

"I brought it in a little basket, wrapped up in a towel, because there's fluid that might leak out. It's a very good hand still. It's just that I can't put it back on."

"I understand."

"Marl says there's a shop, though I'd think it would have to be a big place, really, way over past the crooked bridge, where they make taluses and fix them. Mostly it's fixing, he said, because it takes so long to make one, and so much money. We chems aren't really like taluses. We were made in the Short Sun Whorl, and we can think and see a great deal better, and we don't burn fish oil," she laughed nervously, "or anything like that. But Marl thought they might be able to do this for me—put it back—if I had the money. It wouldn't be like making a chem or even a talus, just a simple repair."

"Yes. Yes, of course. I should have thought of something like that, Maytera. Welding? Is that what they call it?"

Hossaan said, "That's what they call it when they fix a floater."

"It's not just reuniting the metal, Patera. There are little tubes in there, tiny tubes, and wires, and things like threads—fibers, they're called—that pipe light. Look." She held up her useless right arm, pushing back the sleeve so that he could see the sheared end. "Marl thought they might be able to do it. He's as old as I was, Patera, and I don't think he always reasons correctly anymore. But . . ."

Silk nodded. "It's your only chance. I understand."

"Marl would have given me the money if he'd had it, but he's very poor. This Fulmar doesn't pay him, just clothes and a place to live. And even if I had money, they might not want to try it, Marl said, unless I had a great deal."

"Believe me, I'll help you, Maytera. We'll go as quickly as we can. You have my word on it."

She had taken a large white handkerchief from her empty sleeve. "I'm so sorry, Patera." She dabbed at her eyes. "I can't really cry, not for a long, long time. And yet I feel that way. There's so much work, with you gone and Patera Gulo gone, and Maytera Mint gone, and my granddaughter to take care of, and just one hand for everything."

Silk reached another decision. "I'm going to take you away, too, Maytera, for the time being at least. You and Mucor both. I need you both, and it's too dangerous for you—and for her, particularly—to be here alone. Will you come with me if I ask you to? Remember, I'm still the augur of this manteion."

She looked up at him with a new glow behind the scratched, dry lenses of her eyes. "Yes indeed, Patera, if you tell me to. I'll have to straighten up first and put things away. Put a notice on the door of the palaestra so the children will know."

"Good. There's a Caldé's Palace on the Palatine, as well as the Prolocutor's. I'm sure you must remember when the caldé lived there."

She nodded.

"I'm reopening it. I've slept in the Juzgado the past few nights, but that's never been more than an expedient; if Viron's to have a new caldé, he has to live in the Caldé's Palace. I'll need a place to entertain Generalissimo Siyuf when she arrives, to begin with. We'll want an official welcome for her and her troops, too, and I'll have to notify Generalissimo Oosik as soon as possible. Thousands of fresh troops are certain to change his plans."

Silk turned to Hossaan. "How long do we have? Can you give me some idea?"

"Not an accurate one, Caldé. I'm not sure when she left Trivigaunte, and Siyuf's a famous hard marcher."

"A week?"

"I doubt it." Hossaan shook his head. "Three or four days, at a guess."

"Patera." Maytera Marble touched Silk's arm. "I can't live in the same house with a man, not even an augur. I know nothing will—but the Chapter . . ."

"You can if he's ill," Silk told her firmly. "You can sleep in the same house to nurse him. I've a chest wound—I'll show it to you as soon as we get there, and you can change the dressing for me. I'm also recovering from a broken ankle. His Cognizance will grant you a dispensation, I'm sure, or the coadjutor can. Hossaan, can you take us back to the Juzgado? There will be four of us."

"Sure thing, Caldé."

"I don't have a floater at present, except for the Guard floaters, and Oosik needs those. Perhaps I could hire you and your floater—we'll talk about it.

"Maytera, do whatever you must, and tack up that note. I was hoping to sacrifice here and go to the Cock when I left, but both will have to wait. Tomorrow, perhaps.

"Hossaan, I'm going into the manse for a moment while she does all that; then we'll collect Mucor and a young woman who came here with me, and pay off my litter."

"I heard you had a pet bird," Saba said, eyeing Oreb; she was a massive woman with a marked resemblance to an angry sow.

Silk smiled. "I'm not sure pet's the correct word. I've been trying to set him free for days. The result has been that he comes and goes as he pleases, says anything he wants, and seems to enjoy himself far more than I do. Today we went back to my manteion, mostly to enlist Maytera Marble's help in airing this place out. I got some important news there, by the way, which I'll give you in a moment."

"That's right." Saba snapped her fingers. "You holy men are supposed to be able to find out the gods' will by looking at sheep guts, aren't you?"

"Yes. Some of us are better at it than others, of course, and no one's ever suggested that I'm much better than average. Don't you have augurs in Trivigaunte?"

"No cut!" Oreb required reassurance.

"Not you, silly bird. Positively not." Silk smiled again. "I got him as a victim, you see; and though I've ruled that out, he's afraid I'll change my mind. What I wanted to tell you is that I went into the manse to see if I'd left my beads there Phaesday night. I should have said earlier that he'd flown off when I got out of my litter.

"Well, I went into the kitchen because I empty my pockets on the kitchen table sometimes, and there he was on the larder. 'Bird home,' he told me, and seemed quite content; but he rode out on my shoulder when I left."

"He sounds like a good trooper." Saba leaned back in her ivory-inlaid armchair. "You have so many male troopers here. I'm still getting used to them, though most fight well enough. I have news for you, too, Caldé, when you've given me yours."

"In a moment. To tell the truth, I'm afraid you'll rush off the minute you hear it and I want to ask about augury in Trivigaunte. Besides, Chenille's making coffee, and she'll be disappointed if we don't drink it. She wants to meet you, too—you helped save her; she was one of the hostages at Blood's." Seeing that Saba did not understand him, Silk added, "The villa in the country."

"Oh, there. You were the one we came after, Caldé."

"But you saved Chenille too, and Patera Incus and Master Xiphias—you and Generalissimo Oosik, and several thousand of General Mint's people, I ought to say."

Saba nodded. "We were a little part, but we did what we could. Where's Mint, anyhow?"

"Trying to turn courageous but untrained and undisciplined volunteers into a smoothly running horde, I assume. I've tried to do that sort of thing myself on a much smaller scale—with the mothers of the children at our palaestra, for example. I don't envy her the task."

"You've got to get rough with them, sometimes," Saba told him, looking as if that were the aspect she enjoyed. "There's times to be pals, all troopers together. And there's times when you need the *karbaj*."

Silk wisely refrained from asking what the *karbaj* was. "About augury. From what you said, I take it that it's not practiced in Trivigaunte? Is that correct?"

Saba inclined her head, the movement barely perceptible. "You try to make the gods like you by cutting up animals. We don't. I'm not trying to offend you."

"Not at all, General."

"I'm a plain-spoken old campaigner, and I don't pretend to be anything more. Or anything less. A simple old trooper. The way things are here makes me try and act like an ambassador, so I do my best." She laughed loudly. "But that's not too good, so I'll give it to you straight. Your customs seem backwards to me, and I keep waiting for them to turn around. Take her, now." Saba pointed to Chenille, who had entered with a tray. "Here's a woman and a man talking, and a woman waiting on them. I'm not saying you never see that at home, but you don't see it often."

"But to get back to—" Silk accepted a cup. "Thank you, Chenille. You didn't have to do this, and I'm not sure General Saba realizes that. Goodness and servility look alike at times, though they're very different. Won't you sit down?"

"If I won't bother you."

"Of course not. We'll be happy to have your company, and I know you were anxious to meet General Saba. She's the commander of the Rani's airship."

"I know." Chenille gave Saba an admiring smile.

"She was one of your rescuers. Generalissimo Oosik told me afterward that he'd be delighted to see the kind of efficiency her pterotroopers displayed in a brigade of our Guard."

"They're picked women, every one of them," Saba told Silk complacently. "The competition to get in is fierce. We turn away ten for each we take."

"I want to get back to augury. If I seem to be harping on it, I hope you'll excuse me; I was trained as an augur, and I doubt that I'll ever lose interest in it entirely. But first, would it be possible for me to go up in your airship sometime?"

Saba winked at Chenille, her brutal face briefly humorous.

"One of the students—his name is Horn, and he's acting as a messenger here for the present—told me not long ago that he'd dreamed of flying. So have I, though I didn't admit it to Horn, or even to myself when I spoke with him."

"Bird fly!" Oreb proclaimed.

"Exactly. We can scarcely look up without seeing a bird; and there are fliers every few days, proving it can be done. When I was a boy, I used to imagine they were shouting, 'We can fly and you can't!' up there too high to be heard. I knew it was foolish, but the feeling has never left me entirely."

"Wing good." Hopping onto Silk's head, Oreb displayed it.

"He couldn't fly for a while," Silk explained. "Before that I doubt that he took much pride in it."

"I'm going to surprise you, Caldé," Saba announced. "You are welcome to visit my airship anytime. Just let me know when you're coming so I can get things trooper-like for you."

"Of course." Silk sipped from his cup, pausing to admire the delicate porcelain, brave with gilt and holding a painted Scylla as well as coffee.

"If that were wine, I'd tell you I was going to fit you up with wings like my girls'," the teeth of Saba's underjaw showed in a savage grin, "and shove you out. But sham diplomats don't get to make that sort of a joke."

Silk sighed. "I'd thought about it. I'm not at all sure I have the courage, but perhaps I might try."

"Don't. You'd be crippled for life if you weren't killed. My girls start with a platform that would fit in this room. I—who's that!"

"Who?" Silk glanced at the doors; so did Chenille.

"There was a face in that mirror." Saba stood up, her cup still in her hand. "Somebody that isn't in here, somebody I've never seen before. I saw her!"

"I'm sure you did, General." Silk put down his coffee.

"You've only just reopened this palace, isn't that right?"

"Less than an hour ago, actually. Maytera Marble and—"

"A secret passage." Saba's tone brooked no contradiction. "The mirror's a peephole, and somebody's spying from in there already. One passage at least, and there could be more, I've seen some at home. What's that girl doing?"

Chenille had gone to the mirror and grasped the sides of its ornate frame with both hands. "It's dusty," she told Silk. "They had dust covers over all this, but dust got in anyhow." With a grunt of effort, she lifted the mirror from its hook; behind it was featureless plaster, somewhat lighter in color than that to either side.

Silk had risen when Saba did. He limped to the wall and rapped it with his knuckles, evoking solid thuds. Saba stared, her wide mouth working.

"Want me to put this back, Patera?" Chenille inquired.

"I don't think so. Not yet, at least. I'll do it, or Master Xiphias can. Can you put it down without dropping it?"

"I think so. I'm pretty strong."

The heels of Saba's polished riding boots came together with a click. "I apologize, Caldé. I'm leaving. Again, I regret this very much."

"Don't go yet," Silk said hastily. "Your Generalissimo Siyuf is bringing us thousands of—"

Saba's cup fell to the costly carpet, splashing it and her gleaming boots with black coffee. "That's the news I was going to tell you! You—you learned that from animal guts?"

Chapter 3

THE FIRST THEOPHANY
ON THELXDAY

Three busy days after Saba had dropped her coffee, Marrow the green-grocer abandoned the pleasant anticipation of the parade that was to close the market early to stare at the weary prophet nearing his stall. "Auk?" Marrow smoothed his fruit-stained apron. "Aren't you Auk?"

"That's me." The prophet stepped out of the wind to lean against a table piled with oranges.

"You're a friend of the caldé's. That's what they say."

"I guess." Auk scratched his stubbled jaw. "I like him, anyhow, and I brought a ram when Kypris came. I don't know if he likes me, though. If he don't, I don't blame him."

Marrow wiped his nose on his sleeve. "You're a friend of General Mint's, too."

"Everybody is now. That's what I hear."

"Scleroderma told me. You know her? The butcher's wife."

Auk shook his head.

"She knows you, and she says you used to come to Silk's manteion, on Sun Street."

"Yeah. I know where it is."

"She says you'd sit in a little garden they've got and talk to her. To General Mint. Would you like an orange?"

"Sure, but I don't have the money. Not that I can spend."

"Take some. Wait a minute, I'll get you a bag." Marrow hurried to the back of his stall, and Auk slipped a peach into his pocket.

"Now you're going around talking about the Plan of Pas. Would you like some bananas? Real bananas from Urbs?"

Auk looked at the price. "No," he said.

"Free. I'm not going to charge you."

Auk straightened up, filling his barrel of a chest with air. "Yeah. I know. That's why I don't want any. Listen up. I'd steal your bananas, see? That's lily. I'd steal 'em and riffle your till, 'cause that's the kind I am. I'm a dimber thief, and Tartaros needs cards for something we're planning to do. Only I won't let you give me bananas. They cost you too much, and it wouldn't be right."

"But—"

"Muzzle it." Auk had begun to peel an orange, pulling away bright cusps of rind with strong, soiled fingers. "I got a mort back in the Orilla I'm supposed to take care of. She's hungry, and she's not used to it like me. So if you want to put oranges and maybe a couple potatoes in that sack, I'll thank you for 'em and take 'em to her. No bananas, see? But nab the gelt off these that want to buy first. I'll take the sack when you're done, if you still want to give it."

"That's Auk the Prophet," Marrow whispered to the crowd around his stall. "A dozen yellow apples, madame? And two cabbages? Absolutely! Very fresh and very cheap."

A few minutes later he told Auk, "I want to take you over to Shrike's as soon as my boy gets back. Scleroderma's husband? He'll let you have a bite or two of meat, I'm sure."

There were two hundred, if not more, waiting for Auk in the Orilla, and another hundred following him. Tartaros whispered, "You are fatigued, Auk my noctolater, and cold."

"You got the lily there, Terrible Tartaros."

"Therefore you are liable to be impatient."

"Not me. I been tired and cold up on the roof, when they were looking with dogs."

"Be warned. This time the prize is greater."

Auk shouldered their way through the crowd, halted at the door of the boarded-up shop that had been his destination, and put down the bags he carried. "Listen up, all you culls."

The crowd hushed.

"I don't know what you want, but I know what I want. I want to leave this stuff with the dell inside. She's hungry, and some cullys in the market gave me this for her. If you want to see me, you've done it. If you want to hear me, you've done that, too. If it's something else, let me give her these and we'll talk about it."

A voice from the crowd called, "We want you to sacrifice!"

"You're abram. I'm no augur." Auk pounded on the warped door. "Hammerstone! Look alive in there!"

The door opened; at the sight of the towering soldier, the crowd fell silent. "This ain't one of the Ayuntamiento's," Auk shouted hastily. "He's working for the gods like I am, only when we were coming here . . ." He tried to remember when they had come; although he vividly recalled watching Hammerstone free himself from tons of shattered shiprock, he could not shut his mind upon the day. "It was when the Alambrera gave up. Anyway all these trooper culls were taking shots at him, so we figured it was better for him to pull it in."

Behind him Hammerstone hissed. "Ask if Patera's here." It was like receiving confidences from a thunderhead.

"Patera Incus!" Auk shouted. "We're looking for this real holy augur named Patera Incus. Somebody said something about a sacrifice. Is Patera Incus out there?"

Voices from the back of the crowd: *"You do it!"*

From behind Hammerstone, Hyacinth inquired urgently, "Is there food in those? I want it."

Tartaros whispered, "Tell them you will," by some miracle overcoming the clamor of the crowd.

Auk was so surprised he turned to look. "What the shaggy—I mean yeah, dimber, Terrible Tartaros. Anything." Passing both sacks to Hammerstone, he cupped his hands around his mouth. "I'll sacrifice. You got it!"

"When?" Four men lifted a terrified brown kid over their heads; its unhappy bleats were visible, although inaudible.

"Now, Auk my noctolater."

"Now!" Auk repeated.

A thin man whose coat and hat had once been costly asked, "You say you're doing the gods' will. Will a god appear?"

Auk waited for assurance from the blind god at his side, but none was forthcoming.

Others took up the question. *"Will a god come?"*

"What do you think?" Auk challenged them, and a hundred arguments broke out at once.

From behind Hammerstone's green bulk, Hyacinth inquired, "Where're we going to do it?"

"I thought you were eating."

"She is," Hammerstone rumbled. "I can hear her."

The noise grew as fifty men and a dozen loud-voiced women shouted demands. Auk muttered, "Terrible Tartaros, you better tell me what to tell 'em or we could have a problem here."

"Have I not, Auk my noctolater? You are to sacrifice, to me or to whatever god you wish."

Auk turned to Hammerstone. "Get out of the door. I got to tell both of you, and I ain't going to talk to her through you."

The soldier emerged into the street, evoking another awed silence. Revealed, Hyacinth chewed and gulped, wiping her hands on her soiled gown. "That was a nectarine, I think, and I think I swallowed the pit. I can't remember spitting it out. Maybe I chewed it up. Thelx, was it good!"

"You take care of this stuff," Auk told her, "I got to go to Sun Street."

"I'm coming!"

Auk shook his head. "I ain't no augur—"

Tartaros whispered, "Bring the soldier and the woman."

"But I got to sacrifice. Scalding Scylla wanted me to, too. She was going to make me give her Dace, probably."

"I'll need a coat and a bath, makeup—don't you hit me! If you hit me again I'll—I'll—"

"You're coming all right," Auk told her, "and we're going now." He strode into the crowd. "Listen here! Slap a muzzle on it, you culls. Listen up!"

Hammerstone fired his slug gun into the air.

"No god's coming! You want me to sacrifice, we'll go over to Sun Street and do it right. Only no god!" Under his breath he added, "You couldn't see one anyhow, you cank cullys."

They followed him through the narrow street nonetheless, cowed by him more than by the menacing soldier beside him who never relaxed his hold on the shivering, disheveled young woman in the red silk gown.

From the highest step of Silk's manteion, Auk addressed them again. "I told you there ain't going to be a god. You jerk me around, don't you? Sacrifice right this minute! Show us a god, Auk! All your clatter. You think you could jerk me around like you do if I could jerk the gods around? I can't. Neither can you. What I'm telling you is, it's time."

He drew his brass-mounted hanger. "I can cut your goats with this. That's nothing. Can I cut myself out of the whorl? That's what matters. Think about it. Nobody but you can make you think, not even gods."

"Sacrifice!" someone shouted.

"Not even the gods!" Auk bellowed. "Only they can snuff you if you don't, see? Or just leave you to die, 'cause this whorl's finished! Tartaros told me!"

The crowd stirred.

"Ever see a dead bitch in the street? And her pups still trying to suck? That's you! And that's me!" Over his shoulder Auk added, "Open these doors, Hammerstone."

The soldier hooked a finger as thick as a crowbar through one wrought iron handle and rattled the door until it seemed it must leave its hinges. "It's locked."

"Then bust it down. We'll use the wood."

Hammerstone released the door and drew back his fist, but Hyacinth exclaimed, "Wait! Somebody's coming!"

In a moment Auk heard the rattle and squeak of the old iron lock, and the solid *thunk* as the bolt slid back. He grasped the handle and pulled.

"Patera!" Hammerstone knelt as a father does to embrace a boy who does not like being lifted, and hugged Incus in arms that could have splintered the ribs of a bull.

Even Auk smiled. "Hi, Patera. Where you been?"

Hyacinth, torn between the opportunity for flight and the deliverance she sensed was almost at hand, nudged Auk. "Is this him? The one Hammerstone talks about all the time?"

"Yeah. You want to argue with him? Me neither."

Pointing to Incus he announced, "This's the augur I asked you about. Now we can have a regular augur, and maybe he'll let me help. We'll need wood for the altar, you scavy? Some of you got to go get us some. Cedar if you can find any, any kind if you can't."

From Hammerstone's embrace, Incus protested, *"Auk,* my son!"

"We got to, Patera. You like for lots of people to see you sacrifice? I got you three or four hundred here. Hammerstone, loosen up or you'll chill him."

Speaking so quickly her racing words flashed past like frightened linnets, Hyacinth gabbled, "Patera, I know what I look like, I know how awful, but I'm not the sort that would ever set her cap for a cully like this or even let him, you know, talk to her even if he just wanted to talk, you know how they do, and that's not me, and I've got money and good clothes even if you wouldn't think it to look at me and jewelry, and I know people, I've got, you know, bucks that would do me favors any time, commissioners and brigadiers, and I know the caldé, I really do, he's a particular friend of mine and this man and the soldier have been making me stay in a dirty freezing place with rats, and you've got to help me, Patera, you've got to tell—"

Auk clapped a hand over her mouth. "She goes on like that quite a bit, Patera, and we ain't got time for it all. Let him go, Hammerstone. Get him inside there and up to the altar. You can carry him, I guess, if it makes you feel better."

"I've *prayed,*" Incus managed to gasp as Hammerstone hoisted him, "all morning, prayed upon my *knees* with tears and *bitterest groans*—don't drop me, Hammerstone my son, your shoulders are slippery—for a sign of *favor* from Surging Scylla or any other god, the smallest *morsel* of *assistance,* the most humble *crumb* of *succor* in my *divinely ordained* mission."

"I'd say maybe you got it," Auk told him. "What do you think, Terrible Tartaros?"

Briefly, the blind god's hand tightened on his. "Release the woman, Auk my noctolater. I am about to leave you. I have mended your mind, insofar as I am able."

Auk turned, although he knew he could not see the god.

"It will heal itself soon of the damage that remains. I have explained your task, and you have learned better than I could have hoped. Direct your gaze to the Sacred Window, Auk my noctolater."

"This's the Plan, Terrible Tartaros. Emptying the whole whorl. I can't do that by myself!"

"Look at the screen, Auk. At the Sacred Window. This is the last instruction I shall give you."

Auk sank to his knees. Faintly, through the open door, the silver glow shone from the far end of the manteion. "Get out of my way, Hammerstone! I got to see the Window."

"Farewell, Auk. May neither of us forget the prayers you offered nightside, while I hearkened invisible in your glass."

Auk stood up, alone.

"You're crying." Hyacinth stepped closer to peer at him. "Auk, you're *crying.*"

"Yeah, I guess I am." He wiped his streaming eyes with his fingers. "I never had any father."

"I do, and he's a pig's arse." Worshippers pushed past them carrying armloads of wood; some paused to stare.

"I got to get up there and do it. You want to go, go on. I won't stop you."

"I can leave anytime I want to?"

"Yeah, Hy. Beat the hoof."

"Then I'm going to—no, that's abram. G'bye, Bruiser." Her lips brushed his.

"*Auk* my son!" Incus stood beside the altar, directing the laying of the fire. "We've more wood than we require. Tell them to *desist.*"

He did, happy to have something to do.

At Silk's ambion, Incus drew himself up beyond his full height, rising on his toes. "A holy *augur's* blessing upon each and every one of you, my children. *Silence,* back there! This is a *manteion,* a house sacred to the *immortal gods.*" It was the hour he had dreamed of since childhood.

"*Hammerstone,* my son. It is best to offer our *pious gifts* upon a fire kindled *directly* from the *beneficent* rays. This is not accorded us on this *day of darkness.* If you will look in the sacristy, behind the *Sacred Window,* you may discover a *firekeeper,* a vessel of metal or even lowly *terra cotta* safeguarding the *holy spark* against such an hour as *this.*"

"I'm on it, Patera."

Incus returned his attention to the congregation. "*At this point,* my children, I am severely tempted to *discover* to you my *own* identity, and the *multifarious vicissitudes* and *tribulations* through which I come to you *today.* I *refrain,* however. I am an *augur,* as you see. I am *that* augur whom *Surfeiting Scylla* has designated *Prolocutor-to-be,* charged with the *utter destruction* of the *Ayunta—*"

For half a minute, their cheers silenced him.

"I am *in addition*—might I say *comrade,* Auk? A *fellow sufferer* at least of Auk's."

From the manteion floor Auk shouted, "A dimber mate!"

"Thank you. Beset, as you should know, by *woe* and eager for a *situation* of *venerational tranquility,* I bethought me of this manteion, the *new caldé's own* as a place to which I might retire, pray and contemplate the *inscrutable* ways of the gods. I had not seen it and had heard much of it during the *brief days* since Auk, my dear friend *Hammerstone*—"

"I got it right here, Patera." Hammerstone displayed a pierced clay pot from which a feeble crimson glow proceeded.

"Auk, are you to *assist* me? Is that to be our *procedure?"*

A seemingly disembodied voice called, "He has to kill 'em!"

"Then he *shall,* and with my blessing. What of the *liturgy,* however? *Auk?"*

Auk had climbed the steps to the altar. "I don't know the words, Patera. You'll have to do it."

"I *shall.* And if *Auk* is to assist, why need my dear friend *Hammerstone* be excluded? Put the *sacred flame* to this fuel, if you will, Hammerstone.

"I obtained the *key,* journeyed *hence,* and locked myself in, counting the lock's *blessed squeakings* among the *treasures* of my *spirit.* I came, I say, in search of *quiet,* resolved upon *prayer and supplication.* I *found* it, as I had hoped, and spent hours upon my *knees,* the least supplicant of the *immortal gods.* It is a practice I recommend to you *without reservation."*

A tongue of fire had sprung up where Hammerstone fanned the wood piled on the altar.

"I was safe from all *interruption.* Or so I thought. Then *you* arrived, a *tumultuous throng,* elevating me to this *sacred* ambion. How *clearly* the gods speak! *Surmounting Scylla* had *lifted* me to the *Prolocutorship.* Now was I *cautioned* that the *Prolocutor—I*—can be no *holy recluse,* however he may *long* for peace. *Pray* for me, my *children,* as I pray for *myself.* Let me *not* forget my *lesson!*

"Auk, my son. Have you the *knife* of *sacrifice?"*

Auk drew his boot knife. "This's all I got, Patera."

"Then it must *suffice.* Bring it to *me* and *I* shall *bless* it." Incus did so, tracing the sign of addition over the blade. Before he finished, Hammerstone had been forced to step back from the leaping flames.

"In a *sacred ceremony* more regular, I should now ask their presenters to which of the *Nine,* or other *immortal gods,* they wished to offer the *fair victims. Today,* however—"

Someone shouted, "To Tartaros! He's always on him!"

"They ain't black," Auk told the speaker.

Incus nodded solemnly. "In the *present instance* that must be *dispensed* with. None are *white.* Nor are any *black,* as my erstwhile comrade has *rightly* said. Therefore *each* shall be offered to *all* the *gods.*"

After glancing at the first victim, Incus faced the Sacred Window, his arms and his voice raised dramatically. "*Accept* all you gods, the sacrifice of this fine *piglet.* And speak to us, we beg, of the times that are to *come. What* are we to do? Your *lightest* word will—will—"

He got no further.

The silver radiance showed flecks of color, faded pastels that might have been shadows or phantoms, the visual illusions of disordered sight, dabs of rose and azure that blossomed and withered, shot with pearl and ebony.

Poised beside the young pig, Auk dropped his knife and fell to his knees. Momentarily it seemed that he could make out a face on the left. Then another, wholly different, on the right. A voice spoke, such a voice as Auk had never heard, filled with the roar of mighty engines. It praised him and urged him to seek something or someone. Now and again, though only now and again, he heard or at least believed he heard, a term he knew: *ghost, augur, plan.* Then silence.

Incus, too, was on his knees; his hands were clasped, his face that of a child.

The piglet had vanished, drawn perhaps into the Window, or perhaps merely fled through the dim manteion and out into the windy winter morning.

Hammerstone stood at rigid attention, his right hand raised in a salute.

For a time that might have been long or short, after the voice spoke no more and the half-formed colors had gone, all was silence; the congregation might have been so many statues, there in the old manteion on Sun Street, statues with starting eyes and gaping mouths.

Then the noise began. Men who had been sitting sprang to their feet; men who had been kneeling jumped up to dance upon the pews.

Some howled as though in agony. Some shrieked as if in ecstasy. A woman fell in a fit, thrashing, contorted as a swatted fly, belching bloody foam as her teeth tore her tongue and lips; no one noticed her, or cared.

"He's gone." Auk rose slowly, still staring at the now-empty Window. More loudly, loudly enough to make himself heard by Hammerstone, he said, "He ain't here, not any more. That was him, wasn't it? That was Pas."

Hammerstone's steel arm crashed to his steel side, a sound like the clash of swords.

"Did anybody . . . You understand him, Patera? It sounded like he was talking about—about—" A man Auk did not know reached out and touched Auk's coat as he might have touched the Sacred Window.

"He liked me," Auk concluded weakly. "Kind of like he liked me, that was what it sounded like." No one heard him.

Incus was on his feet. He tottered to the ambion; although his mouth opened and shut and his lips appeared to shape words, no words could be heard above the din. At last he motioned to Hammerstone, and Hammerstone thundered for silence.

"It is my task—" Incus's voice had risen to a squeak; he cleared his throat. "My task to *explicate* for you the *utterance* of the god." The recurrence of something near his accustomed singsong restored his confidence. "To *gloss* upon his *message* and *relay* his *commands*."

A man in the second row shouted, "It was Pas, wasn't it?"

Incus nodded, his cheeks trembling. "It *was*. Lord *Pas,* the *Father* of the *Whorl* and the *Builder* of the *Gods*." Neither he nor his hearers noticed his mistake.

"He talked to me," Hammerstone told Auk. His voice held a dawning joy. "I seen him once, way off, reviewing the parade. This time he talked to me. Like I'm talking to you, and he gave me a order."

Auk nodded numbly.

"Patera will have heard, won't he? Sure he will. We'll talk about this years from now, how Pas talked to us and gave me the order. Me and Patera."

"Ere I *commence* my *exegesis*," his voice was stronger, and carried an authority that stilled the congregation, "I shall *confide* to you something not generally known, which I *myself* learned only *today*. There has been no *announcement*, but I was not sworn to *secrecy*. On *Molpsday* Great *Pas* granted a *theophany* to the—the *aged worthy augur* who has for *innumerable decades* served us as *Prolocutor*. His office has been *attorned* to me by *Saving Scylla,* who would doubtless see his *protracted devotion* rewarded with that *freedom* from *concerns* which is the *perfumed ointment* of *superannuity*. It was that, I *confess,* which sent me in search of *tranquility,* as I have *related*. The *disquieting intelligence* that the *Father* of the *Seven* had *manifested* himself to one whom I have been *only too ready* to reckon a *rival*."

"Did he say something about me?" Half pleading and half threatening, Auk closed upon the ambion. "He said something, didn't he? What was it?" Hammerstone interposed himself.

"I *prayed* to *Pas,*" Incus continued, wondering. "I urged the *justice* of my *cause* with *tears*. Now how *clearly* do I see this lesser *plan,* the *plan* that is to set in motion his *greater Plan*! First he *bestowed* his *benefaction* upon the *Prolocutor* that was, then upon the *new*." Incus indicated his own stomach. "It is the *hallmark* of the *actions* of the *gods* that, however *unanticipated* they may be, once done they are seen to be both *perfect* and *inevitable*.

"And *now* I confide the *divine utterance* that *Great Pas* has *vouchsafed* to us."

High above the mummy-colored bead that was General Saba's airship, but five hundred cubits below the low winter clouds, Fliers whom Caldé Silk was just then likening to a flight of storks rode the blustering north wind.

From their center, Sciathan studied his companions. Their eyes were on the clouds, as he had expected, or else the sere brown fields, the silver threads of streams, or the shrinking lake; no mere emergency could overcome the habits of years, no urging—not even a god's—bring them to consider the teeming Cargo below relevant.

Sciathan himself glanced up at the clouds and scanned his instruments before abandoning both. A long yellow-brown column of marchers was approaching the city from the south. He had glimpsed similar parades often, giving little thought to them and what they might portend; soldiers and troopers could be halted by avalanches, turned aside by floods and forest fires, and dispersed by storms not much less readily than flotillas. No host had ever succeeded in crossing the Mountains That Look At Mountains; and in all likelihood, none ever would. Here in the hold, hordes like the one below would be a different matter.

Chapter 4

SWORDS OF SPHIGX

Standing stiffly in his official cloak of tea-colored velvet, Caldé Silk cursed himself mentally for not providing chairs—or rather, for not seeing to it that chairs were provided. He had supposed (such, he told himself, had been his lamentable innocence, his utter unfitness for the position thrust upon him) that he, with Quetzal, Oosik, and Saba—and Maytera Mint, if she could be found—would take their places on this platform, at which the force dispatched by Trivigaunte to the aid of Viron would appear.

The fact, of course, was otherwise. The fact was that even Generalissimo Siyuf's highly disciplined horde of seventy-five thousands remained a mass of seventy-five thousand women and men—to say nothing of thousands of horses and none but the Nine knew how many camels.

Camels!

As a precociously pious boy, he had considered Sphigx the least attractive goddess, a tawny-maned virago, more lioness than woman. Now it appeared that real lions had nothing to do with real warfare; horses, mules, and camels were the pets of Stabbing Sphigx, and he would have accepted them happily (or even gerbils, guinea pigs, and geese) if only they would appear in reality.

A freezing gust shook the triumphal arch. It had been hastily erected, and would almost certainly collapse if this winter wind blew even a trifle harder; indeed, it was liable to collapse in any event if Siyuf's troopers did not put in an appearance soon.

Surely there ought to be somebody in the crowd around the platform who could and would fetch chairs. First, he decided, he would ask that a chair be provided for Quetzal, who was of advanced years and had been standing for the better part of an hour; then, as if it were an afterthought, he could order chairs for Oosik and Saba, and himself as well. Five minutes more and he would leave the platform, collar a commissioner, and demand chairs. He must and he would—that was all there was to it.

The wind rose again, and he clenched his teeth. Yellow dust gave it a score of visible bodies, whirling devils that skated over the Alameda. A streamer of green paper tore free of the arch to mount the wind in sinuous curves, vanishing in a few seconds against the heaving bulk of the tethered airship.

From that airship, he reflected, it should be simple to gauge the advance of Siyuf's troops. Given just one more day, he might have arranged for signals: a flag hung out from the foremost gondola when her advance guard entered the city, or a smoke-pot lit for an unanticipated delay. To his own surprise, he found that he had lost none of his eagerness to board that airship, in spite of multiplying duties and the winter wind. Like Horn (just the person to find chairs, or boxes at least) he longed to fly as the Fliers did.

There were a lot of them today. More, he decided, than he had ever seen before. An entire flock, like a flight of storks, was just now appearing from behind the airship. What city sent them to patrol the sun, and what good could such patrols do?

A fresh gust roared along the Alameda, shaking its raddled poplars. To his right Saba stiffened, while he himself shivered shamelessly. The Cloak of Lawful Governance tossed like Lake Limna about his shins, and would have streamed behind him like a banner if he had not been holding it with both hands. Hours ago, when he had put it on in the Juzgado, it had carried in its long train a sensation of oppressive and almost suffocating warmth; he had been sorely tempted to substitute a cheap (and therefore thin) augur's robe for the luxuriously thick one he was wearing under it, although Master Xiphias and Commissioner Trematode had dissuaded him. By this time it should have been soaked with his perspiration; instead he found himself wishing fervently for a head covering of some kind. Saba had her dust-colored military cap, and Oosik a tall helmet of green leather. He had nothing.

The old broad-brimmed straw hat he had worn while repairing the roof was gone—lost at Blood's, like Maytera Mint. The new broad-brimmed straw he had bought at the lake was gone too, left in the room from which the talus had snatched him. Patera Pike's cap, the black calotte that Patera had worn in winter, was back at the manse—he had scarcely dared to touch it after Patera's ghost had dropped it on the landing.

All were dead now, Pike, Blood, and the talus. The second and third by his own hand.

Would this Siyuf and her troopers never come? He searched the clouds beyond the airship for a glimpse of the sun. The dying Flier had said they were losing control. With what chains did one control the sun? With what tiller was it steered?

But no doubt the sun was merely masked by the threatening clouds; it would be childish to complain because winter had come at last when the calendar declared it half over.

Spring soon, unless this winter proved to be as protracted as the summer that had preceded it. If the rains failed then, so would he; if the new corn sprouted and died, Viron's new god-appointed caldé would surely die with it. He pictured himself and Hyacinth fleeing the city on fast horses, but Hyacinth was as lost as Maytera Mint, and he knew nothing about horses save that they might be offered to Pas without impropriety. This though Pas was dead.

Was Hyacinth dead as well? Silk shivered again.

A band struck up in the distance, and ever so faintly his ears caught the clear, brave voices of trumpets and the clatter of cavalry.

Someone, it might have been Oosik, said *"Ah!"* Silk felt himself smile, happy in the knowledge that he had not been alone in his misery and impatience. On his right Saba murmured, "I can identify the units as they approach, if you want, and tell you a little about their history."

He nodded. "Please do, General. I'd appreciate it very much." He was tempted to ask her about the Fliers, as commander of the airship, she might know something of interest—possibly even of value. But it would be the height of bad manners for him to display curiosity about anything other than the military might of Trivigaunte at this moment.

A young woman's dark face (after a brief uncertainty he recognized Horn's sweetheart, Nettle) appeared at the left side of the platform. Loudly enough for him to overhear, she asked, "Wouldn't you like to sit down, Your Cognizance? There's a man renting folding stools."

Quetzal beamed. "How kind you are, my daughter! No, I've got my baculus, so I'm better off than the others." (It was not entirely true; Oosik had his heavy sword in front of him and was leaning upon it as if it were a walking stick.) "Patera Caldé isn't as lucky," Quetzal continued. "Would you like this kind girl to rent you a stool, Patera Caldé?"

It would be unthinkable, of course, for him to sit while the Prolocutor stood. Silk said, "Thank you very much, Nettle. But no. It's not necessary."

"I've just decided," Quetzal told Nettle, "That though I wouldn't like *one* stool, I'd like *two*. One for me and one for Patera Caldé. Have you enough money for two?"

Nettle assured him she had, and disappeared in the crowd.

On Silk's right Saba muttered, "You men lack the stamina of women. It's biology and nothing to be ashamed of, but it shows why we make the best troopers." His cheeks burned; a subtle alteration in Quetzal's posture hinted that he too had heard, and was awaiting Silk's reply.

What would Quetzal himself have replied? Saba's remark bordered on inexcusable arrogance, surely, and such arrogance was punished by the just gods—or so he had been taught in the schola. Reflecting, he decided it was one of the few things he had been taught that seemed undeniably true.

He smiled. "You're entirely correct, General, as always. No observer can help noticing that women endure far more than men, and with greater fortitude."

On Saba's right, Oosik muttered, "Our caldé has a broken ankle. Haven't you seen how he limps?"

"It had slipped my mind, Caldé." Saba sounded honestly contrite. "Please accept my apologies."

"You have nothing to apologize for, General. You stated an inarguable fact. Sphigx and Scylla might apologize for facts, I suppose—but a mortal?"

"Just the same, I—here they come."

The first riders, tall women on spirited horses, could be seen through the arch. Each bore a slender lance, and a yellow pennant stood out below the head of each lance. "The Companion Cavalry," Saba told Silk in a low voice. "All are wellborn, and in addition to their regular duties, they supply bodyguards to the Rani."

"I know nothing about these matters," Silk leaned toward her, "but wouldn't slug guns be more effective than lances?"

"You'll be able to see them better in a moment. They have slug guns in scabbards, left of their saddles. Their lances are used in a charge. You can't fire a slug gun with its muzzle at the horse's ears without panicking the horse."

Silk nodded, but could not help thinking that from the accounts he had been given, Maytera Mint and her volunteers had fired needlers when they charged the floaters in Cage Street. Presumably, the moderate crack of a needler did not disturb a horse like the boom of a slug gun. To him at least, it seemed that even a small needler like Hyacinth's, with a capacity of fifty or a hundred needles, would be a superior weapon.

Nettle reappeared, holding up folding stools with canvas seats. Quetzal accepted one, and Nettle went to the front of the platform to pass the other to Silk.

He took it and exhibited it to Saba. "Wouldn't you like this, General? You're welcome to it."

"Absolutely not!"

"We could sit alternately, if you like," Silk persevered. "You could rest a while, then return it to me."

She shook her head, her lips tight; and Silk put down the stool, empty, between them.

The Companions had ridden in threes and had appeared to be scanning the crowd; having kept a rough count, Silk felt sure there had been no more than two hundred. The troopers behind them bore no lances and were neither so regular in size nor so well mounted; but they rode ten abreast, led by an officer in a dusty old cloak on the finest horse that he had ever seen.

"Generalissimo Siyuf," Saba muttered. "She's related to the Rani on her father's side, as well as her mother's."

"Your supreme military commander."

Saba nodded. "A military genius."

Surveying that hawk-like profile, he decided it might well be true, and was certainly true enough to make Siyuf a valuable ally; genius or not, she radiated resolution and intelligence. He could not help wondering what she had been told about him, and what she thought of him now, the insecure young ruler of a foreign city; the urge to comb his untidy hair with his fingers, as he would have in a conversation with

Quetzal, was practically irresistible. For half a second, his eyes locked with hers.

Then Saba saluted, and her salute was returned negligently by Siyuf; at once Oosik saluted her, in accord with the protocol agreed to Tarsday. Behind her, rank after rank of disciplined young women drew sabers and faced right, seemingly oblivious to the swirling dust and biting wind.

"Generalissimo Siyuf rides at the head of her own regiment. She joined eighteen years ago as a brevet lieutenant, and it's known now as the Generalissimo's Auxiliary Light Horse. . . ."

Saba fell silent; shivering, Silk murmured, "Yes?"

"Your people aren't cheering, Caldé. Not nearly enough. The Generalissimo won't be pleased."

He seized the opportunity. "Perhaps they're afraid they may panic your horses." It had been juvenile, but for a minute or more he enjoyed it.

A wide break in what had threatened to become an infinite succession of mounted troopers apparently marked the end of the Generalissimo's Auxiliary Light Horse. It was followed by the yellow, brown, and red flag of Trivigaunte, borne by an officer on horseback and escorted by an honor guard clearly drawn from the Companion Cavalry, and the banner by the band whose martial music had been the first indication that the Rani's troops were near. The musicians, marching with the precision of a picture in a drill book, were all men and all bearded; the onlookers' cheers increased noticeably as they passed.

"They're really very good," Silk told Saba, hoping to restore friendly relations. "Very skillful indeed, and our people seem to love their music."

"I'm an old campaigner, Caldé."

Privately wondering what the campaigns had been, and how Generalissimo Siyuf had revealed her military genius in them, Silk ventured, "So I understand."

"Your people are cheering because they're men. You think we keep our men chained in the cellar, but most of our support troops are men."

"With beards," Silk commented; it seemed safe.

"Exactly. You shave yours off to make yourself look more like a woman. I'm not criticizing you for it, in your position I'd do the same thing. But we don't let our men do it at home. They can trim their beards with scissors if they want to, and these support troops are required to. But they can't shave, or pull the hairs out."

Silk felt himself wince and hoped she had not noticed it.

"We've only let them use scissors for about twenty years," she continued. "When I was a lieutenant they couldn't, and you saw a good many with beards below their waists. We let them tuck them into their belts, and some people felt that was going too far. The idea is that a beard makes it easy to cut a man's throat. You grab it and jerk his head up."

"I see," Silk said. Mentally, he cancelled the beard he had only just resolved to grow.

"These are Princess Silah's Own Dragoons. You'll notice—"

Oosik interrupted. "I do not mean to begin an argument, General, but I question that it is actually done. If it is, it cannot be done often. Men are much stronger than women."

Saba indicated the mounted troopers passing before them. "Horses are stronger than women, Generalissimo."

Silk chuckled.

"Don't you believe me, Caldé?" Saba was holding back a smile. "It's true, I swear, in our city. We've been breeding chargers since Pas laid his first brick, and our horses are stronger than women and—"

"Wiser than men," Silk finished for her. "I don't doubt it for a moment."

"Who is?" inquired a new voice. "Everyone, I think."

Silk turned to look as Generalissimo Siyuf stepped onto the reviewing platform. "Here you are." He offered his hand. "I was afraid you'd be delayed. It's an honor to greet you at last, and a great pleasure. Welcome to Viron. I'm Caldé Silk."

She shook his hand awkwardly, unsmiling; her own was hard and dry, not quite as strong as he had anticipated. "It is my joy to see your lively city, Caldé Silk. Most of my life I have spend in the south. Your Viron is not more than a name on my maps, one week ago. My parade is bad, I know. When they must march they cannot be drilled. When they fight it is the same."

Silk assured her that he had been enormously impressed by what he had seen, and introduced her to Quetzal and Oosik.

"We will see your troops after mine," she told Oosik. "We pass them waiting. Ah, you have a stool for me, Caldé. Thank you." She seated herself between Silk and Saba. "This is most welcome. I have been up since three, in the saddle since five. I have tired two horses. I must have a fresh one for this."

"It was very good of you to join us after you'd marched," Silk told her sincerely. "We've all heard great things about you. We were anxious to meet you."

Siyuf's eyes were on her troops. "I do not come for you, Caldé Silk. I come for me. Soon we fight together. Is this right? Or does this mean you will fight me and I you?"

"No. That's perfectly correct. Together, we'll fight the Ayuntamiento, if we must. I'd much rather we didn't have to."

"And I. Both." Siyuf pulled her cap down and drew her streaked old cloak over her knees.

For a time, no one spoke. Silk pretended to watch the parade as cavalry gave way to infantry, attractive young women who saluted the reviewing platform by holding their slug guns vertically at their left shoulders and marching with a stiff stride that reminded him of sibyls dancing at a sacrifice.

Mostly, he studied Siyuf and reexamined her remarks, and his own. Her cap was clean and well-shaped, but by no means new, her cloak frankly soiled; no doubt she had changed horses as she had said, but she had not changed clothes. Her boots were slightly scuffed, her spurs (he risked a surreptitious glance at Saba's feet) markedly larger than her subordinate's.

She had not hesitated to claim the empty stool. Silk tried to put himself in the place of one of the expressionless women marching past. Would they feel ashamed of their Generalissimo? Would they think her weak?

Would he, if he were somehow a member of Siyuf's horde? After arguing the point with himself, he decided that he would not. Sitting when others had to stand was one of the surest signs of rank, and her clothes proclaimed that she need answer to no one, that no bullying sergeant or trumpeting colonel dared rebuke her. In imagination, Silk soared from the platform to a gondola of the airship, and from it scanned the parade. There was the reviewing platform, on it various dignitaries of Viron and Trivigaunte. Who was in charge? Who commanded the rest?

It was unquestionably Siyuf, who was seated with Quetzal and himself to her left and Saba and Oosik to her right—the civil authorities, religious and civic, on one side in other words; and the military, Trivigaunti and Vironese, on the other. When Viron's own troopers marched past, they would receive the same impression.

"Is it always so cold here in the north?" Siyuf pulled her cloak more tightly about her.

"No," Silk told her. "We had a very long summer this year, and a very warm one."

"I wish we have come to your city then, Caldé. When I was small my teachers told me this north was cold. I learn to write it on examinations, but I do not believe. Why should it be so?"

"I have no idea." Silk considered. "I learned it just as you did, and I don't believe I ever thought of questioning it. To tell you the truth, I accepted just about everything I was taught, including many things I ought to have questioned."

"The sun." Siyuf pointed up without looking upward. "This begin at the east and end at the west. That is only because we say it so, I know. Here you may speak different. But from East Pole to West Pole or West Pole to East. Your day in Viron is soon our day in Trivigaunte. Is that true?"

"Yes," Silk said. "Of course."

"Then what do you do to make your day so cold?"

Saba laughed, and Silk and Oosik joined her.

Quetzal seemed not to have heard, contemplating the ranked women passing before him through half-closed eyes. Studying him sidelong, Silk sensed a need, a longing, that he himself did not feel, and puzzled over it until he recalled that Saba had said that sacrifices were not offered in her city. The Chapter would be different there, quite possibly known by another name; each of the marching women was, in that case, a potential convert to Viron's more dignified mode of worship. No wonder then that Quetzal eyed them so hungrily. To amend the religious thinking of even a few would be a signal accomplishment and a glorious conclusion to his long, meritorious career. Furthermore, there were thousands and thousands of them, the vast majority still young, still malleable, as Saba for example was not.

As if the comparison had stirred her to speech, Saba asked, "What do you think, Generalissimo? A fine body of women?"

Oosik declared that he had been favorably impressed.

"How old are they?" Silk inquired suddenly; he had not intended to speak.

"We take them at seventeen," Saba told him. "There's a year of training before they're assigned to permanent units. After that we keep them four years."

"Do you mean that they have to become troopers? What if one doesn't want to?"

Saba pointed. "See that one with the big feet? And her over there, the tall one with a stripe?"

"At the end of the line? Yes, I see her."

Saba pointed again. "There, that little fat one. None of them wanted to."

"I see. I'm surprised you know these troopers so well, General. Is this group a part of your airship's crew?"

"No, Caldé." Saba glanced across Siyuf's head with the suppressed smile he had noticed earlier. "In weather like this we need everybody on board. I picked them by chance, but that's the truth about them. Who'd want to be a trooper?"

Silk glanced at Oosik, who was looking at him; troopers in Viron served voluntarily.

Another band, then hundreds of saddleless horses herded by mounted men. Seeing Silk's puzzled expression, Saba explained, "They're remounts. When a trooper's horse is shot, she has to fight on foot unless there's a remount for her."

Siyuf looked up at him. "Do you not have remounts for your own cavalry?" He found her steady eyes disconcerting.

Oosik said quickly, "Our practice is to issue two horses to each mounted trooper. He is responsible for their care, and is to ride them alternately unless one goes lame. In peacetime he rides one on one day and the other on the next."

"You, Generalissimo. Were you a horse officer? We say cavalry-woman, but I do not think you will say that here. A cavalryman, I think?"

Oosik made her a small bow. "Correct, Generalissimo. No, I was not, nor are most of our officers. We have only one mounted company per brigade, though the second has two at present. My son is a cavalry-man, however."

For the first time, Siyuf smiled; seeing it, Silk could readily imagine her subordinates risking their lives to earn that smile. She said, "I hope to meet him. Tomorrow or the day after. We shall speak of horses."

"He will be honored, Generalissimo. Unfortunately he is unwell at present."

"I see." She turned back to the parade, and her voice became indifferent. "It is sad that boys must fight here."

Mules hauling cannon followed the horse herd. "I expected camels," Silk told her.

"Horses and camels do not make friends," she said absently. "It is best we hold them apart. Mules are more . . ." She snapped her fingers.

"Easygoing," Saba supplied. "They don't mind camels as much as most horses do."

"Does it really take eight to pull one of these big guns?"

"On your street of fine stones? No. But over our desert where is no road, many more sometimes. Then one must lend to another its mules and wait. I have seen sixteen unable to pull a single howitzer from the mud. That was not on this march, or we would not be here."

Saba asked, "Didn't you notice the mixed gun crews, Caldé? I expected you to ask about them."

Already the last cannon was rumbling past. After it came a long triple line of small carts with male drivers; each cart was drawn by a pair of mules.

Silk said, "I'm accustomed to working with women, General. With Maytera Marble and Maytera Mint at my manteion, before I became caldé—with Maytera Rose as well until she left us. Your mixed crews seem more normal to me than," he groped for an inoffensive phrase, ending lamely, "than the other thing, just women or just men."

"Men drive the mules and hump shells. They do those almost as well as women could. Women lay the guns and fire them."

Siyuf asked, "Where is General Mint? Did you not call her Mother Mint just now? Or are there two of this name?"

"No, they're the same person. She's a sibyl as well as a general, just as I'm an augur as well as caldé." Silk was tempted to add that he hoped to drop the first soon.

"She marches with her troops today?"

"I'm afraid not." A bare-faced lie would serve best, but he was unwilling to provide one. "We're still engaged with the enemy, Generalissimo."

If Siyuf suspected, nothing in her face revealed it. "I am sorry I do not meet her. Next you see camels."

Silk, who had seen camels singly or in small caravans of a dozen or a score, had scarcely imagined that there were so many in the whorl—not hundreds but thousands, innumerable camels tied one behind another in strings of thirty or more, each such string led by a single camel-driver riding its big lead camel. They grunted continually as they walked, peering at everything with haughty eyes in faces that recalled Remora's.

"They carried food, mostly," Saba explained, "and oats and barley for the horses and mules. They're lightly loaded now."

Here was one of the most sensitive points. "You have to realize there's very little food in Viron." Silk picked his way among snares. "We're delighted to have you, and we'll do our best to feed you and your troops; but the harvest was bad, and our farmers have been hoarding food because of the fighting."

"We know your difficulties." Siyuf's dust-colored cap and hunched shoulders spoke. "We will send out foraging parties."

"Thank you," Silk said. "That's extremely kind of you."

Oosik stared.

"Which reminds me," Silk hurried on, "I've planned a small, informal dinner tonight at the Caldé's Palace." (He found he could not bring himself to say, *"At my palace."*) "You're all invited, and I hope that all of you can attend. We haven't got a real kitchen yet, but I've arranged to have Ermine's cater our dinner; Ermine's serves the best food in our city, or at least it has that reputation."

"I must bring with me a staff officer." Siyuf turned to face him. "This our custom demands. May I do this?"

"Of course. She will be very welcome."

"Then I come. Saba also, if you wish it."

"I certainly do," Silk assured Siyuf.

Saba nodded reluctantly.

Oosik said, "You may rely upon me, Caldé."

"Thank you. And you, Your Cognizance?"

With the help of the baculus, Quetzal rose. "I've no food, Patera Caldé. That's what you'll talk about, isn't it?"

"I'm sure we will; we have that to discuss, along with many other things. You have wisdom, Your Cognizance, and we may need it more than food."

"Then I'll be there. I may even have suggestions."

Chapter 5

THE MAN FROM MAINFRAME

A hand signal held the group parallel to the human stream below; Sciathan reinforced it with helmet notification: "Two east." As each agreed, he checked them off mentally: Grian, Sumaire, Mear, and Aer were still willing to accept his leadership. His right arm stiff, he slapped toward Viron's thatch and shingles, palm down. "Going lower." Fingertips to forehead. "You may follow if you choose."

Aer almost certainly would.

Was this man Auk among the marchers' creeping rectangles? One of the spectators whose cheers had dwindled to chirps in the vastness of the sky? Either way this Auk was a lone individual, his fellow citizens a myriad of myriads. As he had from the beginning, Sciathan told himself that he should be bursting with pride; for this daunting, almost impossible mission, Mainframe had chosen them.

The possibility that Mainframe wished to destroy them had to be dismissed unheard, like the equal possibility that he, Aer, and the rest had been chosen because they were expendable.

Right arm pointing, hand cupped. "I fly east."

Four acknowledgments. They were all coming.

He had begun a circuit of the city. They would have to land soon, have to remove and secure their wings, question and persuade its inhabitants in the Common Tongue. Whether he was a miracle worker or a malcontent, his fluency had no doubt been a factor.

Where was there a good, big field, with people near but not too near, close to the city? Below him, a house with a desert-colored peaked roof sprang up like a mushroom.

Right arm extended, palm flat, motioning down. "Lower."

It seemed that he could read the character of each of his companions in their acknowledgments: Grian weighing the odds; Sumaire narrow-eyed, her hands deadly still; Mear frantic for adventure; Aer concerned for everybody except herself.

At this altitude they were within the reach of small-arms fire, and small arms were evident; all the overseers of the bearded men erecting tents seemed to have them. He reminded himself that once they had landed the presence or absence of weapons would make no difference, that any mob of Cargos could kill them with stones or sticks. In fact the weapons that these Cargos had should be an advantage; armed, they would be less apt to feel threatened.

Pointing arm, hand a fist. "North." Two fingers down, separated. "Terminate flight."

"*Aye, Sumaire.*" Taut face, dry lips, hooded eyes.

"*Aye, Mear!*" Descending too fast and glorying in it.

"*Aye, Grian.*" Picking his spot.

"*Aye, Aer.*" Worrying about him, worried not that he would crash but that he would bungle his approach.

Grassy land, a little uneven. No more time for character or planning. Reverse thrust, legs down and feet together, hands braced for a fall that must be straight forward.

Mear was already down, having pulled up at the precise moment and landed striding; reckless though Mear was, no more skilled Flier ever tuned the sun. Now he, too, would have to land without a fall or lose what authority he had. Four cubits, stall, drop into the wind. Did it!

At once a gust nearly blew him off his feet.

Grian, Sumaire and Aer came down as he was taking off his wings and PM, Aer too close, perhaps; Sumaire four-pointing; Grian dropping a full eight, wings bow-bent when he hit.

Big women were running toward them from the tent ground, pursued, overtaken, and surpassed by a lone woman on horseback.

"Peace!" He raised both hands, palms out. "We who serve the gods mean no harm."

The rider reined up, a handweapon drawn. "There are no gods but the goddess!"

Could the database be wrong? "We are her supporters and servitors!"

A dozen towering women surrounded them, some staring, some leveling short, gap-mouthed guns, some clearly waiting for the mounted woman's instructions.

"We come from Mainframe," Sciathan explained. "Mainframe, the home of the goddess. At her order we come to find Auk." Privately he wondered which goddess it was.

"We'll help you, but first you must give your weapons to us." There was calculation in the mounted woman's eyes.

Aer said, "No gun, no knife."

The mounted woman's attention went to her at once. "You're in charge?"

Aer shook her head. "Fliers." She touched her chin. "Aer I am. All fly."

Mear joined them carrying his wings and PM, and accompanied by a gaggle of big women. "Each is one. Five ones."

"Surrender your weapons," the woman on horseback told him.

Coming up behind Mear, Sumaire held out her hands. "Mine. With these I kill."

Calculation again. "You're the leader."

"Yes. My own."

Mear said, "I am mine. No weapon. No gun. You give?" One of the big women laughed loudly and the horse shied, neck bent and hooves dancing.

"Quiet, you!" Pulling up the reins, the mounted woman scrutinized them. *Marhaba! Betifham 'arabi?"*

Aer and Mear looked to Sciathan; he could only shrug.

She holstered her weapon and dismounted; her smile could not vanquish something vindictive that had made her face its own. "We started badly," she told Aer. "Let's start over and be friends. I'm Major Sirka, Flier Aer. I command the advance party of the Horde of Trivigaunte. I can't welcome you to this city, because this city's not mine. Mine's to the south. You have flown over it many times. You must know it."

Aer nodded and smiled. "Beautiful!"

"This man," Major Sirka nodded at Sciathan, "came looking for a Vironese, another man. Are you looking for a woman?"

Sumaire said, "The man. Where will we find Auk?"

Grian, who arrived still wearing his PM, said slowly, "We are not like you are, Woman."

"I wouldn't expect you to be, little man. Now listen to me. You're . . ."

Her voice faded; she had become a painted figure, an image of gray on a featureless plain. Sciathan felt his lips drawn back and lifted in a grin by someone else.

Aer gaped at him, eyes wide as her mouth. Now, when all other color had fled, the blue of her eyes was still bright. Someone else reached out to her with Sciathan's arms, and in a distant place she screamed.

The flash and boom of the shot so startled him that almost he woke; colors were briefly real, the scarlet-daubed thing at his feet Aer. He felt himself thrust violently down and back into a helpless dark at the edge of oblivion.

Sumaire slew with a touch and Mear fought with desperate valor until more shots threw both to the ground in their first embrace. Still carrying his wings, Grian shot straight up. He, Sciathan, should fly too; but his PM was gone, his hands bound. Turning, he saw his wings and kicked and stamped them.

"Let me think, Patera." Maytera Marble cocked her head to one side. "The generalissimo from Trivigaunte and another one, but we don't know her name. I'm assuming it will be a woman."

Silk nodded. "I believe we can rely on it."

"We don't know how much either one eats. Probably a lot. Then there's General Saba and Generalissimo Oosik. I've seen them, and they'll want a whorl of food. Are each of them going to bring some-body, too?"

"That's a good point." Silk considered. "Oosik's almost certain to, because Siyuf said she'd bring one of her staff. Let's assume that they both do. That's six so far."

"All big eaters."

"I'm sure you're right, but His Cognizance and I won't eat much and you'll eat nothing."

"Am I invited?" It was difficult to read Maytera Marble's expression.

"Of course you are. You're the hostess, the mistress of the house—of this palace, I should have said."

"I thought Chenille might do it, Patera."

"She's a guest." Silk settled himself more comfortably in the big wingback chair, conscious that he would have to leave it soon. "She's here only because she may be in danger."

"She's a real help, that girl. She does everything I tell her to and looks for more. There are times when I have to hold her back, Patera."

"Now I understand. You were afraid I wouldn't invite her, that I'd ask her to wait on table or something. She's invited—or she will be as soon as I see her. I want her, and your granddaughter and Master Xiphias; I sent Horn to tell him."

"I teach arithmetic." Maytera Marble sighed. "And now I want to count on my fingers. What's worse, I can't. Only up to five, and we had six with Generalissimo Oosik and all those foreign officers. You and His Cognizance make eight. The old fencing master nine. Chenille, ten. Mucor and me, twelve. If you're going to invite anybody else, you'd better make it two, Patera. Thirteen at table's not lucky. I don't know why, but you're supposed to bring somebody in off the street if you have to, to make fourteen."

Silk stood up. "No, that should be all. Now come with me. I asked Hossaan to bring the floater, and I think I heard it a moment ago."

"Where . . . ? I can't go away, Patera. Not with company for dinner tonight."

Silk had anticipated that; he imagined himself arguing with Siyuf and was firm. "Of course you can. You're going to. Go get your hand."

"No. No." Maytera Marble's one functioning hand gripped the arm of her chair so tightly that the upholstery rose like dough between its metal fingers. "You don't understand. You're a good man. Too good, to tell the truth. Too good to me, as you always have been. But I've a thousand things to do between now and dinner. What time will it be? Six?"

"Eight. I do understand, Maytera, and that's why we're going to that shop the valet—what was his name?"

"Marl. Patera, I can't."

"Exactly. You can't because you have only one hand. You have to tell Chenille, for the most part, and get her to do it. So we're going to get your right hand reattached. As you say, there's a lot to be done, and with two hands you'll be able to do twice as much as Chenille, instead of half as much."

Without waiting for her to reply, he strode to the door. "I'll be outside; I want to ask Hossaan why their generalissimo speaks the way she does. We'll expect you in five minutes, with your hand." As he stepped into the reception hall, he added, "You and Chenille, and your granddaughter. Bring her, too."

Maytera Marble's last wailing *"Patera . . ."* was cut off by the closing of the door. Grinning, Silk limped the length of the reception hall and got an overrobe of plain black fleece from the cloakroom off the foyer.

The outer door swung toward him before he could open it, and Hossaan stepped inside with Oreb perched on his shoulder. "Your bird was out there, Caldé. I guess he couldn't find a window open, so I brought him in."

"Girls fly," Oreb croaked, fluttering. "Bird see."

"Yes, and just in time, silly bird. Come here."

Oreb hopped to Silk's wrist. "Men perch!"

"He's been flying up to the airship," Silk explained. "By now he probably understands it a great deal better than I do. They lower people from it in a thing like an oversized birdcage, and bring people and supplies up; that seems to interest him." He hesitated, then waved toward a long divan. "Let's sit down for a moment. There's something I want to ask you."

"Sure thing, Caldé."

"We could do this in your floater, but I have the feeling there'd be somebody wanting to talk to me, and I don't want to be interrupted. Did you see the parade?"

Hossaan nodded. "I was keeping an eye on you up on that stand, Caldé, in case you wanted me."

"Good. Then you saw me talking to Generalissimo Siyuf and General Saba. Do you know either of them, by the way?"

"Personally, you mean, Caldé? No, I don't. I know what they look like."

"You haven't spoken to them."

Hossaan shook his head.

"But you've traveled. You're from Trivigaunte originally?"

"Yes, Caldé. I was born there. You'd be a fool to take anything I tell you at face value. You realize that, I'm sure."

"Good man!" Oreb defended him. "Men fly. Perch!"

"Of course. I understand that your primary loyalty must be to your native city."

"It is. And you're right, I've traveled more than most men ever do. I can tell you about some of the places I've been, if you like, but I can't always tell you what I was doing there."

Silk nodded thoughtfully. "Here in Viron, we sometimes say that someone speaks Vironese, as if it were a separate language. It isn't, of course. It's just that we have certain idiomatic expressions that aren't used, as far as I know, in other cities. There are words we pronounce differently as well. I know very little about other cities, but I wouldn't be surprised to learn that they have peculiarities of their own."

"That's right. I think I know what you're going to ask me, but go on."

"Is there any reason you shouldn't tell me about it?"

"Not a one."

"All right. I was going to say that there actually are other languages, languages quite different from ours. Latin, for example, and French. We have French and Latin books, and there are passages in the Writings in those languages, which makes them of interest to scholars and even to ordinary augurs like me. Presumably there are cities in which those languages are spoken just as we speak Vironese here."

"The Common Tongue," Hossaan said. "That's what travelers generally call it, and it's what we call it in Trivigaunte."

"I see." Silk's forefinger traced small circles on his cheek. "In that case you, from your foreign perspective, would say that both Viron and Palustria, for instance, speak the Common Tongue? Palustrian is similar enough to Vironese that one might have to listen to a speaker for several minutes to determine his native city. Or so I was taught at the schola."

"You've got it, Caldé."

"Very well then. I can imagine a foreign city in which another language is spoken, Latin let us say. And I can easily imagine one like Palustria, where the Common Tongue is spoken; I can't prove it, but I suspect that there may be more differences between the speech of a Vironese of the upper class and a beggar or a bricklayer than there are between an ordinary merchant from Viron and a like merchant from Palustria. What I cannot imagine is a city in which some citizens speak the Common Tongue, as you call it, and others Latin or another language."

Hossaan nodded, but said nothing.

"Men fly!" Oreb announced, having lost patience with his owner. He launched himself from Silk's shoulder and flapped around the room spiraling higher. "Fly! Fly! Girls! Men!" He extended his wings in a long glide. "Perch!"

"Great Pas guide us!" Maytera Marble was coming down the staircase with Chenille and Mucor. "What's gotten into your bird, Patera?"

"I don't know," said Silk—who thought, however, that he did. "Hossaan, he came to you while you were waiting in the floater, is that right?"

"He landed on the back of the seat, Caldé, and started talking. I couldn't understand him at first."

"Yet another language, or at least another way of speaking the Common Tongue." Silk smiled wryly. "What did he say?"

" 'Bird out, bird out, Silk in.' Like that, Caldé."

Silk nodded. "Go out and wait for us. Put the canopy up. I don't know how long the wait will be, and there's no point in your freezing."

As Hossaan left, Chenille asked, "Aren't we going, Patera?"

"In a moment. Step into the library, please, everybody. Oreb, where are the flying men and flying girls who perched?"

Oreb hopped to a corner occupied by a fat-bellied vase and rapped it sharply with his beak.

"Northeast, Mucor," Silk muttered. "Did you see that?"

Her skull-like face turned toward him as a pale funeral lily lifts its blossom to the sun. "Flying, Silk?"

"Fliers, I believe. The people who fly on wings made of something that looks like gauze."

Chenille added, "Like the Trivigaunti pterotroopers, only their wings are longer and look like they'd be lighter."

The night chough flew to Silk's shoulder.

"One more question, Oreb. Were there houses where the flying people landed?"

"House now! Quick house!"

Silk took a handkerchief from his pocket, shook it out, and draped it over his spread fingers. "Like this?"

"Yes, yes!"

"Sit down, please," Silk told the three women. "Mucor, as a great favor to me, and your grandmother, too, do you think you could find out what these Fliers are doing?"

When she did not answer, he said, "Search the grazing land north and east of the city, where the Rani's men are putting up their tents. I believe that may be what he means when he says quick houses. The Fliers will have taken off their wings when they landed, I imagine, and they'll probably leave at least one of their number to guard them."

"As Patera says, this is for both of us, Mucor." Maytera Marble patted her knee. "I don't know why it's important, but I'm sure it must be."

Chenille remarked, "You know, I've been wanting to have a look at this ever since that Trivigaunti saw her in the mirror, only now I can't even tell if she's doing it. You ought to be chanting and sprinkling perfume on Thelxiepeia's picture."

"The miracle—or magic, if that's what you wish to call it—is in Mucor," Silk told her.

"Auk believes in the gods, Patera. He's really religious in his way, and he knows I had Scylla inside running things. But what I'm seeing wouldn't make him believe in this."

"Auk," Mucor repeated suddenly.

Oreb cocked his head like Maytera Marble. "Where Auk?"

Mucor's toneless voice seemed to emanate from a forsaken place beyond the universe. "Where Auk is . . . Silk? Chain my hands. Feet smash strong wings."

Chapter 6

In Spider's Web

"Are we truly, um, abandoned, Maytera? Solitary? Or are there other ears, eh? In this dark and—er—noisome. That's the question, hum?"

"I don't know. I have no way of telling. Do you?" The question Maytera Mint herself was debating was whether it would be disrespectful to lie down before Remora did.

"I—ah—no. I have none, I confess."

"Do you have a secret that would let Potto and the other councillors return to power in defiance of the gods?"

"I would—um—General. Be safer not, eh? Not to speak upon such, er, topics."

"It certainly would if you had one, Your Eminence. Do you?" She was trying to forget how thirsty she was.

"Positively not. Not privy to military matters, eh?"

"Neither do I, Your Eminence, so let them listen all they want." It was ecstasy to take her shoes off; for half a minute she debated taking off her long black stockings, too, but self-control prevailed. "By now Bison's taken charge. Or someone else has, but probably it's Bison. He was my best officer, absolutely steady in a crisis but not very imaginative. If he can find somebody a little more creative to advise him, Bison should give the Ayuntamiento a very difficult time."

"I am, er, suffused with pleasure at the prospect."

"So am I, Your Eminence. I just hope it's true." She leaned back against the wall.

"You will, um, reproach me."

"Never, Your Eminence."

"You, or others. One never lacks for, um, critics? Patera Feelers.

Faultfinders. You will—um—er—vociferate that as a, um, intermediary I must restrain my partisanship."

She laid her arms on her knees, and her head upon her arms.

"I rejoin, General, by, er, asseverating that I have done so. And do so, eh? In our, um, current instance and beyond, hey? It is not partisanship but reason, hey? I am a man of peace. I have so, um, declared myself. Under flag of truce, eh? Having consulted Brigadier Erne. Having likewise consulted Caldé Silk. Brought the, um, exceedingly significant—hum. You, General. I brought you to discuss, er, armistice. An—ah—feat of diplomacy? Triumph. Is my, er, our persons. Are they respected? They are not!"

"I'm going to stretch out, if that won't upset you, Your Eminence. I'll tuck my skirt around my legs."

"No, no, Mayt—General. I can scarcely make out your, ah, self in this—er—stygian. There is one quarrel that cannot be mediated, hey?"

"We certainly haven't succeeded in mediating this one."

"I refer to the quarrel between good and, um, evil. Yes, evil. As a man of the cloth, an augur erstwhile destined, eh? Destined for—ah—greatness. As that, um, augur, fallible, eh? At whiles foolish, eh? Yet sensible of the ultimate, hey? I cannot mediate all quarrels, for I cannot mediate that one. I have set down my name in the lists, eh? Long since. I am for good. I cannot close my eyes to evil. Will not. Both."

"That's good." Maytera Mint closed hers. The only light in the dark, bare room was a long streak of watery green under the door; closing her eyes should have made little difference, yet she found it deeply restful.

"If—er—ah—um—hum," Remora said; or at least, so she heard him. The façade of the Corn Exchange was falling very slowly, while she waited powerless to move.

She woke with a start. "Your Eminence?"

"Yes, General?"

"Some dreams are sent by the gods."

"Ah—indubitably."

"Has anyone ever proposed that all dreams are? That every dream is a message from the gods?"

"I—um. Cannot recollect, eh? I shall devote thought to the, er, query. Possibly. Quite possibly."

"Because I just had a very commonplace sort of dream, Your Eminence, but I feel that it may have been sent by a god."

"Unusual? Extraordinary. If I do not presume, hey? No wish to, er, intrude. But I offer my, um, if desired."

"I dreamed I was standing on the street in front of the Corn Exchange. It was falling on me, but I couldn't run."

"I—ah—see."

"It actually happened a few days ago. We pulled it down with oxen. I could've run then, but I didn't want to. I wanted to die, so I stood there and watched it fall until Rook carried me out of danger. He was nearly killed, as well as I."

"The—ah—import? I fail to see it, General."

"A god, I think, was telling me that since I'd chosen to die then, I shouldn't be afraid of dying now, that nothing they can do to me could be worse than being crushed by that building, which was the way I'd chosen to die not long ago."

"What god, hey? What god, General? Have you any notion?"

She knew from an alteration in Remora's voice that he had straightened up. She had, temporarily at least, ransomed him from self-pity; she wished fervently that someone would ransom her. "I haven't the least idea which god may have favored me, Your Eminence, assuming one did. I don't recall anything that would furnish a clue."

"No animals, eh?"

"None, Your Eminence. Just the street, and the falling stones. It was after shadelow, and all I remember is how dark they looked against the skylands."

"Not, um, Day-Ruling Pas. Sun god, eh? Master of the Long Sun and all that. Tartaros, hum? Night god. Dark stones, dark god. Bats—ah—flittering?"

Maytera Mint rolled her head so that the tip of her sharp little nose made a small arc of negation. "No animals, Your Eminence, as I said. None whatsoever."

"I shall—ah—prefer. I prefer to, um, suspend? No, table. Table the question, eh? If only for the nonce. In my, er, not inconsiderable experience an, um, signature may be—ah—described by one who, eh? Shall peer about. Let us peer about, Maytera. What day is this, would you say?"

"Now?"

"Ah—yes. And then, eh? What day did you feel it to be in your, um, envisagement?"

"If you mean the night it happened . . . ?"

"No. Did it, ah, seem to you a particular day, eh? Were you, um, conscious of a—ah—the calendar?"

"No, Your Eminence."

"What day is it now? As we, ah, converse."

How many times had their captors halted to eat and sleep? Three? Four? "I can't be sure." Maytera Mint was beginning to regret mentioning her dream; she let her eyelids fall.

"Guess, General. What day?"

"Hieraxday or Thelxday, I suppose."

"Bodies, eh? Vultures?"

"No. Just the skylands, the building and the stones."

"Mirrors, monkeys, deer? Cards, teacups—ah—string? Any colored string? Poultry, nothing of the sort?"

"No, Your Eminence. Nothing of the sort."

"Space—um—largeness? Skylands, eh? You were—ah—not insensible of them?"

"I knew that they were there, Your Eminence. In fact they seemed significant, though I can't say how."

"We, er, progress? Yes, progress. Actually happened, you said? Building fell, eh? You rescued."

"Yes, it was at the beginning of the fighting. I mean to say, Your Eminence, that it was at what we call the beginning now. At the time we felt we'd been fighting a long while, that those of us who'd been fighting from the start had done a great deal of it." Maytera Mint paused, reflecting.

"We were like children who have gone to palaestra for the first time the year before. When the next year starts, children like that feel themselves old hands, veterans. They give advice to the new children and patronize them, when the truth is that their own education has scarcely begun."

Remora grunted assent. "I have observed, um, similar."

"And now—I mean before we went out to that house where the caldé was rescued. Things had quieted down. We had the Fourth penned up, and nobody wanted to go after it right away. We sensed that

Erne was wavering, and you confirmed it. The Ayuntamiento was down in these tunnels, and those of us who thought about it saw how difficult it would be to root them out. We dared hope that some other way could be found. That was why I went out there with you."

She waited for Remora to speak, but he did not.

"People came forward. They would appear, so to speak, to tell us how bravely they'd fought and all they'd done. And I'd think, who are you? Why didn't I ever notice you before, if you were such a famous fighter? Bison had done everything, taken part in almost every fight.

"And Wool, I'd think. Wool has done a great deal, never shirked, not always saying I'll do it, General, like Bison, but when we were repulsed and I'd look back and see one person still there, still shooting when the rest had fallen back and there were hoppies—Guardsmen, Your Eminence, troopers of the Civil Guard—close enough to touch, it would be Wool.

"Then I'd remember that Wool was dead, and think where were the ones who rode with me, where was Kingcup who brought us her horses when her horses were all she had? I hope she's alive, Your Eminence, but I couldn't locate her, couldn't find her, and all these new people telling about the wonderful things they'd done, when I didn't remember them at all. Skink led an attack on the Palatine and had both his legs blown off. Where was he? Where was the giant with the gaps in his teeth? I don't even remember his name, but I remember looking up at them, he must have been twice my height, and wondering who had been big enough to hit him way up there, and what he'd hit him with, and what had happened after he did it."

"What was his name?"

"The giant, Your Eminence? I can't recall it. Cat? Or Tomcat, something like that. No, Gib. That was it. Gib. It means a male cat, Your Eminence, so that would make it Snarling Sphigx, the Patroness of Trivigaunte. Cats are hers, cats and lions. But Gib wasn't in my dream."

"The man who saved you."

"Oh, him. It was Rook, but rooks aren't sacred to any god, are they, Your Eminence? Eagles for Pas. Hawks, too, because hawks are little eagles, or something like them. Thrushes and larks for Molpe, but rooks can't sing. Poultry for Thelxiepeia, as Your Eminence said a moment ago, but rooks—wait.

"I've got it, Your Eminence. I was thinking lists, wasn't I? Thinking about lists instead of animals and what they look like. And a rook looks like a night chough, like the caldé's pet. The caldé got him to give to the god who enlightened him. People think it was Pas, almost everyone seems to think that, but I asked the caldé about it and he said it wasn't, that it was one of the minor gods, the Outsider. I don't know much about him, Your Eminence. I'm sure you must know much more than I, but night choughs must be sacred to him. Or if they aren't, they're associated with him now, because that was the sacrifice the caldé chose. Isn't that correct, Your Eminence?"

Remora did not reply.

Maytera Mint thought of getting up to see whether he had gone. It seemed to her that she had slept even as she spoke aloud; but it was too delicious, far too delicious to lie where she was, with Bison in the other bed snoring softly and Auk to watch over them. "Auk?" she called softly. "Auk?"

Auk would bring them water, would surely bring water if she asked for it, a carafe of cold clear water, fresh from the well, and glasses. More loudly this time: "Auk!"

Yeah, Mother. Right here.

"*Auk,* my son?"

"Sorry Patera." Shivering in the afternoon sunlight, Auk returned his attention to Incus. "Thought I heard something."

"You desired to speak with me?"

"Right. Back in the manteion you explained what he said." Auk felt uneasy among the Palatine's gracious mansions of gray stone; until now he had visited them only to steal.

"I *endeavored* to explain, certainly. It was my *sacred duty* to do so, thus I *strove* to make clear the *divine utterances.*"

"You were clear as polymer, Patera," Hammerstone declared loyally. "I felt like I could understand every word Pas ever said before you finished."

Voices called for them to halt, and they did.

"Bios with slug guns, Patera. I heard them behind us, but I was hoping they wouldn't mess around."

Afraid he was about to be arrested, Auk grumbled, "Can't a man walk uphill any more?"

By then the patrol leader had noted Incus's black robe. "Sorry, Patera. It's the soldier. They say some are on our side. Is he one?"

Hammerstone nodded. "You got it."

"*Indeed,* my son." Incus favored the patrol with a toothy smile. "You have my *sacred word* as an augur and your—well, let us not go into *that.* You have my *sacred word* that Corporal *Hammerstone* longs for the overthrow of the Ayuntamiento, even as I do myself."

"I'm Sergeant Linsang," the patrol leader said. "Are you going to the Grand Manteion, Patera?"

Incus shook his head. "To the *Prolocutor's Palace,* my son. I am a resident *thereof.*" His voice grew confidential. "I have been favored with a *theophany. Great Pas himself* so favored *me.* It is not the first, but the *second* time that I have been thus *favored* by the gods. You will *scarcely* credit it, I know, for I scarcely credit it *myself.* But *both* my companions were present upon the *latter* occasion. They will *attest* to the *theophany,* I feel quite *certain.*"

One of Linsang's troopers raised his slug gun so that it no longer pointed at Auk. "Aren't you Auk? Auk the prophet?"

"That's me."

"He's been going all over the city," the trooper explained to Linsang, "Telling everybody to get ready for Pas's Plan. He says Tartaros told him to."

"He did," Auk declared stoutly. "Pas wants me to keep on doing it, too. What about you, trooper? Are you set to go? Set to give up on the whole whorl?"

Linsang asked, "What did Pas say? That is if I'm not—"

"It is *irregular,*" Incus conceded, "but not *contrary* to the *canon.* Do all of you *desire* to hear the words of the *Father of the Gods?*"

Several assured him that they did.

"And *will* you," Incus pursued his advantage, "permit us to *proceed* upon our *sacred errand* once you have *heard them?*"

Linsang's troopers nodded. They were in their teens, and identifiable as troopers only by their slug guns and bandoliers.

Linsang objected. "I need to get it from this soldier, first. Hammerstone? Is that your name, Corporal?"

"Present and accounted for." Hammerstone's own slug gun was pointed at the skylands, its butt on his hip.

"Are you for the Ayuntamiento or the caldé?"

"The caldé, Sergeant."

"How do you feel about the Ayuntamiento?"

"If the caldé or Patera here said not to shoot them, I wouldn't do it. If it's up to me, they're dead meat."

One of the troopers ventured, "A soldier killed Councillor Potto. That's what we heard."

Hammerstone grinned, his head back and his chin out. "It wasn't me, but I'll shake his hand first chance I get."

"All right." Linsang grounded his slug gun. "You can go on to the Prolocutor's Palace, Patera. Them, too. Only tell us what Pas had to say."

"I fear *not*." Incus shook his head. "You would not *accept* my *sacred word*, my son, but *insisted* that Hammerstone speak for *himself*. As it chanced, though nothing is mere *chance* to the *immortal gods*, but a moment previously he had *declared* that he *comprehends* the god's entire *message*, while my other companion, *Auk*, wished a fuller *exposition*."

Incus turned to the prophet in question. "Is that not *so*, Auk? Am I not *correct*?"

"You got it, Patera. Maybe I'm dumb. There's not many that said so where I could hear 'em, but maybe I am. Only this is important, and some was about me. I got to be sure I got it straight, so I can do what he wants me to."

"*Would* that such *stupidity* as yours were more *widespread*. The *Chrasmologic Writings* assert that the *wisdom* of the *immortal gods* is but *folly* in the ears of *mortal men*. *Persevere* in your *stupidity*, and you will be welcomed to *Mainframe*." Incus nodded to the big soldier. "Tell us, *Hammerstone*, my son, and do not fear that you may *blunder* or omit a *sacred* injunction. I shall *amend* any such *innocent errors*, though I *anticipate* none."

"I can't do it as good as you, Patera, but I'll give it my best shot. Let me get my thinking works going." For eight or ten seconds, Hammerstone was as immobile as a statue.

"All right, I got it. It was when that bio was bringing up the pig. First the colors came on, right? Then his face. He started off by blessing everybody and said that everybody that was there 'cause they came with Auk—that was everybody but you, Patera—he blessed twice, once for coming and once for following Auk. Have I got that right?"

Incus nodded. "*Admirable*, Hammerstone, my son."

"Then he said he was giving us this theophany 'cause his son told him what was coming down in the manteion we were at, only he didn't say which son it was."

"Terrible Tartaros," Auk assured him.

Incus raised an admonitory finger. "He did not *so state*."

"Maybe not, but I'd just been talking to him. That's who it had to be."

"He said his son'd given Auk his orders, and they were the right ones. He and his son were going to see to it everybody got the word. We'd been thinking about his Plan like it was way off, when it was already time to move out. . . ."

"*Continue,* my son."

"I'm sorry, Patera. That's when he started talking about me, and I get kind of choked up. It was the greatest moment of my life, right? I mean, if I was to make sergeant or anything like that I'd feel pretty good. But this was Pas. I got his drift and later you explained, and it was like I'd been feeling it was, just exactly. Hearing you say it was just about like I was hearing it all over again from him. I'm thinking there's a war, and all the good people's on his side. That's this son–"

"Terrible Tartaros," Auk put in.

"And the caldé and Auk and naturally you are, Patera. And it's the side I'm on, too. He said how Auk got hurt when he was underground with us and how hard he'd been working for his Plan, and he was sending somebody from Mainframe to help him out."

"From the *Pole,* Corporal. That is the term which the god *himself* preferred to employ. That *Mainframe* is at the *Pole,* I freely concede."

Auk edged nearer. "To help *me* out? I'm the cull?"

"Yeah, you're the one, only I'm supposed to help too. He said he was going to decorate you for what you've done soon as you do what he wants you to next. Only here's where Patera said something I got to say too, so it'll make sense to these other bios. Pas is us chems' god. He's the god of all the digital, nuclear-chemical stuff. You got to buy that if you want to see where Pas's coming from. Isn't that right, Patera?"

Incus nodded solemnly.

" 'Cause Pas told us what Auk's decoration's going to be. Anytime he sees anything like me, he's going to understand it straight off. How it goes together and what it's supposed to do, and how. Pas means to stick all the data into Auk, 'cause he'll need it to carry out the Plan."

Linsang and his troopers stared at Auk openmouthed. Auk endeavored to appear humble.

"That was when he gave me my direct order, and it wasn't just 'cause I happened to be around. I never thought anything like this would happen to me. I asked Patera about it back at the manteion, and he says if I hadn't been the one Pas wanted, I wouldn't have been there, it would've been some other tinpot. But it wasn't. I'm the one. Patera says it was probably 'cause him and me are, you know, like brothers only closer, and he's a holy augur, and as soon as he said it I knew it was right.

"Pas needs a soldier, so which one? There's thousands. Why, the augur's friend, doesn't that make sense? The friend of the augur Scylla picked to be the new Prolocutor, that's the one you need. A god don't have to think about stuff like that, he just knows. He said, talking to me, Auk might have a little trouble at first. You stick with him and help him over the tough spots. You're a mechanism, help him out and he'll help you. So here we are, Patera and me both, and we're trying to help."

Linsang asked Incus, "Was that all, Patera?"

"*All?* I should say it was more than *enough,* my son. But no. It was *not.* Let us have the *remainder,* Hammerstone."

"He said that a while back, forty years, he said, he knew he was going to die—"

"To die?" Linsang was incredulous.

"That's what he said. He saw it coming, so he sort of took off little pieces of himself and hid them in various bios where they wouldn't be found. Then he died, and he's been dead for quite a while."

Incus cleared his throat. "All of *you,* and I, *similarly,* must comprehend the *difficulties* under which a god seeking to *communicate* with *human kind* labors. He can but speak to us in words mere *mortals* apprehend. Thus by *die,* the *Father* of the *Gods* indicated his own *renewal.* That *noblest* of *trees,* the *goldenshower,* is sacred to *Great Pas.* You cannot be ignorant of so *elementary* a fact."

Linsang and several of his troopers nodded.

"*Suppose* that a *forest* of goldenshowers could *speak* to us. Would it not say, 'That *I,* the *sacred forest,* may remain *young* and *strong,* my *aged* trees must *fall,* though they have *endured* for *centuries.* Let *young* trees spring up in their *places.* I, the *forest, endure.*' Hammerstone?"

"I'm on it, Patera. He said now when his Plan's starting to move, he's putting himself back together. He said right now he was his own ghost, Pas's ghost, but with more of his pieces getting found, he'll be Pas

again. He wants us to help. Auk in particular, but everybody's supposed
to pitch in. We got to find this one particular bio, Patera Jerboa, 'cause
he's got the piece for Viron. There was maybe five or six hundred bios
in the manteion, but after Patera'd explained the whole thing to them,
there wasn't one that knew who this Patera Jerboa was or where we
could maybe find him.

"So Patera told them not to bunch up, but scatter and start asking
people all over, and bring him to Auk when they got him. Then he told
Auk the Chapter's got records about all this stuff, where every augur's
at and what he's doing there, and they're in the Palace, and Patera
knows where and how to read them. He's worked with them for years,
right Patera? So him and Auk and me started off to take a look, and here
we are."

"The *majesty* of diction was lacking, *Hammerstone,* my son, yet the
matter was in *attendance.*" Incus regarded Linsang and his troopers.
"What of *you*? We seek to obey the dictates of the *Father* of the *Seven.*
Can you *assist* us? No *holy augur* can know every other. We are *far* too
numerous. Do you know of a *Patera Jerboa*? Any of you? *Speak.*"

No one did.

Shots woke Maytera Mint. At first, as she lay blinking in the darkness,
she did not know what the sounds had been; she was hungry and
thirsty, vaguely conscious of the cold, and conscious that she had been
cold for a long time, shivering as she slept. Her buttocks and shoulder
blades, pressed by her slight weight to unyielding shiprock, were numb,
her feet freezing.

She sat up. Her room had been the smallest and meanest in the old
cenoby on Silver Street, with a ceiling that dripped at every shower; yet
it had not been too small or too mean for a window past whose threadbare drape wisps of light crept on even the darkest nights.

Three sharp bangs, unevenly spaced. Pictures falling? She recalled
an incident from her childhood: an old watercolor had fallen when its
yellowed string rotted through at last, and had taken another picture
and a small vase down with it. Once she had heard a horse trying to
kick its way out of its stall. The shots had sounded like that.

"Ah, General?"

The voice had been Remora's; his nasal tones brought it all back to her. "Yes, Your Eminence."

"You have, um, familiar with the sound of gunfire, hey? During the past—ah—fighting."

"Yes, Your Eminence. Tolerably so." Against her will, she found herself wondering how many Remoras there had been, how many augurs and sibyls who had responded to Echidna's theophany by going to the safest place they could find and staying there. Patera Silk had not. (But then, he wouldn't.) Patera Silk had been shot in the chest, had been captured, and had contrived, somehow, to turn Oosik and the whole Third Brigade, the act that had done more than any other to determine the course of their insurrection. But how many more—

"Er, General?"

"Yes, Your Eminence. I was considering the matter. The door is thick and rather tightly fitted, and these walls are shiprock. Those factors must have affected the quality of the shots as we heard them."

"You—ah—believe them shots, eh?"

"I'm putting on my shoes, Your Eminence." She groped for them in the dark. "If we're to be taken somewhere—"

"Quite right." Remora sounded cheerful. "Quetzal, eh? Old Quetzal. His Cognizance, I ought to say."

More thirsty than ever, Maytera Mint licked her dry lips. "His Cognizance, Your Eminence?"

"Rescue, eh? He's come for me, er, we. Or—ah—sent somebody. Shrewd, eh? Plays a deep game, old Quetzal. Card sense in both—um—the applicable senses."

She tried to imagine the elderly Prolocutor fighting, slug gun in hand, against Spider and his spy-catchers, and failed utterly. "I would think Bison's sent scouts into the tunnels by this time, Your Eminence. If we're lucky, it may be some of them we heard. But even if they notice this door, they may not be able to get it open."

Another shot, and it was definitely a shot.

"They will notice it, General. I—um—my word on it. My gamma-dion, eh?"

"Your gammadion, Your Eminence?"

"Not you, ah, sibyls. But we augurs. Holy augurs, eh? Wear Pas's voided cross. Comes apart. Use to test a Window, hey? Tighten connections, make adjustments, all that sort of, er, operations. Gold, hey? Mine is. Coadjutor, eh? Stones. Not like old Quetzal's, I, um, but gems. Amethysts, largely. Gold chain. Under my tunic, generally. Out at sacrifice, hey?"

"I'm familiar with them, Your Eminence."

"I've–ah–slipped it beneath the door, Maytera. Push it out, eh? Pull it back in. Moving object, hum? Catches the light, ah, attracts the eye."

She went to the door (almost tripping over Remora) and rapped it sharply with the heel of one shoe.

"Admirable–ah–admirable. Crude, eh? Yet it–ah!"

The latch outside rattled and the door swung in, impeded by Remora. The burly Spider growled, "What's that noise?"

The lights in the tunnel were so dim that Maytera Mint did not blink. "I was pounding on the door with my shoe. We heard shots and hoped we'd be freed."

"Come on." Spider gestured with the barrel of his needler.

"We, um, require food," Remora ventured. "Water or–ah–similar, er, potable."

"You won't if you don't get movin'."

"You don't dare shoot us," Maytera Mint declared. "We're valuable hostages. What would you tell–"

He caught her arm and jerked her through the doorway. "I'm strong, see?"

"I never doubted it." She tested her shoulder, fearing he had dislocated it.

"Strong as a chem. Not one of them soldiers, maybe, but a regular chem. You with me, sib? So I don't have to shoot you. There's twenty, thirty things I could do." One of Spider's men was lounging in the tunnel; he held a gleaming slug gun. "I'm ready to try a couple," Spider continued. "You scavy Councillor Potto's kettle? Wasn't anythin'. He was just playin', he's like that. I don't fool. We get lots of spies."

"I'm delighted to hear it." Maytera Mint had feared that she would not be allowed to resume her shoe; she tightened the bow and straightened up with an odd little thrill of triumph.

"I learned a lot, workin' on them. I never seen one so tough I couldn't get him to tell me anythin' I wanted to know. That way, and keep movin'."

"I, er, weak. Thirsty, eh? What one physically–ow!"

Remora had been prodded from behind by the man with the slug gun, who said, "I kicked a dead cull once till he got up and ran."

"The gods–ah–Pas. Tartaros, eh?" Remora progressed with rapid, unsteady strides, outdistancing Maytera Mint.

"Slow up!"

"I–ah–prayed. Beads eh? The, um, general slept."

"You should have awakened me," she protested, and got a shove from Spider.

"Never! Wouldn't, um, consider–" Remora froze until he was prodded from behind. Somewhat nearsighted, Maytera Mint blinked as she tried to peer ahead through the watery light.

"Dead cull," Spider told her. "One of mine."

"Was that the shooting we heard?"

Spider pushed her forward. "Yeah." Another push. "He was watchin' your door. Sib, you better shaggy learn to drive your shaggy ass or you're going to learn a shaggy bunch you don't want to know."

She whirled, facing him. "I've already learned something, but it was something I wanted to know. That I wanted very much to know, in fact."

He struck her face with the flat of his hand, spinning her around and knocking her down, the blow as loud as the boom of a slug gun. "Pick her up," he told Remora.

Remora did, carrying her like a child as he staggered down the tunnel. When they reached the corpse, the man with the slug gun caught his arm and ordered him to stop, and he set her on her feet. "You're cryin'," Spider told her.

"I am. I shouldn't," she wiped her eyes, "because I know our hour will come. Perhaps I should cry for you instead, but that will come later if it comes at all."

Remora had knelt beside the corpse; he rose shaking his head. "The spirit has, ah, dispensed with its house of flesh."

The man with the slug gun asked, "You were going to say the words over him?"

"I–ah–so intended. It is too late."

"He never believed in it."

Maytera Mint said, "Then I should weep for him. A short life and a violent death in this wretched place. You can write on his stone, here lies one who sought no succor from the gods, and hence received none."

The man with the slug gun chuckled. "Maybe you can. How about it, Spider?"

"Sure, why not? She can do it while we're waitin'."

Remora ventured, "May we be seated? My legs, er, flaccid."

"Go ahead. They'll be along in a minute."

"If you mean Bison's scouts, I feel certain you're right," Maytera Mint told him.

He took off his cap and ran a dirty comb through greasy, graying hair. "You figure Bison's boys chilled him? You're abram."

"I doubt that you even know who Bison is."

"The shag I don't. I got people all through your knot. You think I don't?"

"Thank you very much." She wiped away the last tears with her sleeve. "We appreciate all who come to us."

He laughed. "You appreciate them? They're tellin' us what you do, every move you make."

"Meanwhile they must work and fight for us, if they're not to be detected." She sat down next to Remora. "They would like to rise in our councils, I suppose. To do it, they'll have to work and fight well."

"S'pose all you want to," Spider grunted.

"You are, um, confident it was not one of Colonel Bison's men—er—persons. Troopers. Who shot this, um?"

"Sure. Sib, how come my culls don't faze you?"

"Isn't it obvious? Because we're hiding nothing. You want to learn our secrets, but they're only virtue and prudence. His Eminence and I had hoped to arrange a peace in which your spies and you might live. Now there will be none. We—"

"All right! Muzzle it!"

"Will root you out. We'll go down into this wretched hole and fight, find the underwater boat on which—"

He kicked her.

"You held the caldé—"

He kicked her again, and she screamed.

Remora lurched to his feet. "Really, I cannot—simply, ah, will not tolerate this. Kick me, if you like." Spider pushed him; he staggered, tripped over the corpse, and fell.

"And drop stones on it from the surface or catch it in a net,"

Maytera Mint finished. "If you want our plans, there you have them. Your spies can tell you nothing more."

"You're one tough little girl."

"I'm a gross coward," she told him. "I realized it about an hour after Echidna declared me her sword. We were storming the Alambrera. It might be more accurate to say we were trying to. I—shall I tell you?"

Spider put away his comb. "I'll break you."

"You have already. I screamed, didn't I? What more do you need to complete your triumph? My death?" She threw her arms wide. "Shoot!"

"Another time, maybe." Spider turned his attention to Remora, who was sitting up and rubbing the back of his head. "You, Patera. Your Eminence. Is that what they call you?"

"You may call me either. Or neither, eh? I should, um, opt for neither, given the choice. I—ah—covet no honors from you."

"You can die, too, Patera."

"I, um, well aware. Thinking, hey? Thinking while I, um, bore the general. Not valiant, eh? Not like, er, she."

"Your Eminence, I am *not* brave!"

"You are, Maytera—ah—General. Yes, you are. Not, um, sensible of it, conceivably. I—ah—am not. Was a, um, prisoner of Erne's. I told you, eh?"

"You told me you'd conferred with him, not that you were his prisoner."

Remora looked toward Spider, seeking his permission; Spider said, "Sure, I'd say we got time."

"In the, um, Palace, eh? Eating dinner. Warned, eh? By a page. Guardsmen coming. Thought they wanted—ah—consult me. Waited for my sweet. In they tramped, these, er, troopers. Where's the Prolocutor? That was the, um, term they employed. I endeavored to explain. His Cognizance comes and, ah, departs at his, er, pleasure. Arrested me, hey? Hands bound, all that. Under my robe, eh? I, um, petitioned that favor, and they, er, condescended. Marched me out."

Remora paused to swallow. "Frightened, General. Badly frightened. Horribly, er, affrighted. Coward. Questions, eh? Questions, questions. Read, um, statements I never made, eh? Spoke in my own defense. Struck. Said I'd lied. Struck, eh? On and—ah—more of the, er, like treatment."

Maytera Mint nodded. Her right cheek was beginning to swell, but her eyes were full of sympathy. "I'm sorry, Your Eminence. Truly sorry."

"Said they'd kill me, eh? Needler at my head. All that. Coward, lost control. Bowels, er, voided. Soiled my clothes. Had to speak to the Brigadier. Said that over and over. I—ah—know him. Knew him, eh? In better days. Yes, in better days. Saw him at last. Truce, eh? Truce, cease-fire. I can, er, bring one about, hey? Caldé's an augur. Let me go. Spoke through glass to—ah—Councillor. Loris. Councillor Loris. He said—um—let him go. And they—ah—did. Brigadier Erne did. Fellow I'd—ah—chatted with, hey? Ten, twenty, er, occasions. Parties, dinners, receptions. Gossip, prattle over wine. Beaten, wet—um—stinking. But free. Free."

Spider laughed.

"Back to the Palace, hey? Frightened—ah—terrified. Shooting augurs, eh? Sibyls, too. I, um, didn't see it. For that thank—ah—Tartaros. Thanked Tenebrous Tartaros for it, for, er, shielding my eyes. But I knew, eh? They told me. Felt the—ah—slug. Needle strike my back a score of times in—er—three streets. Roughly, eh? Roughly three. Dead twenty times. Back to the Palace, washed. Listening all the while. Listening for them. Why, eh? Why listen?" Remora's bony fingers laced and loosed, knotting and writhing free to form new knots.

"My—ah—rise. Page as a lad. Schola. Augur. My mother, eh? Be Prolocutor someday, eh? Mother, couple aunts. Father, too, hum? Acolyte, desk in the Palace, higher every year or so, hey? Father died. Careful, hey? Careful, worked hard, hey? Always careful, no enemies, hey? Long hours. Aunt died. Work and wait, eh? Coadjutor died. Younger than old Quetzal, hey? Dead at his table, eh? Lying on his—um—documents. Coadjutor, Mother. Old then, eh? Very. But her eyes shone, Maytera. Er, General. Her eyes shone." Remora's own were full of tears.

"There is no need for you to torment yourself like this, Your Eminence."

Spider told the man with the slug gun, "See what's keepin' them." He rose, nodded to Maytera Mint, and walked away, down the tunnel.

"Mother . . ." Remora coughed, a racking cough deep in his chest. "Sorry. My, um, couldn't prevent it. Mother dead, hey? Mother dead, General. All dead, then. Mother, father, both, er, sisters. Not Mother's—ah—her vision. Vision for me. Prolocutor. Why afraid? Beatings. Blows, eh? 'Fraid of them, too. Most of all—ah—her vision." He fell silent.

Wanting desperately to change the subject, Maytera Mint asked Spider, "Where is that man going? What are we waiting here for?"

"A stretcher." Spider shifted his weight from one foot to the other. "For him." He gestured toward the corpse.

"You're going to carry it away for burial?"

"Cleaned up, hey?" Remora had not been listening. "Lay clothes. Left the Palace. Soon as I could. Went to Ermine's. Caldé might come. I knew. I knew. In the, um, his letter."

Maytera Mint nodded, supposing that the letter had been addressed to Remora.

"Went to Ermine's. Drinking den there. Lay clothing so they wouldn't–ah–shoot. Waited. Porter dropped something in the street. Up like a rabbit. Die, never Prolocutor. Her spirit, eh? Her ghost. Her vision for me."

"It never occurred to me that you were waiting for a means carry the body," Maytera Mint told Spider. "It should have, but I've seen so many left lying where they fell."

He cleared his throat. "We got a place. You'll see it."

"Down here?"

"Yeah. Eight, ten chains from here."

Maytera Mint indicated the corpse. "Did you like him, Spider? You must have."

"He was all right, and I worked with him ten years."

"Then you would not object if I covered his face?"

"Nah. Go ahead."

She did, standing and smoothing the black skirt of her habit, taking short steps to the side of the corpse, kneeling, and spreading a dirty handkerchief she took from her sleeve over its face. "May Great Pas pardon your spirit."

"No more–ah–the vision." Remora was addressing no one. "An, er, administrative post, eh? Finance. Most, er, plausibly. Finance. No."

"Muzzle it," Spider told him. "See, sib, there's this place where they was diggin' one of these tunnels. They put a big door in it like they did. You seen some."

Maytera Mint nodded.

"Martyr, hey? No martyrs since, ah–"

"They went fifty, sixty steps in and quit. I don't know why. Quit in dirt. We're under the city, and it's mostly dirt up here."

"Are we? I thought you were taking us to the lake."

"Maybe we will, but we're takin' you here for now. We meet down here sometimes. Meet with Councillor Potto, and when we get somebody, we generally leave him where you two were. It's an old storeroom, I guess, but I don't–" They heard the thunderous boom of a slug gun, attenuated by distance but unmistakable.

"Guan must of shot somethin'," Spider told Maytera Mint.

"Or he was shot himself."

"He's a rough boy. He can take care of himself. What was I talkin' about?"

"How you bury the other rough boys." She sighed. "It was interesting. I'd like to hear more about it."

"Sure." Spider sat down facing her, his needler still in his right hand. Settled in his place, he held it up. "I could put this away. You aren't goin' to jump me, either of you."

"I–ah–intend it," Remora muttered.

"Huh! I don't think so." Spider thrust the needler into his coat. "Like I said, sib, there's a big door, and I got the word for it. Councillor Potto told it to me a long time back. So you go in and where it ends there's dirt. Down towards the lake, where they run deeper, it's all rock or shiprock, but up this high there's a lot of dirt."

"I understand."

He touched the shiprock wall. "Behind here's dirt. I can tell from how it's made. What we do, when somebody's chilled up in the city and there's nobody for them, we bring them down. Or if somebody dies down here. That happened one time."

Seated again, Maytera Mint nodded toward the corpse.

"Lily. Twice, now. But before, one of my knot got hurt up there and we brought him down, but he died. We dig straight in, like, into the dirt till the hole's long enough. We got rolls of poly. We lay some poly in the hole and wrap them up in some more, and slide them right in." He looked at her quizzically, and she nodded.

"Then we put some dirt back to fill the hole, right? And everybody's got a shiv." He took a big stag-handled clasp knife from his pocket. "We write the name and some stuff about him on a piece of paper, and we stick it up with his shiv so we don't dig there again for anybody else."

"As a memorial, too," Maytera Mint suggested, "Though I doubt that you would admit it."

"That's lily, sib, I wouldn't. It's just somethin' for the older bucks like me. When we go in there again we look at them, and then maybe we tell the new culls. Like we used to have cull name of Titi that would put on a gown and pay his face like they do. Not you, sib. You know what I mean, powder and rouge, and all that. Perfume."

She nodded. "Indeed I do, and I'm not offended in the least. Go on."

"Give Titi a half hour, and he's the best lookin' mort in the city. He kept his hair kind of long, and he could fix it just a little different and it was a mort's hair cut short. Not as short as yours, but short, and soon as you saw it you knew it was a mort's hair. If Titi hadn't paid his dial, that shaggy hair'd make you abram. You'd be talkin' to yourself."

"A person like that must have been of great value to you."

"Lily, he was. He was a bob cull, too. There was this time when we were workin' on a knot from Urbs. We knew who they was and what they was after, and was peery a while to see what they done and who they talked to. We do it in our trade all the time. We'd see they found out things Councillor Potto wanted Urbs to know, and we'd foyst in queer, too, fixed so they'd like it. One came fly. Know what I mean, sib?"

"I believe so."

"We could've done for him. Chilled him, you know. But we don't unless we got to."

Remora looked up. "Um—irrevocable. No—ah—going back after, eh?"

"Slap on, Patera. That's her in a egg cup. You know this one, see? He's a hog grubber, won't spend. Or he's one of them that lushes till shadeup and don't forget a thing. Whatever. Soon as he's cold, it's all down the chute, and Urbs'll send a new cull.

"So what I laid to was to get him nabbed. I got Titi to hook him and go 'round to two, three places so's to get some to say they seen them. Then Titi went to Hoppy and capped I been ramped. The Urber done it. They got him to go along to finger.

"I knew the ken, so'd Titi, and I was keepin' him there. I'd planted books goin', to keep him on top. Not lumb, but lowre enough, you know, to have him sure he'd draw my deck."

"I—ah—dishonest game? You, er, cheated?"

"Yes, Spider. Did you?"

"Sure thing. But not skinnin' him. I'd take his gelt and let him win back and more to the bargain. He had to lose swop, or I'd been shy more'n I had. Larger, he'd got to win so he wouldn't stamp. I'd say haven't you nicked me proper and push my chair, you know the lay, and he'd say one more hand. I knew Titi was goin' to have to let the hoppies carry him two or three places 'fore he steered 'em right.

"In they prance, and Titi fingered the Urber and blubbed like two morts, and the hoppies grabbled him and what's your name, you're for iron."

"Rape is a very serious charge," Maytera Mint protested. "He could have been sent to the pits."

"Sure thing, but Titi wasn't goin' to dock. I wanted him shy of his knot to Pasday, that's all. Well, he broke and run at Titi. Petal, what're you doing to me, and the rest, and he's nabbed a flicker and bashes it on the cat ladder."

"A wine bottle as a weapon, you mean?" This was a foreign whorl to Maytera Mint.

"A glass tumbler, sib, but it's the same notion." Spider chuckled. "Titi fans him so hard he's back across and on my knee if I hadn't hopped. Knocked over my perch and both down together.

"Now right here's where my jabber pays. Titi run to him bawlin' like a calf with the cow in the kitchen, and Hoppy? Never twigged. I was on velvet. Showed me the door. Titi had to stay and cap, which he did, and Hoppy never twigged. I'd like to turn up another, but I've never seen any half so fine, not even on boards."

"Yet he's dead," Maytera Mint said pensively. "He's dead and buried in that place you told us about, because there was no one else who cared enough to bury him. Otherwise we would not be talking about him. How did he die?"

"I was hopin' you wouldn't quiz me, sib."

She smiled. "I'll withdraw the question if you'll call me Maytera. Will you do that for me?"

"Sure thing." Spider's hand massaged his stubbled jowls. "I'm goin' to tell you anyhow. Thing is, some culls nicker. All right, it's abram. But, well . . ."

"But he was your friend."

"Nah. I miss him, though. I brought him in. I found him, and I got

him in, helped him out of a queer lay he was standin' and all that, and
pretty quick he's a dimber hand. Everybody knew, all my knot. They
stood him wide. You wouldn't think, and they didn't to start, but after a
while. I told about how he said the Urber ramped him."

"Yes, you did."

"A buck tried it, see, Maytera? He got down to shag and twigged
Titi's yard, and did for him on account. Squeezed his pipe for him."

"That's sad. I understand perfectly why you dislike it when people
laugh. May I ask about him, too? She gestured toward the corpse.
"What was his name?"

"Paca." While seconds crawled by, Spider stared at the
handkerchief-shrouded face. "He was a pretty good all-round cull, know
what I say? For jabber or a breakin' lay or rags-and-tags, any of the jobs
we do, smokin' or liftin' seals—"

Remora looked up.

"Any game you name, I could name you better. You don't always
know, though, and sometimes that cull's got his plate full or he's crank,
and Paca could take it. Once in a while he'd big my glimms."

Spider spoke to Remora. "I was goin' to ask, Patera, if you'd cap for
him. Think you could?"

"Pray for, um, Peccary? Paca. I, er, have. Privately, eh? While we,
er, now."

"When I slide him in," Spider explained impatiently. "Cut bene
whiddes for everybody."

"I—ah—indeed. Honored."

"What about Guan?" Maytera Mint inquired. "Aren't we going to
bury him, too? Wouldn't you like His Eminence to pray for him as well?
Perhaps we could make it a group ceremony."

"Guan's not for ice."

"Certainly he is." She sighed. "Where is your stretcher?"

"He'll be along in a minute."

"Thirsty, eh? Might we, um, hungry, likewise."

"So am I," Maytera Mint declared. "You have a stretcher somewhere, or so you say, Spider. If there's food and water there, too, may
we not go to it?"

"I, ah—"

"You ate and drank last night, I assume, and this morning. You,
Guan, Paca, and the others. We didn't."

Spider clambered to his feet. "All right, you two, you got it. Come on. I want to see what's keepin' those putts."

"Ah—water? And, um, something to eat?"

"Sure thing. We got prog and plonk. There's a well, too. I ought to of let you have some last night. You need a hand up, Patera? How 'bout you, Maytera?"

"I'm fine, thank you, Spider."

"I—ah—give warning," Remora said as Spider helped him to stand. "The next, um, instance. Strike the General. Or me. I shall attack, eh? Will. Martyr, hey? Gone but—um, er—commemorated. Unforgotten."

"He isn't going to," Maytera Mint told Remora briskly. "We are past all that hitting and hating with Spider. Don't you understand, Your Eminence?"

"Come on," Spider repeated, and started down the tunnel. "You want to eat? I'll bet you anythin' they aren't cold."

"Um, forbidden."

"Wagering is contrary to the regulations of the Chapter," Maytera Mint explained, "but I am prepared to violate them and accept whatever punishment may be meted out to me. I say that they are dead, all of them. The men you sent for the stretcher, and Guan, too. As dead as Paca. Will you take my bet?"

"Sure thing." Spider had drawn his needler again. "I got a card says I'm right."

"I don't want your card. What I want are answers to three questions. You must promise to answer in full. No lies and no evasions. No half truths. What will you have from us if we lose? We haven't any money, or at least I have none."

Spider halted, waiting for her. "I donno, sib. Maytera, I mean. That's better, huh? You call each other sib, though."

She nodded. "We call one another sib, which is short for *sibyl,* because *maytera* is reserved for the sibyl in charge of the cenoby in which we live. There's only one other sibyl in my cenoby since Maytera Rose passed on, Maytera Marble. She is senior to me, so she is in charge. I will call her Maytera when next we meet, assuming that Maytera Rose has been buried."

"You, too, huh? Well, I'm sorry, Maytera. Come on, Your Eminence, shake it up."

"His Eminence has a gold gammadion set with gems," Maytera Mint confided. "He might be willing to make it my stake in our bet. I'll try to persuade him."

Spider shook his head. "I could nab it anytime."

"Certainly you could, but you would have stolen it. Though Tenebrous Tartaros, whose realm this surely is, is the patron of thieves, I doubt very much that he approves of stealing from augurs, and all the other gods surely condemn it. If you won His Eminence's gammadion you would have acquired it honestly, and would have no reason to fear divine retribution."

"Yeah. But you don't think I'll win."

Maytera Mint shook her head. "No, I don't. I will not deceive you, Spider. I am as sure as I can be without having seen them that all those men are dead. If you accept my bet, you'll have to answer my questions, one for each dead man."

"All right, I'll tell you what I want, Maytera. But I'm goin' to call you General. That's who I want to bet with, the rebel general. Can I do that? Patera does."

"Certainly. I'd prefer it, in fact."

"You figure I'm a thief. I can tell by the way you were talkin' a minute ago. That's the lily, isn't it, General?"

"You employ a great deal of cant, Spider, and cant is used principally by thieves. Also by prostitutes, with whom I've spoken now and then, but most of them steal when it seems safe."

"Most everybody will," Spider told her positively.

"Perhaps. If so, it is small wonder that the gods show us no more affection than they do."

"Well, I ain't a thief. I talk like I do 'cause we're with them a lot. Spies don't ken with people like you, General, or this other sibyl you call Maytera. She don't know anythin' they need, see? You do, but if they were to ken with you, they'd need a shaggy good reason or you'd start thinkin', why's he around all the time?" Spider paused for breath.

"You go to some city to look into things, you know, and you want somebody local to help out, what you want's a thief six to one. When we got to have new blood, that's where we look, too. Not always, but mostly."

"I understand, Spider. . . ."

"Out with it."

"Very well." Maytera Mint took a deep breath. "Were you a thief previously? Is that how you came to be a spy-catcher?"

He grinned at her, displaying crooked and discolored teeth. "What makes you think you can believe me, General?"

"I'm a good judge of character."

"I'd lie to you."

"Indeed you would, and you might do it so skillfully, that I would think you were telling the truth. But you won't lie to me about this, not here and not now. Were you? It's none of my affair, and to confess the truth there is a thief I taught when he was a child of whom I'm very fond. His name is Auk."

"I know him," Spider said.

"You do? That hadn't occurred to me, but now that you've mentioned it, no doubt you must. Does he—is he one of your knot, as you call it?"

"That'd feague you, huh? He's not. Auk won't work for anybody else, and he's too peppery for my trade anyhow. I wasn't a thief, either. I was a hoppy. You believe that?"

"If you say it's true, absolutely. May I ask why you left the Caldé's Guard?"

"They callin' it that again? That's what it was when I went in, then they changed it. They kicked me out. Let's not talk about why."

Remora, who had caught up with them and overheard much of their conversation, muttered, "No, ah, never. Only shriving, hey? There—um—solely."

"I won't ask," Maytera Mint promised.

"Pulled off my stripes and put them on my back. I could show you the scars. Cull called Desmid brought me in. He's cold. I been catchin' spies for Viron twenty-two years now. I don't know how many I've nabbed or helped nab, thirty or forty. Could be more, and there's a lot we don't want to nab but could anytime we wanted to. I'm telling' you 'cause of what I want my end of our bet to be. I'm stickin' with Councillor Potto, see? Twenty-two years I been workin' for him, and he took me when I didn't have two bits or a padken. I'm his man, always will be."

"In that case, let us hope a peace can be arranged that will permit Councillor Potto to retain his seat."

Spider nodded. "Sure thing. All right, let's talk about this bet. First off, these three questions. Suppose you were to ask me who my boys are, the ones you think's yours. I can't tell you names. You see that? I won't lie to you, General, but I won't tell, either."

"I understand. I won't ask you to betray your friends."

"All right, here's what I want. If your side wins and you get loose, you don't nab me and my knot for spyin' on you, or for holdin' you like we're doin'."

Maytera Mint started to speak, but Spider raised his hand. "That's not all. You let us keep doin' what we been doin' for Viron. You're goin' to need us worse than you think. If you do that, I'll tell what's gone on before, and give you the files."

"I can't. I would accept that bet if I could, cheerfully and without hesitation. But those are matters for the caldé and the new Ayuntamiento, not for me."

"The, um, terms. He, er, designated? Specified yourself, General. Not the—ah—reconstituted Ayuntamiento or the caldé, hey?"

"But he means our side. The caldé, Generalissimo Oosik, and even the Trivigauntis. Don't you, Spider? For myself, I would give you my word, as I said. In fact, I do, whether I win or lose. But I cannot bind the caldé and an Ayuntamiento that does not yet exist."

"But you'll promise, General? Personally?"

"Absolutely. I have and I do."

Spider indicated Remora with a jerk of his thumb. "Have him flash that gaud. Pas's cross. You can swear on that."

"If you wish. Will you allow me my three questions, when I win? Full, honest answers?"

"Sure thing. I'll swear too, if you want."

"Then it won't be necessary."

Remora had produced his gammadion; Maytera Mint laid her hand upon it. "I, General Mint of the Horde of Viron, called by some the rebel or insurgent forces, I who am also Maytera Mint of the Sun Street manteion, do hereby swear that should we prevail I will not punish nor attempt to punish this man Spider and his subordinates for their activities in collecting intelligence for the Ayuntamiento as presently constituted. I further swear that I will do everything I can to prevent others from so punishing them, short of force. In addition, I will actively support their being retained in their function, that is to say the counterintel-ligence function, in which they have served our city faithfully. I will do these things whether I win my wager with Spider or lose it."

She drew breath. "Is that satisfactory?"

"Ought to cover it."

"Great Pas, bear witness! Ophidian Echidna, whose sword I am, bear witness! Scintillating Scylla, Patroness of Our Holy City of Viron, bear witness!"

"Good enough." Spider held out his hand. "Have we got a bet? Shake on it." Solemnly they shook hands, her own small hand enveloped in a thickly muscled one twice its size.

"All right, I'll tell you right now I got a lock. We're almost there." He gestured. "See that side tunnel up ahead? We go in there, and the old guardroom's only four, five steps. If they were cold, we've have made them before this."

She shook her head. "To the contrary, though I wish you were cor-rect. They would have heard our voices and called out."

A hundred steps brought them to the side tunnel's entrance. As soon as they turned into it, she caught sight of a man's feet protruding from a doorway. "That will be Guan," she murmured.

Spider stopped her, spreading his arms to hold Remora back as well. "That's Hyrax. I always twig a cully's shoes, or a mort's either. Shoes tell more than any kind of kick. A lot know it, but that don't stop it from bein' true."

"Wasn't the other man with Hyrax, Spider? Where is he?"

"In there." Spider's breath rasped in this throat. "Just out of sight, most likely. You don't shoot a cull soon as you see him through the door, not if he's comin' in. You let him get inside. That way you got two tries if he beats hoof."

He turned to Remora. "You first, Patera. Pull out Pas's cross and have it where they can see, and hold your hands up. You're a augur in a robe, not holdin' a slug gun or anything. They won't shoot you, or I don't think they will. Tell them I got the general. Leave us be, or she's cold."

Remora looked stricken.

"You wanted to die down here, didn't you? This's your chance. Go on before I shoot you myself. They won't."

"They must know we're out here," Maytera Mint said. "They will have heard us. If not before, they will certainly have heard that." Spider did not reply; his eyes were on Remora.

"I, er, shall." Remora backed away, raised his hands, and turned toward the doorway.

"Pas's gammadion," Maytera Mint prompted him. "Take it out so they can see it."

If Remora heard her advice, he ignored it. She watched him pause at the threshold, then step through. There was no shot.

"They used to have soldiers down here awake and ready to go if there was trouble," Spider told her. His hoarse voice was close to a whisper. "That was before the Guard. That's what Councillor Potto told me one time, and he ought to know."

They stood side-by-side in silence after that. There was no sound from the guardroom, no sound from any source save the almost inaudible sigh of the cool wind that filled the tunnel.

At length Spider said, "I should of told him to take a look around in there. I guess he's doin' it anyhow."

"I'm going too." Maytera Mint started toward the doorway.

"Hornbuss!" Spider caught her arm. "You're goin' to do what I say, and I say you can't."

"Your Eminence!" she called. "Are you all right?"

For a few seconds her words echoed hollowly from the gray walls, and she felt certain that she and Spider were the only living people within earshot. Then Remora stepped out of the doorway, avoiding the dead man. He held out a bottle of thick, mottled glass. "Water, Maytera! General. Ah—potable. Um, pure, in so far as I can, um, gauge its qualities."

Spider snapped, "Nobody in there?"

"Not—ah—dead men. Two, in addition to the one you, um, observe in the entrance. Shot with slug guns, I—ah—or, um, both with a single such gun. Quite possibly. Our, ah, companions, eh? Yesterday, likewise earlier. One the, um—"

"Guan."

"Er, yes. Ah—the name you gave. Furnished? Supplied." Having come near enough, Remora handed the bottle to Maytera Mint. "He dropped this, I fancy, General. So it appeared, eh? When he—um—attained life's culmination. Some spilt, eh?"

She was drinking and did not trouble to reply. The water was cool and clean and tasted fresh and unspeakably delicious. All her life she had been taught that Surging Scylla, the water goddess, was first among the Seven; she had not realized either how true or how important that insight was until this moment.

Chapter 7

THE BROWN MECHANICS

Silk looked around curiously, finding it hard to believe that this enclosure, this collection of sheds surrounded by a fence, produced taluses. On his shoulder, Oreb croaked in dismay.

"It's starting to rain," Chenille announced; she pushed back raspberry curls to squint at the sky.

"I've been trying to remember where I came from," Maytera Marble ventured. "I don't think it was like this at all." She edged Mucor toward the shelter of the sentry box as she spoke.

If Fliers were a rain sign, what might Fliers who landed presage? The final days of the whorl? Silk decided to keep the speculation to himself. "I should have asked you about that long ago, Maytera. Tell me about it."

"I couldn't remember a thing then, I'm sure. Not till poor Maytera Rose bequeathed me my new parts. I'm sure I must have told you about them."

Silk nodded.

"A week last Tarsday, that was. They're much better than my old ones, but after I'd put them in, it was hard for me to keep straight which memories were Marble's and which were mine."

Chenille corrected her. "The other way, Maytera."

"You're quite right, dear. Anyway, I recollect a big room with green walls. There were pallets, or perhaps metal tables, little ones about as high as a bed."

"Here comes one of the guards." Chenille pointed.

"I was lying on one, and I didn't have any clothes on. Perhaps I shouldn't talk about this, Patera."

"Go ahead. It's not immoral, and it could be important."

"I was trying to boot, and I remember that the girl next to me sat up and said she was naked, which she certainly was. When she did, somebody brought her a dress."

The guard halted with a clash of armored heels, one hand leveled across his slug gun. "Follow me, Caldé."

"No wet," Oreb muttered.

"He has a point," Silk remarked as they set out. "Could we borrow umbrellas? If we're going to have to walk between these buildings, as I expect we will."

"I'll get some while you're talking to the director," the guard promised; he trotted ahead to open the door of a brick structure not much different from a modest house.

"We can wait outside," Chenille told Silk. "I mean, in the hall or whatever, just as long as it's out of the rain."

He shook his head, entering a reception room presided over by a woman rather too large for it. She smiled. "Go right on in, please, Caldé."

"Will there be enough chairs? There are four of us."

From the room beyond, a short man beginning to go bald told him, "Three chairs and a settle. Come in!" He offered his hand. "Swallow's my name, Caldé." Silk shook it and introduced Maytera Marble, Mucor, and Chenille.

Swallow nodded, still smiling. "Sit down, please, ladies, Caldé. You're lame, I hear, and I see you're limping." He shut the door. "Everybody's got some tidbit about you. You're lame, you've got that tame bird, and you predicted the downfall of the Ayuntamiento. I'm sure you've heard it all."

Silk took a leather armchair near Swallow's table. "And now you're surprised to see how young I am, and would like to ask my age."

"Why, that's none of my affair, Caldé."

"I'm twenty-three. You must be," he glanced at Swallow's hands, "in your forties. Forty-five or forty-six. Am I right?"

"I'm glad you're not, Caldé. I'm forty-three."

"Twenty years older than I am, precisely. You must think I'm very young and inexperienced to head the city government. I am, and I realize it. I have to depend on the judgement of more experienced men and women. That's one reason Maytera Marble's with me today; it's also the reason I'm here talking to you, an older man with experience I haven't got but need to draw upon."

"I'll be happy to help you any way I can, Caldé. Would you like something before we get started? Coffee, wine, tea? Would the young ladies? Chamomile can fetch us some."

Chenille shook her head; Silk said, "No thank you. You build taluses here?"

"We do. That's our business and our only business."

Oreb offered his judgement on taluses. "Bad things!"

"Be quiet, silly bird." Silk leaned back, the tips of his fingers together. "I know nothing about business, and this must be a remarkable one."

"Not to me." Swallow smiled. "I grew up in it, working in our shops. But you're right, it's unique. That's the word we like to use. Call it self-promotion if you want, but it fits."

"Because a talus is a person," Silk continued, "both in law and in fact. There are boatyards along the shore of the lake, where I was a few days ago. The boatwrights build a boat there; and when they're through, the fishermen paint eyes on it and call it 'she.' They give it a name, as well."

Swallow nodded.

"A boat has a certain character, just as this chair does. This is comfortable and solid, brown, and so forth. A boat may be a willing or a reluctant sailer, it may be stable or prone to rock. But a boat isn't a person."

Maytera Marble cleared her throat, a rasp like the scraping of a crusted pan. "Are you going to ask how they can build a talus with a certain character, Patera? I don't think they can, really. I've never . . ."

"Go on, Maytera."

"Never built a child. With a man, you know. But—but from what I understand, we can't either. We do our best, give the child all the advantages we can. But after that, it's up to the gods. To Molding Molpe and Lord Pas, principally."

Swallow nodded again. "It's no different here, Maytera. The layman thinks taluses are all alike. That's because they all sound the same to him. When you've spent a while talking to them, you find out they don't really talk alike even if they all sound like taluses. When it comes to ingenuity or honesty, that kind of thing, they can differ pretty widely. As you say, it depends on the spirit they get from the gods."

"They're all boring," Mucor told him; he seemed about to reply, but meeting her corpse-like gaze quickly looked away.

"There is another difference I wanted to inquire about," Silk interposed. "I mean between taluses and boats, or any other man-made object. If I were to go to Limna with a case full of cards, I could buy a boat; and once I had paid for it, it would be mine. I could sail it or leave it tied to a pier. I could burn or sink it if I wanted to, or give it to Maytera here, or to Chenille or anyone I chose. A talus is a person, and I would assume that in cities in which slavery is legal, anyone with sufficient funds could go to a facility such as yours and order a talus built—"

"You can do that here, Caldé," Swallow put in.

"Ah. That's interesting."

"Good thing?" Oreb inquired.

Maytera Marble said, "It seems to me that all this applied to me once as well, Patera. No one owned me. I've always been free, I'm sure, and yet I did what I was told. I still do, for the most part. I respect authority, and when I was younger, I don't think it even occurred to me to question it." She looked thoughtful, her head down and inclined to the left.

To encourage her Oreb croaked, "Talk now."

"Most bio—do you really want to hear this, Patera? I could tell you later, if you like."

"Of course I do. Tell us."

"I was just going to say that most bio children are like that, too. I don't mean that there are no bad children, though foolish people say that because it makes them feel virtuous. But there are really very few. I've taught children for a long time, and most can be controlled quite easily with a few little scoldings and a few words of praise." She paused, lifting her head and squaring her shoulders. "So can most grownups. Not quite so easily, but it isn't a lot more difficult."

Swallow chuckled. "She's right, Caldé. I boss almost two hundred employees here, and as a general thing a good chewing out now and then and a pat on the back for good work are all it takes. Once in a rare while we take on somebody that doesn't work out, stealing tools or whatever, and we've got to get rid of him. But it doesn't happen often."

"I've been thinking about Marl, Patera."

Silk nodded, noting as he did the first large drops of the rain that had been threatening; they were tapping on the window panes tentatively, but with growing urgency.

"Marl doesn't receive any wages at all. I told you."

Swallow raised an eyebrow. "Black mechanics, Maytera? It sounds like it."

"I don't know. I really hadn't considered it. I was just going to say that Marl seems like an extreme instance of—of pliability. I suppose you could call it that. . . ."

Maytera Marble's remaining hand tightened its grip on the handle of the small basket in her lap. "And if you can make use of that pliability to control others as you do, Director, with a little money and scoldings and praise, then it seems to me people like you don't really need slaves, except as sops to their egos. I'm expressing this offensively, I know, but I think you see what I mean. As for black mechanics, aren't they legendary? Largely legendary, I should have said. I know that some people practiced the black art in the past."

"There's still a bit around in my opinion, Maytera. In my business we hear things, and that's one of the things we hear." Swallow turned to Silk. "I'm a blunt man, Caldé, and I'm going to ask you straight out. Are you interested in getting a new talus for the Guard? Is that why you're here?"

"I've been considering it," Silk admitted. "Several, perhaps."

Swallow smiled. "Good. Very good! I'm delighted to hear it. I've been telling our people that this unrest was sure to bring in some fresh business, and I'm glad to see I was right. You're wondering why you should have to pay for something that the city can't own, aren't you?"

"I am. Also how I can be assured that the taluses Viron pays for will be loyal and obedient."

"It's a good question." Swallow hitched his chair nearer his office table, resting his elbows on it. "First of all, if you want absolute assurance, I can't give it to you. Nobody can. I'm told there's an outfit in Wick now that tells people that, but they're lying. Suppose you went to that boatyard in Limna. Could the people building boats there give you an iron-clad guarantee that any boat they sold you would never sink or turn over? Under any circumstances?"

"I doubt it."

"So do I. If they did, they'd be lying exactly like those fellows in

Wick. Here's the guarantee we offer. If one of our taluses betrays your interests or won't carry out a legitimate order, within the first two years you employ it, we will refund the entire amount you paid. When I say 'you' now, I mean the city. For the third year, the amount is cut by a quarter. You get three quarters of what you paid us back. During the fourth you get half, then a quarter."

"Nothing after the fifth year?" Maytera Marble asked.

"That's right. But you will have had five years service from your talus by that time, don't forget."

Silk nodded thoughtfully.

"I'd like to have your business," Swallow continued. "I don't deny that. We rarely receive an order for more than a single talus. And it would be a feather in our cap to be able to say we already had a large order from the new government. So here's what I'll do. I said a full refund if there's any serious trouble during the first two years. All right, for each talus you get over one, I'll increase the guarantee by one year. Say you were to order three. Is that about what you're thinking of, Caldé?"

"Perhaps."

"Then let's say three. That's two over one, so you'd get a full cash refund—we're talking here about the price of the individual talus, not the price of all three."

"I understand," Silk said.

"A full refund on that talus for serious trouble during the first four years. After that, three quarters, then half and a quarter, as I've already outlined it to you. You'll be entirely covered or partly covered for . . . How long, Maytera?"

"Twenty-five percent in the seventh year, Patera," she told Silk. "Nothing after that."

"Good deal?" Oreb tugged a lock of Silk's hair.

"A safe one, at least, I believe. You don't have to pay often, do you, Director Swallow?"

Swallow smiled and relaxed. "No, we don't. If we did, we'd be bankrupt. We paid a quarter-price refund fifteen years ago—no, make that sixteen. I was foundry supervisor then, and I felt it was a pretty dubious case. All of us knew it was, really, and if we'd fought it in court, we'd probably have won. But it was only a quarter, the customer was making a lot of noise, and the director we had then wanted to establish that we keep our promises. I'm not saying he was wrong, just that the talus in question had been abused. The customer'd had it piling bricks, which isn't natural."

"What is?" Silk inquired.

"Fighting and protection, the same things you'd expect from a watchdog." Swallow cleared his throat. "Can I get a little bit personal, Maytera? No disrespect intended, but you brought up an important principle, obedience to authority. What you said made a lot of sense, and I'd like to use you for an example."

Chenille said, "I don't think you ought to. Tell him no, Maytera. I don't think this is a good idea at all."

"Because it will make me more aware of my nature, dear? I don't believe it will, since I'm very much aware of it already. I've spent many, many hours thinking about who I am and what the gods require of me. But if it does, even a little, I'll thank the director very sincerely for the insight."

"No talk," Oreb advised Swallow.

He chuckled. "I won't say what I was going to, I promise. But I will say this. What I was going to say, I could have said about myself or anybody else in this room. I just thought the clothes might make it clearer."

"The clothes that were given to me when I woke? I didn't get to them, but you're right. After a while I sat up too, and another girl gave me my first clothes. Were you going to ask me what kind of clothes they were?"

Swallow nodded. "That's right, I was."

"A little black dress, very simple, with rather a short skirt. Underclothes." Maytera Marble paused to smile. "I was about to say I'd prefer not to describe them, but they were so plain that there's hardly anything to describe. Black shoes with low heels, but I don't think there were any stockings. A pretty little lace apron and a matching cap. It's easy for me to describe those clothes, because people from Ermine's came to Patera's palace just before we left, and there were young women dressed exactly as I was then, except that they had stockings."

"Did they come to clean?" Swallow asked. "Sweep and dust?"

"Dear Chenille and I have done that already. To wash the dishes they'll need tonight and set the table, and wash walls we haven't gotten to. At least I hope they'll wash those walls and the downstairs windows. I asked them to."

Swallow nodded again. "You see, Caldé, each of us is born to do certain things. Maytera was born to sweep and dust, and wash walls and floors, and she's still doing it. Did you have to urge her to?"

Silk shook his head.

"I would have been surprised if you'd said you did, and it shows the important principle I want to explain. When you're born to do a thing, and somebody gives you a chance to do it, that's all it takes. Everybody else is afraid I'll embarrass her, so let's talk about your bird."

"Oreb," Oreb elucidated.

"Nobody's got to make him fly. He flies because it's his nature. Nobody has to make him talk either. He was born to."

"Talk good!"

"There you have it. All right, it's a talus's nature to fight and protect property. Give your talus a chance to do those things, and it will do them. You're afraid the ones we build for you will give you a hard time, but you're caldé, and if they did, you'd give them a hard time, too, wouldn't you? Have them arrested and disarmed? And tried, too, eventually?"

"I suppose so."

"Naturally you would. So why should they make trouble, when what you want them to do is what they want to do? The things they were born to do?"

"I was at a country house guarded by a talus not long ago, and Mucor told me it could be bribed, though it took a great deal of money." Silk looked at her for confirmation.

"Musk said so."

Chenille asked, "What would a talus do with money?" and Maytera Marble ventured, "The same things that you or I would, I suppose, dear."

"You were asking how you could buy something you couldn't own, Caldé." Swallow picked up a pencil, apparently to rap the tablet before him. "Let me tell you about that now, about the financial arrangements. When a talus is finished, it owes us, by law, the cost of its manufacture plus fifteen percent."

"Even though the city has paid for it?"

"Exactly. What the city's doing, you see, is advancing us the money we'd eventually get from the talus. We make no more than we would if we'd built without an order. Which we seldom do, by the way, since by building to order we get our money a lot sooner. What's even more important, we don't have to worry about the talus getting killed before it can pay us."

Silk nodded while his right forefinger drew small circles on his cheek. "I see."

"We require payment in full before the talus is finished. When it's finished, we explain that it has been built because there's an employer anxious to hire it. That's you, Caldé. We also explain the nature of wages, what wages it can reasonably expect, and what bonuses."

"But I don't actually pay it. Isn't that correct?"

"I can see you grasp the idea already. That's right, you don't. Let's say that you and your talus agree on five cards a month, a fair wage. From that, you deduct your expenses for fuel, maintenance, and repairs, if any. Most employers furnish ammo free of charge. It's customary."

Silk nodded again.

"You report the net to us, or you can have the talus do it. We deduct it from the talus's debt. Eventually its indebtedness will be wiped out and it can keep the wages it earns."

"Provided it survives that long."

"You've got it." Swallow glanced over his shoulder at the windows behind him, where the tapping of raindrops had mounted to a steady, insistent pounding. "If you'd rather have a look at our shops another time . . . ?"

"Patera," Maytera Marble began, "I don't—"

She was interrupted by Silk, who stood as he spoke. "I'm eager to see them, and I'm sure a little rain won't hurt me. I was caught in that downpour a week from yesterday, but here I am. I don't want you to feel that you have to take us around in person, however, Director. Someone else can do it."

"Not take the caldé around?" Grinning broadly, Swallow rose too. "I wouldn't miss it for any money. The ladies can wait in here if they like."

"I'm coming," Maytera Marble declared. "My granddaughter can stay here with Chenille."

"Me too," Chenille announced. "I want to see this."

"In that case Mucor will have to come with us, Patera."

"I can fly," she informed Swallow gravely. "Even in the rain. But they can't."

The promised umbrellas had been left on a chair in the outer room. Chenille picked one up. "Here's a black one for you, Patera, if you want it."

Silk shook his head. "Let Maytera have it."

Hanging her basket on her right forearm, she accepted the black umbrella and shook it out. "It's bad luck to open them indoors, they say, but I've already had mine. I can't thank that nice young man for getting these for us."

"One of your guards," Silk explained. "Now that I come to think of it, it seems strange that you've hired bios to protect this place instead of a talus."

"We do have a talus." Swallow accepted a yellow umbrella from Chenille. "As a matter of fact we have two now, because of the unrest. They're in the guard shack."

He went to the door, opening his umbrella. "You went by it on your way here. They have windows so they can keep an eye on the gate, but mostly they listen for shooting or shouting. A lot of the little matters that our guards handle, a good bio can take care of better than any talus. Suppose you had taluses patrolling the streets instead of troopers, Caldé. You'd have a dozen people shot every night, instead of one or two a week."

Opening the green umbrella that Chenille handed him, Silk followed Swallow out into the rain. "I've dealt with taluses once or twice, and I'm sure you're right."

"They protect the plant at night, and we have them there ready to roll in case of serious fighting. So far it's been around the Palatine and the Alambrera. I'm sure you know."

Silk nodded.

"Would you like to look at them? There's the guard shack." Swallow pointed at a weathered wooden shed.

"Not now, thank you." Silk had to raise his voice to make himself heard above the rattle of rain on his umbrella. "Later, perhaps. Right now I'd like to see how they're made."

"Good. That's where I'm taking you. Excuse me a minute, and I'll get the door."

Swallow strode off through the rain; Silk limped after him as rapidly as he could, splashing through deepening puddles in shoes that were already sodden.

The wide wooden door Swallow had opened let them into a cavernous structure whose floor was covered with coarse sand; three men were working in a pit a few steps from the doorway, illuminated by a single bleary light high overhead. "This is the foundry," Swallow announced as Maytera Marble and Mucor entered under a single black umbrella. "I always start visitors here, because it's where I started myself. I sifted, shoveled, ran errands, and the rest of it. It's hard, dirty work, but I was bringing home a little money to help my folks, and I've never felt so good about anything I've done in my life."

Chenille exclaimed, "You make those great big things out of sand? I don't believe it!" Oreb flew off into the darkness at the other end of the building to explore.

"There are some glass parts, and they really are made out of sand, but not by us." Swallow shut his umbrella and thumped its tip on the sand-strewn floor. "This is foundry sand and wouldn't make good glass. But we cast some big parts in sand, which is what these men are getting ready to do."

He pointed with his umbrella. "You see the hollow left by the form when it was lifted out? Those round pieces are called cores. They're made of compressed sand with a starch binder, and if they aren't positioned exactly right, and firmly enough that they stay in place when the iron's poured, the whole piece will be ruined. What they're doing here is preparing to cast an engine block, Caldé." At the last word, the workers looked up.

Silk had been trying to locate Oreb in the darkness. "This seems a very large place for three men."

"When we're going full tilt, which we will be tomorrow if we get your order today, there will be eighteen men and six boys working in here, Caldé. I've had to lay off everybody except my best men, which I don't like to do."

Taking Silk unobtrusively by the elbow, Swallow led him deeper into the building, his voice kindling a second light. "They're all good men to tell the truth, and the boys are smart lads who'll be good men too before long. We can't use anything else. I hate layoffs because I know the people I let go won't be able to find another job, generally. But if they could, I'd hate them worse because I'd lose them, and you can't just bring in an untrained man and have him go to work. It takes years."

Maytera Marble inquired, "How old are the boys?"

"We start them at fourteen nowadays. I was twelve when I started." Silk heard the soft exhalation of Swallow's breath. "We had layoffs then, too, though it wasn't as hard as now. Not usually. I never got to go to palaestra, but there was a woman on our street who had, and she taught me to read and write and figure during layoffs. I'm pretty good with figures, if I do say it. She was a friend of Mother's and wouldn't take anything for it, but I always thought that someday I'd get to where I could pay her. I was just about there, just made leadman here, when she died."

Silk asked, "May I speak as an augur instead of caldé?"

"Go ahead. I'm not religious, but maybe I should be."

"Then I'll explain to you that the woman who helped you out of friendship for your mother had been helped herself, when she was younger, by some earlier person you never met."

Swallow nodded. "I suppose it's likely enough."

"She couldn't repay that person any more than you could repay her, but when she helped you she wiped out her debt. When you help someone, you'll wipe out yours. Possibly you already have—I have no way of knowing."

"I've tried once or twice, Caldé."

"You say you're not religious. Nor am I, though I was very religious not long ago. Because I'm not, I'm not going to say that this passing forward from one generation to the next is the method the gods have ordained for the settlement of such debts, though perhaps it is. In any event, it's a good one, one that lets people die, as everyone must, feeling that they've squared accounts with the whorl."

Maytera Marble said, "Perhaps he already has, Patera, by employing those boys."

Swallow shrugged. "They don't pay, and that's the truth. We pay a card a month, and they're not worth it to us. But we're not doing it from charity. We have to have them so they can learn the work. If we didn't, someday we'd need foundrymen and there wouldn't be any, no matter how much we offered."

"Then it was good of you to . . . Lay them off? Is that what you call it? So they could attend a palaestra. Because I'd think that if you were teaching them, they'd be the last ones you'd want to send home."

"They were," Swallow told her shortly.

Chenille had been looking at the largest ladle Silk had ever seen, a great cup of scaly pottery large enough to hold a man. "Is this what you melt the iron in?"

"That's right." Swallow was himself again at once, brisk and all business. "It's heated in this brick furnace here." He went to it. "It burns charcoal with a forced draft, and it takes a lot. Those bunkers you saw against the wall where we came in were for sand. Every casting we make uses up a little, and they're our reserve. These bunkers hold charcoal and steel scrap. We fill up that crucible with scrap, lower it into the furnace, and put the lid on. When it's been in long enough, depending on how much scrap was in it, we lift it out the same way and pour."

A slightly smaller crucible stood on the other side of the brick furnace; reaching into it, Chenille displayed an irregular scab of shining yellow metal. "This looks almost like gold."

Oreb flew over for a closer inspection.

"It's brass," Swallow told her. "A talus's head requires some pretty complicated castings, and brass is easier to cast than iron, so we use that for the head."

Silk said, "Some taluses wear helmets, I've noticed, while others don't."

"The helmet's actually a part of the head," Swallow told him. "Or you could say it takes the place of the skullplate. Would you like helmets on the taluses we're going to build for the city? I can specify them in the contract."

"I don't know. I was wondering whether a helmet furnished better protection for the head." In his mind's eye, Silk saw the talus he had killed; the shimmering discontinuity that was the blade of the azoth he had thought Hyacinth's had struck it below the eye, vaporizing metal and inflicting a mortal wound.

"Not really." Swallow clapped his hands to brighten the lights. "Over here we have the forms for various head designs. They're made so the parts can be switched. Say you like the nose on one head, but you'd rather have the mouth on another. We can give you both without any additional charge. We cast the nose you want and the mouth you want, and after the castings have been cleaned up, they'll fit together."

"How thick is the metal?" Silk inquired.

"Two to four fingers, depending on where you measure. It has to be at least two, to get enough melt through the space." Proudly, Swallow gestured toward a row of somewhat worn-looking wooden heads, each nearly as tall as he was. "There they are, Caldé, twenty-nine of them. Since all of them trade parts, there's almost no limit to the number of faces we can provide."

"I see. Is two fingers of brass enough to stop a slug?"

"No shoot," Oreb advised from Chenille's shoulder.

"It depends, Caldé. How far away was the trooper when he fired? That can make a big difference. So can the angle it strikes at. If it hits square on, it might go through if the trooper was standing close. I've known that to happen. The talus has its own guns, though, and unless it's out of ammo, an enemy trooper that close isn't likely to be alive."

Chenille grinned. "I'll say!"

"What we've found," Swallow continued, "is it's pretty rare for a trooper to shoot at the head at all. The thorax plate and the front of the abdomen are bigger targets, but they're steel. I'll show you some in the welding shop."

"Will a slug penetrate them?"

Swallow shook his head. "I've never known it to happen. I won't say it can't, I'd want to run some tests. But it's very unusual, if it happens at all."

Silk turned to Chenille. "You and Auk were riding on the back of a talus when it encountered some of the Ayuntamiento's soldiers in the tunnel. You told me about that."

She nodded. "Patera Incus was with us, too, Patera. So was Oreb here."

"Later on, one of the wounded soldiers?"

Chenille nodded again. "The talus stopped to shoot, I guess that's why it stopped anyhow, and Auk got on Patera about not bringing the dead ones Pas's Pardon. We could see a bunch of dead ones in back of us. There were lights in that tunnel, and some of the dead ones were on fire."

"I understand."

"So Patera did. He got off the talus. Auk was just—he couldn't believe it. Then the talus saw what had happened and said for Patera to get back on, and he said only if you'll take this soldier too. That was Stony, we found out his name later."

Maytera Marble asked, "Wasn't this nice talus that let you ride on it killed, dear? I think you told me about its death, and how the holy augur who was with you brought it the Pardon."

Silk nodded. "That's the point I particularly want to hear about, Chenille. How was that talus killed? Where did the slug strike it?"

"I don't think it was a slug at all, Patera. Stony said it was a missile. Some of the soldiers had launchers—I got one myself, after—and they were shooting them."

"You'll have to excuse my ignorance," to relieve the pain in his ankle, Silk backed to the crucible and sat down on its rim, "but I'm not familiar with those. What's the difference between a missile and a launcher?"

"The launcher fires the missile, Caldé."

"That's right. Just almost exactly like a slug gun shoots a slug. Maybe they ought to call a launcher a missile gun, but they don't."

"You had one of these weapons, Chenille? Where is it now?"

"I don't know. Stony took it to shoot at the Trivigaunti pterotroopers. That was while me and Auk were in the pit with Trivigauntis flying all around and you talking at us from that floater up in the air. Somebody yelled for us to get back in the tunnel, and it sounded like a real good idea to me."

Swallow said, "A missile's a very different proposition from a slug, Caldé. A slug's just a heavy metal cylinder. It hits the target a lot harder than a needle or a stone from a sling, but that's only because it's heavier than a needle and going faster than a stone. Missiles carry an explosive charge, and that lets them do a lot more damage."

"Missiles are heavier, I think, too," Chenille told Silk. "I've seen troopers carrying forty or fifty slugs—"

"Cartridges," Swallow corrected her.

"Whatever. They had them on a special canvas strap, and they were walking around fine. I think if you loaded a trooper down with forty or fifty missiles, he couldn't hardly stand up. My launcher was nice and light when I found it, but Stony helped me load it, and it was really heavy after that."

"Director Swallow."

"Yes, Caldé?"

"You mentioned a part called the thorax plate. I take it that's the part covering what I would call the talus's chest."

"Exactly right, Caldé."

"Chenille says the soldier Patera Incus befriended felt that their talus had been killed by one of those things—by a missile fired from a launcher. Are those the terms?"

Swallow nodded; Chenille said, "That's it, Patera."

"But if I understood her, he was on the talus's back at the time that it was shot. How could he have known?"

Swallow fingered his chin. "He lived through this, didn't he? He must of, since the young lady said he took her launcher later. If he had a chance to see the talus afterward—"

"Man see," Oreb announced confidently. "Iron man."

"In that case, Caldé, it wouldn't have been hard for him to tell the difference between a wound from a slug gun and one from a missile."

Silk nodded again, largely to himself. "Was this a facial wound, Chenille? Do you recall?"

She shook her head. "He talked to us after. I'm not sure where he was hit, but lower down."

Silk stood up. "You mentioned your welding shop, Director. I want to see it—and ask a favor. May we go now?"

As they left, Silk lagged to question Mucor. "You told us you could fly in the rain," belatedly he opened his umbrella, "But they couldn't. By 'they' did you intend the Fliers?"

She only stared.

"Is that why it rains after they've flown over? Because they somehow prevent it when they're present?"

"Answer him, dear," Maytera Marble prompted, but Mucor did not speak.

As they splashed along a rutted path between sodden wooden structures that could easily have been barns, Swallow remarked, "I wish you had better weather for this, Caldé, but I hear the farmers need rain pretty badly."

Silk could not help smiling. "They need it so badly that the sight and sound of it fill my heart with joy. All the time we were in your foundry I was listening to it, and the finest music in the whorl couldn't have moved me half so much. I don't suppose Chenille or Maytera like it—I know Oreb here doesn't, and I'm a bit worried about Mucor, whose health is frail; but I'd rather walk through this than the clearest sunshine."

Swallow opened the door of another ramshackle building, releasing a puff of acrid smoke and revealing a large and dirty canvas screen. "Foundry work's pretty crude, Caldé. In the old times they knew a lot we don't, though I've spent a good part of my life trying to learn their secrets. What I'm going to show you now's closer to what you might have seen on the Short Sun Whorl. But before I do, I've got to warn you. You mustn't look at the process. At the blue welding fire, in other words. The light's too bright. It can make you blind."

Silk shook his umbrella. "Smiths join iron by heating and pounding it. I used to watch them as a boy. I wasn't blinded, so what you're doing here must be a different process."

Chenille tossed back wet raspberry curls. "Better make sure Oreb doesn't watch either, Patera."

"I certainly will." For Swallow's benefit, Silk added significantly, "At times we all look at things we shouldn't. Even birds do it."

Swallow blinked and abandoned his study of Chenille's damp gown. "Sometimes people think we do it different because we're working with steel instead of iron, but that's not true. We use this method because it works on pieces your smith couldn't have welded, because they're too big to be hammered." Light showed above the canvas screen, brilliant enough to make the rafters cast sharp shadows on the underside of the roof.

"One of our men's making a weld now. We'll wait here till he's through, if it's all right with you, Caldé. Then we can go in, and I'll show you what he's doing and how he does it. He'll be welding up a thorax plate, I think."

While her remaining hand closed the black umbrella she had shared with Mucor, Maytera Marble gave Silk a significant look.

He nodded. "I want to see it. In fact, I'm very eager to, Director. You spoke of thick pieces in connection with these thorax plates and so on? How thick are they?"

"Three fingers." Swallow held them up.

"I want mine thicker. Six at least. Can you do that?"

Swallow looked startled. "Why . . . ? Could we weld them, do you mean? We could, but it would take longer. It would be a lot more work."

"Then do it," Silk told him.

Oreb whistled.

"Put it in our contract, six-finger thorax plates. What was the other piece? Below the thorax plate?"

"The abdomen front plate?" Swallow suggested.

"That's it. How thick is it?"

"Three fingers, too, Caldé." Swallow hesitated, his eyes thoughtful. "Do you want them thicker? I suppose it could be done, but it may take us a while to find steel that thick and work out a way to bend it."

Oreb exclaimed, "No, no!"

"We cannot afford delay, Director. Viron requires these taluses immediately. I realize you can't supply them today, but if you could, I'd accept them and pay you for them, and thank you. You join steel here— that's what the workman on the other side of this screen is doing?"

Swallow nodded.

"Then make my thorax plates and abdomen front plates out of two pieces of the steel you have, each three fingers thick. Maytera here could make me a robe from doubled cloth, if I had need of such a thing. Why couldn't you do this?"

"We can, I think." Swallow cleared his throat. "There'll be problems. With all respect, Caldé, welding steel isn't as simple as sewing, but I think it could be done. Can I ask . . . ?"

"Why they need it? So they can fight the Ayuntamiento's soldiers in the tunnels, of course. I've been down in those tunnels, Director—I even fought a talus there. There was only a step of clearance between the sides of that talus and the sides of the tunnel. A soldier who got that close would be very close indeed; and the taluses I want you to build will have troopers protecting their backs. The danger will be in front, where it will come from soldiers armed with weapons like the one Chenille had."

"Launchers," she supplied.

"Exactly. Launchers shooting missiles." Silk collected his thoughts. "The heads still trouble me. You say you can't cast them from iron?"

"No, Caldé. We usually paint them black. Nearly always, because it makes the eyes and teeth show up better. If we could cast them from iron we wouldn't have to paint them or touch up scratches, so we've tried it. Iron won't make castings that detailed, not till we learn more about casting it, at any rate."

"Too bad!" The light above the screen had vanished; Oreb flew up to peer over.

"Yes, it is," Silk confirmed.

"But you're worried about strength, Caldé. Resistance to slugs and that sort of thing. And to tell you the truth, iron wouldn't be a lot better. It might even be worse. Cast iron's a wonderful material in a lot of ways, but it's pretty brittle. That's why we use steel plate for the abdomen and so forth."

"Patera? Director?" Maytera Marble looked from Silk to Swallow and back. "Couldn't the talus hold something in front of its face? A piece of steel with a handle like an umbrella?"

Silk nodded. "And look over the top. Yes, that could be done, I'm sure, Maytera."

"There's one other possibility, Caldé," Swallow offered hesitantly. "This is from the old days too. But it was done right here, I understand, though it was before my time. We might try bronze."

Silk looked around at him sharply. "Isn't that what they are now?"

Chenille shook her head. "It's brass, Patera. Remember when I held that piece up? He said brass."

"Bronze would be a lot stronger, Caldé." Swallow cleared his throat again. "Tougher, too. I mean real bronze. This is kind of hard to explain."

"Go ahead," Silk told him. "I'll make every effort to understand you, and it's important."

"Let me start with iron, maybe that will make it clearer. You and I talked about iron. Casting it and so forth."

Silk nodded.

"What people call iron's really three different materials, Caldé. The commonest is just soft steel, any steel that doesn't have a lot of carbon in it. People call that tin when it's rolled out as sheet metal, and some-times it's plated with tin. Most people have never seen a real chunk of solid tin."

"Go on."

"When you watched that blacksmith making horseshoes, that was what he was using. He probably called it iron, but it was really soft steel, iron with just a little touch of carbon. If there's gobs of carbon in it, it's cast iron, the melt we pour in the foundry. You can't pound cast iron the way a smith does. It'll break."

"I remember that you said it was brittle."

"That's right, it is. It has lots of uses, but you can't use it for armor or a hammer head, or anything like that."

Swallow took a deep breath. "Number three's wrought iron, and that really is iron, though there's generally some slag in it, too. We start with cast iron and burn all the carbon out, when we want some. It's pretty soft, and it'll take almost any amount of bending. Mostly it's used for fancy window grills and that kind of a thing."

"You still haven't told me anything about bronze."

"I thought this might help make it clearer, Caldé. You see, there's a couple dozen alloys people call bronze, because they look like bronze. Most have quite a bit of pot metal in them and no tin at all. Tin costs too much. Real tin."

Silk stirred impatiently.

"That makes real bronze cost a lot, too. Real bronze, not the stuff you'd get if you bought a bronze figure of some god, is half tin and half copper."

"Is that all?"

Swallow nodded. "It's a pretty simple alloy, but it's got marvelous properties. It's tougher than steel and almost as strong, and you can hammer and weld it, and machine it easier than anything except cast iron. I know that because we still make some little parts out of it, sleeve bearings mostly, and the worms for the big worm gears. But when I was a boy, the older men said they used to cast heads out of it, and there were still some old taluses around with those bronze heads."

Silk leaned against the doorframe; he was already tired, had been tired before the parade had ended, and there was still the dinner tonight; he resolved to get an hour's sleep before eight, no matter what happened. Aloud he asked, "Can you cast bronze—this real bronze—as well as brass?"

"Better, Caldé. We cast those worms I mentioned, and then machine the bearing surfaces, so I know. It would speed things up too, because the parts wouldn't need so much cleanup. But it would be expensive, because of the cost of the tin."

"Have you got the tin? Here right now?"

Swallow nodded. "Because we still use bronze for the worms and so forth."

"Then do it. Use it."

"I'll have to up the price, Caldé. I'm sorry, but I will. Even if you order two or three."

"Then up it." Longing for the brown leather chair he had occupied earlier, Silk added, "We'll talk about how much when we get back to your office. And don't forget the double-thick thorax and front plates. Obviously you'll need a little more for those, and the steel umbrellas—shields, I suppose you'd call them—that Maytera suggested."

Mucor said, "The storm will pass over soon," surprising everyone; then, "I'm tired."

"She ought to sit down," Silk told Swallow, "and so should I, but first I must ask you about Maytera's hand. She's got it in her basket. Maytera, will you show it to him, please?"

"Man cut," Oreb remarked from his perch on the top of the screen. Silk was not certain whether he meant that Blood had severed it or that Blood himself had been killed—by him—as animals were as sacrifice.

Maytera Marble had passed her basket to Swallow; he took off the white towel that had covered her now-lifeless right hand and held it up, in appearance the hand of an elderly woman. A short cylinder of silvery metal extended from its wrist. "I lost some fluid," she told him, "but not very much. There are valves and things to control that. I'm sure you know."

He nodded absently.

"But the tubes would have to be mended some way. The one that brings the fluid to move my fingers, and the one that takes it back."

Silk said, "We'd appreciate it very much, Director, if you would do everything you can for Maytera. She can't pay you; but I may be able to, if it isn't too much. If it is, I feel sure I can arrange for you to be paid."

"Don't worry about that, Caldé." Swallow returned the severed hand to its basket. "We'd be happy to do what we can for Maytera here as a courtesy to you. We could rejoin those pressure and return tubes, though it'll take delicate work."

Maytera Marble smiled, her face shining.

"The load-bearing part's no problem at all. Or I don't think it should be. It won't look quite as pretty as it did, though. Repairs never do."

"I won't mind a bit," Maytera Marble assured him.

"The difficulty—pardon me, Caldé." Swallow closed the door, the only source of daylight on their side of the canvas screen. "Maytera, will you hold up your arm a minute? I need to show the caldé something."

She did, and Swallow pointed. "Look down in here, Caldé. Maytera, I want you to try to move your fingers. Pretend that you're going to grab hold of my nose."

Minute glimmerings appeared in the shadowy interior of the stump of arm, pin-point gleams that reminded Silk oddly of the scattered diamonds he had seen beneath the belly of the whorl.

"There! See that, Caldé? Those are glass threads, like very fine wires, with light running through them. It's fluid that powers her fingers, like she said, but it's those twinkles that steer them. The twinkles are messages. They're supposed to tell every joint in her hand how to move."

Hesitantly, Silk nodded.

"Suppose you were to put a man on a hilltop twenty miles away, and tell him to ride as soon as he saw a lantern run up the flagpole of the Juzgado. It's the same principle."

"I believe I understand."

"When ordinary wire like we use gets cut, you can fix it by wrapping the ends together. With glass threads like you find in chems, that won't work. You've got to have a special tool they call an opticsynapter. We don't have one here because we don't use glass thread. We haven't any way to make it."

Silk endeavored to ignore Maytera Marble's disappointment. "Then we must locate one of these tools—and someone who knows how to use it, I assume—and tie the glass threads? Is that correct? Then you can complete the repair?"

Swallow shook his head. "If she went around with her hand hanging from the glass string, it would probably break. We can do the welding right now, and we'd better. When you find an opticsynapter she can take off her hand in the usual way. The operator shouldn't have any trouble fishing out the other end of the string."

"Where would we find one?"

"There you have me, Caldé. A doctor who specializes in chems should have one, but I don't know of one here in Viron."

Chenille snapped her fingers. "I know somebody!"

"Do you, dear? Do you really?" Maytera Marble's voice, usually so calm, trembled noticeably.

"You bet. Stony had one of those strings cut where our talus had shot him, and Patera Incus fixed it for him so he could move again. He had a gadget to do it with, and that's what he said it was, an opticsynapter. I was watching him."

Silk turned to Blood's emaciated daughter. "You were gone a few minutes ago, Mucor. Are you back with us? Please answer, if you can."

She nodded. "With the Flier, Silk. Women have him. They want to know about the thing that lets him fly."

"I see. Perhaps it would be wiser for us not to speak of that at present. I want you to search for Patera Incus for me, as well as Hyacinth and Auk. Do you know him?"

After a silence that seemed long, Mucor said, "No, Silk."

"He was a prisoner in your father's house for a while, at the same time I was. He's an augur too, short, with a round face and prominent teeth. A few years older than I. I realize you don't see things as we do, but that is how we see him."

Mucor did not reply, and Maytera Marble passed her working hand before Mucor's eyes without result. "She's gone, Patera. She's looking for him, I think."

"Let's hope she finds all three soon." Silk glanced up at Oreb. "Has the man finished working over there? Joining the iron, or whatever you'd call it?"

"No fire! No more!"

"Thank you. Come along, Director. As interesting as all this is, and potentially valuable, I can't spare more time for it. Your workman must begin Maytera's repair. You and I can discuss our contract while he works. How many taluses could you build at the same time if you called back all of the employees you've sent home? Don't exaggerate."

"I won't. I just wish I had my charts here. The movement of parts, you know, Caldé, and the time required to make them."

"How many?" Silk stepped around the screen into a clutter of metal tables, remembering at the final moment to smile at the leather-aproned craftsman at work there. "Good afternoon, my son. Thelxiepeia bless you."

"Four, Caldé." Behind him, Silk heard Swallow's relieved exhalation. "I want to say five, but I can't guarantee it. We could start a fifth, once the first four are moving along."

"Then the city will order four," Silk decided, "with the double front plates I described, heads of real bronze, and the shields. We must consider armament, too, I suppose, and price. How long will four require?"

Swallow gnawed his lip. "I'm going to say two and a half months. That's the best I can promise, Caldé."

"Six weeks. Hire new people and train them—there are thousands of unemployed men and women in this city. Work day and night." Silk paused, considering. "The city agrees to pay a premium of six cards for each day less than forty-five. You have my word on that."

Swallow licked his lips.

From his perch on the screen, Oreb crowed, "Silk win!"

Chapter 8

TO SAVE YOUR LIFE

Repressing a shudder, Maytera Mint stepped over the dead man's leg, the last to go into the guardroom. Over Hyrax's leg, she told herself firmly. It was only Hyrax's leg, and not a thing of horror; *Hyrax,* a near-homophone of *Hierax,* was a name often given boys whose mothers had died in childbirth.

Now, Maytera Mint reflected, Hierax had come for Hyrax.

"They, the–ah . . ." Remora began, and fell silent.

"Soldiers." Spider seated himself on a stool. "Soldiers got them." He pulled up his tunic and thrust his needler into his waistband, let the tunic fall into place again, and wiped his hands on his thighs. "See how good they got shot, Patera? Dead center, all three. That's soldiers' shootin'."

"I would have thought that Hyrax's body would warn Guan," Maytera Mint ventured. She was looking down at Guan's body as she spoke. "He must have seen it, exactly as we did."

Spider nodded. "That's why he figured there wasn't nobody layin' for him. He figured they'd of moved it if they were, and he had a slug gun, didn't he? I'd want to know more than feet in the door, wouldn't I? So he went in careful and had a look around, see? That's how I would of done, and that's how Guan did. Then he set his gun down, probably stood it in the corner, and got that water. That's when they got him, shot him from in back. See where he's lyin'? He was watchin' the door while he drank. He couldn't shut it without movin' Hyrax, and he hadn't done that yet, but he was watchin', only a soldier was in here with him that he didn't know about, and that's when he shot him."

"May I sit, too?" Maytera Mint had found another stool. "May His Eminence?"

"Sure."

"We—er—arms? Should be armed." Remora was poking about the guardroom. "Slug guns, hey? Slug guns for soldiers, um, chems. Chemical persons, eh? All of them. The slug guns of the, um, departed."

"They're gone," Spider informed him. "They all had slug guns. That's Guan, Hyrax, and Sewellel. A slug gun'll do for a soldier, and soldiers don't like them lyin' around."

"I am sorry," Maytera Mint told him. "Genuinely sorry. You must understand that. I sympathize with your grief, not just conventionally but actually."

"All right. Sure."

"Nevertheless, I have won our bet. You pledged your word to give me honest answers to three questions. If you would prefer to wait, I understand. We may not have long, however."

"I might not," Spider told her. "That's what you're thinkin', isn't it? Say it."

She shook her head. "I'm not, because I don't understand the situation sufficiently. When you've answered my questions, I may. Here is the first. The Army is by no means alone in its possession of slug guns. All Bison's troopers have them, as do many others. Yet you were entirely certain it was not one of Bison's troopers who had killed Paca. Why was that?"

Remora put in, "He's answered already, hey? The—um—um—accuracy. Precision."

"Yeah, that. But we saw them, and the other boys shot at them. You said you heard shootin' when we had you locked up. Well, that was what you heard. It was soldiers, two or three, maybe. If they'd known there wasn't but five of us and me with no slug gun, they'd have shot it out, but they couldn't be sure we didn't have a couple dozen, that's what I think. So they beat hoof figurin' to chill us one at a time." He sighed. "We ought to of stuck together, but I didn't see it like that then."

"Thank you." Maytera Mint laced her fingers in her lap as she considered. "If they have come to rescue His Eminence and me, there would be no reason for us to shoot them if we had slug guns to do it. That's not a question, Spider. It's a comment."

"It's right enough, whichever it is. But if you're tryin' to find out who sent them or why, you're not goin' to get it out of me. I don't know. The Army's ours, the Ayuntamiento's. All the soldiers are supposed to know about us."

"Possibly, um, councillor, eh?" Remora had carried over a stool. "Might not he have come to—ah—dubiety? You have, um, informers? Against the general's forces, eh? Might not the councillor have come to fear that the Caldé, er, likewise? You?"

"Maybe." Spider rose, went to the door, and taking Hyrax's wrists pulled him into the room. "But I don't believe it."

"Nor do I," Maytera Mint murmured as Spider shut the door and bolted it.

"You gamble, eh? Put yourself at hazard. And us. If the soldiers you apprehend are concealed, hey? There are other, um, chambers? In addition to this in which we, er, presently?"

"That's the latrine," Spider told him, nodding toward an interior door. "We got one of those portable jakes in there. The other's the storeroom. Yeah, they could be in either one. Or locked out. I'll take that for now."

He turned to Maytera Mint. "You got two more questions, General. You goin' to ask them? Or you want more water and somethin' to eat? You can eat first if you want to."

Observing Remora's expression, she said, "Why can't we eat while I ask? We're adults."

"Swell. Patera, you're the hungriest, right?"

"I, er, possibly."

"Then you go in and get it. The door's not locked. Go in there, have a look at the prog, and bring out whatever you and the general want. Fetch along some wine, too, and more water if you want it."

Remora gulped. "If they are, hey? Inside?"

"They most likely won't shoot you. Tell them they won't have to shoot me, neither. Tell them all I got's a needler. When we went up to that house, I figured a needler'd be plenty and leave a hand free. Besides, it's what I usually pack."

"I shall emphasize the point, um, assuming." Remora faced about and bowed his head.

"Well, get to it. Open the shaggy door."

"He's praying," Maytera Mint explained. "He knows that he may be shot as soon as he does. He's commending himself to High Hierax and offering the other gods what may be his final prayers as a living person."

"Well, make it quick!"

"Thank you for answering my first question," Maytera Mint said to distract Spider. "I agree that you've answered fully and fairly, as specified. My second may be a bit touchier. I want to point out in advance that it concerns no confidential matters of our city's. Or of the Ayuntamiento's, in so far as the two can be distinguished.

"Before I ask, would you like to pray too? If there are soldiers in there, which you seem to think possible, they are more likely to shoot you than His Eminence. And if they shoot His Eminence, they will certainly shoot us as well."

Spider gave her a twisted grin. "How about you, General? You're a sibyl. Why aren't you prayin'?"

She took out her beads and fingered them while she framed her answer. "Because I have prayed a great deal already during the past few days. I have been in danger almost constantly, and I've sent others into dangers far worse and prayed for them. I would only be repeating the petitions I've made so often. Also because I've told the gods again and again that I'm very willing to die if that is their will for me. If I were to pray, I would pray only that His Eminence, and you, be spared. I do so pray. Great Pas, hear my plea!"

Spider grunted.

"Furthermore, I don't believe there are soldiers hiding in here. I think that what must have happened was that one of them was in here looking for something. He heard Guan come in and hid, then came out and shot Guan after Guan's first and perhaps rather cursory examination failed to find him. Would the water have come from the storeroom?"

Spider nodded. "Right."

"Then I should think that the soldier was in the latrine. Since chems don't use them, he might have thought Guan wouldn't expect him there."

Spider said nothing, sitting with eyes half shut, his back against the shiprock wall.

"Here is my second question. You'll recall that Councillor Potto described the situation on the surface to His Eminence and me, then asked who was master of the city. His description made it clear that he was implying the Rani was. I take it you will concede that. You were present."

"Sure. When her troopers come out of her airship, some of yours took shots at them. You know that?"

"I do. Many died as a result of that tragic error."

"Those troopers thought Viron was bein' invaded, and they were right. Sure, the Trivigauntis are goin' to help you fight us. Sure, they're goin' to make this Silk caldé. But he'll lose his job the first time he balks. What's the question?"

"You've answered it already, at least in part. I planned to ask what you know of the plans of the Trivigauntis."

Remora cleared his throat. "I am—ah—readied. Also resolved. You yourselves, eh? Are you, um . . . ?"

"Go ahead," Spider told him.

Remora took two determined steps to his right and threw wide the door.

"That's the latrine, you putt!"

Calmly, Remora turned. "I am, ah, was aware of it. I, um, eaves-dropped, eh? Couldn't help it. The General, um, indicated that this, ah, necessary room would be the point of greatest, er, greater hazard. I revere her intellect. More than your own, if I may be thus—ah—incivil."

"Usually I do better than this," Spider told him. "Now get in there where you're s'posed to, and don't forget to bring me out a bottle."

"You would—ah—indubitably have had me, um, risk the necessary room as well." Remora opened the storeroom door as he spoke. "I there-fore, eh? Advised by the immortal gods. Or so I would like to, um, have it. The greater risk first."

He stepped into the storeroom. "As for, ah, this . . ." He clapped to brighten the single dull light on the ceiling. "It is equally, um, innocent? Unpeopled."

"In that case, I would like another bottle of water, Your Eminence," Maytera Mint declared firmly, "if it's not too much trouble. And some bread, if there is any. Meat, too. I would be very grateful." To Spider she continued, "I inquired about what you knew, you'll notice, not what you guessed. Do you know this? Or is it speculation?"

"I know it. Now you'll want to know how I know."

She shook her head, marveling to find herself—little Maytera Mint from Sun Street!—haggling with such a man over such a matter. "I won't require you to reveal your sources."

"I'll tell you anyhow. Councillor Potto told me before we went up there. He wasn't just guessin', neither."

Remora emerged from the storeroom with a dusty wine bottle, two even dustier bottles of water, and several small packages wrapped in tinted synthetic.

Spider accepted the wine. "Brown's bread and red's meat. I ought to of told you, but I guess you worked it out yourself."

"It was not—ah—cryptic." Remora sat down. "This, er, packet is unopened, Maytera. I, hum, sampled the other. Somewhat saline, but tasty."

She accepted a red package and unwrapped it eagerly; it held flat strips of what seemed to be dried beef. "We thank all gods for this good food," she murmured. "Thanks to Fair Phaea, especially. Praise Pasturing Pas for fat cattle." She tore the leathery meat with her teeth and thought it sweet as sugarcane.

"Councillor Potto can lie birds out of a tree," Spider drew the cork of the wine bottle with a pop. "I've heard him to where I just about believed him myself. You said while we were talkin' in the tunnel that you figured I could fool you if I wanted to. I'm not so sure, but Councillor Potto could put it over on me, and I know it. Only this wasn't that. He just said it, listenin' to himself. I don't think he cared a sham shaggy bit whether I believed it. But I do, and I've known him twenty years, like I said."

Maytera Mint nodded and swallowed. "Thank you. And thank you, Your Eminence, for this food. I thanked the gods, I fear, but not their proximal agent."

"Quite all right, eh? Um—delighted. Have some bread." Remora handed her a brown-wrapped package. "Strengthening. Ah—fortifying."

"Thank you again. Thank you very much. All praise to Fruiting Echidna, whose sword I am."

She paused as she tore the loaf. "Spider, I'll ask my final question, if I may. I won't be able to, with my mouth full of this good bread. You may not know the answer."

"If I don't know, I don't." He wiped the top of the wine bottle on his cuff and held it out to her. "You want to bless this, too, while you're doin' everythin' else?"

"Certainly." Maytera Mint laid the bread in her lap with the remainder of the dried beef and traced the sign of addition over the bottle. "Praise be to you, Exhilarating Thelxiepeia, and praise to you, likewise, dark son of Thyone."

"Want a drink? Help yourself."

She sipped cautiously, then more boldly.

"I bet that was the first wine you ever had in your life. Am I right?"

She shook her head. "Laymen—they are men in fact, very largely—give us a bottle now and then. When it happens, we have a glass at dinner until it's gone." She hesitated. "We did, I should have said. Maytera Rose and I did, but we won't any more. She passed away last Tarsday, and I've scarcely had a moment to mourn her. She was . . ."

"A, umph, excellent sibyl," Remora put in. He chewed and swallowed. "Doubtless. I did not have the—ah—happiness of her acquaintance. But doubtless, eh? No doubt of it."

"A good woman whom life had treated sufficiently roughly that she struck out, at times, before she was struck." Maytera Mint finished pensively. "Toward the end she struck at others habitually, I would say. It could be unpleasant, and yet her asperity was fundamentally defensive. That's good wine. Might I have a little more, Spider?"

"Sure thing."

"Thank you." She sipped again. "Perhaps His Eminence would like some too."

"Dimber with me."

Maytera Mint wiped the mouth of the bottle and passed it to Remora. "My third question now. As I said, you may not know the answer. But what was the original purpose of these tunnels? I've been wondering ever since our caldé described them to me, and it may be important."

Spider leaned back, his homely heavy-featured face tilted upward and his eyes closed. "That's somethin' I can tell you all right, but I got to think."

"As I say—"

He leaned forward once more, his eyes open and one large hand tugging at his stubbled jaw. "I didn't say I don't know. Councillor Potto told me about them. One thing he said was it wasn't just one thing. There's three or maybe four, and they go under the whole whorl. You know that?"

Her mouth full, Maytera Mint shook her head.

"If you went along the big one we turned off of," Spider jerked his thumb at the door, "far enough, you could get clean to the skylands, maybe. I don't know anybody that ever tried it, but that's what Councillor Potto said one time. You can be way out in the sticks where there isn't any houses or anythin', nothin' but trees and bushes, and maybe there's one right under you. Could be a hundred cubits down or so close you'd hit it puttin' in a fence post."

Hoping her face did not betray the skepticism she felt, she said, "The labor involved must have been incredible."

"Pas built them. It's queer, tellin' you two that. You ought to tell me. But he did. He did it when he was buildin' the whorl, so it wasn't as bad as you'd figure."

The wine returned to Spider, who drank and wiped his mouth on the back of his hand. "His boys did the real work, accordin' to the councillor. When we say Pas made it, it just means he had the idea and ran the job."

"His divine—ah—puissance animated his servants."

"If you say so. But there was a lot, see? He wanted the job done fast. Mind if I have a little of that?"

Spider took two strips of dried meat from Maytera Mint's lap. "I'm with him there, I'm the same way. You got a job to do, you do it. Wrap it up and tie the string. Let one drag, and somethin' always goes queer." He bit through both strips.

"If they were indeed constructed by Pas, it must have been for some good reason. It's one of the paradoxes of isagogics—" Maytera Mint looked to Remora for permission to speak on learned and holy topics, and received it. "That Pas, with all power at his disposal, squanders none. He never acts without a purpose, and educes a multitude of benefits from a single action."

She paused, inviting contradiction. "We sibyls don't go to the schola, but we receive some education as postulants, and we read, of course. We can also question our augurs if we wish, though I confess I've seldom done so."

"All—ah—admirably correct, Maytera. General."

Spider nodded. "Councillor Potto said somethin' like that about the tunnels. We were talkin' about when they got built."

"I'd like to hear it."

"It was while they were buildin' the whorl, like I said. To start it was just a big hunk of rock. You know that?"

"Certainly. The Chrasmologic Writings emphasize it."

"So how could they get in and get the rock out? They dug a bunch of tunnels. Then they had to haul in dirt and trees, and pretty soon a big cart would come out and it'd be tearin' up stuff they just planted. These tunnels are shiprock in lots of places, especially high up. You twig that?"

"Most have been, I believe. Nearly all."

"All right. They made those before they brought in dirt, see? Up on the surface, only it was bare rock then, and now that's maybe ten, twenty cubits down. They set those stretches up and shoveled dirt around them. Then they could cart in more, and the trees, without tearin' up what they'd already finished."

Maytera Mint swallowed bread. "But the deeper tunnels are bored through stone? That's how our caldé described them."

"Sure, that's how they got the rock out. Look up at the skylands next time you're out in the open. Look at how much room there is, just clouds and air, and the sun and the shade, all right? What's a few tunnels compared to that?"

Remora nodded vigorously. " 'How mighty are the works of Pas!' The, er, initial line of the Chrasmologic Writings, eh? Therefore known to—ah—all. Even laymen. We clergy, um, prone to forget."

"He pumped water through them too," Spider continued. "You make the lake. That's a shaggy lot of water. Think if old Pas had to bring it in barrels. So for the little stuff, he just run pipes down the tunnels, but for big ones like the lake, he put in doors to keep the water out of the ones he wanted to stay dry, and pumped. I could show you a cave by the lake with one of those doors in the back. That's where Pas pumped in water to fill the lake, and he put in that door 'cause he didn't want the water to wash back into his tunnels when he was done. That cave used to be under the water when the lake was bigger."

Spider fell silent, and Maytera Mint remarked, "Something's troubling you."

"I was just thinkin' about a couple things. I told you this side one ends in dirt, and that's where we bury them?"

She nodded.

"There's one of those doors in front of the dirt. I guess the big tunnel was one of them they pumped in, and they didn't want water in it. What we're in now was probably put in after. Anyway, talkin' about doors reminded me we're goin' to have to bury these culls. It'll take a lot of diggin'."

"I had assumed we would," she said. "You indicated there were two points troubling you. May I ask what the second was? And what the other uses of these tunnels are?"

"That's the same question two times." Spider shrugged. "You never asked me why the lake keeps gettin' smaller."

"I didn't suppose you knew, and to tell the truth, I've never thought much about it. The water has gone elsewhere, I suppose. Down into these tunnels, perhaps."

"You couldn't be any wronger about that, General."

Remora put his water bottle on the floor between his feet. "You know, eh? Privy to the, um, information?"

"Yes, I'd like to know, too," Maytera Mint said, "if you don't mind. And I've by no means finished eating yet."

"It's all the same. You wanted to know what else they're good for and something else. I forget."

"The second consideration that troubled you."

"Same thing. The sun shines all the time, don't it?"

"Certainly."

"But we get night half the time 'cause the shade's there. It cools things off, right? When it's hot, you're happy to see the shade come down, 'cause you know it's goin' to get cooler. Wintertime, you don't like it so much."

"Primary. Um, puerile. What—ah—the significance?"

"See this room, Patera? Three doors. Let's say they're all shut. No windows, all right? Now s'pose the sun started at that corner there and run over to that one, about as big as a rope. That's the whorl. That's what it's like, see? Goin' to get pretty hot in here, right?"

"I take your point," Maytera Mint told Spider, "but I do not understand it. The whorl is very large."

"Not that big. It's been goin' for three hundred years and over. That's what they say."

"The, um, fact. Provable in a—ah—many ways."

"Good here, Patera. It had to be hot enough for people to live in when Pas started it, see?"

Neither Remora nor Maytera Mint spoke.

"But it couldn't get much hotter or we'd fry. Couldn't get much hotter with the sun goin' all the time. So there had to be some way to get shut of the heat."

"The—ah—outside, eh? Beyond the whorl. The, um, Writings state, hey? A—uh, um—frigid night."

"You got it. Notice how the wind blows all the time down here? It's cold, too, colder than up top, anyhow."

"I, um, fail—"

Maytera Mint interrupted. "I see! Air circulates through these tunnels, doesn't it, Spider? Some of them must be filled with warm air bound for the night outside. The ones we've been in are carrying cold air back to the surface."

"Bull's-eye, General. Well, it's not workin' as good as it did. You said about lake water goin' in the tunnels."

She nodded.

"Suppose it fills a tunnel half up. The wind can't blow as much, see? If it fills the whole tunnel in just one spot, the wind can't blow at all. There's places where the shiprock gave way, too, and wind can't blow there either. So it's gettin' hotter. We don't notice, 'cause it's too slow. But talk to old people and they'll say winters used to be colder, and longer, too." Spider stood. "I'm goin' to start diggin'. You want to eat more, bring it along."

"I do and I will," Maytera Mint gathered up what remained of her bread and meat, picked up her bottle of water, and rose. The bolt of the outer door clanked back; the shadowy side tunnel beyond was deserted.

"They've gone off," Spider told her over his shoulder. "I'd like to know why they started shootin' at my boys."

She sighed. "Because they were Ayuntamientados, I should imagine. Four brave men who had kept Viron secure for years, slain by others who've guarded it for centuries. That's what we've come to."

"Not all, eh?" Remora closed the door behind him. "All the, um. Not, ah, er, fah . . ." His mouth worked soundlessly.

Maytera Mint looked around at him in some surprise. His eyes seemed to have sunk into his skull, and his nose appeared both thinner and smaller. As she watched, his lips drew back, exposing his big, discolored teeth in a frightful grin. Spider exclaimed, "Sphigx shit!"

"He's not the right one," Remora informed Maytera Mint.

She made herself smile.

"This is the one who talks to the one who's not there. The right one was down here with the tall girl. He might be here."

"This is Mucor," Maytera Mint explained to Spider. "She's Maytera's granddaughter. We've spoken before.

"Do you remember, Mucor? You came to tell me our caldé was in danger of capture, and I stormed the Palatine. Afterward, we met in person in the Juzgado."

Remora nodded, his head bobbing like a toy's, lank black hair mercifully concealing his terrible eyes. "Incus is his name. A little augur."

"I don't know him, though His Eminence has told me of him. Mucor? Mucor!"

The death-head grin was fading.

"Mucor, come back, please! If you see Bison or our caldé, tell them—tell either or both—where I am, and that this man is holding us for Councillor Potto."

"You won't be then." The final word was almost too faint to hear. The grin vanished; Remora tossed his hair back as he habitually did, and the eyes his gesture revealed were no longer terrifying. "Not all, hey? Many on our, um, the caldé's."

When no one spoke, he added, "The general's, hey?"

"You want my needler?" Spider asked Maytera Mint.

"Certainly, if you're willing to let me have it."

He presented it butt first. "You wouldn't shoot me, would you, General? Not with my own needler that I gave you."

She accepted it, glanced at it, and dropped it into one of her habit's side pockets. "No. Only if I were compelled to, and perhaps not even then."

"All right. I'm goin' to dig the graves now, see? You two can finish eatin' and watch," Spider stepped out into the empty tunnel, "but if I'm cold 'fore I finish, it's for me. You wrap me and slide me in. Knife's in my pocket."

They followed him down the tunnel until it was blocked by a massive barrier of rusty iron. "Councillor Potto doesn't want anybody to hear," Spider confided, "but I guess it don't matter any more. *Fraus!*"

For a second or longer, nothing happened.

The great barrier shuddered, creaked, and began to creep upward, rolling unpleasantly into itself. Abruptly, Maytera Mint became conscious of the stench of decay, nauseous yet so diffuse that she might almost have believed she imagined it. Remora snorted, sounding surprisingly horse-like, and wiped his nose on his sleeve.

"No fresh air, 'cept when the door's open," Spider remarked as he led them into the dim cul-de-sac the rising barrier had revealed. "It'll air out pretty quick." He stopped to point. "Right here's where the shiprock ends. Have a look."

Maytera Mint advanced to do so, crossing loose earth into which her scuffed black shoes sank. "I'm very glad you let us hear the word for that door. I'd hate to think of our being locked in here, unable to get it open."

"I'm bein' nice to you two so you'll slide me in after it happens. See the rolls of poly?"

"Certainly." She was examining the edge of the shiprock wall. "This is not as thick as I had imagined."

"It's pretty strong, though. There's iron rods in it."

"The—ah—interments." Remora indicated scraps of paper that dotted the sloping earth at the end of the tunnel. "Those, um, are they all?" He counted them silently, his lips twitching. "Eleven in—ah—toto?"

Spider nodded. "Plenty of room left, but we got three in the guardroom, and Paca back in the big tunnel, and me."

"You—ah—depression. A mere, um, state of mind, my son. Emotion, hey?"

"Yes," Maytera Mint agreed heartily. "You mustn't talk as if your death were inevitable, Spider. I mean now, killed by those soldiers. It isn't, and I pray it won't happen."

"That devil you called your sib's granddaughter, General. What'd it say?"

"She is not a devil," Maytera Mint declared firmly. "She is a living girl, one who has been shamefully mistreated."

Spider grunted, picking up a long-handled spade that had lain between two rolls of synthetic.

"This, er, granddaughter, General. An—ah—difficult child?" Remora bit into a strip of dried beef.

Maytera Mint nodded absently, and found herself staring at one of the grim slips of soiled paper. Bending and squinting, she read a name, a date, and a few particulars of the dead man's life. "Is this the most recent one, Spider? The paper seems cleaner than the others."

"Yeah. Last spring."

There was still half a loaf. Deep in thought, she tore away piece after piece, chewing and swallowing slowly, and drank from her bottle.

"I'm about done here." Spider had ceased to dig, leaning on his spade. "Think you two could fetch a cull out for me? Door's not locked."

"I was about to suggest it myself," Maytera Mint told him.

"We—ah—trust, hey? On our honor?"

"I have his needler, Your Eminence. We could go at any time, and I could shoot him if he tried to stop us."

"In that case, um, the circumstances—"

"But he gave it to me, remember? Besides, he knows these tunnels, and we don't."

"Ah—the soldiers."

"I feel certain they'd help us if we could find them, but what if we couldn't? Spider, we'll be happy to bring one of your late friends here for burial. Thank you for your trust in us. It is not misplaced."

He nodded. "Cut off a big hunk of poly. You can lay him on that and drag him, it's real slick. When you get him here, I'll wrap him up in it."

"May I borrow your knife?"

He got it from his pocket and handed it to her, then went back to his digging. Remora held the ends of the smaller roll while she pulled out and slashed free a length twice the height of a man.

As they carried it back to the guardroom, Remora muttered, "You, um, wonders with him, Maytera. I congratulate you."

She shrugged, unconsciously thrusting her hand into her pocket to grasp Spider's needler. "He has no slug gun, Your Eminence, and without one he would be defenseless against the soldiers. He's hoping our presence will make it possible for him to surrender."

"I, ah—" Remora opened the guardroom door and glanced around. Their stools stood in a circle as they had left them, and the three dead men still sprawled on the gritty shiprock floor, untouched. "One can always, eh? Give up? Capitulate. Not, um, that we—"

"One can always raise one's hands and step into full view of the enemy," Maytera Mint told him. "A good many troopers lose their lives doing it. This one nearest the door, I think. If Your Eminence will unfold that synthetic, we can roll him onto it, poor spirit."

"You, er, concerned, eh?" Remora spread the synthetic winding sheet, holding it down with his knees as he wrestled with the dead man's shoulder. "I observed your demeanor in—ah—there. As you ate."

"Puzzled." She forced her gaze away from the dead man's eyes, wishing that it had been possible to roll him so that he lay face down again. "There was fresh earth on the blade of that spade. At least, I think it was fresh, or fairly fresh. Maytera has a little garden back at the cenoby, Your Eminence. I've helped her with it now and then, hoeing, and spading in the spring. I don't think that Spider noticed it."

"I fail to see the, um, import. Someone else, eh? Could be Councillor Potto, another—hum—subordinate."

"I fail to see it too," she told Remora. "Take the other corner, will you?"

Back at the end of the tunnel, Spider had completed the first grave and begun a second. "That's Hyrax." He produced a stump of pencil and a battered notebook. "I'll write, you two cap for him."

They knelt. Maytera Mint found herself, rather to her own surprise, clasping the cold hand. If things had been different, she thought, we might have been man and wife, you and I. We must be nearly of an age.

The drone of Remora's prayer reminded her of the singsong voices of children in the classroom, reciting the multiplication table, memorizing prayers for meals, for betrothals, for the dead. Had she taught girls this year? Or boys. She could not remember.

We would have kissed and held hands, and done what men and women do, and I would have borne you a child, perhaps, my own child. But when I met Bison . . .

"All right, General, let him go. I got to fold this over him." Suddenly Hyrax was no longer a dead man, but a statue or a picture, still visible but blurred and faintly blue through the synthetic.

"His knife." She rose, dusting loose earth from her black skirt by reflex. "You'll need his knife for the paper."

"I already got it. You want to help, Patera? I could do it alone, but it'll be easier with two." They crouched, one on either side, and Spider said, "Lift when I do, see? A-one and a-two and a-*three!*"

Raising the shrouded corpse to waist level, they slid it into its grave; and he began shoveling earth after it, pausing from time to time to tamp the damp dark face of death with the handle of his spade. He said, "You're wonderin' why we don't dig them down the way you usually do, I guess."

"The, um, papers," Remora ventured. "Stepped upon, eh? Trodden."

"There's that. But mostly it's easier to dig here. Then too, we'd have to walk on the old ones to bury the new ones."

As they were leaving the guardroom with Guan stretched on a fresh sheet of poly, laughter, faint and mad, echoed in the main tunnel. "Wait!" Maytera Mint told Remora. "Did you hear that? You must have!"

He shuddered. "I—ah—possibly."

"Will you do me a favor, Your Eminence?" She did not wait for his assent. "Go back in there and get two packages of that dried meat. One for yourself, and one for me. We can put them in our pockets."

"That—ah—merriment . . ."

"I have no idea, Your Eminence. I have a feeling, a presentiment, if you will, that we may need food."

"If we—er—never mind." Remora vanished into the guardroom.

When he returned, Maytera Mint handed him a needler.

"But I am—er—better, perhaps, with you, eh, General? Your, um, forte."

"That isn't Spider's, it's Guan's," she told him. "Spider said a needler was what he usually used, remember? It didn't really make much of an impression at the time, but afterward, thinking about that poor man who dressed as a woman, it struck me that the other spy-catchers must have done the same thing. They would want some sort of a weapon, and before the rebellion nobody but a Guardsman could walk around the city carrying a slug gun. Then I wondered—this was while we were bringing Hyrax—what they did with them when they got their slug guns. It seemed likely that most of them had simply put them in their waistbands, under their tunics, where they were accustomed to carrying them."

"Most, um, sagacious."

"Thank you, Your Eminence. Anyway, whatever that was we heard wasn't a soldier. Do you agree?"

"I, um, indubitably." Remora stared down at the needler in his hand.

"Or a chem at all, any kind of chem. So a needler should work, and we may need them, just as we may need this meat, for which I haven't yet thanked you. Thank you very much, Your Eminence. It was a great condescension for you to oblige me as you have."

"You must know how to, um, operate? Manage this?" Remora might not have heard her.

"It's not difficult. Push that down," she pointed to the safety catch, "when you wish to shoot. Point it, and pull the trigger. If you want to shoot a second needle, pull it again. I won't show you how to reload now. There isn't time, and we don't have any more needles anyway."

Remora gulped and nodded.

"In your waistband under your robe, perhaps. I believe that's where our caldé must carry his."

"I–ah. It would be, er, inadvisable, hey? When we return to the–ah–up there."

"I won't tell anyone if you don't." Maytera Mint stooped for a corner of the sheet of synthetic on which Guan's body lay. "We'd better go now, and quickly, or Spider will wonder what delayed us."

At the end of the side tunnel she knelt as she had before, trying to keep her mind upon appropriate petitions to the gods. Guan had kicked her shortly before Spider had locked her away with Remora so that he and his men could sleep; the right side of her thigh was still sore and stiff. She had scarcely given it a thought since it had happened, or so she had convinced herself. Now that Guan was dead, now that Guan lay before her, she found she could not free her mind from the memory of that kick. It was easy to mouth *I forgive you,* and to ask the gods, Echidna particularly, not to hold the kick against him; yet she felt that her forgiveness did not reach her heart, however hard she tried to bring it there.

The transparent sheet covered Guan as a sister sheet from the parent roll had covered Hyrax, and Maytera Mint got to her feet. What was the third man's name? He had been the quietest of their captors; she had thought him sullen and marked him as potentially the most dangerous. She would never know, now, whether she had been correct.

"How 'bout if you dig for Sewellel, Patera? I'll go back with General Mint here and fetch him."

"Why, ah–"

She saw Remora assure himself that his needler was in place with a touch of his forearm, and said, "He's not going to attack me, Your Eminence. He would like to speak to me in private, I imagine."

Remora managed to smile. "In that, um, circumstances, I shall—ah—comply. With all good will."

"What it really is," Spider told him, "is I want to see if you can do it right. You'll have to dig for me, see? You seen me do it. Now you do for Sewellel and Paca, and that'll be two for each of us. Let's move out, General."

Obediently, she followed him down the side tunnel. "What I told Patera's lily," Spider said as they walked. "You know that word? Means the truth."

"Yes, I do, though I've always considered it children's slang. My pupils use it sometimes."

"But that you said, General. That was the lily too."

She nodded, striving to make her nod sympathetic.

"I'm sorry about the way I talk. Sometimes I swear when I didn't mean to. It's just that I always do."

"I understand, believe me."

He stopped abruptly. "Thing is, I don't believe you. Or him, back there. Patera What'shisface."

"Remora."

Spider waved aside Remora's identity. "Echidna made you a general? She talked to you about it?"

"She certainly did."

"Could you see her like you're seein' me now? Could you make out what she was sayin'? She talked to you out of one of those big glasses they got in manteions?"

"Exactly. I can repeat everything she said, if you wish. I'd be happy to." This was a return to familiar ground, and Maytera Mint felt more confident than she had since she and Remora had passed through the ruined gate of Blood's villa.

"I know somebody that says he couldn't really hear the words. He just knew what she meant."

"He had known woman," Maytera Mint explained, hoping that Spider would understand what she intended by *known*. "Or else he had . . . Excuse this, please. The indelicacy."

"Sure thing."

"He had known another man, or a boy, as men know women. That man you told us about? Titi? I should imagine—"

"Yeah, so do I, and the other way, too. Sure he did. Is that the only reason?"

"It is. By Echidna's will, those who have enjoyed carnal knowledge of others may not behold the gods. Nor may they hear them distinctly, though in most cases they understand them. It varies between individuals, and several reasons have been put forward for that. If you don't mind, I won't explain those in detail. They concern the frequency and the specific natures of various sexual relations. You can readily construct them, or similar theories, for yourself."

"Sure, General. You can skip all that."

"I have never known Man. Therefore I saw the face of the goddess exactly as I see yours. More clearly, because her face was very bright. I heard each word she uttered, and can repeat them verbatim, as I said. When I have known Man . . ."

The guilty words had slipped out; she hurried on, conscious that her cheeks were reddening. "I shall no longer be able to see Echidna. No more than your friend could. In the event that I know Man—I mean, have relations with a—with a husband. My husband. Then I won't be able to repeat the words of the gods any more than you could."

"That was the thing I was wanting to talk to you about."

"The words of the goddess? She said—"

Spider waved Echidna's words aside. "You gettin' married and knowin' a man, like you said. I got to tell you."

Her hand closed about the needler in her pocket. "Do you mean yourself, Spider? No. Not willingly."

He shook his head. "Bison. I'm fly, see? I can tell from how you talk about him. It got you worried when I said I got culls you think's yours. You were scared Bison was one."

"Certainly not!" Maytera Mint took three deep breaths and relaxed her hold on the needler. "I suppose I was, a little."

"Yeah, I know. You kept tellin' yourself it couldn't be like that, on account of stuff he's said to you."

She had taken a step backward; she found that her shoulders were pressed against the tunnel's cold shiprock. "I haven't said anything to him, Spider, nor has he said a single such word to me. Nothing! But I've seen—or believed I saw . . . And he, Bison, no doubt has—has. Seen me. And heard me, too. My voice. In the same fashion."

"Yeah, I got you, General." To her surprise, Spider leaned against the wall next to her, sparing her the embarrassment of his gaze. "How old are you?"

"That is none of your affair." She made her voice as firm as she could.

"Maybe it is, and maybe it isn't. How old'd you say I am?"

She shook her head. "Since I decline to confide my age to you, it would be completely inappropriate for me to speculate on yours."

"I'm forty-eight, and that's lily. I'd say you're about thirty-three, thirty-four. If that's queer I'm sorry, but you wouldn't tell me."

"Nor will I now."

"I just want to say it goes awful fast. Life goes by awful fast. You think you know all about that now. The shag you do. I remember all kind of things that happened when I was a sprat."

"I understand, Spider. I know precisely what you mean."

"You just think you do. I've had maybe a hundred women. I wish I'd kept count, but I didn't. There was only two I didn't have to pay, and one was abram once you got to know her."

"It's quite normal for men to think women—" Maytera Mint sought for a diplomatic word. "Irrational. And for women to think men irrational as well."

"Handin' you the lily, I had to pay the other one, too. I didn't give her the gelt, but she cost a shaggy lot more. More than she was worth." Spider shot Maytera Mint a sidelong look. "I got something important to say, but I don't know how to make you believe me."

"Is it true, Spider?"

"Shag, yes! Every word."

"Then I will believe you, even if you don't believe me about the gods. What is it?"

"This isn't it. This's what I should of said back there, see? There was a time when I might of got a woman like you, but that's over. Over and done up, see? Just slipped away. Last year I met one I thought I might like and sort of shaved her a little, you know? And she shaved me back. Then she seen I was gettin' to be serious, and she just froze up.

She'd look at me, and her eyes kept sayin' *too old, too old*. It goes so fast. I didn't feel like I'd got old. I still don't."

For a half minute or more, his silence filled the tunnel.

"All right, about this buck Bison."

Maytera Mint forced herself to nod.

"I'm goin' to die. Probably it won't be very long at all. Back there where we bury, I kept hopin' they'd shoot me and I'd get to say it before I went cold, 'cause then you'd believe me. But they don't shoot like that. The way my culls got it, you're chilled straight off, so I got to say it right here. He was one of mine, see? Bison was. A dimber hand."

She could not be certain she had spoken; perhaps not.

"He was supposed to check in every night. I'd meet him, see, in this certain place. But he only come the first time, the first night."

It was possible to breathe again.

"So I sent somebody. I sent this cully we're fetchin', Sewellel. Bison, he told him he was out. He wouldn't tell you anything about us, but he wouldn't tell us anything about you, neither. That's the lily, General. That's how it was. I don't blame you if you don't believe it, and in your shoes maybe I wouldn't. But I'm goin' today and know it, and I'd like you to cap for me when I'm cold."

"Pray for your spirit." She was still trying to wrap her understanding about the fact.

"Yeah. So it's lily. I told you I wouldn't tell you who mine was, the ones you thought was yours. But he's not mine any more. That's what I'm tellin' you."

She found herself entering the guardroom again, with no memory of having resumed their walk. "Shall I go back and cut off a piece of synthetic?" she asked. "I forgot entirely that we'd need another one. If you carry Sewellel on your shoulders, you'll have blood all over you."

"I got it right here," Spider told her. He held it up.

"But I have your knife. You gave me that so . . ."

"I used Guan's, 'fore I wrote for him." Spider smiled, a small, sad smile heart-wrenchingly foreign to his coarse face. "It don't really take three. It don't even take two, see? I been down here by myself and buried a couple times, and that's what I do, 'cause I start by findin' the dead cull's knife."

"Yes," she said. "Yes, I'm certain you must have been the only mourner that those men had, more than once." She thrust her hands into her pockets, found his needler and her beads, and at last his knife. "Take it, please. I don't want to bury you, Spider. I won't. I want to save your life, and I'm going to try. I'm going to try very hard, and I'll succeed."

He shook his head, but she forced the rough clasp knife into his hand. "Close the door, please. I think it would be better if we didn't startle His Eminence."

Striding purposefully now, she crossed the guardroom and entered the storeroom. "I should have gone in here before," she told Spider over her shoulder. "I let His Eminence do it both times, and it was cowardly of me. This locker—I suppose that's what you call it—with the sign of addition on it in red. Is this where the stretcher's kept?"

Behind her, Spider said, "Yeah, that's it."

She turned, drawing his needler. "Raise both your hands, Spider. You are my prisoner."

He stared at her, his eyes wide.

"He may be able to see us. I can't be sure. Raise them! Hold them up before he kills you."

As Spider lifted his hands, the front of the locker swung open; a soldier stepped out and saluted, his slug gun stiffly vertical, his steel heels clashing. Maytera Mint said, "You aren't Sergeant Sand. What's your name?"

"Private Schist, sir!"

"Thank you. There's a dead man in the outer room. I take it you killed him?"

"That's right, sir."

"Take the synthetic this man's holding and wrap him—the dead man out there, I mean. Wrap the dead man's body in that. You can carry it for us."

Schist saluted again.

Spider said, "You knew he was in there all the time."

Maytera Mint shook her head, finding herself suddenly weak with relief. "I wish I were that . . . I don't know what to call it. That godlike. People believe I am, but I'm not. I have to think and think."

She paused to watch Schist through the doorway as he knelt beside Sewellel's corpse. "And even then I ask Bison's advice, and the captain's. Often I find they've seen more deeply into the problem than I have. I suppose it's useless to ask whether you were telling me the whole truth about Bison now. You can put down your hands, I think."

"I was, yeah." From his expression, Spider was relieved as well. "How'd you figure he was in there?"

"From the earth on the spade. There was fresh earth on the blade. Didn't you notice it?"

He shook his head.

From the guardroom, Schist announced, "I got him, sir."

"Good. You'd better walk ahead of us, Spider, and put up your hands again. There are more, you see. They could have rushed you hours ago, but they must have been afraid you'd kill His Eminence and me."

A hundred thoughts crowded her mind. "Besides, if we let you walk behind us, you might decide that your duty to Councillor Potto compelled you to run. Then this soldier would fire."

"I'd hit you, too," Schist said. "I don't miss much." He patted Sewellel's swathed corpse, slung over his left shoulder.

"Can I put my hand down to open the door?"

"Certainly," Maytera Mint told him; and Schist, "Sure."

"I ought to explain that I've spoken with Private Schist's sergeant," Maytera Mint continued as they left the guardroom. "That was on Sphixday, the day after our caldé was rescued. His name is Sand, and he has come over to our side, to the caldé's side, with his entire squad. Or rather, with what remains of it, because several were killed by a talus."

"I know how it feels."

"I realize you do, Spider. Neither you nor I, nor Sergeant Sand, created war. What I was going to say is that our caldé and I, with Sergeant Sand himself and Generalissimo Oosik and General Saba, conferred upon how we might make the best possible use of Schist here and the rest. Of the few soldiers we had. It wasn't a lengthy debate, because all of us found the answer rather obvious. The soldiers knew these tunnels, and none of us did, though our caldé had spent some time in them. Furthermore, down here they might encounter other soldiers whom they could bring over to our side. Plainly then, the best use that could be made of them was to send them back here to scout the enemy's dispositions, and augment their number if they could."

"All right, but how'd you know he was in there from the dirt on my spade?"

"It was fresh, as I said. Still somewhat damp. I asked about the grave that looked most new, and read the date on the paper, and it wasn't nearly new enough. So somebody else had been burying something. I thought of an ear, as they're called, or something of the sort, though to the best of my knowledge Sand didn't have one." She fell silent, listening to their echoing footsteps.

"Go on," Spider urged her.

"Eventually I realized that room back there was a better place. A soldier as intelligent as Sand would surely anticipate that we would stop there to eat and talk. He'd want to know what we said, since you might say something that would be of value to him. He was right, because as soon as we arrived I began asking my questions. At any rate, he had Schist hide and listen, and when we left we were going here."

Already, too soon as it seemed to Maytera Mint, they had passed beneath the great iron door, and Remora was staring at Schist. She called, "It's all right, Your Eminence! We have been rescued, and Spider is our prisoner."

The earth around Remora erupted as two more soldiers freed themselves from it.

Chapter 9

A Piece of Pas

Auk pounded on the door of the old manse on Brick Street with the butt of his needler. Behind him, Incus cleared his throat, a soft and apologetic noise that might have issued from a rabbit or a squirrel. Behind Incus, twenty-two men and women murmured to one another.

Auk pounded again.

"He's in there, trooper," Hammerstone declared. "Somebody is, anyhow. I hear him."

"I didn't," Auk remarked, "and I got good ears."

"Not good enough. Want me to bust the door, Patera?"

"By no means. Auk, my son, allow *me."*

Wearily, Auk stepped away from the door. "You think you can knock better than me, Patera, you go right ahead."

"My *knock* would be no more effectual than *your own,* my son, I feel quite confident. *Less so,* if anything. My *mind,* however, may yet be of *service."*

"Patera's the smartest bio there is," Hammerstone told the crowd, "The smartest in the whole *Whorl."* They edged forward, trying to peer around him.

Incus drew himself up to his full height, which was by no means great. *"Blessed* be this *manse,* in the *Most Sacred Name* of *Pas, Father of the Gods,* in whose name *we* come. Blessed be it in the name of *Gracious Echidna, His Consort,* in those of their *Sons* and their *Daughters* alike, this day and until *Pas's Plan* attains *fulfillment,* in the name of *Scylla,* Patroness of this Our Holy City of Viron and *my own* patroness."

Hammerstone leaned toward him, reporting in a harsh stage whisper, "They stopped moving around in there, Patera."

Incus filled his lungs again. "Patera *Jerboa!* For you we have the *highest and holiest* veneration. *I* who speak am *like you* a *holy augur.* Indeed, I am *more,* for I am *that augur* whom Scintillating Scylla *herself* has *chosen* to lead the *Chapter* of *Our Holy City.*

"Accompanying *me* are two *laymen* who *themselves* have the greatest of claims to your *revered attention,* for they are *Auk* and *Hammerstone,* the bio-chemical person and the *chemical* one, *cojoined,* selected by Lord Pas *himself* to execute his will at a *holy sacrifice* at which *I* presided, this very—"

The door opened a hand's breadth, and the pale, affrighted face of Patera Shell appeared. "You—you . . . Are you really an augur?"

"I *am,* my son. But if *you* are *Patera Jerboa,* the augur of this man-teion, you are the *wrong* Patera Jerboa, one whom we do *not* seek."

From behind Hammerstone, the foremost of Auk's followers declared, "He ain't no augur! Twig his gipon."

Incus turned back to address him, one small foot blocking the door. "Oh, but he *is,* my son. Do *I* not know *my own kind?* No mere *tunic* can deceive *me.*"

"Yeah," Auk put in, "he's an augur right enough, or I never seen one. C'mere, Patera." Catching Shell's wrist, he jerked him through the doorway. "What's your name?"

Shell only stared at him with wide eyes, his mouth opening and shutting.

"He's Patera Shell, my acolyte," announced a white-bearded man who had taken Shell's place; his antiquated voice creaked and groaned like the wheel of an overloaded cart, although he wore a brilliant blue tunic intended for a young man. "I'm Patera Jerboa, and I'm augur here." His rheumy eyes fastened upon Incus. "You're looking for me. I don't hear much any more, but I heard that. Very well." Jerboa stepped through the doorway and traced the sign of addition between Incus and himself, making it both higher and wider than was currently customary. "Do what you came to, but let Shell go."

Auk already had. "You're the cull, all right. You got a Window in your manteion, Patera?"

"It would not be a manteion without one. I've—" Jerboa coughed and spat. "I've served my Window for sixty-one years. I'd . . ." He fell silent, sucking his gums as he looked from Auk to Incus and back. "Who's in charge here?"

"I am," Auk told him, and offered his hand. "I'm what you call a theodidact, Patera. Patera Incus there ought to have told you. I been enlightened by Tartaros. Right now, I'm doing a job for his pa. So're they." He jerked his thumb at Hammerstone and Incus, then held out his hand again.

Jerboa clasped it, his own hand dry and cold, with a grip that seemed oddly weak for its size; for a moment his eyes were bright. "I was going to say that I'd like to die in front of my Sacred Window, my son, but you haven't come to kill us."

" 'Course not. Thing is, Patera, you got a piece of Pas."

Shell, who had relaxed somewhat, stared again.

"He wants it back now. He sent us to get it for him."

"My son–"

"That's the job I been talking about, Patera. That's what he asked me to do for him at the theophany."

One of Auk's followers called, "This afternoon, Patera! We were there!"

"There has been another?" Jerboa lifted his raddled old face to the vanishing thread of gold that was the long sun, and seemed at that moment nearly as tall as Auk.

"At Silk's manteion!" the same follower called.

Auk nodded. "Only this time it was Pas, Patera. You know about that, don't you? You seen him one time yourself, that's what he said."

"He did," Shell announced unexpectedly.

"Dimber here." Auk felt the last lingering doubt melt away, and grinned. "That's good, Patera. That's real good! People talk about how long it's been since any god come to a Window, or they did 'fore Kypris told us we could solve any place we wanted that night. Only they don't never say when last time was, or who it was that got the god to come. Pas said it was you and gave your name, but we didn't know where to find you."

Shell looked beseechingly at Incus. "I don't understand, Patera. The Peace of Pas? Patera's brought the Peace of Pas to thousands, I'm sure, but–"

"A chunk of him," Hammerstone explained. "Like a slice, sort of, or if I was to unscrew one of my fingers."

"We need some animals for him," Auk announced, raising his voice. "A whole herd of 'em. *Listen up, you culls!* We found him. This right here's the holy augur that's got a piece of Pas in his head, a piece that Pas wants back. Our job was to find him. I mean mine and Hammerstone's, and Patera's here."

A sibyl, herself stooped and old, appeared like a shadow at Jerboa's side. "Are they going to hurt you, Patera? I came through the manse. I broke the rule, but I don't care. If you are—if they're going to do something bad to you . . ."

"It will be all right, Maytera," the old augur assured her. "Everything's going to be all right."

Still addressing his followers, Auk told them, "We did our job, and it's your turn. You want to be part of this? Part of the biggest thing that's ever happened yet? You want to bring Pas back for people everywhere in the whorl? You get us those animals now, good ones. Get 'em any way you can, and bring 'em back to this manteion."

"You can't answer your own door," Maytera Marble scolded Silk. "You simply cannot!"

He resumed his seat, vaguely unhappy that the longed-for respite from the stacks of paper before him would be postponed. The city's various accounts at the Fisc totalled—he tapped his pencil in unconscious imitation of Swallow—not much over four hundred thousand cards. In private hands it would have been a vast fortune; but the Guard had to be paid, as did the commissioners, clerks, and other functionaries, to say nothing of the contractors who sometimes cleaned the streets and were supposed to keep them in repair.

His mouth twisting, he recalled his promise—so lightly given—to reward those who had fought bravely on either side.

All four taluses would have to be paid for as well before Swallow would deliver even one; it was in the contract he had signed less than an hour ago. Long before those taluses were finished, the Guard would need food, ammunition, and repairs to five armed floaters. (For the tenth or twelfth time that day, Silk considered using those floaters in the tunnels and rejected it.) Meanwhile, both the taluses the Guard employed currently, the remnant of those it had when the fighting began, would have to be paid as well.

Maytera Marble reentered, bowing. "It's Generalissimo Oosik, Patera. He desires to speak with you at once." Oosik's bulky form was visible in the reception hall beyond the ornate doorway, rocking back and forth with impatience.

"Of course," Silk said heartily. "Show him in, please, Maytera. I apologize for asking you to get the door."

"It was no trouble, Patera. I was glad to do it."

Behind her, Oosik was already marching into the room; he halted before Silk's work table and saluted with a flourish and a click of polished heels. "I trust that your wounds are not too troublesome, Caldé."

"Not at all, Generalissimo. Thank you, Maytera—that will be all."

"Coffee, Patera? Tea?"

Oosik shook his head.

"No, but thank you." Silk waved her away. "Pull up a chair, Generalissimo. Sit down and relax. Have you found—?"

Oosik shook his head. "I regret not, Caldé."

"Sit down. What is it, then?"

"You watched the parade, as I did." Oosik carried over an armless chair that looked too small for him.

"The Guard detachment was amazingly trim, I thought, for having just been taken from the fighting."

"Pah!" Oosik blew aside the detachment. "I thank you, Caldé. You are gracious. But the Trivigauntis? That was the thing to see, Siyuf's horde."

Silk, who had been wondering how to bring up the matters that had occupied his mind earlier in the afternoon, tried to seize the opportunity. "It was what I didn't see that seemed most significant. Sit down, please. I don't like having to look up at you like this."

Oosik sat. "You saw their infantry. I hope you were impressed, as I was."

"Of course."

"Also their cavalry. A great deal of that, Caldé. Twice what I had expected." Oosik wound one end of his white-tipped mustache around his finger and tugged.

"The cavalry was beautiful, certainly, but I was struck by their guns; I'd never seen big guns like that. Do we—do you have any, Generalissimo?"

"A few, yes. Never as many as I would like. What did you think of their floaters, Caldé?"

"There weren't any."

"What of the taluses? I should like your opinion, Caldé."

Silk shook his head. "You won't get it, Generalissimo. There weren't any of those either. That is a matter—"

"Precisely so!" Oosik released his mustache and waved his forefinger to emphasize his point. "I do not seek to embarrass you, Caldé. Every man knows much upon some subjects, little or nothing on others. It cannot be otherwise. No one can predict what will happen in war, yet a commander must try. What sort of fighting does Siyuf anticipate here? A horde shapes itself as a man dresses, at one time to hunt, at another to attend the theater. I have seen her horde now, and I will tell you."

Silk, who had been about to speak at length himself, said, "Please do, Generalissimo."

"She will fight above ground, not in tunnels. Not in the city, either, or little. Infantry, Caldé, for fighting in a city, and to defend one. The guns that so impressed you are for defense also. Mostly she will attack. Thus she brings cavalry, which can go swiftly to a place chosen by herself in her airship and strike without warning. She spoke of mules to free her guns from mud. I overheard your talk, for which I hope you will forgive me."

"Of course you did; you were standing beside General Saba."

"Exactly so. Why not taluses, Caldé? In your Guard, we use our taluses to free mired guns and even wagons, and a talus is stronger than thirty mules. Why will she not use taluses, and tell you so?"

"Because she hasn't got any. I noticed it at the time, and before the parade was over I became very conscious of it. It may be that no one in Trivigaunte knows how to make them, though I'd think unemployed taluses would go there seeking work if that were the case."

"They have kept their taluses at home to defend their city, Caldé. Their floaters, too. Those are best for forcing a city street, however. I would think them best for tunnels, also."

"I agree."

"They would have been destroyed in the tunnels, fighting the soldiers and taluses of the Ayuntamiento. You see."

Silk, who feared that he saw only too well, said, "Not as clearly as I'd like. Go on, Generalissimo."

"My wife visits a woman who professes to reveal the future to her." Oosik tugged his mustache again. "She says she does not believe this, but she does. I have upbraided her without effect. A man without a wife is spared a full half of life's unpleasantness."

"We augurs," Silk said carefully, "profess to reveal the future, too. That is to say, we profess to read the will of the gods in the entrails of their sacrifices. I admit that the intestines of a sheep seem like an unlikely tablet even for a god, but history records many striking instances of accurate predictions."

A slight smile elevated Oosik's mustache. "My change of topic did not discomfit you, Caldé."

"Not at all."

"Good. I mentioned this woman because she and many like her are false, and I do not wish you to think me a false prophet like them. If I predict, with success, the next event of the war, will that increase my credit with you?"

"It can go no higher, Generalissimo."

"Then this will demonstrate that I deserve the confidence you repose in me. Siyuf will send a force of substance into the tunnels. It will bravely engage the enemy, and there will be terrible fighting. You, I think, Caldé, will be taken to see it, if you will go. You will find a tunnel choked with bodies."

Silk nodded thoughtfully.

"Once more in the Juzgado, you will insist that the force be withdrawn, those gallant young girls. Soon it will be, and after that, Siyuf will fight in the tunnels no more."

"You are a false prophet, Generalissimo," Silk told him. "Having heard your prophesy, I won't permit that to happen."

"In which case we must fight there, and because they are narrow, a hundred or two at a time. One by one we will lose our floaters and taluses, and with them scores of troopers. It will be slow work, and while it is done our numbers will grow less each day. These thousands and thousands of troopers of General Mint's, who constitute so formidable a force. Can you afford to pay them?"

Silk shook his head.

"Then what will there be to hold them, if there is little fighting for them? A trooper fights for honor, Caldé, whether he is General Skate's trooper or hers. Or from loyalty. Or for loot sometimes. But he waits for pay. He will not wait without it, because when there is no fighting there is no honor to win, no flag to die for, no loot to gain."

"The Trivigauntis are stronger than we are already," Silk said pensively. "I think so at least, after what I saw today."

Oosik shook his head. "Not yet, Caldé, though Mint's ranks have begun to thin, perhaps. By the end of the winter—" Oosik was interrupted by chimes, and Horn's hurrying footsteps.

The three augurs had agreed that Jerboa would offer the first victim and the largest. The rest—eight had been led through the chill dusk into the old manteion on Brick Street, and more were expected momentarily—would be divided between Incus and Shell, with Incus offering the second, fourth, sixth, and eighth, and each choosing freely from those available, as long as he did not choose the largest.

Auk, who had been a silent witness to their discussion, watched with interest as Jerboa tottered to the ambion; this feeble frame, this snowy-haired, half-naked skull, contained a tiny fragment of Great Pas, Lord of the Whorl and Father of the Seven. Did it know it was about to be reclaimed?

Shag yes, Auk told himself, it was bound to. He, Auk, had explained the whole thing to old Jerboa, hadn't he? How gods could tear chunks off themselves without getting smaller, and how they could slip those into a cull. The chunk could be jefe then if it wanted to, but it didn't have to. It could, as he had been at pains to make clear, just go along. It was like a buck on a donkey. Sure, he could order it around, make it trot or stop, turn one way or the other—only he didn't have to. Maybe he'd just let go of the reins, hook a leg over the pommel, and snoodge, letting his donkey graze or look for water, or whatever it wanted to. That was what Pas had done for years and years, but how long would he keep it up?

"My very dear new friends," Jerboa began, "I know you have not, any of you—" He coughed and clearly wished to spit, but swallowed. "That you haven't come out here and brought the gods more fine offerings than we've seen since . . . I don't know."

Benevolently, he looked toward the sibyls gathered about the fire that the youngest was kindling on the altar. "Maytera Wood, you've a better memory. They just brought another calf. That makes three. No, four. Four nice calves and four lambs, and a colt. We'll have a bull before we're done, I declare . . . What was I going to ask you about, Maytera?"

"When we'd had better animals," the oldest sibyl told him. "It was when you came from the schola, Patera. Your parents and your aunt bought a bullock and a peacock, and—oh, dear. It was Maytera Salvia who told me. What else did she say?"

"A monkey," Jerboa informed her. "I recollect the monkey, Maytera." He had not liked offering the monkey, and something of that showed in his face after sixty-one years. "It doesn't matter. There were nine, one for each of the Nine."

As if they were a backward class, he fixed his eyes on Auk and Hammerstone, and those of Auk's followers who had returned. "There are nine great gods, as all you young people should know. That's Pas and Echidna, and their children. What my father and my aunt did was to buy a gift for each, for me to give them the first time I sacrificed. On that altar right over there it was. Most were small. Some kind of a singing bird for Molpe, and a mole for Tartaros, and the monkey. I recollect those."

Incus, waiting with Shell, stirred impatiently.

If Jerboa noticed, he did not betray it. "What they were doing was a very important thing. They were starting a young man off—" He coughed again. "Excuse it. The gods' will, I'm sure. I just want to say it's a more important thing that we're doing tonight. A god, not just any god but Lord Pas himself, they say, has told these new gentlemen and Patera—Patera—?"

"Incus," Hammerstone prompted from a front seat.

"What's an incus anyway? I don't think I've offered an incus in all my years. Well, never mind. One of those little things that live in trees and eat the birds' eggs, I imagine." Another cough. "Told them if they'd find me . . . Is that right?"

Incus, who had been on the point of objecting violently a moment before, exerted self-control. "*You* are indeed the augur whom Pas *himself* designated, Patera, if you are that *Jerboa* whom he intended."

Shell added encouragingly, "I'm sure you are, Patera."

"If they'd find me and sacrifice, he'd come again, he said. Have I got that right?"

Hammerstone, Incus, and even Shell nodded confirmation, as did most of those assembled; there was a stir at the back of the manteion as an immensely tall worshipper led in a tame baboon.

"What I wanted to say while our good sibyls get the fire going is that it's not a little thing. Not a little thing at all. Theophanies over on Sun Street lately, and this you've come from makes three. But I'm no stranger to them, not what you could call a stranger at all."

He turned, shuffling around behind his ambion to address Incus. "You talked to Pas, did you?"

"I *did*." Incus swelled with pride.

Jerboa faced about again. "He said he was going to come. Well, we'll see. It'll be a great thing, a tremendous thing. If it happens."

Maytera Wood presented him with the knife of sacrifice, the signal that the sacred fire was burning satisfactorily. "I'll have that black calf with the white face," he decided.

"Bird back!"

Bison halted before Silk's table and saluted at the very moment that Oreb, who had been riding on Horn's shoulder, landed upon Silk's head; no slightest twitching of Bison's thick black beard betrayed amusement, although it seemed to Silk that there had been the briefest possible flicker of hilarity in Bison's dark and darting eyes. "I'm early, Caldé," Bison confessed. "I came beforehand because I want to talk to you. If you object, I understand. Go ahead and tell me. But I have to talk to you, and I hope you'll let me when you're through."

"We could have talked at dinner." Silk was thinking about Bison's salute. Bison had not tried to imitate a Guardsman's click, snap, and flourish, which would almost certainly have rendered him ridiculous; yet the salute had conveyed respect for order and the office of caldé, plainly and even attractively.

"Not alone. Part of what I'm going to say . . ." Bison let the thought trail off.

Oosik rose. "We must speak more upon our topic, Caldé. Not now, but soon. I hope you agree."

Silk nodded, causing Oreb to hop from his head to his left shoulder.

"With your permission, I shall look in on my son. I hope he is well enough to attend. I will return at eight."

Silk glanced at the clock; it was after seven. "Of course. Tell your son, please, that all of us hold high hopes for his recovery." Oosik saluted and made an about face.

Stepping aside for Oosik, Horn put in, "Willet's back with Master Xiphias, Caldé. He asked me to tell you."

Silk was on the point of instructing Horn to call Hossaan by his true name, but thought better of it. If Hossaan had called himself Willet, Hossaan had no doubt had a reason.

"Master Xiphias's in the Blue Room. He says he doesn't have to see you before dinner unless you want to see him."

"That's good." Silk smiled. "I'm in dire need of people who don't have to see me. I wish that there were more. You'd better go home now, Horn, or you'll miss supper."

"Nettle and me are going to help. We'll get something."

"Fish heads?" Oreb inquired.

"If there are any, I'll save them for you," Horn promised.

"Very well, Horn, and thank you." Silk returned to Bison. "When I heard you were here early, I hoped that you had come to tell me you'd found Maytera Mint. I take it you haven't."

"No, Caldé, but that's what I want to talk to you about."

"Then sit down and do it. I don't have long before dinner—the other guests will be here soon—but we can finish up afterward if we must."

Bison sat; like Oosik, he seemed too large for the chair. "You've talked to Loris and Potto on a glass, Caldé."

Silk nodded.

"They won't talk to me. I know, because I tried before I came here. But they talked to you, and they might talk to you again. I want you to ask them to let you see General Mint for yourself. They say they've got her. Make them prove it."

"Why do you doubt them, Colonel?"

Bison sighed and leaned back. "I knew you'd ask that. I don't blame you, I would too. Just the same, I kept hoping you wouldn't."

"Poor man!" Oreb commiserated.

"When I ask to see her, they'll want to know why. I must have something to tell them, and the more compelling it is, the more likely it will be that they'll show her to us—assuming that they have her."

"You'll let me watch?"

"Certainly." Silk paused, his forefinger tracing circles on his cheek.

"You're emotionally involved. Oreb senses it, and so do I. I hope you won't let your attachment to Maytera Mint, one that I feel myself, goad you into acting rashly."

"I hope so, too, Caldé." Bison clenched hairy fists that looked as big as hams. "You've been down in the tunnels. You said so during that meeting."

"Bad hole!"

"Well, so have I. Maybe I should've told you then, but I didn't because it didn't seem relevant and I didn't want you to think I was showing off. There's a way down in the Orilla, and I'm pretty sure there's more, besides the one under the Juzgado that Sand and his soldiers used."

Silk nodded. It had not occurred to him that Bison might be a thief, and he adjusted his mind to the new information as Bison spoke again.

"I got a hunch after a while. I remembered a place down there, an old guardroom that they used when there were soldiers underneath the city all the time. I had a feeling they might have taken her there, and went in with thirty of my troopers to check it out myself."

"Bad hole!" Oreb repeated; and Silk nodded again. "It is a bad hole, and I'm not in the least sure that what you did was wise, Colonel. I understand why you did it, however."

"We found the place all right." The big hands clasped and seemed intent upon pulling each other's fingers off. "The door was open, and there were bloodstains all over the floor. Fresh blood, Caldé."

"Which could have been anybody's." Silk hoped that his expression did not reveal the dismay he felt. "Horn! Horn, would you come back in here for a moment, please?"

"When we got back to the surface, I tried to talk to the Ayuntamiento on a glass," Bison continued. "There used to be one in that old guardroom, I think, but it was stolen a long time ago, if there was. Anyway, I tried to talk to Potto, and when he wouldn't, to Loris. Then to Tarsier or Galago. None of them would speak to me. That was when I came here."

"Did you ask your glass to find Maytera for you?"

Bison shook his head. "It didn't occur to me. Do you think they might have her where there's a glass?"

Horn burst in. "Yes, Patera? I mean Caldé."

"It's late," Silk said, "and I'm getting tired. It seems to me that I've been inviting people to dinner all day long, and relying on Maytera to keep track of everybody. Would you ask her, please, as soon as she has time, to write me a complete list of the guests we expect?"

"I can tell you, Caldé. Or write it out for you if you'd rather. I wrote the placecards and put them around."

"Tell me then. If I need a written list afterward, I'll have you do it."

"You, Caldé, at the head of the table. On your right will be Generalissimo Siyuf. Maytera said we had to put her there because the dinner was to welcome her to the city."

Silk nodded. "Quite right."

"Then His Cognizance. She'll be between you and him."

Oreb fluttered uncomfortably; Silk said, "Go on."

"Then General Saba, she's the captain of their airship. Then Colonel Bison."

"I'm Colonel Bison," Bison explained. "I came a little early to speak to the Caldé."

"Good man!" Oreb assured Horn.

"Horn is one of the boys at our palaestra," Silk told Bison. "The leader of the boys at our palaestra, I ought to say, and he's been worth a hundred cards to us. Continue, if you please, Horn."

"Sure. Colonel Bison, then Generalissimo Siyuf's staff officer, whoever she is. And then Maytera at the foot of the table, only I don't think she's going to sit down there much and talk to people, Caldé. She's too excited and worried about something going wrong in the kitchen. That's the chair closest to the kitchen."

"Of course."

"On her right there'll be General Saba's staff officer, then Chenille, then Master Xiphias."

"I'm beginning to lose track," Silk told him. "Where will Generalissimo Oosik sit?"

"On your left, Caldé. Then his son. When he got here, he said please put his son right beside him, because he's been so sick. He's worried about him."

"Naturally," Silk said.

"Then Master Xiphias on the Generalissimo's son's left."

"If I've been following you, there should be five people on the right side of the table and five on the left." Silk counted on his fingers. "Right–Siyuf, His Cognizance, Saba, Colonel Bison here, and Siyuf's staff officer. Left–Oosik, his son, Xiphias, Chenille, and Saba's staff officer."

"That's right, Caldé, and you and Maytera make twelve."

"Bird eat?"

"Yes indeed." Silk smiled, glancing sidelong at Oreb. "I wouldn't think of dining without your company. Unfortunately you'd make thirteen at table the way things stand; you won't, however, because I'm asking Horn to ask Maytera to set one more place to my immediate left–a place for General Mint. Please letter a card for her as well, Horn, and set her place exactly like all the others. It will make the left side a trifle more crowded than the right, but the guests on that side will have to bear it."

"It's a real big table, Caldé. It won't be bad."

"I know, I've seen it. Perhaps General Mint will come. Let's hope so. She'll certainly be welcome if she does."

"Very welcome," Bison rumbled.

"So they–no, wait a moment. What about Mucor? Surely she isn't going to help you in the kitchen. Isn't she going to eat with us?"

Horn looked slightly embarrassed. "Maytera thought it'd be better for her to eat in her room, Caldé. She isn't always–you know."

"Maytera Marble's granddaughter," Silk explained to Bison. "I don't believe you've met her."

Bison shook his head.

"She must certainly eat with us. Tell Maytera I insist upon it. She had better be close to Maytera, however. Put her on the right side, between Maytera and Generalissimo Siyuf's staff officer. That gives us six on each side, and fourteen places–fifteen diners in all, including Oreb. Be sure to letter a placecard for Mucor as well as one for General Mint."

Silk heaved a sigh of relief, feeling better than he had since early that morning; his informal dinner no longer seemed a mere formality, and when the dinner was over the formalities (which he had come to detest) would be over as well. "She may be dead," he told Bison. "With all my heart, I pray she isn't, but she may be."

Bison nodded gloomily.

"Even if she is, however–even if we were to find her body, even if we knew beyond doubt that she was dead–we dare not let the Trivigauntis know it, or even suspect we think it. She has won more victories than any other commander we've got, and the better chance they think we have of winning, the more help they will provide us. Am I making myself clear?"

Bison nodded again. "We mustn't let her troopers know, either. Half would go after her on their own, if they knew the Ayuntamiento's got her."

"Or your troopers. Quite correct." Silk pushed back his chair and stood up. "Come with me; there's a glass in the next room."

The gauntleted hand of old Jerboa withdrew the knife of sacrifice, and the calf fell to its knees and rolled over on its side, its spurting blood captured in an earthenware chalice held by one of the younger sibyls. With more dexterity than Auk would have believed he possessed, Jerboa cut off the calf's head and laid it on the fire. The right rear hoof gave him some difficulty, but he persisted.

A fleeting fleck of color in the Sacred Window caught Auk's eye. He gasped, and it was gone.

The impact of the calf's final hoof sent up a fountain of scarlet sparks; Jerboa faced the Window, hands aloft. "Accept, O Great Pas—" He coughed. "Pas who art of all gods . . ."

The Window bloomed pink, violet, and gold. As Auk watched open-mouthed, the dancing hues coalesced into a face of more than human beauty—one that he saw as plainly as he had ever seen any other woman's. "You seek my lover," the goddess said.

"We do, O Great Goddess." Jerboa's reedy old voice was weaker than ever. "We seek him because we seek to do his will."

Auk blurted, "He said he'd come if we'd find Patera."

The goddess's violet eyes left Jerboa. "So much love . . . So much love here. Auk? You are Auk? Find her, Auk. Clasp her to you. Never part."

"All right," Auk said, and repeated, "All right." It was difficult to argue with a goddess. "I sure will, Kindly Kypris. Only Pas gave us this job. We had to find Patera, so we did. Now we got to find Pas, got to get the two together, like."

"The Grand Manteion. Auk." The goddess's shining eyes left him, opening their bottomless lakes to Jerboa once more. "Will you go, old man? Dear old man, so filled with love . . . ? Will you find my lover and your god? Jerboa?"

The old augur struggled to speak. Shell said, "I'll take him, Great Goddess. We'll go together." His voice was stronger than Auk had ever heard it.

Although he could not tear his gaze from hers, Incus, on his knees, scuttled backward. "I am *pledged* . . ."

"To prevent my mischief." Kypris's laughter was the peal of icy bells. "To kill fifty? A hundred children. Or more, that little Scylla may heed you. Homely little Scylla, with her father's temperament and her mother's intellect."

Incus seemed incapable of speech or motion.

"You'll require a sacrifice . . . Auk? Not children."

"Not children," Auk repeated, and felt an immense relief.

"My lover. Pas? My lover is engaged with his wife. At present." This time the precious bells were warm and merry. "Not in making more . . . Brats? You call them sprats. No. Oh, no. Wiping her out of core. Do you know what that means? Auk?" Kypris's smile found Shell. "Tell him. . . ."

"He don't have to, Kindly Kypris. I got it."

"You will need a victim. To get my lover's attention. Not a child . . . Auk? Something unusual. Think upon it."

"A victim in the grand Manteion," Auk repeated numbly.

"Several. Perhaps. Auk. I offer no . . . suggestions. But tonight. As quickly as you can." For a half second her high, ivory-smooth brow wrinkled in thought. "The piece the old man has may aid him in the fight. I hope so."

As Silk limped into the room, one of the waiters provided by Ermine's pulled out his chair for him. He halted behind it, his hands resting on the back. Bison, smiling broadly, made his way down the table to his seat near the foot.

"Welcome," Silk said. He had intended to welcome them in the name of the gods, but the words died unspoken. "Welcome in the name of the City of Viron, to all of you. I deeply regret that I was unable to welcome most of you when you arrived; but I was engaged with Colonel Bison. Maytera will have welcomed you, I feel sure, in Scylla's name."

At the other end of the table, Maytera Marble nodded.

Xiphias whispered, "Sit down lad! Want your leg worse?"

"In which case," Silk continued, "I welcome you in the name of him who enlightened me, the Outsider, the only god I trust."

"He is right, Caldé." Oosik pushed back his chair. "If you will not, my son and I must rise. We cannot remain seated while our superior stands." The pale cornet on his left was struggling to get to his feet already.

"Of course. That was thoughtless of me, Generalissimo. I beg your pardon, and your son's." Silk sat, finding his inlaid rosewood chair rather too high. "I was about to say that I do trust him, now, though it's very hard for me to trust any god."

"We are like children, Patera Caldé," Quetzal told him, and Oreb flew from Silk's shoulder to perch upon the topmost level of the crystal chandelier. "A child has to trust its parents, even when they're not to be trusted."

The pale cornet looked up with a flash of anger that seemed as much a symptom as an emotion. "What are you two implying!"

"Nothing, Mattak. Nothing at all." His father's big hand covered his.

Siyuf's laugh was clear, pleasant, and unaffected. "So we feel of Sphigx, Caldé. But are we fighting among ourselves so quick as this? At home we make a rule that there is allowed no fighting until the fourth bottle."

"That's a good rule," Bison put in, still smiling. "But the tenth might be better."

The young officer had already relaxed, slumping back in his chair; Silk smiled, too. "I don't know what the proper form is, but this is a thoroughly informal dinner anyway. Generalissimo Siyuf, have you met your fellow diners? I know you know His Cognizance and Generalissimo Oosik."

"There is one I should particularly like to meet, Caldé Silk. That very promising girl who sits with Major Hadale."

The major, a gaunt, hard-faced woman of about forty, said, "Her name is Chenille, Generalissimo. She's living here in the palace temporarily."

Siyuf cocked an eyebrow at Silk. "I am surprise that you have not seated her next to you. She could fit in very easily here between you and me."

"Good girl!" Oreb assured Siyuf from his lofty perch.

"Major Hadale is correct," Silk told Siyuf. "Her name is Chenille, and she's a close friend. So much has happened since we met that I could call her an old one. She has been helping Maytera here, haven't you, Chenille?"

She stared down at her plate. "Yes, Patera."

"Is there anyone else? What about Master Xiphias?"

"I have not this pleasure." Siyuf's eyes remained upon Chenille.

"Master Xiphias is my fencing teacher and my friend, as well as the best swordsman I have ever seen."

"Rich, too, lad! Rich! You asked me to open the window, remember? Up there in Ermine's! Everybody heard you! Think they'd stay away after that? Breaking my door down! Doubled my charges Molpsday, tripled them yesterday. It's the truth!"

"I am happy for you," Siyuf told him. "Your Caldé speaks of swordsmen. He has never seen a swordswoman, perhaps. Soon we must cross blades for him."

Silk recalled Hyacinth's feigned fencing with the azoth; to hide what he felt, he said, "We are neglecting the cornet. Neither Generalissimo Siyuf nor I have met you, Cornet. That is our loss, beyond doubt. Are you a swordsman? As a cavalry officer, you must be."

"I am Cornet Mattak, Caldé," the young officer announced politely. "My sword has been drawn against you. I'm sure you know that. Now I long to draw it again, in your service."

"You must recover your health first," his father told him.

Quetzal murmured, "I will pray for him, Generalissimo. We augurs teach others to pray for their foes. We try, at least. We seldom get a chance to pray for ours, because we have so few. I'm grateful for this opportunity."

Maytera Marble was equally grateful for the opportunity to turn the talk to religion. "It's Lord Pas who teaches us that, isn't it, Your Cognizance?"

"No, Maytera." Quetzal's hairless head swayed from side to side above his long, wrinkled neck.

Mattak said, "I want to apologize, Your Cognizance. I've been feverish . . ." His voice faded as he met Quetzal's gaze.

"My son has horrible dreams," Oosik explained to the table at large. "Even when he is awake—" He was interrupted by the arrival of the wine, a huge bottle rich with dust and cobwebs.

"We've an extensive cellar here," Silk told Siyuf, "laid down by my predecessor. Experts tell me a good deal of it may have soured, however. I know nothing about such things myself."

The sommelier poured him a half finger, releasing a light aroma suggestive of wildflowers. "Not this, Caldé."

"No, indeed." Silk swirled the pale fluid in his glass. "I really don't need to taste it. No ceremony could mean less." He tasted it nonetheless, and nodded.

"Except these introductions," Bison said unexpectedly, "if the generalissimo's intelligence is as good as I imagine. I'm Colonel Bison, Generalissimo."

"They are not," Siyuf told him, "yet I hear of you, and I receive a description I find accurate." She let the sommelier half fill her wineglass, then waved him away. "You are Mint's chief subordinate. Not long ago you are upon the same footing as many others. Now you are their superior, answerable to her alone. Is it not so?"

"I'm her second in command, yes."

"So well regarded that Caldé Silk closets himself with you before this dinner. I congratulate you."

Siyuf paused, glancing around the table. "There is but one other I do not know. That thin girl beside my Colonel Abanja. She is also of the caldé's household? Pretty Chenille, you must know her. Tell me."

"Her name's Mucor, and she's Maytera's granddaughter," Chenille explained. "We take care of her."

"This is by adoption, I take it."

Chenille hesitated, then nodded.

"Hello, Mucor. I am Generalissimo Siyuf from Trivigaunte. Are we to hope that you will soon be a fine strong trooper? Or a holy woman like your grandmother?"

Mucor did not reply. The sommelier paused, his bottle poised above her wineglass. Maytera Marble put her left hand over it, and Silk shook his head.

"I see. This is not fortunate. Caldé Silk, you know of my General Saba, and you have heard the names of Colonel Abanja and Major Hadale, also. Will you not tell me of the empty chair at your left? I did not read the little card before sitting.

"Wait!" Siyuf raised her hand. "Let me to guess. Mine is the place of honor. I am your distinguished guest. But in the second is not Generalissimo Oosik as I expect, but another. It is then for someone deserving of exceptional honor, and not one of us, for Crane who saved you from the enemy is now dead."

Surreptitiously, Silk made the sign of addition.

"Tell me if I am right as far as I have gone. If Crane is living and I am wrong, I like to know."

"No, he's dead. I wish it weren't so."

A waiter whose livery differed from the others came in with a tray of hors d'oeuvres; as he set the first small plate before Siyuf, Silk recognized him as Hossaan.

If Siyuf herself had recognized him as well, she gave no indication. "Then Crane must be dismissed. Each officer here was permitted a subordinate. That is our custom, and I think it a good one. For me, Colonel Abanja, for my General Saba is Major Hadale, and for your own generalissimo his son. But there is here also Colonel Bison. Mint herself is not present."

"You're entirely correct," Silk told Siyuf, still studying Hossaan out of the corner of his eye; he handed Maytera Mint's placecard to Siyuf. He had invited Bison himself and forgotten to tell him that he could bring a subordinate, but there seemed little point in mentioning it.

"Bird eat?" The hors d'oeuvres included clams from Lake Limna, and Oreb regarded them hungrily.

"Of course," Silk told him. "Come down and take whatever you fancy."

Oreb fluttered nervously. "Girl say."

"Me?" Chenille looked up at him. "Why Oreb, how nice! I'm flattered, I really and truly am. I always thought you liked Auk better." She gulped, and Maytera Marble directed a searching glance at her. "Only I don't blame you, because I do too. I'll get a bunch of these, and you can have anything you want, like Patera says." Oreb glided from the chandelier.

Siyuf asked Silk, "He is dead, this Auk?"

Silk shook his head.

"He is not, and so this card," Siyuf held it up, "should be for him. Is that not so? He is alive, you say. But your General Mint is as dead as my Doctor Crane."

Quetzal asked, "Are you sure, Generalissimo? I have good reasons for thinking otherwise."

"You have cut open some sheep."

"Many, I fear."

"A god speaks to us, also. Sublime Sphigx cares more for us than any other city. She alone of the gods speaks to us in our ancient tongue, speaking as we did in my mother's house, and as we speak in mine."

Silk said, "The High Speech of Trivigaunte? I've heard of it, but I don't believe I've ever heard the language itself. Could you say something for us? A prayer or a bit of poetry?"

Siyuf shook her head. "It is not for amusement at dinner parties, Caldé. Instead, I shall say what I set out to say. It is that no other city is so close to its goddess as we. Look at you. You have a goddess, you say. Scylla. Yet your women are slaves. If Scylla cared for you, she would care for them."

Mattak started to protest, but Siyuf raised her voice. "We who are near the heart of Sphigx do not butcher beasts to read her will in offal. Each day we pray to her, and do not tease her with questions but offer sincere praise. When we wish to know a thing, we go and find it out. Your Mint has been shot." She looked at Saba for confirmation, and Saba nodded.

"This is not pleasant," Siyuf continued, "and I would like that I am not the one to say it. She went to treat with the enemy, is that not so?"

From Saba's right, Bison answered, "Yes. It is."

"With a holy man to safeguard. The enemy has killed both. Captured, they say, but I have spoken to their leader, this man Loris, and he cannot produce either." Siyuf waited for someone to contradict her, but no one did.

"Your Mint was of greatest spirit. I would have liked to speak to her. Even a bout with practice swords, this old man to see fair play. All I have heard says plainly that she was of greatest spirit, and I am sure that when she, who had come to talk peace, was made prisoner she would resist. Some fool shot her and her holy man also, a filthy crime. I learned of this after our parade and already I have set our Labor Corps to dig. We will find these tunnels, make a new entrance near the big lake, and soon find one that shall lead us to this Ayuntamiento of Viron. Then Mint will be avenged."

Bison glanced at Silk; Silk nodded, and Bison said, "I must tell you, Generalissimo, that the caldé and I saw General Mint in his glass before we sat down. The caldé had a place set for her originally as a sort of signal, I'd say. He wanted to show that we hoped she was still alive."

"That she would return to us soon," Silk added.

"Now that chair," Bison gestured, "is more than a symbol. Caldé Silk got a monitor to show us what it had seen before we questioned it, and it was General Mint, with four other people and some soldiers and animals hurrying along a tunnel. She may join us before the evening's over."

Siyuf pursed her lips. "If your Mint was in the hands of soldiers, is not that the enemy?"

Saba put down her wineglass. "Vironese soldiers protected the caldé when some private guards tried to kill him, sir. I mentioned that . . ." Her voice altered and her mouth assumed a ghastly grin. "I found her, Silk. She was in the market. She bought a little animal that talks. She's taking it where they kill them."

Chapter 10

A Life for Pas

Sergeant Sand had scrambled up first. Maytera Mint, exhausted and practically suffocated by the ash that filled the air of the tunnel, thought it strange that it should be large enough to admit his bulky steel body. She had purified the altar of the old manteion on Sun Street many times, and although she told herself that she must surely be mistaken, it seemed to her that its chute had been scarcely half as large as this one.

"These victims, eh?" Remora coughed, eyeing the yearling tunnel gods Eland had taken charge of. "For, hem!, Pas. His—er—ah—ghost?"

Schist nodded. "That's what the Prolocutor says."

"You're saying that Pas is dead." Maytera Mint was by no means sure she believed such a thing possible, still less that it had taken place. "He's come back as a ghost?"

"That's it, General."

Shale added, "We're not sayin' it happened, but that's what he says." He jerked his head toward the chute into which Sand's heels had vanished. "Sarge believes him. So do I, I guess."

Urus edged nearer Maytera Mint. "They're abram, lady, all these chems. Look, we're bios, all right? You 'n me, 'n Spider 'n Eland here. Even the long butcher."

She could scarcely make out Urus's features in the ash-dimmed light; yet she could picture his wheedling expression only too vividly.

"We got to stick, us bios. Got to make a knot, don't we? The way they're talkin', we'll all be cold."

"Good riddance," Spider muttered.

Sand's voice ended the conversation, hollow-sounding as it echoed down the chute overhead. "The augur next. Hand him up."

Remora was peering up the chute. "It's a manteion, eh?"

"Big one, Patera. Pretty dark, too. Wait a minute."

Slate had crouched at Remora's feet. "I'm goin' to grab you by the legs, see, Patera? I'm goin' to lift you up 'n in. Get your arms up over your head to steer yourself. When you're in good, I'll push on your feet 'n get you up as far as I can. Maybe you'll have to wiggle up a little more before Sarge can grab hold of you." Abruptly the dark mouth of the chute became a rectangle of light.

It is big, Maytera Mint thought; it has to be. They have a lot of victims, burn a cartload of wood at every sacrifice.

Sand's voice returned. "They got oil lamps here. I lit a couple for you."

"Thank you!" Remora called. "My most, um, deepest—ah—sincere appreciation, my son." He looked down at Slate. "I am ready, eh? Lift away."

"You'll be fine, Your Eminence," Maytera Mint assured him.

"You think—ah—fear me apprehensive." Remora smiled, his teeth visible in the light from the chute. "To, um, revisit the whorl of light, Maytera, I should—umph!"

Slate had grasped his ankles and was rising. For a moment Remora swayed dangerously and it seemed he must fall; but Spider pushed his hips to right him, and in another second his arms and head were out of sight.

"Here he comes, Sarge!"

"What it is, see," Urus was nearly at Maytera Mint's ear, "is they think they ought to give Pas somethin'. He put that in their heads, your jefe did."

"His Cognizance." Coughing, she turned to face Urus. "I cannot imagine His Cognizance in these horrible tunnels, though I know he was here with the caldé."

"Me neither. Only, see—"

"Be quiet." Maytera Mint was studying Eland's beasts. "How are we going to get these animals up there, Slate?"

"I been thinkin' about that," Slate said. "Watch this."

Crouching again, he sprang into the chute and scrambled up.

"You two'd better stay here to lift the general and me up," Spider told Schist and Shale.

"Sure thing." With Slate gone, Schist leaned back against the shiprock wall. "We'll pass 'em up just like the slug guns. You'll see."

Shale indicated the opening with a contemptuous gesture. "He's buckin' for another stripe, Slate is. We used to have this corporal from 'H' Company, only he bought it in the big fight with the talus the other day. This time probably they'll promote from inside, and Slate figures he'll cop it."

Slate's voice came from the chute. "Knock off jawin' down there 'n pass them guns."

Schist said, "Sure thing," and lifted the bundled slug guns into the chute. Shale explained, "I strapped 'em together with one of the slings. Makes 'em easier to handle."

The bundle of guns vanished amid scrapings and bumpings. Schist tilted his head back and to the left to grin at Maytera Mint. "He's hangin' in there, see? Sarge's got his feet."

Spider coughed. "Maybe you'd like to go next, General."

"I would," she confessed, "but I'll go last. It is my place as the senior officer present."

"I don't think you can jump up there," Schist objected.

She turned on him. " 'I don't think you can jump up there *sir.*' Or *'General.'* I give you your choice, Private, which is more than I ought to give you."

"Yes, sir. Only I don't think you can, sir, and I'd be glad to stay down here and help you, sir."

"That won't be necessary." Maytera Mint turned to the other soldier. "Private Shale."

"Yes, sir!" Shale snapped to attention.

"You were very ingenious with that sling. After you and Private Schist have passed these beasts up and helped Spider, Urus, and this other convict—"

"Eland," Eland put in, speaking for the first time since they had reached this darkest stretch of tunnel.

"Thank you. And Eland, to climb up, you will contrive a rope of slug gun slings, making a loop at the bottom into which I can put one foot. Can you do that?"

"Sure thing, sir."

"Good. Do it. Than you can pull me up. Last."

Spider ventured, "You're goin' to be down here all alone, for a minute or two, anyhow."

"These—" She was wracked by a paroxysm of coughing. "These animals. I don't know what to call them."

"Bufes," Eland supplied.

"Thank you." Turning her head, she spat. "I will not call them gods. That must stop. More bufes may come, though I hope they won't. I pray they won't. But if they do I'll shoot them. If I don't see them in time, or don't aim well, I will die."

"I'll stay with you," Spider told her.

She shook her head. "Only one—"

From the chute, Slate called, "Gimme a god." Shale lifted a squirming beast over his head and thrust its hindquarters into the opening in the ceiling; its eyes were wild, and blood ran from the sinews binding its muzzle.

"I dunno if I could of trained 'em as big as that," Eland muttered, "only it seems like a shame to waste 'em."

"I caught 'em, sir," Shale explained to Maytera Mint. "The bios and me were back by that dead bio you left behind. We knew the smell would fetch 'em."

Schist added, "That was why Slate and Sarge jumped out of the dirt when they did, probably, sir. Sarge thought you might scare 'em off if you went back for the dead one."

"Perhaps. I can understand how a soldier could capture such an animal. What I cannot understand is how you, Eland, were able to capture others without the help of one."

"Mine was littler when I got 'em." He watched the second beast vanish up the chute. "We killed the big 'uns, we had to. I got behind the little 'uns and got a noose over their mouth."

"It must have been dangerous just the same."

He shrugged, the motion of his skeletal shoulders barely visible. "I want to go up next. Be with 'em. That all right?"

From the chute, Slate called, "Pass up them other bios."

"Certainly," Maytera Mint told Eland. She gestured toward the chute, and Schist lifted him.

"You can't get 'em to like you," Eland said as his head vanished into the chute, "only maybe mine did, a little."

From nearer the top, Slate told him, "Grab on."

"If the bufes don't bring Pas, lady, 'n they won't, I know they won't–"

Maytera Mint shook her head. "You cannot know."

"Then it's us. Me 'n Eland. Him, too," Urus pointed to Spider, "if you let 'em. That sergeant–"

"My son." Maytera Mint stepped so close to Urus that the muzzle of the needler she held gouged his ribs. "I have been most remiss with you. I have let you call me 'lady' or whatever you wished. I must remember to bring it up at my next shriving, if there is a next shriving. In future, you are to address me as Maytera. It means *mother*. Will you do that?"

"Yeah. Dimber here, Maytera."

"That is well." She smiled up at him; she was a full head shorter than he. "As your mother, your spiritual mother, I must explain something to you. Please pay strict attention."

Urus nodded mutely. From the chute, Slate called, "Gimme another one."

"Go, Spider," Maytera Mint said, and turned back to Urus. "I haven't had much time in which to form my estimate of your character, yet I think it accurate. It is not an estimate very favorable to you."

When he did not speak, she added, "Not favorable at all. I will not compare you to such a man as Sergeant Sand. Though not pious, he is resolute, energetic, loyal, and reasonably honest. To compare him to you would be grossly unjust to him. Nor will I venture to compare you to His Eminence. His Eminence has less physical courage, I think, than many other men. Yet he has more than a casual observer might suppose, as I have seen, and his assiduity and piety have justly earned him a high position in the Chapter. He is intelligent as well, and he labors almost too diligently to put the mental acuity that he received from the gods at their service."

"Have you got the safety on that thing, lady?"

"Call me *Maytera*. I insist on it."

"All right, all right!" His voice shaking, Urus repeated, "Have you got the safety on?" and added, "Maytera?"

"No, my son, I do not." She took a deep breath. "Stop talking and listen. Your life hangs upon it, and we haven't long. I am a general and a sibyl. As a sibyl I try to find good in everyone, and though it may sound less than modest, I generally succeed. I find a great deal in His Eminence, as I would expect. I find more than I expected in Sergeant Sand.

There is good in Private Slate, too, and in Private Shale and Private Schist here. Not good of a very high order, perhaps, but abundant in its kind. I have tried to find good in Spider and found more than I dared hope for. The glimmers of good in Eland are hardly discernible, yet unmistakable." She sighed. "I talk too much when I'm tired. I hope you've followed me."

Urus nodded. There was a faint play of light across one cheekbone; it was half a second before she understood that he was sweating, cold perspiration soaking the gray ash black and running down his face like rivulets of fresh paint.

"As a general, it is my duty to defeat the enemy. I must do it by killing men and women. I find that repugnant, but such is the case. You are the enemy, Urus. Do you follow me still?"

From the chute, Slate called, "Ready for the next one."

"That will be you," Maytera Mint told Shale. "Remember what I told you about those slings."

He saluted with a clash of steel. "I'll get right on it, sir."

She returned her attention to Urus. "You are the enemy, I say. Should I, who have been called the Sword of Echidna, let you live when I have you at my mercy?"

"You're fightin' the Ayuntamiento, right? General, I swear by every shaggy god there is that I never done nothin'—"

"Be quiet!" Angrily, she poked him with the muzzle of the big needler that had been Spider's. "What you say is true, I'm sure. You never served the Ayuntamiento. But ultimately the enemy is evil. Evil is the ultimate enemy of us all."

She fell silent, listening to the faint rattle as Shale was helped up the chute, to the sighing of the ever-present breeze, and to Urus's feverish breathing. "The ash is not so thick in the air as it was," she said.

Schist nodded. "Not so many stirrin' it up, sir."

"I suppose so, and those ugly beasts were struggling." She jabbed Urus as hard as she could, and he yelped.

"This one, too. I'm tired, Urus. I'm awfully tired. I've slept on floors, and walked for leagues and leagues. I forget, sometimes, what I've said, and what I intended to say. You were thinking of snatching my needler a moment ago."

Schist chuckled, a hard dry metallic rattle.

"No doubt you could. No doubt you can. Taking a needler from a tired woman much smaller than yourself, a woman so close that her needler is within easy reach, should be simple for you. For anybody." She waited.

"If you're not going to, you'd better raise your hands. Otherwise some small motion may cause me to pull the trigger."

Slowly, Urus's hands went up.

"As you say, you haven't served the Ayuntamiento. I've talked with Councillor Potto, Urus. Did you know that?"

He shook his head.

"I have. Also with Spider, who served the Ayuntamiento and would serve it still if he could. With a number of Guardsmen, Generalissimo Oosik particularly, who served it for many years. I've questioned prisoners, too. In not one of them did I fail to discover some gleam of good. Councillor Potto is the worst, I think. But even Councillor Potto is not entirely evil."

From the chute, Slate called, "How about the general and that other bio?"

Maytera Mint backed away, then motioned toward the area under the chute. "I give you fair warning. I must see some good in you, Urus, and soon."

His smile was at once pitiable and horrible. "You're goin' to let me get out, lady? Let me go up there?"

"Call me Maytera!"

"M-maytera. Maytera, I figured, see, I'd made it out. Only it w-w-was just the pit, the shaggy pit, 'n then we run back down 'n got into it with the old man—"

Schist lifted him by his ankles. "He ain't got no sores on his legs like that other one, sir. Maybe you saw 'em."

Looking down at the needler, Maytera Mint felt herself nod.

"I had to sorta wash off my hands with ashes." Somewhat violently, Schist shoved Urus's head and shoulders into the chute. "After I lifted him, sir. I got pus on 'em, sir."

"No doubt he'd been nipped from time to time by the beasts he had earlier," Maytera Mint said absently. "Those would be the ones our caldé says Patera Incus killed, perhaps." Eland and Urus might have encountered Auk, in that case; she made a mental note to ask them about it, adding as an afterthought that she must not kill Urus before she had a chance to question him.

"You're goin' to stay, sir?"

"Until Private Shale lets down his slings. Yes, I am. Go ahead, Schist. Anytime they're ready for you."

The safety had been off, as she had said. Did that make her better, because she had told the truth? Or worse, because she had practically nerved herself to killing Urus? Dropping the needler into one of the big side pockets of her torn and soiled habit, she watched Schist's feet disappear into the chute, then sat down in the ash to await Shale's slings, or the beasts that he called gods, and Eland bufes.

Bison put down the untasted leg of a pheasant. "Two cards to every one of them, Caldé?"

Silk nodded, his eyes upon Mucor. "Yes. I hadn't meant to tell you tonight, Colonel. To be more exact, I hadn't planned to make my decision until morning."

Saba began, "I submit—"

"But if Mucor can locate the manteion to which the woman I've had her looking for is bringing her offering, I'll be busy tomorrow. Besides, it's better that I announce it now, so that Generalissimo Oosik and Generalissimo Siyuf can hear it. We'll send the volunteers home tomorrow, each with a letter of credit worth two cards at the Fisc."

"Caldé . . ." Oosik reached across Maytera Mint's vacant place to touch Silk's arm. "It will take longer than one day merely to collect their weapons."

Silk shook his head. "We won't collect them. They're to keep whatever they have—those are their weapons now."

Saba looked at Siyuf, and when Siyuf did not speak, said, "That's unheard-of. It's folly. Insanity." Chenille caught Silk's eye and nodded. "She's right, Patera. It's abram."

He spoke to Maytera Marble, at the far end of the table. "You told me something earlier that weighed heavily with me, Maytera; there's no one whose judgement I value more, as you know. Would you repeat it for us?"

"I can't, Patera. I don't remember what it was."

Xiphias put in, "Couldn't you just let them keep their swords, lad?"

"I could scarcely take those, could I? Those are their own property already. Chenille, you agree that I shouldn't do this. Why not?"

Saba snapped, "Because they're men, ninety percent of them, and unstable, like all men." Chenille added, "They'll kill each other, Patera."

"Of course they will—they always have." Silk addressed Siyuf. "My manteion is in what we call the Sun Street Quarter. I should explain that our city counts many more quarters than four; a quarter in our sense really means no more than the area served by a manteion."

If she inclined her head, the motion was too slight to be seen. "Fifty thousand, Caldé Silk? All with slug guns?"

"There are more than fifty thousand certainly, but not all of them have slug guns. Fifty thousand slug guns, perhaps, or a little over."

When she put no further question, he said, "It's a violent quarter; most augurs would say it's the worst in the city. It borders on the Orilla, which is what we call an empty quarter—one without a manteion. A few people from the Orilla come to our manteion, however, just as a few from our quarter go into the Orilla to buy stolen goods. What I was going to say is that there's seldom a week without a killing or two, and there are often three or four. When one man decides to kill another, he does it. If he has a slug gun or a needler, he may use it; but if he doesn't, he uses a dagger or a sword. Or a hatchet, an axe, or a stick of firewood."

Recalling Auk, Silk added, "A big, strong man may simply knock down a weaker one and kick him to death. A group of men could clearly do the same thing; and I know of one instance in which a man who had raped a child was killed by a dozen women, who beat him to death with their washing sticks and stabbed him with kitchen knives and scissors."

Hadale told him, "One woman can kill a man, Caldé. It's common at home, and there's a woman at this table who's killed several."

"It isn't uncommon here, either, Major; and that bears on the thing Maytera told me that impressed me so much. A woman from our quarter came to see her this afternoon, and Maytera asked if she wasn't afraid to walk so far through the city when just about everyone has a slug gun or a needler. The woman said she wasn't, because she had one, too."

Silk paused, inviting comment, and Saba growled, "They'll overthrow you, Caldé, in half a year or less."

"You may well be right." He spread his hands. "But not by force, since they won't have to—I haven't the least desire to retain this office if our people don't want me. That's the chief difference between the Ayuntamiento and our side, really. But I think you've hit on something important. The reason the Ayuntamiento didn't let our people have slug guns or launchers like the one Chenille told me about this afternoon was that they are effective means of fighting soldiers and troopers in armor. The Ayuntamiento believed that if our people didn't have those weapons it could rule as long as it retained the loyalty of the Army and the Guard."

"Very sensible," Saba declared.

"Perhaps, but it didn't work very well. A few days ago, our people overwhelmed hundreds of Guardsmen and took their weapons. I see I have not convinced you."

Saba shook her head.

"Then let me say this. Generalissimo Oosik says that he would need more than a day to collect the weapons of General Mint's volunteers."

Bison added, "If they'd surrender them."

"Exactly. The best troopers would give their weapons up when they were ordered to, but the worst would hide theirs—the precise opposite of the situation we'd prefer. Furthermore, it would take at least as long to reissue those weapons, and we may need the volunteers again any day."

Quetzal, who had been nodding over his untouched plate, murmured, "One hundred thousand cards is a large sum, Patera Caldé. Can you afford that much?"

Silk shook his head.

Xiphias exclaimed, "Then don't, lad! Don't do it!"

"We can't afford to do it, Master Xiphias." Silk smiled wryly. "But we cannot afford not to, either. In the first place, I promised to reward those who fought bravely on either side, and I've done nothing thus far. There may be a thousand things we cannot afford. No doubt there are. But the thing we cannot afford above all—the thing we dare not risk—is to have people come to believe that my promises are worthless. So tomorrow, as I say, every trooper that General Mint and Colonel Bison have is to receive two cards, and permission to return to his or her home and occupation. Those who were given slug guns or other weapons are to be told that the weapons are theirs now. No one will be able to complain that those who fought on our side went unrewarded, at least."

Siyuf smiled. "Like you, Caldé Silk, I think we may need the horde of Mint again, and soon. When you call for them they will come, having been rewarded handsomely for the first time."

"Thank you. Most of our financial troubles result from various businesses—"

Hossaan had entered as he spoke, carrying a huge roast upon a magnificent golden platter. "The people from Ermine's can see to that, Willet," Silk told him. "Please get your floater ready—I'll want it soon."

Oreb flew up the table, circling warily before perching on Silk's shoulder. "Bird too!"

"Of course, if you wish."

"Let me hear the rest, Caldé Silk. I am most interested."

"I was about to say that if the overdue taxes were paid, our city government would be rolling in wealth, Generalissimo. General Mint's troopers will spend the cards they receive very quickly for the most part, and that should produce a wave of prosperity. If we make forceful efforts to collect the overdue taxes then, we may be able to meet our other obligations."

Siyuf looked down the table to Saba. "You have tell me he is mad. He is not mad. He is only more clever than you. It is not the same."

Might not the dead rise and walk again? There were tales of such things, and they flitted through Maytera Mint's mind as she was drawn up the chute.

I was sacrificed, she thought. I should have realized it when Councillor Potto had Spider bend me over his knee. A drop struck me, too. How wonderful it would be if all the rest could come back up through these the way I am!

The top of the chute was a glaring rectangle above her, light so bright that it seemed to her it must surely be noon, with the whole of Pas's long sun pouring golden radiance through the windows of the manteion into which she rose. Fascinated, she watched Slate's metal hands in silhouette as they slowly and steadily hauled her up, each grip succeeded by the next.

Then a hand of flesh, Remora's long blue-veined hand, was reaching for her; she caught it and let him help her climb from the looped slings to a mosaic floor. "There you are, Maytera. I, um, we have been waiting for you. The sergeant is most, er, desirous to proceed, eh?" Remora's face was clean, his soiled overrobe was gone, and his costly robe had been replaced by one more costly still.

She looked for the windows she had pictured, expecting to find them glowing with sunshine; but there were no windows, only scores of rock-crystal holy lamps surmounted by long, bright flames, and a fire blazing upon the altar.

"I—ah—kindled the, um," Remora ventured, following the direction of her eyes. "It seemed provident."

"Certainly. You've cleaned up, too. May I ask where, Your Eminence?" Catching sight of Urus edging toward the back of the manteion, she shouted, "Sergeant! Stop that prisoner!"

"An, er, dressing chamber? Cubiculum. Off the sacristy, eh? For sibyls. Cabinets—ah—wardrobes in there. So I, um, given to understand."

"I'll want water and soap," she told him. "Warm water, if that's possible. You've washed, clearly."

Spider interjected, "The sergeant wants to sacrifice right away. He—" From his position between Urus and the door, Sand himself rasped, "The Prolocutor told us Pas would come, sir. I reported that. It's the Plan, and standing orders say it's got higher priority than anything else." Slate nodded agreement.

"Indeed it does. But Pas may *not* come as well. We must be prepared for that eventuality, too. I say that, though I hate putting myself on the same side as Urus, who feels certain Pas won't. But if he comes, as we hope, we must be fit to receive him. Not only I, but all of you as well." She followed Remora onto the sanctuary elevation and past the fire-crowned altar.

"The, um, locality, hey?" Remora was almost grinning.

"What about it, Your Eminence? If you're asking whether I know where we are," she glanced around her, "I haven't the least idea. I didn't know that a manteion like this existed."

They entered the sacristy, thrice the size of Silk's on Sun Street; a shelf held a long row of jeweled chalices, and on a block of fragrant sandalwood a dozen sacrificial knives whose gold or ivory handles flashed with gems.

"I have officiated here, er, innumerable," Remora informed her. "Five hundred, eh? A thousand? I should not contest even so lofty a figure as that. It is the, um, oratorium abolitus, the private chapel beneath the Palace. For His Cognizance's use, hey? And augurs who have—ah—administrative duties, eh? We, er, offer our—ah—seldom-seen? Obscure services to the gods."

He was about to go; she caught the voluminous sleeve of his robe.

"The room where I can wash? Where there may be a clean habit I can borrow?"

"Oh, yes, yes, yes! Right—ah—door." He opened it for her. "Should be a bolt, eh? Inside. No doubt, no doubt. Water likewise. Tank, eh?" He pointed at the ceiling. "Under the—ah—in the west cupola."

The room was twice as large as her longed-for bedroom in the cenoby. Gratefully, she shut its door and shot the bolt. Two large wardrobes and a wash basin; a pierced copper hamper, presumably for laundry; a full length mirror on one wall and a glass on another. A table in a corner.

Opening one of the wardrobes, she found half a dozen clean habits of various sizes; she draped the biggest over the glass, then emptied her pockets onto the table, took off her own habit, and dropped it into the hamper. It was probably beyond saving, and the Chapter owed her a round hundred new ones at least.

Grimly stepping out of her soiled underdrawers and removing her chemise and bandeau, she resolved to collect those habits and distribute them to sibyls as poor as she.

It was Mainframe itself to take off her shoes and stockings, although she had to sit on the floor to do it, which made it seem likely there were no clean stockings. She rinsed the ones she had taken off, wrung them as dry as she could, and hung them over the open door of the wardrobe.

The tap to her left gushed water that was at first tepid, then pleasantly steaming. There was a boiler somewhere in the Palace, presumably; Maytera Mockorange, whose family had been wealthy, had spoken of such luxury, although Maytera Mint had never dreamed it might be available to sibyls.

She had to wash her hands three times (with scented soap!) before the suds that streamed from them were no longer black with filth. Even so, small crescents remained under her nails. The point of one of the little projectiles called needles attended to those.

Her small, tired face seemed to her equally dirty, if not worse; gingerly dabbing at the bruises and burns, she washed it again and again, washing her short brown hair too, then sponged her entire body, heedless of the pools that formed on the red-tiled floor.

Remora's querulous voice penetrated the heavy wooden door. "The . . . Sergeant Sand. Sergeant Sand wishes—"

She felt her sly little smile, although she struggled to repress it. "Tell him that I myself wish for sandwiches, Your Eminence, and ask what he knows about court-martials."

"*You . . . chaff.*"

"Not at all. Tell him that and ask him." Her image in the mirror appalled her. If Bison were ever to see her like this!

Not that he or any other man ever would, presumably; but men did not like skinny legs, narrow hips, or small breasts, all of which she possessed to a degree that seemed appalling. Yet she had been pretty twenty years ago; many people had told her so, many of them men.

A pretty girl whose long curls had bordered upon chestnut. Some of those men might have been lying, and no doubt some had been. But all of them? It seemed improbable.

The other wardrobe was divided into pigeonholes; most were empty, but one held two clean chemises and two pairs of clean underdrawers. The underdrawers were several sizes too large, but wearable with the string pulled tight. She could rinse her bandeau as she had her stockings—

In a flurry of rebellion, she flung it into the hamper. A bandeau to cover up what? To hold in what? She had worn one because her mother, and subsequently Maytera Rose, had said she must; she looked no different now in this yellowed chemise than she had in her own in the cenoby.

Snatching the habit from the glass, she clapped her hands. "Monitor? Monitor?" She had used glasses during the past few days, but was not completely comfortable with them.

"Yes, madame." The floating gray face was at once detached and deferential.

"Look at me. I'm lacking an essential item of feminine apparel. What is it?"

"Several, madame. A gown, madame. Hose, and shoes."

"Besides those." She turned sideways and stood on tiptoe. "What is it?"

"I am at a loss, madame. I might offer a conjecture."

"You needn't bother." She took the smallest habit from the first wardrobe. "Do you know who I am?" For an instant she was wrapped in darkness before it settled into place. Still no coif, she thought. Still no coif.

"I recognize you now, madame. You are General Mint. I was ignorant of your identity, previously. Would you prefer that I address you as General?"

"As you like. Has anyone been trying to contact me?"

For perhaps a second, the monitor's face dissolved into darting lines. "Several, madame. Currently, Captain Serval. Do you wish to speak with him?"

She sensed that the name should have been familiar, yet it meant nothing to her. She nodded. Better to find out who he was and what he wanted, and be done.

The monitor's face revised itself, gaining color, a round chin, and a debonair mustache. "My General!" A brisk salute, which she returned almost automatically.

"My General, I have been ordered by Generalissimo Oosik to make you aware of the situation here."

She nodded. Where was "here"?

"It is a detachment of the Companion Cavalry, My General. They have posted sentries who are standing guard with mine as we speak. I have requested that their officer explain this to Generalissimo Oosik, but she refuses."

"I see." Maytera Mint took a deep breath and found herself wishing for a chair. "Let me say first, Captain, that it's good to see you again."

"For me it is a great pleasure, My General. An honor."

"Thank you, Captain. I'm sorry to find that you're still a captain, by the way. I'll talk to the generalissimo about that. You mentioned Companion Cavalry. That is the name of the unit?"

"Yes, My General."

The memory of Potto's boiling teakettle returned. "You'll have to forgive me, Captain. I've been out of touch for the past few days." It had seemed like weeks. "I was told that a Trivigaunti horde was marching toward the city. Am I to take it that this Companion Cavalry is theirs?"

"Yes, My General. An elite regiment."

Regiment was a new term to her, but she persevered. "What was it you wanted this officer from Trivigaunte to explain to the generalissimo?"

"I wish her to explain why she and her women are mounting a guard on our Juzgado, My General, when it is already guarded by my men and myself." (That was "here" then, almost certainly.) "I wish her to explain who has issued these orders and to what purpose."

"I take it she won't tell you either."

"No, My General. She will say only that her instructions are to protect our Juzgado until relieved. No more than that."

"Generalissimo Oosik asked you to make me aware of this situation. Where is he?"

"At the Caldé's Palace, My General. He is dining with the caldé. He
informs me that the caldé has seen you, My General, in his glass, and
that he has ordered a place set for you at his table. Generalissimo Oosik
instructed me to request that you join them there if I reached you,
should this be convenient."

"I need sleep more than food." It had slipped out.

"You drive yourself too hard, My General. I have observed this
previously."

"Perhaps. Can you tell me what orders you received from Generalissimo Oosik regarding these Trivigauntis?"

"He is of the opinion that they have learned of a threat to the Juzgado, My General. I am to cooperate. There is to be no friction between
those of my command and theirs." The captain paused, a pause preg-
nant with meaning. "Or as little as may be. I am to explore the situation
and report once more, should I discover facts of significance."

"And notify me."

"Yes, My General. As I do."

"Also Colonel Bison, I hope. If Generalissimo Oosik did not tell you
to notify Colonel Bison, I am ordering you to now. Tell him I consider
Generalissimo Oosik's position prudent."

Someone was tapping at the door.

"Colonel Bison is also at the caldé's dinner, My General. Generalissimo Oosik stated that he would inform him."

"Good. That will be all, then, Captain. Thank you for keeping me
abreast of things." She returned his salute.

"Monitor, was Colonel Bison one of the people who have been trying to reach me?"

The captain's face grayed and sharpened. "Yes, madame."

"I want to speak to him now. He's at the Caldé's Palace." Vaguely,
she recalled seeing it the year before on her way to sacrifice at the Grand
Manteion, a huge house upon whose façade files of shuttered windows
had risen like stacks of long and narrow coffins; she had shuddered and
turned away. "I'll be out in a moment, Your Eminence!"

EXODUS FROM THE LONG SUN

The monitor said, "I am aware of it, madame. I will ask someone to bring him to the glass there, madame."

She would see him—and he would see her: the tired eyes and blood-less mouth that the mirror had shown her, the wet hair plastered to her skull, the face black-and-blue with bruises, surmounted by a scab. "Monitor?"

"Yes, madame."

"Let me speak to whoever comes to the glass." This was the hardest thing she had ever done, harder even than shutting her eyes during Kypris's theophany. "I needn't speak to the colonel in person."

"Yes, madame."

A minute, then two, passed. The gray features melted and flowed, becoming those of a lean man with hooded eyes. "Yes, General Mint," he said. "I'm Willet, the caldé's driver. How may I serve you?"

General Saba spoke, looking less like an angry sow than a dead one. "She's coming up here with it, Silk. Coming up the hill you're on."

"This is warlockery," Siyuf declared.

"I disagree, but I haven't time to discuss it now." Silk stood so abruptly that Oreb fluttered to maintain his balance. "Leaving you is the height of bad manners; I know it, and all of you are entitled to be furi-ous with me. I'm leaving just the same. Maytera Marble will remain as my representative. I beg your forgiveness sincerely and fervently, but I must go." He was already halfway down the table,

Xiphias sprang to his feet as Silk strode past his chair. "Alone," Silk said. Undeterred, Xiphias hurried after him, and the door slammed behind them.

Saba's head jerked. She looked around self-consciously.

"We must speak of this," Siyuf hissed. "You must describe to me. Not now."

Major Hadale drained her wine. "I'll remember this dinner as long as I live. What entertainment!"

Maytera Marble whispered to Chenille. "I should have gone, too. He's hurt, and—"

Smoothly, Siyuf overrode her. "General Saba has say to me he suf-fer a broken ankle, Maytera. Maytera? It is how you are addressed?"

She nodded. "Yes, he did. He does. A week ago Phaesday, I think it was. He fell. But—but . . ."

"He limp. So I observed. He was in greatest haste, he took big steps. No so big of the right leg, however. The old swordswoman—sword-man. He, also, but the left."

"The caldé was shot." Maytera Marble indicated her own chest with her working hand. "That's much worse."

"Not a slug gun, which would have kill there. A needler?" Siyuf glanced around the table, seeking information.

Oosik shrugged and spread his hands. "Yes, Generalissimo. A needler in the hand of one of my own officers. We strive to prevent these terrible mistakes. They occur in spite of all we do, as you must know."

"This is a remarkable young man. We do not breed like him in Trivigaunte, I think. Do you know the—what is this word? The ideas of Colonel Abanja?"

Oosik nodded to Siyuf's staff officer. "I would like to hear them, particularly if they concern our caldé. What are they, Colonel?"

"I am something of an amateur historian, Generalissimo. An amateur military historian, if you will allow it."

"Every good officer should be."

"Thank you. I'm accused of shaping my theory to flatter Generalissimo Siyuf, but that is not the case. I have studied success. Not victory alone, because victory can be a matter of chance, and is frequently a matter of numbers and materièl. I search out instances in which a small force has frustrated one that should have defeated it in days or hours."

Saba had regained her self-possession. "I still say that it is brilliance that's decisive. Military genius."

Maytera Marble sniffed decisively, and Siyuf said, "Colonel Abanja does not think this. Brilliance, it is well enough when the execution of the so-brilliant orders is brilliant also. I do not speak of genius for I know nothing. Except it is rare and not to be relied on."

Bison said, "I have a theory of my own, based on what I've seen of General Mint. I'll be interested to see how it compares to the Colonel's."

"I mention Abanja's," Siyuf continued, "because I think Caldé Silk so fine an example of him. She believe it is not this genius, not any quality of the mind. That it is energy, by clearest thoughts directed. Tell us, Abanja."

"Successful commanders," Colonel Abanja began, "are those who are still acting, and acting sensibly, on the fourth day. They endure. We have a game that we play on horseback. I don't think you play it here, but I've won a good deal of money by betting on the games during the past year."

The ends of Oosik's mustache tilted upward. "Then you must tell us by all means, Colonel."

"It imitates war, as most games do. A cavalry skirmish in this case. The players may change mounts after each goal, but the players themselves can't be changed, or even replaced if one is hurt." Both Oosik and his son nodded.

"There is a twenty-minute rest for them, however, and so we speak of the first half of the game and the second, divided by this rest. What determines the result, I have found, is not which team scores the most goals in the first half, because there's seldom much disparity. The winning team will be the one that plays best and most aggressively in the second. When I see the team I've backed doing that, I double my bet, if I can."

Siyuf nodded. Her head moved scarcely one finger's width, but the nod announced that the time for controversy had ended. "Let us move from the fields where *killi* is played to this city of Viron, where is a so illustrative struggle. Who is winner? It is not too soon to say. One side hide in holes. Above prowl and roars the host of Viron and my horde of the Rani. For the second time I ask you that listen." She paused dramatically. "Who is winner here?"

No one spoke.

"A man? This man Caldé Silk? Can that be? Observe the leg broken, the wound to the chest of which Maytera our hostess speak. Yet he hunt by magic for a woman he require, and when by magic she is found, he leave food and friends and seek her out. Most women, even, would not do this."

Chenille said, "He's going to need a lot more help than one old man. I wish I'd made him take me along."

Across Xiphias's abandoned plate, Mattak said, "Two old men. His Cognizance has gone, too." Surprised, Siyuf stared at the empty chair next to her own.

Under his breath, Mattak added, "I'm glad."

. . .

Sergeant Sand spoke for them all. "He didn't come."

Kneeling by the headless, pawless body of Eland's second beast, Remora looked up. "I shall—ah—proceed. I have, um, led astray myself. Enthusiasm. Contagious, eh? But I, um, coadjutor, have not, eh? Seen a god. Possibly the victim will enlighten us."

As the holy knife laid open the beast from breastbone to pelvis, Spider said, "Sure, read it for us, it can't hurt."

It hurt the poor brute, Maytera Mint thought; but its death was swift, at least, and now the pain is over.

Sand had brought his slug gun to his shoulder before she saw Urus, halfway up the convoluted iron stair at the back of the manteion and taking its steps three at a time. She shouted, "Don't fire!" and Sand did not. A moment later the door at the top of the stair slammed shut. "He thought we were going to offer him," she explained to Eland. "Do you? We won't. I will not permit it."

Remora, who had been kneeling by the second victim, rose and strode to the ambion. "Extraordinary, eh? Extraordinary, my, er, sons. And daughter. Nothing, er, initially, and now this." Sand resumed his seat, his head bowed.

"An—ah—preface. Necessary, I think. The offering of persons was practiced in the past in—ah—here. Many of you aware of it. Have to be. Forbidden within, um, by the present holder of the baculus."

O you gods, Maytera Mint thought, he's going to say the entrails order us to sacrifice Eland. What am I to do?

"In practice, children, hey? Almost always. No sense sending a messenger who cannot see the, er, the recipient, eh? The offering of, um, persons, children, by no means usual even then, eh? In dire need. Only then."

Slate shifted his position until he stood behind Eland.

"Before my time. As an augur, eh? I would have—ah——delared . . ." Remora paused, his bony hands gripping the edges of the ambion, his eyes on the headless carcass.

"Never, eh? Couldn't do it. Not a child. Not even, um, Urus. Now—ah—two sides to the entrails. You follow me? One for the congregation and the city. Other the presenter and the augur. For the—ah—Our Holy City, war, death, and destruction. Bad. Calamitous! For the, um, myself, I shall. Offer a person, er, human being. Man. So Pas warns us. Me."

Maytera Mint said firmly, "Eland, can you see the gods?"

He looked at her in mild surprise. "I dunno, General. I never saw any."

There was no time for delicacy. "Have you had a woman? You must have!"

"Sure. Lots of times 'fore I got throwed in the pit."

She turned to Remora. "He is not suitable. I can see that, Your Eminence, and you must—"

Sand stood up. "I am." He jabbed his steel chest with a steel thumb; the noise it made was like the clank of a heavy chain.

"You can't mean it!"

"Yes, sir, I do." With oiled precision, Sand mounted the steps to the sanctuary. "He came. Great Pas came to the Grand Manteion."

Maytera Mint nodded reluctantly.

"He talked to the Prolocutor, and he told him to talk to us. To me. He said for us to get you out, 'cause it's part of the Plan. The Plan's the most important thing there is, sir."

"Certainly."

"You say that," he advanced on her, formidable as a talus, five hundredweight metal. " 'Cause they taught you to in some palaestra. I say it 'cause I know it in my pump. He said get you and sacrifice, and he'd come and tell us what to do next. Pas said that."

Meekly, she nodded again.

"So we caught the bios, and then I thought maybe it's not enough so I made them catch the two gods."

"Bufes, Sergeant."

"Whatever. Only the bufes aren't any good, and now you and him say the bios are no good either, sir." Sand wheeled to face Remora and pushed his slug gun into Remora's hands. "I knew, Patera. 'Fore you read it, I knew. You ever want to die?"

"I? Ah—no."

He's lying, Maytera Mint thought. I know what it is, and so does he.

"I do." Sand gestured toward Schist, Slate, and Shale. "So do they. Maybe they won't say it, but they do. I want to die for Pas, and I'm going to right now." He knelt, staring at the floor, and Remora looked helplessly down at the slug gun.

Maytera Mint murmured, "If you would prefer not to, Your Eminence, it would certainly be permissible for someone more familiar with the weapon to act for you."

"You, er, concur, General?"

She sighed. "Sometimes generals need sergeants to recall them to their duty. So it seems. Whether I learned it in a palaestra or not, Sergeant Sand is right. The Plan is the most important thing in the whorl, and the victim consents."

Still on his knees, Sand muttered, "Thanks, sir."

She knelt beside him. "I've heard it's possible for chems to—to reproduce. You've never done that?"

Slate said, "None of us have, General, and there's hardly any fem chems left." And Sand, "No. Never."

She turned back to Remora and held out her hands for the slug gun. "I've never fired one either, Your Eminence, but I know how they work and I've seen it done thousands of times since this began."

"No, Mayt—No, General."

"Please, Your Eminence. For your own sake."

He silenced her by raising Sand's slug gun and pointing it awkwardly at Sand. "Precisely. Ah—to the point. For my sake, General. If I must, um, officiate, the—ah—holy and um, self-sacrificing. Sole responsibility. Do you follow me? Criminal penalties, hey? Religious, likewise. Removed from the—ah—active clergy."

His wheezing breath seemed to fill the manteion. "But for him—ah—highest god. For Pas!" He jerked at the trigger.

"Not like that, Your Eminence. There's a safety, and if you hold it that way the recoil will cripple you. Or so I'm assured." She positioned the slug gun in his hands. "Grasp it firmly, tight against your shoulder. Then it will merely push you backwards. If you hold it loosely and try to keep it away, it will fly back and strike you like a club."

Sand said, "In the head, Patera. That's the best."

"I am augur here," Remora told him, and fired.

The crash of the shot was deafening in the enclosed space of the manteion. Sand rose; for an instant Maytera Mint could not see where the slug had hit him. Spinning to face the Sacred Window, he threw up both arms. There was an uncanny sound that might have been a cry of pain or harsh laughter. Black liquid spurted from his throat, spattering the clean black habit she had just put on.

And the Holy Hues began before Sand fell.

She blinked and stared, then blinked again. Not one face but two crowded the Window, one gaping and gasping, the other radiant with power and majesty, just—and more than just—pitiless and nurturing. "My faithful people," intoned Twice-headed Pas, "receive the blessing of your god."

"I see him!" From the voice she thought it must be Spider, although she could not be sure.

Pas's was thunder and a destroying wind. "Carry this most noble of my soldiers to the Grand Manteion. I shall speak—"

Both his faces faded. Tawny yellows and iridescent blacks filled the Window on Mainframe. Serpents writhed across it as scorpions scuttled over their backs; behind them all, Spider and Maytera Mint, Eland and Remora, Slate, Shale, and Schist saw the agonized face of Echidna.

Pas returned as if Echidna had never been. "There our prophet Auk will restore him to us."

Chapter 11

LOVERS

As the floater rose, Hossaan said, "I've a dozen things to tell you, Caldé. I know there won't be time for all of them. It's only four streets."

"I know where it is," Silk snapped. "Hurry!" Xiphias laid a hand on his arm. "Easy, lad!"

Hossaan glanced at the small mirror above his head, and his eyes met Silk's. "So I'm going to tell the most important one first. You think there won't be anybody at the Grand Manteion when Hy gets there, and you're afraid she'll leave."

"Yes!"

"That's not right. I told you I had to talk to General Mint on your glass, and that was what made me late." Heeling like a close-hauled boat, the floater swerved around a gilded litter with eight bearers.

"I said we'd discuss it later."

"Right. Only because of what she said, I thought it might be smart to have a look at the Grand Manteion. There's three augurs in there and a couple thousand people."

"Did you see Hyacinth?"

Hossaan shook his head. "But I could've missed her pretty easily, Caldé. She's not as tall as the redhead, and there was a bunch of women with animals."

Orb muttered, "No cut."

"She's probably still outside, Caldé. If she was climbing the Palatine when Mucor said she was, she can't have gotten to the Grand Manteion yet."

Xiphias asked, "Why's everybody there, lad?"

"There's been another theophany—there must have been. Do you know about Pas appearing to His Cognizance?"

"No, lad! Never heard about it!"

"I have," Hossaan said. "There's a rumor, anyhow. Do you think that's brought them?"

Silk shook his head. "It was Molpsday, and would be stale news now." Half to himself he added, "What does it mean, when a dead god rises?"

No one answered him. The floater sped on.

A surging crowd filled Gold Street. "Stop!" Silk ordered Hossaan. "No! Higher if you can. I saw her. Turn around."

"Near us, Caldé?" They rose, blowers racing.

"Cut!" Oreb exclaimed. "Cut cat!"

"Two or three streets down the slope. Turn!"

The floater darted forward instead. "Your bird's right," Hossaan told Silk. "It would take too long to get through that mob, but we can duck down here—" He swerved onto a steep and narrow street bordered by high walls. "And cut across to Gold so we come up behind her. We'll be moving with them, and that will make it a lot faster."

Silk drew breath and exhaled. The aching weakness in his chest was fading, but it seemed to him that he had not filled his lungs properly for days. "You told Horn that your name was Willet, Willet. Also you found clothing—somewhere in the Caldé's Palace, I suppose—similar to the waiters', so that you could help them serve."

"I like to be useful, Caldé."

"I know you do, and it may be useful for you to tell me why you did those things before we locate Hyacinth—if we do. You say you have a dozen items to relate. That should be the next."

Still steering their floater expertly, Hossaan glanced over his shoulder at Xiphias.

"If Master Xiphias and Maytera Marble can't be trusted, no one can. If I explain your actions—I believe I can, you see—will you tell me whether I'm correct?"

They spun around a corner as though it were an eddy. "I'm afraid not. General Mint says Siyuf's surrounded the Juzgado. That's why I thought I ought to check on the Grand Manteion."

"Where was she, and how did she learn of it?"

"I don't know, Caldé. She didn't say, and I didn't ask. She said one of Oosik's officers told her. Oosik had told him to try and get in touch with her."

Xiphias said, "He left when Willet here was handing out those appetizers, lad! Another waiter fetched him, remember?"

"Later than that—after I had asked Mucor to find out to which manteion Hyacinth was bringing her offering."

Their floater tacked on Gold, pushing through chattering pedestrians.

"You know what she looks like," Silk muttered. "She had on a black coat, and was carrying a large rabbit, I believe."

"Cat talk," Oreb informed him. "Talk bad."

"The bird's right, lad! The skinny girl said it talks!" Before Xiphias had finished speaking, their floater was slowing and stopping; the canopy slid into its back and sides.

For the space of a breath, Silk thought there had been a mistake. The hurrying young woman with something orange-furred tucked under her arm seemed too tall and too slender until she turned with their cowling nudging her leg, and he saw her face.

"Hyacinth!" He stood up by reflex, and for a moment he was half outside the floater (and she more than half in it) as they kissed.

When that kiss ended, they lay face-to-face on the soft leather seat, she crowded against its back and he practically falling off, with Xiphias standing over them and waving his saber to force passersby to keep their distance. They sat up, but their hands would not part. "I was afraid you were dead," Silk confessed.

And Hyacinth, "I shaggy near was, and I—but I . . ." Her eyes swam with tears. "Can't we put up the top?"

"I don't know how."

"I do." She freed her hand, and with a flurry of skirt and ruffled underskirt, and a flash of legs and spike-heeled scarlet shoes, was in Hossaan's seat. Xiphias ducked, and the canopy flowed up and darkened until it was nearly opaque.

She wiped her eyes. "Now I'm coming back. Catch me." She rolled over the back of the front seat so that Silk had to, and lying in his arms kissed him again. With no need of speech, her kiss said, *Beat me, shame and starve me. Do as you want with me, but don't leave me.* I'll never do those things, he thought, and tried to make his own kiss tell her so.

When they parted, he gasped, "Where do we start?"

She smiled. "That WAS the start. I love you. Let's start from there. I haven't felt this way since—since you jumped out my window."

He laughed, and she turned to Xiphias. "This time I know you from a rat. You teach sword fighting, and I want lessons. Do you always go around with him?"

"Much as I can, lass!"

Silk asked her, "Where have you been? I've had people searching everywhere."

"In a horrible old building in the Orilla, with a soldier as big as this floater watching me for Auk. You must know Auk, he says he knows you. Tartaros turned me loose." Hyacinth grinned like a twelve-year-old. "You believe in the gods, but you won't believe that. I don't, and I know it happened. Do you mind if I don't call you darling?"

Silk shook his head. "Not in the least."

"I've called too many men that. I'll find something else, something good enough, but it may take a while." She turned back to Xiphias. "There's jump seats that fold down out of the back of that one. You'd be more comfortable."

"Feel better outside, lass! Know how to get this plaguey door open?"

She laid her hand on his. "You stay in here or we'll get all naked and sweaty, and we ought to do that someplace nicer. Where's the driver?"

"Hunting!" Xiphias jerked down a seat, sat, and contrived to sheath his saber. "Hunting your cat with Silk's bird!"

"That's right, I dropped Tick, and he cost five cards."

Silk said, "When you got free—and I'll be grateful to Tartaros for-ever—you should have come to me."

Hyacinth shook her head.

"I understand. You didn't know where I was, either."

"No, you don't. I did. I knew exactly where you were. At the Juz-gado or the Caldé's Palace. Everybody I asked wanted to talk about you, and everybody said one place or the other. But I looked, well, like every other slut in the Orilla, only worse, and I stank. I couldn't wash, or only a little. I tried, but when the water's dirtier than your face it doesn't help much. I wanted perfume and powder, and a comb to hold my hair, except I had to wash it first and dry it. I tried to go back to Blood's. Do you know about Blood?"

"About your trying to go back there? No."

"And clean clothes, clean underwear and a bunch of other things. You know what I'd look like without all this stuff?"

"Yes," Silk declared. "Like Kypris herself."

"Thanks. Like a boy, only with tits down to my waist. You saw me naked."

Silk felt his face flush. "They weren't. Not nearly."

"That's the trouble with big ones," Hyacinth explained to Xiphias. "The bigger they are the lower they go, unless you've got something to hold them up. Will that make it hard for me to sword-fight?"

"Will if they bounce, lass! But there's ways! Think I don't know 'em, long as I've been at it?"

"I put myself in your hands, Master Xiphias." She gave him a sly, sidelong smile, then brushed Silk's cheek with a kiss. "I was going to see about lessons that time I came to meet you, I mean before I found out it was so bad here, before we left Blood's. When we got out of bed I said wouldn't I be a good sword-fighter, and you said you'd back a dell with shorter legs that wasn't so fond of her looks, or something like that. So I thought I'd learn and surprise you."

He nodded, speechless.

"I'm a good dancer, I really am, and I never had lessons, so I think with lessons I could learn. Only it's a long way to Blood's and Auk took my money, and I looked like a slut, so I turned around and went to Orchid's. She loaned me gelt and let me wash and, you know, fix up. But she says Blood's for ice. This was only about, oh, before I went to the market. Did you know? That Blood was dead? Since Phaesday, she says."

"Yes. I killed him." Hyacinth's eyes widened, and Silk felt pride, coupled with a deep shame in it. "I killed him with a sword Master Xiphias had loaned me, and destroyed the sword in the process. I'd rather not discuss the details. I understand why you wanted to return, or at least I believe—"

"All my things are out there! My clothes, my jewelry, everything I've got!"

"Also, you thought your driver would have gone back there, I'm certain. I also understand why you went to Orchid's; you anticipated help from her, and you received it. I went there myself for the same reason a few days ago, and I was helped as well–I found Chenille there. Which brings me to a point I ought to have raised sooner. What was the soldier's name? The one who watched you for Auk?"

"Hammerstone." Two tiny lines had appeared on Hyacinth's forehead. "It was Corporal Hammerstone, and he had stripes on his arm like a hoppy corporal, but painted on. All of a sudden you're worried, I can see it. What is it?"

"It would take an hour to explain it all." Silk shrugged. "I'll try to be brief. I love you very, very much."

"I love you, too!"

"Because I do, I have something to lose, someone–you–I must protect. Most men live their entire lives like this, I suppose, but I'm not accustomed to it."

"I'm sorry. I'll try to help. I really will."

"I know you will. You'll put yourself at risk, and that worries me more than anything else."

There was a tap on the canopy.

"You see, I've forgotten some of my obligations already. I promised Chenille I'd help her find Auk, and Auk took you from me. Do you know where he is, or where this Corporal is? Patera Incus is anxious to locate him, I know."

Xiphias interjected, "Don't you think that's that Willet outside knocking, lad?"

"Let him in, please."

"I don't know how to work this soggy door!"

"Then that will give us a little more time. You'll solve it soon, I'm sure."

Hyacinth giggled. "You've been around people like me too much. That's what Auk says about houses. And I know where he is, too, or anyway I know where he was, at a reedy old manteion on Sun Street. Was that yours? That's what somebody said when we were going over there."

"It was." Silk found that he was smiling. "It's old and run down, just as you say; but I used to love it, or thought I did. In a way I suppose I still do."

Scarcely visible on the other side of the darkened canopy, Hossaan tapped again. This time his taps were followed by a series of sharper ones.

"That's where Kypris came to your Window? Orchid told me. It was at Orpine's funeral, she said. I knew Orpine, and I wish I'd been there. I've got a shrine for Kypris . . ." Hyacinth paused, teeth nibbling her full lower lip. "Or I did. Is the house really wrecked? That's what Orchid said."

Silk recalled Blood's villa as he had seen it during his rescue. "It's badly damaged, certainly."

"If it was just damaged we've got to go there!"

He gestured toward the canopy. "Even with Willet outside knocking? Willet used to be one of Blood's drivers. You must know him—he drove you to the city so that you could meet me at Ermine's."

"That's wonderful! He can take us."

Xiphias exclaimed. "Think I've got it! Want me to let him in, lad?"

Silk nodded, and the door opened. Hossaan reached through it to unlatch the one in front, and Oreb shot past him to land upon Silk's shoulder, a-flutter with excitement and indignation. "Bad cat! Cut cat!"

Hossaan slid into the driver's seat as the orange-and-white animal he held spat, "Add word!"

"He led us quite a chase, Hy," Hossaan said, "but we got him in the alley trying to wriggle through a hole."

"You're bleeding!"

"He put up a fight. If somebody else will hold him, I'll get out the aid kit."

"Add, add word!" the little orange-and-white catachrest reiterated. "Pack! Itty laddie, peas dun lit am kilt may!"

"She won't, for an hour or two at least," Silk told him. "Willet, I want you to take us out to Blood's and help us collect Hyacinth's belongings." For a moment, Silk paused to gaze upon Hyacinth. "Then to the Prolocutor's Palace." As the floater slid forward, he added, "We may well need weapons, but we'd have to go back to the Caldé's Palace, and we can't afford that. I'd never get away."

Xiphias accepted the small catachrest from Hossaan. "I've my sword, lad!"

Silk nodded absently as the song of the blowers strengthened to a muted roar. "Let's hope it will suffice."

·   ·   ·

"We might have these drinks I wish in the bar, perhaps," Siyuf told Chenille, "but in my lodging would be more nice, do you not think also?"

"I had three with dinner." By intent, Chenille spoke too loudly. "If I'm going to start falling down and taking off my clothes, I'd a whole lot rather do it in private." She looked around Ermine's sellaria with interest. "Only we've got to get a room, don't you?"

"My staff has arrange this for me while I watch our parade with your friend the caldé." Siyuf stopped a liveried waiter. "My lodging will be up the big stairs, I think? Number seventy-nine?"

He shook his head. "We don't have a room seventy-nine at Ermine's, General."

"Generalissimo. Wait, I will show you." While Chenille smiled and strove to appear innocent, Siyuf fished a key from her pocket.

"Ah!" The waiter nodded. "Number seven nine. That's a double room, we call it the Lyrichord Room, Generalissimo. On your right at the top of the Grand Straircase. You can't miss it."

"A room you say. More, I understood."

The waiter lowered his voice confidentially. "Our suites are four, five, or six rooms, depending. We call them rooms for convenience. Your room, the Lyrichord Room on account of the instrument in the music room, is a double suite with eleven rooms and three baths, besides balconies and so forth. Three bedrooms, sellaria, cenatiuncula for formal dining, breakfast cosy, drawing room—"

She waved him to silence. "You have here a wine waiter, one good and knowing?"

"The sommelier, Generalissimo. He's at the Caldé's Palace just now, I believe."

"I come from there. He too, I think. Send him to me when he arrive."

Siyuf turned away, motioning to Chenille. "Men are so stupid, do you think also? It is what renders them less than attractive, even the most fine. One thing, better I had say, one thing from many. Men are duty. So we are taught in my home. Girls are pleasure."

Chenille nodded meekly, blinking to show that she was assimilating this information. "In Trivigaunte, you mean? That's where your home is? I still can't get used to liking somebody from someplace so far away."

"This is natural. I have a house there bigger than this Ermine of your Viron's, the house which was my mother's. Also outside our city, a farmhouse made large for rest and educating my horses. For the hunt two houses also, one in a cave where is more cool. Do you perhaps hunt? I will show it to you. You will be very delighted I think, but there are places where you could not stand so straight, perhaps."

"I'd like to learn. Only I thought all of you were east of here. The caldé, I call him Patera, said something about tents out there. Anyway, it's really nice you've got this suite too, only I never would have guessed."

Arms linked, they started up the broad staircase. "I have my tent outside your city, and my headquarters, which I bring closer soon. Also this is convenient, as we see. I have good hunting there, so perhaps I will not have to take you home to teach. Already we kill three wing people and catch one also."

"Four Fliers?" In her astonishment Chenille forgot to sound admiring. "I didn't think anybody could."

Siyuf laughed. "Nine years in Trivigaunte another kill a wing person, but she does not catch the round thing on the back that push forward. I forget this word."

"I have no idea."

"By this we put wings on my pterotroopers. This time it is me that kill and I have catch the things that push also, but he does not yet tell me how it go."

Siyuf moistened her lips, and for the first time Chenille felt frightened. "Not yet he will not tell. But soon. He is like all men stupid, and not fine even but small and thin. We take his clothes and do other things until he is our friend. This is not confusing to you, I hope?"

"I think I get it."

"We take the clothes, and look, he is nothing. I have five husbands, all are more fine. Perhaps you would like him? When we have finish, I will give him to you."

"Oh, no! I don't want him, Siyuf."

"Good."

"I really don't like men at all, except Patera and one other one."

They had reached the top of Ermine's sweeping and richly carpeted Grand Staircase. Siyuf glanced to her right and down at her key. "My husbands I like sometimes, but so one like a hound. For me, tall girls and strong over all else. I enjoy, you see, at first a certain resistance."

Maytera Marble paused to stare at the strange procession crossing Manteion Street; although it was some distance away, Maytera Rose's legacy had improved her eyes out of reckoning. In the streetlights' glow, she saw a large and rough-looking man, accompanied by a smaller man so thin that he seemed a mere assemblage of sticks. After them, three soldiers, large and handsome like all soldiers, two of whom appeared to be carrying a fourth. Behind the soldiers, a tall augur and—and . . .

"Sib! Oh, sib! General, General Mint! It's me, sib!" In her joy Maytera Marble actually sprang into the air. The diminutive sibyl walking beside the tall augur looked around, and her mouth dropped open.

Maytera's eyes were not the only things Maytera Rose's legacy had improved; Maytera Marble dashed up Manteion Street as though winged, and Oreb himself could not have covered the distance more rapidly. Her good hand clutching her coif, she shot between the rough men, collided with the leading soldier with a clang and a fluster of elided apologies, and threw her arms about Maytera Mint.

"It's you, it's really you! We've been so worried! You don't know! You can't, and when Patera said you were all right I thought that's just when it happens, when everyone's saying the danger's over, that's when they get killed, and, and—oh, Hierax! Oh, Scylla! Oh, Thelxiepeia! I simply couldn't stand it. You were the light of my existence, sib. I know I never told you but you were, you were! If I'd had to live by myself in the cenoby with just Maytera Rose and that chem I couldn't have stood it. We'd have gone mad!"

Maytera Mint was laughing and hugging her and trying to lift her off the ground, which was so ridiculous that Maytera Marble exclaimed, "Stop, sib, before you hurt yourself!" But it really did not matter at all. Maytera Mint was right there, laughing, and was the same dear Maytera Mint but better because she was the Maytera Mint who had come back from Tartaros knew where and there was no mother and daughter, no grandmother and granddaughter half so close as they, and no child or grandchild half so dear.

"I'm happy to be back, Maytera," Maytera Mint declared when she could stop laughing. "I hadn't really known how happy till now."

"Where have you been? Dear, dear sib, dear girl! Patera said they'd got you, they had you in some horrible place under the city, and then they didn't, you were with soldiers, but the generalissimo, not the fat one, the other one, said you were dead and—oh, sib! I missed you so much! I wanted you to meet Chenille. I still do, because Chenille's been a second granddaughter to me, but nobody, nobody in the whole whorl can ever mean as much to me as you!"

The tall augur said, "The—ah—all Viron. Feels as you do, eh, Maytera? Just look at them."

Already heads were turning and people pointing.

"You—ah—speak to them, General? Or, um, I myself—"

Maytera Mint waved both hands and blew the onlookers half a dozen kisses; then the silver trumpet sounded, the trumpet that Maytera Marble had heard in Sun Street on that never to be forgotten Hieraxday when the Queen of the Whorl had manifested during her final sacrifice, ringing from every wall and cobble like a call to battle: "I am General Mint! His Eminence and I have been down in the tunnels where the Ayuntamiento's hiding, and Pas himself has given us instructions. We're going to the Grand Manteion! All of you are going there, too, aren't you?" She pointed with a wide gesture that was like the unsheathing of a sword.

There were cheers, and several voices shouted, *"Yes!"*

"Lord Pas's prophet, Auk, will be there. We know, because Lord Pas told us. Please! Do any of you know him?"

A giant, taller even than Remora, waved. He held a ram under his left arm, and a tame baboon trotted after him as he pushed through the crowd; Maytera Marble thought that she had never seen so big a bio, a bio nearly as big as a soldier.

"I do." His voice was like the thudding of a bass drum. "I know you, too, General. Know you a dog's right, anyhow, but me an' Auk's a old knot." Legs like two pillars devoured the distance between them with swinging strides.

For a second time, Maytera Mint's small face went blank with surprise. "Gib! You're Gib! We charged the floaters on Cage Street together!"

"Pure quill, General." The giant dropped to one knee, eliciting an enraged bleat from the ram. "I'm Gib from the Cock, an' I was tryin' to stick by you, but that sham horse couldn't keep up. Too much weight's what Kingcup says. Then he took a slug an' down we went." He held up his free arm to show a cast, then touched the ridge above his eyes with the fingertips protruding from it. "So I can't salute like I'd like to, but Bongo here can. Salute the General lady, Bongo. Salute!"

The baboon rose on his hind legs, his forepaw seeming to shade his startlingly human eyes.

Maytera Mint demanded, "But you know Auk, Gib? I mean Pas's prophet named Auk?"

Maytera Marble sensed her uncertainty. "She knows a man called Auk who went to our palaestra; but I don't believe she's sure he's the one Pas—Pas told you about this Auk, sib?"

"Yes!" Maytera Mint nodded so hard her short brown hair danced. "Just now, a few minutes ago, down in a chapel under the Palace. He came to the Window there, Maytera, and all of us could see him, even Spider and Eland. It was wonderful!"

The soldier carrying the feet of the fourth soldier said, "He talked about our sergeant. We gave him to Pas."

The third soldier objected, "He gave himself, that's how it was. Now Pas wants him fixed. Not 'cause he don't want him but 'cause we need him. Pas don't want to scrap him."

The augur tossed back a lock of lank black hair. "It—ah—*gave*. Sense of the word, hey? I myself—"

Maytera Mint was not to be distracted. "Do you know Auk the Prophet, Gib? Yes or no!"

"Sure do, General."

"Describe him!"

"He's part owner in my place, he's maybe forgot but he is. Pretty big cully." Gib waved his cast toward the larger of the rough-looking men. " 'Bout like him, only not so old. Got more hair than he needs an' ears that stick out of it anyhow."

"A strong, forthright jaw!" She was fairly dancing with anxiety and impatience.

"That's him, General. You could hang your washing on it." Gib chuckled, the laughter of a happy ogre hiding in his barrel chest. "I was wantin' to say he looks like Bongo here. Auk's my ol' knot an' wouldn't mind. Maybe you would of, though, an' maybe the god that's tapped him. Tartaros is what he says."

"This, er, hiatus, General . . ."

Maytera Mint nodded vigorously. "He's right, Gib. Stand up. You needn't address me as if I were a child, just because I'm not tall."

She trotted forward, drawing the giant behind her like a magnet. "Let's see . . . You don't know anybody here except me. Neither does poor Maytera, whom I ought to have introduced. Or have you been introduced to His Eminence, Maytera?

"Your Eminence, this is my senior and my dearest friend, Maytera Marble. Maytera, this is His Eminence the Coadjutor, Patera Remora."

Maytera Marble, hurrying after them, paused long enough to bow in approved fashion.

"An honor, eh? For me, Maytera. For me. Very much so. Um—privilege. We begin our acquaintance under the most—ah—propitious circumstances. You, um, concur?"

"Decidedly, Your Eminence!"

Maytera Mint never broke stride. "This is Gib, as you heard, a friend of Auk's and a comrade-in-arms of mine. The soldier with his slug gun pointed at our prisoners— Slate, you really don't need to do that. They're not going to run."

She glanced back at Maytera Marble. "Where was I? Oh, yes. That's Acting Corporal Slate. I've put him in charge of his fellow soldiers till Great Pas, as he promised, restores Sergeant Sand to us by Auk's agency."

Catching up to her, Maytera Marble ventured, "That must be poor Sergeant Sand they're carrying?"

"That's right, and Schist and Shale are carrying him. Our prisoners—they're friends now, friends of mine at least, and His Eminence's too, I'd say—are Spider and Eland." She had reached the milling crowd before the Grand Manteion and stood on tiptoe in the hope of catching a glimpse of Auk.

.   .   .

Xiphias had found a candle and lit it; Silk drew Hossaan away from its light and out into the darkness of the corridor. "Master Xiphias can help her look—hold the light, at least, which is all she needs. You and I have things to talk about."

"Good man!" Oreb assured Silk.

"I employed you—knowing you are an agent of the Rani's—because you Trivigauntis are our allies. You realize that, I'm sure."

"Certainly, Caldé."

"You owe nothing to Viron, and nothing to me. But if you want to remain, you'll have to be more forthcoming than you've been thus far."

"Only because the old man was listening, Caldé. I know you trust him, and you probably can. But I'm not you. I try not to trust anybody more than I've got to."

"I understand. Do they trust you? I mean the officials to whom you report."

There was a momentary silence; it was too dark for Silk to see Hossaan's face, but he sensed that it would have done little good. Then Hossaan said, "No more than they have to, Caldé. I don't mind, though. I'm used to it."

"I'm not. No doubt I must become used to it, too; but I'm finding that difficult. You're deceiving them. That was the reason you had Horn—and others, no doubt—call you Willet, the name you had used here. That was also why you helped serve dinner. You wanted to show someone at my table that you had penetrated my household—someone who would recognize you at once. Isn't that correct?"

Hossaan's only answer was an eerie silence. On Silk's shoulder, Oreb croaked and fluttered uneasily.

"That person will assume, of course, that I am not aware you're a Trivigaunti—"

"Let's not dodge words, Caldé. I'm a spy. I know it and you've known it since you spotted me on the boat."

"You will be applauded and rewarded."

Hossaan started to speak, but Silk cut him off. "I'm not finished. While you took us out here, I was thinking about your deception and your position as my driver. Please don't tell me that your lie is essentially the truth because I'm the only one who knows and you intend to inform your superiors that I do. It would only be a further lie."

"All right, I won't."

"Then I say this. You may tell your superiors everything you learn. I've assumed that you would from the start, and since I haven't the least intention of betraying the Rani, it can do Viron no harm. But you must afford me the same courtesy Doctor Crane did—you must tell me everything I want to know about what you're doing and reporting. In return, I'll keep your secret."

A second crept by, then two. "All right, Caldé. But I've always been willing to tell you whatever you needed to know."

"Thank you. Earlier I asked whether Generalissimo Siyuf or General Saba knew you by sight. You said neither did, and I believed you." For a moment, it seemed to Silk that something stealthy moved through the darkness. He paused to listen, but heard only the sudden flapping of wings as Oreb launched himself from his shoulder.

"I ask again—was it the truth? Does either know you?"

"It is, Caldé. I've never spoken with them, and I doubt that they know what I look like, either one of them."

"There was someone at my dinner who does. Who was it?"

"Colonel Abanja. Didn't you ask what she does on Siyuf's staff? She's intelligence officer."

"Do you report to her?"

"I will now, probably. You still don't see—"

Soft candlelight had appeared in Hyacinth's doorway. Oreb announced, "Cat come!" from Xiphias's shoulder.

Silk asked, "How are you faring, Master Xiphias?"

The old man shook his head. "Not a thing, lad! Want a bit of silver chain? Ring worth half a card?"

"No, thank you."

"Me neither! But we found 'em! Think she'd keep 'em? Threw 'em on the floor! Fact!"

Oreb confided, "Girl cry."

"You shouldn't have left her in the dark," Silk muttered.

"Chased me out, lad! Candle and all!"

Feeling the pressure of Hossaan's hand on his back, Silk said, "You're right, of course, Willet. I must go in to her. I don't know that I can help, but I must try."

Alone, he walked down the dark corridor and turned into the darker doorway of what had been Hyacinth's suite. Here there had been a dressing table inlaid with gold and ivory, wardrobes crammed with expensive gowns and coats, and a summonable glass. Only darkness remained, and the melancholy sweetness of spilled perfume. One door had led to Hyacinth's balneum, Silk reminded himself, another to her bedchamber. In vain, he tried to recall which was to the left and which to the right, although with her sobs to guide him he did not really need to know. By touch, he located the correct door and found that it was open.

After that, there was nothing for it but to walk in, with the ghost of the Patera Silk that he had been.

"Halt!" The voice was male, accompanied by the rattle of sling swivels and the click of the safety; Siyuf's intelligence officer raised her hands while trying to make out the sentry in the cloud-dimmed skylight. "I am Colonel Abanja, in the Rani's service."

Whispering. There were two or more sentries, clearly. "Advance and give the password."

Abanja moved forward slowly, hands still in the air. If these nervous men were from the Caldé's Guard, they were (or at least ought to be) disciplined troopers. If they were General Mint's volunteers, they might fire without warning.

"Halt in the name of the Rani!"

Abanja stopped again and identified herself a second time. Somewhere behind her, a voice hissed, "They're shaggy shook up, lady. I wouldn't stand between 'em."

"Thank you," she murmured. "That's good advice, I'm sure."

A lanky trooper of the Companion Cavalry stepped from a shadow; Abanja was happy to see that the muzzle of her slug gun was lowered. "You must give to me our password also, Colonel."

"Boraz." Now she would see whether this trooper's lack of familiarity with the Common Tongue, with its implication of aristocracy, was real or feigned.

"You can pass, sir."

Feigned.

"Halt!" It was the calde's men again. Abanja said, "I've already halted for you once."

"Do you have our password?"

Inwardly, she sighed. "I didn't know one was required. I have to speak with the officer in charge of our detachment."

"You can't go in the Juzgado without our password."

"Then you must give it to me."

Another whispered conference. "It's against regulations, Colonel."

Her eyes were adapting to the darkness; both male sentries were visible to her now, skylight gleaming on their waxed armor. "If it's against regulations to give it to me, you can't expect me to know it." She spoke to the cavalry trooper. "Go get her. You have my permission to leave your post."

Too softly for the men to overhear, the voice behind Abanja hissed, "There's a nice place, Trotter's. A street down 'n turn west. We can have a drink. Tell these hoppies to send her when she comes."

Abanja shook her head.

"Lady, you need me worse'n I need you."

Without looking around Abanja murmured, "Do I? I hadn't realized it."

"I could of got you in without a hitch. Shag, I still will. Tell 'em *Charter*. This's for free."

"Sentry!" Abanja called. "I remember your password now. Your caldé told me at dinner."

Both advanced with leveled slug guns. "Give it."

She smiled. "Unless someone's changed it without notifying your caldé, it's Charter."

"Pass, friend."

"Thank you again," Abanja murmured.

The hiss was scarcely audible. "Back room. Name's Urus."

"All g-gone." Slowly, Hyacinth's sobs had subsided into sniffles. "All the times. All that smiling. Cream and lotion. Beggar's root and rust, do this and do that. N-nothing left." The sobs returned. "Oh, K-k-kypris! Have pity!"

Silk muttered, "I think perhaps she already has."

"Bake here shop!" It was the catachrest. "Cuss-cuss."

He did, kissing Hyacinth's ear and the nape of her neck, and when she raised her face to his, her lips.

"Niece! Mow cuss!" The little catachrest attempted a smacking that emerged between the intended kiss and a squall.

The third cuss was not yet over. When it was, Hyacinth said, "Wipe your face. I got snot all over you."

"Tears." Silk took out his handkerchief.

"B-both. I was crying so hard my nose ran. Don't think I can't cry pretty when I w-want to."

"Itty laddie, done! Shop!"

"I've got certain things I think about, and here it comes. Know what I had when I left h-home?"

He shook his head, then said, "What was it?" realizing that she could not have seen the motion.

"Two gowns M-Mother made and her umbrella. She didn't have a-anything else to give me, so she gave me that. A big green umbrella. I kept it for years, and I don't know what happened to it. H-Here's what I've got now. The clothes I've got on and a gown Orchid promised to get cleaned, Tick here, and one card. But I owe her seven. That's w-way too much for what I got, but what could I say?"

Silk stood. "That you'll repay her later. You can say that again, too."

"Y-y-you know . . ." A stifled sob. "You're learning, you really are. Listen, I'm not through crying about all this yet. I'll cry m-m-more—cry some m-more . . ."

"Shop!"

"Tonight. Before I go to sleep. I just about always cry then, and when I'm asleep, too, s-sometimes. Well, by Thelx!"

"What is it?" Silk inquired.

"Go stand in the doorway. Shut it behind you. Don't ask, do it quick."

He did, and heard voices in the dark: "Tick? Tick, are you still in here?" "Puck Tuck ape no!" "All right, quit pulling my skirt." "Nod heavey." "Did I say why I got him? You can open the door again. I was going to give him to Kypris and ask her to give me you."

Once more, Silk was speechless.

"The market was closed, but some animal culls are always in there, and I gave the watchman a card to let me in and got Tick. The cull said talking animals are the best."

"So I've been told—by the same seller, I'm sure."

"I had a string around his neck, and I held it while I was looking for my things. Sometimes I held it in my teeth. When I got to crying I put my foot on it, but he got it off. Untied it or got it up where he could bite it, I guess."

"Nod rum."

"No, you didn't run, and I know you knew what I was going to do, 'cause you kept on begging me not to." To Silk, Hyacinth added, "Then everybody was going to that big manteion uphill, so I did, too."

"I understand."

"But when he got loose he didn't beat hoof. Why not, Tick?"

"Say wharf laddie."

"I guess." Abandoning Tick, she addressed Silk. "What I'm trying to say is I know you're really religious. I'm not, but you could teach me."

He could not escape the thought that it would be better if she taught him. "I'm far from being the best possible teacher, but I'll try if you wish it."

"You said we'd go to the Prolocutor's when we were done here. If it was for me, we don't have to."

He smiled. "You're not going to offer Tick?"

"I will if you want me to."

Tick protested, "New!"

"I see no point in it." Something large and soft pressed Silk's leg; he groped for it in the dark, but there was nothing there. "You want me to teach you. The gods—this is what I've found—aren't greatly influenced by our gifts. When they give us what we ask—" The soft pressure resumed, practically pushing him off his feet.

"What is it?"

"That's what I was wondering myself, but now I believe I know. Oreb tried to tell me out in the hall; and I should have guessed when he flew the first time I heard it. Mucor calls them lynxes. There's one in the room with us."

"Are they like bats?" Hyacinth sounded alarmed.

"They're cats."

"Have—something touched me. As big as a big dog."

"That's it; but there's no point in my describing them, when you could see this one for yourself." Silk raised his voice. "Master Xiphias, bring your candle, please."

"Are they the big cats the talus used to let out at night?" Hyacinth sounded more frightened than ever.

"Mucor controls them, to her benefit and ours." Silk tried to sound reassuring. "I'd imagine that this one would like us to bring it to the Caldé's Palace, where she is."

There was a muted yowl, far too deep and reverberant to have proceeded from Tick.

Abanja glanced around Trotter's, which seemed deserted except for an old man asleep at a table and a fat man washing earthenware mugs. "Barman?"

"Yeah, sister. You need a drink?"

She shook her head. "I'm addressed as Colonel. Since I want something, you may call me sister. When you want something from me, call me Colonel. You might get it if you do."

The fat man looked up. "Hey, I'll call you Colonel right now, sister."

"Though I don't think so. You have a patron named Urus."

"Couple, anyhow," the fat man said. "Three I can lay hand to, only one got the pits."

"Urus is in your back room, and he's expecting me. Show me where it is."

"Nobody's in my back room, sister."

"Then I'll wait there for him. That yellow bottle." She pointed. "I take it that's sauterne?"

The fat man shrugged. "S'posed to be."

"Bring it, and two clean glasses."

"I got some that's better, only it's twenty-seven bits. That up there's sixteen."

"Bring it. You keep accounts for patrons? Start one for me. My name is Abanja."

"You mean you'll pay later? Sister, I don't—put that thing away!"

"You men." Abanja smiled as she stepped behind the bar. "How are you to face lances if one small needler terrifies you? Get the good sauterne and the glasses. Are you going to send for the Caldé's Guard when you leave me? They won't arrest an officer of the Rani's, but I don't think my friend Urus will like it."

"I never do that, sister."

"Then it won't be necessary for me to have you arrested when they come. Nor will I have to shoot you. I admit I had thought about it." Abanja smiled more broadly, amused by the clinking of the glasses in the fat man's hand. "Lead the way. If you don't misbehave, you have no reason to be frightened."

With her needler in his back, he pushed aside the dirty green curtain that had concealed the entrance to a dark and narrow hall. She said, "You know, I think I understand this Trotter's of yours. Are you Trotter?"

He nodded.

"Your courts meet in the Juzgado, and this is where the accused drink before they go there. Or if they're discharged. It's empty because your courts are not in session."

"The back room's empty, too." Trotter had stopped before a door. He gulped. "You can wait if you want to, only I close—"

She shook her head.

"When you leave. After that, all right? If anybody called Urus comes in, I'll tell him you're here." Trotter opened the door and gaped at the filthy, bearded man at the table inside.

With exaggerated politeness, Urus rose and pulled out a chair for Abanja. As she sat, Trotter mumbled, "I forgot the caldé let 'em out. A lot can't hardly walk."

"I sprung myself," Urus told him. "Get me somethin' to eat. Put it on her tab."

Still smiling, Abanja nodded.

When the door had closed behind Trotter, Urus said, "Thanks for gettin' the bottle 'n standin' me a meal. You're the dimber damber, lady." His voice became confidential. "What I got to tell you is I'm all right too. You treat Urus brick 'n he'll treat you stone. Ain't you goin' to put your barker up?"

"No. Trotter didn't know you were in here."

"He'd of wanted me to drink, 'n I didn't have the gelt. Lily with you, see? Yeah, I been in the pits. I just got out. Yeah, I'm flat. Only you need me, lady, so you're goin' to give me ten cards—"

She laughed.

" 'Cause I'm goin' to tell you a lot. Then I'm goin' to find out a lot more, 'n you 'n me'll knot up again, see?"

"Open that and pour yourself as much as you want," she told him. "I feel sorry for you, so I'm giving you a drink, and food if the barman has any."

"You know who Spider is?"

"Should I?"

"Shag yes. You got spies here. Spider knows 'em all. He knows me, too, only he don't know I'm workin' for you."

"You aren't. Not yet. To whom does this Spider report, assuming that he exists?"

"Councillor Potto. He's Potto's right hand. You ever hear of Guan? How 'bout Hyrax? Sewellel? Paca?"

Abanja looked thoughtful. "Some of those names may be familiar to me."

"They're dead, all of 'em, 'n I know what happened to 'em. Spider was their jefe, 'n he ain't. I know where he is 'n what he's doin'. I could bring you. I don't scavy you'd want me to, only I could. You twig they nabbed General Mint?"

"She's free now." Abanja holstered her needler. "That's what I've been told."

"You don't cap to it."

"I believe what I see."

Urus grinned. "Pure keg, lady. All right, it's the lily, she's loose. I could show her to you 'n throw in Spider, 'cause they're together. Only I'm like you, see? 'N what I want to see's gelt."

Abanja took a card from her card case and pushed it toward Urus, across the stained and splintered old table.

With a furtive glance into the next room, Chenille tapped the surface of the glass with her forefinger. A floating gray face appeared. "Yes, madame."

"Keep your voice down, all right?" Chenille herself was whispering. "There's somebody asleep in the big bed."

"Generalissimo Siyuf, madame. She is well within my field of view."

"That's right, and you wouldn't want to wake her up, would you? So keep it down."

"I shall, madame. I suggest, however, that you close the door. It would provide additional security, madame."

Chenille shook her head, her raspberry curls bobbing. "I got to know if she's waking up. Pay attention. You know the Caldé's Palace?"

"Certainly, madame."

"I've asked three or four times on the glass there, see? He let me, the caldé did, I'm a friend of his. What I want to know is are you the same one? The monitor I talked to there?"

"No, madame. Each glass has its own, madame, though I can utilize others, and consult their monitors if need be."

"That's good, 'cause he couldn't find Auk for me, ever, and I saw this glass of yours when me and Generalissimo Siyuf came in, and I've been wanting to try it ever since, only not where she could hear 'cause I'm looking for Auk. I know there's a lot of Auks. You don't have to tell me that. The one I want's the one that lives in the Orilla, the one they call Auk the Prophet now. Real big, not too bad looking, broken nose—"

"Yes, madame. I have located him. It was a matter of no difficulty, the word *prophet* being a sufficient clue. Do you wish to speak with him?"

"I—wait. If I speak to him, he can see me, right?"

Like a floating bottle disturbed by a ripple, the gray face bobbed in nothingness. "You might postpone your conversation until you are dressed, madame. If you prefer."

"That's all right. Just tell me where he is."

"In the Grand Manteion, madame. It is two streets north and one west, or so I am informed."

"Yeah, I know. Listen, he's there now? Auk's there right now, in the Grand Manteion?"

"Correct, madame."

"Is he all right? He's not dead or anything?"

"He appears somewhat fatigued, madame. Otherwise I judge him in excellent health. You do not care to converse?"

"I think it would be better if he didn't know about me and the generalissimo. Better if I don't shove it at him, anyhow, and even if I close the door he's bound to want to know what I'm doing here."

The gray face nodded sagely. "Prudent, madame."

"Yeah, I think so. Wait up, I got to think."

"Gladly, madame." For nearly a minute, there was no sound in the Lyrichord Room save Siyuf's hoarse respiration.

At last Chenille announced, "This is going to be one tough job for you, Monitor."

"We thrive upon adversity, madame."

"Good, I've got some for you. I want to get word to a lady named Orchid. Get her, or get anybody that might be able to get a message to her. What time is it?"

"Two twenty-one, madame. It is Phaesday morning, madame. Shadeup is less than four hours distant."

"That's what I was afraid of. If you can't do it, just tell me. I won't blame you a bit."

"I shall make the utmost effort, madame, but *Orchid* is also a widely employed appellation. Additional information may be of assistance."

"Sure. This Orchid's got a yellow house. It's on Lamp Street. Music runs right in back, and there's a pastry shop across the street. Across Lamp Street, I mean. She's a big fat woman, I guess forty or forty-five."

"That is sufficient, madame, I have identified her. There is a glass in her private apartments, and she is preparing for bed in the room beyond. Shall I summon her to her glass?"

"I know that glass and it doesn't work."

"To the contrary, madame, it is fully operational, though it was out of service for . . . eighteen years. Would you care to speak with Orchid?"

Chenille nodded, and in half a minute saw Orchid standing in front of her own glass in lacy black pantaloons and a hastily assumed peignoir. "Chen! How'd you get this thing turned on?"

"Never mind, it just is. Orchid, I need a favor, only there'll be something for you. Maybe a card. Maybe more."

Orchid, who had been eyeing the rich furnishings of the Lyrichord Room, nodded. "I got my ears up."

"All right, you see the mort in doss in the next room? She's the Trivigaunti's generalissimo. Her name's Siyuf."

"You always were lucky, Chen."

"Maybe. The thing is, I got to beat the hoof. Is Violet riding pretty light?"

Orchid shrugged, plump shoulders rising and falling like pans of dough. "Pretty much. You know how it is, Chen. Where are you?"

"Ermine's. This's Room Seven and Nine, get it? It's a double room, so seven and nine too. Right at the top of the big stairs. Siyuf likes tall dells, she would've given me five easy. Five's nothing to her. Violet ought to get more if she soaps her. Tell her to come uphill and play spoons, tell Siyuf she's my pal and I told her what a nice time I'd had, so she thought she'd drop by and party. I'll leave the door unlocked when I go out." Chenille's voice hardened. "Only I get half. Don't think you're going to wash me down."

"Sure thing, Chen."

"The way I'm set with the caldé—" groping the carpet at her feet, Chenille found her bandeau, "I ought to be able to throw something your way pretty often. Only don't try to wash me, Orchid. The word from me could shut you down."

Under her breath, Hyacinth asked, "Do you really want to go through with this?"

It seemed too foolish to require a reply, but Silk nodded. "Your Cognizance, you and His Eminence, with Patera Jerboa and Patera Shell, are more than sufficient, surely."

From Echidna's dark chapel behind the ambulatory, Maytera Marble called, "Just one moment more, please, Patera. Patera Incus is working as quickly as he can, and—and . . ."

Like a rumble of thunder, Hammerstone's deeper voice added, "She wants to be there, and there's another reason. Hold on, Caldé. Patera's about finished."

Hyacinth whispered, "We really don't have to. We could just go somewhere and do it all night. It doesn't matter to me, honest." Tick added, "Goo no!" from her arms.

"I've revoked your vow of chastity," Quetzal said; it was impossible to say whether he had overheard her. "You're still an augur. Is that clear?"

"Perfectly, Your Cognizance."

Remora smiled in a way he meant to be reassuring. "Can't, eh? Not even Quetzal. Indelible, hey?"

The Prolocutor himself nodded. "I could enjoin you from augural duties, but you'd still be an augur, Patera Caldé."

"I understand, Your Cognizance."

"I'm not doing it. You're relieved of the requirements. You need not say the office and sacrifice, but you can if you want to. You can and should wear the robe. Our citizens have chosen an augur, believing the gods chose for them. We must keep it so. We must sustain their faith. If necessary, we must justify it."

He glanced at Maytera Mint, who said, "Your Cognizance is wondering whether I retain mine after Pas failed to appear. I don't know, and it may be weeks before I do. Years, even. I wish Bison were here."

Spider nodded. "Me, too."

Spokesman for his master, Oreb croaked, "Do now!"

Hoping his bird had been understood, Silk said, "You told me what took place, General, but I'm afraid I wasn't listening as closely as I should have been. I couldn't think beyond my need to obtain His Cognizance's permission and persuade Hyacinth to accept me. Did Pas actually say that he would grant you a second theophany when you got here?"

"I . . ." Maytera Mint sighed, her face in her hands. "To tell you the truth, I don't remember. I thought so."

Slate put in, "No, he didn't, sir. He said you take the sarge to the Grand Manteion, 'cause my prophet Auk's there and I mean to tell him how to fix him up. He didn't say nothing about right away."

Remora nodded.

Auk said, "He told me he'd teach me, and he will. Only he ain't yet." Auk cleared his throat. "This was as queer for me as for Maytera. Worse, when I had to watch what it did to her. Pas had us fetch Patera Jerboa there—that's Hammerstone and me, and Patera Incus. All right we did, only nothing's happened yet. I had all my people up here and they're not here any more, so I guess you know what they think about me after this."

Oreb sympathized. "Poor man!"

"Only that don't matter." Defiantly, Auk looked around at the rest of the impromptu wedding party. "They still think more of me than what I do myself. It's what they think about the Plan, and that's what's hardest, harder even than Maytera. But I'm sticking. If everybody goes, that's all right, only not me. I'm here, like Pas said, and I'm sticking."

From deep within the vast nave, far from the light of the dying altar fire, a voice rumbled, "This's my fault, Caldé." A man taller even than Auk rose, and as he did a misshapen figure sprang to the top of the pew before him.

From his position behind and to the right of Quetzal and Remora, old Patera Jerboa quavered, "My son . . ."

"Probably you don't remember me, Caldé, only I gave you one on the house once, 'cause you said Pas for Kalan. I'm Gib from the Cock."

Silk nodded and smiled. "Of course I remember you, Gib; though I admit I didn't expect to meet you here, and I thought we'd met everyone. Have you been praying?"

"Tryin', anyhow." Gib strode down a side aisle, his tame baboon leaping from one pew to the next.

Auk said, "Muzzle it, Gib. You didn't do anything."

Silk nodded again. "If by 'fault' you mean this delay, the fault certainly isn't yours, Gib. If anyone is at fault, I am the person. I should have acted much more expeditiously to have Maytera's hand repaired."

Tick said, "Ale rat, nod rung." And Hyacinth, "You always blame yourself. Do you really think you're the only one in the whorl that makes mistakes?"

"I tagged along after Auk when he went to your place over on Sun," Gib explained. "Me an' him's a old knot. I'd got Bongo here when I broke my flipper, see, Caldé? I can't pluck proper. He'll do for anybody I say. I figured to sell him when it was fixed."

"I believe I'm beginning to understand," Silk said.

"Then Auk says to fetch animals, so I fetched him. Bongo here, that is. Then comin' up here I thought maybe—"

Jerboa's trembling hand motioned him to silence. "It was I, Caldé. I—" his thin old voice trembled and broke, "have an aversion to offering them. Just an old fool."

"It isn't, Patera," said a sibyl who seemed at least as old. "Caldé, they remind him of children. I don't feel that way, but I know how he feels. We've talked about it."

Patera Shell stepped forward. "Someone brought one once for Thelxiepeia, Caldé, a little black monkey with a white head. Patera had me offer it."

Silk cleared his throat. "In your youth—I understand, Patera Jerboa. Or at least I believe I do. Let us say that I understand as much as I need to. You dissuaded Gib."

"While we were walking—" Jerboa coughed. "It's a long, long way. He helped me along. He's a kind man, Caldé. A good man, though he doesn't look it. I asked him to refrain for my sake. He said he would, and left us to buy a ram. I offered it for him tonight."

Gib said, "Only I think that's why Pas won't come. They kill stuff at weddin's, don't they? So you—"

"Auk!" Silk recognized Chenille's voice before he saw her. "Auk, is this a wedding?" Holding up her skirt, she sprinted down an aisle. "Hello, Patera! Hi, Hy! Congrats! Are you going to marry them, Your Cognizance?"

Quetzal did not reply, smiling at Hammerstone and Maytera Marble as they emerged from Echidna's chapel. She knelt before him. "I begged your predecessor, Your Cognizance . . ."

Quetzal's hairless head bobbed upon his long, wrinkled neck. "My predecessor no longer holds the baculus, Maytera."

"I begged him to. I implored him, but he wouldn't. I should tell you that."

Maytera Mint looked down at her in amazement.

"Your Eminence, you said a moment ago, I overheard you, that not even His Cognizance can unmake an augur. It's true, I know. But— but . . ."

"Their vow, eh?" Remora spoke to Silk. "Not indelible, hey? Not as—ah—serious."

Quetzal inquired, "Do you want me to free you from your vow, Maytera? Yes or no will suffice."

"Yes, but I really ought—"

"To explain. You're right. For your own peace of mind, you must. You've good sense, Maytera, I've seen that. Doesn't your good sense tell you I'm not the one to whom you owe your explanation? Stand, please. Tell your sib Maytera Mint. Also Maytera Wood and her sibs. Be brief."

As Maytera Marble got to her feet, Hammerstone said, "We knew each other a long time ago. You remember, Caldé? I told you before you gave me the slip. Her name was Moly then."

Maytera Marble spoke to Maytera Mint and the other sibyls in a voice so soft that Silk could scarcely hear her. "I was the maid, the sibyls' maid, when the first bios moved into the city. I got our cenoby ready for them, and in those days I used to look like—like Dahlia, I nearly said, sib, but you never knew Dahlia. Like Teasel, a little." She laughed nervously. "Can you imagine me looking like Teasel? But I did, then."

Still staring, Maytera Mint managed to nod.

"There were six then. Six sibyls on Sun Street. I didn't have a room, you see. I don't really need one. But there were never more than six, and as time went on, fewer. Five and then four, then three. And then—and then only two, as it was with us, dear, dear sib, after I died."

The youngest sibyl from Brick Street started to object, glanced around at the others, and thought better of it.

Maytera Marble displayed a string of yellowed prayer beads. "Just Maytera Betel and I. These were hers. They're ivory." She lifted her head, a smile and a plea. "The chain is silver. She was a fine, fine woman."

"Girl cry," Oreb informed Silk, although no tears streaked Maytera Marble's smooth metal face.

"We couldn't do it all. There was just the two of us and young Patera Pike. And ever so many children, and so Maytera called—called upon . . ."

Hammerstone explained, "She drafted Moly."

"Upon me. I knew arithmetic. You've got to, to keep any sort of house. How much to buy for so many, and how much you can spend, that sort of thing. I kept a—a diary, I suppose you call it, to practice my hand, which was really quite good. So I could teach the youngest their sums and letters, and I did. Some parents complained, and . . . There wasn't any reason not to. I put my hand on the Writings and promised, and Maytera and Maytera Rose witnessed it and kissed me, and—and then I got new clothes."

She looked at Hammerstone, begging his understanding. "A new name, too. I couldn't be Moly any more once I was a sibyl, or even Maytera Molybdenum. We all take new names, and you were gone. I hadn't seen you in years and years."

"He *slept*," Incus told her. "He was so *ordered*."

"Yeah, I did," Hammerstone confirmed. "For me a order's a order. Always has been. Only now Patera says it's all right. If he'd of said no—" Slate slapped him on the backplate, the clang of his hand startlingly loud in the religious hush of the Grand Manteion.

Xiphias nudged Silk. "Double wedding, lad!"

"Your Cognizance must think this terribly strange," Maytera Marble ventured.

"Perfectly natural," Quetzal assured her.

"We—we're not like bios about this. It matters terribly to you how old somebody is. I know, I've seen it."

"Her and me are really about the same age," Hammerstone confided. "Only I slept so much."

"What matters to us is—is whether we can." Maytera Marble raised her right hand to show Quetzal the weld that had reattached it, and moved her fingers. "My hand's well again, and I've got a lot of replacement parts, and I can. So we're going to. Or at least we want to, if—if Your Cognizance—"

"You are released," Quetzal told her. "You are a laywoman again, Molybdenum."

"Like a story, right, lass?" Xiphias edged toward Hyacinth and spoke in a tone he intended as confidential. "Must be the end! Everybody getting married! Need another ring!"

Chapter 12

I'M AUK

It was, Silk thought, no time to be wakeful.

Or more persuasively, no time to sleep. Careful not to awaken Hyacinth, he rolled onto his back and put his hands behind his head. How many times had he daydreamed of a night like this, and thrust the dream away, telling himself that its reality could never be his? Now . . .

No, it was no time to sleep. As quietly as he could, he slipped from their bed to bathe and relieve himself. Hyacinth, who wept before sleep, had wept that night; he had wept too—had wept in joy and pain, and in joy at his pain. When tears were done and their heads rested on one pillow, she had said that no man had ever wept with her before.

Two floors below them, their reflected images knelt in the fishpond at Thelxiepeia's feet, subsistent but invisible. There she would weep for him longer than they lived. He lowered his naked body into a rising pool, warm and scarcely less romantic.

Ermine's, Silk discovered when he rose from it, provided everything. Not merely soap, water, towels, and an array of perfumes and scented powders, but thick, woolly robes: one pale and possibly cream or pale yellow, and a longer, darker one that might have been blue had he dared clap and rouse the dim sparks that circled one another on the ceiling.

After drying himself, he put on the longer robe and tied its belt, returned to their bedroom, and covered Hyacinth's perfect, naked body with infinite gentleness. Then, standing outside upon air, watched himself do it, a darker shadow with tousled hair pulling up sheet and blanket to veil his sleeping wife's long, softly rounded legs and swelling hips—Horn and Nettle huddled in a musty bed in a small, chill room in the Caldé's Palace.

—Patera Pike cutting the throat of a speckled rabbit he himself had bought.

—a ragged child weeping on a mattress of straw.

—a blind god metamorphosised from a blind man who remained a blind man still, and was struck.

—a man scarcely larger than the child lying naked on the ground, his stark ribs and emaciated face black with bruises, his arms chained around a tent pole.

—a madman among tombs, howling that the sun would die.

—Violet embraced by Siyuf in the room below.

—Auk asleep on his back before the smoking, unpurified altar of the Grand Manteion.

"Auk? Auk?"

He sat up blinking, and rubbed his eyes. Chenille slept at his side, her head pillowed on muscular arms, her skirt hiked to her knees. Sergeant Sand slept in death at the foot of the Sacred Window; about him lay Pateras Jerboa, Incus, and Shell, Incus face up and snoring.

On the farther side of the lofty marble ambion, Spider and Eland slept as well, watched by three soldiers; Slate nodded in friendly fashion and touched his forehead. In the third row of pews, Maytera Mint knelt in prayer.

"Somebody call me?" Auk asked Slate softly.

Slate's big steel head swung from side to side. "I'd of heard. Must of been a dream."

"I guess." Auk lay down again; he was as tired as he could ever remember being, and it was good not to have been called.

Sciathan soared above a leafless plain at sunset. Far ahead, Aer flew a little higher and a little faster. He called to her aloud, knowing somehow that her helmcom was out or had been turned off. She looked back, and he glimpsed her smile, the roses in her cheeks, and a tendril of flaxen hair that had escaped her helmet. *Aer!* he called. *Aer, come back!* But she did not look back at him again, and his PM was overheating. Moment by moment, over a long hour of flight, he watched her dwindle into the dark sky ahead.

"Auk? Auk!"

He sat up stiffly, conscious that he had slept for hours. The great arched windows of the Grand Manteion, which had been featureless sheets of black by night, showed vague tracings now—gods, animals, and past Prolocutors half visible.

He stood, and Maytera Mint looked up from her vigil at the scrape of his boots on the floor. Leaving the sanctuary, he knelt beside her. "Did you call me? I thought I heard you."

"No, Auk."

He considered that, rubbing his chin. "You been awake all this time, Mother?"

"Yes, Auk." (A tiny spark of happiness appeared in her red-rimmed eyes; it warmed him like a blaze.) "You see, Auk, I swore I would wait here in prayer until Pas came, or shadeup. I'm keeping that vow."

"You've kept it already, Mother. Look at those windows." He gestured. "I was so tired I lay down with my boots on, see? I bet you were just as tired, but you haven't slept a wink. You know what I'm going to do?"

"No, Auk, how could I?"

"I'm going to lay down again and sleep some more. Only first I'm going to take off my boots. Now you lay down and sleep too, or I'm going to make a fuss and wake up everybody. The job's done. You did it just like you promised."

Hyacinth woke and went to the open window to examine her ring in the faint gray light of morning—a tarnished silver ring like a rose with a woman's tiny face at its heart, framed by petals. She had bought it because a clerk at Sard's had said it resembled her, never guessing that she was buying her own wedding ring. She had worn it once or twice, tossed it into a drawer, and forgotten it.

It didn't really look like her at all, she decided. The woman in the rose was older, at once more come-on and more . . . She groped for a word. Not just pretty.

Though Silk thought her beautiful, or said he did.

She kissed him as he slept, went into the dressing room, and tapped the glass.

"Yes, madame."

"Show me exactly the way I look right now. Oh, gods!"

Her own face, puffy-eyed and retaining traces of smeared cosmetics, said, "You are actually quite attractive, madame. If I might suggest—"

She waved the suggestion away. "Now look at this face in my ring. See it? Make me look just a tiny little like that."

For a few seconds she studied the result, turning her head left, then right. "Yes, that's good. Hold that." She picked up the hairbrush and began a process that Tick the catachrest watched approvingly.

"Auk! Auk!"

He sat up and stared at the Sacred Window. The voice had come from there—this time he was certain of it. He got up, grasping his hanger to keep the brass tip of the scabbard from rattling on the floor, and padded across the sanctuary. Shell and Incus were clearly sound asleep, but Jerboa's eyes were not quite closed. Old people didn't need much sleep, Auk reminded himself.

He squatted beside Jerboa. "It's all right, I wasn't going to nip your case or anything, Patera. Is that what you thought? Anything you got you can keep."

Jerboa did not reply.

"Only somebody over here's been calling me. Was that you? Like when you were dreaming, maybe?"

Shell grunted something unintelligible and turned his head away, but Jerboa did not stir. Suddenly suspicious, Auk picked up Jerboa's left hand, then slid his own under Jerboa's tunic.

He rose, wiping his hands absently on his thighs; it would be well, certainly, to move the old man's body to some private spot. The sibyls were sleeping in the sacristy; that, at least, was where Maytera Mint had gone when he had persuaded her to lie down for an hour or two, and Auk thought he recalled old Maytera Wood and the others—sibyls whose names he had not learned—going in there at about the time he had stretched himself on the terrazzo floor.

Squatting again, he picked up the old augur's body and carried it to the ambulatory. Schist straightened up as they came into view. "He dead?"

"Yeah," Auk whispered. "How'd you know?"

Schist's steel shoulders rose and fell with a soft clank. "He looks dead, that's all."

Shale asked, "How's Pas supposed to get his part back if he's dead?"

Without answering, Auk carried the body into the chapel of Hierax and laid it on the altar there.

Slate inquired, "You goin' back to sleep?"

"Shag, I don't know." Auk discovered that he was wiping his hands again and made himself stop. "I think maybe I'll fetch my boots and walk around outside a little."

"I thought maybe you could wake the rest of 'em up." Slate waited longer for his reply than a bio would have, then asked, "What you lookin' at over there? Must be shaggy interesting."

"Him."

Slowly, Slate clambered to his feet. "Who?"

"Him." Auk turned away impatiently, striding toward the Sacred Window. "This soldier. He got it in the autofunction coprocessor, see?" Auk knelt beside Sergeant Sand. "Only his central could handle that stuff if it had to. There's lots of redundancy there. His voluntary coprocessor could, even."

He fumbled for his boot knife, discovered that he was not wearing his boots, and got it. "Look alive, Patera!" He shook Incus's shoulder. "I need that gadget you got."

"Up!" A boot prodded the captive Flier's ribs. "Reveille an hour ago. Didn't you hear it?"

Blinking and shivering, Sciathan sat up.

"You speak the Common Tongue well," the uniformed woman looming over him said. "Answer me!"

"Better than most of us, yes." Sciathan paused, struggling to clear his brain of sleep. "I did not hear it, that word you used. I know I did not since I heard nothing. But if I heard it, I would not know what it was."

The woman nodded. "I did that to establish a point. Any question I ask, you are to answer. If you do, and I like your answer, you may get clothes or something to eat. If you don't, or I don't, you'll wish you'd been killed, too." She clapped. "Sentry!"

A younger and even taller woman ducked through the door of the tent and stood stiffly erect, her gun held vertically before her left shoulder. "Sir!"

The first woman gestured. "Get him off that pole and lock the chain again. I'm taking him to the city." As the younger woman slung her gun to fumble for the key, the older asked, "Do you know my name? What is it?"

He shook his head; a smile might have helped, but he could not summon one. "My name is Sciathan. I am a Flier."

"Who questioned you yesterday, Sciathan?"

"First Sirka." His hands were free. He held them out so that the younger woman could refasten his manacles.

"After that."

"Generalissimo."

"Generalissimo Siyuf," the older woman corrected him. "I was there. Do you remember me?"

He nodded. "You did not speak to me. Sometimes to her."

"Why did your people attack Major Sirka's troopers?"

Here it was again. "We did not."

She struck his ear with her fist. "You tried to take their weapons. One escaped, three were killed, and you were captured. Why did you break your wings?"

"It is what we do."

"How did you disable your propulsion module?"

He shrugged, and she struck him on the mouth. He said, "We cannot do it. Mechanisms have been proposed, but would increase weight."

She smiled, surprising him. "Aren't you going to lick that? My rings tore your lip."

He shrugged again. "If you want me to."

"Get him a rag he can tie around his waist," she ordered the taller, younger woman. Turning back to him, she said, "I'm Colonel Abanja. Why did you attack Sirka's troopers?"

"Because they were shooting at us." He could not actually remember that, but it seemed plausible. "I made a face. I do not know why."

"Did you now?" For a fraction of a second Abanja's eyes widened. "What kind of face?"

He was able to smile when he reflected that this was vastly preferable to talking about the propulsion modules. "With lips back."

"You don't know why you did that. Perhaps I do. Are you saying we shot your people because you grimaced? You yourself weren't shot at all."

"Aer saw it and screamed. They shot her then. We tried to take their guns so they could not shoot."

Abanja stepped closer, peering down at him. "She screamed because you made a face? Most people wouldn't believe that, but I might, and perhaps Generalissimo Siyuf might. Let's see you make a face like that for me."

"I will try," he said, and did.

The click of booted heels announced the younger woman's return. When Abanja turned toward her, she held up a scrap of cotton sheeting that had been used to clean something greasy. "Will this do, sir?"

Abanja shook her head. "Get the coveralls he was wearing. Bring a winter undershirt and a blanket, and tell the cooks to give you something he can eat on horseback."

She returned to Sciathan. "Stop grinning, it's making your lip bleed. You came here looking for a Vironese, a man. That's what Sirka told us. You gave his name, and it was one I think I heard last night. Say it again for me."

"Auk," Sciathan said. "His name is Auk."

Sergeant Sand's arm stirred, then struck the floor of the Grand Manteion hard enough to crack it. Chenille shouted a warning. "Don't worry," Auk told her, "just a little static, like. I got it fixed already."

Behind him, a voice he did not recognize said, "I only wish Patera Shell could watch. He'll be *so* disheartened when we tell him what he missed."

"So will His Eminence," Maytera Mint murmured. "But it's his fault for going back to the Palace, if that can be called a fault. We're certainly not going to wait to carry out Pas's instructions, nor would His Eminence want us to. You didn't see Pas, Auk? Are you certain?"

"No, Maytera, I ain't." Auk squinted, still bent over his work.

" 'Cause he must've showed me this stuff some way, after I talked to you, probably." Inspiration struck. "Want to know what I think, Maytera?"

"Yes! Very much!"

"I think it was you keeping your promise the way you did that swung it. I think he was asking himself if we were worth all the trouble he was taking, till then. Wait a minute, I got to tie in his voluntary."

Auk made the last connection and leaned back, easing aching muscles. "Think you could fetch one of those holy lamps over here, Patera? I'm going to need more light."

Incus scurried away.

"Patera Shell is hoping to engage a deadcoach to return Patera's body to our manteion." The owner of the unknown voice proved to be a young and pretty sibyl. "Maytera said nothing would be open, but he said they *would* be by the time he got there, or if they weren't he'd wait. It was a great temptation, Maytera admitted this to me, to ask His Cognizance to permit Patera's final sacrifice to take place right here in the Grand Manteion, since he ascended to Mainframe from here. But the faithful of our quarter would *never*–"

Incus, returning, knelt beside Auk. "Is this *sufficient*? I can pull up the *wick,* should *more light* be needed." He held up a flame-topped globe of cut crystal.

"That's dimber," Auk told him. "I can see the place and the register, and that's all I got to see." Delicately, he eased the point of his knife into Sand's cranium. "Muzzle it, everybody. I got to think." He counted under his breath.

And Sand spoke, making Maytera Mint start. "V-fifty-eight, zero. V-fifty-eight, one. V-fifty-nine, zero. V-fifty-nine, one."

"Those are *voluntary* coprocessor inputs," Incus explained in an awed whisper. "He's *enabling* them."

When Auk showed no sign of having heard, the young sibyl from Brick Street whispered, "I simply can't believe that your Maytera–she was, I mean. That Molybdenum and that soldier are going to do all this, and where are they going to buy these coprocessor things?"

"They must *make* them, Maytera," Incus explained, "and *I* shall assist them." Maytera Mint shushed him.

Auk returned his knife to his boot. "Don't froth, Maytera. He's all right. He just don't know it yet."

As if on cue, Sand raised his head and stared around him.

"Hold that right there," Auk told him. "I got to put your skull plate back. How was Mainframe?"

The crack-crack-crack of a needler was followed by a savage snarl, more shots, and the boom of a slug gun. In the choir high above them, a nephrite image of Tartaros fell with a crash.

"Is that warm?" Abanja asked as she watched Sciathan pull on his flight suit.

Smiling was easy now. "Not as warm as I wish, sometimes."

"Then you better put the undershirt over it. It's wool and should be a lot warmer than that thing. Once you're on your horse you can wrap the blanket around you." She fingered the needler in her holster. "Can you ride?"

"I never have."

"That's good," Abanja told him. "It may save your life."

In the cutting wind outside, two bearded men held a pair of restive horses. Abanja said, "That's mine," and to Sciathan's relief pointed to the larger. "The other one's yours. Let's see you mount."

She watched him for five minutes while the bearded men struggled to contain their mirth. At last she said, "You really can't ride, or you're a marvelous actor," and ordered them to help him. As they lifted him into the seat, she swung herself up and onto her own tall horse with a practiced motion that seemed almost miraculous. "Now let me explain something." She leveled her index finger. "It's two leagues to the city, and when we're halfway you're liable to think that all you've got to do to get away is clap your heels to that horse."

He shook his head. "I will not."

"I could chain you to your saddle, like you were chained to that pole. But if you fell, you'd probably be dragged to death, and I don't want to lose you. So listen. If you start that horse galloping, you're going to fall and you could be killed. If you're not I'll catch you, and I'll make you wish you'd died. Don't say I didn't warn you." She slapped her horse with its own control straps, and it stalked away a great deal faster than Sciathan had ever wanted a horse to go.

"I will not ride quicker than you," he promised.

For a moment it appeared he would not ride at all. Then one of the bearded men shouted, *"Hup!"* and struck the horse with something that made a popping sound, and he felt that he was being blown about by the wildest gale in the *Whorl*.

Abanja pulled up and looked back at him. "Another thing. This is a good horse. Yours isn't. Yours is old, a common remount nobody wants. Your horse couldn't gallop as fast as mine if a lion were after it."

Shaken too hard to nod, he clutched his blanket.

"If you're fooling me—if you really can ride, and you gallop off when you see your chance—I'll shoot your horse. It's not easy to bring down an animal as big as a horse with a needler, but half a dozen ought to do it. I'll try not to hit you, but I can't promise."

He gasped, "You are a kind woman."

"Don't count on it." After a moment she laughed. "It's just that you may be useful. Certainly it will be useful for you to show Siyuf what you showed me. I take it women aren't kind among your people."

"Oh, no!" He hoped his shock showed in his face. "Our women are very kind."

"That Aer who screamed, wasn't that a woman? You said, *her.* Stand in the stirrups if you're getting bounced."

He tried. "Yes, a woman. A kind woman."

"You loved her." There was a note in Abanja's voice he had not heard before.

"Very much. If I may say this, Mear loved Sumaire also. In the tent last night I thought about them. How stupid I was! I did not know they loved until they died."

"Mear, was that the woman who killed the troopers?"

For the first time since his capture, Sciathan felt like laughing. "Mear is a man's name. It was Sumaire who killed the women with guns, and they killed her."

"Just trying to take away their weapons."

Aer had been shot before Sumaire killed the troopers, but arguing would be worse than useless. Sciathan remained silent.

"She was your leader?" Abanja slowed her horse.

"Thank you." He was genuinely grateful. "We do not fly like that. Each flies for himself. Sumaire was the best at *gleacaiocht,* the best at fighting with hands and feet. I do not know your word."

"I saw her body," Abanja told him, "but I didn't measure it. I wish I had. The blonde?"

By now Sciathan was able to shake his head. "Dark hair. Like yours."

"The little one?"

He nodded, recalling how cheerful Sumaire had always been, most cheerful when storms roared up and down the hold. When Mainframe had needed information and not excuses, it had sent Sumaire.

It would send her no more.

"Answer me!"

"I am sorry. I did not intend to be rude." Unconsciously, Sciathan looked down the unpaved track and over the wind-scoured fields, seeking something that would render his loss bearable. "The small one, yes. Smaller than Aer."

"But taller than you."

He looked at Abanja in some astonishment.

"Was she smaller?"

"Yes, much." He considered. "The top of Aer's head came to my eyes. I think the top of Sumaire's head would have come to Aer's eyes, or lower. To my mouth or chin."

"Yet she killed troopers a long cubit taller."

"She was a fine fighter, one who taught others when she was not flying."

Abanja looked thoughtful. "What about you? Do you know this kind of fighting? I forget the word you used."

"*Gleacaiocht.* I know something, but I am not as quick and skillful as Sumaire was. Few are."

When Abanja said nothing, he added. "We all learn it. We cannot carry weapons as you do. Even a small knife would be too heavy." Now that he was no longer being shaken so much, he had begun to feel the cold. He shook out the rough blanket he had held onto so desperately and wrapped himself in it as she had suggested, contriving a hood for his head and neck.

"In that case you can't carry food or water, can you?"

"No, only our instruments—" He had been on the point of saying "and our PMs." He substituted, "and ourselves."

"Have you seen our pterotroopers? Troopers with wings who fly out of the airship?"

"I have not seen these. I was told, and I have seen your airship if it is what I think."

"You can see it now." Abanja pointed. "That brown thing catching the sun above the housetops. Our pterotroopers carry slug guns and twenty rounds, but no rations or water. We tried field packs, but they left them behind whenever they could."

"Yes," Sciathan said.

"You would too, you mean. So would I, I suppose, though I've never flown. I doubt that our wings are much better than yours, and they may not be as good. I hadn't thought about how you'd fight, but I should have. Do you have to break your wings if you're forced down? You said that."

He nodded. "We must."

"The others didn't. We've got them. Siyuf is sending a pair back to Trivigaunte for study, the blond woman's wings and her propulsion module. Is that what you call it?"

"In the Common Tongue? Yes."

"What about in your language?"

He shrugged. "It does not matter."

Abanja stopped her horse and drew her weapon. "It does to you, mannikin, because I'll shoot if you don't answer. What do you call it?"

He chose the least revealing word. "The *canna*."

"Her *canna*. You don't know how they work, you say."

"I do not. Shoot me and end it."

Again, her smile surprised him. "Shoot you? I've hardly started on you. Who makes them?"

"Our scientists. I do not know the names."

"You have scientists."

"That may not be the correct term." He had said too much, and knew it. "Makers. Mechanics. Is that not what it means?"

"Scientists," Abanja said firmly, then changed the subject with an abruptness that startled him. "You loved Aer. Were you planning to be married?"

"No, she was a Flier."

"Fliers don't marry? Here the holy women don't, which seems pointless to us."

"Marriage is so that there shall be children, new Fliers, in the next generation." He was floundering. "I do not talk of you or, or–" He pointed. "People in the house upon this small hill. But for us, for Crew, it is for children. A Flier woman cannot, because she could not fly. She may when she no longer flies. Some give up wings for marriage." He hesitated, remembering. "They are not happy soon."

"But you can marry. Are you?"

"Yes. One wife." If he had succeeded in this, he would have been given one more at least, and perhaps as many as four; he thrust the thought aside.

"But you loved Aer. She must have been handsome when she was alive, I could see that. Did she love you?"

He nodded slowly. "When she was alive, I wondered. She did not like to say. She is dead, and I know she did."

"I know this must mean a whole lot to you, Patera, and I really am sorry." Chenille's face, framed by the metal margins of the glass, was almost comically apologetic.

"Why?" Silk seated himself in the low-backed chair facing it. "Because my egg will get cold? The kitchen here will send up another if I want it, I feel sure."

"We all got together," Chenille drew breath, her formidable breasts heaving like capsized boats. "That's Auk and me, and General Mint and Sandy and the other soldiers, and Spider and Patera Incus, and those sibyls. Maytera Wood and Maytera Maple, and the rest of them. I don't remember who most of them are."

"I doubt that it matters," Silk told her. "What were you getting together about?"

"Everything, but especially the shooting. So much's been—oh, hi, Hy! I'm sorry about this, truly I am, only Patera said you were finished and having breakfast."

"Bird eat," Oreb announced from Hyacinth's shoulder; Tick countered with, "Ma durst, due add word!" She hushed them, setting Silk's plate and the toast rack before him. "Hi, Chen. Did you and Auk get married too?"

"We talked about it, but we want Patera to do it, so just Moly and her soldier."

"I know that soldier," Hyacinth positioned Silk's egg cup, "and I know your Auk, too. Kypris's kindness on both of you. You're going to need it."

"Auk's all right." Chenille winked. "You've got to know how to handle him."

Silk cleared his throat. "You mentioned shooting, and that sounds very serious. Who was shot?"

"Eland. Only I'd better start at the beginning, Patera—"

He raised his hand. "One question more, before you do. Who is Eland?"

"This cull General Mint nabbed when she was down in the tunnels where me and Auk were."

Oreb whistled. "Bird see!"

"Yeah. Oreb, too. She had these culls, Spider and Eland, and the soldiers were watching them for her. Spider's the fat cull, and the skinny one was Eland, only he's dead."

Silk's forefinger drew small circles on his cheek. "I said I would ask only one question, but I'd like a point verified as well. When you listed those who participated in your impromptu conference, did you include Sergeant Sand?"

"That's the pure quill, Patera. Auk brought him back, just like General Mint says Pas said he would."

"I see. I ought to have had more faith in Pas, though at the time it appeared to me that Maytera Mint had originally had more than enough for both of us, and had been disappointed."

"Yeah, Auk was too. He got all these culls sold on him and said Pas would come, so after the animals were used up and Pas never did, they cleared out. Except Gib. Then when you and Hy went, and Moly and Hammerstone, Gib did too. I said I'd start at the beginning. I guess I have already."

Silk nodded. "Tell me everything, please."

"When you and Hy went, the old man sort of followed you. Master Xiphias, only I don't think he went home. I think he's probably hanging around there to watch out for you. Then His Cognizance and the augur that talked to us that time in your manse left. Maybe it would be easier if I said who didn't, who was still there."

"Go ahead."

"I'll try not to make it so long. Auk stuck, so I did too. We slept on the floor and didn't do anything. Everybody from Brick Street stayed, and Patera Incus, like I said, and General Mint and the soldiers, only

Sandy was dead, and those culls the soldiers were watching. I think that's everybody.

"It was a soldier shooting that woke me up, Slate his name is. There was somebody way up in the balcony, and he'd shot Eland. Patera Incus said Pas for him. Slate saw him up there and took a shot at him, only he doesn't think he got him. He broke a beautiful statue, is all. Auk went up there with him to look, and they brought back a great big dead cat. I thought it was Gib's baboon at first, but it wasn't. It was spotted, sort of like a big house cat only with a little beard and a little short tail."

Hyacinth said, "We brought it in the floater," to which Tick added, "Add cot!"

"I was sort of scared of it," Hyacinth continued, "but Silk said it wouldn't hurt us, and it didn't." He put down his cup. "His name was Lion, and he belonged to Mucor. We stopped at the Caldé's Palace and let him out, thinking he would go to her; it's only a few streets from the Grand Manteion, of course. Am I to take it that Lion was with the person who shot Eland, and that this Slate hit Lion when he fired at Eland's murderer?"

Chenille shook her head, her raspberry curls dancing. "It wasn't a slug gun that did for it, it was a needler. We think when it saw this cully shoot Eland it went for him and he shot it, too. Auk says he heard it before Slate shot, and a needler shooting four or five times up there. That's what got everybody worked up, mostly. That and Pas, only nobody saw him, and Auk bringing back Sandy. Only Sandy's kind of mixed up, on account of being dead."

"I would like to speak to him," Silk said. "I will, at the first opportunity. Before you proceed, did you know Eland, other than as a prisoner of Maytera Mint's? Did you, Hyacinth?"

Both said they had not.

"Since Maytera Mint captured him, I assume he was one of our citizens who remained loyal to the Ayuntamiento. If that's the case, he may have been shot by someone who considered that treachery; but there are a dozen other possibilities. What took place after that?"

"Did I tell you the old augur from Brick Street's dead? He'd gone to Mainframe when I woke up, only he wasn't shot or anything. It looked like he'd just gone to sleep."

"When Pas came," Silk murmured.

"I guess it could've been, yeah. Auk says Pas showed him that stuff about Sandy, only he doesn't remember seeing him."

Silk broke the corner of a slice of toast, and dipped it into his egg. "Others have been visited by gods, though they did not see them. Patera Jerboa was safeguarding a fragment of Pas—or so Hyacinth and I were told."

Hyacinth said, "Something's bothering you. What is it?"

Much as Sciathan was just then shrugging in response to a question from Abanja, Silk shrugged. "I was thinking that the fragment of Pas which Patera Jerboa was safeguarding may have been responsible for his long life, and that its retrieval may have been responsible in his death—not because Pas willed it, but simply because that fragment of Pas was no longer present to maintain him in life."

Silk put the egg-soaked toast into his mouth, chewed it reflectively, and swallowed. When neither woman spoke, he said, "After that, logically enough, I began to wonder which god it is who maintains the rest of us. I believe I can guess, but we have other things to talk about. Naturally you were agitated, Chenille. No doubt all of you were."

"That's right, and General Mint said we ought to find you and tell you, only we thought you'd come here. The sibyls from Brick Street—"

"Wait. You're at the Caldé's Palace?"

"Right. We thought you and Hy probably came here, so we walked over, except the sibyls. They stayed to watch the old man's body, and there's a deadcoach supposed to come. Only you and Hy weren't here. I went in here where this glass is because I thought the monitor would probably know where you went."

Hyacinth exclaimed, "It couldn't!"

"Last night Hyacinth instructed our monitor not to reveal our whereabouts to anyone," Silk explained. He looked to her for confirmation, and she nodded vigorously.

"It didn't, Violet told me. See, the one here couldn't find you, so I tried to figure out where you'd go, you and Hy. You're not going to like this, Patera."

"I won't be angry, I promise."

"The first place I thought of was back to Sun Street, that little three-cornered house where I waited for you. Only the monitor where the sibyls live didn't think you were around." Chenille hesitated, unwilling to meet Silk's eyes. "So then I thought where could they have gone? It was still pretty early. It was about the time the market opens when we came over here."

He said, "I can think of one other place, though I can't imagine why you suppose I might be insulted because you thought of it as well—my rooms in the Juzgado. I slept there before we reopened the Caldé's Palace."

Chenille shook her head again, the dance of her fiery hair wilder than ever. "I knew you wouldn't go there, Patera. You wouldn't want somebody bothering you like I am now, so it would be the very last place. Only I thought maybe Orchid's, and it couldn't hurt to try. I figured she'd be asleep, but I could ask the monitor and maybe go down there and get something at the little bakery across the street and wait for you and Hy to come out. So I tried, only Orchid was awake. You remember Violet?"

"Of course."

"She sort of spent some time with Generalissimo Siyuf last night. Not at Orchid's but up there at Ermine's. Orchid was kind of lathered about that because it was Siyuf, so she got up and waited for Violet to hear how it went."

Hyacinth put in, "And would she want somebody for tonight, maybe somebody new, and did she have any friends who might want somebody, and did you remember to tell her we're available for private parties. I can imagine."

"Yeah, all that stuff. Well, I sort of thought, hey, this is interesting, so I talked to Violet some myself." Chenille sounded apologetic.

"Sure," Hyacinth said. "Why shouldn't you?"

"So it pops out that the Trivigauntis caught a Flier. Maybe you don't know about this, Hy, but I do because I was there when Patera found out. Remember, Patera?"

Silk smiled ruefully. "Yes. It was something that I had hoped to discuss with Generalissimo Siyuf over dinner."

"Only you didn't know they killed three, did you? Three Fliers. That's what Siyuf said, Violet says."

"No." Silk pursed his lips. "I certainly did not know that. I thought only one had landed, for whatever reason, and the Trivigauntis had him. You're correct, Chenille, this is serious as well as unpleasant."

"I haven't even gotten to the worst stuff yet, Patera. Violet figured it might be good to know where this Flier was. You know, something somebody might pay to know."

"She'll be rewarded if she's entitled to it, and it sounds to me as though she is."

"Only she told Orchid, and Orchid didn't try to hold out for money, she just wanted me to tell you, and say where I got it. Then Violet lets out she spotted you and Hy at Ermine's. It was when she'd just got there herself, and that's how I knew where to find you."

"That's not so bad, surely."

"It's where they put this Flier, Patera." Chenille gulped. "He's in our Juzgado, and Siyuf's moving her headquarters there. They're taking it."

Silk sat in stunned silence.

"And Violet spilled something about me and Auk, Patera, just making conversation, she says, with Siyuf. She says as soon as she said Auk's name Siyuf wanted to know all about him. I think maybe that was why she was so nice to me last night at dinner. Violet thinks Auk's mixed up with this Flier somehow, and now the Trivigauntis are looking for him."

The formidable breasts heaved again. "So the Juzgado's the main thing for you, Patera, but Auk's the main thing for me and I'm scared. Not for me, but for him."

The little catachrest sprang onto the dressing table for a better view of Hyacinth. "Shop, itty laddie! Wise rung?"

She wiped her eyes. "It was just such a short honeymoon, that's all, Tick."

Sciathan opened his eyes as the key squealed in the lock, then resolutely closed them. The newcomer was twice his height and three or four times his weight, brawny, dirty, and bearded. This freezing cell had been a haven of peace for the past few hours, Sciathan reflected; the interlude was over, and troubles of a new kind had begun.

Outside the warder said, "I can get you clean sheets if you want 'em."

"Fetch my prog," the newcomer rumbled. As the iron door swung inward: "You upstairs! You hungry?"

"I am not." Sciathan turned his face to the shiprock wall. "Thank you very much."

"I am." The newcomer seated himself heavily on the lower bunk.

"Shaggy hungry and shaggy tired. I been hungry so long I forgot I'm hungry. I'm just sort of empty. I was up shaggy late last night and up shaggy early this morning, and between times I slept on the floor. It was a stone floor, too, but I was so shaggy tired it felt better than this."

He lay down, his position attested by the creaking of the bunk straps. "This's the easiest I've had it all week."

"A pleasant sleep to you," Sciathan suggested politely.

"Oh, I ain't going to sleep. I slept on the floor anyhow, like I said, and I got eating to do." The newcomer chuckled, "How 'bout you? Have a good night?"

Sciathan risked a quick look over the side at the big man below. "I have rested more comfortably."

"Somebody's been dusting your dial, too, so I'm better off than you."

Ten minutes or more crawled by until curiosity tweaked Sciathan. "You are Vironese? You are of this city?"

"Born on Wine Street," the newcomer declared sleepily. "You're scared I'm Trivigaunti, I guess. Been three or four days since I shaved is all. I been too busy."

"I, myself, am a stranger here," Sciathan ventured.

"Yeah, Peeper told me."

At once Sciathan was on guard. "Who is Peeper?"

"Out there with the keys. He's sort of a friend of mine. I been in a couple times, and it helps. I got gelt, too. That always helps. We're not going to pluck, anyhow."

"I understand you," Sciathan said, and fell silent.

"People think it's a nickname, like, 'cause he looks in to make sure we're not chilling each other." The newcomer yawned. "But it's his right tag. A peeper's a kind of a little frog. They're frogs mostly in his family, I guess, and toads and such. Twig him coming? Smells dimber."

Sciathan sniffed. "It smells good, the first good odor I have smelled in this place."

"Beef brisket and noodles. They got some kind of a sour cream sauce they put on it. Sour cream and red peppers dried and pounded up, butter, and some other stuff, I guess."

The warder's keys rattled against the cell door; outside it, the warder himself said, "Here's your lunch."

"My breakfast," the newcomer told him. "I ate something sometime yesterday, some kind of a fruit, I forget what." The key squeaked in the lock, and the newcomer chuckled as though the squeak amused him.

"I did the best I could with what you give me," the warder declared. "I said who it was for and you were real hungry, and half a card but make it good. I've seen you eat, only I doubt you can wrap yourself around all this."

"I mean to try." The newcomer sat up.

"This big one here—" A faint chime sounded as the warder lifted the lid from a covered dish; Sciathan, watching from the corner of his eye, saw a cloud of fragrant steam waft toward the ceiling. "Your beef brisket and the noodles, enough for three's what he said. Then this little one's extra sauce."

There was a somewhat softer chime, followed by an aroma indescribably delicious. Sciathan sat up in time to see the warder lift the lid from a third dish.

"This here's pickled cabbage. He says you like it."

The newcomer rubbed his big hands together. "Yeah, I do."

"Good and hot, he says, and it'll stay hot a long time. Only it's about as good cold, so if you can't finish you can keep it to eat later." The warder paused. "Hoppies didn't rough you up much."

"You're a hoppy yourself," the newcomer told him.

"They don't think so."

"Sure you are. You just don't get the green clothes." The newcomer craned his neck to look up at Sciathan. "Remember what I said about his name? It's 'cause his whole family's hoppies, just about. They want their sprats to be hoppies, too, so they give 'em those names, Peeper and like that."

The warder said, "I got a brother named Buffo and he's a hoppy all right, but not me."

"Pardon." Sciathan leaned over the edge of the upper bunk to look at the laden tray that held the newcomer's meal. "I do not understand."

"He's foreign," the warder informed the newcomer. "They got queer ways in Urbs and places like that."

The newcomer was unwrapping napkins to reveal a loaf as long as Sciathan's arm. "What's itching you, Upstairs? You figure they don't feed everybody this good?"

The warder laughed.

"Your food was not prepared here."

The newcomer shook his head. "There's a place over on the other side of Cage Street. Peeper went over there for me and told 'em what I wanted, then after he locked me up he went back and got it. I fronted him a card, and he gets half for doing it for me. That's how we do here."

"You have just arrived," Sciathan objected. "There could not be time to prepare so much."

"He was in the hot room," the warder explained, "only they made it easy for him, it looks like, and they let me come in to see if he wanted anything."

"They know me, too," the newcomer said.

Sciathan glanced at the snowflakes drifting down beyond the small, barred window, and drew his blanket about his shoulders. "It is warmer in there?"

Both big men laughed, and the newcomer said, "It's where they ask you questions, only they're pretty easy on everybody today, I figure."

"On myself as well. It may be so. It will be worse the next time, I am sure."

The newcomer was spreading butter over a quarter of the long loaf. He said, "They have you in the hot room today?"

The warder shook his head.

"I do not think the hot room. I was questioned on a horse by Abanja, which was not as bad as I feared. Afterward here by Siyuf, Abanja, and others whose names are not known to me. It was worse then. Siyuf is a hard woman."

"That's this Trivigaunti that's taking over," the warder explained to the newcomer. "Generalissimo Siyuf, and she's got the caldé doing everything she says."

"They're supposed to be here helping us out," the newcomer protested.

"They're helping themselves, if you ask me."

The newcomer raised his buttered quarter-loaf. "Here, try some, Upstairs. You hear what we just said?"

"Thank you. I could not fail to do so."

"Well, that's why the hoppies made it easy for me. They ain't sure where they stand yet."

"This is your police? Vironese police?"

"Yeah. Only all of a sudden they're working for the Rani, maybe. They don't know, and neither do we."

The warder cleared his throat. "Anyhow, it's all here. Red in the bottle, and here's your tumbler on top. There's pigs' feet, too, in the square dish, and lots of other stuff. Yell if you want anything."

"I sure will," the newcomer told him, and chuckled as the iron door closed behind him. "Keep a sharp eye on me, Peeper. Make sure I don't get out."

"This is good bread," Sciathan said. "Very good. I thank you for it."

"Sure." The newcomer was heaping noodles and brisket onto his plate.

"I wish that I could repay you. I have no means."

The newcomer looked up at him. "You been in clink before?"

"Last night. My arms were chained about a pole, and I was made to sleep upon the ground. There was grass, not as hard as your floor, I am certain."

"Only a lot colder. Had to be. I was pretty warm, even on the floor."

"Cold, yes." Sciathan took another bite of bread; it was soft and white, with a thick brown crust that required chewing.

"I had my mort with me, too, and she kept me warm. You say you ate already?"

It was a moment before Sciathan was able to swallow. "On a horse. A slice of gray meat between bread, bread not as good as this. We had spoken about the Common Tongue, Abanja and I, this language in which you and I converse. She said that my meat was also common tongue, which she thought amusing."

"Wait a minute." The newcomer poured the extra sauce from its small side dish into his plate. "Want me to put you some noodles in here? You'll have to eat 'em with your fingers. We only got the one fork."

"I should not." Sciathan wrestled against temptation. "I must tell you there have been many, many days on which I have eaten less than the gray meat. Always we eat little, and often we do not eat at all." He swallowed again, this time only his own saliva. "But, yes. I would like these noodles very much, and it will not trouble me to eat them with my fingers."

"You got it." The newcomer forked noodles into the sauce dish. "You know, I been wondering why you're so weedy, and I hear the rice is bad in Palustria. You come looking for food?"

"Eating makes one heavy." The concept was so simple and so basic that Sciathan had trouble formulating it. "One no longer flies well. I am a Flier. That is your term."

The newcomer gave him a sceptical look. "They don't never come down, and they're spies anyhow, everybody says."

"I am not a spy. Even Siyuf does not think that."

"Then you better muzzle that clatter about being a Flier. Somebody might believe you." The newcomer passed the sauce dish up to Sciathan. "I put a little bit of smoked turtle on top there for you. They give me a little bit of that, too, smoked turtle and onions. If it makes you too thirsty, we can get Peeper to fetch water."

"I have never eaten this." Sciathan dipped up the brown concoction with two fingers and tasted it. "It is delicious."

"Maybe I ought to try some myself."

"I have spoken of becoming heavy," Sciathan muttered, "but why should I not? My wings will not fly again."

The newcomer peered at him. "You really are a Flier, huh? They go up in the big airship and catch you?"

Sighing, Sciathan shook his head. "We landed to question them. I knew that it would be hazardous." More swiftly than a conjuror's transformation, his wizened face twisted to display a corpse's rictus. "Hello, Auk."

"Hi. You really can do this. Jugs and Patera swore you could, but I guess I didn't believe 'em."

"Do you need help?"

"Nah." Finding the empty stare that had become Sciathan's unsettling, the newcomer returned to his plate. "Tell 'em it's going fine, and I'll give a signal when I know which one." He mopped up sauce with a piece of beef, hoping she would be gone before he finished. "I'll send Peeper to fetch something, too. Be better to get him out of the way."

"So hungry, this tiny man."

The newcomer chewed brisket into submission. "He's got more meat on him than you."

"I'd like some soup. I'll ask Grandmother."

"Do that," the newcomer said.

Sciathan blinked and grabbed, discovering that the sauce dish was about to slide off his lap. He made himself breathe deeply. "This is not expected."

The newcomer nodded without looking up. "What's that?"

"When one flies too high, one grows faint. Now too I felt faintness. Could your food be drugged?"

"No," the newcomer said.

"You spoke to me several times. I replied, but I do not recall what you said, or what I said."

"Doesn't matter."

Sciathan finished his smoked turtle and started in on his noodles. "I have no reason to trust you. You might be a spy."

"Sure."

"I have received good food from you, for which I thank you very much. It is better to be spied upon than beaten."

"You can say that again."

"There is nothing I know that I have not told Siyuf and Abanja. Why am I confined?"

The newcomer lifted the lid of another dish. "You like cheese? He gave me some of that, too."

"I have eaten more than suffices already. I have not even finished the bread you gave."

"Here." The newcomer offered a blue-streaked, whitish lump. "Try some of this with it."

"Thank you. We make good cheese in my home, but I have not eaten any in a long while."

"Now you listen up, Upstairs." The newcomer poured four fingers of brandy into his tumbler. "These Trivigauntis you talk about, Abanja and Siyuf? I never seen either one of 'em. I don't know 'em from dirt, but I know about this place here, and the hot room, and the courts and beaks, and all that. If you want to tell me what you did and what's going on with you, I just might be able to scavy you a couple answers. If you don't want to, dimber here. Only don't ask me stuff I don't know, why I'm confined and that clatter."

"You desire to know my crime. I have done nothing wrong."

"Then if they're keeping you here, it's 'cause they're afraid of what you'd do if you got out. What's that?"

"I would resume my searching for the man called Auk. That is all. They know this."

"You going to chill him when you find him?"

Sciathan leaned over the side of his bunk to look down at the newcomer. "Is this equivalent to *kill*? The softer sound instead of the hard sound at the top of the mouth?"

"Yeah. It's what this holy sibyl that taught us would say was an alternate pronunciation."

"No, I would not chill him. I would tell the masters of the airship above this city that they must take me, with this man Auk and those he chooses, to Mainframe."

"Wait up." The newcomer cleaned his ear with the nail of one forefinger. "To Mainframe? I ain't sure I heard you right. Say it again."

"I am from Mainframe. This is where we live, we Crew. It is our director, it shelters us and we repair it as it directs, when repairs are needed."

"A real place." The newcomer sipped brandy.

"Mainframe is where we live. Viron is where you live."

"If you live there, why are you shaggy flying over here all the time making it rain?"

"Because Mainframe directs it. It is the director of the *Whorl,* not ours alone. If rain did not fall, you Cargo would perish. Or if too much falls. Mainframe has many sources of data. We are one, not the least."

"You want some red?" The newcomer offered his tumbler. "You still feel like fainting, it might be good for you."

"No, thank you."

"All right, what's this about cargo? Like on a boat?"

"You people, the animals, and the plants. It is the same as a boat, yes, because we are in a boat, we as well as you."

"We're the cargo?" Staring up at Sciathan, the newcomer tapped his own chest. "Me, and everybody I know?"

"That is it with precision." Sciathan nodded emphatically. "Abanja and Siyuf also. So you see that I would not chill Auk. It is our duty to preserve the Cargo, not to chill it."

"Mainframe told you to do this?"

"To preserve the Cargo? Yes, always." Sciathan's voice dropped. "It is increasingly difficult. The sun no longer responds well, not even so well as in my father's day. Heat accumulates, another difficulty, because the cooling no longer functions efficiently. Mainframe may be compelled to blow out the sun. Is that how you say it? Interrupt its energy. It has warned us, and we have done what we can to be ready."

The newcomer put down his tumbler. "You're getting me dizzy enough without this." He rose, stepping to the small barred opening in the iron door. "Hey! Peeper!"

"You think that I am deceiving you. You will seek to have me removed."

The newcomer turned to face him. "Cost me two cards to get this pad, and now I scavy you're cank. It's getting too hot, you said. The whole whorl's getting too hot."

Sciathan nodded. "There are other difficulties, but that is worst."

"So you're going to shut off the cooling–"

"No, no! The sun. Until the *Whorl* can be cooled. I will not do this, you must understand. I could not. Mainframe must, if it must be done. It will be a terrible darkness."

" 'Cause the whorl's getting too hot." The newcomer strode to the window. "You take a look out there. That's snow."

"You will not credit me." Sciathan sighed, studying the newcomer's coarse, bearded face for some sign of belief. "I cannot condemn you, but you have fed me and been kind. I would not deceive you. It was difficult to make the winter this year. Mainframe struggled, and we flew many sorties."

"It had to make winter. Mainframe had to make it?" The newcomer pointed to the window. "I always figured winter was just natural."

"Nature is a useful term for processes that one does not understand," Sciathan told him wearily. "Once already the sun has blown out because Mainframe was trying to make this winter. This was not intended."

"Yeah. I heard about that." The newcomer sounded less argumentative. "Then the sun came back, only real bright for a minute. It set fire to some trees and stuff. A cull I know asked Patera about it. Caldé Silk. He said it was another god talking and he knew which one, only he didn't say."

"It was not a god," Sciathan asserted. "It was the sun's restarting. Restarting must be at maximum energy."

"Anyhow, that's not why you're here." The newcomer pulled his tunic over his head, revealing a red wool undershirt that he removed as well. "Mainframe told you to find this cully Auk."

The warder's face appeared in the opening in the door. "What you need?"

"I want you to go to Trotter's for me," the newcomer told him, and handed him two cards. "You tell him any friends of mine that come in, the first one's on me. Have him tell 'em I'll be back real soon, and I'll see 'em at the Cock. You got it? You got to go straight away."

"Sure. You too hot in there?"

"I got a itch is all. You tell Trotter, then maybe I'll have another little job for you."

When the warder had gone, Sciathan began, "Is it known here . . . I do not wish to offend religious sensibilities."

"You won't," the newcomer told him, " 'cause I ain't got any. I got religion, and that's different."

"Is it known that all the gods are Mainframe?" Sciathan awaited an explosion with some anxiety; when it did not come, he added, "Equally is Mainframe all gods. Mainframe in its aspect of darkness, which in this tongue is termed Tartaros, issued my instructions."

After knotting its sleeves around one of the bars, the newcomer pushed his undershirt out the window. "You know, I wish you'd told me that sooner, Upstairs."

He picked up his fork, bending its tines with powerful fingers. "What's your right tag, anyhow?"

"I am Sciathan. And you?"

"I ain't going to tell you, Sciathan. Later I will, only not now, 'cause I scavy it might slow us down. You know where the keyhole is in this door? About where it is, anyhow?"

Sciathan nodded.

"Dimber. Look here. See how I twisted the one funny and bent the other two up out of the way? I want you to stick your arm through the peephole there. I could maybe do it if I was to rub butter on my arm, but you can do it easy. Sort of feel around for the keyhole with your kate, that's the funny-looking one. When you find it, stick your kate in and twist."

Sciathan accepted the fork. "You are saying this will open the door. You cannot know it."

"Sure I do. I seen the key when he was letting me in, and I know how these locks work. I know how everything works soon as I see it, so get cracking. I don't want to keep 'em waiting outside."

Slowly, Sciathan nodded again. "Then you will be free, and I free to pursue my search for Auk, but clothed as I am, and ignorant of the customs of this city."

"We're going to take care of you," the newcomer told him briskly. "Clothes and everything, and we'll teach you how to act, all right? Do it!"

Standing on tiptoe, he was able to thrust his arm through the space between two bars. The strangely bent tine scratched the door for the lock plate, then scratched the lock plate for the keyhole. "I am fearful that I may drop it," he told the newcomer, "but I will try to–" He had felt the bolt retract. "It is unlock!"

"Sure." As Sciathan withdrew his arm, the newcomer pushed the door open. "Come on. There's a couple mort troopers on the outside door already, so we best bing. Wrap that blanket so they can't see your kicks."

He led Sciathan along the corridor and down a stair to a massive iron door. "They ought to of had 'em inside too," he whispered, "only they figured it was all rufflers and upright men, so nothing would happen. It don't matter what's afoot, it gets queered when some cully figures nothing's going to happen."

"I understand this," Sciathan told him; and wanted to add: *Yesterday that was I.*

"Only that's the way I'm figuring too, 'cause I got to. They'll have slug guns out there, and if we beat hoof they'll pot us sure. So we're going to walk easy going out, and just keep going till we're 'cross the street. And maybe nothing will happen. If they holler or say something, don't you stop or even look back at 'em. You got it?"

"I will try. Yes."

"Dimber." The newcomer pressed his ear to the iron door. "Long as you do, you don't have to worry. We'll take care of the rest."

There followed a lengthy silence; at last the newcomer said, "Pretty quiet out there. Get set."

The motion of the door seemed much too quick as Sciathan stepped, half blinded by winter sunlight, through the doorway at the newcomer's side. From the corner of his eye he glimpsed the towering woman whose thick sand-colored greatcoat his blanket brushed.

The wide street was freezing mud, rutted by the wheels of carts and wagons, and almost empty. Snowflakes whirled before his eyes, a few sticking to their lashes.

"You two!" a woman's voice bawled. *"Halt!"*

So fast that it seemed sure to strike them, a black vehicle swooped toward them, roaring like a storm. He was airborne once more, out of control and without wings. For an instant he saw the startled face of a man in black with whom he collided full tilt, after which something huge and heavy struck his back.

A bang—like a slamming door—and the roar mounted to a deafening crescendo. Acceleration pushed him backward into two obstacles he did not at first realize were the shins of the man in black. As though by some mysterious device of Mainframe's, the roar was muffled; above and behind him the newcomer growled, "Just the one shot. Pretty good."

A new voice, that of the man in black, said, "Even one is too many."

And then, as the pale hands of the man in black and the muscular hands of the newcomer lifted him onto a padded seat, "Welcome to Our Holy City of Viron, in the names of its people, its patroness, the Outsider, and all the other gods. I'm sorry we couldn't do this with less violence and more ceremony. Are you hurt? I'm Caldé Silk."

Sciathan wiped his mouth with his fingers, finding to his surprise that it was not bleeding. "I am somewhat bruised, but from blows and not from this escaping. I am Sciathan." Beyond their enchanted tranquility, snow swirled and homely blank-faced buildings raced like camels. He blinked, looking from this pale Cargo to the newcomer and back. "Are we safe?"

"For the time being at least," the pale Cargo called Caldé Silk assured him.

"I am your prisoner, instead of that of the tall women?"

Caldé Silk shook his head. "Of course not. You may come and go as you wish."

The newcomer added, "Anyhow, we like you."

Sciathan smiled; it was very good now to smile, he found. "Then I am free to search again?"

"Yeah," the newcomer told him, "only it ain't going to take you long. I'm Auk."

Chapter 13

MAKING PEACE

"Good man!" Oreb assured everyone at the table.

"This is Sciathan." Silk indicated the tiny man on his left. "Sciathan landed near the Trivigaunti camp on Thelxday, with four of his fellow Fliers—I believe while the parade was still in progress. The Trivigauntis shot three of them and captured him. One escaped."

Potto nodded, his round, cheerful face mirrored in the waxed and polished wood. "And he escaped yesterday with your help. I won't congratulate you on that operation, just on its success. We could have managed it much better."

Halfway down the table, Spider concurred. "Shag, yes!"

"It was hastily improvised," Silk admitted. "We knew only that Sciathan had come to find Auk; we couldn't even guess why he wanted him. Fortunately Generalissimo Oosik was able to get through to the Guardsmen on duty in the Juzgado—"

Loris interrupted. "They've been replaced."

"That's good. I'm glad nothing worse was done to them. On Generalissimo Oosik's instructions, they pretended that they had arrested Auk, and he was able to bribe a turnkey to put him in Sciathan's cell. Quite frankly, we thought it likely that Auk would leave him there after he had talked to him, at least for the time being. We were extremely reluctant to worsen our relations with the Trivigauntis."

Silk scanned the faces beyond Hyacinth's. Maytera Mint looked angry; Bison, beside her, angrier still. Oosik, eager and expectant, a slug gun across his lap; he had wanted both councillors killed, and might conceivably have a subordinate stationed somewhere to kill them.

"If things had gone as we expected," Silk continued, "The rest would have been easy. Auk would have been escorted out by Guardsmen, and Siyuf's sentries would have assumed that he had been questioned and was being released."

Auk himself said, "Only I couldn't. We got to get to Mainframe. That's him and me and everybody that's going with me." He glanced at Quetzal and Remora, seeking support.

Potto smiled more broadly than ever. "I congratulate you again on the outcome. It was all we could wish for and more. Just the same, our enemies retain four propulsion modules, and three undamaged pairs of wings."

Hyacinth said loudly, "You're the enemy!"

Maytera Mint shook her head. "They were the enemy, up to Thelxday night. Now we've been betrayed, and we're no longer sure. I doubt that the Trivigauntis are either. We're all Vironese here, everybody except the Flier. If Councillor Loris is really here to make peace, we ought to welcome it."

She closed her eyes. "I do. Echidna, forgive me!" On the other side of the table, Remora nodded emphatically.

Silk asked, "Have you come to make peace, Councillor Loris? Councillor Potto?"

"Our azoths have been confiscated." Potto giggled. "I was searched! Me! It was absolutely hilarious, but calling this a peace conference is funnier."

"I didn't say it was a peace conference," Maytera Mint snapped, "I implied it could become one. It should, if there's any chance for peace. As for taking your weapons, His Eminence and I went to parlay without any, and you know what you did to us. Because of that, this parley is being held on our ground with us armed and you disarmed. I will insist upon the same arrangements for any future parleys as well."

Loris snarled, "Your troops are melting away as we speak!" to which Potto added, "It was worth it to see your face, my dear young General, when I threatened you with the teapot. I'd do it again, just for that. But you have no right–"

Oosik interrupted him, drawing his needler and holding it up. "Here is one of my weapons. It will kill me, or General Mint, or even Caldé Silk. Do you want it?" He laid it on the polished tabletop between them, and gave it a push that sent it past the middle of the table.

While Silk counted three beatings of his heart, no one spoke. Potto stared at the needler before him, and at last shook his head.

"Then do not complain to us about your weapons," Oosik told him.

Silk rapped for order. "Like you, Generalissimo, I do not believe that Councillor Potto is entitled to complain about the loss of his weapons. We are entitled to complain about the projected loss of ours, however, and I'm not at all sure that Councillor Potto—although he is inclined to be proud of his information—knows about that. Councillor Loris seems to be less than current with regard to General Mint's volunteers."

He addressed Potto directly. "Councillor Loris said they were melting away. Colonel Bison reports that they've melted altogether. We had to hurry it, and hurry it we did. Do you know why?"

Loris said, "He doesn't, but he'll never admit it. I'm not so pigheaded. Why, Caldé?"

Silk nodded to Bison, who said, "Generalissimo Siyuf has ordered the Guard to collect our peoples' slug guns and store them in the Juzgado." Bison leaned forward, his eyes on Loris and his face tense. "It was exactly—exactly!—the right order to split the Guard and our people, and she didn't even try to route it through Generalissimo Oosik. She sent it to the individual officers in command of the brigades."

Potto put in, "Except Brigadier Erne."

"Except for Erne. That's right. We were lucky, in that the brigadiers wanted to clear those orders with Generalissimo Oosik. He countermanded them, naturally. Now we've dispersed our people so that it will be impossible for the Triviguantis to disarm them themselves."

Potto's giggle mounted to a shrill laugh. He slapped his thigh. "You can't use them against us unless you call them up again. And you won't dare call them up because your friends from Trivigaunte will disarm them. You're in a pickle!"

Maytera Mint told him, "Yours is worse."

She glanced at Silk, who told Potto, "We have a strategy, you see—one that you cannot frustrate. The Trivigauntis are preparing to mount a vigorous offensive against you. You know that, I'm sure."

Loris nodded.

"I listened to Generalissimo Siyuf outline her plans last night, and I've been thinking about our options all day. In order to win, all that we have to do now is sit back and let them carry out those plans. She is a rigid disciplinarian, and she's never been down in those tunnels. Furthermore, she's not greatly concerned about the lives of her troops, especially her infantry, which consists largely of conscripts."

Silk leaned back, his fingers joined in a pointed tower. "As I said, all we have to do is to let her do as she plans. There will be a terrible war of attrition, fought underneath the city between foreigners and soldiers most of the men and women who live in it have scarcely seen. In the end, one side or the other will triumph, and it won't make much difference which it is, since the winner will be too weak to resist General Mint's horde when we reassemble it. Either way, we'll be masters of the city. And either way, you will both be dead."

Potto sneered. Loris said smoothly, "A few minutes ago somebody was saying we're all Vironese here, with a single exception. Was it you, General? You, whose troops are to complete the destruction once Viron's army has defeated the Trivigauntis for you?"

"Yes," she told him. "It was."

Silk said, "There are at least three major objections to the strategy I have just outlined, Councillor, though I do not doubt that it would succeed—that it will, if we choose to employ it. You've voiced the first yourself: it entails the destruction of Viron's army. The second is that it will take at least half a year, and very possibly several years; either would be too long, as we'll explain in a moment. The third is that there is one part of Siyuf's force that we must have, and it is exactly the part that would almost certainly escape us. I refer to General Saba's airship.

"Sciathan, will you please tell these councillors what you told me?"

The Flier nodded, his small, pinched face solemn. "We of Mainframe, we Crew, were visited by the god you call Tartaros. It was the morning of the day on which I was captured."

Auk put in, "Right after he left me, see?"

"His instructions were urgent. We were to find this man Auk," Sciathan pointed, "and bring him and his followers to Mainframe, so that they can leave the *Whorl* to journey to a short-sun sphere outside." Sciathan turned to Silk. "They do not believe me."

"They need only believe that I believe you," Silk told him, "as I do. Continue."

"This very wise man Caldé Silk has spoken to you of the airship, the great vessel that flies without wings, stirring the air with wooden arms. The god also spoke to us of this airship. We were to employ it to carry back this man who is my friend now, and those who wish to accompany him."

Profound conviction lent intensity to Sciathan's voice. "It cannot be accomplished otherwise. No, not though a god should demand it. He cannot fly as we do, nor can the others who wish to accompany him. For them to walk or ride animals would consume many months. There are mountains and deserts, and many swift rivers."

"We'd need enough bucks with slug guns and launchers to fight our way past anybody that tried to stop us," Auk added. "We ain't got them." Seeing Chenille enter with a tray, he inquired, "What you got there, Jugs? Tea and cookies?"

She nodded, "Maytera thought you might like something. She's busy with Stony and Patera, so Nettle and I baked."

"There is too much eating here," Sciathan protested in a whisper, "also, too much drinking. Behold that one." He indicated Potto with a nod.

"I agree," Silk said, accepting a cup of tea, "but we must consider hospitality."

"In short," Loris was saying, "you want us to help you take over the airship. I won't argue about your reason for wanting it, though I might if I thought we could do it. I doubt that we can."

Potto rocked from side to side, bubbling with mirth. "I might. Yes, I might! Silk, I'll make you an offer on behalf of my cousins and myself, but you'll have to trust me."

Maytera Mint shook her head, but Silk told her, "This is progress, whether we accept it or not. Let's hear it."

"I'll seize the airship for you within a month, capturing as many of the technicians who operate it as possible. I'll turn them over to you after they've agreed to cooperate with you in every way." He tittered. "They will, I promise you, when I've had them for a few days. Ask the general there."

He turned to Chenille, who was serving Remora. "May I have a cup of your tea, my dear? I can't drink it, but I like the smell."

Maytera Mint snorted.

"I do, my dear young General. You think I'm mocking you, when I'm simply indulging the only pleasure of the flesh left to me." As Chenille poured, he added, "Thank you very, very much. Five bits? Would that be acceptable?"

Chenille stared. "Is this . . . I don't—"

Silk said, "Councillor Potto is merely using you to make a point, Chenille. He prefers to make his points in the most objectionable way possible, as General Mint and I can testify. What is it, Councillor?"

"That even trivial things are seldom free." Potto smiled. "That there is a price to pay, even when it's a trivial price. Want to hear mine for the airship?"

Silk nodded, feeling Hyacinth's hand tighten about his.

Loris said, "I've no idea what he has in mind, but I'm going to attach one of my own first. You're to do nothing to interfere with us during the month specified. No attacks on any position of ours, including Erne's."

Silk said, "We wouldn't, of course—if we accepted. But it's your cousin's price that concerns me."

"Two men." Potto held up two fingers. "I want to borrow one and keep the other. Can't you guess which they are?"

"I believe so. Perhaps I should have made it clear that I haven't the least intention of accepting. Even if you had offered to do it for nothing, as a gesture of goodwill, I still could not have accepted."

Auk started to protest, but Silk cut him off. "Let me say this once and for all, not just to you, Auk, and not just to these councillors; but to everyone present. Trivigaunte is our ally. There has been friction between us, true. I daresay that there is always friction in every alliance, even the small and simple alliance of husband with wife."

Hyacinth's lips brushed his cheek.

"I did not ask the Rani to send us help, but I welcomed it with open arms when she did. I have no intention of turning against her and her people now, because of a little friction. Maytera Marble often tells me things she's learned from watching children's games, and I received the greatest lesson of my life during one such game; now I want to propose a game for us. Let us pretend for a few minutes that I'm Generalissimo Siyuf. Will all of you accept that, for the sake of the game?"

His eyes went from face to face. "Very well, I am Siyuf. I understand that some of you are nursing grievances in spite of my long and swift march to your rescue, and in spite of the aid I brought you. Let me hear them now. There is not one I cannot dispose of."

Loris said, "I hope you're not so deep in your part as to shoot me."

Silk smiled and shook his head.

"Very well then, Generalissimo Siyuf. I have a complaint, exactly as you said. I'm speaking as the presiding officer of the Ayuntamiento, the legitimate government of this city. You and your troops are interfering in our internal affairs. That is an act of war."

Silk heaved a sigh, and his gaze strayed to Chenille, who was pouring tea for Maytera Mint. "Councillor, your government was never legitimate, because it was established by murdering your lawful caldé. I can't say which of you ordered his murder, or whether you acted jointly. For the purposes of discussion, let's assume it was Councillor Lemur, and that he acted alone. You nevertheless—"

"I didn't intend to get into this," Loris protested. His craggy face was grim.

"You introduced the subject yourself when you referred to yours as the legitimate government, Councillor. I was about to say that though you searched for the adopted son Caldé Tussah had named as his successor, as your duty required, you did not hold elections for new councillors, as your Charter demands. My ally Caldé Silk governs because the people of your city wish it, and so his claim is better than yours. Aid given by a friendly power is not an act of war. How could it be? Are you saying that we of Trivigaunte attacked your city? It welcomed us with a parade."

Silk waited for a response; when none came, he said, "You have already heard that I know the contents of your previous caldé's will. I found a copy in your Juzgado. Let me say, too, that in my opinion the adopted son you searched for with so much diligence did not exist. Caldé Tussah invented this son to draw your attention from another child, an illegitimate child who may or may not have been born before his death. If she had already been born, referring to an adopted *son* was doubly misleading, as he doubtless intended it to be." Silk sipped his tea. "Don't go, Chenille."

Potto sprang to his feet. "You!"

"Did you kill my father, Councillor?" Chenille's dark eyes flashed. "The real one? I don't know, but I don't think it was really Councillor Lemur. I think it was you!"

Oosik raised his slug gun, telling Potto to sit down.

"If you did and evidence can be found," Silk continued, "you will have to stand trial. So far we have none."

"Are you Silk or Siyuf?" Potto demanded.

"Silk at present. I'll resume the game in a moment. Your Cognizance, will you speak? I ask it as a favor." Upon Silk's shoulder, Oreb fluttered uneasily.

"If you want me to, Patera Caldé." Quetzal's glittering gaze was fixed on Potto. "Not many of us knew Tussah. Patera Remora did, and Loris. Did you, Generalissimo?"

Oosik shook his head. "Twenty years ago I was a captain. I saw him several times, but I doubt that he knew my name."

"He knew mine, eh?" Remora cleared his throat. "I had, er, was coadjutor in those—um—happier days. Ah—mother still living, eh, General? It, um, sufficient in itself, hey? Though there were other favorable circumstances."

Chenille, who had stopped pouring tea, murmured, "I wish I knew more about him."

"I, um, disliked him, I confess," Remora told her. "Not hatred, you understand. And there were times, eh? But I was, er, substantially alone in it. Wrong, too, eh? Wrong. I, um, concede it now. Loud, brawling, vigorous, and I was—um—determined, quite determined secretly, to be offended. But he, er, put the city first. Always did, and I—ah—accorded insufficient weight to it."

"He wouldn't flatter my then coadjutor, Patera Caldé," Quetzal explained. "He flattered me, however. He flattered me by confiding in me. He never married. Are you both aware of that?"

Silk and Chenille nodded.

"Clergy take a vow of chastity. Even with its support, chastity is too severe for many. He confided to me, as one friend to another, that his housekeeper was his mistress."

"Not—ah—under the Seal, eh?"

Quetzal's hairless head swayed on its long neck. "I don't and won't speak of shriving, though I shrove him once or twice. This was at dinner, one at which only he and I were present. If he were alive I wouldn't speak of it. He's dead and can't speak for himself. He introduced the woman to me. He asked me to take care of her should he die."

Chenille said, "If that was my mother, you didn't."

"I did not. I couldn't find her. Though she was good-looking in her way, she was an ignorant woman of the servant class. I know she disliked me, and I think she was afraid of me. She was guilty of adultery weekly, and unable to imagine forgiveness for it."

Silk said, "You searched for her as soon as you heard Caldé Tussah was dead?"

"I did, Patera Caldé. Not as thoroughly as I should, since she was alive and I failed to find her."

Loris said, "I remember her now. The gardener's wife. She oversaw the kitchen and the laundry. A virago."

Quetzal nodded frigidly. "She was the type he admired, and he was the type she did."

Auk began, "This gardener cully—"

"A marriage of convenience, performed by my prothonotary in five minutes. There would have been talk if Tussah had a single woman in this palace. His gardener wasn't intelligent, though a good man and a hard worker. He was proud to be seen as married, as a man who'd won the love of an attractive woman. I imagine she dominated him completely. I thought they would look for new employment when Tussah died, and I planned to make places for them on our staff. They didn't. I know now, thanks to Patera Caldé, that they became beggars. At the time I assumed they'd known something about Tussah's death, and had been silenced."

Chenille said, "We sold watercress. But if somebody wanted to give us money, we took it. I used to ask for money, too, and run errands. Do little jobs." She swallowed. "After a while I found out there were things men would give me half a card for. It was a fortune to us, enough food for a week." She stared at her listeners, challenging them.

Loris smiled. "Blood will tell, they say."

"Blood won't," Silk declared. "Blood's dead—I killed him. But if Blood were alive, he might tell you that it was good business to give rust, at first, to the young women at Orchid's, and to sell it to them afterward—to keep them in constant need of money, and thus keep them there for as long as he and Orchid let them stay. The Ayuntamiento let him bring rust and other drugs into our city, in return for what I must call criminal services."

Hyacinth said, "I use it sometimes, and I've been telling myself that if Chen can kick it so can I, and I hope it's true. But it's hard, don't ever believe anybody who says it's not."

Quetzal gave Loris a lipless smile. "Blood does tell, my son."

"Watch out!" Oreb advised; it was not clear to which he spoke.

Maytera Mint asked, "Do you know why they didn't try to find another situation, Caldé?"

"I don't; but I believe I can guess. Chenille's mother had recently given birth to the caldé's child, or if she had not, she was carrying that child—and it was her child, too. She must have guessed, or known, that the caldé had been murdered. At that time, the Ayuntamiento was searching everywhere for the adopted son mentioned in the caldé's will; and she would have supposed, as I believe most people did, that it would kill him if it found him. She needn't have been an educated woman, or an imaginative one, to guess what would happen to another child of the caldé's, if it learned that she existed."

Silk filled his lungs, feeling a twinge from his wounded chest. "We've gotten far off the subject, but since we're here, let's finish what we've begun. Caldé Tussah left a substantial estate. I have it now as trustee for his daughter; I'll turn it over to Chenille as soon as she reaches twenty, the legal age of maturity."

"Good girl!" Oreb assured everyone.

Loris told Silk, "That will have to be adjudicated by the courts, I'm afraid."

He shook his head. "Our government is sorely in need of funds, Councillor. We have a war to prosecute, in addition to all the usual civic expenses; and we gave each of General Mint's troopers two cards, as well as his or her weapon, before we sent them home."

Loris said, "You're generous with the taxpayers' money."

"In order to do it, we've taken control of the Fisc; the city assumes responsibility for inactive accounts, and for the accounts in trust, such as Caldé Tussah's. We've sequestered the accounts of the members of the Ayuntamiento, as you know. Do you want to talk about it now?"

Sciathan said, "We must speak more of the airship. It is urgent. This Potto says he will get it, but in one month. We have a few days at most. Not more."

"Why?" Hyacinth asked him, speaking across Silk.

Auk told him, "Let 'em jaw about the money first. If you don't, they'll keep going back to it."

"Wise man!" Oreb exclaimed.

Silk rapped the table. "Which will it be, the airship or your accounts? Personally I'd prefer to deal with Generalissimo Oosik's complaints against Generalissimo Siyuf, and General Mint and Colonel Bison's. It's usually best, I've found, to consider minor matters first and get them out of the way. Otherwise they cloud everyone's thinking, as Auk says."

"We knew you'd stolen our money," Loris told him, "but we also knew it would be useless to protest the theft."

Maytera Mint declared, "You want to make peace after all."

"Hardly. But we're prepared to offer you new terms of surrender, much more liberal terms than those I proposed at Blood's, which were intended merely as an opening point for negotiations."

"You said at the time that they were not negotiable," Silk reminded him.

"Certainly. One always does. You were willing to listen to Potto's proposal. Will you hear ours as well? Our joint proposal?"

"Of course."

"Then let me first explain why you should accept it. You assert that you have a strategy that will assure your victory, though you are loath to follow it. You are mistaken, but we are not. We have a strategy of our own, one that will assure your defeat in under a year."

Oosik said, "Clearly you do not, or you would follow it," and Silk nodded.

"You have been assisting us with it," Loris continued, smiling, "for which we are appropriately grateful."

Potto grinned. "We're giving away slug guns too!"

"We are," Loris confirmed, "and other weapons as well, needlers mostly. We still have access to several stores of weapons. I hope you will excuse my keeping their locations confidential."

"Giving them to who?" Bison inquired.

"In a moment. Some preparation is necessary. You were underground not long ago, Colonel. The tunnels are extensive, are you aware of it? You saw not a thousandth part of them."

"I've been told the caldé went into them from a shrine by the lake, and that General Mint went in from a house north of the city and came out on the Palatine. If those she saw and those he saw belong to the same complex, it's pretty large."

Maytera Mint told him, "Much larger than that, according to what I've learned from Spider."

"I want him," Potto put in. "I want him and the Flier. I offered the airship and you refused it. Name your price."

Silk sighed. "I said that trivial points tend to obscure discussions. This is just such a point, so let's dispose of it. Spider is our prisoner. We will exchange him for one of equal value, during this truce or another. Have you a prisoner to offer us? Who is it?"

Potto shook his head. "I will have, soon. Give him back, and you'll get double value as soon as I have it."

"No!" Maytera Mint struck the table with her small fist, and Hyacinth's catachrest thrust his furry little head above the tabletop, saying, "Done bay saw made, laddie."

"Of course not," Silk told Potto, "but may I propose an alternative I believe workable?"

"Let's hear it."

"In a moment. You also want Sciathan."

"Only temporarily." Potto giggled. "I'll pay you a fine for every day I keep him over a fortnight, how's that? Like a library book. I still have a lot more money than you stole."

Auk declared, "I heard about you from Maytera, and you ain't taking him."

"Auk speaks for me as well," Silk said, "and for all of us. Sciathan is a free individual—"

"A free *man,*" Loris amended.

"Precisely. He is not mine to give or keep. He is here in this palace as my guest, and nothing more—nothing less, I ought to say. If you believe he's under restraint, ask him."

Remora tossed back his lank black hair. " 'Sacred unto Pas are the life and property of the stranger you welcome.' "

"Furthermore, he would disappoint you. He's been beaten and interrogated already by Generalissimo Siyuf, who hoped to learn how the Fliers' propulsion modules operate. Councillor Lemur killed Iolar, who was another Flier, for the same reason; I shrove Iolar before he died. Since Lemur himself died soon after, you may not be aware of it. Are you?"

Loris shrugged. "We were aware of his capture, of course. What Lemur learned from him died with Lemur, unfortunately."

"Lemur learned nothing from him; that was why Lemur killed him. I discussed the propulsion modules with Sciathan today. He freely conceded that their principle is important; that it would be valuable to our city or any other is obvious; but he doesn't have it, and neither did Iolar.

"The scientists who make them remain in Mainframe, safe from capture. The Fliers who use them are kept ignorant of the principle, for reasons they understand and approve. It's an elementary precaution, one that you and your fellow councillors ought to have anticipated. It would have been anticipated, surely, by anyone not blinded by the itch for power. If you want to find out how they operate, you might capture one of those the Trivigauntis have and take it apart; but I doubt that I could tell leaf from root."

"Naturally you couldn't." Potto giggled. "Have you got one? Name your price for Spider. A hundred cards? I want to hear it, and the price of the propulsion module, too, if you've got one."

"We don't. Councillor Loris, Councillor Lemur told me that he was a bio, not a chem. Are you?"

"Certainly."

"Despite the marble bookend you crushed at Blood's?"

"This is not my natural body. Physically, I'm on our boat, well out of your reach. This body," Loris touched his black velvet tunic, "is a chem, if you like. To simplify matters, I won't object to your calling it that. I manipulate it from my bed, making it move and speak as I did when I was younger."

Maytera Mint told Silk, "I explained all this, I think."

"Yes, you did, Maytera; I'm very grateful. Spider should be grateful as well."

"If it gets me loose," Spider grunted.

"It very well may. From what General Mint has reported, counterintelligence has been your chief concern. I'm not so naïve as to think that your organization—what remains of it—could not be put to other uses, however; and I noticed that Councillor Potto wanted you back when he was planning to seize control of General Saba's airship."

Potto said, "I do anyhow. He's valuable to us."

"Clearly. Primarily in frustrating spies?"

Loris said, "Primarily, yes."

"Spider, General Mint says you're a decent man, a patriot in your way. If I were to release you to Councillor Potto, as you wish, would you be willing to give me your solemn promise that in so far as our forces are concerned, you would confine your activities entirely to counterintelligence? By 'our forces' I intend those headed by Generalissimo Oosik and Auk—not only the Guard, but General Mint's volunteers, including those commanded by her through Colonel Bison."

Spider licked his lips. "If Councillor Potto don't tell me I can't, yeah, I will."

Potto raised a hand. "Wait. I think I heard something funny. Does your friend Auk have a private horde now?"

Auk grinned. "The best thieves in the whole city, the ones that's going with me and Sciathan. A month for the airship, you said. I figure we might nab it a whole lot sooner."

Sciathan stood up. "We must! If the Cargo will not leave the *Whorl,* Pas will drive everyone out as one drives a bear from a cave. He will starve and afflict Crew and Cargo until we go."

Loris's icy blue eyes twinkled. "A rain of blood. The Chrasmologic Writings speak of such things, I'm told."

Remora nodded solemnly. "Ah—worse, Councillor. Plagues, hey? Famine, er, likewise."

"Listen to me!" Sciathan's excited tenor cracked. "If a landing craft leaves, even one, Pas will wait for more. But if none leave, everyone will be driven out. Do you understand now? We Crew have a craft ready, but so much Crew cannot be spared so early in the Plan. For this reason Tartaros has readied Auk for us, and we must have them!"

"Me and my knot," Auk explicated.

Chenille added, "That's me. I hope you don't mind that I stayed to listen, Patera. But when Auk goes, I go too."

"With my blessing," Potto chortled. "Oh, yes! Very much so. I'll be delighted to lose my accuser, and have the enemy lose its airship."

He turned to Silk. "Will Spider be free to act in any way we choose against your cherished allies? That's what it sounded like. You didn't expect me to miss that, did you?"

"No." Silk's expression was guarded. "But if you had, I would have mentioned it to him. You may not be aware of it, but Maytera Mint left the tunnels with two other prisoners. One was a convict named Eland. Eland was murdered yesterday morning in the Grand Manteion."

"A mystery!" Potto clapped his pudgy hands like a happy child. "I love them!"

"I don't. I try to clear them up when I can, and I've been trying to clear up this one. My first thought was that this man Eland had been killed by some old enemy, most plausibly someone who had attended the sacrifice there the previous night and had seen him. I asked Auk to find out who that enemy might be, and had one of General Skate's officers inquire as well."

Silk shifted his attention from Potto to Spider. "The harder they looked, the less probable it appeared. Eland had not been a thief, as I had assumed, but a horse trainer who had killed his employer in a fit of rage. Presumably there was some public sympathy for him, since he was not executed. Auk could find nobody who knew of anyone who bore him a murderous grudge."

Maytera Mint asked, "Did you consider Urus, Caldé?"

"We did, but we quickly dismissed him. Eland had been a useful subordinate in the tunnels, where Urus would have had any number of opportunities to kill him in complete safety. Why wait? Why run the risk of being shot by Acting Corporal Slate, as the killer very nearly was? Besides, I've gotten a sketchy description of the killer, and if it's even roughly correct, he was neither dirty nor dressed in rags. I'll tell you later how I obtained it."

"Got to protect his sources," Spider explained. "That's how it is, Maytera."

"Most of Eland's friends and relatives had assumed he was dead long ago," Silk continued, "yet someone with a needler had quite deliberately climbed into the choir of the Grand Manteion to shoot him. Why? After I'd turned over the question for an hour or two, it occurred to me that someone might have made a mistake—that he might have intended to shoot another person entirely, and mistaken Eland for that person. Chenille here was able to tell me in considerable detail how everyone present had been dressed, and Auk and Spider appeared to be the only possibilities."

Eyeing Spider, Oreb whistled.

"There were a number of sibyls present. All wore habits, and could be dismissed at once. So could Patera Incus and the body of Patera Jerboa—both were robed in black, as I am. No one could mistake a man for Chenille, and so on. If an error had been made, the intended victim was clearly Auk or Spider."

Auk said, "I don't think he was shooting at me."

"Neither do I," Silk told him. "You were near the altar, and thus somewhat nearer the killer. Furthermore, you were in a relatively well lit area. Spider and Eland were in a chapel behind the sanctuary, a more distant area as well as a more dimly lit one. I would guess that the killer had been given a verbal discription of Spider, and had been told that he was being guarded by soldiers."

Silk turned back to Spider. "Were you and Eland awake when he was shot?"

Spider nodded.

"Were you standing up?"

Spider shook his head. "We were sittin' on the floor. That soldier wouldn't let us get up unless we had a reason."

"There you have it." Silk shrugged. "At least, you have as much as I do. Sitting would tend to conceal the difference in size. Slate was guarding both of you, and from what I've heard, neither of you had been given an opportunity to wash and change clothes, as General Mint and Patera Remora did. In the dim light of the chapel, the killer may not have seen you at all. Or he may simply have felt that Eland corresponded more closely to the description he had been given.

"The question then became, who would want to kill Spider? Plausibly, the Ayuntamiento or the Trivigauntis. The first because he knows a great deal about its espionage and counterespionage activities, and about the tunnels under the city, information that he might pass on to Generalissimo Oosik, to General Mint, or to me."

"I'd know about it. I'd have ordered it." Potto giggled. "I didn't."

Silk nodded. "And you could easily have found an assassin who knows Spider by sight, I would think. The Trivigauntis are our allies— but they are Spider's enemies, and he is said to know a great deal about their spies in Viron." He fell silent.

Maytera Mint said, "You can't be sure this is true."

"No, I can't; but I believe it very well may be. We stole a prisoner from Generalissimo Siyuf. Is it absurd to suppose that she might try to kill one we had? Since that may have been the case, it would be manifestly unjust to limit Spider's activities with regard to Siyuf and her horde."

"They went after me, so I can go after them," Spider said.

"Exactly."

Hyacinth touched Silk's arm. "I don't understand. Are we for them or against them?"

Maytera Mint was staring at Silk. "I feel this is almost ancient history, but before all this started—before poor Maytera Rose passed on, I felt that I understood you, just as I felt I understood myself. In the past ten days or so you've become somebody else, somebody I don't understand at all, and so have I. You're married now, I witnessed the ceremony, and I'm thinking about marrying too."

A change in her expression told Silk that Bison's hand had found hers.

After a moment of silence she added, "You've lost your faith, or most of it, I think. What's happened to us?"

Potto laughed loudly.

Quetzal, seated between Oosik and Loris at the other end of the table, murmured, "Circumstances have changed, Maytera. That's all, or nearly all. There is an essential core at the center of each man and woman that remains unaltered no matter how life's externals may be transformed or recombined. But it's smaller than we think."

Silk nodded his agreement.

"If I—ah—permitted." Remora pushed back the errant lock of lank, black hair. "The General and I were companions in, um, adversity. The—ah—spirit. The inalterable core, as His Cognizance has, um, finely. The spirit that survives even death. It grows when trod upon, like the dandelion. I have learned it, eh? So may you, if you—um—reflect."

He stared down at his long, bony hands. "Wouldn't have killed Spider, hey? In those tunnels? Would've, er, failed. But I wish now I had tried, or very nearly. And here, eh? No longer coadjutor. Got my own manteion, hey? After all these years. Moved in today."

He spoke to Silk. "I, er, necessary that I talk to you about it, eh, Caldé? Sun Street. Accounts and so on. When we're, um, we've adjourned."

Silk managed to say, "Gladly, Patera."

"Stripped of, er, power. That's the expression. Smaller, outside, growing, inside. I—ah—feel it." He held up the gammadion he wore; it was of plain iron.

As much to cover his embarrassment as her own, Maytera Mint asked Silk, "You said everything Siyuf's done since her horde arrived could be defended, and she's our ally, and yet you're letting Spider go? Free to attack her and the rest of the Trivigauntis in any way Potto chooses?"

Potto rocked with merriment. "Be her again, Silk, and you can shoot yourself."

He shook his head. "I'm not being asked to defend Siyuf's actions now, but my own. I have changed, I suppose, General, as you say; but I don't think I've changed as much as you may imagine. The faith I had, I had learned as one learns other lessons—from reading and lectures and my mother's example and conversation. I'm in the process, I believe, of replacing it with new faith gained from experience—from circumstances, as His Eminence says. You have to wreck the old structure, or so it seems to me, before you can build the new one; otherwise, it's always getting in the way."

He held out his hand to Hyacinth, who took it.

"We're married, as you say. I don't believe my mother ever was. Did I tell you that?"

Maytera Mint shook her head.

"I told Maytera Marble, I'm sure. I know now, or think I know, how—how I came to be, as a result of something that happened to me in the tunnels, or at least underground. You don't understand me, I know."

"Certainly I do! You don't have to talk about that, Caldé, or anything. But I certainly wasn't asking about that."

Silk shook his head. "You don't, you merely suppose you do. Councillor Potto, here's a mystery for you. Can you solve it? I've lied about it once already tonight, I warn you; and I'll lie again if I must."

Maytera Mint objected, "You don't tell lies, Patera."

Silk shook his head. "We all do when we must. When we're asked about something we heard in shriving, for example. We say we don't know. This is something I have to lie about, at least until it no longer matters, simply because everyone would think I lied if I told the truth."

Maytera Marble's voice surprised him. "Not I, Patera."

He turned in his chair to look at her.

"Chenille brought in tea and cookies, the ones she and Nettle baked, and she never came back. Horn seems to have disappeared, too. I thought something might be wrong."

"A great many things are, Moly," Silk told her, "but we're trying to set a few right. Do you remember what I told you about my enlightenment? I saw Patera Pike praying, praying so very hard year after year for help for his manteion, remember?"

She nodded.

"Until the Outsider spoke in his heart, telling him his prayer was granted. When I had seen that, I waited, waited full of expectation, to see what help would be sent to him."

Maytera Marble nodded. "I remember, Patera."

"It arrived, and it was me. That was all it was. Me. Laugh, Councillor."

Potto did not oblige.

"But for a moment, ever so briefly, I saw myself as Patera Pike had seen me then. It was a humbling experience. Better, it was a salutary one. I'm emboldened by the memory now, when I find myself having to reckon with councillors and generalissimos, people whose company is alien to me, and whose opposition I find terrifying."

Maytera Marble nodded, "As they find yours, Patera."

"I doubt it." Shaking his head, Silk addressed Loris. "We're prepared to offer you a very good bargain, Councillor—an exceptional one. Spider has promised he'll confine himself to counterespionage as regards our forces if we will release him. We ask no oath on the Writings, no ceremony of that kind; a man's word is good or it isn't, and General Mint has indicated that his is. In exchange, we ask only your present self. I emphasize *present*—the Councillor Loris here with us. You can divert your consciousness to another such body as soon as we're through conferring, and I assume that you will; it won't be a violation of our bargain. Do you agree to the exchange?"

"No," Loris said. "I have no second body available."

Potto exclaimed, "I will!"

"I'm afraid not, Councillor. When you have a prisoner of similar importance, an exchange can be effected. Until then, Spider must remain with us. Councillor Loris, are you certain you won't reconsider?"

Loris shook his head—then stared at Remora, who was seated to Potto's right.

Quetzal murmured, "He has these fits occasionally, poor fellow. I think Patera Caldé witnessed one last week."

"I did, shortly before my bride and I were reunited at Ermine's."
Longing to embrace her, Silk tore his gaze from Hyacinth's.

"They're coming, Silk." Remora announced in a flattened voice. "A
colonel and a hundred cavalry troopers."

Oreb whistled sharply.

"Thank you. Auk, I'm afraid this means we have very little time.
You and Sciathan must leave at once by a side door. Your followers are
meeting at the Cock? Warn them that Trivigaunti patrols may search for
them. Chenille had better go with you; otherwise they're liable to take
her to get you."

Loris stood. "We'd better leave, too."

"Not with us," Auk snapped. "Out the front, if you're going.
C'mon, Upstairs. C'mon, Jugs."

Potto rose, giggling. "He doesn't share Silk's love for you, Cousin
Loris."

Silk motioned for both to sit again. "You have come under a flag of
truce. They'll respect that, surely."

"So did we," Maytera Mint told him.

He ignored it. "You and Colonel Bison are affronted now because
Generalissimo Siyuf wished to confiscate the weapons you gave your
troopers. If she were here, she might explain that she acted in support of
our government, the one opposed to the Ayuntamiento that Echidna
ordered you to establish and that you have established. She probably
feels sure, as General Saba and Chenille did Thelxday night, that once
freed of the restraint of discipline your troopers will use their weapons to
overturn it. Remember that, when we talk to these Trivigauntis."

Silk addressed Oosik. "You, Generalissimo, are piqued because
Generalissimo Siyuf bypassed you and Skate, issuing orders to the commanders of the brigades."

Oosik nodded, his face grim.

"Bear in mind that when she tried to collect those weapons she was
doing what you would have, had you not been restrained by my orders;
and that she's shown clearly that she thinks it useless to try to suborn
your loyalty."

"I–er, um?" Remora gaped at Quetzal's vacated chair.

"His Cognizance has left us," Silk explained. "I suppose he went
with Auk. You dozed off for a moment, I believe.

"Councillor Loris, Councillor Potto, you said you'd come to

demand my surrender, with new terms. Let's not trouble about the terms now. Explain briefly, if you will, how you know that we and our allies will be defeated."

Loris nodded. "Briefly, as you ask. Siyuf's been sending patrols into the countryside to forage for food. They take whatever our people have and leave promissory notes in which our people have no confidence. Notes that are almost certainly valueless, in fact. Our farmers have begun hiding what food they have and organizing bands to resist—"

Oosik interrupted him. "You gave your permission, Caldé, at the parade. I was thunderstruck."

Hyacinth said, "You think you're terribly clever, don't you, Oosie. What would you have done?"

Oosik started to speak, but thought better of it.

"He would have told Generalissimo Siyuf that she'd have to buy what our farmers brought her—or so I imagine." Silk shrugged. "They wouldn't have brought enough, or nearly enough, and they wouldn't have accepted promises to pay later. Soon she would have had to send out patrols, as she's doing now, or shut her eyes to the fact that unit commanders were foraging for themselves. In either case, we would have had to stop them, or anyway we would have had to try. Within a short time we'd have been fighting Trivigauntis in the streets. I hoped to prevent that, or at least postpone it; but I'm afraid that I gained very little time for us, and it may be that I gained none at all."

"We could have sent out foraging parties of our own," Bison suggested.

Maytera Mint shook her head. "Then the farmers would have hated us instead of them. If they must hate somebody, it's far better that they hate Siyuf and her Trivigauntis."

"The point," Loris interposed, "is that they're beginning to resist. You've helped them, and we're helping them more."

Potto grinned at Silk. "Cementing their loyalty to us, you see. We're the government of the good old days, coming up out of the ground with armloads of slug guns, and giving them away." He tittered. "We get food aplenty for our bios. It's mostly chems with us down below, and they don't need it."

"We estimate that fifteen thousand of General Mint's fifty thousand odd were countryfolk," Loris continued. "They're armed now, thanks to you. We've armed another four thousand thus far, and we continue to distribute arms. This sibyl—"

"I'm a laywoman again," Maytera Marble told him.

"This officious laywoman once boasted that though others might be tempted to lie, her figures were accurate. So are mine. Inside of three months, Siyuf will be unable to feed her troops, to say nothing of her horses, mules, and camels. Having no alternative, she'll return to Trivi-gaunte. By then half the city will have abandoned your rebellion. We came to inform you of that, and demand that you restore our personal accounts."

"And keep your hands off the Fisc," Potto subjoined.

"That will be guaranteed by their surrender." Loris looked around the table, a councillor so rich in wisdom and experience that even Maytera Mint was inclined to accept everything that he said. "Would you care to hear our terms?"

"No." Silk paused, listening to the sounds of hurrying feet in the foyer. "We haven't time. I accept. We surrender. We can discuss terms when we have more leisure. That was why I hoped you'd remain, Councillor. It would have facilitated—"

At that moment Horn burst into the room. "They're coming, Caldé, like you said. A couple of hundred, some on horses."

"Thank you, Horn." Silk smiled sadly. "They'll knock, I believe—at least I hope they will. If they do, delay them as long as you can, please."

Potto was on his feet again. "We accept your surrender. Let's go, Cousin!"

Maytera Marble stepped into their path. "Let me remind you of what I told you at my son's. Caldé Silk's surrender is valid and binds everyone. Patera Silk's means nothing at all. Do you accept him as Caldé? For life?"

The door to the kitchen flew open then, and Hossaan strode in with a needler in each hand; behind him came a dozen women brandishing slug guns. "That life may be short," he told Silk. "It will be, unless you get your hands up. The rest of you, too."

One by one Hyacinth, Silk, Remora, Potto, Spider, and Horn complied, Maytera Marble and Bison raising their hands last, and together. Silk said, "You realize, I hope, that this is fundamentally a misunder-standing, a falling out among friends. It can be smoothed over, and soon will be."

"Spread out," Hossaan told the women who had entered with him. "Each cover a prisoner." He smiled at Silk, a smile that did not reach his hooded eyes. "I hope you're right, Caldé. On the personal level, I like you and your wife. I'm carrying out Colonel Abanja's—"

The crack of a needler cut him off. Ragged fire from the slug guns ended in a choking cloud of plaster dust and an ear-splitting roar as most of the west wall fell, severed from its foundations by the azoth Silk had received from Doctor Crane and given to Maytera Mint.

Chapter 14

The Best Thieves in the Whorl

"Patera?" Horn inquired softly. "Caldé?"

Silk sat up. "What is it?"

"Nettle's asleep. Just about everybody is, but I knew you weren't. I could see your eyes."

Silk nodded, the motion almost invisible in the darkness of the freezing tent. "You're right, I wasn't; and you're afraid, as we all are, and want reassurance. I'll reassure you as much as I can, though that isn't very much."

"I have some questions, too."

Silk smiled, his teeth flashing in the gloom. "So do I, but you can't answer mine. I may be able to answer a few of yours. I'll try."

Nettle whispered, "I'm not asleep. Horn thought I was, but I was pretending so he'd sleep." Horn took her hand as she said, "I've got a question too."

"Reassurance first," Silk told them. "You may need it more than you realize. It's quite unlikely that Generalissimo Siyuf will have you executed or even imprisoned. Hossaan—that's Willet's real name, he's a Trivigaunti—knows that you and Horn were at the palace to help Moly. Besides, you're hardly more than children. Siyuf's a harsh woman, but not a cruel one from what I've seen; she wouldn't command the loyalty she does if she were. I can only guess, but I believe that you and Horn will be questioned and released."

Horn asked, "Is there anything you don't want us to tell?"

"No, tell them everything. Nothing you can say can harm Hyacinth or Moly or me. Or Patera Remora and Patera Incus, or even Spider. Nor can anything you say harm you. The better they understand your place in all this, the more likely it is that you'll be set free once they've learned all they can from you—or so it seems to me."

In a whisper, Nettle asked, "Does this mean we've failed, Patera?"

"Of course not. I'm not sure what you're asking about—whether you're afraid we've failed as human beings—"

"Failed the gods."

"No." There was resolution in Silk's voice. "How old are you?"

"Fifteen."

"I'm eight years older. It seems an enormous separation to me, as no doubt it does to you. How does it appear to His Cognizance, do you think?"

Horn said, "Like nothing. His Cognizance was an old, old man when we were born."

"When I was, too. Consider then how young we must appear to Pas, who built the whorl—or to the Outsider, who shaped our forebears from the mud of the Short-Sun Whorl." Silk fell silent, listening to the slow pacing of the sentries outside, and Remora's soft snores.

"Since the Outsider began us, let us begin with him. I've never seen him, except in a dream, and even then I couldn't see his face clearly; but he's seen me from the beginning—from before my own beginning in fact. He knows me far better than I know myself, and he chose me to perform a small task for him. I was to save our manteion from Blood.

"Blood is dead. Musk, who was the owner of record and who I once considered worse than Blood, is dead too. Patera Remora over there is the new augur on Sun Street—I believe that may be the Outsider's way of telling me the task is done. You both helped do it, and I'm sure he's grateful, as I am."

Horn muttered, "We didn't do anything, Patera."

"Of course you did—but listen. I may be wrong, wrong about having saved our manteion, and wrong about the sign. I may fail after all; I can't be sure. But I can be sure of this—he will forgive me if I fail, and he would surely forgive you. I know him more than well enough to be certain of that."

Nettle said, "I was mostly thinking about Echidna. I saw her, when she talked to Maytera Mint? I was there."

"So was I. Echidna told her to destroy the Alambrera. It has been destroyed, and the convicts have been freed. I freed them."

"Yes, but—"

"Echidna also ordered the destruction of the Ayuntamiento. It is still in existence, if you like, but consider: Lemur, who headed it so long, is dead; so is Loris, who succeeded him."

"Maytera says that wasn't really him," Nettle objected. "She says Maytera Mint said Potto just works the councillors that we see, like you'd work a puppet."

Silk chuckled, a small, cheerful sound in the darkness. "Like the wooden man that Horn had when you were small."

"Yes, Patera."

"That's true, I'm sure; and I'm equally sure that at one time it was true of all five councillors. Before Doctor Crane killed Lemur, however, we learned that the real Lemur had died some time before—years before, probably. The manipulated body had become Lemur, the only Lemur in existence, though it thought itself still manipulated by the corpse in Lemur's bed. Do you follow this, Horn? Nettle?"

Nettle said, "I think so, Patera."

"When I had time to think about that, which wasn't until Doctor Crane and I had been pulled out of the water, I wondered about the other councillors. If Councillor Loris had remained with us as I asked, and if he had found it impossible to divert his consciousness to another chem, I would have known—and we would have held the presiding officer of the Ayuntamiento. As it was, I would guess that Loris himself knew before he came to treat with us; if he hadn't, he wouldn't have snatched up the needler Generalissimo Oosik offered to Councillor Potto and begun firing. He understood Generalissimo Siyuf well enough to realize that she would have him executed on some pretense, and knew he had his life to lose like any other man. In the event, he lost it sooner; but he had the satisfaction of a combatant's death, which may have meant something to him."

"One of those women shot him?"

Maytera Marble's voice reached them out of the darkness, spectrally reminiscent of old Maytera Rose's. "Yes. I watched it. I saw him fall."

Silk told her, "I've been expecting you to join us, Moly. I would have invited you, but I wasn't sure where you were, and it wouldn't do to go stumbling around waking up people."

"Certainly not, Patera."

Nettle said, "I'm glad you're here, Maytera. I want to ask something. Everybody says we run things in Trivigaunte. The Rani's a woman and so's Generalissimo Siyuf. I saw her. So who were the women that Willet let in, the ones that shot Councillor Loris? Why did they take orders from him?"

Maytera Marble sniffed. "You've a great deal to learn, Nettle. Doesn't Horn do what you tell him, sometimes, even when he doesn't want to?"

"I don't believe I can improve on that," Silk said, "but I'll enlarge upon it a trifle. They are spies, of course—agents of the Rani's, as Hossaan himself is. I'm reasonably sure that they're Vironese as well. Hossaan has told me that he and Doctor Crane were the only Trivigauntis in the ring they built up here, and I believe he was telling the truth."

Horn began another question, but Silk stopped him. "I ought to tell you that before I went into the tunnels by the lake I saw someone ahead of me. Later I saw footprints, and still later I came across the body of someone who Hammerstone told me had been a woman."

"Don't even talk about that place," Nettle said, "every time I hear about it, it sounds so awful."

"It is. But if I may talk about the dead woman, I would imagine she traveled here from Trivigaunte from time to time, probably in the guise of a trader. Chenille carried messages to a woman in the market, and the dead woman I found may well have been the same person. Hossaan wouldn't have counted her as a part of Doctor Crane's ring, since she wasn't subject to Doctor Crane's orders. I'd imagine she stayed here no more than a few weeks—a month at most—when she came."

"Does anybody know about him?" Nettle inquired. "About Hammerstone? Is he, you know, all right?"

Maytera Marble murmured, "You want to know if I'm a widow so soon. I don't know, but I doubt it. He was away searching for materials when Willet and his women came in, but he might have saved us all if he'd been there. He would certainly have saved Patera Incus and me, and the daughter we had begun to build, if he could."

Horn said, "There were two hundred Trivigauntis coming,

Maytera. Patera had me out in the street watching for them. They would've killed Hammerstone, unless he gave up."

"We'll never know." Maytera Marble seated herself beside Nettle.

"He may rescue you still," Silk told Maytera Marble. "He may well rescue us all. From what I've seen of him, he will surely try, and that worries me—but I'd like to return to Nettle's question.

"Because women have more power than men in Trivigaunte, Nettle, most people would expect that most or all of the Rani's agents would be women—that's as good a reason for employing men as I can think of. But it would be natural for male agents from Trivigaunte to recruit women here. Women would be more sympathetic to their point of view—Hyacinth said something like that when we first met—and men from Trivigaunte would naturally seek out courageous, assertive women like the ones among whom they had lived at home.

"We all tend to generalize too much, I'm afraid. If most augurs are pious and naïve, for example, we imagine that every augur is, though if we were to reflect we would see immediately that it cannot be true. In the same way, there are bound to be bold men in Trivigaunte and brave and forceful women here—in fact there is a fine example of the latter sitting with us now. As for those women following Hossaan's instructions, it really doesn't matter if they were Vironese or Trivigauntis. If they wouldn't obey, they would have been of no value to Doctor Crane and Hossaan, and would have been eliminated long ago."

"I want to ask about something else, Caldé, but I'm afraid Maytera will be mad at me."

"That's the risk you run, Nettle dear."

Horn said, "Tell me and I will."

"No. If those women could spy and shoot a councillor, I can do this. Caldé, I was listening at the door. Maytera caught me and made me quit, but when she went to work on her child again I came back."

"I'm not angry," Maytera Marble told her, "but you should be angry with yourself. It was wrong, and you knew it."

Silk said, "It hardly matters now."

"Yes, it does. Because I heard something right at the end, and it's why I got up when I heard you talking to Horn. You—you just . . . Gave up. The councillor they shot? Loris? He was talking about giving away slug guns. . . ."

"And I said that we could discuss terms later. That we surrendered."

"Uh-huh."

Horn objected, "We were winning. Everybody said so."

"Horn, he said *they* were, because the farmers would fight the Trivigauntis and they'd have to leave. Then the Caldé said all right we give up, we'll settle the arrangements when we've got more time. Only Maytera said he had to be caldé, because if he wasn't it wouldn't mean anything."

"Patera Silk has never been vindictive, dear."

"I know, Maytera, and I know that word, but I don't know what you mean by it. Didn't you want to kill the councillors, Caldé?"

"Of course not. As far as our insurrection is concerned, what I've always wanted to do is end it. I want peace, and a reunited Viron. Echidna ordered Maytera Mint to destroy the Ayuntamiento and return the city to Scylla. Haven't you ever thought about what that last instruction meant, Nettle?"

"Not enough, I guess."

"Then think now." Silk's fingers groped for his ambion. "Returning to Scylla means returning to our Charter. Scylla wrote it, and no quantity of prayers and sacrifices would be a convincing demonstration of loyalty as long as we violate it. The Charter demands an Ayuntamiento. Did you know that?"

Horn said, "I did, Patera."

"From that, it's clear Echidna does not want us to do away with the institution of the Ayuntamiento. There can be nothing wrong, surely, with a board of advisors elected at three-year intervals, which is what the Ayuntamiento is intended to be—a council of experienced men and women to whom the caldé can turn in time of trouble. Echidna was demanding that the present and quite clearly illegitimate Ayuntamiento be dissolved, a demand entirely in harmony with her implied demand that our government return to the Charter.

"That being the case, the way to peace was clear, as I had seen from the beginning. I would remain as caldé as long as the people wanted it. I could declare the present Ayuntamiento ended, announce an election, and urge everyone to support the surviving members of the previous Ayuntamiento. Those who still favored their cause would vote for them as well, and they would be reelected. Would have been, to be realistic."

"You sound so sad, Caldé." Nettle shivered, snuggling against Horn. "It might happen yet."

"Yes, it may. I was thinking of the time at Blood's when Councillor Loris presented a list of demands to Moly and me."

"Absurd demands," Maytera Marble declared.

"Extreme demands, certainly. He wanted hostages from the Rani, and he would have put Generalissimo Oosik and the other high-ranking officers on trial. I defied him."

"You offered to resign, too," Maytera Marble said. "You were very brave, Patera."

"I was very stupid, very tired, and very frightened. If I hadn't been, I would have realized that the thing to do was to agree, stop the fighting, and go to work on the details. Have you ever talked with the clerks in the Juzgado, Nettle?"

"No, Caldé."

"I have. I made it a point to, because I knew Hyacinth's father was a head clerk; she hates him, yet she will always be his daughter. I located him, and while we were talking about reforming the Fisc he said that the devils are in the details."

Silk chuckled, cheered by the memory. "Later, one of the officers of the Fisc made the same remark; and I recalled what we were taught in the schola—that the malice of devils is such that they destroy even evil people. My teachers didn't really believe in them, as Patera Pike did; but I believe what they said was true, and that what Hyacinth's father and the official from the Fisc said was true as well.

"All right, let the Ayuntamiento accommodate the devils. Peace would mean that nine-tenths of Siyuf's horde could go home. Thousands of innocent women would be spared horrible deaths in the tunnels, we could buy enough food for those who remained here, and the Ayuntamiento's chief weapon would be snatched from its hands—let it give our farmers slug guns, those guns would only make us stronger."

"You were going to win by giving up?"

Silk shook his head. "No one wins by giving up, Nettle, though many fights are not worth winning. I was going to gain what I wanted—peace—by persuading my enemy that he gained by letting me have it, which happened to be the truth. I still hope to do it, though the prospect isn't bright at the moment."

Horn said, "General Mint and Colonel Bison got away. So did Generalissimo Oosik." Nettle added, "The fat councillor did, too, I think. Is there going to be peace now because of what you said?"

"I don't know, but I doubt it." Silk sighed. "It will depend mostly on the Trivigauntis; and as long as they hold us, Generalissimo Oosik and General Mint are liable to regard them as enemies as bad as the Ayuntamiento, if not worse."

Maytera Marble sniffed. "I don't see why they want us."

"His Cognizance is fond of giving short and long answers," Silk told her. "In this case, he'd probably say that the short answer was that Siyuf has a bad conscience. She came to Viron as an ally, ostensibly, but with the secret hope of making it dependent upon Trivigaunte—a servant city."

"Did she actually say that, Patera?"

"Of course not; but she was quick to believe that we were plotting against her, and people who always suspect they're being cheated are generally trying to cheat. When General Mint and Patera Remora tried to treat with the Ayuntamiento, Siyuf feared we'd come to an agreement unfavorable to Trivigaunte. By taking our Juzgado, she showed clearly that she intended to govern Viron. Today—though that's yesterday now, I suppose—I made the mistake of telling Councillor Loris that he and Potto could confer in person with us, since that was what they wanted. I thought it was safe, because Hossaan would report everything we said to Colonel Abanja, and I was resolved to say nothing that Siyuf could object to."

"I don't think you did, Caldé, except there at the end."

"Thank you. There at the end it no longer mattered. Horn and Mucor had told me the Trivigauntis were on their way, and I knew I'd overplayed my hand just by letting the councillors into the Caldé's Palace. Unfortunately, Hossaan overplayed his as well. If he and his spies had simply kept us from leaving until the troopers arrived, something might have been gained. I doubt it, but it might have been. As things are, a great deal has been lost—peace first of all. Peace is always a great deal, but now it's more urgent than ever, because of Pas's threat."

Silk wiped his eyes. "Having saved our manteion, I tried to save Viron and the whorl, Nettle; and now all I can do is sit here crying."

"That's a awfully big job for just one man, Caldé, saving the whorl. Do you really think Pas is going to destroy us?"

As if he had not heard her, Silk said, "We were talking about those who escaped, and no one mentioned Oreb. Did he get out? Did anyone see him?"

A horse voice croaked, "Bird here!"

"Oreb! I should've known. Come down here."

Wings beat in the darkness, and Oreb landed with a thump.

"His Cognizance reminded me once that there are people who love birds so much they cage them, and others who love them so much they free them. Then he said that Echidna and the Seven were people of the first kind, and Pas a person of the second kind. When I bought Oreb, he was in a cage; and when I freed him I smashed that cage—never thinking that it might have seemed a place of refuge to him."

Horn said, "I never thought of the whorl being a cage."

"I never had either, until the Outsider showed me what lies outside it."

"Maybe Auk and Chenille can steal General Saba's airship, Caldé, and take Sciathan back to Mainframe like he wants."

"Good man," Oreb informed them. "Man fly."

"He is, Oreb, in both senses, I believe. So is Auk, and even Chenille is a very competent person in her way. But to tell you the truth I have no confidence in them at all when it comes to this—less than I would have in Potto and Spider, if anything. Frankly, I've never imagined that there was any way to get Auk and his followers to Mainframe other than getting General Saba and her crew to fly them there.

"That was another reason for wanting peace, and in fact it was the most pressing one—as long as there was war, Siyuf would want to keep the airship here. It couldn't be used in the tunnels, of course, but eventually the Ayuntamiento would have to send troops to the surface if it hoped to win, and the airship would be a terrible adversary.

"With the war ended, it might—I say might—have been possible to persuade her to do what we wanted. Now we'll have to wait for it to end, I'm afraid, or at least for Pas to do whatever he plans to do first to drive humanity out. I can think of a dozen possibilities, none pleasant."

Silk awaited another question, but even Oreb was silent. At length he said, "Now let's sleep if we can. We'll have a trying day tomorrow, I'm afraid."

"Ah—Caldé?" Remora's nasal voice floated out of the darkness.

"Yes, Patera. I'm sorry we woke you. We tried to keep our voices down."

"I have listened with great, um, edification. Sorry I did not wake sooner, eh? But there is one, um, point. Eland, eh? I knew him. You said—ah—"

"I said I had a vague description of his killer. Vague from our point of view, anyway. I believe it was Hossaan, whom you may have met as Willet, my driver. I won't tell you at present how I obtained it. Let us sleep, Patera."

"Good girl," Oreb confided.

"Add cot end add word," Tick commented sleepily from his place at Hyacinth's side.

Staring up at the still-distant airship, Silk clenched his teeth, determined equally that the icy wind that whipped his robe would not make them chatter and that the airship would not make him gape, though so immense a flying structure seemed less an achievement than a force of nature. Ever so slowly, it edged its vast, mummy-colored bulk across the gray midday sky, lost at times among low clouds dark with snow, always reappearing nearer the winter-wet meadow where he and his companions waited under guard.

Maytera Mint's grip on his arm tightened, and she uttered a sound like a raindrop falling into a scrub bucket, then another, and another. He turned from his contemplation of the airship to her. "Why are you making that noise, Maytera?"

Hyacinth whispered, "She's crying. Let her alone."

"Wise girl!" Oreb approved.

"You won't be able to take your bird, Caldé." Dismounting and dropping her reins, Saba strode over to them, her porcine face sympathetic and severe. "I'm sorry, but you can't." She indicated Hyacinth with her riding crop. "You had some sort of animal too, girly. Where is it?"

"A c-catachrest," Hyacinth told her through chattering teeth. "I gave him a little of my food this morning and sent him away."

Silk said, "You'll have to leave, Oreb. Fly back to the place where you were caught if you can."

"Good Silk!"

"Good bird too, but you must go. Go back to the Palustrian Marshes, that's where the man in the market said you came from."

"Bird stay," Oreb announced, then squawked and took wing as Saba cut at him with her quirt.

"Sorry, Caldé, I didn't try to hit it. Have a nice breakfast?"

"Baked horse-fodder," Hyacinth told her.

"Horde bread, you mean. We turn little girls like you into troopers with it."

Silk said, "I had assumed that we would be questioned by Generalissimo Siyuf."

Behind him, Incus began, "We are holy *augurs*. You *cannot* simply—" He was jointed by Remora, and Remora by Spider.

"Quiet!" Saba snapped. "I'll have the lot of you flogged. By Sphigx, I'll flog you myself!" She counted them, her lips twitching. "Eight, that's right."

She raised her voice. "You're going up in my airship. The caldé said he'd like to see it, and he's going to. So are the rest of you, as soon as they drop the *'ishsh*. We're taking you home so the Rani and her ministers can have a look at you, but anybody who gives us trouble might not get there. She might sort of fall off first. Understand? If you—if . . ."

Seeing Saba's eyes sink and grow dull, Silk took his arm from Hyacinth's shoulders. "Can you and I walk a step or two, General? I'd like a word with you in private."

Saba's head nodded like a marionette's. "I've been in here all morning, Silk. She thinks you won't come back."

"I see." He drew Saba aside. "But she isn't going to kill us, or she wouldn't have threatened to. I'm not worried about myself, Mucor; the Outsider will take care of me in one way or another. I'm worried about Hyacinth, and about you."

"Grandmother will take care of her, Silk."

"At the moment, Hyacinth's taking care of her; but no doubt you're right. With your grandmother gone, however, there's no one to take care of you."

Saba laughed, a mirthless noise that made Silk shudder even as he worried that the watching troopers had heard it. "I'm going with you, Silk, way up in the air. The man who broke his wings is there already."

"You can't! Can't you understand? You absolutely cannot!" Assistant Day Manager Feist trotted at Sand's side, snapping and yelping.

"It's right up there, Sarge." Hammerstone waved toward the sentries before Siyuf's door. "See the twist troopers? Got to be it." The "Twist troopers" in question were moving the safety catches of their slug guns to the FIRE position.

Ignoring them, Sand grasped the front of Feist's tunic and separated his highly polished shoes from Ermine's three-finger-thick stair runner. "You say we can't go barging in, right?"

Feist gasped and choked.

"Fine, we've got it. So you're going first. You've got to talk your way past those girls and get inside."

Sand paused at the top of the stair, displaying Feist to the sentries while covering them with his slug gun, gripped in one hand like a needler. "When you get in, tell the Generalissimo we got big news to trade real cheap, and if—"

The intricately carved sandalwood door of the Lyrichord Room had opened; a tall and strikingly handsome brunette in a diaphanous gown peered out. "Hi. You want to see Generalissimo Siyuf?"

"You got it, Plutonium." Sand strode toward the door, as an afterthought tossing Feist over the ornate railing. "You tell her the First Squad, First Platoon, Company 'S,' Army of Viron's here. You got all that?"

The handsome young woman nodded. "Close enough, Soldier. I'm Violet."

"Sergeant Sand, pleased. You tell her we won't take much of her time and we aren't asking much, and she'll be shaggy glad she talked to us."

"Wait a minute, she's getting dressed." The door closed.

"What do you think?" Slate asked Hammerstone. "She goin' to see us?"

"One way or the other," Hammerstone told him; almost too swiftly for the eye to follow, his hands shot out, grasped the barrels of the sentries' slug guns, and crushed them.

At length, when repeated knockings had produced no result, Maytera Marble's friend Scleroderma employed the butt of her new needler to pound the rearmost door of the Caldé's Palace. A second floor window flew open with a bang, and a cracked male voice called, "Who's there? Visitor? Want to see the Caldé? So do I!"

"I'm here to see Moly," Scleroderma announced firmly. "I'm going to. Is she all right?"

"Mollie? Mollie? Good name! Fish name! Relative of mine? Don't know her! Wait."

The window slammed down. Scleroderma dropped her needler into the pocket of her winter coat, drawing the coat so tightly about her that for a moment it appeared buttonable.

The door flew open. "Come in! Come in! Cold out there! In here, too! Wall's down! Terrible! No Mollie. You mean Mucor? She's here, skinny girl! Know her?"

"I certainly do, she's Moly's granddaughter. Maybe—"

"Won't talk," the lean old man who had opened the door declared. "Asked about Mollie. She talk to you? Not to me! Upstairs! Want to see her? Maybe she will!"

Scleroderma, whose weight gave her a pronounced aversion to stairs, shook her head emphatically as she pushed the door shut behind her. "She'll catch her death up there, the poor starved little thing. You bring her down here right away." Waddling after him through the scullery and into the kitchen, she called to the old man's fast-vanishing back, "I'll build a fire in the stove and start her dinner."

High above the Trivigaunti airship, Oreb eyed the cage-like enclosure swinging below it. The question, as Oreb saw it, was not whether he should rejoin Silk, but when. It might be best to wait until Silk was alone. It might also be best to find something to eat first. There was always food at the big house on the hill, but Oreb had a score to settle.

Bright black eyes sharper than most telescopes examined the good girl pressing herself against Silk without result, then scanned the orderly rows of pointed houses. The target sighted, Oreb began a wingover that quickly became a dive.

"You," Pterotrooper Nizam told her new pet, "are going to have to be as quiet as a mouse in this barracks bag."

"Ess, laddie."

"As quiet as *two* mice. As soon as we get aboard—"

A red-and-black projectile shot between them with a rush of wind and a hoarse cry. The new pet bared small teeth and claws in fury. "Add, add word! Laddie, done by scarred."

.   .   .

Sand's soldiers filled the Lyrichord Room's luxurious sellaria with polite clankings as Siyuf returned his salute. "I have hear of you, Sergeant. Why do you come?"

"You got a couple prisoners—" he began.

"More than this."

"Two I'm talking about. This's Corporal Hammerstone."

Hammerstone stiffened to attention.

"He's married, only you got his wife and his best buddy. We want 'em back, and what we got to tell you's worth ten of 'em. So here's what I say. We tell you, and we leave it up to you, sir. If you don't think it's worth it, say so and we'll clear off. If you do, give 'em back. What do you say?"

Siyuf clapped her hands; when the monitor appeared in her glass she said, "Get Colonel Abanja.

"To begin, Sergeant, I do not know that I hold the wife or the friend of this soldier. Violet my darling, bring for me the list that was last night from Colonel Abanja."

Violet grinned and winked at Hammerstone. "Sure thing."

"The wife, the friend, they are soldiers also?"

Hammerstone said, "No, sir. My wife's a civilian. Her name's Moly. She's no bigger'n you, sir, maybe smaller. My friend's a bio, a augur, His Eminence Patera Incus. People think he's the coadjutor. Really he's the Prolocutor, only people don't know yet."

The monitor's face gained color, reshaping itself to become that of Siyuf's intelligence officer.

"There is here too much of warlockery, Colonel. You see here soldiers, marvels we should have in museums but here fight us, and for us also. They are come to offer a bargain. Am I not a woman of honor?"

Violet nodded enthusiastically and Abanja said, "You are indeed, Generalissimo."

"Just so. I do not cheat, not even these soldiers. So I must know. Do we have the holy man Incus? Violet, my darling, read the names. How many now, Colonel?"

"Eighty-two, sir. There were some other holy men besides the caldé, and I suppose this might be one of them." Abanja leafed through papers below the field of her glass.

Leaning over Violet's shoulder, Hammerstone pointed with a finger thrice the size of hers.

"I don't really read so good," she whispered. "What's that second word? It can't— Sweetheart, there's a Chenille in here. Is that the Chen we know?"

Abanja looked up. "The paramour of the Vironese who was plotting to steal our airship, sir. She was seated across the table from me at that dinner at the calde's residence."

Hammerstone said, "It says, 'Maytera Marble a holy woman,' on here, sir. That's my wife, Moly. Patera's here, too. You got them all right."

"Then you must give me your information," Siyuf told Sand. "If it is worth their freedom, I will free them as soon as I can. I do not say at once. At once may not be possible. But as soon as is possible. You do not betray your city when you do this?"

Sand shook his head. "Help it, is what we figure. See, if you're smart you'll let the calde go when we tell you. And with us, it's him. He's the top of the chain of command, and we know you got him."

"Sir, the airship. . . ." Abanja's face was agitated.

Siyuf motioned her to silence. "We speak of that later, Colonel. First I must learn what this soldier knows."

She turned back to Sand. "I will release your calde, you say. I do not say this. With regard to Calde Silk, I give no promise. You do not bargain for him. I notice this."

"Because we know you wouldn't, sir. You'd say you were going to keep him, and dismissed. But you'll let him go if you're smart. It'll be better for us and better for you, too. You're going to, is what we think. Only we want to see to it Hammerstone's wife and his buddy get loose too."

Sand hesitated, glancing at Abanja's face in the glass, then back to Siyuf. "The insurrection's over. That's what we're here to tell you, sir. Give us your word on Moly and Patera What'shisname—"

"Incus," Hammerstone prompted.

"And Patera Incus, and we'll give you the details. Have we got it?"

"I will release both as soon as I am able. Have I not said? Bring to me the image of the sole great goddess, and I swear on it. There is not one here, I think."

"Your word's good enough for us, sir." Sand glanced at Hammerstone, who nodded.

"All right. You want me to tell you, or you want to ask questions, sir?"

"First I ask one question. Then you tell, and after I ask more if I wish. When I am satisfied, I give the order, and if there is a place to which you wish them brought, we will do it. But not more than a day's travel."

Hammerstone said, "The Caldé's Palace. That's where me and Moly have been living." Shale asked, "You got any problem with that, sir?"

"No. This is within reason. My question. You say I will let go your caldé, the head of your government. I do not think so, so I am curious. Why do you say this?"

" 'Cause out of all the people you got to deal with here, he's the one that likes you the most," Hammerstone told her. "I know him pretty well. Me and Sarge picked him up one time on patrol, and I shot the bull with him before he gave me the slip. Then too, I been living in his palace like I said, and I heard a lot from Moly."

"I helped Councillor Potto interrogate him the next time we got him," Sand said, "so I know him pretty well too. He's big for peace. He was trying to stop the insurrection before you got here."

For a second or more, Siyuf studied Sand as if she hoped to find a clue to his thoughts in his blank metal face. "You have kill this man Potto. After, I suppose? This Mint tells. But you have not kill him well. He is now back."

"I been dead too," Sand told her, and Violet gasped. "I could give you the scoop on that, but it'd take a while."

"Rather I would hear of the end of the insurrection. This you proposed."

"Good here. Last night there was a confab at the Caldé's place. None of us were there, but we heard from General Mint. Your people tried to grab everybody, only four made it out, and Councillor Loris is K. The ones that gave you the slip was her and Colonel Bison, and the Generalissimo and Councillor Potto."

"I know of this." Siyuf delivered a withering glance to Abanja's image in the glass.

Schist said, "Tell her about surrendering, Sarge. That's pretty important."

"Yeah, he did. The caldé did. Maybe you don't know that, sir. It was before your people came in."

Siyuf nodded. "Colonel Abanja have report this. She has had an informant in your caldé's household, a most praiseworthy accomplishment."

Abanja said, "Thank you, Generalissimo."

"So the four that got clear put their heads together, see? Our generalissimo, he'd come in a Guard floater, and they piled in and took off, Councillor Potto too. Naturally he said, well, your caldé's called quits so we're in charge again. Councillor Loris's dead so I'm the new presiding officer. You're working for me, and if you do what I say maybe I won't shoot you."

Schist interjected, "He figured they all had it coming, I guess. What we figure is, not just them. He'll probably stop Sarge's works real good."

Violet said, *"Ah!"* and Siyuf laughed. "Shadeup, after so long a night. Potto is not friend to this soldier who not one month past shoot him. Potto has the . . . What is this word?"

"He'll have it in for him."

Sand nodded. "But he can't hand out anything that I can't take. I been dead already, just like I said. You want to talk about me, or you want to hear the rest?"

Hammerstone said, "They went around quite a bit, to hear Colonel Bison tell it. Only there was one thing they didn't have any trouble with. Tell 'em, Sarge."

"You foreigners, sir." Sand leveled his huge forefinger at Siyuf. "Councillor Potto's mean as a bad wrench, and he hates you worse'n dirt in his pump. General Mint, she hates Councillor Potto, but you're number two on her list."

"She is the central, to be sure. The sole woman." Siyuf looked thoughtful. "Colonel, what is it you say of this?"

In the glass, Abanja's image shrugged. "It doesn't run counter to any information I have, Generalissimo."

"You have leave off two, Sergeant. What of those?"

"I didn't leave 'em out, sir," Sand protested, "I hadn't got to 'em yet. Colonel Bison's General Mint's man. If she says spit oil, he says how far?"

"I grasp this. Proceed."

"We haven't seen Generalissimo Oosik, but Corporal Slate here chewed things over with his driver this morning, the one that brought him and got them clear. Tell her, Slate."

"He brought a slug gun to the meetin', sir," Slate began. "That's what his driver says, 'n he says he don't usually have nothin' but a needler 'n his sword, see? So who was that for? Then when they was talkin' in back—you know how them armed floaters are laid out, sir? There's no wall or nothin' between the seats up front and the back, so he tuned in. General Mint said somethin' about how Councillor Loris was the head of the Ayuntamiento, and it was Generalissimo Oosik that said he was dead. He thinks maybe Generalissimo Oosik did it himself, he seemed so happy about it."

Sand looked from Violet to Abanja, then at Siyuf. "Only Councillor Potto's got it in for him, and he knows it. He was like a brigadier back before the insurrection, so he had to be one of the Ayuntamiento's floor bolts. But when Caldé Silk came along, he went over right away and got made head of the whole host of Viron. He knows Councillor Potto, so he's got to know how pissed off he is about that."

Siyuf, who had been slouching in her chair, straightened up. "You desire me to set free your caldé to save your Viron, so much is plain. I do not care about your Viron."

Violet said, "I do, a little. Besides, I know his wife."

"You're thinking it's going to go back the way it was," Sand told Siyuf. "Them in the tunnels and us on top. Stuff it. Like we say, there's one thing they're together on."

He paused and Abanja said, "That we must return to our own city, I'm sure. He's probably right, Generalissimo."

"I am, only you're not. What they're saying, all four of them, is that they can't let you go back. Or won't. To start off, they don't think you'll go."

Sand wanted for Siyuf to speak, but she did not.

"So they're thinking let's take care of this, wipe 'em out—that's you, sir—before they can get reinforcements from Trivigaunte."

Hammerstone declared, "The caldé wouldn't do that, or I don't think so, sir. They're getting set now, getting General Mint's troopers together again, and lining up the Guard and getting the Army into position. If we weren't detached, we'd be with it this minute. You got maybe a day, maybe two. But if you let the caldé go, he'll put a lid on it."

"You are wise," Siyuf said. "I agree. Colonel Abanja, you have our friend Caldé Silk? Bring him to my Juzgado, I meet him there. This holy woman Marble, and the holy man, also. Saba's airship have not depart?"

"I'm afraid it left an hour ago, Generalissimo," Abanja sounded regretful. "I'll contact General Saba on the glass, however, and convey your request that she return to Viron."

Hammerstone edged closer, his hard features and scratched paint incongruous among so much satin, porcelain, and polished rosewood. "We don't want a request. We want a order. Tell them to turn around!"

"This I cannot do," Siyuf explained. "When the airship has leave Viron, it come under control of our War Minister in Trivigaunte. She will send it back, I think, when I ask."

"Get her now. Tell her!"

"This I cannot either. Monitor, this is sufficient of Abanja. She know what she is to do."

Siyuf turned back to Sand and Hammerstone. "Abanja must speak to General Saba, then Saba to our War Minister. While they speak I must make prepares for this attack. It may be we attack first. This we see."

As Abanja's face faded to gray, Violet murmured, "I'd help if I could, only—"

"Sure, Plutonium." Slinging his slug gun, Sand stooped, grasped an astonished Siyuf about the waist, and tossed her headfirst onto his broad steel shoulder. "You come too. You can keep her company."

Shale caught Violet's arm. "You make one more for us to trade, see? That don't ever hurt."

Sitting crosslegged on one of the ridiculous bladders that served as mattresses aboard the airship, Silk found it almost impossible to remain upright without holding onto the swaying, whispering bamboo grill that substituted for a floor. "You're wonderfully cheerful," he told Auk. "I admire it more than I can say. Cheerfulness is a sacred duty." He swallowed. "A cheerful agreement with the will of the gods is a—a—"

"I been sick already," Auk told him. "Had the dry heaves, too. Worst thing since I busted my head down in the tunnels."

The Flier smiled impishly. "I heard no cheerful agreement to the wishes of Mainframe at that time, however. Cursing is not a new thing to me, and my own tongue is a superior vehicle to this Common Tongue we speak. But never have I heard curses such as that."

Face down and miserable behind Auk, Chenille muttered, "Just don't talk about it, all right?"

"I do not. Instead I talk of cursing, a different thing. Should I say in this Common Tongue, may your pubic hair grow longer than your lies and become entangled in the working of a mill, it is but laughable. In my own tongue, it soars to the sun and leaves each hearer awed. Yet the cursing of Auk was new to me, grand and hideous as the birth of devils."

Silk managed to smile. "I have been sick, actually. I was sick in the cage that swings so horribly in the wind, and we were so tightly packed into it that I couldn't help soiling myself and Hyacinth, and Patera Remora, too; they bore it with such fortitude and good will that I felt worse."

Hyacinth smiled as she sat down beside him. "You didn't get a whole lot on me, but you filled up one of his shoes. If you're feeling better now, you should take a look around. Gib showed me, and it's pretty interesting."

"Not yet." Silk found his handkerchief and wiped his nose.

"It's not like the Juzgado at all, no bars on the windows."

"Sure." Auk winked. "We can climb right out."

"I opened one and looked outside. Not long, because it's so cold. I wish you could see better through the white stuff."

"That's sheep's hide stretched and scraped till it's real thin," Auk told her. "When you get it the way you want it, you rub fat on it, and it lets the daylight in. They use it in the country 'cause they can make it themselves, but glass costs. It's a lot lighter, too, so that's why they got it here.

"See, Patera, even with this as big as it is, everything's got to be real light, 'cause it's lifting the guns and those charges they blew up the Alambrera with, and food and water, and palm oil for the engines. That's going to make it easy for us."

"To do what?"

Gib sat down so violently that Silk feared the grill would give way. "To hook it, Patera. We got to. Only I wish I had Bongo here. He'd be abram about this place."

Chenille groaned. "You're all abram. Me, too."

"This ain't bad," Auk told her. "See, Patera, after they loaded us on in the city, it had to go northeast to get you, lousewise into the wind. It was doing this." He illustrated with gestures. "We all got pretty sick. Only now—"

"I did not," Sciathan objected. "I am accustomed to the vagaries of winds."

"Me neither," Hyacinth told Auk. "I never have been."

"You weren't on it then. This is nicer, 'cause there's a north wind and we're heading south. That's why you can't hear the engines much. They don't have to work hard."

"We're out over the lake," Hyacinth told Silk, who felt (but did not say) that it would be a blessing if the airship crashed into the water.

"Thing is, Patera, Terrible Tartaros is setting this lay up for us. It's like we got somebody inside. The fat councillor said they'd do it in a month, remember? Then I said I got the best thieves in the city, we can do it quicker. I was thinking two or three weeks, 'cause we'd have to get clothes like these troopers' and get pals up so they could pull up the rest—"

Spider joined the group around Silk, sliding across the woven bamboo as he shook his head.

"You got a better way? Dimber here. I don't say mine's best, just that's how I was thinking. The queer was it'd have to be mostly morts, likely all morts. Wouldn't be rum, finding morts that wouldn't up tail if there was a row up here."

"We'd be too sick." Chenille sat up, pale under her tan.

Silk began, "If this is indeed the hand of Tartaros—"

"Got to be. What I was saying, I was figuring maybe three weeks, and the fat one maybe a month. Then Upstairs here says we only got a couple days."

Sciathan nodded.

"Tartaros heard it and he says, Auk needs a hand. Willet, you tell the Trivigauntis Auk's knot's going to be at the Cock. They nab us and haul us up. How long was it? Under a day. So right there's the difference between a god and a buck like me. Twenty-one to one."

For a moment there was silence, filled by the distant talk of the other prisoners, the whispered complaints of the bamboo, the almost inaudible hum of the engines, and a hundred nameless groanings and creakings. Silk said, "They have slug guns, Auk. And needlers, I suppose. You—we—have nothing."

"Wrong, Patera. We got Tartaros. You watch."

Chenille stood up; sitting at her feet, Silk found himself a trifle shocked by her height. She said, "I'm feeling better, I guess. Want to show me around, Hy? I'd like to see it."

"Sure. Wait till you look outside."

He made himself stand. "May I come? I'll try not to . . ." He groped for words, reminding himself of Remora.

"Puke," Chenille supplied.

"See their beds?" Hyacinth kicked the side of a bladder. "There's four rows, and twenty-five in a row, so this gondola's meant for a hundred pterotroopers. Gondola's what you call this thing we're in, Gib says."

Silk nodded.

"Look through the floor and you can see the guns. Their floor's got to be solid, I guess, so it's iron or anyhow some kind of a metal. There's three on each side, and the barrels stick out through those holes. That's why it's so cold here, it comes up through the floor."

"How do you get them open?" Chenille was wrestling with the fastenings of a port.

Silk rapped the wall with his knuckles. "Wood."

"You've got to pull out both pins, Chen. You're right, they're wood, bent like on a boat, but really thin."

Chenille slid back the frame of greased parchment to reveal what looked like a snow-covered plain bright with sun.

"There's another gondola ahead of ours," Hyacinth told her, "and two in back. You can see them if you stick your head out. I don't know why they don't just have one big, long one."

"It would break, I imagine," Silk told her absently. "This airship must bend a good deal at times." He looked out as she had suggested, peering above him as well as to left and right.

"Remember when we were up in the air in that floater? I was scared to death." Her thigh pressed his with voluptuous warmth, and his elbow was somehow pushing her breast. "But you weren't scared at all! This is kind of like that."

"I was terrified." Silk backed away, fighting with all his strength against the thoughts tugging at his mind.

Chenille put her head through the port as he had; she spoke and Hyacinth said, "Because we're blowing along, or that's what I think. Going with it, you can't feel anything."

Chenille retreated. "It's beautiful, really beautiful, only I can't see the lake. You said we were over it, but I guess the fog's too thick. I was hoping to see the place Auk and me bumped out to, that little shrine." She turned to Silk. "Is this how the gods see everything?"

"No," he said. The gods who were in some incomprehensible fashion contained in Mainframe saw the whorl only through their Sacred Windows, he felt sure, no matter what augurs might say.

His sweating hands fumbled the edge of the open port.

Through Windows and the eyes of those whom they possessed, although Tartaros could not even do that, Auk said; born blind, Tenebrous Tartaros could never see.

Over the snowy plain the long sun stretched from Mainframe to the end of the whorl—a place unimaginable, though the end of the whorl must come very soon.

Through Sacred Windows and other eyes, and perhaps through glasses, too. No, certainly through glasses when they chose, since Kypris had spoken through Orchid's glass, had manifested the Holy Hues in Hyacinth's glass while Hyacinth slept.

"The Outsider," he told Chenille. "I think the Outsider must be able to see the whorl this way. The rest of the gods can't—not even Pas. Perhaps that's what's wrong with them." A shoelace had knotted, as it always did when he tried to take off his shoes quickly. He jerked the shoe off anyway.

Hyacinth asked, "What are you doing?"

"Earning you, I hope." He pulled off his stockings and stuffed them into the toes of his shoes, recalling the chill waters of the tunnels and Lake Limna.

"You don't have to earn me! You've already got me, and if you didn't I wouldn't charge you."

He had her, perhaps, but he had not deserved her—he despaired of explaining that. "Doctor Crane and I shared a room at the lake. I doubt that I've mentioned it."

"I don't care what you did with him. It doesn't matter."

"We did nothing. Not the way you mean." Memories flooded back. "I don't believe he was inclined that way; certainly I'm not, though many augurs are. He told me you'd urged him to give me the azoth, and said something I'd forgotten until now. He said, 'When I was your age, it would have had me swinging on the rafters.' "

Hyacinth told Chenille, "Half the time I don't understand a thing he says."

She grinned. "Does anybody?"

"One does, at least. I looked out the window of that room just as we've been looking out this opening." Silk put his foot on its edge and stepped up and out, holding the upper edge to keep from falling. "I was afraid the Guard would come."

He had feared the Civil Guard, and had been willing to try to pull himself up onto the roof of the Rusty Lantern to escape it; yet very little had been at stake: if he had been taken, he would have been killed at worst.

The roof of the gondola was just out of reach; but the side slanted inward, as the sides of large boats did.

Much, much more was at stake now, because Auk's faith might kill them all. How many pterotroopers were on this airship? A hundred? At least that many, and perhaps twice that many.

Hyacinth was looking out at him, saying something he could not understand and did not wish to hear; her hand or Chenille's grasped his left ankle. Absently, he kicked to free it as he waited, gauging the rhythm of the airship's slight roll.

Auk and his followers would wait, biding their time until shadelow probably, if shadelow came before the airship reached Trivigaunte—break the hatch that barred them from its body, climb the rope ladder through the canvas tube that he could just glimpse, and strike with a rush, breaking necks and gouging out eyes. . . .

At the next roll. It was useless to wait. Hyacinth would have called for help already; Auk and Gib would grapple his legs and pull him inside.

He jumped, caught the edge of the top of the gondola, and to his delight found it a small coaming. In some remote place, someone was screaming. The noise entered his consciousness as he scrambled frantically up the clinker-laid planks, hooking his leg over the coaming when the slow roll favored him most.

A final effort, and he was up, lying on the safe side of the coaming and almost afraid to look at it. Rolling onto his back put half a cubit between him and the edge; he pressed his chest with both hands and shut his eyes, trying to control the pounding of his heart.

Almost he might have been on top of Blood's wall, with its embedded sword blades at his shoulder. Almost, except that a fall from Blood's wall would have been survivable—he had survived one, in fact.

He sat up and wiped his face with the hem of his robe.

How foolish he had been not to take off his robe and leave it with his shoes! The gondola had been cold, the draft from the port colder still; and so he had kept his robe, and never so much as considered that he might have lightened himself by some small amount by discarding it. Yet it was comforting to have it now, comforting to draw its soft woolen warmth around him while he considered what to do next.

Stand up, though if he stood he might fall. Muttering a prayer to the Outsider, he stood.

The top of the gondola was a flat and featureless deck, painted mummy-brown or perhaps merely varnished. Six mighty cables supported the gondola, angled out and stabbing upward into the airship's fabric-covered body. Forward, the canvas tube snaked up like an intestine; aft was a hatch secured with lashings, a hatch that would return him to the gondola—that would, equally, permit those inside it to leave. Once again he pictured the stealthy advance and wild charge, a score of young pterotroopers dead, the rest firing, disorganized at first.

Soon, shouted orders would render them a coherent body. A few Vironese would have weapons by then, and they might kill more pterotroopers; but they would be shot down within a minute or two, and the rest shot as well. Auk and Chenille and Gib would die, and with them Horn and Nettle and even poor Maytera Marble, who called herself Moly now. And not long after that, unless he and Hyacinth were lucky indeed—

"Hello, Silk."

He whirled. Mucor was sitting on the deck, her shins embraced by her skeletal arms; he gasped, and felt the pain of his wound deep in his chest.

She repeated her greeting.

"Hello." Another gasp. "I'd nearly forgotten you could do this. You did it in the tunnel, sitting on the water—I should have remembered."

She bared yellow teeth. "Mirrors are better. Mirrors scare more. This isn't, is it? I'm just here."

"It was certainly frightening to hear your voice." Silk sat too, grateful for the chance.

"I didn't mean to. I wanted to talk to you, but not where there were so many people."

He nodded. "There would have been a riot, I suppose."

"You were worried about me with so many people gone. My grandfather came to see if I was all right. The old man and the fat woman are taking care of me. He wanted to know where Grandmother and the little augur went, and I told him."

My grandfather was Hammerstone, clearly; Silk nodded and smiled. "Does the old man have a beard and jump around?"

"A little beard, yes."

Xiphias in that case, not His Cognizance; no doubt the fat woman was a friend of Xiphias's, or a servant.

"I've been eating soup."

"That's very good—I'm delighted to hear it. Mucor, you possessed General Saba, and there's something that you can tell me that's very, very important to me. When does she expect us to arrive in Trivigaunte?"

"Tonight."

Silk nodded, he hoped encouragingly. "Can you tell me how long after shadelow?"

"About midnight. This will float over the city, and in the morning they'll let you down."

"Thank you. Auk intends to try to take control of this airship and fly it to Mainframe."

Mucor looked pleased. "I didn't know that."

"He won't be able to. He'll be killed, and so will others I like. The only way that I've been—" He heard voices and paused to listen.

"They're in there." Mucor looked over her shoulder at the dangling canvas tube.

"Going down into the gondola? Can they hear us?"

"They haven't."

He waited until he heard the hatch thrown back. "What do they want?"

"I don't know."

His forefinger traced small circles on his cheek. "When you go, will you try to find out, please? It may be important, and I would be very, very grateful."

"I'll try."

"Thank you. You can fly, I know. You told me so in that big room underground where the sleepers are. Have you been all over this airship?"

"Most of it, Silk."

"I see. The only way that I could think of to stop Auk from trying to take it and being killed was to disable it some way—that was why I climbed up here, and you may be able to tell me how to do it. In a moment I'm going to try to tear the seam of that tube and climb up."

"There's a trooper up there."

"I see. A sentry? In any case, I must find a way to open the seam first. I should have gotten new glasses; I could have broken them and cut it with a piece of glass. But Mucor," Silk made his tone as serious as he could to emphasize the urgency of his request, "you've given me another way now, at least for the time being. Will you possess General Saba again for me?"

She was silent, and as seconds crept by he realized that she had not understood. "The fat woman," he said, but Mucor would surely confuse that with the woman Xiphias had found to care for her. "The woman that you frightened in the Caldé's Palace. She spilled her coffee, remember? You talked to me through her before Hyacinth and I went into the cage."

"Oh, her."

"Her name is General Saba, and she's the commander of this airship. I want you to possess her and make her turn east. As long as it's going in the direction that Auk—"

Mucor had begun to fade. For a second or two a ghostly image remained, like a green glimmer upon a pool; then it was gone and he was alone.

Condemning himself, he rose again. There had been half a dozen things—eight or ten, and perhaps more—he should have asked. What was taking place in Viron? Was Maytera Mint alive? What were Siyuf's plans? The answers had melted into the fabled city of lost opportunities.

He walked forward to the tube and examined it. The canvas was thinner than he had feared, but looked strong and nearly new. His pockets yielded only his new prayer beads and a handkerchief, the only items that his captors had let him retain. He detached an arm of Pas's voided cross and tried to tear the canvas with it, but its sharpest corner slipped impotently along the surface. Many men, he reminded himself angrily, carried small knives for just such occasions as this—although any such knife would presumably have been taken from him.

Even if he had possessed a knife, there was a sentry at the top of the ladder. If he was able to poke a hole in the canvas and enlarge it enough to climb through, he would almost certainly be captured or killed by that sentry when he emerged from the tube. Saba had no doubt worried that her prisoners might break one of the hatches; but a single pterotrooper there would be able to hold her position until she exhausted her ammunition, and her shots would have brought reinforcements long before then. Saba's prisoners had not escaped through either hatch—not yet. But Saba's logic confined him as though he had been its object.

Shaking his head, he crossed the deck of the gondola to the nearest cable. Woven of many ropes, it was as thick as a young tree, and its surface was rougher than the bark of many. Still more significantly, its angle, here where it was bent through a huge ringbolt, slanted noticeably off the vertical.

Removing his robe, he put it over his shoulder and tied it at his waist. Once he had finished praying and begun to climb, he found it relatively easy; as a boy he had climbed trees and poles far more difficult. The key was to fix his eyes on the surface of the cable, never stealing even a glance at the snowy plain of cloud so achingly far below.

He had boasted of his climbing to Horn, while conceding only that he had climbed less adroitly than a monkey; it was time to make good that boast. . . .

Gib missed the companionship of his trained baboon—what would Bongo think, if Bongo could see him crawling upward with chattering teeth and sweating palms! Could baboons laugh?

The airship was, just possibly, turning ever so slightly to its left. To look down was death, but to look up?

The whir of the engines sounded louder, but of course he was somewhat nearer them. He reminded himself sharply that he had not yet climbed far. . . .

The airship's southward course must necessarily have put its long axis across the great golden bar of the sun. If he looked up—if he risked it, and it was not much risk, surely, he might be able to catch sight of the sun to one side of the vast hull from which the gondola hung. . . .

Momentarily, he halted to rest the aching muscles in his thighs, and glanced upward. Scarcely ten cubits overhead, the cable entered the monstrous belly of the airship proper; beyond the opening, he glimpsed the beam to which it was attached.

·   ·   ·

"Done try, laddie."

"Tick!" Hyacinth stared, blinking away tears. "Tick, how in the whorl—"

Auk handed him to her. "Came in through the window, didn't you, cully? A dimber cat burglar, ain't you?"

"My see, wears she putty laddie?" Tick explained. "An Gawk sees, hue comb wit may. Den my—add word!"

" 'Lo, girl." Flapping in advance of Silk, Oreb ignored the little cat-achrest. " 'Lo, Auk."

Auk swore. Hyacinth dropped Tick (who landed on his feet) and Silk embraced her.

To him, so lost in the ecstasy of her kiss that he scarcely knew that her right leg had twined about his left, or that her loins ground his, Horn's distant shout meant less than nothing.

"So what?" Auk inquired from the West Pole. *"Let 'em come."*

After what seemed an eternity of love, something tapped Silk's arm and Hyacinth backed away.

"Caldé Silk!" The harsh voice belonged to a gaunt, hard-faced Trivigaunti officer of forty or more; he blinked, certain that he should recognize her.

"You're Caldé Silk. Let's not waste time in evasions."

"Yes, I am." She had clicked into place in his memory, her hand around a wineglass, her back straight as a slug-gun barrel. "Major Hadale, this is my wife, Hyacinth. Hyacinth, my darling, may I present Major Hadale? She's one of General Saba's most trusted officers. Major Hadale consented to join me for dinner Thelxday, before we were reunited."

Oreb eyed Hadale apprehensively. "Good girl?"

The major herself addressed the lieutenant on her right. "You were in here an hour ago looking for him. Are you saying he wasn't here then?"

"No, sir." The lieutenant's face was set like stone. "He was not. I'm familiar with his appearance, and I examined every prisoner in this gondola. He was not present."

Hadale turned to a trooper with a slug gun. "How long have you been on post?"

Silk began, "If I may—"

"In a moment. How long, Matar?"

The trooper had stiffened to attention. "Almost my whole watch, sir."

Auk spoke into Silk's ear; but if Silk heard him—or anything—he gave no indication of it. "You're going to ask her if anyone left this gondola," he told Hadale. "She'll say no, and then I suppose you'll call her a liar, or the lieutenant will. Can't we—"

"Before we came down here I asked if she'd seen anybody," Hadale interrupted. "She said she did. She saw a Vironese holy man. He went down into this gondola, and he had an order from General Saba that let him. Is that right, Matar?"

"Yes, sir."

Silk fished a folded paper from his pocket. "Here it is. Do you want to see it?"

"No!" Angrily, Hadale took it from him. "I want to keep it. I intend to. Caldé, you were careful to remind me that I've been your guest. You welcomed me and fed me well. That puts me in an uncomfortable position." She glanced at the crowd that had formed around them. "Get out of here! Go to the other end of the gondola, all of you."

Auk smiled and shook his head. Sciathan tugged the sleeve of Silk's robe. "Now you wish it? If not, you must stop it."

"You're right, of course." Silk raised both hands. "Auk! All of you! Go to the other end. You're very brave, and there are only three of them; but there are at least a hundred others on this airship." He took Hyacinth's hand.

"Go 'way!" Oreb seconded him.

Maytera Marble added her voice to theirs, the crisp tones of a teacher bringing her classroom to order. "Hear that bird? He's a night chough, sacred to Tartaros. Trust Tartaros!"

"*I* speak for the *gods.*" Incus stood on tiptoe, making wide gestures. "We must *obey* the caldé, whom the *immortal* gods have chosen for all of us."

"Thank you," Silk told the little Flier. "Thank you very much. Moly—thank you. Thank you, Your Eminence."

Hadale exhaled, a weary sigh that recalled Maytera Marble. "And I thank you, Caldé. They wouldn't have succeeded, but there would've been a lot of killing. By Scarring Sphigx, I don't like this! A few days ago, we were drinking toasts."

"I like it less," Silk told her. "I propose that we put an end to it. May I speak with General Saba?"

Hadale shook her head. "Lieutenant, you and Matar go over there and keep an eye on those people. They may try to jump you. Shoot if they do."

Silk watched them go. "I'd imagine you've got a glass on this airship. If you won't let me speak with General Saba, may I use it to speak to your generalissimo?"

"No." Hadale paused to listen. "We just lost an engine."

"The second one," Hyacinth told her. "That was what Auk whispered to my husband, that the first one had stopped. I've been paying attention to them ever since."

"Auk's the man who was talking to my wife and me when you came," Silk explained. "I apologize for not introducing you."

"I should be in the cockpit, they'll be going crazy up there. Caldé, are you doing this?"

"Good man!" Oreb assured Hadale. "Good Silk!"

She gave him a look intended to fry him. "Your bird's an oracle of Tartaros, so if he says you're good that settles it. Don't you know that many of us don't believe in Tartaros, Caldé? We have a faction that teaches that Sphigx is the only true god, and Pas and the rest are just legends. A lot of us believe it."

Silk nodded, looking at the dangling ladder behind her. "I can sympathize with that—no doubt it's nearer the truth than many of our beliefs. May I offer a suggestion, Major?"

"I've got one, too, but let's hear yours. What is it?"

He showed her his hands. "We're unarmed. You may search us if you wish; and we won't attack you—we'll swear to that by Sphigx or any other god you choose. If you were to hand your needler to Hyacinth or me, we wouldn't employ it against you—though of course I'm not asking you to do anything of the kind. That said, I suggest we go to the place from which this airship is commanded. Where the tiller is, or whatever you call it. Is that the cockpit?"

Hadale nodded, her eyes suspicious.

"First, because we'd like to see it—that's a selfish reason, I admit, but we would. Second, because they may need you there, you're clearly anxious to go, and we can talk there as well as anywhere. Third—"

Hadale pointed to the dangling ladder. "That's enough. All right. You two first, and stay in front."

"So," Siyuf began as she sat down in the wooden chair the round-faced stranger pulled out for her, "are we today at war? I hope you are lose, General Mint." Without evident curiosity, her quick, dark eyes surveyed the spartan room, and the snow-splotched drill field and leaden sky beyond its windows.

Oosik nodded as he took his seat. "That was a point we planned to discuss, Generalissimo. Events have overtaken us."

"Trivigaunte declared war on Viron an hour ago," Maytera Mint said briskly. "We feel we owe it to you to explain the situation. Our caldé thinks you care nothing for the lives of your troops. He's told me so. I'm doing something here that's quite foreign to me, I'm assuming he's wrong. If he isn't, no harm will be done by this meeting. If he is," she smiled, "some good may come of it. Are your troopers' lives precious to you?"

The elevation and decline of Siyuf's epaulets was scarcely visible. "Valuable is certain. Precious we must speak about, I think. Do you know how greatly I have desire to meet you, Mint? Do they tell this? Is Bison to sit in one of these empty chairs? He know of this."

A new voice exclaimed, "So do I! I vouch for her, my dear young general. She's expressed the wish many times."

Siyuf turned to the fat man who had come in. "You I know from a picture. You are Potto of the Ayuntamiento, that would make war on my city. You have win, I think, if we are at war."

Potto sat gingerly, unsure of the strength of his chair. "If only a declaration were all it took!"

"I'm Councillor Newt," the round-faced stranger explained, "The newest member of the Ayuntamiento." He offered his hand.

She accepted it. "I am your prisoner Siyuf."

"Not a badly treated one, I hope."

Potto giggled. "A very well treated one, so far, Cousin. Since you're a councillor now, I've appointed you an honorary cousin. Do you mind?"

Oosik cleared his throat. "Perhaps I should outline the entire situation, Generalissimo."

"We are at war, you say. I believe this. I therefore give my name and rank. These alone, no other fact. Do you desire to exchange me? I will go."

Maytera Mint said, "We do, very much."

"Then I will fight you, after. It is to be regretted, but it is so. You cannot make me answer your questions—"

Potto giggled again.

"No more can I make you to answer mine. I ask anyway. Do you fight me together, Mint? Or do you fight each other also? When I return to my horde, it would be good that I know this."

"Viron's reunited. It's been our caldé's dearest wish, and I'm delighted to say we've realized it."

Potto rocked with mirth. "Wait till he finds out we're on the same side! I can't wait to see his face."

"He'll be radiant with joy. If you understood him as I do, you'd know it." Maytera Mint spoke to Siyuf. "Let me explain, because all this hinges on your understanding what your troops are up against. We've not only made peace among ourselves, but given the city a new government. There are two main provisions to our agreement. One is that ours is a Charterial government, which means there must be a caldé and an Ayuntamiento. We agree mutually that Caldé Silk is—"

"My prisoner," Siyuf interrupted.

"Hardly." Oosik leaned forward, his elbows upon the old deal table, his bass voice dominating the room. "He may be a prisoner of your city. We don't know that yet. It is one of the things we need to discuss."

Siyuf looked back to Maytera Marble. "You wish to tell me of the Charter of your city, before this man have interrupt you. I find this of interest."

"I think it's vital. If we're to secure the favor of the gods, we have to govern according to the Charter they gave us. We've been trying from the start. Now we've succeeded."

"I would ask who it is who rule this government, but you say Silk, who is not here. Who is commander here? You?"

Maytera Mint shook her head. "In military affairs, my own superior, Generalissimo Oosik. In civil, Councillor Potto, the Presiding Officer of the Ayuntamiento."

"In this case you are not needed," Siyuf told her, and turned to Newt. "Neither you, I think. Yet both sit at this table where is one chair more. You take our custom that each bring a subordinate? Is that the explanation I require? You for Potto, Mint for Oosik, Violet for me, perhaps? I do not think this I have say."

"I'm breaking in," Newt told her. "I'm the new boy." He sounded anything but humble.

"I'm here," Maytera Mint explained, "because we think you may listen to a woman when you won't really hear a man."

Oosik rumbled, "You've the quickest mind I know. You are present because we are likely to succeed because you are here."

"I'm less apt to kill him, too," Potto confided.

"He's only joking," Newt assured Siyuf.

"Not, I hope. You are a new councillor, you say. Where is it they find you?"

Maytera Mint said, "In the Juzgado. Councillor Newt was a commissioner there, the one who bought supplies for the Caldé's Guard, made out the payroll, and so forth." She paused.

"When I began, when Echidna called me her sword, I thought all we had to do was fight. I'm learning that fighting is the smallest part of it, and in some ways the easiest."

Smiling, Siyuf nodded.

"Quite often it's the other things that count most. You have to get supplies to the people who need them, and not just ammunition but food and bedding, and warm clothes. At any rate, part of our agreement was an acknowledgment by all of us that the Charter demands an Ayuntamiento."

Potto made her a seated bow.

"But not *just* an Ayuntamiento, an elected one with a full compliment of councillors. We can't hold elections because of the state things are in, so we've promised them after a year of peace. Meanwhile the present members will continue to serve, with Councillor Potto as Presiding Officer. New councillors are to be appointed as necessary by the caldé, or in his absence by a de facto board of those who have his confidence. It consists of the current Ayuntamiento, including Councillor Newt now, with Generalissimo Oosik, His Cognizance, and me. I wanted a woman councillor—"

"You will not have her," Siyuf put in. "They are all men."

"So we appointed Kingcup. She's not here because she's out explaining all this to our people. I felt we needed—" Maytera Mint groped for words. "An ordinary woman with extraordinary gifts. Kingcup's from a poor family, but she built a successful livery stable from scratch, so she's used to managing. Besides, she's the bravest woman in Viron."

Oosik muttered, "No one but you would say that, General."

She brushed the compliment aside. "So Kingcup for the people and Newt for the Juzgado."

"With such as these you prepare to fight me," Siyuf mused, "but I am not there. This is sad. I beat you, I think. Does my General Rimah beat you also? I do not know. She is a good officer. You ask of love for my horde. Why is this?"

"Because we hope that you will want to preserve it," Oosik told her, "as I want to preserve the Guard. There has been some skirmishing already. If we fight in earnest, your horde will be destroyed and my Guard decimated." Maytera Mint added, "To say nothing of what will happen to our city," and Oosik nodded.

"We wish victory. None but cowards count life more high."

Maytera Mint started to speak, but Oosik silenced her with a gesture. "I am confident General Rimah is an able officer. You're not the sort to tolerate anything less. There is a gulf, however, between an able officer and an exceptional leader. The ranks sense it at once, and the public almost as quickly. I will not ask if you care about your troops. We're too close for that, you and I, so close I can hear my own voice in everything you've said. You long for victory, and you know, as I do, that it would be more probable if you were in command of your troops. Wouldn't you agree that for any other—"

Potto interrupted. "A subject of the Rani's."

"That for another citizen of your city," Oosik continued, "To prevent you from resuming your place would be treason? It is not an idle question."

"You think someone does this? I wish to know."

"Let me." Maytera Mint's small, not uncomely face shone with energy and resolve. "You want to fight me, Siyuf, because of what you've heard about me. I don't want to fight you, and in fact it's the last thing I want. I want peace. I want to end this foolish fighting and let everybody in our city and yours go back to their proper lives. But it's been clear ever since your spies tried to arrest us that as long as you have our caldé there can be no peace. I'm going to assume you understand that, because if you don't there's no use talking."

"I am captive also." Siyuf touched her chest.

"Exactly! You've saved me a lot of time. We've got you, but in a very important way we don't want you, since your city will fight to get you back. Clearly the sensible thing is to exchange you for our caldé. Peace would be possible then, but if we still couldn't make peace, you and I would be fighting each other, which is what you want. Now if—"

Siyuf made a quick motion, the gesture of one accustomed to instant obedience. "I have pledged to your Sand that I will free Incus the holy man and Marble. She is your friend?"

"Yes, she is." Maytera Mint glanced at Oosik, but he did not speak. "You cheated Sergeant Sand and Corporal Hammerstone. You know you did. You knew those prisoners were already on your airship when you promised to let them go."

"Over this we fight a duel, perhaps, if I am free. It may still be so. I did not know, Mint. If you have deal with Saba and her airship as I, you know that what is to be at shadeup may not be until midday, or not this day or the next. Let me go. I get them again and free them. Caldé Silk also."

For a second or two Maytera Mint studied her with pursed lips. "All right, I'll accept that. I apologize."

Potto tittered.

"But your airship doesn't seem to have reached Trivigaunte yet. Does that bother you?"

Siyuf shook her head. "Tonight, or I think the morning."

Oosik rumbled, "Suppose I were to say tomorrow afternoon, Generalissimo. Your knowledge, I contend, is not so deep as you pretend. Tomorrow afternoon!"

Siyuf shrugged. "If you say. Perhaps."

"In that case I proffer a further supposition. Not before shadelow next Phaesday. What would you say to that?"

"That you are a fool. The airship could be here once more in such a time."

"Just so." Oosik wound his white-tipped mustache about his finger.

"We have contacted Trivigaunte by glass, Generalissimo. We have spoken to your Minister of War. We have explained how things stand here, and offered to exchange you for Caldé Silk."

"They won't," Newt declared. "Won't do it or even talk about it, by Scylla! We invite your comments."

"I offer what is better. Let me speak with her."

Potto roared, slapping his thigh. "This is too, too rich! My dear young General, you're not even smiling. How do you do it?" He turned back to Siyuf, speaking across the empty chair. "You already have, and it didn't help a bit."

"I have not. Abanja for me, perhaps."

Maytera Mint said, "We think it's politics. By we I mean Generalissimo Oosik and I. The internal politics of your city. We'd like confirmation of that, and some suggestions about what to do about it."

"If this you say is true . . ." Siyuf shrugged again.

Oosik muttered, "Every city has its feuds, Generalissimo."

"Mine also. Our War Minister, you do not say her name. This is Ljam? A scar here?" Siyuf touched her upper lip.

Newt and Maytera Mint nodded.

"This is not possible. My city have politics, as your generalissimo say. Feuds, plottings, hatreds. Of these very many. But Ljam is with me most near. If I fail here she fail also. You understand? Lose her ministry, perhaps her head."

Oosik regarded Siyuf through slitted eyes. "You're saying it is impossible for her to betray you, Generalissimo?"

"She cannot unless she is betray herself!"

Potto sang, "I told you! I told you!"

"He thinks your airship's wrecked, or it's gone off course somehow." Maytera Mint looked somber. "Naturally they won't say so, and Generalissimo Oosik and I thought it was more likely they were playing some game, though Councillor Potto received a report implying it's gone. Now it seems he must be right. This is truly unfortunate."

"But we're going to let you go anyhow," Potto told Siyuf. "Isn't that nice of us?" He bounced from his chair and went to the door calling, "You can send them in!"

It was opened by a soldier; and Violet and a second Siyuf entered, Violet with her arm linked with the second Siyuf's. She stared at the first in open-mouthed amazement.

"You'll have to go now, my dear young strumpet," Potto told her. "We don't want you, though I'm sure many do. Have a seat, Generalissimo. I'll be with you in a half a moment."

"I am to sit beside this bio?" the second Siyuf inquired. "This I do not like. You say you send me to my horde, I think. When is it you do this?"

"You'll escape," Newt explained to the first Siyuf. "Or rather, she will."

"Too much warlockery for me." Hadale dropped into one of the cockpit's black-leather seats. "Too much in your city, and too much on our airship now that you're here. People at home say you're all warlocks, but I discounted it. I should have tripled everything. You're a warlock, Caldé, and I'd call you the chief warlock if I hadn't met the old man who sat between our generalissimo and General Saba."

"She refers to His Cognizance," Silk told Hyacinth; awed and delighted, he tried to stare at everything at once. "Like a conservatory . . ."

Oreb croaked "Bad thing" as Tick squirmed in Hyacinth's grasp. "Add word, dew!"

"Three engines gone." Hadale peered morosely through the nearest rectangle of glass at the parting clouds and the rocky sandscape that they revealed. "What do you want? Surrender? I'll shoot you first and take my chances with the desert."

"Then we don't want it," Hyacinth declared.

"We don't in any case," Silk said, "and I'm no warlock; the truth is that I'm hardly an augur any more—I certainly don't feel like one."

"General Saba told me the other day that you read about our advance in sheepguts. Do you deny it?"

"No, though it isn't true. Denying it would waste time, so you may believe it if you like. There are five engines still in operation. Is that enough to keep us in the air?"

The navigator looked up from her charts, then returned to them; Hadale pointed to the ceiling. "None are needed to keep us up, the gas does it. Are we going to lose all our engines?"

Silk considered. "I can't promise that. I hope so."

"You hope so."

"No shoot," Oreb advised Hadale nervously. "Good man."

"It was what I intended." For a moment, Silk allowed his eyes to feast on Hyacinth's loveliness. "The risk that gave me most concern was that Hyacinth might be killed as a result of what I was doing; I hoped it wouldn't happen, and I'm very glad it won't. I betrayed my god for her—I was horribly afraid that it would recoil on me, as such things do."

She brought his hand to the soft warmth of her thigh. "You betrayed the Outsider for me? I'd never ask you to do that."

Hadale turned to the pilot, "We've still got five?"

The pilot nodded. "Can't make much headway against this wind with five, though, sir."

Hyacinth asked, "Aren't we going south anyway? Isn't the wind blowing us south to Trivigaunte? Somebody said something like that."

"It's blowing us south," Hadale told her bitterly, "but not to Trivigaunte. We turned east for about an hour before the first one quit."

"Veering north-northwest, sir," the pilot reported.

Having freed himself from Hyacinth's grasp, Tick stood on his hind legs to pat Hadale's knee. "Rust Milk, laddie. Milk bill take hit hall tight."

"He says you can trust my husband," Hyacinth interpreted. "He's right, too, and I don't think you ought to pay too much attention to what my husband says about betraying a god. He—oh, I don't know how to explain! He's forever blaming himself for the wrong things. He's sorry for holding me too tight when I wish he'd hold me tighter. See?"

"Your catachrest's an oracle of our goddess, so I have to trust him implicitly. Is that it?"

"I didn't say that." Hyacinth sat down. "I guess I would have, though, if I thought you'd believe it. Maybe it's right, and she isn't telling us."

"Hat's shoe!" Tick exclaimed.

Silk smiled. "I take it that General Saba's no longer in charge. Where is she?"

"In her bunk, with three troopers to watch her. I won't ask how you drove her mad. I'm sure you wouldn't tell me."

"I didn't." He leaned over the crescent-shaped instrument panel for a better view of the desert below. "I arranged for her to be possessed, that's all. You saw the same thing at our dinner. Are you in charge now? There's no one over you?"

"The War Minister. In a moment I'm going to have to report this situation to her."

"No talk," Oreb advised.

"By 'this situation' you mean—"

"Three engines out. I've told her about Saba turning east already. I had to. I was hoping you'd agree to repair the engines before I had to report them, too. That's why I let you come up here. Will you?"

"I can't." Silk took the seat next to Hyacinth's. "Nor would I if I could. We'd be back where we began, with Auk's people trying to seize control, and everyone—all of us, I mean—dying. I said I betrayed the Outsider because that was how I felt—"

"Wind's due west now, sir," the pilot reported.

"Course?"

"East by south, sir. We might try dropping down."

"Do it." Hadale considered. "A hundred and fifty cubits." She turned back to Silk. "You were afraid we'd crash. We may. It's dangerous to fly that low in weather as windy as this. If a downdraft catches us, we could be finished. But the wind won't be as strong down there."

Hyacinth gasped, and Silk said, "I can feel the airship descend. I rode in a moving room once that felt like this."

"You want to go east. That was how you had General Saba steering us."

He nodded, and smiled again. "To Mainframe. Auk wants to carry out the Plan of Pas, and the Outsider wants it, too, which is why I felt I was betraying him when I did what I did to your engines. But letting Auk try to take your airship wouldn't have achieved anything, and this was the only way I could think of to prevent him."

"So now that we don't have enough engines to fight the wind, you're working your magic on that."

Silk shook his head. "I can't. All that I can do is pray, which isn't magic at all, but begging. I've been doing it, and perhaps I've been heard."

He drew a deep breath. "You want your engines back in operation, Major. You want to preserve this airship, and to deliver me to your superiors in Trivigaunte; the rest of your prisoners don't matter greatly, as you must know. I do."

Slowly, Hadale nodded.

"We can do all that, if only you'll cooperate. Take us to Mainframe, as Pas commands and the Outsider wishes. Auk and his people can leave the whorl and thus begin carrying out the Plan. Hyacinth and I will return—"

"Shut up!" Hadale cocked her head, listening.

The pilot said, "Number seven's quit, sir." The absence of all emotion in her voice conveyed what she felt.

"Take her up fast. Just below the cloud cover."

Hyacinth asked Silk, "Won't the wind be stronger there?"

Hadale was on her feet, scanning the desert below. "A lot stronger, but I'm going to set her down and try to fix the engines. Even if we can't, we won't be blowing farther from Trivigaunte. We want a big level stretch to land on, and an oasis, if we can find one."

"No land!" Oreb advised sharply; Hyacinth began, "If you'll go to Mainframe like he—"

Hadale whirled. "He can't fix them. He admits it."

Silk had risen, too; almost whispering, he said, "You must have faith, Major."

"All right, I've got faith. Slashing Sphigx, succor us! Meanwhile I need a place to set us down on."

"I said I couldn't repair your engines. I said it because it's the truth. I should have added—as I do, now—that if only we were doing the gods' will instead of opposing it, a way to repair them—"

"Sir!" The pilot pointed.

"I see them. Can you get us over there?"

"I think so, sir. I'll try."

Silk leaned forward, squinting. Hyacinth said, "Something like ants, but they're leagues and leagues away."

"That's a caravan," Hadale told Silk, "could be one of ours. Even if it isn't, they'll have food and water, and a few of us can ride to the city to guide a rescue party."

"I just hope they're friendly," Hyacinth murmured.

Rubbing her hands, Hadale looked ten years younger. "They will be soon. I've got two platoons of pterotroopers on board."

Chapter 15

To Mainframe!

"Silk say." Settling on Auk's extended wrist, Oreb whistled sharply to emphasize the urgency of his message. "Say Auk!"

"All right, spill it."

Matar prodded Auk's ribs with the muzzle of her slug gun. "The lieutenant says for you to stop leaning out of this port. She's afraid you'll jump out."

Auk withdrew his head and arm. "Not me. I could, though. With our gun deck—that what you call it?"

Both Matar and Chenille nodded.

"Shaggy near on the ground like this, it's maybe eight cubits. That's sand down there, too, so it'd be candy."

Matar was studying Oreb. "Where did you find that bird? I thought your caldé had it."

"Girls go," Oreb reported hoarsely. "Say Auk."

"He just flew down and lit on me," Auk explained. "Me and him's a old knot." Gently, he stroked Oreb with his forefinger.

Chenille told Matar, "We were together down in the tunnels under our city. It was pretty rough."

"It *was*, my daughter." Incus joined the group. "It was *there*, however, that *I* received the divine *favor* of Surging *Scylla*, our patroness."

From her seat at the front of the gondola, the lieutenant called, "What are you talking about back there?"

"Tunnels, sir." Matar was a lean young woman two fingers smaller than most.

"There," Incus elucidated, "I learned to load and *shoot* a needler." He approached the lieutenant, his plump face wreathed in smiles. "It is an *accomplishment* of which very few augurs *indeed* can boast. I had a most excellent *teacher* in my faithful *friend* Corporal Hammerstone."

"Girls go," Oreb repeated. "Camels. Girl take."

"Matar!" the lieutenant called. "Get over here." Matar hurried to obey.

Maytera Marble caught Auk's sleeve. "There's something else," she whispered. "That little cat creature Patera's wife had is back."

Auk nodded absently. "He's got word from Silk, I'll lay."

"Something about milk and mammals," she explained, "and strong twine off caramels. I can't quite make out what it's so excited about. Gib has it."

"That's camels in a caravan," Auk said under his breath. "I saw 'em, and I saw troopers going after 'em. Now I got to take the dell and her jefe before that flash little butcher does it and nabs the credit."

The flat crack of a needler came from the front of the gondola; a woman screamed.

Silk had been watching two distant Trivigauntis probe the desert sand for soil with enough cohesion to hold a mooring stake. As the faint thuddings of the heavy maul reached the cockpit, he turned to the pilot. "Could we take off without untying those ropes?"

"The mooring lines?" The pilot shook her head.

"That's unfortunate. It might have saved lives." He sat down beside Hyacinth again and took her hand, listening to the moan of a winter wind that raised sand devils in the distance.

"We ought to have half a dozen more," the pilot told him. "We will, too, pretty soon. We use twenty-four at home."

"You have five already." The number suggested Hyacinth's five fingers; Silk raised them to his lips, kissing them and the cheap and foolish ring that had been the only ring they had. His padded leather seat lifted sharply beneath him, a forceful upward push like that of Blood's floater rising from the grassway. "Feel that?" the pilot said.

Hyacinth pointed. "Something flashed way over there." She swung wide the pane they had opened for Tick.

"Don't do that," the pilot told her. "We've got plenty of cold air in here already."

Silk put his own finger to his lips. Almost beyond the edge of hear-

ing, faint, irregular booms filled the intervals between the blows of the
maul. "They're firing," he informed the pilot. "I know the sound from
the fighting in our city."

Then the gondola heaved beneath them again, faster than the moving room had ever moved, and wilder even than Oosik's armed floater—
rocked and shook them as it soared into the air.

Nearer than the besieged caravan, a slug gun boomed, loud among
the gondola's tormented creaks and groans. Reeling, the pilot jerked out
her needler. Hyacinth knocked it from her hand and rammed both
thumbs into her eyes, kicking savagely at her knees until both she and
the pilot fell.

"What are you doing?" Auk inquired.

"Dropping ballast." Silk pointed. "If you'll look down there, you
should see something like smoke falling from under the rear gondola."

Auk thrust his head and shoulders through the opening left by a
shot-out pane of glass. "Yeah."

"That's desert sand," Hyacinth explained. "They started shoveling
more on as soon as we got down, and the pilot told us about it. You can
make this go up with the engines, or pull it down with them. That's
what we did when we landed. But if you want to fly high up for a long
while, the easiest way's to drop sand like he's doing."

Chenille said, "This floor's about level now."

Silk nodded, pointing toward the bubble in a horizontal tube on the
instrument panel.

Auk took the seat nearest him. "If you want me to, I can get somebody else to do this. Even that pilot. I'd have one of ours sit here to
watch her."

"She's blind," Silk told him. He threw a lever on the instrument
panel. "Hyacinth blinded her. I saw it."

"She's just got sore eyes, Patera. She'll be dandy."

Hyacinth sat on Silk's left. "You like this, don't you?"

"I love it—and I'm terrified by it at the same time. I'm afraid I'm
going to kill us all; but the pilot or another Trivigaunti might do so
intentionally, and I certainly won't. But . . ." His voice trailed away.

"Even if we had a pilot we could trust, you'd want to."

He cleared his throat. "We do have a pilot we can trust—me. I'm not very experienced as yet, but there must have been a time when that woman wasn't either."

Chenille sat down next to Hyacinth. "You poke her glims?"

Hyacinth nodded. "She was going to shoot us, Chen."

"No shoot!" Oreb sailed into the cockpit.

"Right," Hyacinth told him. "That's what I thought, but we had shooting anyway when Auk's culls fought it out with the troopers watching the general."

"Only Patera's still sort of bothered by what you did to her. I can tell."

Silk glanced at Chenille. "Am I so transparent as that?"

"Sure." She grinned. "Listen, Patera. Do you think us dells at Orchid's were always really polite? Do you think we always said please and thank you, and excuse me, Bluebell, but that gown you've got on looks a whole lot like one of mine?"

"I don't know," Silk admitted. "I would hope so." From his shoulder, Oreb eyed him quizzically.

"You think I'm rough because I'm big, and you think those dells from Trivigaunte are because they don't wear makeup, and they had needlers and slug guns. I never had to fight a lot at Orchid's because I was the longest dell there. You know where Hyacinth comes on me?"

"I believe I do, yes."

"Without those heels she always wears, the top of her head doesn't even hit my shoulder. She's beautiful, too, like you always say. The whole time she lived there, she was the best-looking dell Orchid had, and Orchid would tell you so herself. You know who looks the most like Hy now? It's Poppy, and Poppy looks like Hy about as much as a sham card looks like a lily one. You know how that is? They look the same till you look hard, but when you do you know it's not even close. The gold in the sham one looks brassy, and it feels greasy. You look at Hy, at her eyes and nose. Look at her chin. Just look! The first couple weeks I knew her I couldn't see her chin without feeling like a toad in the road." The huskiness that affects women's voices when they speak of matters of genuine importance entered Chenille's. "Poppy's cute, Patera. Hy's real gold."

"I know."

"So just about everybody hated her." Chenille coughed. "I nearly did myself. The second or third day—"

"Second," Hyacinth interjected.

"She came to the big room with a mouse under both eyes. Orchid threw a fit. But you know what?"

Silk shook his head; Hyacinth said, "That's plenty, Chen," and he swiveled his seat to face Chenille. "Please tell me. I promise you that I won't hold it against her, whatever it is."

"No talk," Oreb croaked.

"I was going to tell you what happened next, but I'll skip it. She doesn't want me to, and she's probably right. Only she learned fast. She had to, or she'd of been killed. A couple days after that I saw a dell shove her, and Hy tripped her and wapped her with a chair. A lot of the other dells saw it too, and they left her alone. Are you wanting to ask something?"

Silk said, "No."

"I kind of thought you were, that you were about to ask me if Hy and I ever got into it."

Hyacinth shook her head.

"If I could've worn her clothes, maybe we would. Or if she could've worn mine. We weren't a knot, either, I'd be lying if I said we were. For one thing, she wasn't there long enough. I didn't like her a whole lot, even, but there were things I liked about her. I told you one time."

Auk said, "Sitting in that thing they got for the grapes back at your manteion, Patera. I was there."

Silk nodded. "Yes, I remember. I could tell you what you said, Chenille, almost word for word—not because my memory's remarkable, but because Hyacinth is so important to me."

He turned away to scan the instrument panel and the cloud-smeared sky, then turned to Auk. "As a favor, would you please bring Sciathan?"

"Sure." Auk rose. "Only I got to talk to you about those engines, see? I need you to tell me what you did to 'em, and if we're going to lose any more."

"I'll get him," Hyacinth said, and left the cockpit before Silk could stop her.

Chenille leaned nearer Silk. "She thinks you ought to be proud of her. I do too."

He nodded.

"Only you're not, and it hurts. The first time you saw her she had an azoth, and you had to jump out the window to get away. Isn't that right? Moly told me."

"It was terrifying," Silk admitted. Although he was not perspiring, he wiped his face with the hem of his robe. "The azoth cut through a stone windowsill. I don't believe I will ever forget it."

Auk said, "You think she was just some village chit after that, Patera?"

"No. No, I didn't. I knew exactly what she was."

He was silent then until Sciathan came into the cockpit and bowed, saying, "Do you desire to speak to me, Caldé Silk?"

"Yes. Have you flown an airship like this one?"

"Never. I have flown with my wings many times, but we crew have nothing like this save the *Whorl* itself, and that is flown by Mainframe, not by us."

"I understand. Just the same, you know a great deal about updrafts and downdrafts and storms; more than I'll ever learn. I've been flying this airship since a gust dispatched for our benefit by Molpe—or the Outsider, as I prefer to believe—returned us to the air. Now I want to leave the controls for a while. Will you take my place? I'd be extremely grateful."

The Flier nodded eagerly. "Oh, yes! Thank you, Caldé Silk. Thank you very much!"

"Then sit here." Silk left his seat, and Sciathan slid into it. "There are no reins, nor is there a wheel one turns, as there is in a floater. One steers with the engines. Do you understand?"

Sciathan nodded, and Auk cleared his throat.

"A west wind is carrying us toward Mainframe. We could fly faster, but it may be wise to conserve fuel. These dials give the speeds of all eight engines; as you see, four are no longer operating."

As quickly as he could, Silk outlined what he had learned of the functions of the levers and knobs on the panel; as soon as the Flier seemed to comprehend, Silk turned to Auk. "You wanted to know what I did to the engines. I did very little. I climbed up there into the cloth-covered body."

Auk said, "Sure. I knew you must of."

"Most of the space—it's enormous—is occupied by rows of huge balloons. There are bamboo walkways and wooden beams."

"I been on some."

"Yes, of course; you'd have had to in the fighting. What I was going to say is that there are tanks and hoses, too. I'd found a clamp, a simple one such as a carpenter might use."

Silk paused to glance at the bird on his shoulder. "It was then that Oreb joined me; I'd just picked it up. Anyway I put it on a hose, I suppose a fuel hose, and screwed it closed as tightly as I could. I doubt that it stopped the flow entirely, but it must have reduced it very considerably. It shouldn't be hard to find when you know what to look for."

Auk rubbed his chin. "Don't sound like it."

"For my conscience's sake, I should tell you that I lied to Major Hadale—or anyway, I came very close to lying. She asked whether I could repair the engines; and I said, quite honestly I believe, that I could not. One speaks of repairs when a thing is broken. To the best of my knowledge, the engines we've lost aren't; but if they were, I wouldn't have the faintest notion how they might be repaired—thus I told her truthfully that repairing them was beyond my power. It was not a lie, though I certainly intended it to deceive her. If I'd said I might be able to set them in motion again, she would have had me beaten, I imagine, to compel me to do it."

Without turning toward them, Sciathan nodded vigorously.

"I'll ask Patera Incus to shrive me later today. Will you excuse me now? I . . . I would like very much to be alone."

As he left the cockpit, Auk told his back, "Get him to tell you how he charmed the slug gun."

A flimsy door of canvas stretched over a bamboo frame was all that separated the cockpit from a narrow aisle lined with green-curtained cubicles. Hearing a familiar voice, Silk pushed aside the curtain on his right.

The cubicle seemed overfilled by a bunk, a small table, and a stool; Nettle occupied the stool, holding a needler, and Saba smiled in a way that Silk found painful from the bunk.

"Poor girl," Oreb muttered.

Silk traced the sign of addition in the air. "Blessed be you, General Saba, in the Sacred Name of Pas, Father of the Gods, in that of Gracious Echidna, His Consort, in those of their Sons and their Daughters alike, in that of the Overseeing Outsider, and in the names of all other gods whatsoever, this day and forever. So say I, Silk, in the name of their youngest, fairest child, Steely Sphigx, Goddess of Hardihood and Courage, Sabered Sphigx, the glad and glorious patroness of General Saba and General Saba's native city."

"Gracious of you, Caldé. I thought you'd come to gloat."

Nettle shook her head. "You don't know him."

"I came—or at least I left the cockpit—to escape my friends," Silk told Saba. "I had no more than stepped out when I heard you and looked in. 'When neither our fellows nor our gods spoil our plans, we spoil them ourselves.' I read that when I was a boy, and I've learned since how very true it is."

Nettle said, "She was telling me about Trivigaunte, Caldé. I don't think I'd want to live there, but I'd like to see it."

"We go in for towers." Saba smiled. "We say it's because we build such good ones, but maybe we build good ones because we build so many of them. Towers and whitewash, and wide, clean streets. Your city looks," she paused, searching for a telling word, "squatty, like a camp. Squatty and dirty. I know you love it, but that's how it looks to us."

Silk nodded. "I understand. The interiors of our houses are clean, I believe, for the most part; but our streets are filthy, as you say. I was trying to do something about it, and a great many other things, when I was arrested."

"Not by me," Saba told him. "I didn't order it."

"I never thought you did."

"But you were talking to the enemy without telling us. If—" Saba's voice broke, and Oreb croaked in sympathy.

"We each have our sorrows." Silk let the green curtain fall behind him. "I won't ask you to palliate mine, but I may be able to ease yours. I'll try. What were you about to say?"

"I started to say I'd put in a word for you back home, that's all. Because we'll get you again when we get back this airship. If Siyuf's not running your city yet, she soon will be." Saba chuckled wryly. "Then I remembered where I stand. I'd forgotten, talking to this girl. I'm the general who went crazy and turned the airship east when it ought to have been headed home. That's what Hadale told them at the Palace, that I'd gone crazy. They'll think it was treachery and she was covering for me."

"You weren't insane," Silk told her. "You were possessed by Mucor, at my urging. You were possessed in the same way at my dinner. Others must have told you about it—Major Hadale, particularly, since she is your subordinate."

"I didn't want to hear it. Is Hadale your prisoner too?"

Silk shook his head. "She left the airship with most of your pterotroopers to capture a caravan. That let Auk and Gib and their friends overcome the rest."

Nettle held up her needler. "We fought too, Horn and me both. We'd fought hoppies already for General Mint, but a lot of Auk's people had never fought before. Hardly any of the women." To Saba she added, "Your pterotroopers were good, but our hoppies were better. You couldn't panic them."

"I'm sure you acquitted yourself creditably," Silk told her. "I, unfortunately, did not. Hyacinth knocked a needler from the pilot's hand and subdued her. I picked it up and held it, feeling an utter fool. I couldn't fire for fear of hitting Hyacinth, and with the needler in my hand I couldn't think of anything else to do. Then someone back here started shooting. Slugs came into the cockpit, and it was only by the favor of a god that all three of us weren't killed."

Silk paused, reflecting. "Have I thanked you, General, for your obvious goodwill? I should, and I do. I'll see to it that you're not mistreated, of course."

Saba shrugged. "That man Auk said I could stay in here, which was nice of him. Those were my jailers that almost shot you. I like this girl better."

She fell silent, and Silk found himself listening to the hum of the engines.

"My pterotroopers fought alongside Mint's when we were the only Trivigrauntis in Viron, Caldé. We fought beside your Guard to get you out of that place outside the city, too. If I said I was planning to put in a good word for you already when we left Viron, would you believe it?"

"Of course."

"I wasn't, but I should have been. I was thinking about covering my own arse, as if that mattered."

"Don't torment yourself, General, I beg you." Silk pushed back the curtain that served the cubicle as a door. "In the second gondola there was a hatch toward the rear that opened onto the roof. Is there a similar hatch here?"

"Sure. I'll show you, if it's all right with her."

"That won't be necessary." Silk stepped back and let the curtain fall.

A rope ladder rolled and tied at the ceiling marked the hatch. Pulling a cord released the ladder. The light wooden hatch was held shut by a simple peg-and-cord retainer. Silk removed the peg, threw back the hatch, and climbed out onto the open, empty deck.

With a glad cry Oreb left his shoulder, racing the length of the gondola, shooting ahead of the airship until he was nearly lost to Silk's myopic vision, wheeling and soaring.

More circumspectly, Silk followed until he stood at the gondola's semicircular prow, the toes of the scuffed old shoes he had never found time to replace hanging over the aching void. He looked down at them, seeing them as if he had never seen them before, noting as items new and strange small cracks in their leather, and the ways in which the shoes had shaped themselves to his feet. Beside his left shoe there was a brass socket set into the deck. Presumably a flagpole would be put in it when the airship took part in military ceremonies in Trivigaunte.

Even more probably, similar sockets ringed the entire deck. Light poles would support railings of rope, used perhaps when dignitaries stood where he was standing now, bemedaled women in gorgeous uniforms waving to the populace below. It was even possible that the Rani herself had stood upon this very spot.

He recalled then that he had wished for flags to be raised on this airship to signal the approach of Siyuf's horde. The signalmen (who would more plausibly have been signalwomen) would have kept watch from here with telescopes, would have run their flags up one of the immense cables from which the gondola hung. Below them—

Some minute motion of the gondola, some response to a tiny variation in the wind, nearly caused him to lose his balance; he came very close to putting his right foot forward to regain it, and would have fallen if he had, ending the persistent pain in its ankle.

It would not have been such a bad thing, perhaps, to have fallen. If one did not dread death, it would be an experience of unparalleled interest; to fall from such a height as this, a height greater than that of the loftiest mountain, would provide ample time for observation, prayer, and reflection, surely.

Eventually his body would strike the ground, probably in some unpeopled spot. His spirit would return to the Aureate Path, where once he had encountered his mothers and fathers; his bones would not be found—if they were found at all—until Nettle's children were grown. To the living he would not die but disappear, a source of wonder rather than sorrow. All men died, and all died very quickly in the eyes of the Outsider. Few died so well as that.

He peered upward to study the Aureate Path as it stretched before the airship's blunt nose, and again felt himself—very slightly—lose balance. If his parents waited there for him, they were not to be seen by the eyes of life.

One father had been Chenille's father as well. He, Silk, who had possessed no family save his mother, had gained a sister now. Although neither Chenille nor Hyacinth nor any other woman could take his mother's place. No one could.

Recalling the unmarked razor he had puzzled over so often, he fingered his stubbled cheeks. He had not shaved in well over a day; no doubt his beard was apparent to everyone. It was better, though, to know to whom the razor had belonged.

He looked down at his shoes again. Beneath them, Sciathan sat at the controls, steering a structure a hundred times larger than the Grand Manteion with the touch of a finger. There was no Sacred Window on the airship—that would have been almost impossible—but there was a glass somewhere. Idly Silk found himself wondering where it was. Not in the cockpit, certainly, nor in Saba's cubicle. Yet it would almost have to be in this gondola, in which the Rani's officers ate and slept, and from which they steered her airship. Perhaps in the chartroom; he had climbed to this deck from that chartroom without seeing it—but then he had been occupied with his thoughts.

Too much so to do anything to relieve Saba's depression. Yes, too self-centered for that. Saba and her pterotroopers might be outnumbered at present, but—

Hands upon his shoulders. *"Don't jump, Caldé!"*

He took a cautious step backward. "I hadn't intended to," he said, and wondered whether he lied.

He turned. Horn's pale face showed very clearly what Horn thought. "I'm sorry I frightened you," Silk told him, "I didn't know you were there."

"Just come away from the edge, please, Caldé. For me?"

To soothe Horn, he took a step. "You can't have been up here when I came—I would have seen you. You weren't on the roof of our old gondola either, because I looked back at it. Nettle told you I asked about a hatch, of course."

"A little farther, Caldé. Please?"

"No. This is foolish; but to reassure you, I'll sit down." He did, spreading his robe over his crossed legs. "You see? I can't possibly fall from here, and neither can you, if you sit. I need someone to talk to."

Horn sat, his relief apparent.

"When I was in the cockpit, I wanted to leave it in order to pray—that was what I told myself, at least. But when I was up here alone and might have prayed to my heart's content, I did not. I contemplated my shoes instead, and thought about certain things. They weren't foolish things for the most part, but I feel very foolish for having thought so much about them. Are you going with Auk when he leaves the whorl? That's what he's going to do, you know. The Crew, as Sciathan calls the people of his city, have some of the underground towers Mamelta showed me—intact underground towers—and they're going to give Auk one. I forget what Mamelta called them."

"You never told me about towers, Caldé."

Silk did, striving unsuccessfully to make his description concise. "That isn't all I can recall, but that's all that's of importance, I believe; and now that you mention it, I don't think I've ever told anyone, except for Doctor Crane while we were fellow-captives, and Doctor Crane is dead."

"I never even got to see him," Horn said. "I wish I had because of the way you talk about him. Is the underwater boat like this airship?"

"Not at all. It's all metal—practically all iron, I'm certain. There's a hole at the bottom, too, through which the Ayuntamiento can launch a smaller boat. You'd think that would sink the big one, wouldn't you? But it didn't, and we got away through that hole, Doctor Crane and I." Silk paused, lost in thought. "There are monstrous fish in the lake, Horn, fish bigger than you can imagine. Chenille told me that once, and she's quite correct."

"You wanted to know if I was going with Auk. Nettle and me, because either way we'd do it together."

"Yes, of course."

"I don't think so. He hasn't asked us, but I don't think Nettle would want to if he did. There's my father and mother back home, and my brothers and sisters, and Nettle's family."

"Of course," Silk repeated.

"I like Chenille. I like her a lot. But Auk's not what I call a good man, even if Tartaros did choose him to enlighten. You remember what I told you about him that time? He's still the same, I think. The people he's got with him aren't much better, either. He calls them the best thieves in the whorl, did you know that, Caldé? Because of stealing this airship."

"They're not all thieves," Silk said, "Though Auk may like to pretend they are. Most are just poor people from the Orilla and our own quarter. I doubt that many real thieves have the sort of faith something like this requires." He fell silent, by no means sure that he should say more.

"What is it, Caldé?"

"I doubt that all of them will go. Chenille will, I think, though she would be a wealthy woman in Viron; but I wouldn't be in the least surprised to see more than a few of the others hold back."

"You're not going, are you, Caldé?"

Silk shook his head. "I would like to. I don't believe Hyacinth would, however; and these are Auk's people when all is said and done. Not mine."

"Then Nettle and me will come home with you and Hyacinth. Moly wants to go back, too. She wants to find her husband and get back to building their daughter. And there's Patera Incus and Patera Remora."

Silk nodded. "But we will not be numerous enough to keep the Trivigauntis we have on board from reclaiming their airship, even so. Had you thought of that, Horn? Not unless a great many of Auk's followers desert him at the last moment. It had just occurred to me when you laid hold of my shoulders."

Horn frowned. "Can we leave the Trivigauntis in Mainframe, Caldé? I can't think of anything else we can do."

"I can. Or at least, I believe I have, which gave me a very good reason not to step off the edge. Perhaps I needed one more than I knew." Noticing Horn's expression, he added, "I'm sorry if I distress you."

Horn swallowed. "I want to tell you something, sort of a secret. I haven't told anybody yet except Nettle. I know you won't laugh, but please don't tell anybody else."

"I won't, unless I believe it absolutely necessary."

"You know the cats' meat woman? She comes to sacrifice just about every Scylsday."

Silk nodded. "Very well."

"She likes Maytera. Moly, I mean. She came to see her one time at the palace. I wouldn't have thought she'd walk all the way up the hill, but she did. They were sitting in the kitchen, and the cats' meat woman—"

"Scleroderma," Silk murmured. His eyes were on the purple slopes of faraway mountains. "It's a puffball—it grows in forests."

"She was the one that held General Mint's horse for her before she charged the floaters in Cage Street," Horn continued. "She told Moly, and naturally Moly wanted to know all about it, so they talked about that and the fighting, and how Kypris came to our manteion for the funeral. Then she said she was writing all about it, writing down everything that had happened and how she'd been right in the middle of all the most important parts."

Silk tried not to smile, but failed.

"So she wants her grandchildren to be able to read about everything, and how she met you when you were just out of the schola, and how she walked up to the Caldé's Palace and they let her right in. I thought it was pretty funny too."

"I think it heart-warming," Silk told him. "We may laugh—I wouldn't be surprised if she laughed herself—and yet she's right. Her grandchildren are still small, I imagine, and though they've lived in these unsettled times themselves, they won't remember much about them. When they're older, they'll be delighted to have a history written by their own grandmother from the perspective of their family. I applaud her."

"Well, maybe I should of thought like that too, Caldé, but I didn't. To tell the truth, I got kind of mad."

"You didn't play some trick on her, I hope."

"No, but I started thinking about what had happened and if she'd really been in the middle like she said. Pretty soon I saw she hadn't at all, but you'd been there more than anybody, more even than General Mint. And what Scleroderma said about meeting you when you got out of the schola? Well, I met you then too. You used to come into our class and talk to us, and naturally I'd see you helping Patera Pike at sacrifice.

So I decided I'm going to write down everything I can remember as soon as I get some paper. I'll call it Patera Silk's Book, or something like that."

"I'm flattered." This time Silk succeeded in suppressing his smile. "Are you going to write about this, too? Sitting up here talking to me?"

"Yes, I am." Horn filled his lungs with the still, pure air. "And that's another reason for you not to jump off. If you did, I'd have to end it right here." He rapped the deck with his knuckles. "Right up here, and then maybe I'd wonder a little about why you did, and then it would be over. I don't think that would be a very good ending."

"Nor would it be," Silk agreed.

"But that's the way you were thinking of ending it. You were standing too close to the edge to of been thinking about anything else. What's the trouble, Caldé? Something's—I don't know. Hurt you somehow, hurt you a lot. If I knew what it was, maybe I could help, or Nettle could."

Without rising, Silk turned away; after a moment, he slid across the varnished wood so that he could let his legs dangle over the edge. "Come here, Horn."

"I'm afraid to."

"You aren't going to fall. Feel how smooth the motion of the airship is. Nor am I going to push you off. Did you think I might? I won't, I promise."

Face down, Horn crept forward.

"That's the way. It's such a magnificent view, perhaps the most magnificent that either of us will ever see. When you mentioned your class, you reminded me that I'm supposed to be teaching you—it's one of my many duties, and one that I've neglected shamefully since you and I talked in the manse. As your teacher, it's my pleasure as well as my duty to show you things like this whenever I can—and to make you look at them as well, if I must. Look! Isn't it magnificent?"

"It's like the skylands," Horn ventured, "except we're a little closer and it's daytime."

"A great deal closer, and the sun has already begun to narrow. We haven't much time left in which to look at this. A few hours at most."

"We could again tomorrow. We could look out of one of those windows. All the gondolas have them."

"This airship may crash tonight," Silk told him, "or it may be forced to land for some reason. Or the whorl below us might be hidden by clouds, as it was when I looked out of one of the windows earlier today. Let's look while we can."

Horn crept a finger's width nearer the edge.

"Down there's a city bigger than Viron, and those tiny pale dots are its people. See them? They look like that, I believe, because they're staring up at us. In all probability, they've never seen an airship, or seen anything larger than the Fliers that can fly. They'll speculate about us for months, perhaps for years."

"Is it Palustria, Caldé?"

Silk shook his head. "Palustria doesn't even lie in this direction, so it's certainly not Palustria. Besides, I think we've gone farther than that already. We were hoisted up early this morning, and we've been flying south or east ever since. A well-mounted man can ride there in less than a week."

"I've never seen off-center buildings like those," Horn ventured. "Besides, there aren't any swamps. Everybody says Palustria's in the middle of swamps."

"They've turned them into rice fields, or so I'm told—if not all of them at least a large part of them, no doubt the part closest to their city. Their rice crop's failed this year because of the drought. They say it's the first time the rice crop's failed in the entire history of Palustria." For a while Silk sat in silence, staring down at the foreign city below.

"Can I ask you something, Caldé?"

"Certainly. What is it?"

"Why isn't it windier up here? I've never been up on a mountain, but Maytera read something about that to us one time, and it said it was real windy just about all the time. Looking down, it seems like we're going fast. It's not taking us very long at all to go over this, and it's big. So the wind ought to be in our faces."

"I asked our pilot the same thing," Silk told him, "and I was ready to kick myself for stupidity when she told me. Look there, up and out, and you can see one of the engines that's still running. Notice how slowly it's turning? You can almost make out the wooden arms; but when the engines were going fast, those were just a blur, a shimmer in front of each engine."

"Like a mill."

"Somewhat; but while the arms of a windmill are turned by the wind, these are turned by their engines to create a wind that will blow us wherever we wish. They're making very little wind at present—just enough to keep us from tumbling about. We're being carried by a natural wind; but because we're blown along by it, like a dry leaf or one of those paper streamers the wind tore off our victory arch, it seems to us that the air is scarcely moving."

"I think I understand. What if we turned around and tried to go the other way?"

"Then this still air would at once become a gale."

The smooth wooden deck on which Silk was sitting tilted, seeming almost to fall away from under him.

"Patera!"

He felt Horn clutch his robe. The sound of the remaining engines rose. "I'm all right," he said.

"You could've slid off! I almost did."

"Not unless the gondola were to slope much more steeply." A vagrant breeze ruffled Silk's straw-colored hair.

"What happened?" From the sound of Horn's voice, he was far from the edge now, perhaps halfway to the hatch.

"The wind increased, I imagine. The new wind would have reached our tail first; presumably it lifted it."

"You still want to die."

The plaintive note in Horn's voice was more painful than an accusation. "No," Silk said.

"Won't you tell me what's wrong? Please, Caldé?"

"I would if I could explain it." The city was behind them already, its houses and fields replaced by forbidding forests. "I might say that it's an accumulation of small matters. Have you ever had a day when everything went amiss? Of course you have—everyone has."

"Sure," Horn said.

"Can you come a little closer? I can scarcely hear you."

"All right, Caldé."

"I also want to say that it has to do with the Plan of Pas; but that isn't quite right. Pas, you see, isn't the only god who has a plan. I've just understood this one, perhaps while I was still in the cockpit, as it's called, guiding this airship and thinking—when I didn't have to think much about that—about Hyacinth's overpowering our pilot. Or perhaps only when I was talking with General Saba, just before I came up here.

It might be fair to say that I understood in the cockpit, but that the full import of what I had understood had come only when I was talking with Nettle and General Saba."

"I think I get it."

"On the other hand, I could say that it was about facts that the Outsider confided on my wedding night. You see, Horn, I was enlightened again then. Nothing I learned at the schola had prepared me for the possibility of multiple enlightenments, but clearly they can and do take place. Which would you like to hear about first?"

"The little things going wrong, I guess. Only please come back here with me, Patera. You said it was hard to hear me. Well, I can hardly hear you."

"I'm perfectly safe, Horn." Silk discovered that he was grasping the edge of the deck; he forced himself to relax, placing his hands together as if in prayer. "We might begin anywhere, but let us begin with Maytera Marble. With Moly, as she asks us to call her now. Do you think her name was really Moly—Molybdenum—before she became a sibyl? Honestly."

"That's what she says, Caldé." Horn was moving closer; Silk heard the faint scrub of his coat and trousers against the planking.

"I don't. She hasn't told me she's lying, but I hope she will soon."

"I—I don't think so, Caldé." Horn's tones grew deeper as he asserted his opinion. "She's really careful about that kind of thing."

"I know she is. That's why it's such a torment to her. I'm going to ask Patera Incus to shrive me. I hope that it will lead her to ask him—or Patera Remora, though Incus would be better—to do the same."

"I still—"

"Why are there so few chems now, Horn? There the Plan of Pas has clearly gone awry. He made them both male and female, and clearly intended them to reproduce and so maintain their numbers—perhaps even increase them. Let us assume that he peopled our whorl with equal numbers of each sex, which would seem to be the logical thing for him to do. What went wrong?" It was becoming colder, or Silk more sensitive to the cold. He drew his thick winter robe about him.

"I don't know, Caldé. The soldiers sleep a lot, and naturally they can't, you know, build anybody then."

"Ours do, at least. Most of the soldiers in most other cities are dead.

Most have been dead for a century or longer. Pas should have made female soldiers, like the troopers from Trivigaunte. He didn't, and that was clearly an error."

"You shouldn't say things like that, Patera."

"Why not, if I think them true? Would Pas like me better if I were a coward? Some male chems were artisans and farm laborers, from what I know of them, and a few were servants—butlers and so forth. But most were soldiers, and the soldiers fought for their cities and died, or slept as Hammerstone did. The female chems, who were largely cooks or maids, wore out and died childless. Nearly every soldier must have courted a cook or a maid, three hundred years ago. And nearly every such cook and maid must have loved a soldier. How likely is it that such a couple would be reunited by chance after centuries?"

"It could happen." Horn sounded defiant.

"Of course it could. All sorts of unlikely things can, but they rarely do. Something has been troubling her ever since she and Hammerstone were married, and I believe I know what it is. Let's leave it at that."

"Even if you're right," Horn said, "That's not a very good reason to want to die."

"I disagree, but let's move on. In the cockpit, I realized that Chenille and Hyacinth had fought when both of them were at Orchid's—she was the woman who paid for the funeral at which Kypris spoke to us, not that it matters. My sister—"

"I didn't know you had a sister, Caldé."

Silk smiled. "Forget I said that, please; it was a slip of the tongue. I was about to say that Chenille blacked Hyacinth's eyes, which isn't surprising since she's considerably larger and stronger. Nor do I blame her. If Hyacinth has forgiven her, and she clearly has, I can do no less. But they lied about it, both of them, and I found it very painful. I can't prove they lied, Horn; but if you'd been there, you would have caught the lie just as I did. Hyacinth identified an incident to which Chenille was about to refer before Chenille specified it. That could only mean that Chenille was much more closely involved than she pretended."

A wide river dotted with ice divided the forest below. Silk leaned forward to study it. "You'll say that what I've told you is not a good reason to die. Again, I disagree."

"Caldé . . . ?"

"Yes. What is it?"

"You don't look like her. Like Chenille. She's got that red hair, but it's dyed. Underneath her hair's dark, I think. Your eyes are blue, but hers are brown, and like you said she's real big and strong. You're tall and pretty strong, but . . ."

"You need not proceed, Horn, if it embarrasses you."

"What I mean is she'd be a lot like Auk if she was a man. You'd be a better runner, but—but . . ."

"We are alike in certain ways, I suppose."

"That's not it." Horn was less at ease than ever. "Since you've been caldé everybody talks about the old one. Then last night before those women came you were talking about his will. Nettle told me, and this's her idea, really. He said he had an adopted son, and this son was going to be the next one. What Nettle says is he didn't say to make it happen, he just said it would. Is that right?"

Silk nodded. " 'Though he is not the son of my body, my son will succeed me.' "

"Chenille's his real daughter, Nettle told me that too. And you're the next caldé. So if she's your sister—"

"We will go no further with this, Horn. It has nothing to do with our topic."

"All right. I won't tell anybody."

"There are so many lies in the whorl that it's not likely anyone would credit you if you did. May I instance one more? Hyacinth subdued our pilot, Hyacinth alone. I mentioned it."

"Yes, Caldé."

"I've been trying to think of an enlightening analogy for you, but I can't. Suppose I were to say that it was like seeing Patera Incus overpower Auk. The analogy would be flawed because I've never supposed that Patera Incus could not fight, only that he would fight badly. I had imagined Hyacinth would be helpless in the face of violence; she spoke of taking fencing from Master Xiphias once, yet I never . . ."

"I can't hear you. Can't you turn around this way?"

"No. Come closer." Silk found Horn's hand and drew him nearer the edge.

"Nobody thought you could fight either, Caldé."

"I know, and they had almost convinced me of it. That was a part of the reason I broke into Blood's—I needed to prove I wasn't the milksop everyone took me for. Nor was I, though I was badly frightened most of the time."

"Maybe that's how Hyacinth felt about the pilot." Greatly daring, Horn sat up, his legs stretched before him and his feet on the edge of the deck. "Hyacinth's real girly when you're around. We got lots of it this morning. She smiles whenever you look at her and holds on like she can't stand up. She wants you to like her. Caldé, you know that big cat Mucor's got?"

Silk was staring down at a mountain valley, following the snowy rush of a young river over red stones. "You mean Lion?"

"I don't know the name, but Lion sounds like a boy. This was a girl cat, I think, kind of gray, with long pointed ears and a little short tail. I saw it one time when I brought up Mucor's dinner. It really liked her. It would rub up against her and smile. Cats can smile, Caldé."

"I know."

"It kept putting its paw in Mucor's lap so she'd pet it, but it wasn't too sure about me. It showed me its teeth, pulling its lips back without making any noise. I was pretty scared."

"So was I, Horn. I shot two of those horned cats once; I'm very sorry for that now." Silk leaned forward again. "Look at that cliff, Horn. Can you see it?"

"Sure, I saw it just a minute ago. I don't think I could climb it, but I'd like to try." Horn made himself speak more loudly. "I know what Hyacinth seems like to you, Caldé, but she seems a lot like Mucor's cat to Nettle and me. She's respectful to Moly, though."

Silk glanced over his shoulder. "You're right, there is a great deal of good in Hyacinth, though I would love her even if there were none."

Horn shook his head. "I was going to say she sort of hits it off with Hammerstone. He can be awful rough."

"Yes, I'm well aware of it."

"He likes Moly and Patera Incus, so he's nice to them. But he treats Nettle and me like sprats, and with other people he's like Auk. Hyacinth won't give him half a step, and once when she got mad she called him all kinds of names. I thought I knew all those. I learned most of that stuff when I was little, but she had some I never heard. If the pilot pulled a needler on Mucor, what do you think her cat would do?"

"Come here," Silk told him. "Sit with me. Are you afraid I'll take you with me if I jump? I'm not going to, and I'd like you beside me."

"I'm still pretty scared."

"You would have climbed that cliff, given the chance. You would be no more dead falling from here."

"All right." Gingerly, Horn edged forward until his legs dangled over the abyss of air. Oreb settled on his shoulder.

"As I said, I've neglected my duty to teach you. Now I can actually show you part of the Plan. I find it enlightening, and you may, too. See the city ahead? The mountains we crossed isolate it from the west. Soon we'll see what isolates it from the east; and if we were to turn north or south, we'd come upon barriers there as well. Some are more formidable than others, of course."

"Their houses are like people, Caldé. Look, there's Pas, with the two heads. Even the little ones are like people lying down, see? The thatch makes it look like they've got blankets."

"Good place." Oreb bobbed on Horn's shoulder.

"It is," Silk agreed, "but if we weren't used to seeing Pas pictured like this, we'd think this image the more horrible—and it is horrible—for being so large. I won't ask if you've lain with a woman, Horn; it's too personal a matter to broach save in shriving, and I know you too well to shrive you. Should you wish to be shriven, I hope you'll go to Patera Remora."

"All right."

"I had not until my wedding night. Indeed, it remains my only such experience. You needn't tell me that Hyacinth has lain with scores of men. I knew it and was acutely conscious of it; so was she. I can't say what our experience meant to her, and perhaps it meant little or nothing. To me it was wonderful. Wonderful! I came to her as one starving. And yet—"

Still very frightened, Horn jerked his head. "I know."

"Good. I'm glad you understand. There was a taint that came from neither Hyacinth nor me, but from the act itself. After two hours, or about that, I rested. We had done what men and women do more than once, and more than twice. I was happy, exhausted, and soiled. I felt that Echidna, particularly, was displeased; and I doubt that I would have had the courage if I had not rejected her in my heart after her theophany. You were there, I know."

Horn nodded again. "She's a very great goddess, Caldé."

"She is. Great and terrible. It may be that I was wrong to reject her—

I won't argue the point. I only say that I had, and felt as I did. As I've said, the Outsider enlightened me a second time then. I won't tell you all that he told me—I couldn't. But one thing was that he created Pas. The Seven, as everyone knows, are the children of Pas and Echidna; it had never occurred to me to wonder whence they themselves came. Why do you think Pas built barriers between our cities, Horn?"

The sudden question caught him off guard. "To keep them from fighting, Caldé?"

"Not at all. Not only do they fight, but he knew that they would; if he hadn't, he wouldn't have provided them with armies. No, he erected mountains and dug rivers and lakes so they could not combine against him. More specifically, so they couldn't combine against Mainframe, the home he was to set over them."

"Did the Outsider tell you that, Caldé?"

Silk shook his head. "Hammerstone did, and Hammerstone is right. The Outsider, as he showed me, has no reason to fear our leaguing against him. We've done it innumerable times, just as we betray him daily as individuals. His fear—he is afraid for our sake, not his own—is that we may come to love other things more than we love him. When I was at your manteion on Sun Street, foolish people used to ask me why Pas or Scylla permitted some action that they regarded as evil, as if a god had to sign a paper before a man could be struck or a child fall ill. On my wedding night, the Outsider explained why it is that he permits what people call evil at all—not this theft or that uncleanness, but the thing itself. It serves him, you see. It hates him, yet it serves him, too. Does this make sense to you, Horn?"

"Like a mule that kicks whenever it gets a chance."

"Exactly. That mule is harnessed like the rest and draws the wagon, however unwillingly. Given the freedom of the whorl—and even of those beyond it—evil directs us back to the Outsider. I told you I rejected Echidna; I thought I did it because she is evil, but the truth is that I did it because he is better. A child who burns its hand says the fire's bad, as the saying goes; but the fire itself is saying, 'Not to me, child. Reach out to him.' "

"I think I see. Caldé, I'm getting pretty cold."

"Fish heads?" Oreb inquired.

Silk nodded. "We'll go in soon, so you and Oreb will be warm and can get something to eat; but first, have you been looking at our whorl,

Horn? This is winter wheat below us, I believe. See how the sunlight plays on it, how it ripples in the wind, displaying every conceivable shade of green?"

"You still haven't told me—maybe I shouldn't ask you—"

"Why I was tempted to jump? It's obvious, isn't it?"

Oreb squawked, "Look out!"

Already, Horn was sliding from the edge of the deck; the face he turned toward Silk displayed Mucor's deathly grin.

"You know where Silk is?" Auk stepped into the cockpit and shut the flimsy door behind him.

Sciathan pointed to the ceiling, his urchin face all sharp *V*'s. "Upstairs, which is what you call me. I saw shoes and stockings, and the legs of trousers at the top." He gestured toward the slanted pane before him. "The trousers were black, the shoes and stockings the same, the legs too long for the smallest augur. The tallest, I think, would not do this."

"They ain't there any more." Auk bent, craning his neck to peer upward. "I ought to tell you, too. Number Seven ought to work if you start it."

Sciathan flicked two switches and nodded appreciatively as a needle rose. "You have removed his clamp."

"There was more to it than that. We're working on Number Five now. They got 'em out on booms, see?"

"I have observed this. In a moment I shall tell you what else I have observed."

"Only you can haul the booms in to fix the engines. It's a pretty good system. We had to yank the heads and beat on the pistons some, but we didn't hurt 'em much. What'd you see?"

"Another seated beside Silk. It is hazardous to sit thus."

"You said it."

"The other was almost chilled . . ." Sciathan paused, his head cocked. "Caldé Silk comes now to General Saba's cabin. I hear his voice."

Leaving the cockpit, Auk saw that Saba's curtain was drawn back. Silk stood where it had hung, and a perspiring Horn had crowded into the cubicle beside Nettle.

"–don't know how to put this, exactly," Silk was saying. "I ought to have given that more thought while I was up on the roof a moment ago." He glanced over his shoulder. "Hello, Auk. I'm glad you're here; I was going to send Nettle for you. We're about to return her airship to General Saba."

Oreb bobbed in assent as Auk stared.

"I don't mean, of course, that we're not going to take you to Mainframe–you and Sciathan, and the rest. We are. Or rather, she is; Hyacinth and I will accompany her, with Nettle, Horn, His Eminence, Patera Remora, and Moly."

Saba grinned at Auk. "I don't understand this either, but I like it."

"Of course you do," Silk told her, "and so will Auk. We all should, because it will help every one of us."

He turned back to Auk. "A small ceremony at which you return General Saba's sword might be appropriate. Would you like that?"

Auk shook his head.

"It wasn't taken from her, in any event. It's still in that box at the foot of her bed, she tells me."

Nettle displayed her needler. "Can I put this up?"

Auk snapped, "Keep it!"

"A very small ceremony, then–here and now. Would you get out your sword for me, General? I'll give it to Auk, who will give it back to you. You should wear it thereafter. It will hearten your troopers, I'm confident."

Auk declared, "We're not giving the slug guns back."

"Not now, at least. That will depend upon whether there are arms on the craft the Crew provides you, though I imagine there will be."

Horn mopped his forehead. "Nobody understands this except you, Caldé."

"It's simple enough. Neither General Saba nor I desire a war between Viron and Trivigaunte. We Vironese have seized this airship, the pride of its city."

Horn looked to Nettle, who said, "They'd seized *us*."

"Exactly. Another reason for war, which General Saba and I wish to prevent. The solution is obvious–our freedom for the airship."

"We're free now!"

"Nobody can be truly free without peace. Consider the alternative. When we returned to Viron, Generalissimo Siyuf would try to recapture this airship by force, while General Mint and Generalissimo Oosik tried to prevent her; it would cost five hundred lives the first day—at least that many, and perhaps more."

Saba told Nettle, "You're going to have to wait a little before you get a tour of Trivigaunte. When he wanted to know if I'd take you home if I got my airship back, I was too surprised to say anything. But I will, and let Auk here and the rabble we loaded first out at Mainframe, if that's what he wants." She bent over her footlocker. "Some of you are afraid I'm going to cross you. All of you, except your caldé, most likely."

Auk grunted.

She straightened up, holding a sharply curved saber with a gem-studded hilt. "This is the sword of honor the Rani awarded me last year, and I'm proud of it. Maybe I haven't worn it as much as I ought to for fear something might happen to it."

Oreb whistled, and Nettle told Saba, "It's beautiful!"

Saba smiled at Auk. "The girl let me keep it. I told her about it, and she said leave it where it is, Auk won't mind."

He muttered, "I'd like mine back. That Colonel's got it."

"If you come back with us, I'll try to get it for you."

"No cut!" Oreb hopped from Silk's shoulder to Saba's to examine the sword more closely.

She drew it and took a half step backward, holding it at eye level with both hands grasping the blade. "By this sword I swear that as long as Caldé Silk's on my airship, I'll do whatever he tells me, and when I land him and his friends at their city it will be as passengers, and not prisoners."

Silk nodded. "On the terms you have described, General, we return command to you."

"You're going to let me talk to the Palace on the glass and tell them what we're doing?"

"If you choose to. You are in command."

Saba lowered her sword. "Then if I break my oath, you can take this and break it."

She led them through the gondola to the airy compartment from which Silk had climbed to the deck. It held cabinets, a sizable table, and two leather seats; there was a glass on the wall, next to the door. "This is the chartroom," Saba told Silk, "The nerve center of my airship, where our navigational instruments and maps are. There's a speaking tube that runs through officers' quarters to the cockpit. Do you know about those? Like a glass, but only to the one place and all you can do is talk."

"This's where you ought to be," Auk said, but Silk shook his head.

Saba pointed. "Right up there's the hatch. We go up to take the angle between the ship and the sun, mostly. Now it should be zero." She swallowed. "I'll check it as soon as I talk to the Palace."

Horn touched Silk's arm. "Don't go back, Caldé. Please?"

Auk asked, "You were up there, huh? Somebody nearly got killed is what I heard."

"He was going to jump off," Horn told Auk. "I grabbed him and I guess I got him back, only I don't remember, just sort of wrestling, and the roof gone, and music." Puzzled, he stared at Silk. "Someplace down there was having a concert, I guess."

"I saw the evil in the whorl," Silk explained. "I thought I knew it, when I actually had no idea. A few days ago, I began to see it clearly."

He waited for someone to speak, but no one did.

"An hour ago, I saw it very clearly indeed; and it was horrible. What was worse was that instead of focusing on the evil in myself, as I should have, I gave my attention to the evil in others. I would have told you then that I saw a great deal in Horn, for example. I still do."

"Caldé, I never said—"

"That was utterly, utterly wrong. I don't mean that the evil isn't there—it is, and it always will be because it is ineradicable; but seeing it alone, not merely Horn's evil but everyone else's too, did something to me far worse than anything Horn himself would ever do, I'm sure—it blinded me to good. Seeing only evil, I wanted with all my heart to reunite myself with the Outsider. That would itself have been an evil act, but Horn saved me from it."

"I'm so glad." Nettle looked at Horn with shining eyes.

"Just by coming up on the roof of this gondola, really. For Horn's sake, I won't go there again, though it's such a marvelous thing to stand in the sky smiling down at the whorl that I find it difficult to renounce it; merely by standing there, I came to understand how Sciathan feels about flying."

Auk cleared his throat. "I want to tell you about that clamp. All right if I do it now, before she talks to 'em back in Trivigaunte?"

"You found it, I assume."

"Yeah, only that wasn't a fuel hose. It was a lube hose."

Saba's eyes opened wide. *"What!"*

Auk ignored her. "The clamp cut the flow to where they got hot and seized. It didn't show on the gauge up front 'cause it just measures tank temperature. The tank was all right and the pump was running, but there wasn't much getting through. We got Number Seven busted loose, and maybe we can fix the rest."

"They'll never be as good as they were." Saba sounded disgusted.

"They weren't anyhow," Auk told her. "I made a couple little improvements already."

Oreb eyed them both. "Fish heads?"

"I feel the same way myself," Silk announced. "If I'm to live after all, I'd like something to eat."

Saba stepped to the glass and clapped; it grew luminous, as the monitor's gray face coalesced. At once dancing flecks of color replaced it—peach, pink, and an ethereal blue that deepened until it was nearly black.

Silk fell to his knees; for him the sunlit chartroom and its occupants vanished.

"Silk?" The face in the glass was innocent and sensual, preternaturally lovely. "Silk, wouldn't you like to be Pas? We'd be together then . . . Silk."

He bowed his head, unable to speak.

"They can scan you at Mainframe. As I was scanned, Silk, with him. He held my hand. . . ."

Silk found that he was staring up at her; she smiled, and his spirit melted.

"You'll go on with your life. Silk. Just as it is. You'd be Pas too. And he would be you. Look . . ."

The face lovelier than any mortal woman's dispersed like smoke. In its place stood a bronze-limbed man with rippling muscles and two heads.

One was Silk's.

Chapter 16

EXODUS FROM THE LONG SUN

They floated in an infinite emptiness lit by a remote, spool-shaped black sun: Sciathan the Flier, Patera Incus and Patera Remora, the old woman who called herself Moly, Nettle and Horn, the caldé's wife, and the caldé. The shrinking red dot that was the lander winked out.

"Good-bye, Auk my noctolater." The speaker seemed near, though there was a note in his voice that had traveled far; it was a man's voice, deep, and heavy with sorrow.

"Good-bye, Auk," Silk repeated; until he heard his own voice, he did not realize he had spoken aloud. "Good-bye, sister. Good-bye, Gib. Farewell."

Maytera Marble murmured, "Heartbroken. Poor General Mint will be simply heartbroken."

"He goes to a better place than any you have seen."

"I *disliked* him, though the harlot *Chenille* was not devoid of *pre-eminent qualities. Notwithstanding,* I feel *bereft . . .*"

So softly that Silk supposed that only he could hear her, Hyacinth inquired, "Is that where? Those little dots?"

"To one or the other," the god replied. "The blue whorl or the green. Auk's lander cannot carry them to both."

"Auk—ah. Devoted to you, eh? As we, um, all. He was, er, reformed? Devout. If you are not, um, hey?"

There was no reply. The distant sparks faded. Hyacinth gripped Silk's arm, pointing to the black, spool-shaped sun behind them, from which light streamed. "What *is* that? Is it–is it . . . ? The lander came out of it."

"That is our *Whorl.*" Sciathan wiped his eyes.

"That little thing?"

Already the little thing was fading; Silk relaxed. "You liked Auk, didn't you? So did I. If I live as long as His Cognizance, I won't forget meeting him in the Cock, sipping brandy while I tried to make out his face in the shadows."

"When I saw Aer die, I did not weep. That pain was too deep for weeping. Auk is not dead, but no one will call me Upstairs any more. I weep for that."

"Wish that he stated, um, unequivocally, eh?" Remora had already activated his propulsion module and was drifting toward the circular aperture. "Is–um–Great Pas satisfied? Is this adequate? Sufficient?"

Silk and Hyacinth followed him. Silk said, "If he were, we Cargo would return to our herds and fields. Auk has bought us a brief respite, that's all. Pas will not be satisfied until the last person in the whorl has gone. It has served its purpose."

They emerged into the penumbra, shade that seemed blinding light after the darkness. "I don't see how Tartaros showed us the whorl from outside," Hyacinth murmured. "There can't be an eye out there, can there?" When Silk did not reply, "I don't like not walking. My thighs are getting fat, I can feel it."

Maytera Marble overtook them. "They can't be, dear, you don't eat anything. I'm worried about you."

"I don't like people seeing up my gown, either. I know it sounds silly, but I don't. Every time I feel like somebody's looking up there my thighs swell up and never go back down."

"There is no *up,*" Incus called as he accelerated toward them, "nor is there *any down.* All is a realm of *light.*"

"The, um, deceased." Remora glanced back at him, vaguely worried. "How shall we explain that, Your Eminence? The, um, faithful, eh? They expect the–ah–dear decedent."

"Do you desire a visitation by your dead?" Sciathan asked.

Silk said firmly, "No." Hyacinth's jaw dropped, and for a moment her sculptured face looked foolish.

Silk decelerated to allow Sciathan to catch up. "I speak only for myself. I've met mine, and know and love them. The temptation to rejoin them would be too great. I know your offer was well intended—but no, I do not."

"There is no physicality," the little Flier explained. "Mainframe recreates them and beams the data to one's mind."

"Moly, would you escort Hyacinth back to the airship for me, please? I have to confer with Sciathan." Silk took the Flier's arm.

Horn asked, "Can we come?" Silk hesitated, then shook his head; Oreb launched himself from Horn's shoulder to flap after them upside down.

One by one the pilot was testing the engines; Horn counted as each coughed, roared to life, and declined to a hum.

Nettle asked, "Aren't you going to knock?"

He would have preferred that she do it, but could not say so. "What on?"

"On the frame, I guess. They're pretty solid."

Silk pushed the curtain to one side as Horn raised his fist. "Hyacinth isn't here. Were you looking for me?"

Both nodded.

"Very well, what can I do for you?"

Horn cleared his throat. "You promised me you wouldn't go up on the roof again, Caldé. Remember?"

"Of course. I've kept my promise."

"Me and Nettle have been up there," Horn said, and Oreb applauded with joyful wings.

Nettle said, "It's not scary when you can float." Her eyes appealed to Horn, who added, "We want you to go up with us."

"You're releasing me from my promise?"

Horn nodded. "Yeah."

"Say *yes,* Horn." Silk looked thoughtful. "You bear the repute of your palaestra."

"Yes, Caldé. Caldé, is Patera Remora really going to be our new augur?"

"No." Absentmindedly, Silk glanced around the cubicle for his propulsion module before remembering that he had returned it. "He cannot become your new augur, since he is augur there already. He'll take up his duties when we get home. How do you keep from floating away? That might not be frightening, I'll allow; but I would think it serious."

"Bird save!"

"Yes, if I'm adrift you must tow me to safety."

"There's supplies in the last gondola," Horn explained as Silk pushed off from the doorway. "We found a coil of rope in there. The table in the chartroom's bolted down, so we tie onto the legs."

"It's better than having that thing on your back," Nettle told Silk. "You just float around without having to worry about anything. When you're tired of it, you pull yourself in."

Horn added, "But I don't get tired of it."

"There's something you want me to see." They had floated through the officers' sleeping quarters; Silk stopped, bulging the canvas partition, and opened the door to the messroom.

"Just—just everything you can see from out there."

"Something to ask, in that case."

In the chartroom, Silk knotted the finger-thick line about his waist in accordance with Horn's instructions and pushed off from the table, out through the open hatch.

The airship had revolved, whether from the torque of its engines or the pressure of some passing breeze, until Mainframe stood upright as a wall, its black slabs of colossal mechanism jutting toward them and its Pylon an endless bridge that dwarfed the airship and vanished into night.

Horn gestured. "See, Caldé? We don't have to sit on the edge, but we can go over there if you want to. Way, way down you can see the Mountains That Look At Mountains, I guess. It's kind of blue at first, then so bright you can't be sure."

Nettle emerged from the hatch. "I still don't understand what Mainframe is, Caldé. Just all those things with the lights running over them? And why do they have roofs here if it can't rain? How would they get the rain to come down?"

"This is Mainframe," Silk told her. "You are seeing it."

"The big square things?"

"With what underlies its meadows and lawns; Mainframe is dispersed among them all. Imagine millions of millions of tiny circuits like those in a card—billions of billions, actually. The warmth of each is less than the twinkle of a firefly; but there are so many that if they were packed together their own heat would destroy them. They would become a second sun. As things are it is always summer here, thanks to those circuits."

"That's what you call the little wiggly gold lines in card?" Nettle inquired. "Circuits? They don't do anything."

"They would, if they were returned to their proper places in a lander. We will have to return some ourselves soon."

Horn was watching Silk narrowly. "Did Sciathan tell you all that?"

"Not in so many words, but he said enough to let me infer the rest. What was it you wanted to ask?"

"A whole bunch of stuff. You know, Caldé, for my book. Is it all right if I call you Caldé?"

"Of course. Or Patera, or Silk, or even Patera Caldé, which is what His Cognizance calls me. As you like."

"I heard Chenille tell Moly that when she was Kypris she made you call her Chenille anyway. It must have seemed funny."

Nettle said, "I'm not writing a book, Caldé, but I've got stuff I want to ask, too. I'm helping Horn with his, I guess. I'll have to, probably. Did you make the dead people come back and talk to us like they did?"

"Mainframe did that, Nettle." Silk smiled. "Believe me, I'm unable to compel it to do anything. I asked Sciathan to ask it on our behalf, but he explained that it was unnecessary. Mainframe knows everything that takes place here; as soon as I formulated my request, Mainframe took it under consideration. I'm delighted that it was granted, immensely grateful."

"But not back home." Nettle waved vaguely at the deck some ten cubits below. "It doesn't hear everything there."

"No, it doesn't; but it discovers more than I would have believed. Since Echidna's theophany, I've assumed the gods knew only what they saw and heard through Sacred Windows and glasses, which seems to be very near the truth. Those are Mainframe's principal sources, too; but it has others—the Fliers' data, for example."

Horn said, "I've got a tough one, Caldé. I'm not trying to show you up or anything."

"Of course not. What is it?"

"Tartaros told Auk the short sun whorl would be like ours, only there wouldn't be any people, or no people like us. Auk told Chenille, and I asked her. She said it means there'll be grass and rocks and flowers, only not like we're used to. Why is that?"

Nettle shook her head in disbelief. "That's not hard at all. Because Pas picked them out for us to make it easy."

"Or difficult," Silk muttered.

"I don't understand."

"Suppose there were no plants or animals—we'll leave the rocks aside. Auk's lander is stocked with seeds and embryos, as you saw. He'll be able to grow whichever ones he wants; and if the whorl he chooses had none of its own, those would be the only plants and animals with which he would have to deal. As things are, he'll have a much more interesting time of it—as well as a much harder one."

The hum of their engines deepened, and the three of them drifted toward the prow of the second gondola until the ropes that united them with the first were taut. "We're under way," Horn announced. Oreb agreed: "Go home!"

"As soon as we're gone, I don't think I'll believe I was here." Nettle sighed. "Grandma came for a talk. I said stay with me and we'll take you back, but she said she couldn't."

"Patera Remora's mother came to see him," Horn told Silk. "He's been smiling at everybody. He told her he had his own manteion now, and he'd sacrifice and shrive and bring the Peace, and wouldn't have to work in the Palace any more. And she said it's what she'd wanted for him all the time."

"Hyacinth's mother visited her, too."

Nettle looked surprised. "I didn't think her mother was dead, Caldé."

"Neither did Hyacinth."

Hand over hand they pulled themselves forward again, until they were standing on the deck, although standing very lightly; Silk freed himself from the loop of rope.

Nettle said, "Caldé, you never did answer my question about the roofs. And I wanted to know why the shade's so close here, and we can't see the sun."

"The Pylon makes it," Horn declared, "or anyhow it shoots it into the sky. Isn't that right, Caldé? Then the sun burns it but instead of smoke it turns into air. If the Pylon didn't shoot out more, the shade would burn up and there'd be daylight all the time. Only Mainframe would fry, because it's so close. The sun starts at the top of the Pylon and goes all the way to the West Pole."

"Long way," Oreb elaborated.

"We, too, have a long way to go," Silk said, addressing neither Horn nor Nettle, "but at last we've begun."

"I understand about the roofs now," Nettle said.

He looked around at her. "Do you? Tell me."

"We used to go to the lake every summer when I was little. Then ... I don't know, something happened, and it seemed like we never had enough money."

"Taxes went up after the old caldé died," Horn told her. "They went up a lot."

"Maybe that was it. Anyway, one year when I was nine or ten we waited till everybody else had gone home, and went when it was cheaper, and after that we never went any more."

Silk nodded.

"It would be nice, sometimes, in the afternoons, and we'd swim, but it was pretty cold in the morning. One morning I got up when everybody else was still asleep and walked to the lake just to look at it. I think I knew this was the last year, and we wouldn't come any more. Maybe we were going home that day."

"This isn't about roofs," Horn said; but Silk put a finger to his lips.

"The lake was all covered with ghosts, white shapes coming up out of the water and reaching for the air, getting bigger and stronger all the time. I was thinking about ghosts a lot then, because Gam had, you know, gone to Mainframe, the one I talked to today. We were supposed to say she was in Mainframe, but we didn't think it meant anything. Aren't you going to say that it wasn't really ghosts, Horn?"

He shook his head.

"It wasn't, it was fog. There was an old lady fishing off the pier, and I guess she liked me because when I asked she said there was water in the air over the lake, and when it got cold enough it came together and made tiny little drops that take a long, long while to fall, and that was what you saw. I'd never wondered where fog came from before then."

"Fog good."

"That's right, you're a marsh bird. Don't they come from Palustria, Caldé? The swamps around there?"

Silk nodded. "I believe so."

"What I was going to say was that the fog got thicker and thicker that day, and got everything wet. So if they have a lot of fogs here . . .

We're not hardly there, though, any more. But you know what I mean. Only you wouldn't want it inside, so you'd have roofs, and they do."

Horn said, "The fountains get the grass wet, too, like it does at home on a windy day. It's not as much as you'd think, because there's a thing that sucks in air at the bottom and takes the water out for the pump. If they shut that off, it would water everything."

Silk tossed aside his rope and watched it settle to the deck. "We have weight once more."

"Yeah, I know. I mean yes."

"I should consider this better before I speak, Horn, but I find it exhilarating. When we arrived and could float—could fly, after a fashion, after Sciathan secured propulsion modules for us—I found that exhilarating as well. I'm contradicting myself, I suppose."

Horn looked to Nettle, who said, "I don't think so."

"It's not easy for me to sort out, and even less easy for me to explain. Sciathan is a Flier, in love with flight and pardonably proud of his wings and his special status among the Crew. Until we got here, I was confident that I understood his feelings."

Horn looked puzzled. "Everybody flies here, Caldé."

"Exactly. They have to, and we flew in the same way. Or floated. *Floated* may be the better term. It's easy, so much so that all three of us floated here without modules; but we floated under a lowering shade that never brought night or rose to bring a new day."

"It's getting to be daylight here." Horn gestured toward the sky-filling brown bulk of the airship.

"We've reached the foothills of the Mountains That Look At Mountains," Silk said, "and if we had tried to float this far, we'd have settled to the ground. But Sciathan flies over these hills, and across the mountains, too—or soars from valley to valley, if he chooses."

"Bird fly!"

"Yes. Sciathan flies like Oreb here, or the eagle that brought down poor Iolar. I had a taste of that when I piloted this airship." For a moment Silk's smile was radiant.

Saba's head emerged from the hatch. "Hello, Caldé! Going to take a reading?"

"I wouldn't know how."

She swung herself easily onto the deck. "I do, and I've got the pro-tractor so I can show you. It's early yet, but I wanted to climb up here while it didn't take so much lifting." She chuckled. "I heard you talking about flying. I command a thousand pterotroopers, but I can't fly like they do. Neither could you, we're both too heavy. Even this girl would have to lose a little to be much good."

"I was about to explain to Horn and Nettle that while wings are wonderful–and they are, truly, truly wonderful–feet are wonderful too. Doctor Crane, if he were still alive, could amputate my legs, and then I'd be light enough to fly the way your troopers do, and perhaps even as Sciathan does; but as much as I envy them, I wouldn't want him to. It would be marvelous to fly as they do, so it's not surprising that we envy them; but imagine how much someone without legs must envy us."

"I don't have to imagine. Some of my dearest friends have lost their legs."

Horn asked, "Are you going to be pilot some on the way back, Caldé? You like it so much I think you ought to. You were good at it, too."

Saba said, "For somebody without training, he was better than good. He'll be taking over in four hours."

Horn looked relieved.

"When we're past the mountains," Silk told him, and walked forward to the prow of the gondola.

Saba trotted after him. "I wouldn't do that, Caldé. We still haven't got all the altitude we want, and mountains can give you some tricky winds."

"I'll be fine; but you must remain where you are."

Behind Saba, Nettle called, "Horn's afraid you're going to jump, Caldé. That's all it is."

"I'm not."

"When General Saba said you were going to be the pilot, he felt a lot better, because he thought you wouldn't want to miss it. We both did."

Looking down upon the green and rising slopes far below, where hillside meadows yielded to forested heights, Silk smiled. "You don't have to worry. I love life and Hyacinth too much to jump. Besides, if I jumped I wouldn't be able to wrestle with your questions, Nettle– though that might be good for both of us. Have you more?"

"I was going to ask you about the mountains." Timorously, she edged past Saba to grasp Silk's hand. "It scares me to look at them. You know how lampreys look in the market? Those round mouths with rings and rings of teeth? These look like that to me, under us and up in the skylands too. Only a million times bigger."

"Were you going to ask me why they exist? Because Pas built them to guard Mainframe; but that's sheer speculation. I don't know any more than you do."

"If anybody lives there. And—and why there's snow on the tops. The tops are closer to the sun, so they ought to be warmer."

"I don't believe that the sun heats air," Silk told her absently, "not much, and perhaps not at all. If it did, the sun's heat couldn't reach us. If you think about it, you'll soon realize that sunlight doesn't illuminate air either; we could see air if it did, and we can't."

Behind Silk, Horn said, "No kind of light does then."

"Correct, I'm sure. The warmth of the sun heats the soil and the waters, and they in return warm the air above them. Up here where there are only widely separated peaks, the air must be cold of necessity. Hence, snow; and in the Mountains That Look At Mountains, snow has weight enough to fall."

Silk paused, considering. "I never asked Sciathan who lived in the mountains, or whether anyone did. I've seen no cities, but I would think a few people must, people who fled the cities or were driven out. It must be a wild and lawless place; no doubt many like it for just that reason."

From the hatch Hyacinth called, "Silk, is that you?" and he turned to smile at her.

"I've been looking all over for you, but nobody'd seen you. Oh, hello, General." As gracefully as ever, Hyacinth stepped from the ladder onto the deck. "Hi, sprats. Got a better view from up here? It's bigger, anyway."

"You can leave me to my own devices now," Silk told Horn.

It was snowing in Viron, a hard fall that converted misery to unrelieved wretchedness, snow that rendered every surface slippery and made every garment damp, and rushed into Maytera Mint's eyes each time she faced the wind.

"We have done what we can, My General." Under stress of weather, the captain stood beside, not before, her. Both had their coat collars turned up against the wind and cold; his uniform cap was pulled over his ears like her striped stocking cap, his right arm inadequately immobilized by a bloodstained sling.

"I'm sure you have, Colonel. They'll start dying in a few hours, I'm afraid, just the same."

"I am not a colonel, My General."

"You are, I just promoted you. Now show me you deserve it. Find them shelter."

"I have tried, My General. I shall try again, though every house in this quarter has been burned." He was not a tall man, yet he seemed tall as he spoke.

That about the houses had been unnecessary, Maytera Mint thought, and showed how tired he was. She said, "I know."

"This was your own quarter, was it not? Near the Orilla?"

"It was, and it is."

"I go. May I say first that I would prefer to fight for you and the gods, My General? Viron must be free!"

She shivered. "What if you lose that arm, Colonel?"

"One hand suffices to fire a needler, My General."

She smiled in spite of her determination not to. "Even the left? Could you hit anything?"

He took a step backward, saluting with his uninjured arm. "When one cannot aim well, one closes with the enemy."

He had vanished into the falling snow before she could return his salute. She lowered the hand that had not quite gotten to her eyebrow, and began to walk among the huddled hundreds who had fled the fighting.

I would know every face, she thought, if I could see their faces. Not the names, because I've never been good with names. Dear Pas, won't you let us have even a single ray of sun?

Children and old people, old people and children. Did old people not fight because they were too feeble? Or was it that they had, over seventy or eighty years, come to appreciate the futility of it?

Something caught at her skirt. "Are they bringing food?"

She dropped to one knee. The aged face might almost have been Maytera Rose's. "I've ordered it, but there's very little to be had. And we've very few people we can spare to look for it, wounded troopers mostly."

"They'll eat it themselves!"

Perhaps they will, Maytera Mint thought. They are hungry, too, I'm sure, and they've earned it. "Somebody will bring you something soon, before shadelow." She stood up.

"Sib? Sib? Mama's over there, and she's real cold."

She peered into the pale little face. "Perhaps you could find wood and start a fire. Someone must have an igniter."

"She won't . . ." The child's voice fell away.

Maytera Mint dropped to one knee again. "Won't what?"

"She won't take my coat, Maytera. Will you make her?"

Oh, my! Oh, Echidna! "No. I cannot possibly interfere with so brave a woman." There was something familiar about the small face beneath the old rabbit-skin cap. "Don't I know you? Didn't you go to our palaestra?"

The child nodded.

"Maytera Marble's group. What's your name?"

"Villus, Maytera." A deep inhalation for words requiring boldness. "I was sick, Maytera. I got bit by a big snake. I really did. I'm not lying."

"I'm sure you're not, Villus."

"That's why she won't, so tell her I'm well!" The small coat stood open now, displaying what appeared to be an adult's sweater, far too large.

"No, Villus. Button those again before you freeze." Her own fingers were fumbling with the buttons as she spoke. "Find wood, as I told you. There must be a little left, even if it's charred on the outside. Make a fire."

As she stood, the wind brought faint boomings that might almost have been thunder. Distant, she decided, yet not distant enough. It probably meant the enemy had broken through, but it would be worse than futile for her to rush back knowing nothing. Bison would send a messenger with news and a fresh horse. These two . . . "Are you all right?"

"We'll keep." An old man's voice, an old man with his arm around a woman just as old. The old woman said, "We're not hurt or anything." "We been talking about that." (The man again.) "We'd stay warmer moving around." "We were pretty tired when we got here."

"I'm trying to get you some food," Maytera Mint told them.

"We could help, couldn't we, Dahlia? Help pass it out, or anything you want done."

"That's good of you. Very good. Do either of you have an igniter?"

They shook their heads.

"Then you might look for one, ask other people. I set a little boy to gathering fuel a moment ago. If we could build a few fires, that would help a great deal."

"All this burned." The old man made an unfocused gesture with his free hand. "Should be coals yet." His wife confirmed, "Bound to be, snow or no snow." "I smell smoke." Sniffing, he struggled to stand, and Maytera Mint helped him up. "I'll have a look," he said.

Here I am, Maytera Mockorange. I am the sibyl I dreamed of becoming, moving among sufferers and helping them, though I have so little help to give.

She visualized Maytera Mockorange's severe features. The girl who would soon assume the new name *Mint* had yearned for renunciation and pictured herself walking through the whorl she would give up like a blessing; Maytera Mockorange had warned her of missed meals and meager food, of hard beds and hard thankless work. Of year after year of loneliness.

They had both been right.

Maytera Mint fell to her knees with folded hands and bowed head. "Oh Great Pas, O Mothering Echidna, you have given me my heart's desire." A feeling she had never known thrilled her: her body alone knelt in the snow; her spirit was kneeling among violets, baby's breath, and lily-of-the-valley, in a bower of roses. "I have won life's battle. I am complete. End my life today, if that is your pleasure. I shall rush into the arms of Hierax exulting."

"We tried, Maytera."

It had been a woman's voice to her left, and its words had not been addressed to her. To another sibyl then? Maytera Mint got to her feet.

"Cold," the woman was saying, *"and there's not a scrap of flesh on her poor bones."*

Three—no, four people. Two fat people sitting in the snow, with a starved face between the round, ruddy ones. The figure in black bending over them was the sibyl, clearly. What had been that young one's name? "Maytera? Maytera Maple? Is that you?"

"No, sib." She straightened up, turning her head farther than seemed possible, eyes glowing in a tarnished metal face. "It's me, sib. It's Maggie."

"It—it—I—oh, sib! Moly!" And they were hugging and dancing as they had on the Palatine. "Sib, sib, SIB!"

Another distant boom.

"Moly! Oh, oh, Moly! May I call you Maytera Marble, just once? I've missed you so!"

"Be quick. I'm about to become an abandoned woman."

"You, Moly?"

"Yes. I am." Maytera Marble's voice was firm as granite. "And don't call me Moly, please. It's not my name. It never was. My name's Magnesia. Call me Maggie. Or Marble, if it makes you happy. My husband will—never mind. Have you met my granddaughter, sib? This is she, but I don't think she'll talk right now. You must excuse her."

"Mucor?" Maytera Mint knelt beside the emaciated girl. "Our caldé described you to me, and I'm an old friend of your grandmother's."

"Wake up." Mucor's pinched face grinned without meaning. "Break it." There was no hint of intelligence in her stare. She said nothing further, and the silence of the snow closed about them until the fat woman ended it by saying, "This's my husband, General. Shrike's his name."

"Scleroderma! Scleroderma, I didn't recognize you."

"Well, I knew *you* right off. I said that's General Mint and I held her horse when she charged them on Cage Street, I did, and if you'd gone like you ought to you'd know her too."

The fat man tugged the brim of his hat.

"I went up to the Caldé's Palace to see Maytera, only she wasn't home and half the wall down, so I've been taking care of her granddaughter ever since, poor little thing. Did those bad women carry you off, Maytera? That's what I heard."

"You'd better call me Maggie," Maytera Marble said, and pulled her habit over her head.

"Maytera!"

"I am not a sibyl any more," the slender, shining figure declared. "I have become an abandoned woman, as I warned you I would." She dropped the voluminous black gown over Mucor's head, and pulled it down around her. "Put your arms into the sleeves, dear. It's easy, they're wide."

"There was an old man that helped me with her," Scleroderma explained, "but he went to fight, then the bad women came and we had to scoot."

If it had not been for the shock of seeing Maytera Marble nude, Maytera Mint would have smiled.

"I think it means he's dead, but I hope not. Aren't you cold, Maytera?"

"Not a bit." Maytera Marble straightened up. "This is much cooler and more comfortable, though I'm sure I'll miss my pockets." She turned to Maytera Mint. "I've been consorting with other abandoned women, a dozen at least. I'm afraid it's rubbed off."

Maytera Mint swallowed and coughed, wanting to bat the snowflakes away, to sit down with a mug of hot tea, to awaken and find that this lithe pewter-colored creature was not the elderly sibyl she had thought she knew. "Did they capture—"

With nimble fingers, Maytera Marble wound the long top of Maytera Mint's blue-striped stocking cap about her neck like a scarf. "This way, dear, then you won't be so cold, that's what it's for. You tuck the end in your coat." She tucked it. "And the tassel keeps it from coming out. See?"

"These women!" Maytera Mint had spoken more loudly than she had intended, but she continued with the same vehemence, telling herself, I *am* a general after all. "Are you referring to enemy troopers or Willet's spies?"

"No, no, no. Dear Chenille, who's really quite a nice girl in her way, and the caldé's wife. She's no better than she ought to be if you know what I mean. And the women our thieves brought. They were more interesting than the poor women, though the poor women were interesting too. But the thieves' women didn't mind taking their clothes off, or not very much. Dear Chenille actually enjoys it, I'd say. Her figure's prettier than her face, so I find it understandable."

Scleroderma said, "So's yours, Maytera," and her husband nodded enthusiastically.

Another explosion punctuated the sentence. Cocking her head, Maytera Mint decided it had been nearer than the last; there had been something portentious about the sound.

". . . Cognizance told us," Scleroderma finished.

Maytera Mint asked, "Did you say His Cognizance?" Then, before anyone could answer, put her finger to her lips.

The stammering popping reports seemed to come from above her head. They were followed after an interval by the remote crash of shells.

"What is it, General?" Scleroderma asked.

"I heard guns. A battery of light pieces. You don't often hear the shots, just the whine of the shells and the explosions. These are near, so they may be ours."

Maytera Marble took Mucor's hand and got her to her feet. "Will you excuse us? I want to take her to the fire."

"Fire?" Maytera Mint looked around.

"Right over there. I just saw it. Come along, darling."

Scleroderma and Shrike were getting to their feet as well, not swiftly but with so much effort, scrambling, and grunting that they gave the impression of frantic action.

The messenger should be here by now, Maytera Mint told herself, and stepped in front of Scleroderma. "You said His Cognizance was here? You must tell me before you go. But before you do, have you seen a mounted trooper leading another horse?"

Scleroderma shook her head.

"But His Cognizance was here?"

The fat man said, "Stopped an' had a chat, nice as anybody. I wouldn't of known, only the wife, she knows all that. Goes twice, three times most weeks. Just a little man older'n my pa. Had on a plain black whatchacallit, like any other augur." He paused, his eyes following Maytera Marble and Mucor. "Crowd around any harder, an' they'll shove somebody in."

"You're right." Maytera Mint trotted through the snow to the fire. "People! This little fire can't warm even half of you. Collect more wood. Build another! You can light it from this one." They dispersed with an alacrity that surprised her.

"Now then!" She whirled upon Scleroderma and Shrike. "If His Cognizance is here, I must speak to him. As a courtesy, if for no other reason. Where did he go?"

Shrike shrugged; Scleroderma said, "I don't know, General," and her husband added, "Said we'd have to leave this whorl, then the caldé come an' got him. First time I ever seen him."

"Caldé Silk?"

Scleroderma nodded. "He didn't know *him* either."

The Trivigauntis had released their prisoners, as General Saba had promised; no other explanation made sense, and it was vitally important. Maytera Mint looked around frantically for the messenger Bison would surely have dispatched minutes ago.

"He was lookin' for the caldé," Shrike explained, "only it was Caldé Silk what found *him*."

"There aren't as many as there were." Maytera Mint stood on tip-toe, blinking away snow.

"You told 'em to go find wood, General."

"General! General!" Beneath the shouted words, she heard the stumbling clatter of a horse ridden too fast across littered ground. "This way!" She waved blindly.

Scleroderma muttered, "Just listen to those drums. Makes me want to go myself."

"Drums?" Maytera Mint laughed nervously, and was ashamed of it at once. "I thought it was my heart. I really did."

Through the snow, Bison's messenger called, *"General?"*

She waved as before, listening. Not the cadent rattle of the thin cylindrical drums the Trivigauntis used, but the steady *thumpa-thumpa-thump* of Vironese war drums, drums that suggested the palaestra's big copper stew-pot whenever she saw them, war drums beating out the quickstep used to draw up troops in order of battle. Bison was about to attack, and was letting both the enemy and his own troopers know it.

"General!" The messenger dismounted, half falling off his raw-boned brown pony. "Colonel Bison says we got to take it to 'em. The airship's back. Probably you heard it, sir."

Maytera Mint nodded. "I suppose I did."

"They been droppin' mortar bombs on us out of it all up and down the line, sir. Colonel says we got to get in close and mix up with 'em so they can't."

"Where is he? Didn't you bring a horse for me?"

"Yes, sir, only the caldé took it. Maybe I shouldn't of let him, sir, but—"

"Certainly you should, if he wanted it." She pushed the messenger out of her way and swung into the saddle. "I'll have to take yours. Return on foot. Where's Bison?"

"In the old boathouse, sir." The messenger pointed vaguely through the twilit snow, leaving her by no means certain that he was not as lost as she felt.

"Good luck," Scleroderma called. And then, "I'm coming."

"You are not!" Maytera Mint locked her knees around the hard-used pony, heedless of the way the saddle hiked her wide black skirt past her knees. "You stay right here and take care of your husband. Help Maytera—I mean Maggie—with the mad girl." She pointed to the messenger, realizing too late that she was doing it with the hilt of her azoth. "Are you certain he's in the boathouse? I ordered him to stay back and not get himself killed."

"Safest place, sir, with them bombs droppin' on us."

A floating blur resolved itself into two riders in dark clothing upon a single white horse. A familiar voice shouted, "Go! Follow that officer— he'll take you to shelter. Get away from that fire!"

The voice was Silk's. As she watched in utter disbelief, he galloped through the fire. For a moment she hesitated; then the boom of slug guns decided her.

"I like this part though," Hyacinth whispered, hugging Silk tighter than ever, "just don't let it trot again."

He did not, but lacked the breath to say so. Reining up, he shielded his eyes with the right hand that snatched at the pommel whenever he was distracted; the group he had glimpsed through the snow might be a woman with children, and probably was. Gritting his teeth, he slammed his heels into the white gelding's flanks. It was essential not to trot—trotting shook them helpless. More essential not to lose the stirrups that fought free of his shoes whenever they were not gouging his ankles. The gelding slipped in the snow; for an instant he was sure it would fall.

Behind him, Hyacinth shrieked, *"Up, stand up! That way!"* She sounded angry; and briefly and disloyally, he wished that she possessed the clarion voice that Kypris had bestowed upon Maytera Mint—though it would have been still more useful to have it himself.

"My Caldé!" A snow-speckled figure had caught the bridle.

"Yes, what is it?"

"All are within, My Caldé. They are gone. You must too, before you die."

He shook his head.

"But a few remain, I swear. I shall send them. You must compel him, Madame."

Then the captain was running and the gelding trotting after him, and they were being shaken as if by a terrier.

"Here is the entrance, My Caldé. I regret I cannot assist you and your lady to dismount."

Too shaken even to think of disobeying, Silk slid from the gelding's back and helped Hyacinth down. The captain pointed to a deep crater almost at his feet; its bottom gleamed with greenish light.

Too sharply for comfort, Silk recalled the grave he had been shown in a dream. "We got to ride on a deadcoach the first time," he told Hyacinth. It was difficult to keep his voice casual. "That was a lot more comfortable, but there was dust instead of snow." She stared at him.

"You must climb down." The captain pointed again. "The climb is somewhat difficult. Several have fallen, though none were injured seriously." He produced a needler, fumbling the safety with his left thumb.

Silk said, "You're about to join the fighting."

"Yes, My Caldé. If you permit it."

Silk shook his head. "I won't. I have a message for you to give to General Mint. Do you know where Hyacinth and I are going?"

"Into this tunnel below the city, My Caldé, to preserve yourself for Viron, as is proper."

Hyacinth smoothed her gown. "We're supposed to leave the whole whorl with thousands and thousands of cards. If we get to whatever it is, we'll be rich." She spat into the snow.

"I've taken all the funds I could out of the fisc," Silk explained, "and His Cognizance has emptied the burse—the Chapter's funds. I'm telling you this so you can tell General Mint what's become of us, and what's happened to the money. Do you know which Siyuf you're fighting?"

A voice called, *"Caldé!"*

"Is that you down there, Horn?"

"Yes, Caldé." Horn climbed toward him, his feet loosening stones that rattled down the slope to fall into the tunnel.

"Go back down," Silk told him.

"My Caldé, we have been so fortunate as to chance upon this refuge opened for the defenseless by the enemy's bombs. I thank the good gods for it. You and your lady must employ it as well. Her airship cannot but see the fire."

Horn caught Silk's hand and joined them.

"As for this boy," the captain finished, "I shall procure a weapon for him."

"If we're going we'd better go," Hyacinth declared.

"You inquire concerning the two Siyufs, My Caldé. I have heard only rumors. Are they true?"

"I spoke to General Mint on a glass before we returned," Silk told him. "One of the councillors—Tarsier, I imagine—has altered a chem to look like Siyuf. She was supposed to mend relations between Trivigaunte and Viron, or see to it that the Trivigauntis lost if she could not. She appears to have chosen to occupy Siyuf's place permanently and conquer Viron for herself instead. Generalissimo Oosik has freed the real Siyuf in the hope—"

The final words were lost in an explosion. Silk found himself half in the crater, with Horn beside him and Hyacinth clinging and sobbing. After a few seconds he managed to gasp, "That was too near. Near enough to ring my ears."

"Where's the captain?" Horn asked. From the bottom, Nettle shouted, *"Horn!"*

"I don't know." Silk raised his heat to look around. "I can't see him, or—are those horses?"

"Our horse." Hyacinth staggered but managed to stand. "It must have been killed."

"Unless the captain mounted it and rode away. In either case, we'd better go."

She glared at him; then turned abruptly and slid down the slanting wall of the crater, pushing past Nettle and vanishing into the tunnel.

Horn caught Silk's arm. "You were sort of waiting here with the captain, Caldé. Like you didn't want to."

"Because I wasn't sure all the people who fled the battle had gotten inside."

Silk coughed and spat. "That explosion blew dirt into my mouth. I suppose it was open, as it usually is—I shouldn't talk so much. At any rate, I wanted to tell him I was resigning my office, and General Mint is to succeed me. Don't feel you have to chase after him with the message."

Nettle called, "I'm going inside with Hyacinth. Are you coming?"

"In a minute," Horn told her. "No, Caldé, I won't. But I promised His Cognizance I'd find you and bring you down there, and I'm going to as soon as . . ." He paused, shamefaced.

"What is it, Horn?"

"It's a long way, he says, to the big cave where the people are asleep in bottles, and when we get there we'll have to wake them up. Maybe we'd better get going."

"No, Horn." With the air of one who intends to remain for some time, Silk seated himself on the edge of the crater. "I asked Mucor to awaken the strongest man she could find and have him break the cylinder before the gas inside it killed him. If I could break one with Hyacinth's needler as easily as I did, I'd think a very strong man might break one from within with his fists. They'll be coming to meet us—or at least I hope they will—and may be able to show us a shorter route to the belly of the whorl, where the landers are."

He studied Horn with troubled eyes. "Now, why did you stop me from following Hyacinth? What is it?"

"Nothing, Caldé."

Like noisy spirits, troopers on horseback thundered past, their faces obscured and their clothing dyed black by the snow.

"Those were Trivigauntis, I believe," Silk said. "I don't know whether that's good or bad. Bad, I suppose. If I say it myself—tell you what I believe you were about to say—will you at least confess I'm right?"

"I don't want to, Caldé."

"But you will, I know. You were going to tell me why you and Nettle took me up on the roof of the gondola, where General Saba and Hyacinth joined us, pretending that they hadn't—"

"I was going to tell you about falling off the time before, Caldé. You said you tried to kill yourself and I stopped you, but it was the other way. I started to slide off on purpose. I don't know what got into me, but you grabbed me. You were just about killed too, and now I remember. I'd be dead if it weren't for you."

Silk shook his head. "If I hadn't acted foolishly, you wouldn't have been in danger at all; I provoked your danger and very nearly occasioned your death."

He sighed. "That wasn't what you came so close to telling me, however. Hyacinth had been in General Saba's cabin, though both pretended they had not been together. The walls of those cabins are cloth and bamboo, and you and Nettle were afraid I'd overhear them and realize they were doing the things that women do, at times, to provide each other pleasure."

Seeing Horn's expression, he smiled sadly. "Did you think I didn't know such things occur? I've shriven women often, and in any event we were taught about them—and worse things—at the schola. We're far too innocent for our duties when we leave it, I'm afraid; but our instructors ready us for the whorl as well as they can." He looked down at the object that Horn was offering him. "What is that?"

"Your needler, Caldé. It used to be the pilot's, I guess. Hyacinth knocked it out of her hand, you said, and you picked it up. You must have left it there in the cockpit, because the Flier found it there and gave it to me."

Silk accepted it, tucking it into his waistband. "You want me to kill Hyacinth with it. Is that the plan?"

"If you want to." Wretchedly, Horn nodded.

"I don't. I won't. I'm taking this because I may need it—I've been down there, and I may have to protect her. Haven't I told you about that?"

"Yes, Caldé. On the airship, for my book."

"Good, I won't have to go over it again. Now listen. You feel that Hyacinth has betrayed me, and unnaturally. I want you to at least consider, as I do, that Hyacinth herself may feel differently. Isn't it possible—in fact, likely—that she feared that General Saba might regain her airship in fact as well as in name? That in that case it would be well for us—for Hyacinth and me, and every Vironese on board—if she were as friendly toward us as we could render her?"

Horn nodded reluctantly. "I guess so, Caldé."

"Furthermore, Hyacinth knew that I meant to return General Saba's airship when we returned to the city. May not Hyacinth have considered that General Saba might at some future date be a good and strong friend to Viron?"

Through the break in the tunnel wall, Hyacinth called, "Aren't you coming down?"

"Soon," Silk told her. "We're not finished here."

"Caldé, she's the one dropping mortar bombs on us. General Saba is. That's her up there in the airship right now."

"It is indeed; but she's dropping them because she's been ordered to, as any good officer would. I doubt very much that Hyacinth cherished any hope of suborning General Saba from her duty; but there are many times when an officer, particularly a high-ranking one, may exercise discretion. Hyacinth tried, I believe, to do what she could to make certain any such decisions would favor us—more specifically, my government."

"But we're going. You said so on the airship, and before we found this way, we were going to have to walk all the way to the Juzgado. On the Short Sun Whorl, it won't matter whether General Saba likes us or not, will it?"

"No. But Hyacinth could not have known aboard the airship that we would be leaving this soon, and she may even have hoped that we would not leave at all. I think she did."

"I see." Horn nodded; and when Silk did not speak again, he said, "Caldé, we'd better go."

"Soon, as I said. There's one more thing—no, two. The first is that whatever that act might mean to me, or to you, or even to General Saba, it meant next to nothing to Hyacinth; she has performed similar ones hundreds of times with any number of partners. With Generalissimo Oosik, for example."

"I didn't know that."

"No. But I do—he told me. When she had to leave the house of the commissioner who had obtained her from her father—I don't even know which it was—she lived for a time with a captain. Eventually they quarreled and separated."

"You don't have to tell me all this, Caldé."

"Yes, I do. Not for your book—which you will probably never complete or even begin—but for guidance in your own life. Who was that captain? Would you care to guess?"

Horn shook his head.

"I think I can. He was very formal with her, but I saw his eyes—particularly when he stopped our horse. I don't believe he meant much to her; he was a protector and provider when she needed one. She meant a great deal to him, however—no doubt she always will."

Horn whispered, "She's climbing back up," and pointed.

Silk scrambled halfway down the crater to meet and assist her. "I won't say I'm not delighted to see you—I'm always overjoyed to see you, Hyacinth, you know that. But Horn and I were about to join you down there."

Entering the crater from the tunnel, Nettle called, "You wouldn't believe all the people down here, Caldé. Half the quarter. Marrow the greengrocer, and Shrike the butcher, and even the new augur that was with us on the airship. Moly's here, and he's making her wear his robe. The Prolocutor made everybody sit down."

Horn offered his hand to Hyacinth, and the other to Silk. "My mother, and my brothers and sisters. That's what I care about, only . . ." Something caught in his throat. "Only that sounds like I don't care about my father."

"But you do," Hyacinth muttered. "I know how it is."

"Yeah, I guess so. He made me work in the shop every day after palaestra, and—and we'd fight about that, and lots of other stuff."

"I understand."

"I'm the oldest," Horn said, as though that accounted for everything.

Silk called, "If half the quarter's down there, what about our manteion? The congregation, I mean, the people who came to sacrifice on Scylsday and the children from the palaestra?"

"They're just about all here," Nettle told him. "Not some of the men, they're off fighting for General Mint. But, oh, Goldcrest and Feather and Villus, and my friend Ginger. Wait, let me think. Teasel is, and her sisters and brothers and her mother. And Asphodella and Aster. And Kit—he's Kerria's little brother, and she's there too. And Holly and Hart. He's wounded. And the cats' meat woman, and that old man that sells ices in the summer, and a whole lot more."

Silk nodded, then smiled at Hyacinth. "I've done it—saved it from the dissolution of the whorl. Or at least I will have when we reach the new one. I was to save our manteion; and that is the manteion, all of those people coming together to worship. The rest was trimming, very much including me."

Hyacinth could not look at him.

"When you came back up, I was explaining to Horn that in the end it is only love that matters. The Outsider once told me that though he's not Kypris, she cannot help becoming him. The more she becomes a goddess of love in truth, the more they will unite—it was before we met in Ermine's by the goldfish pool." He smiled again. "Where Thelx holds up a mirror."

Hyacinth nodded; and Horn saw that her eyes were filled with tears. He asked, "Did you really see him there, Caldé? The Outsider?"

"Yes, in a dream, standing upon the water. I had only this left to say, Horn, and there's no reason I shouldn't say it now, or that Hyacinth and Nettle shouldn't hear it. It is that love forgets injuries. I know that Hyacinth would never betray me, just as you know that Nettle would never betray you; but if she did—if she did a thousand times—I would still love her."

Almost violently, Hyacinth pushed herself away from the crater. "I can't listen to any more of this. I don't want to, and I won't." She stood up.

Silk said, "Then let us go," and began to climb down to the break in the tunnel wall.

"I'm not going!" Hyacinth shouted. Her lovely face was savage. "You told me about that place, and I've seen it, and it's horrible! All the landers are broken, you said, not like Auk's, and you're just hoping to fix them. And you're giving up the whole *city!*" She turned and dashed away, vanishing in the swirling snow before she had taken five strides.

Silk tried to scramble back, but in his haste set off a slide that carried him almost to Nettle, who followed him when he began to climb again.

When he reached the surface and started after Hyacinth, Horn and Nettle went with him. A bomb burst near enough to shake the earth beneath their feet, and he stopped. "You have to go, both of you, and you must go together."

His eyes flashed even in that snowy twilight. "Nettle, do you understand? Do you, Horn? I'll find her, and enough cards to repair another lander. Get down there, find His Cognizance, and tell him. We'll meet you at the landers, if we can."

Nettle took Horn's hand, and Silk said, "Make him go. By force, if you must." He offered her his needler, but she drew her own, the one that had been Saba's. He nodded, put his back in his waistband, and disappeared into the snow like a ghost. Overhead, the harsh voice of his bird sounded again and again: *"Silk? Silk? Silk?"*

For a score of poundings of their hearts, Nettle and Horn stood together, staring after him and wondering what the future held for them; until at length they smiled as one, she gave him Saba's needler, and hand-in-hand they returned to the crater and scrambled down to the opening that a bomb had made in the tunnel wall, and went into the tunnel, where Horn's mother was waiting for them.

MY DEFENSE

With the account you have now read, I had intended to conclude *The Book of Silk,* for we never saw him again. I am adding this continuation in response to criticisms and questions directed to us by those who read the earlier sections, sections which Nettle has corrected, and transcribed in a hand clearer than mine.

Many of you urge me to tell the story in my proper person, relating only what I saw, and in effect making myself my own hero. I reply that any of you might write such an account. I invite you to do so.

My purpose is not (as you wish) merely to describe the way in which we who were born in Viron reached Blue, but to recount the story of Patera Silk, who was its caldé at the time we left and was the greatest and most extraordinary man I have known. As I have indicated, I had planned to call my account *The Book of Silk,* and not Starcrossers' Landfall or any of the other titles (many equally foolish) that have been suggested. In the event, it has become known as *The Book of the Long Sun,* because it is much read by young people who do not recall our Long Sun Whorl, or were born after Landing Day. I do not object. You may call it what you wish as long as you read it.

To our critics, I say this: Patera Silk was personally known to Nettle and me; I recall his look, his voice, and his gait to this day, and when young I was punished for imitating him too well, as you have read. Nettle knew him as well as I.

We knew Maytera Marble (who also employed the names Moly, Molybdenum, Maggie, and Magnesia, the last being her original name) at least as well. Until we reached our teens, she was our instructress in the palaestra on Sun Street, as Maytera Mint and Maytera Rose were subsequently. Silk loved her and confided in her; in fact, I have often thought that she had been given the child she longed for, although she was not conscious of it. She in turn confided in us during the time we worked in the Caldé's Palace under her direction, during the time we were together on the airship, and during our passage through the abyss, and here on Blue. To prevent confusion, I have called her Maytera Marble throughout my account. There was never a more practical woman, nor a better one.

On the flight to Mainframe, we had many opportunities to see and hear Auk, though he was not generally communicative. Chenille, with whom we had worked at the Caldé's Palace, often spoke of him as well. Silk did not, as some readers assume, confide to us the content of Auk's shriving, although he told me that he had shriven him upon meeting him in the Cock. That Auk had kicked a man to death was known throughout the quarter, and it seems probable that it was one of the offenses of which he was shriven. Chenille confided to Nettle that he had struck her on two occasions, and described them.

More than one reader has taxed me with whitewashing Auk's character. It is more probable that I have painted it too dark; I disliked him, and even after so many years have found it hard to treat him fairly. As I have tried to make clear, he was a big man and an extremely strong one, far from handsome, with a beard so heavy that he appeared unshaven even when he had just shaved; although he was said to be courageous and a free spender, few besides Silk, Chenille, and Gib ever spoke well of him.

If I found it hard to be fair to Auk, I found it harder still to be fair to Hyacinth, whose extraordinary beauty was at once her blessing and her curse. She had little education, far too much vanity, and a savage temper. When Nettle was present, she displayed herself to me, posing, bending over to exhibit her décolletage, raising her skirt to adjust her hose, and so forth. In Nettle's absence, she cursed me if I so much as glanced at her. She saw all human relationships in terms of money, power, and lust, and understood Silk less well than Tick understood her.

Very few of us, I would say, have known such a woman as General Mint; and it is almost impossible to convey an accurate impression of her to those who have not. She was small, with a smooth little face, a sharp nose, and a dart of brown hair that divided her forehead almost to the eyebrows. In conversation her voice was the soft and timorous one we recalled from her classroom; but when the need for quick, decisive action arose, the little sibyl was cast off immediately. Her glance was fire and steel then, and at the sound of her voice wounded troopers who had seemed too weak to stand snatched up weapons and joined the advance. Unless restrained by her subordinates, she led her troops in person, striding boldly ahead of the boldest and never slackening her pace as she shouted encouragement to those behind her. If it had not been for Bison and Captain Serval, she would certainly have been killed by the second day.

As a tactician, she understood better than most the need for a simple workable plan which could be put into effect before conditions changed; that and the astounding loyalty she inspired were the keys to her success. Although she is better known as General Mint, I have titled her Maytera, just as I have referred to her sib as Maytera Marble throughout my account. Fewer than I had expected have found fault with Silk's assertion that she took her warlike character from the Goddess of Love, although it seems implausible to me. Nettle suggests that many women, thus inspired by love of their city and their gods, might exhibit the same dauntless courage. Certainly love will face the inhumi at midnight, as we say now.

Although neither of us spoke to Blood, both of us saw and heard him when he visited the manteion, and saw him and Musk when they offered their white rabbits. Blood's conversations with Silk and Maytera Marble were detailed to us by them; they, I would guess, saw more good in him than Nettle or I would have.

Neither of us ever saw Doctor Crane, but Maytera Marble had met him and liked him, as Silk had. Chenille, who had known him intimately, said that he looked on injury and illness as a butcher looks on pigs and steers; and I have tried to convey something of that. From what Silk said of him, he believed in Sphigx no more than any other god, and had her reality been proven to him, he would only have turned from ridiculing those who credited it to ridiculing her.

I have taken Incus's character from Remora's description and our own observations during the flight to Mainframe. He was physically unimpressive, and perhaps for that reason frequently impelled to assert his importance, but not lacking in courage. On the airship I watched him "enchant" a slug gun by slipping his finger behind the trigger, then snatch it from the trooper as she struggled to fire it.

Many readers have demanded that I include an account of our passage through the tunnels to the lander and our flight through the abyss.

Again I invite them to pen their own, as Scleroderma did. (Her grandson has it and permits visitors to copy it.) I intend to say no more here than is necessary to illuminate the character of the inhumu Nettle and I knew as Patera Quetzal, His Cognizance the Prolocutor of Viron. No doubt many will object to my writing *character* in such a context, urging that a monster of that kind can no more have character than a hus; but those who trap hus and tame them have told me they differ at least as much as dogs.

To us Quetzal was not an inhumi, but a venerable old man, wise and compassionate, Silk's supporter and steadfast friend. When Nettle and I returned to the tunnel it was to him that we brought Silk's message. When they had heard it, many wanted to return to the surface to look for Silk and help him search for Hyacinth. Quetzal forbade it, pointing out that it was contrary to Silk's own instructions, and led us down the tunnel in the direction of the lake.

Then I remembered something that Remora had told me on the airship: how Quetzal had vanished when Spider forced him into the cellar of Blood's ruined villa. When we had walked a long way down the tunnel and even the hardiest had grown weary, and Quetzal himself had fallen behind nearly all of our straggling company, I was able to ask about it.

"Walk beside me, my son." He put a hand on my shoulder; I recall how light and boneless it felt through the thin jacket I wore, as if he had laid a strip of soft leather beside my neck. "I can't keep up any more. Will you support me? You're young and strong. Patera Caldé likes you, did you know that?"

I said I hoped he did, and that he had always been kind to me.

"He likes you. He speaks of you warmly, and of you, my child. You're both good children. Good children, I say. But men and women with children are children to me. No fool like an old man! You women are wiser when you're old, my child. You're grown, both of you. I doubt you know it, but you are."

We thanked him.

"I can hardly get along. Like the fat woman. Can't leave her, can we? Can't leave them back there, and she's too heavy to carry." He was wearing an ordinary augur's robe; but he bore the baculus, his rod of office, which he used as a staff.

I said that we would have to stop soon for Scleroderma's sake, and many others, and offered to go ahead if he would tell me what to look for.

"I want you to sleep, my son." He seemed to suck his gums and reconsidered. "No, to keep watch. Can you stay awake?"

I assured him that I could.

"Good. Someone must, and I can't. I'm always nodding off, ask young Remora. I can't keep up this pace myself, but I have to keep urging everybody to walk faster. What tricks the gods play! Have you a weapon, my child?"

Nettle shook her head; I explained that she had brought a needler from the airship but had given it to me, and offered to return it to her.

"Keep it. Keep it! You'll need it when you stand guard." He turned his head. He had a long and very wrinkled neck that would have betrayed his true nature at once had I known then of the hooded inhumi. As it was, I was suddenly frightened because there was nothing of warmth or kindness in his look. It was as though I were seeing a mask, or the features of a corpse propped erect. He said, "You won't shoot me, will you?"

Naturally I assured him that I would not.

"Because I'll walk. I always do. They see me around the Palace all night long. They say it's my spirit, that I step out of my skin and walk all night. Do you believe it, my child?"

Nettle nodded. "If Your Cognizance says so."

"I don't." I had the impression that he was leaning most of his weight upon my shoulder, yet he was certainly not heavy. "Never believe such stuff. I can't sleep, and so I wander about dazed and tired, that's all. My son, would you tell those in front to go faster? I haven't the breath."

I shouted, "His Cognizance says we must walk faster!" or something of the kind.

"Thank you. Now we can stop. Let the fat woman and her man catch up." He turned, motioning to them urgently.

Nettle whispered, "We're in danger down here. We must be, or he wouldn't be in such a hurry."

She had spoken in my ear, and I myself had hardly heard her, yet Patera Quetzal (as I thought of him) said, "We are, my daughter, but I don't know how much. When you don't know, you have to act as though it were great."

Wishing to return to my question, I asked him, "Were you in very much danger from Spider, Your Cognizance?"

He shook his head, not as a man does, turning it from side to side, but swaying it while holding it nearly upright. "From him? None. No, a lot, since he would have wasted my time. I'd a lot to do, so I left." He laughed, an old man's high-pitched cackle. "Vanished in the darkness. Is that what young Remora told you? He told somebody that, I know. Want to know how to do it?"

He turned his back and raised his black robe to cover his head, standing with his hands and the baculus out of sight in front of him. That stretch of tunnel was as well lit by the creeping green lights the first settlers brought as any, yet he seemed almost to have disappeared, baculus and all. I said, "I see, Your Cognizance. I mean, I don't."

Scleroderma and her husband caught up with us then, she waddling very slowly and dolefully, he limping in a way that showed how his feet hurt. Nettle told them that Quetzal was worried about them.

"I'm worried about him," Scleroderma said, and holding onto her husband and me as though we were a couple of trees lowered herself to the shiprock floor and kicked off her shoes. Her husband said, "You sprats walk too fast. How's His Cognizance supposed to keep up?" He sat down beside his wife and pulled off his as well.

Recalling that Quetzal had been concerned for their safety, I motioned for Nettle to sit and sat down myself. Scleroderma said accusingly, "I heard you yell at them in front, trying to get them to go faster."

I explained that Quetzal had instructed me to, and Nettle asked, "Where is he? He was here with us a minute ago."

"Up ahead," Shrike told her. "Haven't seen him in a quite a while."

We rested for perhaps an hour, during which Nettle and I worried that we were becoming permanently separated from the rest. For a long way, however, it was impossible for our route to diverge from theirs; the tunnel ran nearly straight, slanting gently, and in fact pleasantly, downward. At length we came upon a side tunnel; but we found a note there signed by Hart, saying that His Cognizance had instructed him to write it, that they would follow the main tunnel, and that anyone who found the note was to leave it to direct others.

After another half league or so, we heard a baby crying and faint snores; and soon we caught up with our friends from the quarter and my mother, brothers, and sisters, all of them sound asleep. Scleroderma and her husband lay down at once, and I got Nettle to lie down as well, telling her to sleep if she could. She had no more than pillowed her head on my jacket than she was sleeping as soundly as Scleroderma.

I sat down, took off my shoes and rubbed my feet, and tried to decide what I ought to do. I had promised Quetzal I would stay awake, and I recalled very clearly what Silk had told me about the dog-like creatures the soldiers called *gods* and the convicts *bufes*. But I was tired and hungry, and longed to rest; and though Quetzal had asked me to protect the company, which by then numbered more than four hundred, he had said nothing about anyone's protecting me while I slept an hour or two.

After turning the matter over for what seemed a very long while in the dilatory fashion in which I weigh problems when I'm fatigued, I decided I would watch faithfully until someone woke, charge him or her to take my place, and sleep myself.

Then it almost seemed that I was asleep already, because it seemed that I could hear the soft sigh of wings, as if a big owl were flying along the tunnel a considerable distance from where I sat. I sat up straight and listened with all my might, but heard nothing more. Soon afterward, it struck me that Quetzal had said he often had difficulty sleeping. Thinking he might watch for me if he were wakeful, I stood up and padded among the sleepers looking for him; but he was not there.

I cannot describe the consternation I felt. Over and over I told myself that I must surely be mistaken, that someone had lent him a blanket or coat that covered his black robe; and so I peered into the same faces that I had peered into a few minutes before, until I sincerely believe that I could have described everyone present and said where each of them lay. We had among us a dozen infants, a large contingent of children, and a good many women; but not more than forty men, including Patera Remora and Shrike. I told myself very firmly then that a woman or even a girl could guard us as well as I could. She would only have to wake me if danger threatened.

Eventually it occurred to me to ask myself what Silk would have done in my situation. Silk would have prayed, I decided, and so I knelt, folded my hands and bowed my head, and implored the Outsider to take pity on my plight and cause one at least of those sleeping around me to wake up, very carefully specifying that a woman or a girl would be entirely acceptable to me.

When I raised my head, someone was sitting up in the midst of the sleepers; when I saw her dark and deathly eyes, I knew at once the mocking fashion in which the Outsider had answered my prayer. "Mucor," I called softly. "Please come over here and talk to me."

Her face floated upward like a ghost's and seemed almost to drift along the tunnel; she was wearing a sibyl's black gown.

"Mucor," I inquired, "where is your grandmother? She was here before." Very tardily it had occurred to me that Maytera Marble rarely slept, and would be the ideal person to relieve me so that I could.

"Gone," Mucor said. I expected to get nothing more out of her, having learned at the Caldé's Palace how seldom she spoke. But after a few seconds she added, "She went with the man who isn't there."

It was encouraging, but there seemed little use in asking who the man who wasn't there was. I asked instead if she would send her spirit to learn where her grandmother was and whether she was in need of help. Mucor nodded, and we sat side-by-side in silence for what I felt sure was at least a quarter hour. I was nearly asleep when she said, "She's carrying him. Crying. She'd like somebody to come."

"Your grandmother?"

I must have spoken more loudly than I had intended, because Nettle sat up and asked what was wrong.

Mucor pointed down the tunnel, saying, "Not far."

Nor was she. We had hardly lost sight of our friends when we met Maytera Marble, more or less dressed in an augur's robe so long it swept the tunnel floor, with Quetzal in her arms. Her face could not display emotion, as I have tried to make clear; but every limb expressed the most heart-rending anguish. "He's been shot," she told us. "He won't let me do anything to stop the bleeding." Her voice was agonized.

As slowly as a flower's, Quetzal's face turned toward us; it was terrible, not merely swollen or sunken, but misshapen, as if death's grip had crushed his chin and cheekbones. "I am not bleeding," he said. "Do you see blood, my children?"

I suppose we shook our heads.

"You can't stop my bleeding if I'm not bleeding."

I offered to carry him, but Maytera Marble refused, saying he weighed nothing. Later I was to find that she was not far wrong; I had lifted younger brothers who weighed more.

Nettle asked who had shot him.

"Troopers from Trivigaunte." He tried to smile, achieving only a grimace. "They're down here now, my child. They were digging trenches east of the city looking for a tunnel near the surface, and found one. They think Silk's with us." He gasped. "But they'd try to stop us anyway. Sphigx commands it."

I said, "We have to do the will of Pas."

"Yes, my son. Never forget what you just said."

By that time we had nearly reached the sleepers. Nettle ran ahead and woke up Remora, knowing that where there is no doctor an augur makes the best substitute; but Quetzal would not let him see his wound. "I'm an old man," he said. "I'm ready to die. Let me go fast." Yet he did not die until the following day, when we had begun to cross the abyss.

Remora brought him the Peace, and when it was over Quetzal gave him his gammadion, saying, "Your turn now, Patera. You were cheated by Scylla, but you'll have to guide the Chapter in the Short Sun Whorl."

(So it came to be. Although there are many other holy men here, His Cognizance Patera Remora heads what people from other cities call the Vironese Faith. I am adding this note because I know that not all of my readers came from Viron, and as Nettle's copies are themselves copied, still more will be unfamiliar with the Chapter.)

But I am running ahead of my account. When Quetzal would no more answer our questions than permit us to treat his wound, we asked Maytera Marble what had happened.

"I was lying awake," she said, "Thinking things over. How we'd seen Mainframe, and about dear Chenille and Auk, and Patera Silk and Hyacinth. Wondering, too, whether my husband was still alive, and, well, various things.

"I saw His Cognizance get up and start down the tunnel, so I told Mucor not to worry, I'd be back soon, and went after him and asked where he was going. He said he was afraid there might be danger ahead, so since he couldn't sleep he was going to see. I said he shouldn't risk himself like that, that he should send Macaque or one of the other boys."

She broke down at that point, sobbing uncontrollably, and cried for so long that many of her listeners left to talk among themselves; but Nettle and I stayed, with Remora, Scleroderma, and a few others.

When she had regained her self-possession, she continued, "I wanted him to send someone else. He ordered me to go back, and I said thanks be to Pas that I'm a laywoman now and don't have to obey, because I'm not going to let you run off alone like this, Your Cognizance, and get killed. I'm going with you. He said he knew these tunnels because he'd come down here alone to make the Ayuntamiento talk to him when they didn't want to, and he knew the dangers. But I wouldn't leave."

Nettle said, "This isn't your fault, Maggie. I don't know how it happened, but I know you, and it can't be." The rest of us seconded her.

Maytera Marble shook her head. "After we'd walked a long, long way we came to a crossing where four tunnels met. I asked which way we were going, and he said he was turning right, but I had to go back. Then he went into the right-hand tunnel. It was the darkest, the one he went into was. I followed him, and for a little while I saw him up ahead, but he wouldn't slow down. We were both practically running. Then I really did run as fast as I could, but I lost sight of him. I walked on and on, and there were these tunnels off to the side but I always kept to the one I was in. Then there was a big iron door and I couldn't go any farther, so I went back. I got to the place—"

She choked and sobbed. "Where the tunnels crossed, and I could hear him walking. Not the way he had been when I'd been following him, but slowly, stumbling every step or two. He was a long way off, but I had good ears and I gave them to Marble."

Nettle looked puzzled; I signaled her not to speak.

"So I ran some more." Maytera Mint looked up at us, and it seemed worse to me than any weeping that her eyes were not full of tears. "He'd fallen down when I got there. He was bleeding terribly, like the animals do after the augur pulls his knife out, but he wouldn't let me look at it, so I carried him."

We ourselves carried him after that, carrying him in our arms like a child because we had no poles from which to make a stretcher. He directed us, for he knew where the Trivigauntis were, and down which tunnel the sleepers were coming.

(I will say nothing of our brush with the Trivigauntis; it has been talked about until everyone is tired of listening. Shrike, Scleroderma, and I had needlers, as did certain others. Scleroderma risked her life to get our wounded to safety; and as the fighting grew hotter, she was wounded and wounded again, but she continued to nurse us when her skirt was stiff with her own blood.

(She has been dead for years now; I very much regret that it has taken me so long to pay her this well-deserved tribute. Her grandchildren are very proud of her and tell everyone that she was a great woman in Viron. Nobody in Viron thought her a great woman, only a short fat woman who trudged from house to house selling meat scraps, an amusing woman with a joke for everyone, who had dumped a bucket of scraps over Silk while he sat with her on a doorstep because she felt he was patronizing her. But the truth is that her grandchildren are right, and we in Viron were wrong. She was a very great woman, second only to General Mint. She would have ridden with General Mint if she could, and she fought the Guard in Cage Street and nursed the wounded afterward, and fought fires that night when it seemed the whole city might burn. In the end, she and Shrike lost their home and their shop, all that they possessed, to the fire that swept our quarter. Even then, she did not despair.)

Quetzal had brought hundreds of cards from the Burse. He had already entrusted most of them to Remora, and he gave him the rest when we reached the landers. Some of us had thought that he had refused to have his wound bandaged for fear his cards would be stolen, but when they had been turned over to the sleepers, he still refused.

With the sleepers, we filled two landers. It was thought best to have some of them on each, because they knew much more about their operation than any of us did. As has been told many times, the monitor who controlled our lander appeared in the glasses, displayed Blue and Green to us, and asked which was our destination. No one knew, so we consulted Quetzal, although he was too weak almost to speak.

He asked to be carried to the cockpit, as we called that part of our lander which Silk had called the nose. The monitor there displayed both whorls to him, as it had to Remora, Marrow, and me; and he chose Green, and choosing died. Remora then personally carried his body back to the small sickbay; it was no easy task, because our engines were firing as never before, not even when we had left the Long Sun Whorl. As it chanced, there was a glass in this sickbay, I suppose to advise those who cared for the sick.

There was a woman named Moorgrass on board whose trade it had been to wash the bodies of the dead, and perfume them, and prepare them for burial. Remora asked her to wash and prepare Quetzal's, and Maytera Marble and Nettle volunteered to help her. I shall never forget their screams.

We did not know then that the inhumi live on Green, nor that they fly to Blue when the whorls are in conjunction, nor that they drink blood, nor even how they change their shapes. Or in fact anything about them. Yet everyone who saw Quetzal's body was deeply disturbed; and Marrow and I urged that we come here to Blue instead of going to Green as he had advised.

Remora heard us out; but when we had finished, he affirmed his faith in Patera Quetzal, whose coadjutor he had been for so many years, and declared that we would remain on the course he had recommended. It was not until three days later, when it had become apparent to anyone who went into the cockpit, that we were really on course to Blue, that we learned that the monitor had overruled him. No one questions its decision now.

Here I close my defense, having (as I hope) satisfied the demands of my critics. Whether I have or have not, having compromised my principles more than I wished, I repeat that I set out to tell Silk's story, and no other.

It may be that he is dead, having been killed in the Long Sun Whorl. It may also be that he and Hyacinth later boarded a lander that carried them to Green, and died there.

But it also may be that he is still alive, and in my heart I feel that he is, either in the Long Sun Whorl or—as I hope—on another part of this Short Sun Whorl we call Blue. The years will have changed him as they change all of us; I can only describe him as he looked on that overheated summer afternoon when he snatched the ball from my hand as I was about to score, a man well above average height, with a clear, somewhat pale complexion, bright blue eyes, and straw-colored hair that would never lie flat. A slender man, but not a slow or a weak one. He will have a scar upon his back where the needle left it, and may have faint scars on his right arm, left by the beak of the vulture Mucor called the white-headed one.

My own name is Horn. My wife Nettle and I live with our sons on Lizard Island, toward the tail, where we make and sell such paper as this. We will be grateful to anyone who brings us word of Patera Silk.

AFTERWARD

Horn wiped the point of his quill with a scrap of soft leather and corked the ink that he and his wife had concocted from soot and sap, pushed back his chair, and stood. It was done. It was done at last, and now perhaps the ghost of the boy he had been would leave him in peace.

Outside, the short sun's fiery rim had touched the sea. A golden road—an Aureate Path—stretched westward across the whitecaps toward a new Mainframe that almost certainly did not exist. He walked to the beach where Hoof and Hide were playing and asked where Sinew was.

"Hunting," Hide declared; Hoof added, "Over on the big island, Father." Hoof's wide, dark eyes showed plainly how deeply he was impressed.

"He should be home by this time."

Nettle called from the kitchen window as he spoke.

"Go inside." When the twins objected, he gave each a push in the direction of the sturdy walls.

From the summit of the tor, he had a clear view of the strait. Still, a half minute passed before he could be certain of the coracle, lifted upon distant waves only to vanish from sight.

Night had come already to the eastern sky, scattering the short suns of other whorls across its black velvet. Soon Green would rise, almost a second sun, yet baleful as a curse; it had brought a succession of storms and monstrous tides—

There!

Horn watched and waited until he was sure the faint gleam was actually moving against its glittering backdrop. Within that point of light he had been born, and had grown almost to manhood. Within that point of light Sinew had been conceived, in all probability, in the Caldé's Palace. It did not seem possible.

Almost too quickly to be noticed, something dark flitted between Horn and the whorl that had been his; and he shuddered.

ABOUT THE AUTHOR

GENE WOLFE was born in New York City and raised in Houston, Texas. He spent two and a half years at Texas A&M, then dropped out and was drafted. He was awarded the Combat Infantry badge during the Korean War: afterward he attended the University of Houston on the GI Bill, earning a degree in mechanical engineering. His engineering career culminated in an editorship on the trade journal *Plant Engineering*, which he retained until his retirement in 1984.

He first came to prominence as a science fiction writer as the author of *The Fifth Head of Cerberus* (1972); in 1973 *The Death of Doctor Island* won a Nebula for best novella. His novel *Peace* won the Chicago Foundation for Literature Award in 1977; his poem "The Computer Iterates the Greater Trumps" was awarded the Rhysling for science fiction poetry.

His four-volume *The Book of the New Sun* quickly established itself as a classic in the field. The first volume, *The Shadow of the Torturer* (1980), won the World Fantasy Award and the British SF Association Award; the second, *The Claw of the Conciliator* (1981), won the Nebula Award; the third, *The Sword of the Lictor* (1982), won the Locus Award; the Fourth, *The Citadel of the Autarch* (1983), won the John W. Campbell Memorial Award and the Prix Apollo. A coda to the sequence, *The Urth of the New Sun,* appeared in 1987.

Other novels include *Operation Ares* (1970); *The Devil in a Forest* (1976); *Free Live Free* (1984); *Soldier in the Mist* (1986) and *Soldier of Arete* (1989); *There Are Doors* (1988); *Pandora by Holly Hollander* (1990); and *Castleview* (1990). He received widespread acclaim for his four-volume *The Book of the Long Sun,* comprising *Nightside the Long Sun* (1993), *Lake of the Long Sun* (1994), *Caldé of the Long Sun* (1994), and *Exodus from the Long*

Sun (1996). His most recent work is the three-volume *The Book of the Short Sun,* comprising *On Blue's Waters* (1999), *In Green's Jungles* (2000), and *Return to the Whorl* (forthcoming).

His 1988 short story collection *Storeys from the Old Hotel* won the World Fantasy Award; other collections include *The Island of Doctor Death and Other Stories and Other Stories* (1980), *Endangered Species* (1989), *Castle of Days* (which also includes essays), and *Strange Travelers* (2000).